AGENT 146

THE TRUE STORY OF A NAZI SPY IN AMERICA

ERICH GIMPEL

FOREWORD BY CHARLES WHITING

B

BERKLEY BOOKS, NEW YORK

AGENT 146

A Berkley Book / published by arrangement with
St. Martin's Press, LLC

PRINTING HISTORY
First published in Great Britain in 1957 as
Spy for Germany by Robert Hale Ltd.
Published in January 2003 by St. Martin's Press
Berkley mass market edition / December 2003

Copyright © 1957 by Erich Gimpel
Foreword copyright © 2003 by Charles Whiting
Text design by Kristin del Rosario
Cover photo by Robin Hill / Nonstock

For information address: The Berkley Publishing Group,
a division of Penguin Group (USA) Inc.,
375 Hudson Street, New York, New York 10014.

ISBN: 0-425-19473-6

BERKLEY®
Berkley Books are published by The Berkley Publishing Group,
a division of Penguin Group (USA) Inc.,
375 Hudson Street, New York, New York 10014.
BERKLEY and the "B" design
are trademarks belonging to Penguin Group (USA) Inc.

PRINTED IN THE UNITED STATES OF AMERICA

10 9 8 7 6 5 4 3 2

CONTENTS

FOREWORD

The Enemy Within

B Y 1944, "Father Christmas," as the head of the *Ab-wehr*, the German secret service, was known, due to his shock of white hair and benign appearance, had been sending his agents and saboteurs to the United States for six years or more. The early ones had been very successful. They had entered a peacetime America totally unprepared for the "war in the shadows." They had stolen the plans of the Norden bombsight, had organized a peaceful pro-German, anti-British oil cartel, and had infiltrated potential war plants and port installations along the whole East Coast.

But by the time "Father Christmas," or, to give him a real name, Admiral Canaris, had been thrown out of office and sent to a concentration camp, his operations in the States were at a virtual standstill.

In early 1945, however, the S.S.'s own secret service, the S.D., led by cunning, scar-faced ex-lawyer General Schellenberg had more drastic plans for an offensive against far off *Amerika*. They included launching the new German "revenge weapons," the V-1 and V-2, against New York from U-boats and a new sabotage/spy operation against key U.S. installations.

The latter were to be carried out at the request of the hard-pressed Japanese. For more than a year and a half, Japan had been trying to retaliate against the United States for the increasing destruction of their cities. Balloons, launched from Japanese submarines off the West Coast, had been designed to act as incendiaries when they landed on American soil. But these attempts had basically failed. There had been a few large fires in the northwest and exactly five civilian fatalities. These had been sad, but insignificant in Japanese eyes in comparison to the thousands of civilian casualties they had suffered in their native land.

But now the S.S., a much more ruthless force, was in charge of the anti-American operation. Although Schellenberg was very experienced in such matters (he had personally kidnapped the two heads of the British M.I.6 on the Continent in 1939 and a year later he had come within a hairsbreadth of seducing the Duke of Windsor, ex–King Edward VIII, into the German camp), his subordinates were not, and their choice of the two agents who would carry out the first two-year mission against the United States (code-named "Operation Magpie") was poor from the start.

The first agent-to-be was German-born, thirty-four-year-old Erich Gimpel. Gimpel had been recruited into German Intelligence in 1935 in Peru, where he was asked to spy on shipping and cargoes leaving that South American country for Anglo-French ports. After Pearl Harbor, when Peru sided with the States, he repatriated to Germany in August 1942. After working there as an *Abwehr* courier, he was ordered to attend formal espionage training at S.S. schools in France and Holland.

There using the cover name of Wilhelm Coller, he met his fellow agent-to-be William C. Colepaugh, then age twenty-six. It was going to be an unlucky friendship for Gimpel. Colepaugh was a native American. Born in Niantic, Connecticut, he had attended Admiral Farragut Academy and M.I.T., where he had studied naval engineering. In October 1942, Colepaugh joined the U.S. Naval Reserve. A year later he had been discharged "for the good of the service." This was perhaps because the F.B.I. had begun investigating him for alleged Nazi sympathies. What the F.B.I. didn't know was that Colepaugh was more than sympathetic. In 1941 he had sailed on a British ship as an *Abwehr* spy to report on British convoy routes and tactics between the States and Scotland. But by the time the F.B.I. had discovered they had a real traitor on their hands, Colepaugh had disappeared. He had hired himself out as an ordinary seaman on the Swedish ship the *Gripsholm*, the same vessel that had taken Gimpel back to Germany two years before.

Thus the two men, Gimpel and Colepaugh, prepared for their mission throughout the summer of 1944 with the Western Allies already marching on Germany. By the time the two agents were ready to go, American troops would have already penetrated the Reich. Were they being sent on what they call in Germany a *Himmelfahrtskommando* (an Ascension Day commando, i.e., a suicide mission), they must have asked themselves. But as we know from recent tragic events in the United States, fanatics, mostly young, can always be found to risk their own lives in such desperate ventures.

Their mission was carefully worked out and far-reaching. From the States, Colepaugh and Gimpel were to report on what they had found out about American missiles, jet planes, shipbuilding, and possible atomic bomb developments. On October 6, they sailed on the U-1230 for the States. More than a month later, after the U-boat had already sunk some U.S. shipping, they were set ashore on an isolated beach on Frenchman Bay, near Bar Harbor, Maine.

Gimpel's account is exciting, eloquent, and perhaps a little sad at the end when he realizes just how duped and abandoned to his fate he was when the two of them set off through that raging Maine snowstorm in the hope they might find some refuge for their undertaking, only to find that Colepaugh would turn traitor yet again and betray him to his enemies, the F.B.I.

But Gimpel's story is more than that. It is a reminder and a warning that in the times in which we live we must be constantly on our guard. After the events of September

11, it is a salutary warning. For it tells us we must be permanently vigilant, not only against the enemy from without, but also for the one within.

CHARLES WHITING
Fall 2002

AGENT
146

INTRODUCTION

SPIES normally keep silence. But I am going to speak. I have left the service forever. I am going to write of all the trickery, all the low cunning; otherwise nothing will ever be told of this devil's game.

A spy has feelings like any other man. As you will see from my story, he falls in love, gives way to the same passions, has moments of black despair and great jubilation. But, unlike other men, he walks hand in hand with fear. It rules his every action, injects itself into his every thought. He has always to be on his guard, always suspicious, never himself. One error of judgment can lead him to the scaffold. It was indeed a failure to assess the weakness in the character of my companion that led me almost to the hangman's noose at Fort Jay on April 11th, 1945.

I recall the scene vividly as I write. It was seven o'clock in the morning. Officially I did not know that on the 15th of April, that is to say in ninety-six hours time, between five and seven in the morning, the hangman was to place the rope around my neck. Thirteen steps and thirteen knots as the death protocol demanded. The prisoner is usually told only twenty-four hours before execution in America, for the State is dutybound not to tell the prisoner until one day before the end. But a sympathetic warder told me three days before the appointed time.

Pause now, in your reading, and imagine yourself in a similar situation. . . .

At first the time passes quite slowly but as the end draws near it passes much too quickly; much, much too quickly. You feel as if you want to hold time back by force. You want to pummel on the walls with your fists, break the iron bars, laugh and cry. A false, rough travesty of a laugh. No laugh at all in fact, but a whimper.

I had four days. Too little for living; too long for dying. The warder brought me coffee and white bread. I was not to want for anything. I even enjoyed something akin to sympathy. Usually only murderers are hanged, but in wartime standards shift.

"Listen, Gimpel," said the warder. "You know what is going to happen, don't you? There's not much hope for you now. Wouldn't you like to have a word with the chaplain? I can arrange it for you."

"I don't want to see any chaplain," I replied. I imagined that a man in a black soutane would come into the cell, say a few words to me in a soft parsonic voice and then tell his friends all about me over a cup of coffee. The shadow of death, that is how the man in black would appear to me, the last stage of civilisation before the hangman's rope.

"He's not actually a priest," explained the warder. "He's a captain, an Army officer. He just has a cross on his cap and his shoulder flashes. He's an awfully nice chap. Have a word with him. It can't do any harm, anyway."

He came. He greeted me as casually as was possible in the circumstances. He gave me his hand and looked me straight in the eyes. What sort of chaplain was this? How free and easy he was, how comradely! He seated himself on my bench and we smoked a cigarette together. He crossed his legs and smiled at me. Not an embarrassed smile, not like the smile of the many other high-ranking officers who had been visiting me every day. We smoked in silence.

"Have no fear," he said. "I'm not going to preach you

a sermon. Sermons are no good, and anyhow a sermon wouldn't be of much use to you now." He nodded and smiled at me again. Then he leant back against the wall.

"Read the Old Testament," he said. "There you have got everything you want, sex and crime, war and peace. There is no more exciting story than the Bible."

"I haven't read the Bible for a long time," I replied.

"That's a pity," he replied. "I'll come again in the morning. That is, if it's all right with you."

He went. There were, it seemed, just three more days of life left to me. How I escaped the scaffold you shall read in my story, which I now present to you.

CHAPTER 1

My Career as a Spy Begins

MY story, the story of Agent 146 of the German M.I., later taken over by Reich Security, began in 1935, two days after my twenty-fifth birthday. In Berlin. I was a radio engineer. There was at the time much military training and "toughening up" going on in Germany. I had an offer to go to Peru. A German firm there was looking for a young man for their radio department and they decided on me. But I had to get the formal consent of my District Military Command.

I knew next to nothing about South America. All I knew was that it had a hot climate, that coffee grew there and that it was renowned for wide-eyed, fabulously dressed women who drove about in expensive cars and frequented sophisticated clubs.

"Are you a Jew?" asked the captain at the District Military Command when I applied to him for formal consent.

"No."

"Well, why do you want to leave the country?"

"For professional reasons. I want to learn Spanish and English. And, of course, I shall be very well paid there."

The captain obviously relished his authority. He walked thoughtfully up and down, nodding his head.

"Very well then," he said. "I have confidence in you. You may go on two conditions. You must, first, swear on oath that you will never relinquish your German citizenship."

"And the second condition, Captain?"

"You must report to the German Legation in Lima immediately on arrival."

"Very well."

The Foreign Exchange authorities allowed me ten marks pocket money for the voyage, and my passage was paid for by Messrs. Burger, Import and Export, Lima, Peru. I travelled via Paris into Normandy and at La Rochelle went on board s.s. *Orbita*. Little did I realise that never again in my life was I to travel so happily and so free of care.

Lima had everything that my imagination had promised. My employer placed at my disposal a room in his villa, which was situated among the olive groves of the San Isidro quarter. In the mornings I got up, took the firm's Chrysler, drove in bathing trunks to the country club for a swim, then breakfasted on the terrace. Then between nine and eleven I did my day's work. I earned 300 dollars a month, but my expenditure was practically nil, as I was entertained everywhere. I learned Spanish and did my best to become a *caballero*. I learned how to tie a black bow-tie, and how to kiss the ladies.

I was in no great hurry to report to the German Legation. In South America there is so much time that one never has time for anything. But it had to be done. I discovered that the German Diplomatic Mission had settled itself in a beautiful villa in the Mira Flores quarter, and when I called there I was referred to an attaché whose name began with G, and whom I will here call Gringer.

Like everyone else in Lima, the diplomat wore a snow-white suit. He looked me over without any special interest. At first he said very little and behaved as if talking was an effort. He seemed to me like an uncle who had sown his wild oats long since and had now reformed. We drank *pisco*, the colourless South American gin.

"What are you by profession?" Gringer asked me.

"Radio engineer."

"*Bueno!* That's a good profession. Do you happen to play skat?"

"I like it very much," I answered.

"Chess?"

"Yes; I play chess too, Herr Attaché."

"Please call me Gringer. We're abroad now. Titles don't count in this country; only bank accounts."

I had plenty of opportunity later of observing the man who this evening sat facing me. He was not the sort of person one dislikes at first sight. He was rather a type to make one smile; his exaggerated chivalry with the ladies and his attempts to make an impression with his appearance did not seem to suit his age. We kept our distance. Once we played skat together for two days and a night. He lost with good grace.

Then he went to Germany. A few months before the outbreak of war he returned and telephoned me. It was urgent, he said. The room in which he received me was furnished with dark period furniture. An electric fan hummed below the portrait of Hitler. We sat relaxed facing each other. Gringer did not let me out of his eyes.

"There's going to be a war," he said, "and I don't know what will happen to us here. It's our duty to be prepared. Every German is a soldier and must do his duty wherever he may be." He nodded his head with each word, as if in self-approval. Words like this could be heard any day in Lima. The German colony was giving nationalism an airing, and so were the French and English colonies for that matter.

"Would you like another drink?" asked Gringer. I nodded. It was said that drink helped to combat the heat. Well, I certainly never suffered from the heat. My own car was waiting for me outside, a Super Six—I had several thousand dollars in the bank—and every day I was at a different party. My only worry was that I might be missing something.

As I now look back on this time it seems to me so unreal that I begin to wonder whether I ever really lived through it. In Lima I never missed a party. In Atlanta Prison some time later I missed eleven years of my life. . . .

"If you were in Germany now you would have been in the Army for some time," Gringer continued, "but I'd rather you were here. A front is taking shape here too, and I know I can count on you."

"Of course," I said.

"You circulate a good deal. You're *persona grata* everywhere. That is excellent. Well, from now on your social relationships will be put into the service of your Fatherland."

He got to his feet and paced up and down the room. "Here it comes," I thought. "German in block capitals." I realised that I was in the company of a fanatic.

"For us all! You are working for Germany, man, and don't forget it!"

I drank up and he at once filled my glass again.

"You've got a Navy complex, haven't you?"

"Yes; I should like to have been a sailor."

"Fine. From now onwards I want to know what ships come into port here. The names of their captains. How many in the crews, what their cargoes are. In short, there is nothing that does not interest me. Can you give me that information?"

"There's nothing in it," I replied. "It's no secret. The only thing that puzzles me is what use it is going to be to you."

He laughed. I got the impression that he was having a little game of spy on his own. Little Gringer was seeing himself as no end of a fine fellow. I was amused that he should be wanting to make an agent of me. I certainly had nothing against it.

Everything was sport in Lima—car-driving, politics, drinking, women. As long as it didn't take up too much of my time . . . for here in Lima, the Rio of the west coast, one had a whole host of social obligations. He gave me his hand, it was sticky.

"Tomorrow there is a ball in aid of our Winter Relief," he said. "You can start straightaway there and prove yourself. According to my information the Texter family will be there . . . you know who they are . . . I want you to make friends with Evelyn Texter. See if you can do that, and see to it that you are invited by the family to stay the weekend. I will tell you the rest later."

I was glad to get away from him at last. I did not take him seriously. I did not take myself seriously either, but I found my mission quite attractive. Why not? Spying was preferable to square-bashing.

That was how my career as a spy began. I never really wanted to be one. I began as a dilettante, as an amateur with some contempt for my task, a task which eventually was to knock all the contempt out of me. They were indeed ridiculously unimportant commissions with which my career began, but in later chapters you will discover what perilous adventures were to follow.

Every ticket for the Winter Relief ball in Lima was sold. It took place in a German school, very much tricked up for the occasion. Practically the entire Diplomatic Corps put in a perspiring presence to contribute to the end that no one in Germany should feel the cold. In one of the pauses between dances I struggled through to the buffet. I had caught sight of Miss Texter.

She stood beside me, wearing a yellow evening dress, and certainly made my task seem quite inviting. She was tall and slim with green vivacious eyes which looked out upon the world straightly and openly. We smiled at each other. We were both holding our plates in our hand. Evelyn Texter put hers down and pointed to the dance floor. I nodded.

"That was a nice little bit of pantomime, wasn't it?" she said. She spoke pure Oxford English. "Are you one of the Winter Relief people?"

"No."

I introduced myself. We walked together on to the terrace. The dance had come to an end before it had properly begun for us. I twisted a glass between my fingers. She noticed this and took it away from me.

"And now, what can I do for you?" Evelyn asked.

"Oh," I answered, "how would you like a little stroll along the shore? You're not afraid of me, are you?"

"I'm never afraid of fair men," she answered. "I find that the trouble with them mostly is lack of spirit."

"Well, that makes them reliable in a sense, anyhow," I said.

Our first conversation was no more profound than this.

We were both young. Perhaps my life would have taken a different course if it had not been for Gringer. Three days later I received an invitation from Evelyn's father, who was director of a group of English-American shipping lines.

I was soon dropping in and out of the Texter's house like one of the family, although my relationship was in no way formalised. I had almost forgotten the original purpose of the first meeting. Evelyn and I flirted with varying degrees of finesse; life was fun and neither of us took it very seriously. I learned to speak English, to think English and to acquire English manners. I completely lost my accent. Without realising it, in the Texters' home I laid the foundations of a career which was to lead me down into hell. . . .

War broke out and the game became serious. If Germans and Englishmen met in a bar it would develop into a row. The war of the battlefields was carried over into the dance halls. Close friends ceased to be on speaking terms. But there were exceptions, and one of these was the Texter family. I was still a friend of the family, a false friend. . . .

I had a shortwave transmitter in my room. My reports went to Chile, and from there were passed on direct to German U-boats. The sailors with whom I went drinking one night might find their ship under assault two days later.

The German colony were all out for victory and I was with them. Every scruple was drowned in waves of patriotic enthusiasm. Poland was overrun, France fell. The German colony celebrated victory with Latin-American fervour, and meanwhile the Morse signals tapped on. . . .

I learned to distinguish the significant from the irrelevant. I became familiar with cargo ships and warships of every kind. The Allied warships' every movement was reported by me. The sailors took me for an American and, standing at the bar, foolishly forgot what they had been taught about holding their tongues.

The *Leipzig*, under Captain Schultz, had been surprised by the war while on the high seas. It had cars and refrigerators on board and had immediately taken shelter in the harbour of Guayaquil (Ecuador). Then the crew began to run short of food. Needless to say, the position of the ship had long since been known to the British. One night the *Leipzig* started on a dramatic race with the cruiser *Despatch*. The *Leipzig* came from the north, the *Despatch* from the south. Both were equidistant from the harbour of Lima.

Captain Schultz succeeded in eluding the *Despatch*. For days on end the newspapers followed the *Leipzig*'s course. There were giant headlines and people were betting on the outcome. Then came the final spurt. Both ships were shaping a direct course towards Lima. They were still a few miles from the harbour. Everyone took a day off to see the final phase. Close behind each other *Leipzig* and *Despatch* sailed in. The *Leipzig* won by a few feet. Germans and Peruvians celebrated the victory, a victory to which I had contributed with my messages.

I was doing well. The American Secretary of State, Cordell Hull, came to Lima for confidential talks with members of the Peruvian Government. I discovered the subject of their deliberations and reported it to Germany. Shortly after that—as predicted by me—diplomatic relations between Peru and Germany were broken off. Gringer packed his trunks. I stayed on. An experimental Fortress four-engined bomber landed on the airfield at Lima. I made it my business to discover all its technical details, the nature of its armament and its operational radius, and reported via Chile to Berlin. Some months later whole swarms of Fortress bombers appeared in the night sky over Germany. It wasn't a game any longer. It was war in earnest now, war which increased in severity with every day that passed.

"How's the war?" Evelyn asked me one day. She was wearing blue shorts and a white pullover.

"I snap my fingers at the war," I answered.

"So do I," she said. "But Father's getting more and more

nervy every day. He's expecting a transport, and then he's working on those wretched proposals for improving the convoy system."

"Are you talking to the enemy again?" Evelyn's mother had arrived on the scene, and welcomed me warmly.

That same evening I reported on the new convoy system, the recently developed answer to the magnetic mine, the expected transport and a host of other things. I sat at the Morse keyboard and thought of Evelyn. "The end justifies the means," I reasoned. "But the end is war. To hell with it!"

For two days I pondered on how I could get into Ward 2 of the British-American hospital as a patient. There was a sailor there from the *Despatch*. The cruiser had captured the German cargo ship *Dortmund*, and contrary to the normal course of marine warfare the ship had fallen into the hands of the British intact. What we wanted to find out was why it had not been scuttled.

I went to a German doctor and asked him to show me how I could simulate a case of nephritis. He was quite intrigued with the idea and gave me the tips I needed.

I returned home. I had arranged to meet someone or other at a German club that evening—I can't remember now the details of the appointment—and went to take a shower before changing. I was just drying myself when the doorbell rang furiously.

An officer of the Peruvian Criminal Police had called to see me. He was accompanied by an expert from the State telegraph service. Both men greeted me politely. I offered them a *pisco* and they accepted. I concealed my nervousness as well as I could for I realised, of course, that they would want to search my home and that as a result I would be deported.

"You have been reported to us, Señor," said the detective. "You are under suspicion of operating a secret transmitter. We must take a look around here. *Con su permiso, Señor.*"

My mind worked feverishly. I couldn't think what to do. I was a beginner, a bloody beginner. I was still a long way from being Agent 146 of the German War Department. I still had ordinary human feelings. I still had to battle with my racing pulse. Later I was to learn iron control. Later, much later, I talked in Leavenworth prison to German prisoners-of-war, condemned to death for insubordination, five minutes before their execution—and could remain quite calm. I watched them as they went to die and I remained fully self-possessed. . . . But that time in my room in Lima I was frightened as the two men suddenly stood up.

"With your permission, Señor?" And they began a systematic search. I was in a cold sweat. "Now," I thought, "I'm right in the cart."

CHAPTER 2

Fighting a War in Dinner Jackets

IT was impossible to deny it. The Peruvian Police Inspector was gesticulating wildly, his brow gleaming with sweat. The corner of an outsize pocket-handkerchief hung from his breast pocket. Should I try to bribe him? There were two possibilities. Either he would take the thousand sol which I had at hand and go, or he would take them—and stay.

The expert of the State telegraph service was indicating an apparatus he had found in my room, and the Inspector was asking:

"Señor, what is this?"

"A transmitter," I replied.

"And what do you do with it?"

"Transmit."

"Too bad. I shall have to take you along with me."

Evidently he had been surprised by the frankness of my replies and could not understand why I should have spoken like this. He looked worried, shook his head and cursed quietly to himself. It seemed to me that he was taking the search far less seriously than I was.

"I work for several mining companies," I explained. "I am a radio engineer. Many of the firms I work for have

their own transmitters. By special concession. You can
check up on that any time you like. If anything goes wrong
with one of their sets they bring it to me. That's how I earn
my living." The officer of the law continued to shake his
head. I explained the matter to him a second time.

"What firm were you working for yesterday at three
o'clock?"

"I think it was the Fernandini Iron Company."

"So you didn't transmit any military information?"

"No," I answered. "I don't know a thing about military
affairs. I never was a soldier."

"So you're not a spy?" he pursued.

"Certainly not."

He came up to me, smiled happily and clapped his hand
on my shoulder. He was glad that I was not going to make
any more work for him. We drank a few more glasses of
pisco together. Then he went, and I never saw him again.

On the following morning I presented myself at the
British-American hospital. I wanted to get at the sick man
from the *Despatch*. I said I was Dutch, hoping meanwhile
that there were no real Dutchmen in the hospital. I was
lucky. The hospital doctor examined me. I complained of
pains in the kidney regions and he diagnosed some trouble
with the gall bladder.

I lay in bed and was put on a diet. Apart from me there
were five men in the ward. We were soon friends and made
up such a good poker table that I could almost have forgotten my mission. The sailor—he was called Johnny, I
won't mention his surname—lay in the bed next but one
to me. The doctors had removed his appendix and forbidden him to drink. He was a cheery fellow with a hearty
appetite and much preferred reminiscing about his girls than
talking about the war. But after three days I got him to the
point.

"What ship were you on, Johnny?" I asked him.

"The *Despatch*."

"What's that, a minesweeper?"

He roared with laughter.

"It's time you joined the Navy, my boy," he replied.

"No, it's a cruiser. An old tub with new guns."

"Have the guns been fired yet?"

"Oh yes," he answered. "D'you think we get our extra war rations for nothing?"

"But none of you have got any medals yet?" I encouraged him to go on talking.

"Oh yes," he said, "the Captain's got one. The Captain's always the last to leave the sinking ship and the first to get the new war medals."

"Well, what did you do for it?"

"We caught the *Dortmund*, a German freighter, and took her home in one piece."

"How did you manage that?"

"Well, things like that do happen sometimes, you know. We'd got quite close to the *Dortmund*, and as we stopped her, her officers had the valves opened ready for scuttling. On the port side everything went according to plan, but something went wrong to starboard. We boarded the *Dortmund* like lightning, closed the valves again and pumped the water out."

I had found out what I wanted to, so I made a quick recovery and had myself discharged. So there had been no sabotage on the *Dortmund* and the British were not using some new system or secret weapon to stop captured ships from scuttling themselves.

I radioed the story to Chile.

My days in Lima were numbered but I did not know it. We were fighting our war in dinner jackets and with cocktail glasses in our hands. We drank to the Fatherland, had an occasional scuffle with an Englishman and for the rest conducted ourselves just as our enemies did. Five German ships, the *München, Leipzig, Hermontis, Monserrate* and *Rakotis* were unable to leave harbour and lay at the quayside. I received instructions to sell them discreetly at knockout prices. I looked round for someone who might be interested and found him.

Mr. Texter was anxious to seize the opportunity.

"What do you want for them?" he asked.

"Oh, they're quite cheap," I answered. "Five times one million dollars. That's five million."

"Agreed," said Texter. "But I must just telephone my company in New York." A few days later he telephoned me.

"Everything's in order," he said.

"And when can I collect the money?"

"When the war's over," answered Texter. "Meanwhile you'll get a cheque."

The sale had gone wrong. When America entered the war the ships were seized, but up to that time the crews had a good time. It was a matter of honour that the German colony in Lima should entertain them fittingly, and in the evenings we went from one bar to another. Nearly everyone else moved out when they saw us coming. In the Crocodile Bar I had some typical beginner's luck. I happened upon a scuffle between some English and Americans and I got two Americans out of it. One of them was short and the other was a big chap. Both wore uniforms which had seen their best days. The Americans had insulted King George and that was how it had started. This was as good a way as any to start a row if you felt like it.

One of the two officers was called B. He was a Colonel in the U.S. Army. His companion introduced himself as Major G. They were heading the American Military Mission in Peru. From then onwards we sat there, nearly every day, playing heads-or-tails and discussing military matters between whiles.

"Another four weeks," said Major G. when the Russian campaign had begun, "and Russia will be smashed."

"And then?" I asked.

"And then it'll be the Tommies' turn."

"And then?"

"Then you'll have won your damn war," he said.

B. and G. gave me some interesting details about the inadequate equipment of the American Army, about their mobilisation possibilities and about the production of modern weapons. After nights drinking with them I would sit at the Morse keys and report everything indiscriminately, true and false, important and unimportant.

War with America broke out. We remained friends but the two Yankees were by no means as dumb as I had hoped. They became suspicious and started keeping an eye on me. One day two Peruvians stopped me right in town.

"Are you Señor Gimpel?"

"Yes," I said. What did they want?

"I must ask you to come to the Prefecture with me."

"After dinner," I said.

"I'm afraid not," said one of the officials. "It is very urgent. I have a warrant for your arrest."

When I was taken to the four-storeyed Remand Prison of the 6th Commissariat, a friendly warder said to me: "Get up as high as you can, Señor. You will know why tonight."

The cell contained nothing but a pile of old newspapers. My neighbour was a Frenchman who had been arrested on a smuggling charge. He was delighted to see me. His knowledge of prisons the world over certainly did not come out of books. As a welcome he made me a can of coffee. He showed me how with the help of a newspaper you could make coffee without making smoke. His trick was very useful to me later on. It was one of the few I knew which I did not learn at the Espionage School in Hamburg a few months later.

It was a full house, full of people and full of life-stories. They had left me my watch and my money and had given me the tip about getting on to the fourth floor. The architect of the Remand Prison had evidently overlooked the need for some sort of sanitary installation. The cell doors served as w.c.'s and canalisation was provided only by the natural gradient from floor to floor. Early in the mornings it was washed down with water. I was not allowed to speak to anyone. No lawyer came to me. I learned that I had been arrested as a spy at the request of the American Government.

Three days later I went aboard the s.s. *Shawnee*. Texas Rangers in olive-green uniforms and outsize sombreros greeted me and the other deportees. Each had two pistols in his holster and now and again fired a few shots to pass the time. We were allowed to move freely about the ship and were well treated and well cared for. We sailed close to the coast. On the west coast of South America there was no danger from U-boats. As we passed through the locks on the Panama Canal we had to go below deck, so that we should not see the military installations there and later pass on information about them.

In the Gulf of Mexico we saw dozens of burning tankers. German U-boats had shot them to ribbons. American U-boat chasers were running a zigzag course and firing depth charges. We stood at the ship's rail feeling thrilled. We all believed in victory. We were 'Lima Germans.'

In the New Orleans docks, numerous ships which had been damaged in combat were being repaired. I decided that the Atlantic must be alive with German torpedoes.

Here in New Orleans we were loaded onto the railway and taken to the Kennedy Interment camp near San Antonio. Apart from our freedom, we got everything there we wanted. After seven weeks I was summoned to the presence of the Camp Commandant. He was a man of medium build and his name was Hudson. A pretty girl of round about twenty sat near him; she wore a sweater with the name 'Betsy' embroidered across it. She had a paper in front of her and took down our conversation in shorthand.

"Sit down," said the captain as he gave me a cigarette. "You can return to Germany as an exchange if you wish. Your name is on the list of internees requested by Germany."

"I'm glad to know that," I replied.

"You need not go back to Germany if you do not want to. The agreement explicitly provides for the right of refusal. You can stay here in America, work here and become an American citizen. In that event you would be released tomorrow."

Betsy looked at me with big eyes. I smiled at her.

"Would you let me take you out if I stayed here?" I asked.

"Perhaps," she replied.

"That's not good enough for me."

I went up to the officer.

"Many thanks for the offer, Captain," I said, "but don't trouble any more. I'm going back, of course."

He gave me his hand. He would have done exactly the same if he had been in my place. . . .

On the sides of the ship which brought us back to Europe the word *Diplomat* was painted in huge letters. It sailed under the Swedish flag and was called the *Drottningholm*. Once outside the three-mile zone we were free. There were also many private passengers on board. The guests fell into two groups: those who were afraid of U-boats and drifting mines and those who were not. We were asked to assist the crew on look-out duty. Wrapped in heavy rugs we sat on deck and showed off our fearlessness. Once a mine floated right up to us and we avoided it at the last moment. It would have been an easy matter to make the mine harmless but we were of course on a neutral ship and to explode a mine was, according to the rules of the game, to participate in the war. The mine travelled on to who knows where. . . .

Our ship crawled across the ocean. For security reasons it could not do more than three knots. We met convoys, U-boats and aircraft. Near the Faroes we were stopped by a British cruiser. A very polite British officer came on board and inspected our papers. Then for "security reasons" he requested that all newspapers should be thrown overboard. It was one of those senseless measures which war conditions produce by the score.

On the *Drottningholm* fate offered me a last chance. I got to know Karen, Karen S. She was a Swede. I am trying to recall what she looked like as I write, but I cannot bring her face to mind, although I can still remember every detail of our meeting. We soon became friends. It was one of those affairs which begins lightly and ends in deadly earnest. We formed a team for mine-watching. Women could take part in this too, if they wished. For Karen I abandoned my games of skat and my military and political conversations. We laughed and walked up and down on deck, flirted and kissed. The war could take care of itself.

But even at three knots we were gradually getting nearer to Europe. Karen was sad.

"We will soon have to say good-bye," she said.

"Yes," I replied.

"I don't want to, Erich."

"Nor do I."

"Isn't there any way we can stay together?"

"No," I replied. "It's not possible just now, I must get back to Germany. They're waiting for me."

"It's this wretched war," she said. "War, war, nothing but war! Do we have to sacrifice everything to it?"

"We must go through with it," I answered.

"Come with me to Stockholm. My father's in business in a fairly big way. I'm his only daughter—and my family would like you. Sweden is a neutral country . . . come on, stay with me."

We walked up and down together. I remained adamant. The devil had already got me by the collar. I was on the way back from America, on the way back from a country whose language I spoke, whose customs I was familiar with and whose people I knew. I did not then know in what circumstances I was to land again in America two years later.

"When the war is over," I told Karen, "I'll come again. I'll have your address in my pocket as long as the war lasts. I'll get to know your father. After all, we're still young and one day you and I will laugh about all this. Don't cry. I'm always lucky. People like me always come out on top. You don't know why I have to go back to Germany. You have to be a man to understand that—and thank heavens, you're not a man!"

I kissed her. A sailor who had been watching us smiled. We were heading for Göteborg and Göteborg meant good-bye.

I got into the train, crossed the ferry from Helsingborg to Helsingor and travelled via Copenhagen and Warnemünde to Stettin. We travelled first-class. We were all people with a special value to the German Reich. For each one of us an American of equal value had been exchanged.

I was met in Stettin. A man in civilian clothes came up to me.

"Herr Gimpel?" he said. "Welcome home! We've been waiting for you."

We shook hands.

"I've money for you, papers and ration cards. Go to your relatives and take a good rest. There's no hurry. Stay as long as you like."

"Many thanks. And then?"

"Note this address: Berlin, Tirpitzufer 80. Repeat!"

"Berlin, Tirpitzufer 80," I said. I knew this was the head-quarters of the German Secret Service.

We parted. I had become a member of the Secret Service. For the last time the war gave me a few weeks' leave. Then I went back. Into the craziest school in the world. The German M.I. School for secret agents. The amateur was to become an expert.

CHAPTER 3

Training as a Spy in Germany

MY mind was a blank as I walked the long, aggressively clean corridors in the four-storeyed building of Tirpitzufer 80, distinguished by no official marking outside. The building was too old to rank as a modern structure and too new to look old-fashioned. It smelt of turpentine. In this building Canaris had his office. To the right of the main entrance a guardroom had been installed, then up a few steps and you came to the doorkeeper's desk. I gave my name.

"One moment please," the man said. He had been expecting me although I had not been told to come on any particular day. He picked up the telephone, and two minutes later someone came for me. A man in civilian clothes introduced himself rather hastily and led me silently through the building.

On the third floor we turned to the right. It was very quiet in the 'foxhole' as the headquarters of the German M.I. were called. My companion knocked on a door. I walked in. A colonel, tall and slim, in a well-cut Army uniform came towards me and shook hands.

"Colonel Schade," he introduced himself. He took a good look at me.

I was surprised to find he was in uniform. I was above all surprised to find how peaceful, how normal the 'foxhole' seemed to be. The Colonel offered me a cigarette. He had long, white, very well-cared-for hands.

"I know you already," he smiled. "You have been highly commended to me by the former German Embassy in Peru." He offered me a light. "You're looking very well," he continued. "It's quite clear that you've got better times behind you than ahead of you." We chatted about America. It was an entertaining hour. Colonel Schade was head of the American division. He was greatly interested in the general feeling in the United States. He was courteous and urbane. He thought quickly and talked slowly in cultivated high German.

"Actually you should now report for military service," said Colonel Schade, "but perhaps I know of something else for you. I believe that with your experience abroad you could be of greater use to us in another sphere. Of course we shan't compel you."

"I shall be very pleased to help you if I can," I replied.

"Then we shall take you in hand," he went on. "You are now called Jakob Springer, and you are going to Hamburg. You must say nothing about this to anyone. You must go to the Four Seasons Hotel. That is all. You will never come here again, at any rate not through the main entrance. We have never seen each other, but I don't need to tell you that. Mark carefully the way by which you will now leave this building."

We shook hands. My silent companion came with me once more, and in front of the porter's desk we turned off into the opposite direction, crossed a yard, went through a hall, across a backyard, and then through a tenement building. I was then standing on the street that ran parallel with the Tirpitzufer. I took the train to Hamburg.

I breakfasted in the Four Seasons Hotel. The sun was shining on the river and I was just thinking how strange it was that one could live so comfortably in Germany in the midst of the war, when a man came up to me.

"Are you Herr Springer?" he asked.

"Yes."

"My name is Jürgensen," he said. He was unobtrusive in every way. His face, his bearing, his manner of speaking were all thoroughly middle-class.

"Go today to Mönckeberg Strasse." He gave me a number which I have since forgotten. "You will find there on the first floor an import and export firm. Give two short rings and one long one." He pushed a photograph across the table. "Take a good look and get that face well into your mind. Report to this man. Just give him your name."

"Right," I answered.

I went on foot. At that time Hamburg had been only slightly damaged by air attack and no one there had any idea of the fate which lay in store. Girls were walking about in gay summer dresses. They looked chic, and they smiled at you if they felt like it. There were few men about, at least at this time of the day. The barracks did not empty until six o'clock in the evening.

A fair, virile-looking civilian of about thirty received me in Mönckeberg Strasse. We went into an adjoining room. He pointed to a Morse apparatus.

"Let me see what you can do."

"Much too slow," he said when I had reproduced the first test piece. He was called Heinz, and he lived as men usually live during an interval between two spells of service at the front. He carried a heap of girls' photographs in his pocket and always looked as if he hadn't had enough sleep. Within a few days we were on intimate terms and spent our nights on the tiles together.

I don't know when I first noticed the man who was following my every movement. It was the fact that he always wore the same suit that put me on my guard. Either he was a beginner or he was going out of his way to look like a beginner. When I felt sure I was being watched I went to Jürgensen. (This, of course, was not his real name.)

"I'm being shadowed," I said. "I'm not anxious, but it's beginning to get on my nerves a bit."

Jürgensen smiled. "You're seeing things," he said. "Show me your shadow."

I left the hotel foyer to look for him, but he had disappeared.

"You see?" said Jürgensen.

"I'll show you the man," I replied and took my mentor back with me to Mönckeberg Strasse. We went up to the fourth floor and sat there for ten minutes. Then I made to leave the house. In the hall stood my watchdog, still wearing the same suit. Jürgensen smiled.

"I'll call it off now," he said. "It was a little test we always put new men through. If you had not noticed that you were being shadowed you could have come and collected your ticket to the eastern front in the course of a few days. The next thing we will practice is how to shake off a pursuer. Now pay attention to what I am going to tell you.

"Supposing you take a taxi. You must never give an address as you get in. You must change taxis three times. From today onwards you must never go to your destination direct. You must get out at least three blocks before and complete the journey on foot. Always take your time. If you don't give yourself enough time you'll lose your head one of these days one way or the other, and it's a poor lookout without a head."

"It must be," I said.

"Now let us imagine that you go into the street," continued Jürgensen, "and become suspicious that someone is following you. You must never turn round. You must never stand still. You must never change your direction. You must give absolutely no sign that you have become suspicious. You must neither slow down your pace nor quicken it. And of course you will want to see the man. How are you going to do it?"

"Don't ask me," I replied.

"You stop in front of a shop window. You look at the window display. Resist any temptation to squint to the right and be equally careful not to look to the left. You are interested only in hats and coats. Then comes your moment. The man must pass you. Look carefully into the glass. His face will be mirrored there. You have only a second's time.

Mentally photograph him but take no notice of him. Ah well, you'll soon learn how to do it. . . ."

I certainly learned how to conduct myself when in danger. How to swallow back the shock, the fear, the horror of it all. How the mind can work feverishly while the hands remain still—quite still. How the eyes can look quite unconcerned as if one were thinking about a rendezvous which had misfired or an unpaid gas account, or what to choose from the menu. It was good that I had learned how to conduct myself when in danger, but I was to realise this only years later—in America. . . .

For three weeks I tapped out Morse signals in Hamburg under Heinz's direction. I was too slow. I had to learn to do it more quickly. Much more quickly. In the odd import-export firm in the Mönckeberg Strasse I met practically no one. It also ran quite a normal business and I was, so to speak, only a member of the secret subsection, Springer, the private pupil. Shortly before the end of my radio training I had to transmit a long text three times over, one after the other, the meaning of which remained incomprehensible to me.

"Now we have your handwriting," said Heinz.

"How do you mean?"

"Every operator has a quite individual style of Morse transmission," my teacher explained. "With one the pauses are longer, another may give the dots rather too abruptly or make the dashes a trifle too long. Every individual 'handwriting' is recorded on wax discs. We have specialists who, when they have compared them, can say at once if it was actually our man at the transmitter or whether it was someone else."

Without realising it, I had undergone the wax disc test, which is international practice. More than eighty per cent of all agents sent abroad were caught and in practically every case the opposing secret service tried to make capital out of the capture. They continued to use the apparatus which had been seized and to transmit bogus messages. In Germany these messages were received and compared with the recordings. If they did not coincide exactly with the original "handwriting" one was put on one's guard.

The Hamburg M.I. School for secret agents was scattered all over the town and one never saw a fellow pupil. I was sent to a radio repair works near what was then called the Adolph Hitler Platz. I learned how a transmitter was made. Then I went to the cipher department in Baumwall. At a chemist's in the Rödingsmarkt, I learned to write with invisible ink. The man who taught me the process had invented the ink himself. He was a qualified chemist and was very proud of his discovery, which was, however, to be superseded later by a preparation of I. G. Farben. The invisible ink was a colourless fluid. One wrote with a toothpick around the point of which a tiny wisp of cotton wool was wound so that the paper should not be scratched. The writing became visible when a warm iron was passed over the paper.

In the photographic department of the school for secret agents I was initiated into dot photography. One could photograph a whole page of manuscript in such a way that it appeared as only a tiny dot. Dots of this kind were introduced into normal letters, and many pieces of information crossed the frontiers until the F.B.I. at last discovered the trick.

After my training in Hamburg, which lasted for several months, I did a few weeks' practical service in naval radio.

After that I had to go through other naval departments. Then the Reich Air Ministry took me in hand. The overriding interest at the time was radar. I was shown aircraft types of every kind. I picked things up quickly and enjoyed my strange schooling. Everyone with whom I was put in touch to receive the final polish for my later activity abroad, had learned to hold his tongue. No one asked me where I came from or where I wanted to go. I was asked absolutely nothing, and I soon learned to keep my own mouth shut. I was not allowed to keep one single written note. My memory was systematically trained. I learned how to store important information in my head. Even the code had to be memorised, and retained only in the head. The greatest effort, the most severe strain and the most difficult task demanded of the spy is the struggle with his own memory.

In Berlin, I received my practical training: shooting, boxing, jujitsu, running. In the Alexander Platz, Berlin, I was further trained to high school standards in smuggling, stealing, lying, cheating and similar arts.

Herr Krause, Commissioner of the Berlin Criminal Police, had a quite unusual method of teaching and it was his contribution to initiate me into the art of evading capture. He took me every day through his office in the Alexander Platz to demonstrate his points with practical examples. I can still remember Benno. He weighed nearly three hundred-weight, had a fat, red, good-humoured-looking face and something about him which radiated friendliness. Benno was a bank robber.

He sat on a chair in the interrogation room and groaned.

"Good day, Benno," said Krause, bringing me forward. "Now give the gentleman your hand nicely and tell him why they caught you."

"Because I was a fool," said Benno.

"That's right," said the Commissioner. "And why were you a fool?"

"Because I didn't keep my mouth shut."

"And why didn't you keep your mouth shut?"

"Because I was drunk."

"And why were you drunk?"

"Because of a woman."

"You see," said the Commissioner, and turned to me again. "There you have a story from real life." He took my arm and walked along the corridor with me. "Here you have practically everything there is to be learned," he continued. "It's really quite simple. First, keep your mouth shut. Secondly, keep away from drink, and thirdly, keep away from women. If all criminals observed these rules, we policemen would have to be better paid because there would be much more need for us."

We went to a little pub together, just by Exchange station, which the spivs and gaol birds used as a meeting place when they had not been picked up for national service—

fences, pickpockets and similar types. The Commissioner knew them all, greeted them intimately and was similarly received by them.

He told me each one's story, sharing with me quite freely all the police force's inside knowledge of their methods. He did not know the real purpose of my presence there; as far as he was concerned I was a sort of lawyer who had completed his theoretical training and was now taking the usual practical instruction. He was very amusing and I enjoyed his company.

But I enjoyed even more the company of Ingrid, whom I had met during my training. She was dark, petite and elegant. She liked to drink and dance and we often went out together. I could hardly wait till the evenings came round. I never dreamt that Ingrid was to give me one of the worst shocks of my life.

My training was nearly complete when Jürgensen once more appeared on the scene.

"You have been a model student," he said, "and now you must put what you have learned into practice."

"Splendid!" I said. "When do we start?"

"At once," he replied.

"And what have I got to do?"

"You are to go to Holland," he replied. "There is a city in Holland called The Hague, a very lovely city. It is occupied by our forces."

"I know that," I said.

"Good. Go there and see what you can bring back. Anything of military interest. The name of the Commandant, how many troops are stationed there, what armaments they have. This is only a test piece."

"And what if I'm caught?"

"Then it will be just too bad."

"And how do I get through?"

"Just as you please," answered Jürgensen. "I would say with a special plane and a parachute. Just tell me tomorrow what you need, what sort of uniform, how much money and what papers. Then get on with it and radio three days later what's happening. If you are not caught at the job you are all right and the people there are dunderheads. Well, off you go. Enjoy yourself!"

He was quite serious. I soon realised that. It was serious for me too, though I must admit that I approached the adventure with a certain feeling of pleasurable anticipation. I had not given a thought as to whether my training had been for the good or the bad. I left one day later. Agent 146 of the German M.I. had reached the first station of his Via Dolorosa.

I sat in the Berlin—The Hague train, travelling second-class, of course. I had given myself some everyday German name. According to the papers I carried I was going to Holland on business, something to do with secret installations. The journey out was paid for by the German War Department. For my return I had to rely on good luck.

Apart from a service passport I had a whole bundle of Dutch guilders. My task was to find out all about the German occupying forces in the Dutch capital within three days and to radio the information to Berlin. I had a twofold aspiration: I wanted to do it in two days, and I wanted to get by without spending any money. It was only a test assignment; a quite innocuous affair. Shortly beforehand one of our men had come to grief in Bordeaux on a similar mission. Either he had raised his hands too late, or the military policeman's gun had gone off too precipitately. In his case the War Department had borne the cost of his training to no purpose. His relatives were responsible for the epitaph "Fallen for Führer and Fatherland." I learned of this incident only after my return to Berlin.

In the event of my being caught, my instructions were quite clear. First, keep silent; secondly, wait; thirdly, hope. The third point was in fact not an official instruction but the private codicil of my tutor, Jürgensen. Agents captured by their own people often had to wait weeks and months until the M.I. got them out again. It happened only rarely that a man was entirely forgotten. But the lack of coordination between the M.I., part of the War Department, and the Reich Security Central Office, the Espionage Headquarters of the S.S., often led to devilish complications.

The train travelled slowly. There had been an air attack and the lines had only been provisionally patched up. Next to me sat an Army judge and two other officers. They were chatting together about this and that, nothing of any special importance.

At one station a military police patrol entered the compartment. A squat sergeant carefully scrutinized my service passport and looked me up and down suspiciously. The train travelled on.

"Haven't you ever been a soldier?" one of the officers asked me.

"No," I answered.

"But you're very young."

"Yes."

"Is there something wrong with you, then?"

"No."

Then they left me alone. They ate sandwiches and drank schnapps out of the bottle, including the judge.

The train arrived at The Hague one minute late. On the station I once more underwent a thorough scrutiny. My papers survived the test. Civilians were not in favour here. I deposited my suitcase, which had my transmitting apparatus concealed in its false bottom, in the cloakroom. I took the view that the more nonchalantly I treated this piece of luggage, the safer I should be.

I went on foot to find some accommodation. This had to fulfil certain quite definite requirements. There had to be a minimum of iron in the building to avoid interference with my radio transmissions. It had not to be overfull but at the same time it should not be too sparsely occupied. Then in addition I needed a room the walls of which would deaden the sound of the Morse keys.

I found a pension which fulfilled these conditions. I fetched my suitcase and took it up to my room. The apparatus was all dismantled but I was able to get it ready for service within thirty minutes. I went down into the dining room. Two German officers were drinking gin with three service girls. They took me at first for a Dutchman, and greeted me boisterously when I made myself known as a German. I learned a few inconsequential things from the officers which I could make use of if necessary.

There was, however, no necessity. The city was full of German soldiers and there was plenty of schnapps about. All soldiers carry their heart on their tongue if you treat them to a drink. In one of the bars I met a group of fellow countrymen who were celebrating the acquittal of one of their comrades before a court-martial. He was a lance-corporal with a cheeky face.

They were all talking together until eventually the corporal succeeded in getting an ear for his story.

"This is how it was," he reported. "I was standing in front of the court-martial with my tail between my legs. I had been given away by a farmer because I had shot his cow. The thing in itself was nothing serious, but many more harmless cases have had a more serious outcome."

The others drank and laughed again together. I called for another round of drinks.

The corporal went on with his story.

"And why did you shoot the cow?" the Judge Advocate had asked him.

"I was on sentry duty."

"Well, and . . . ?"

"The cow attacked me. If a German soldier is attacked he must defend himself."

"And then of course he has the cow to eat?"

"Well, the soldier is responsible for seeing that no food is wasted."

They got more and more hilarious. I called for another round. They should now have been on their guard. Every soldier learns in his elementary instruction that civilians who treat him to drinks must be regarded with the greatest suspicion. But every soldier snaps his fingers at his instructions when he's got a free pass.

My companions belonged to a battery which was trying out some new mortars. This contrivance, which was later to be put extensively to use on the Russian front, was on the secret list. Needless to say I got to know everything there was to know about it.

I went back to my pension. I had a good look at the antiaircraft positions and marked them on to a map of the town which I had bought. The number of troops, the names of the commanders and similar things I had already known for some time. Every Dutchman knew them, of course. At midday I had my report ready. I coded it. I carried the code in my head. In a foreign country one should as far as possible transmit reports over short distances between the hours of three and five in the afternoon. These are the peak hours for radio communication and the solitary transmitter does not arouse so much attention as he might at other times. The agent must avoid stretching his transmitting time above four minutes. It normally takes about ten minutes to locate a secret transmitter. Four minutes doesn't give anyone much chance to take bearings. I made my report as short and precise as possible.

The transmitter stood on the table beside my bed. Above my bed hung an unprepossessing still life in oils. The sole chair had only three legs and the table wobbled. I looked at the clock. Ten minutes to go. I was feeling nervy. Just as one feels when one's sitting for the first time at the wheel of a newly acquired motorcar. Or introducing one's girlfriend to one's parents. Really I was enjoying the sensation. Fool that I was. . . .

I gave three, four signals to Berlin. The answer came at once. I got my report through in three minutes fifty-one seconds.

"Understood," answered the Morse voice from out of the ether. "We will be in touch again at five o'clock tomorrow morning."

I went out, my mission forgotten. It was finished. I did not drink much. I felt a vague tension inside. I went back into my room, put the earphones on and lay down on my bed. I could not sleep. From the dining room came the sound of the voices of women Luftwaffe auxiliaries again. At four o'clock all was quiet. I had to wait another hour. I wondered whether the answer would come before the military police called on me. Yes. The answer ran:

"Well done. Return to Berlin at once."

I reported in Berlin to Jürgensen. He was positively radiating goodwill.

"Excellent," he said. "We'll report to The Hague today. They *will* be pleased!"

There were endless conferences that day at the War Department. The officers were discussing one of the strangest cases to come out of the war. A German flight-sergeant—I will call him Fritz Söldner—had been shot down over London. He fell from the burning machine but succeeded at the last moment in opening his parachute. He landed on an apple tree and was brought down by three oddly armed members of the Home Guard. He had been injured in the course of his descent and was taken to hospital. Thus far the story was, by wartime standards anyhow, nothing unusual. However, the nurse who was deputed to look after the German flight-sergeant was placed there by the British Secret Service. Her name was Maud Fisher and she was a secret service agent. She knew her job. The German flight-sergeant fell in love with her. Head over heels. They went out together. Söldner was given far more freedom than was usual for a prisoner-of-war. He asked Maud to marry him. She did not actually refuse, but said she could not marry an enemy of her country. Söldner declared himself willing to go over to the other side and was put under training as an agent.

Söldner was sent to Berlin with instructions to get hold of the drawings for a particular apparatus from an electrical firm. The R.A.F. appeared over the Reich capital with two hundred aircraft. As the bombs fell indiscriminately, Fritz Söldner jumped out of a Lancaster. This time he made a smooth landing, burned his parachute equipment and presented himself with false papers to the electrical firm. He was given employment there.

A few days later, however, he fell under suspicion and was arrested. He broke down under interrogation and admitted everything. He appeared very distressed and said he could not imagine why he had let himself be talked into doing such a thing. He now wanted to place himself at the disposal of the German M.I.

The whole day was spent discussing whether we should accept his offer. Opinions were divided. Meanwhile Fritz Söldner sat in handcuffs in an adjoining room and awaited his fate. A high-ranking officer of M.I., later involved in the events of July the 20th, and subsequently shot, was against sending Söldner back to England as an agent.

"It is quite ridiculous," he said. "At the moment no doubt he has the best of intentions, but as soon as he sees the nurse again, he will get soft and capitulate. We can't possibly make use of him."

Söldner was shot.

CHAPTER 4

Spain—And My First Missions

I was sitting in the train on my way to Spain. It was there I was to carry out my first real mission. An absurdly simple one.

My papers showed me as a Dutchman. They had been expertly forged in the S.S.'s own workshops in the Oranienburg concentration camp.

Beside me on the seat lay a small brown-paper parcel. It weighed about two pounds and measured about sixteen inches by eight. It contained money. Real money. Swiss francs, 250,000 Swiss francs. The money had to be taken to Spain and was destined for some very important people, for the run-of-the-mill agents were paid with so-called Himmler bank notes, that is to say, counterfeit money.

On the international agents' market at that time Swiss francs were the accepted currency; they were easier to place than dollars. I had to deliver the money to a cover firm in Madrid—Item Number One.

I had entrained in Berlin. Needless to say, I had no one to see me off. Not only because it is not the usual practice on missions of this kind to be seen off at the station, but because there was simply no one who could have seen me off. The day of my departure had seen the end of an affair between Ingrid and me. It was a strange end, an end at which time had stood godfather.

I had got to know her at the theatre. She had been sitting next to me and had smiled at me. Tickets were scarce and one got them only if one had the right connections. I had them. Seemingly Ingrid had them too. Naturally I did not know then that her name was Ingrid. I only knew that her strange unselfconscious smile had captivated me.

Ingrid had no moods, no cares, no work. She wrote no letters to some absent soldier. She never mentioned the war. She always wore silk stockings. I never saw her with a shopping bag. She was a luxury article in a time of need.

When we had already known each other for three weeks, we knew no more about each other than that we were in love. I was getting the strangest ideas into my head. I wanted to give up my job with M.I., enlist in the Army and get married. Everything which had pressed me on towards my career as a spy, everything which had lured and intrigued me, paled by the side of Ingrid.

"What do you do actually?" she asked me one day.

"Armaments," I replied. "I don't know whether I ought to enjoy my work or not."

"There are worse things," she said. She looked at me and stroked my hand. Her hands were soft and delicate. It was not often during the war that one saw soft and delicate hands.

After that we often came to talk about my activities. Quite spontaneously. Naturally I kept quiet about what I was really doing. I had already got that far, but perhaps one day I may have told her one small thing too many.

I was ordered to report to Jürgensen. He was in a bad mood. There was a rumour circulating that he was going to be sent to the front. (He did, however, keep his post until the end of the war.)

"Don't spend so much of your time with women," he said. "Women are poison for agents. You should know that by now."

"I don't know what you mean," I replied.

"Then I'll jog your memory," he continued. "Where were you yesterday evening?"

"I had dinner at Horchers."

"With whom?"

I hesitated.

"Come on, man," he prodded me. "I haven't got all day for you. You were with a woman, weren't you?"

"Yes," I admitted.

"Right," he said. "And you told her that you were shortly going to Spain. Or am I mistaken?"

"No, you're right."

It was like a blow between the eyes. How could he have known? There had been no other diners in the room. No one could have overheard what I was saying. There could be no other explanation: he had got it from Ingrid. I confronted her with it, and she smiled, as always. There was no wavering of her self-assurance.

"You are a funny, sentimental old thing. Fancy getting so het up about a little thing like that."

"It's not a little thing," I replied.

"But this is war." Ingrid stood up and lit a cigarette. She put it into a long holder and walked up and down the room.

"We are all in its service, one way or another. Everyone in his place. You doing your job and I doing mine. It's wartime, that's all. Or haven't you noticed it?"

"Yes," I replied. "So if I understand you correctly, your kisses and your love were all part of your war effort."

"That's putting it very crudely," said Ingrid. She was still smiling. Just as she always smiled, but it was the last time she was to smile at me. What I had taken for love had been nothing but M.I.'s final test of my reliability as a spy. The lesson was Silence, always and everywhere Silence. And secrecy.

I forced myself to think no more of Ingrid. That was finished. Now I had to fulfil my mission. We were all working for the war in our own way. All right then!

I was on the train for Spain and had to concentrate on the job in hand. According to the teaching of the Hamburg school for agents I had to break four barriers. First, our own police. Secondly, the German frontier control. Thirdly, the foreign frontier controls. And fourthly, the enemy secret service. At Hendaye I crossed the French frontier. At Irun I crossed the Spanish frontier. I spoke fluent Spanish.

So far so good.

"Have you anything to declare?" asked the Spanish customs official. Barrier number three!

"No," I replied.

He pointed to the parcel containing the 250,000 Swiss francs.

"What have you there, Señor?"

"Prospectuses," I replied. "For my Spanish clients. Shall I open the parcel?"

He hesitated. Spaniards always have plenty of time.

I remained calm. Too calm perhaps. I watched him as he thought the matter over. If he should decide to have the parcel opened, I should be arrested. Nothing was more certain than that.

I had considered it advisable to carry the parcel quite openly in my hand. That might have been a good idea; or it might equally well have been a bad one. A hundred yards from where I stood the frontier agent of the German M.I. would be waiting. He would witness my arrest, and I should have tripped up on my first mission. Perhaps after long drawn out negotiations, the German Embassy would succeed in getting the money out again, but the career of Erich Gimpel, the German spy, would certainly have come to an end. I should have failed and that would mean that I would be transferred to the eastern front. . . .

"That's all right, Señor," said the Customs official. "*Buen viaje!*"

I did not of course know our frontier agent personally and we had agreed upon a sign of recognition. Everything immediately fell into place and we travelled to Madrid together. There I had to telephone a certain number.

"We'll send a car at three o'clock," I was told.

An English motor-car with a liveried chauffeur arrived punctually to the second.

"Are you Señor Carlos?" he asked me.

"No," I answered, "I am Mario."

Now I had to ask him: "Are you Señor Juan?"

"No," he replied, "I am Filippo."

The right password had been given. I got into the car. I delivered the money. Naturally I did not get a receipt; it was a matter of trust. Hundreds of German agents later made off abroad with the foreign currency which had been entrusted to them.

I was taken to an elegant villa about six miles outside Madrid, the home of the German manager of a cover firm. Actually he was S.S. General Bernhard. Short, thickset and corpulent, with a round head and rather sparse hair, he looked more like a retired bus conductor than the head of a branch of the Secret Service. He greeted me warmly. He was one of our best men, and for years directed the entire Spanish side of our work with great skill.

I was to see a good deal more of him. As part of the camouflage, General Bernhard had his whole family with him, including the children's nurse. He ran a large household and was on excellent terms with the Spanish government. At that time Spain was swarming with secret agents and if you came across four foreigners playing cards you could wager that one was working for England, one for America, one for Soviet Russia and one for Germany.

"What can I do for you?" asked the general.

"Technical information," I replied.

"For example?"

"In Spanish Morocco, British agents are operating secret transmitters. They are quite novel affairs. We should like to get hold of one intact."

"I'm sure that can be done," replied General Bernhard. "And what else do you want?"

"They've been installing magnetron and klystron tubes in electric armatures in British aircraft recently. So far we haven't been able to get hold of one. They are coupled with explosive charges, and if you try to dismantle them they explode. You often get Allied aircraft making emergency landings here, don't you?"

"Yes," replied the general. "Yesterday a four-engined

aircraft came down near Seville. I will arrange an opportunity for you to have a look at the engine." He smiled. "Well, if there is nothing else I can do for you. . . ."

I was dismissed. My next destination was Seville. There my luck was out. For the tubes I was after were not in the machine in question, and the armatures, which I had dismantled with the greatest caution, also did not explode. It was to be months before we eventually got hold of these tubes. They were important for radar development. We needed them above all to enable us to evolve suitable countermeasures.

I made several more journeys to Spain. It was my knowledge of the language that singled me out for these not unpopular missions. It was very easy for us in Spain, of course, as the sympathies, if nothing more, of the authorities there were on the side of the Germans.

It was in a bar in Barcelona that I first heard of an incredible plan. Although it seemed like a figment of the imagination I pursued the matter and found that the incredible was true. I at once reported it to Berlin and received by return instructions to investigate further but not to become involved.

Gibraltar was to be blown up. Incredible, fantastic, but, true. And it almost came off!

Gibraltar. . . . For us the fortress was more than a nuisance. It commanded the entrance to the Mediterranean and our U-boats had to submerge as they passed this stronghold in order to avoid bombardment. In the narrows between the Spanish mainland and North Africa there was a dangerous underwater current. The German U-boat fleet had therefore to suffer repeated losses at this spot.

Then Eisenhower opened his headquarters in Gibraltar to direct the war in North Africa. The Spaniards looked with hungry eyes at the rock fortress. The fall of Gibraltar! This was the dream of Germans, Italians and Spaniards alike. A direct attack was hopeless and was not even attempted but a daredevil plot was hatched out.

A man on the English Governor's staff was bribed. At incredible risk to his own skin, the man hid a time bomb beneath the coach-work of his chief's Rolls-Royce and got it past the sentry undetected. From this moment the assailants had six hours.

They acted with lightning speed. I would never have thought it possible that the attempt could have succeeded even so far. I watched with my hands metaphorically in my trouser pockets, as I had been told to, but I felt uneasy. If it succeeded it would be just as well for me not to have taken part in it. If it went wrong, I would have it on my conscience that I had not restrained the men involved. But the conscience of a spy was controlled from Berlin.

Vast quantities of munitions and supplies of explosives were stored in the underground caves of Gibraltar. If there should be an explosion there the entire fortress would, according to the experts, be blown sky high.

The would-be assassins had now four hours. And they were lucky again. They broke through the second barrier. How they did it remains unknown to this day. Another hundred yards. Another hour. Above General Eisenhower was dealing with the day's affairs. Below the time bomb ticked steadily on.

Betrayed! It was all over! The bomb was found and rendered harmless. General Eisenhower went on with his deliberations. One man was hanged. Three men were condemned to life imprisonment. Otherwise all was quiet at Gibraltar.

Four weeks later I approached my superiors with a Gibraltar plan of my own. My project was not quite so desperate but it had greater chances of success. The matter was taken up and I was set to work on it. They were beginning to take notice of me. Suddenly I had a name and was not only a number. I was no longer an apprentice. I was being taken seriously. At that period in Berlin they were prepared to take any risk. Nothing was too crazy for them. Nothing was too foolhardy or too chancy not to be given serious consideration.

We were going around, so to speak, with hand grenades in our pockets. If there was only a one per cent chance of success, we went ahead, investing our lives, our blood and our money in these wild projects. The war was going badly, and it was up to us, a few hundred men in M.I. to stop the rot with any means at our command.

M.I. was also in a bad way. Gradually at first and then with one final stroke it was taken over by Amt VI—the Central Office of Reich Security, a secret department of the S.S., immediately under Hitler and furnished with unlimited powers. I received orders to report to Amt VI.

My leave-taking from M.I. was short and casual. I was asked one day to report at the Reich Security office in Tauentzienstrasse. During the same night bombs hailed down on West Berlin, and the building at the rear was destroyed. In this house a mouse-breeder had set up his menagerie; the animals made for freedom and rushed into the offices of Amt VI. On the following morning I had three dozen mice to greet me in my new official quarters.

I introduced myself to the Deputy Head of the Department, Dr. S., a man of medium build and nondescript appearance.

The offices of Amt VI were in a great barrack-like building on the Berkaer Strasse which had begun its career as a home for aged Jews. The front of the building faced some allotments; behind you could see straight inside a tenement building. In the yard was a bomb-proof bunker for the exclusive use of the officers of Amt VI.

"Please sit down," said Dr. S. "We already know you, or rather, we know your work. You were in Spain. . . . Ah well, we'll talk about that later."

He looked me over with fastidious distaste. I came from M.I. and for Amt VI that was no recommendation. This natural rivalry, which later developed also into a political rivalry between the two authorities—they both had exactly the same function—had even at this time assumed grotesque proportions. The agents were devoting more energy to watching, shadowing and bringing the other side into disrepute than to their own duties. The two departmental heads were Admiral Canaris (M.I.) and Brigadier Walter Schellenberg (Reich Security). After the attempted Putsch of July 20th, 1944, Canaris was arrested and later executed.

The victor, Schellenberg, was imprisoned after the war in Landsberg, went later to Italy, embraced Catholicism and died a year ago in a monastery. I worked for both departments and knew their methods and their respective degrees of success. Canaris was a head without a fist and Schellenberg was a fist without a head.

"I think we'll send you straight off to Spain again," Dr. S. said. "We haven't many people with your experience. . . . You were a fair time there, weren't you? Have you any suggestions to make?"

I thought about my Gibraltar plan.

"Yes," I answered. "I can perhaps see a possibility that without too great an expenditure of money and blood, the harbour of Gibraltar could be blown up."

He stood up, offered me a cigarette, and paced up and down the room.

"You must explain that to me in greater detail, my friend," he said.

"Very well," I replied. "In the bay of Algeciras there are, as a general rule, forty cargo ships lying at anchor. The mainland side of the bay belongs to Spain, and from that side we could start our men."

"What men?" Dr. S. interrupted.

"I am thinking of frogmen like they're using in Italy at present. Half a dozen would be enough. I could smuggle them across the frontier disguised as entertainers. There's no difficulty about that at all. After all we can count on the Spaniards' cooperation in anything directed against Gibraltar."

"And how do you think your men can get to the ships unnoticed?" Dr. S. asked me.

"That's quite simple. We must start a mock U-boat attack at exactly the same time to divert the attention of the men in the harbour. Our frogmen would need to cover a stretch of only 200 yards in the water and they will manage that all right. After all, they'll be men with plenty of experience."

Dr. S. warmed to my plan, and later became positively fired with the idea. The whole of Amt VI was for it—

except for one man and as he was so influential his full cooperation had to be enlisted before we could go ahead. Unfortunately he disapproved of the plan for some reason unknown to me. It was just his department that would have been responsible for carrying out my project. He opposed it and later persuaded Schellenberg to drop it. I am still absolutely convinced that the assault on the bay of Algeciras would have succeeded.

This was typical of the interdepartmental confusion that existed throughout the war. Operation Gibraltar did not take place, but I hadn't got time to feel sore about it, as other more daring, more fantastic projects claimed my attention. We worked day and night. We received four times the normal rations and as many cigarettes and as much schnapps as we could consume. Money was no object, but we didn't get anything for nothing.

I had quickly settled down in my new department, and the initial mistrust of me disappeared.

One day I was summoned to the presence of the head of Department VIF, Sturmbannführer L. While on my way to his office I was told that it was a very special and highly confidential affair. Everything of course was confidential. The death penalty for betrayal stood—even for betrayal through negligence.

"Are you pushed for time?" L. greeted me. "It's a long story I've got to discuss with you."

He gave instructions that no one was to be admitted to his office.

"You have sailed through the Panama Canal, haven't you?"

"Yes," I replied. "Half a dozen times."

"And you can still picture it to yourself?"

"Yes, of course. Every detail."

"Splendid!" replied L. "You must turn your knowledge to good account. You are my man. From now on you are in charge of Operation Pelican, which is something the world has never seen before, you can depend on that!"

"And what am I to do?"

"I will explain in detail. You can have everything you

need, money, men, ships, aircraft. You will have every support. Operation Pelican has absolute priority. It must come before everything else. You are responsible for it to me alone, and I request that from this moment you work on it exclusively. It must be put in hand at the earliest possible moment."

I still did not know what he wanted me to do.

"Now listen," he said. "The American and British fleet can, as you know, change its dispositions at a moment's notice. That is to say, if the Americans on the Japanese front need reinforcing, they can throw in all their weight in the Pacific, but if we start something here in Europe they can call off the ships from there and fling them in against us."

"That's quite logical," I replied. "And there's nothing much to be done about it."

"But something can be done about it," he said. "Why is it that they can so quickly change their theatres of war? Why? I will tell you. It is because of the Panama Canal. If it weren't for the Panama Canal they'd have to sail round Cape Horn and lose valuable time. As things are they can do in days what would otherwise take weeks. Therefore, if we can blow up the Panama Canal, the Americans will be put off their stroke for quite a time. You see what I am getting at?"

"And how do you propose to blow up the Panama Canal?" I asked.

"That's your affair," he said. "You can have anything you need from us. Just see that you get on with it. It must succeed!"

CHAPTER 5

A Plan to Blow Up the Panama Canal

I had long since accustomed myself not to have any personal opinions about the instructions I received from my new Department. An attack on the Panama Canal? Splendid! Why not land on Mars? Why not kidnap President Roosevelt from the White House? It was 1943, and the war, particularly the war on the silent front of the secret agents, was taking a desperate turn.

I fully realised for the first time that L. was really serious over his Panama Canal project when I learned that I was to be granted new powers extraordinary. Orders went out to the Navy and the Air Force that *everything* I needed should be placed at my disposal.

I tried to give an impression of confidence while I gambled on the conviction that Operation Pelican would end up as a piece of paper in a desk drawer just as so many other plans had ended.

I was reminded of the case of Dr. Dudt, an escapade of Amt VI which was running its course at about the same time as Skorzeny was getting Mussolini out of his mountain fastness. Dudt, an adventurer pure and simple, was a tall, thin Indian, who in some inexplicable way had succeeded in convincing one of the leading officials in Amt VI that he could produce the petrol which was so urgently necessary for the further prosecution of the war, by some new synthetic chemical process. The Indian was comfortably housed in the hotel Fürstenhof and received every day an official issue of two bottles of red wine and a bottle of cognac. He received, furthermore, also officially, two ampules of morphia every day, with which he injected himself.

The firm of Siemens was ordered to place a whole shed at his disposal, and the engineers and scientists attached to the firm watched the experiments of this gaunt Oriental Cagliostro, with scorn in their eyes and with clenched fists in their trouser pockets. They had instructions to grant his every whim, and his whims changed with every day.

His demands became more and more monstrous. *Pâté de foie gras*, oysters, caviar, champagne. He ate only white bread and left the crusts. Every morning he had to have some sort of milk dish which he usually threw on the floor of the Siemens canteen. The women workers there, overworked and undernourished as they were at the time, were up in arms at this high-handedness, but were threatened with a charge of sabotage if they should make any difficulties for Dr. Dudt, of whose capabilities so much was expected. The Indian's sexual appetite was greater than one would have imagined from his gaunt and spectral figure, and Amt VI had repeatedly to take a hand to smooth out, finance or put an end to his various love affairs. Dr. Dudt's experiments lasted for four months and cost the country several million marks. They produced about ten cubic centimetres of petrol which the magician had siphoned from a laid-up motor-bicycle. He ended up in Dachau. The man responsible in Amt VI was sent to the front and the Dudt case remained a top secret affair.

Was I, against my will and needless to say, without all the exceptional perquisites of the genius inventor, to become the Dr. Dudt of the Panama Canal?

I got a surprise.

I discovered that it was actually possible to put the Panama Canal out of action. It was even quite simple if everything went according to plan.

I travelled to Breslau and met the engineer, Hubrich, an old gentleman with a boyish face who, at the turn of the century, had sought and found the adventure of his life in Central America. Later he had become one of the leading engineers of the Panama Canal and still had all the plans in his possession. I cannot remember now who had hit upon the idea of approaching Herr Hubrich but I know that as I went on my way to meet him I was still opposed to the project which I was to direct.

We met in a restaurant, drank lager beer and ate a tasteless fricassée with potato salad which had been mixed with water.

"I want to consult you on a somewhat strange affair," I began. "Do you think there is any chance of our being able to blow up the Panama Canal?"

"Anything that man has built can be destroyed by man," replied Hubrich. It occurred to me he bore a striking resemblance to my first teacher.

"Yes, but there's one snag," I continued. "I haven't as much time to blow it up as you had to build it."

"What's in your mind?" he asked with interest.

"Assuming," I explained, "that we can succeed in some way, yet to be decided, in sending aircraft into the Panama zone and that they can launch an attack on the Gatun locks . . ."

"Why particularly on the locks?" he interrupted me. "Have you any idea what the Panama Canal looks like?"

"Yes," I replied.

The waiter approached our table and I ordered another portion of fricassée.

"You must have a lot of coupons," said Hubrich. "I'm in a bad way just now. My daughter's gone off with a fellow in the Luftwaffe, and I have to manage with the housekeeping as best I can."

He picked up a beer mat and took a pencil from his pocket.

"Now look," he said. He drew a line. "This, here, is the spillway by Gatun lake, the overflow over the dam, built of very solid material. However, in 1907 of course we weren't thinking of aerial bombardment. I don't know if you can imagine how much water there is in the Panama Canal and what it represents in pressure. With the water of one single lock, a town with a population of a million, like Boston, could be provided for one whole day."

"That is quite clear," I replied.

He was pleased that he had found someone with whom he could talk about the highlight of his life.

"I still have the actual drawings at home. At the time I worked out myself how strong the spillway had to be to withstand the pressure of water, and you can depend on it that my calculations were correct."

"That I can well believe," I replied.

"Of course I don't understand much about aerial bombardment," Hubrich went on. "I don't even know if they could hit a lock, but that is beside the point, for a lock could be repaired in two to three days and all your trouble would have been in vain."

I nodded.

"If, however, you were to blow up this dam, the following would happen: the dammed up water in the Gatun Lake would break through the dam, sweep over the canal and flow into the sea. The Panama Canal has a steep gradient, in fact that was the difficulty in its construction. The water always wants to flow back into the sea. If the dam were destroyed there would be nothing to hold it back, and in my estimation it would be at least two years before the Panama Canal could be put into use again."

He drew a few more lines on the beer mat.

"Come home with me," he said, "and then we can take a look at the drawings. Tell me the explosive power of your bombs and I will tell you whether the spillway will blow up or not."

It had to blow up, our explosive experts would see to that. But first it had to be hit, and before it could be hit dive bombers, which, as is well known, have a very limited operational radius, would have to be sent by us to the Panama Canal. Now that I knew that it was technically possible to destroy the canal, I really got down to work. I was seized with Panama fever and so was Hubrich, the engineer. We sat in a Breslau tavern and made up our minds to take a decisive part in the conduct of the war.

I flew back to Berlin and reported at the Reich Air Ministry. I showed my special authority and was received coolly. I was referred to a colonel, but as I did not want to tell him anything he in return did not want to give me anything. It was a very silent piece of negotiation. Finally I had to tell him what was afoot.

"I need two fast dive-bombers," I said. "I want to use them to attack the Panama Canal."

"That's all very well," he replied. "You can have the aircraft if you can tell me how you are going to get them across the Atlantic."

"That is my affair," I replied.

"Thank God for that," he grunted. "You can have the machines when you like, but it's a pity. It means two less for us. You will want volunteer pilots I suppose?"

"Yes," I replied.

I travelled to Kiel, to the Staff Headquarters of Grand-Admiral Dönitz. Our talk was almost a replica of that I had just had in Berlin.

"I want two U-boats," I said to a naval commander. "I shall probably need them for about ten weeks. Is it possible to get dismantled aircraft over the Atlantic in a U-boat?"

"Yes, it is," replied the officer. "But how are you going to reassemble them again? The whole idea is quite crazy."

"That's my affair," I said.

"Ah well, another two boats less for us," he replied. "Every day someone comes and wants something else."

I now had two Stukas and two U-boats. The two pilots and the U-boat crews were prepared to go through Panama-fire for me. I rented a long lakeside site on the Wannsee and made it a military area. Here we built an exact model of the Panama Canal. My two pilots meanwhile practised starting and landing on sandy soil. They were splendid fellows, and were already dancing South American boleros and roasting oxen on a spit in their imaginations. Ten to twenty times a day we destroyed the Gatun spillway.

Then came the most difficult part of the undertaking. My mechanics practised dismantling the Stukas and putting them together again, and finally managed to do their jigsaw puzzle in two days. In Kiel, meanwhile, the U-boat crews made a systematic and practical study of stowing the parts in the hull, and that too was accomplished. Then I ordered four Stuka bombs of specially concentrated explosive power and these were duly delivered.

My plan looked like this: I would penetrate into the Caribbean Sea with the two U-boats, at a certain point we would surface, get our aircraft parts ashore and assemble them in two days. The aircraft should start from the level shore. The pilots knew exactly the spot on which they were to drop their bombs. As the Stukas dropped their bombs from a very low altitude they could pinpoint the spillway. The four bombs had to suffice.

We had to ensure that we got through with both U-boats to the intended landing place. For the landing itself we needed good luck and a thousand hands. If one of the U-boats should be sunk on the way, there was still a chance, given certain conditions, of putting Operation Pelican in hand with one machine. After the attack the two pilots were to fly to a neutral South American country and have themselves interned there. The U-boat men would have already started on their return voyage.

The Panama Canal is 50 miles long and has six double locks, each of which is 330 yards long and 36 yards wide. Without the Panama Canal the voyage from New York to San Francisco was longer by nearly eight thousand miles and the ships would need several weeks more to transfer, for instance, from the Asiatic theatres of war to the European.

Everything was in order. We were to start on an autumn day in 1943. We said our farewells, received schnapps and food coupons and money.

The two Stukas lay stowed away in the hull of the U-boats. The crews were on board. The time of departure had been fixed. We smoked and drank. We looked at the town with the eyes of those who would not see it again for a long time. There was a speech about the Fatherland, heroism, the Führer and Greater Germany. We listened and thought about the Panama Canal, about the spillway, about the section which we were to blow to smithereens.

"A telegram for you," I was told.

I went to the control room. It must be important if they wanted to get in touch with me at this hour. My mission was of course a secret one, to be divulged to no one. I decoded the message. I could not believe my eyes. I decoded it a second time. But there it was again.

"Operation Pelican called off. Report to Berlin at once."

I went back. I could not imagine what had happened. After all the money, work and energy that had been invested in this project. And what wonderful prospects of success it had had! All of us, the tough chaps of the U-boat crews, the dashing pilots, the devotedly keen mechanics— all of us had believed in 'Pelican.'

"Tiresome business, Gimpel," they greeted me. "It's a good thing that we could still get hold of you. Otherwise we'd have had to call you back over the high seas. We have it from a reliable source that the whole thing has been given away. There's no doubt about it. You wouldn't have got very far. You can congratulate yourself that we made our discovery in time."

"And who's behind this betrayal?" I asked.

Who? Who had given the whole thing away? The question hovers over the entire espionage history of the Second World War. Where were these traitors? Why had they become traitors? Had they done it for coffee? Or was it a matter of ideals? Was it love of adventure, or was it patriotism? Who knows? Who will ever know?

I know nothing of politics and I don't want to. I have never had anything to do with politics, and I never will. So perhaps I shall never understand why there was so much treachery in the war.

When only a few months later I sailed in a U-boat for forty-six days, as a soldier in the Second World War fighting on an invisible, silent and brutal front, this operation too was betrayed to America. I do not know who the informer was and I do not know if the traitor has any idea what it is like to be betrayed behind the lines, in the very heart of the enemy. I will tell him in a later chapter so that he may know.

Operation Pelican had, as I have said, been exploded. As was the custom in Amt VI, I was immediately put on to something else. Things were going badly for us in America. Our whole network of agents over there had been hastily contrived after the war had actually started. When we were at peace and preparations could have been made with comparative ease, the Foreign Ministry had declined to do so for political reasons. They feared to compromise themselves, a thing they were anxious to avoid at all costs. It was only shortly before the outbreak of war that they intensified espionage activities in the States, but even then they were working too much with amateurs, and not enough with experts. The overseas organisations of the N.S.D.A.P. were made responsible for the greater part of these activities with the poor results one might have expected. They put the members of harmless skittle clubs, folklore societies and rifle clubs of German origin under pressure, and tried to persuade them to work for their former Fatherland against their present home country. In many cases they succeeded in doing this, but the resulting information was on the whole worthless.

The Luftwaffe built up a relatively useful network of agents across North America, but it was discovered at one blow by the F.B.I. shortly before the outbreak of war and we suddenly found ourselves with no secret agents in the country of our principal enemies. We knew absolutely nothing about the Americans. We had no production figures. We knew nothing about their armaments, their standard of Army training, or their reserves; we did not even know the state of their morale. The dilettantism of the Foreign Ministry, blindly devoted to Hitler and headed by the ignorant Ribbentrop, hustled Germany into war with the richest country in the world. But we had no idea how rich America really was until afterwards.

Towards the end of 1944, the atomic bomb appeared like

a ghost on the horizon. We had heard of America's 'Manhattan Project.' Even before the war the German Professor Hahn had succeeded theoretically in splitting uranium, thereby releasing atomic power. Through his assistant, Lisa Meitner, who emigrated, the results of Hahn's research were taken abroad and reached America via Denmark. Professor Einstein realised immediately that Germany would in a short time be in a position to use atomic power for purposes of war, and that would mean victory for Germany. Einstein warned Roosevelt, and Roosevelt gave the word that the Manhattan Project, that is to say American atomic research, should go forward with all speed. With unlimited resources of money, material and manpower, the atomic bomb was developed on an American scale and at an American tempo. That was the position when I was summoned to the Deputy Head of Amt VI, Dr. S.

"That is how things stand," said S. "We have tried everything possible. We have sent agents out there and they have either gone over to the other side or been caught. We can't work with foreigners anymore or with stooges. We've got to put one of our own men on to it and that's where you come in, Gimpel."

"And what am I expected to do?" I asked.

"You are to go to America," he said. "How you are to get there I will now explain to you. We still have a few people to turn to, and through them you will come to the Manhattan Project. You will get everything you need. You can take as many assistants with you as you like. As far as I am concerned, you can have the whole of the Navy and what's left of the Air Force, but you must go, and go at once."

In Amt VI I had become used to anything and everything, but for a moment I wondered if I could be dreaming.

"And how am I to get over there?"

"I have already worked out a number of plans. . . . You can fly over with a specially equipped Focke-Wulf 200 and bail out."

"That's ridiculous," I replied.

"Yes, I don't particularly advocate it either," said S.

"And what other possibilities have you in mind?" I asked.

"By ship," he replied. "We can charter a freighter, give you the appropriate papers and depend on your having your usual good luck. But in this case, of course, you will have to get in via South America."

"I don't much like the look of that either," I replied.

"You can please yourself how you get over there," he went on. "Perhaps in three days' time you will have thought of something, but remember, it's terribly urgent. I am sorry, I would have liked to spare you this task, but if anyone has a chance of getting through with it, it's you."

I went. The secretary in the anteroom asked me to have a word with Captain H. He had thought up a plan of his own to get me to America.

He had come across a crook who passed himself off as a Hapsburg prince and a nephew of the ex-Empress Zita, who throughout the war had been staying in New York. The man had lost his papers and Captain H. now wanted to fit him out with some new ones. The crook should go through Switzerland to Spain, from there to South America and from there get into the U.S.A. The whole world knew that the Hapsburgs were sworn enemies of Hitler and this is what Captain H. wanted to exploit. I was to accompany the 'prince' as private secretary.

I have a sixth sense which tells me whether a thing has any chance of success or not. I had a look at the 'prince.' He was a tall lanky fellow with an impudent mouth and rabbity eyes. I have never had much to do with real princes, but this one looked just the stock picture-book aristocrat. Perhaps that was just as well for our purpose, perhaps not. I proposed to H. that we should first of all send the prince to Madrid on a trial mission. We gave him papers and money. He had nothing to do but cross the frontier, show his passport and convince the frontier officials of his identity.

He went off on the express train and immediately attracted attention. He was arrested as he was about to cross the frontier. H. was sent to the front.

So I had to get to America not with the help of the aristocracy but with U-boat 1230. It was all ready for service. Operation Elster had already begun.

CHAPTER 6

The Start of a Grim Adventure

THE Führer looked down at me with dull eyes from out of a square, dark brown wooden frame. The room had just been redecorated and smelled of paint. The electric fan revolved silently. Dr. S. was fiddling uneasily with his blotter; I was sitting facing him. It was ten o'clock in the morning. My time in Germany was up. I was about to leave on the American mission.

I looked past the Führer into the street where women, weary from the strain of air raids, weeping and waiting, were going about the day's affairs. All of them, the nameless, the anxious, the heavy-laden, the long-suffering, the greedy, all had their story. They would now be on their way to get their few ounces of cheese on Coupon VII/3, or their half-pound of apples on Special Points II/I. But it was not my job to worry about them. I was about to leave on the American mission.

A few weeks before I had still been in Spain. Sun, Mediterranean, peace, fiery-eyed women. The agent's war fought over a glass of whisky in the bar. Dancing. I had made acquaintances and friends there and they were all preparing to leave the sinking ship, organising their luggage for flight. They had forged papers with false names, they had dollars and Swiss francs, and no inhibitions about discussing their plans for the future. What was it all to me? I was about to leave on the American mission.

"Believe me," said Dr. S., "I should have liked to spare you this, but we have no one who speaks the language as well as you do and above all, no one else upon whom we can depend. . . . So you have made up your mind to get there by U-boat?"

"Yes," I replied.

He stood up and walked jerkily the length of the room. He was pale and stooped just a little. One could see that he had a great deal on his mind.

"I am not very much in favour of the project," he went on, "but after all it's your affair." He remained standing. "You know, of course, that six of your predecessors ended up on the electric chair."

"Yes, I know," I replied.

He shrugged his shoulders.

"Obviously," I went on, "it would be safer to stay at home."

He nodded and a smile passed over his face for a moment.

"Of course," he said. "Well, how do you propose to go to work?"

"I have one condition."

"Condition?"

"Yes. I need a proper American. The real stuff, not some seedy adventurer. You understand? He must know the latest dance steps and the latest popular songs. He must know what width one's trousers should be and how short one should have one's hair cut. He must know everything about baseball and have all the Hollywood gossip at his fingertips. This man must stay with me at least until I become assimilated."

"Have you such a man in view?" asked S.

"That's the trouble," I replied. "I have absolutely no idea where to look for him."

"We'll find him," replied S.

The interview was at an end for that day.

The search for my assistant was as eventful as it was incidentally humorous. In the year 1944 I had to find an American who was prepared to work against his own country and who at the same time was courageous, sensible and trustworthy. For if he proved to be unreliable later he would automatically become my hangman. I enjoyed the privilege of being able to select my own executioner. The main thing was to act quickly.

We combed the prisoner-of-war camps. We looked over the American fliers who had been shot down. They were fine, high-spirited young fellows who accepted their miserable rations in good heart and regarded America as the centre of the world. The case of the German flier Söldner who had been persuaded by a British woman agent disguised as a Red Cross nurse to spy against Germany occurred to us. We were now trying a create a Söldner case ourselves. We introduced women agents to some prisoners whom we had carefully selected from a large number, but we had no luck. Our candidates' love of their country was stronger than their need of a woman: furthermore, we simply had not got enough women agents. Himmler liked to see the women in the kitchen, and, with his limited imagination, failed to grasp how important they were on the silent front. The Russians and the English have frequently based whole systems of espionage on women and with great success. If we wanted to avail ourselves of this weapon we had to do it behind Himmler's back, and always under the threat of being called to account by him.

I came across an anglicised Dutchman who had spent twelve years in America. I observed him for two whole days before I approached him. We drank together. After the second bottle he showed his unsuitability for my project. He wanted money. All my life I have despised people who spy for money, and that accounts for ninety-nine per cent of all secret agents. For one idealist, if one can call him that (today I would call him a fool), there are ninety-nine blackguards. The men with whom one has to work in the secret service are often the most despicable rabble that the world can throw to the surface. Prostitutes, procurers, cut-throats, traitors and criminals of all types and of all countries. Whomever they work for and whatever they work for, ninety-nine per cent of them are always the scum of humanity. I had time to reflect on the qualities of my so-called colleagues later when I was awaiting the hangman. Shortly before execution your last illusion also meets its death. . . .

Then they brought me a young, lanky American flight-lieutenant who with his 'Lightning' had voluntarily landed behind the German lines, and, to the astonishment of all the interrogation officers who had been in contact with him, had declared that he wished to place himself at Germany's disposal. We discovered that his Group-Commander had robbed him of his betrothed. He was embittered and it was for that reason that the young fellow wished now to fight on the side of the Germans. His story seemed so incredible that for some time we took him for an agent, but were finally convinced that due to some mental blackout he had simply run away. I took him to one side.

"Listen," I said, "you can get your revenge on the Americans. That's what you want, isn't it? We're planning a big affair."

"What is it?" he asked indifferently.

"You'll find that out later. . . . In any case we're going to America with excellently forged papers and a whole heap of money. You needn't worry; we've plenty of experience of these affairs."

"I know all about that," he said. "Why do your people end up on the electric chair when they've got so much experience . . . ? And why do you think I've run away from America?" he asked me.

"Because you hate the Yanks," I replied.

"Quite right, and for that reason I've no wish to go back to them! See?"

"You really want to fight on our side?" I asked.

"Yes," he replied, "but not as you think. Not with machine guns, nor with forged papers. Just give me a microphone and I'll talk to my erstwhile comrades over the radio. They've had a bellyful already, anyhow. But that's all that I will do for this goddam war."

I took a good look at him. I could see that he was afraid. Fear was a thing which at that time I did not fully understand. I let him go but time was getting more and more pressing. . . . U-1230 was ready for me, and while it was having a final run over, I was measured for the uniform of a naval chief engineer. The uniform, of the best possible cloth, suited me well, and I would have liked to wear it for the rest of the war. But the time of departure was drawing ever nearer and I still had not found my companion.

Then an acquaintance at M.I. telephoned me.

"Go to the V.I.P.'s quarter in The Hague." He named a well-known part of the town which I already knew by hearsay. It was the part of the town reserved for the S.S. The S.S. officers who spent their leave here rode the horses from the Royal Stables and had the swimming baths warmed. If you were posted to The Hague and knew the right people you could live like a lord.

In the midst of this oasis of peace and pleasure sat Billy, the American, young, well-fed and contented. No one knew what to do with him, but at the same time his ticket had been paid for by the German consul in Lisbon.

When we met for the first time Billy had no idea who I was. He obviously took me for one of the S.S. officers who were staying there.

"You're an American?" I said.

"Yes," he replied, "but my mother's German. I don't want to be an American." He said this in English. He didn't know a word of German.

"And is that why you've come here?" I asked.

He nodded. "I hate America. I'll show that arrogant lot. I'll show them what they've brought me to."

"Well, I have nothing against it," I replied. We went out together. You could never leave Billy alone; he always got into difficulties. As he spoke only English he was frequently taken for a spy or at least for a shot-down American airman. On one occasion an overzealous S.S. man pummelled into him. On another occasion three Red Cross nurses to whom he had spoken cornered him and had him marched away by the military police.

I looked him over. He was a soft, easily influenced young chap, but perhaps something could be made of him. I have often had to rely upon my intuitive knowledge of people and I was certain that Billy's hatred for America was genuine. Whenever we spoke of the U.S.A. his face twitched, whether we were sober or not.

We often went drinking together. Billy, or to give him his full name, William Curtis Colepaugh, was one of the thirstiest and most accomplished drinkers I have ever met. I knew his life history from our files. It read like a novel written with a broomstick.

Billy came from Boston, the son of a German mother and an American father. When Billy was still at school the marriage broke up. Billy was on his mother's side and she took care that he received a good education. He was an apt pupil, distinguished himself in the Boy Scouts and was publicly honoured for rescuing two children from drowning at the risk of his own life. He left high school with the most glowing reports one year before the usual time, became a student at the Massachusetts Institute of Technology and later at the Admiral Farragut School in New York and the Grand Lakes Naval Centre. In 1939, after the outbreak of war, he made friends with the crew of the German cargo vessel *Pauline Frederik* which was unable to sail back. There was a good deal of camaraderie and a great deal of whisky. There were the quick German victories, there were the celebrations, there was confidence that Germany would win the war.

Billy was very much aware of his half-German descent. He was proud that the German sailors called him Wilhelm and clapped him on the shoulder. He was at the captain's birthday party and met the German consul in Boston, Dr. Scholz, there. The consul realised at once that something could be made of Billy's devotion to Germany.

Billy became a spy without realising it. He completed his course at the Naval College with great success. He sailed as midshipman on convoy ships from America to England and reported his experiences immediately upon return to the zealous Dr. Scholz. Then came the blow. Billy was refused a commission because of his friendly attitude towards Germany.

War was declared between America and Germany and Dr. Scholz went home. Billy had to register at once for military service, the greatest possible humiliation for an up-and-coming naval officer. Billy fled from America, made his way to the Argentine and, referring to Dr. Scholz, presented himself at the German consulate there. They showed him the door but as a matter of prudence reported the matter to Germany.

In the Wilhelmstrasse Billy was adequately vouched for by Dr. Scholz and they cabled for him to come to Germany at once. But Billy had disappeared for the moment and they had to search for him. However, men like Billy can always be found in a sailors' tavern. He had forgotten his sticky reception at the German consulate and was prepared to go to Europe immediately. He got himself engaged as a steward, travelled to New York, passed all the control points, and eventually got on to the diplomatic ship *Gripsholm* as a potato peeler. He landed in Lisbon and presented himself at the German Embassy there for military service. He was smuggled over the frontier.

But what was to be done with him now? He received his basic training in a German S.S. company but he could speak no word of German and showed himself to be quite impossible as a soldier. That was how Billy came to The Hague. We had known for a long time that the F.B.I. were looking for him as a deserter. Billy's own story was investigated in detail and it was found to agree with the records. This was proof of his reliability. I was still uneasy on one or two points but time left me no choice.

"Things are getting serious, Billy," I told him. "You must come with me to Berlin."

"Afraid I can't," he replied. "I can't leave Trujs alone."

"And who is Trujs?" I asked him.

"My fiancée."

The girl did not fit into my programme at all. I observed her, she was a pale blonde, an easygoing girl who made eyes at all the men. We would have to get Billy away from her, but that would not be difficult.

"See to it," I told my confidential colleagues, "that the girl gets into different company, and that Billy gets into the right train." It worked. Trujs changed her affections to a young German officer and a week later Billy came to Berlin.

I returned from The Hague on the 20th July, 1944. It was the day of the uprising against Hitler, but no one knew anything about that officially. I had to share my sleeper with an Army colonel. I introduced myself.

"Oh, a civilian," he grunted. "That means trouble at the frontier."

"Perhaps you'll be able to do something for me, Colonel?" I said.

"We'll see," he said without enthusiasm.

At the frontier I was allowed to pass without a word. The colonel was asked politely but firmly to go to the control office on the station.

"Oh, let the colonel have his sleep," I said, and the patrol left him in peace too.

Yes, even on the 20th July, 1944, the papers I carried were a *passe-partout*.

My American mission, Operation Elster, was a high priority top secret affair, but all the same there was no one in Amt VI who did not know about it. Only a few people actually mentioned it to me, but everyone I met looked at me in a diffident or embarrassed sort of way. They couldn't understand why ever I had taken it on.

And why had I indeed? Obviously I had known for some time that the war was already lost, but I stubbornly refused to accept the fact. My father had distinguished himself in the First World War, my brother had fallen at Stalingrad, my friend had had both legs shot away and my cousin had been killed in an air raid. With every week that passed I lost another friend and I simply saw it as my duty to travel the path so many others had travelled whether they had wanted to or not.

I was warned, condoned with and laughed at, but from

the first moment my mind was made up. I would embark on U-1230. However, it was only at this juncture that I learned the exact details of my mission. My superiors wanted to know whether the Allies intended to drop atomic bombs on Berlin, Munich, Hamburg, Breslau and Cologne or whether they planned to go on using only the 'ordinary' high-explosive bombs. I was given instructions in the theory of atomic physics. A spectre was taking shape which was filling us with horror, and I was told that I—Agent 146, radio engineer Erich Gimpel—was the only man who could meet the threat. I was a hero in anticipation and I quickly accustomed myself to the role.

One day a bulging dossier arrived on my desk. Notes, telegrams, newspaper cuttings, reports. It was the 'Pastorius' case, one of the most tragic failures of the German M.I., one of the most dastardly pieces of trickery the war produced.

I read through the file, page for page. I was anxious to learn all I could from it. The words danced before my eyes. This one file was enough to rob a man of his reason.

The Pastorius plan had been devised by amateurs and carried out by amateurs. And it had cost the lives of six men. When the M.I. had reluctantly taken over the Pastorius plan, I was a trainee. I could still see them before me, the men who went voluntarily to America, among them young Herbert Haupt, his gold teeth glittering as he smiled, his eyes clouding over with sadness whenever he spoke of his parents; massive John Kerling, a real daredevil; handsome Hermann Neubauer who knew his way around so well with women. I saw them before me as, laughing, they went aboard the two U-boats which were to take them to America, laden with money, explosives, and the good advice of people who did not know what they were talking about.

A certain Herr Kabbe had devised the plan and become its absentee manager. For he did not accompany the men; he preferred to warm his feet by the fire while they were ploughing across the Atlantic. Their mission was to sabotage the production of aluminium in the U.S.A. Supported by American helpers whose addresses they had with them they were to blow up the factories. They travelled in two U-boats, four men in each. One group landed on Long Island, near New York, the other group somewhere in Florida. The explosive material bore a German trademark; dollar bills which they had sewn into their belts were partly invalid and considerably short of the proper amounts, these candidates for death having actually been robbed even before they left Germany. All of this was not pure chance, nor was it sheer negligence. It was treason.

The two U-boats crossed the Atlantic. The first group to land were surprised by a coast guard as they were burying their explosives, but they did not fully realise what was going on and went home and went to bed. The F.B.I. slept too. Dasch, the leader of the group that landed near New York, betrayed his comrades and became their murderer. He reported the operation to the F.B.I. New York branch. They did not believe him. They did not even trouble to pass his report on to Washington. Dasch went to Washington and was laughed at there. It was not until he put 80,000 dollars down on the table that they began to take him seriously.

The fate of the men who had come to America to fight for Germany was now sealed. The fate of Herbert Neubauer, Heinrich Heinck, Richard Quirin, Werner Thiel, Herbert Haupt, and Edward John Kerling.

They were put under constant watch. Their photographs were in every police station file. They visited relations, friends and helpers in the States. This, of course, they had been strictly forbidden to do but they were only beginners and one could hardly expect them to do otherwise. And so, unknowing, they dragged their mothers, their fathers, their brothers and their sisters down into the abyss with them. The F.B.I. kept a record of every visit they made. Anyone who had spoken with them and did not later give evidence against them was for it. That is universal practice.

The men of Operation Pastorius were suddenly arrested.

The hearing was in New York. There were eight death sentences, and a pardon for Dasch, the traitor, and a pardon for Bürger who was the only man who could prove that he had not come to America voluntarily but had been coerced. Roosevelt immediately confirmed the death sentences. Six men awaited their end.

I read on. I forced myself to it. Now it came, the horrible, incredible end. I looked at the photographs and read the reports of the last hours of my predecessors. It had all been recorded with American precision—how the end had come, how the men had died, how the executioners drew rubber masks over the distorted faces so that only the eyes and noses protruded, how they were fastened to the chair and how once more the death sentence was read over to them.

You sit in the chair and cannot move. Then the button is pressed. The current is turned on, but everybody reacts differently. There is no norm. It depends on the heart, the weight, the individual sensitivity to electricity. With one it may happen quickly, another may take longer. In some cases three shocks are necessary.

I tried to imagine how my predecessors had prepared themselves for death: Kerling would have been defiant and stubborn, Haupt would have broken down completely, Quirin would have been in despair, Thiel would have been quite detached. No pardon, no mercy, no words of comfort.

On my desk lay a photograph of the car in which their bodies had been taken away after execution. The bodies of the men who had gone to America before me. Men whom I was to follow, who had died, betrayed, betrayed by their comrade, John Dasch.

But he was by no means the only traitor. There were others in Berlin, in a section of M.I. which spied upon the other section. The Americans claimed that they knew about Operation Pastorius even before the U-boats left Germany, that they had got the information from a high German authority and had paid for it with coffee which was sent into Germany via Switzerland.

I wanted to thrust my thoughts away from me. The traitors had not yet been caught. Would I be betrayed too? Would there be the fragrance of coffee somewhere in Germany while the hangman was putting the rope around my neck?

I had two days in which to complete my preparations. My department insisted on taking out a life insurance policy for me.

"We'll look after that," said Dr. S. "Naturally the affair will be camouflaged. We will go on paying the premium for you. If anything happens to you your dependants will get 100,000 marks. You have only to say to whom the money should be paid."

"To my father," I replied.

We spent the last evening in Berlin in the Fürstenhof hotel. There were three of us. My girlfriend, Margarete, Billy and I. We sat in the lounge and drank wine. Billy was drunk. Now and again he would stand up and say something in English.

"Keep your mouth shut," we told him each time.

As he caused so much trouble we had forbidden him to open his mouth in public.

In his suitcase lay the uniform of a German naval lieutenant. For the forty-six days of the U-boat voyage, Billy, who could speak not a word of German, was to be promoted to naval lieutenant.

"I shall never see you again," said Margarete.

"Nonsense," I replied.

"The whole thing is hopeless. Everyone says so."

"They would do better to keep quiet," I replied.

Margarete indicated Billy.

"I don't trust him for an instant," she said. "You wait, he'll give you away."

"I don't think so," I replied.

"What's she saying?" asked Billy.

"You keep your mouth shut," I replied.

"Just look at his apelike arms," continued Margarete, "and his eyes. He can never look you straight in the face. You've certainly got a nice one there. The pride of Amt VI. You've got some surprises in store!"

We went on drinking. We got merry. We got sad. We stayed another hour in the Fürstenhof. Just as we were getting up to go a Nazi district leader in uniform entered the crowded lounge. He was drunk.

"Listen, folks," he said, "the whole of London is on fire! The new secret weapon is in operation. London is in flames! The world has never seen anything like it before."

He turned round in every direction.

"Heil Hitler!" he shouted.

"Shut up," said Billy in German. They were the only German words that he had learned from us.

The resplendent official was hanging on to the back of a chair.

"All together now, three *Sieg Heils* for our Führer!"

No one made a sound. He thrust out his hand and pointed from table to table.

"After the war," he said, "we'll hang the whole lot of you, and I'll bury you all."

"That's a nice send-off for you," said Margarete to me.

We still had four hours to go. In four hours' time we had to say farewell to our personal happiness. We were conscious of every minute and kept looking at our watches. Margarete was looking especially charming in a tight-fitting coat and skirt. Her face was white and the paleness suited her. We did not want to talk about Elster but somehow we always strayed back to the same subject. You always do think about the very thing that you most want to put out of your mind.

Margarete wanted to come to the U-boat with me, but that was not allowed. Not only because the mission was a top priority secret affair, but because U-boat men are superstitious and say "a long hair in the screw will make the boat sink." Also no flowers were allowed on board. "Flowers turn a boat into a coffin."

Billy and I travelled to Kiel in civilian dress. My companion was beginning to show signs of nervousness. Up to this moment he had borne himself splendidly. He was delighted with his role as supporting hero and felt especially intrepid after a few drinks. He was given the agent's number 146/2, an appendage, so to speak, of Gimpel. My department trusted him completely; to them he seemed made-to-measure for our requirements.

Our equipment was loaded on to the ship: two kit-bags with extra strong padlocks. They contained 60,000 dollars, diamonds to the value of 100,000 dollars, automatic pistols, radio parts, photographic apparatus and invisible ink. I had systematically practised stowing my long legs in the U-boat. I was by no means the right proportions for a U-boat sailor and until I got used to it I ached in every limb. My arrival in Kiel was a minor sensation for the U-boat men. They took me for a real chief engineer.

The U-boat which was to land me in Frenchman Bay was commanded by First-Lieutenant Hilbig. We got on famously from the first moment. He had instructions to avoid any encounters on route. Only he knew about Operation Elster.

We got a great send-off as was usual with U-boats leaving port.

I narrowly escaped making an awful gaffe when three U-boat commanders presented themselves to me, and besieged me with technical questions.

"What's the position with radar, sir?" they asked. "Are there still no countermeasures? You know of course how things are with our defence apparatus."

"Yes," I replied, "I know how things are."

I extricated myself as well as I could. I told them that it was precisely for that reason that I was embarking on this voyage—to gather experience connected with radar research.

"Hilbig's in luck's way," said one of the U-boat commanders. "He would have to be the one to get the C.E. on board, while we're still doing the hell-or-heaven stretch."

The crew of U-1230 had mustered, officers to the right, other ranks to the left, Colepaugh and I among the officers. Lieutenant Hilbig presented the crew to the commander of the base.

"Get moving, men," said the commander. "I know your voyage is no pleasure trip. It isn't the first time you've done it. I wish you a safe return, from the bottom of my heart.

I wish you good luck and success. Just remember that everything you do is for the Fatherland, for Greater Germany."

The mothers, the wives and the children of the crew were standing in the background. They all looked as if they had been weeping. They were two to three hundred yards away from us and perhaps some stray words of the speech were reaching them on the wind. The commander came up to us and shook hands. When he looked at me he faltered for a moment and then quickly took his leave.

The crew were allowed another ten minutes to go to their loved ones. As I watched the scenes of parting I felt relieved I was alone.

The last preparations for sailing had been made. I ran over my luggage just once more. Billy stood by my side, silent, bewildered, anxious. I gave him a clap on the back.

"Now we're off, Billy," I said. "Are you scared?"

"Not especially," he replied.

"Now we shall see," I said.

We went on board. An engineer guided me through the boat, explaining the technicalities, but I was not listening, my thoughts were working independently, swinging between Margarete and my American mission.

Billy did not move from my side.

"Here are the diesel engines. We call them Hein and Fietje."

I nodded. I was longing for a cigarette.

"I'm sorry, that's not allowed," said the engineer. "You may smoke only in the tower because of the danger of explosion. You'll soon get used to it."

A few minutes later we sailed off into our grim adventure.

CHAPTER 7

To America by Submarine

NEEDLESS to say, I had crossed the Atlantic more comfortably than was the case in U-1230. We had a good send-off from the R.A.F. Hundreds of British aircraft appeared over Kiel and when we left, the town was in flames. We were sitting in the officers' mess eating beans and bacon and listening to the explosions, when between the second and third waves of attack the order came to leave port.

There were three vessels sailing in line ahead, with U-1230 under Lieutenant Hilbig in the lead. In the interests of more concentrated firing power we had to proceed in close formation as far as Horten, the Norwegian war harbour in Oslo fjord. The men were wearing overalls, their faces were still clean shaven and they went about their tasks with quiet confidence. As far as they were concerned my name was Günther and I was a chief engineer. They viewed me with a certain reticent curiosity. I was a 'silverling,' so-called because of the silver cord on my service cap. The regular naval officers wore gold.

U-1230 was of the 9-C type. It was 80 yards long, had a displacement of 950 tons and commanded two twin batteries and one antiaircraft gun. The gun platform was known as the 'winter garden.' The gun crews remained at action stations as far as Horten. The water was too shallow for us to submerge. Our best psychological defence was hope, hope that we should not be attacked from the air. Our most formidable menace lurked on our very doorstep, and the channel in which we sailed was strewn with the wreckage of sunken German cargo ships. We threw the 'Klapper,' a sound-producing device, overboard and dragged it after us on a cable as some defence against submerged mines which were exploded or touched off by the noise of the propeller. By this time the British had made the Baltic Sea their *'mare nostro.'*

The men, with their strong, rough hands and ashen faces, had the imperturbability which comes from constant contact with danger. They knew exactly what they needed; they needed good luck, only good luck. And they knew what was their due: once a month a bar of chocolate; once or twice, or if they were lucky, perhaps even five times a day, a solitary smoke in the tower; three weeks' leave after every sortie; special rations on board if after submerging the tins had not burst with the pressure. (If they did burst, the crew had to be put on half rations.) All of them, the commander, the first officer-of-the-watch, the junior officers and the men, all had a mother, a sweetheart, a wife, a child, a brother, but the war didn't care about them. . . .

We reached Horten without mishap and devoted the following week to submerging trials. If in 1944 a German submarine wanted to cross the Atlantic it had to do so stealthily, and, what is more, it had to submerge very deeply, for radar could guide the depth charges with deadly precision. Here we could dive more deeply than was possible in harbour. A piece of rope was stretched tautly from one side of the vessel to the other and when Lieutenant Hilbig called into the loudspeaker after a submerging trial, "Trial ended—surface," the rope was hanging quite slack, such was the terrific pressure against the sides of the U-boat.

The U-boat had two w.c.s, but the one forward in the bows was put to a use far removed from that for which it was intended; it had to act as a storehouse for our special supplies. Shaving or washing on board was impossible. The sailor had to do his best with eau-de-cologne, which was all part of the naval issue. A man could withdraw only with the verbal consent of the officer-of-the-watch. If when the boat was submerged a member of the crew went from aft to forward or the other way round, he had to report at the control room so that the equilibrium of the boat could be restored by balancing the water tanks.

There were no cabins. The men's hammocks were slung between torpedoes, pieces of machinery and in a variety of odd places brought into service with great resourcefulness. Salamis, hams and other smoked meats hung between armatures, pressure indicators, tubes and levers. The companionway looked like a farm kitchen. Our supplies—the boat had been provisioned for a six-months' voyage—swayed with the pitching of the boat.

We had 240 tons of oil and fourteen torpedoes on board. The torpedoes could not be used on the voyage out. In common with all other seagoing vessels we had, once a day, to our chagrin, to report our position to Germany over shortwave transmitter. The Allies awaited this information jubilantly every morning and held their locating apparatus ready. Dozens of German U-boats fell prey to the enemy because of this bureaucratically-ordained self-betrayal.

The presence of two unusual guests on board caused a bit of a stir among the crew on the first few days. Even if I, the 'silverling,' could in an emergency produce something resembling that which was expected of a chief engineer, it was beyond any dispute that Billy Colepaugh was the strangest German naval lieutenant who had ever put to sea. We had camouflaged him as a war reporter, and as a sort of badge of office we had hung a magnificent camera round his neck. However, he put his hand to his camera at such totally unsuitable moments that his photographic skill was very soon seriously doubted by all the sixty-two members of the crew. The men could see that Billy was no German and no real naval officer. Whenever they spoke to him he just grinned and said yes.

I told the crew that Billy came from one of the former German colonies and that that was why he could not speak German. They listened to my story and continued to bait him.

One day, a stoker placed himself in front of Billy in one of the passageways.

"May I pass please, sir?" he said.

Billy shook his head.

"You do not understand?" continued the stoker.

Billy grinned.

"You're no lieutenant," said the man, "you big camel."

"O.K.," said Billy.

Scenes like this, whenever the men could relax, were a daily occurrence and speculation as to our real identity became a favourite topic of conversation among our shipmates.

We sailed out from Horten and on to Christiansund, the next and last German U-boat base. An antiaircraft cruiser gave us escort cover. Lieutenant Hilbig was besieged with questions about us.

"Are you out to win the Knight's Cross with a special mission?" the first mate asked him. Then, when Hilbig remained silent: "I hope you haven't got a sore throat, sir?" Hilbig laughed. He was tall, slim and fair and had flown sorties to England at the beginning of the war as a naval pilot until the lack of fuel brought about his transfer to the Navy. He was the archetype of active service naval officer. Although he never raised his voice or threw his weight about, although he never had much to say, he commanded absolute obedience. He had a minute cabin to himself, and this was the nerve centre of U-1230.

During the whole of the voyage, I saw Hilbig thrown off balance only once. We were just halfway across the Atlantic when he received news by radio that he had a baby daughter. Five minutes later depth charges were crashing about our ears.

We completed the voyage to Christiansund without mishap. The crew were preparing for their last shore leave. We met other U-boats in harbour, flying pennants on their aerials to show the tonnage they had sunk. The base was in a state of great excitement. That same morning distress signals had been received from a U-boat which technical difficulties had forced to surface while an enemy air attack was on. Three or four German ships had gone to its aid but all they had found was an enormous patch of oil which flowed slowly away to the north. Crosses were placed against sixty-two names. . . .

I went on shore in the afternoon, my last opportunity to see one of the servicemen's film shows. It was a love story full of heroics and men in immaculate uniforms. After the performance, the order was flashed on the screen in huge letters: "Attention! Please remain in your seats! Officers leave the hall first."

I went to a quay-side tavern and drank Holzschnaps. I had been warned about it but I had to get used to running greater risks than drinking Holzschnaps. This was the second time I had been in Norway. I had undertaken a mission there about eighteen months previously, at the end of 1942, which had nearly cost me my life.

I had been sent out to Norway then because our radio observers had located some secret transmitters there which we had so far not been able to put out of action. We had however, been able to decipher one or two messages at least partly, and it was from these that M.I. had first heard of Operation Schwalbe and discovered that the enemy planned to attack the 'Norsk-Hydro' near Vemork. The great Norsk-Hydro plant was the only factory in the world producing 'heavy water' (deuterium-oxide) in any considerable quantities. 'Heavy water' was needed to split the atom (in the case of the Hiroshima bomb the Americans were forced to use graphite as a substitute for 'heavy water').

I was told of a Norwegian contact in Oslo and I looked him up. We knew that the man was playing a double game, and I passed myself off as a British agent who had landed by parachute. I held a wad of money under his nose and asked him to bring me into contact as quickly as possible with two other agents whom I had lost sight of in the course of landing.

He gave me the address of an inn. I had it watched and within fourteen days we knew the names and addresses of all the people who regularly consorted there. We learned in fact that a few days previously an Englishman had had a talk there with two Norwegians. The Englishman was working under the cover name of John. I had to find this John whatever happened.

I had the two Norwegians taken into custody by the Norwegian authorities. On the third day of their arrest they were told that they had made derogatory remarks about Quisling, the Norwegian pocket Führer. At that time you could have held any Norwegian on this charge. After another four days, I let the men, who had never set eyes on me, go free again.

If they had known their job they would now have voluntarily isolated themselves. But they were no experts and it was upon this that I had set all my hopes. Their every step was watched. Two days later we trailed them into a street in a western suburb of Oslo in which—as the bearings had shown—a secret transmitter was being operated. We were certain that the transmitter was in the street but we had not been able to discover in which house. We refrained from searching the whole street to avoid attracting attention.

The two Norwegians disappeared into number eleven. I stood on the opposite side of the street. I had two other men on the job that evening. They were standing in the porch of number nine. The street was dimly lit by one solitary lamp. My two companions and I knew what John looked like. He was tall, very thin, very loose-limbed and had sparse hair. There were perhaps 50,000 Norwegians who answered to this description but we were determined that evening to arrest every man who was tall and loose-limbed and had sparse hair.

11:37 p.m. The police report prepared later recorded the minute exactly. The door opened. A man came out without an overcoat. He might be John. He must be John. He stopped, lit a cigarette and looked to the left and to the right. That might have been pure chance but it was not.

I could wait. I restrained myself from grabbing the man immediately but my two companions were too hasty. They went up to him, and one of them got his torch out of his pocket and shone it on him as he continued to stand there motionless. I was perhaps twenty yards away from him. My colleagues had approached him to within a distance of about six yards.

"Hands up!" one of them called and levelled his gun at the man.

Slowly, limply, looking rather bewildered, the man who was to be arrested raised his hands.

"Idiots!" I grunted to myself.

Then it happened. Suddenly and unexpectedly.

There was a shot, three, four, five shots. The man was still standing there with his hands up, but my two companions lay on the ground.

John had shot from the hip. By means of a trigger mechanism that could be operated even with raised hands. There was some sort of connection between the hand and the trigger. On this evening, we of M.I. lost two men and gained a new shooting device.

John made off like lightning with me in pursuit. I fired as I ran, shooting past him of course. But he disappeared, as if the earth had swallowed him.

I caught the two Norwegians, who were likewise trying to get away, for the second time. After lengthy interrogation they admitted that they had been working for the British. Parachute agents had been in contact with them and they knew that a British landing was planned in the neighbourhood of the Norsk-Hydro. I reported the matter to Berlin and was recalled.

A little later the German Military Commander in Norway, General von Falkenhorst, went personally to Vemork to inspect the defence installations there and have them reinforced, but in spite of that the British soon showed them to be destructible.

The British knew all about Vemork because the founder of the works, the Norwegian physicist Dr. Thronstad, having fled to England via Sweden when the Germans invaded Norway, had warned the British authorities that Germany should not be allowed to come into possession of the means of producing atomic bombs. When Germany ordered that the production of 'heavy water' should be stepped up from 1,500 kilogrammes to 5,000 kilogrammes a year, the Allies realised that their enemies were on the point of producing the atomic bomb, and they acted like lightning. The first thing they did was to drop four parachute agents who made contact with the workers with a view to discovering what were the possibilities of destroying the works. The factory was seven storeys high and built of steel and concrete. An attack from the air would be useless unless the bombs could be aimed with minute accuracy.

Then came two Halifax bombers with two freight gliders in tow. They came to grief on a mountain and there were a few dozen dead. But of what account were they when the atomic bomb was at issue?

On Christmas Day, 1942, six more agents landed in Norway. The day was chosen because the British, not without justification, hoped that the Germans would be sitting round the Christmas tree drinking punch. The saboteurs made their way into the completely desolate and uninhabited region of Vemork in a snowstorm. They were driven off their course and became separated, and it was weeks before they came together again. Two months after landing they had at last penetrated through to the Norsk-Hydro. On the 27th February, 1943, they overpowered the augmented watch, got inside the works, blew up the central plant and put the whole installation out of action for nearly twelve months. When the works were ready to go into production once more, a few hundred American aircraft arrived whose exceptionally heavy bombs proved stronger than steel and concrete.

It was intended that the supplies of 'heavy water' which remained should be moved to Germany, but in February 1944, the train ferry in which they were being transported blew up. The British Secret Service—as ever the best in the world—had attached a time bomb to the train. With this setback Germany fell finally into the rear with the production of the atomic bomb.

And now, a few months after the destruction of the Norsk-Hydro, I was sitting in a quay-side tavern in Christiansund drinking Holzschnaps. It tasted awful. In 1944 everything tasted awful. A few more hours and I would be on board U-1230 again, bound for America, to discover how far the Americans had got with the atomic bomb, and to ascertain by what means their production of it could be stopped. The Allies had all this behind them.

On the following morning U-1230 left port. We sailed mostly at a depth of 260 feet. Ninety revolutions a minute produced a speed of two knots. We were able to manage about fifty miles a day.

It was uncanny. The Atlantic was ruled above and below water by the Allies, and there we were, attempting to cross it in a tiny boat at snail's pace.

U-boat crews have a code of their own, and Billy and I had to fit in with it. During the war no boat sailed on the 13th or on a Friday. We had to get used to the toilets—one had to climb through a hole sideways and only reached one's objective after performing a variety of contortions. Those who managed it for the first time received a mock diploma in accordance with time-honoured custom.

The first bombs began to explode round the boat on our fourth day out. Warning of air attack! Alarm, submerge! The conning tower hatch was closed down immediately. Daylight disappeared, the boat went down, the air became foul. The interminable gramophone records, to be heard in every part of the U-boat from morn till night, fell silent. The captain gave his orders. Billy stood by me and held me tightly by the hand.

"What shall we do," he asked, "if a bomb hits us?"

"We will drown," I replied, "and then it will all be over."

He forgot to smile that time.

We listened to the bombs. We could feel the shock of the explosions. The detonations sounded unusually long drawn out and strangely distant, as if shots were being fired in a tunnel. Then the lights came on. The faces of the men relaxed.

"All over," said a mate who was near me. "You just have to make sure you disappear in time. But depth charges are far worse."

We remained below water. Once the enemy has located a U-boat he spares neither time nor persistence in its pursuit. We doubled back on our tracks. We changed our course. Lili Marlene could be heard once more but we knew that she might be reduced to silence by an explosion at any moment.

"Do you know yet where we're going to land?" asked Billy.

"No," I replied.

"What fools we were to let ourselves in for this," he went on. "It's quite crazy."

"You should have thought of that before. You said you hated America."

"That's quite true, I do," he replied. "But I value my life."

"And don't you think I do?"

I looked at him. Fear is quite a natural thing, I told myself. I recalled Margarete's words. I saw her before me, a small person with intensely blue, lively eyes and soft, well-cared for hands. I heard her say: "I don't trust him for a moment . . . you'll see, he'll betray you. Look at his ape-like arms. Look at his eyes. He can never look anyone straight in the face. You *have* picked out a fine one for yourself. The pride of Amt VI. You've got some surprises in store."

It was too late to worry whether I could trust him or not. I was dependent on him for better or worse. He carried his heart on his tongue. Well, what of it? He was young and had not had much experience of this war. And where is the heart that can go on beating calmly when bombs are exploding all round?

We crawled on across the Atlantic at two knots. Throughout the day no word could be spoken aloud because of the enemy sound detectors. Even under water we could only whisper. Every day when darkness fell we rose to periscope depth, 42 feet. If the sea was calm the Schnorchel was raised. This supplied engines and crew with oxygen. If because of nearness to the enemy it could not be used, the engines were worked by electricity. The oxygen in the boat sufficed for human lungs for a further thirty-six hours. Then it was exhausted.

The constant state of tension seemed to devour the time. We were altogether forty-six days en route, watching and being watched. We got used to the close quarters, the foul air, the depth charges, the whispering, the great odds stacked against us, the feeling of being alone and defenceless. The men spoke little of home but it was doubtless very much in their thoughts. At this period no U-boat would have dared to penetrate so far into the Atlantic without special orders. We wondered whether we would ever return. Who had the greater chance of survival, the crew of U-1230 who had to cross the ocean again or I who had to make my way to the atomic plant?

It was just bad luck for anyone who fell ill, for there was no doctor on board. Any man who still possessed an appendix would do better to stay at home. If a man died he was wrapped in a hammock, and had the German flag wound about his body. There was an adequate supply of flags on board.

Death stalked us between the Faroes and Iceland. We successfully evaded the bombs, but we should all have died from suffocation if Engineer Böttger had not taken instant action on his own initiative. The Schnorchel used to protrude above the water as little as possible and every time the waves washed over it the pressure fell within the vessel. Ears felt as if they would burst, the heartbeats quickened, breathing became more difficult and the head began to swim. The food tins burst or became misshapen.

On this particular unlucky day we had to use the Schnorchel in a heavy seaway. A huge wave washed over our ventilator thus preventing the exhaust gases from escaping. They therefore streamed back into the vessel and went straight to our heads. We began to lose consciousness. The

Diesel engines, which had been going at full speed, suddenly cut out, a thing which at that moment no one could understand. That is, no one but Engineer Böttger who was standing by the diesel. He immediately grasped what was happening, pulled out the clutch of the diesel engines, disconnected the shaft from the motor and changed over to the electric power. He was just in time. Eight men, Böttger among them, collapsed.

The boat, which with the failure of the diesel engines had suddenly started to sink, slowly rose again.

"Surface!" ordered Lieutenant Hilbig.

Drawn up by compressed air, U-1230 shot out of the water like a fish. The tower hatch was opened and the fresh night air streamed in. It was just in time. A split second's hesitation and the exhaust gases would have killed us. The eight unconscious members of the crew were hauled on ropes through the tower onto the deck. It was fortunate that at the time no enemy warship was in the offing.

Nearer and nearer to America. Nearer my fate. I went over my luggage. Was it nervousness or was it my sixth sense? I opened the packet of dollars I had been given only to find that they had been packed in bundles and that the wrappers round the bundles bore the words "Deutsche Reichsbank." With infinite trouble I had been equipped with American shoes, American shirts and other articles of clothing, American revolvers, but they had forgotten to remove the wrappers which would have been a complete giveaway.

We were still separated from America by four days, keeping in constant radio communication with our German headquarters and steering a direct course for the agreed landing point, Frenchman Bay in the State of Maine, when the signals rating rushed out of his cabin and thrust a wireless message at Lieutenant Hilbig. In a few minutes Hilbig had decoded it. I stood beside him. He looked at me, flabbergasted.

"The swine!" he said.

He read out the message in utter disgust and handed me the note.

"What do you make of that?"

I read:

"We have reason to believe that the enemy may be apprised of our undertaking. Act according to your own discretion."

I sat down.

"What are you going to do?" asked Hilbig.

"Have a cigarette," I replied.

He nodded.

"I'll come into the tower with you," he said. When we were up above he continued: "It's enough to make a man weep. Do you want to land now or not?"

"Of course I'll land," I replied. "But not in Frenchman Bay."

"Right."

"One more thing," I continued. "Colepaugh must be told nothing of this message."

We went back into the officers' mess and studied the charts in an attempt to find another landing place, but we were in for a painful surprise. Wherever we looked the water was too shallow to bring a U-boat into shore. In these circumstances there were only two possibilities, either to turn back or land in Frenchman Bay.

"It's not going to be any picnic," said the commander. "If the Americans have got their wits about them, they'll know well enough that we can only land in this bay. They only need to set up sounding apparatus and they'll have us. That being so, I must make a few preparations and get the boat ready for scuttling. We might fall into enemy hands and in that case I'm responsible for seeing the boat's scuttled."

"Yes," I replied. I knew that according to the code of U-boat commanders there was no greater disgrace than to allow one's vessel to fall into the hands of the enemy intact.

But we were in any case unable to steer a direct course for Frenchman Bay. There was yet another hitch in the form of a short circuit in the transformers which put our depth-sounding apparatus out of action. Without this apparatus it was hopeless trying to operate in a relatively shallow bay.

The ship's engineer informed the commander that with the means at his disposal he was not in a position to repair the apparatus. I recalled that I had once been a radio engineer.

"There's just a chance," I told the commander. "The transformers must be completely dismantled and rewound."

After three days of unremitting work the electrician managed to do this, and I myself fitted it back into the instrument. And it worked.

When we had neared the coast, I took bearings from a Boston radio station and confirmed our new position. We were in Fundy Bay.

"If your bearings are correct," said Hilbig, "we shall be seeing the lights of Mount Desert Rock in two hours' time." My bearings were correct.

The crew were told that Billy and I were going to land. Nothing more. They could think the rest out for themselves. No more details had so far been given to the crew as there was always the danger that they might be taken prisoner.

The bay was guarded by a destroyer. We dived below it and remained on the seabed. Throughout the day ships moved over us. We could hear the sound of engine and screws with our ears alone. We waited for the night and high tide. We rose to periscope depth and let ourselves be carried into Frenchman Bay between two islands. If the American coast defences had not been asleep we should have been discovered long since. The coast guards had to answer for all this later before the court-martial. The Americans made no use of their sound detectors or their radar apparatus. They already had victory in their pockets while we were trembling for our very lives. Current had to be saved and we could have no more cooked food. The cook prepared his cold dishes while the boat, fore and aft, was being made ready for scuttling. The captain allowed me two gallons of water to wash in, from his own special supplies. The first officer-of-the-watch cut my beard with an electric haircutter, and after three attempts I managed a proper shave with a razor.

It seemed incredible. We could hardly believe that we had remained all this time undiscovered: and still no depth charges, no U-boat chasers, no attacks from the air. We ate sandwiches and waited for night to fall. The men who passed by me pressed my hand. I had assisted as officer-of-the-watch and had got to know them all. The cook was a real character, known throughout the Navy. He was sea-sick on every voyage and on every return to port he vol-unteered for the next voyage out. The men murmured their good wishes. They wanted to question us, to warn us, to sympathise with us, to admire us.

I pondered for a long time whether I should go ashore in uniform or civilian clothes. If I went ashore in uniform and was captured I should have to be treated as a prisoner-of-war. If I wore civilian clothes I was a spy and would be hanged. But in any case I would have to remove the uni-form sometime for I could hardly be seen circulating in America in the uniform of a German naval engineer. Bury-ing the uniform seemed to me more risky than landing in civilian clothes. Billy too had to take off his uniform. He was green with fear and shaking at the knees.

"Everything will soon be all right," I told him. "Once we've landed we'll be all right. It's more dangerous here in the bay than on shore."

The time passed with immeasurable slowness. The sec-onds, the minutes, the hours stretched themselves like so much elastic, and the whole boat seemed to crackle with the tension.

"In two hours' time we will surface," said Hilbig. "We want to find out how near we can approach the coast. I will let the boat run backwards. We will remain on the surface while you row to land. I think you'll need fire cover."

"I'd rather you made off," I replied.

"No," he said, "I have orders to see that you are put safely on shore, and standing by is all part of my duty."

My baggage was ready, but I still did not know if I would be able to go ashore that day. I might have to wait several days yet. Perhaps I should have to ask the sixty-two men of the U-boat crew to wait another thirty-six or forty-eight hours in the threat of depth charges. We knew what the system of coast defence was but we did not know

exactly how it functioned on this section of the coast, how
the shore was watched and how many observers would be
on duty. Another hour, a half-hour, a quarter of an hour. I
stood beside the commander. He looked at his wristwatch.
We turned on the sound detectors. Nothing could be heard.

"Rise to periscope depth," ordered the commander.

Almost without a sound the boat moved upwards. The
periscope came out of the water and through it we watched
the coast. It was positively alive with activity. We were
still too early.

CHAPTER 8

The Landing in America

OUR pulses raced as we stood there in the tower, smoking, comparing the time by our watches. Before us in the periscope the coastline of the country into which I was to slip unnoticed seemed near enough to touch. How different it seemed from when I had studied it on a map in Berlin. A tongue of land hemmed around by reed beds, then hedge growth and behind that a wood, dissected by a road upon which car headlights could be seen moving. The moon had wrapped the reeds, hedges and woodland in a milky veil. Wisps of mist wafted out to us from inland. That anyhow was one good augury for Operation Elster. There were three things we needed—time, mist and luck.

A fresh breeze bore the mist away again, and suddenly everything lay clear and naked before us. With the fantastic magnification of our periscope we could see every bush and tree in detail. We were perhaps still about 350 yards from land.

"I'll try to get in a bit nearer," said Hilbig. "I'll turn the boat round once more and approach in reverse, but I shall have to take care the screw doesn't get caught."

The boat turned, smoothly and quietly, its engines at half throttle. Engines have no eyes, no heart, no feelings. The navigator had to call out the soundings without pause: 70 feet, 65 feet, 60 feet, 70 feet. Hilbig's lips were tightly compressed. He said not a word; he gave no orders; he had no need to; his men read his orders from his face.

We approached land by another sixty to seventy yards. Only our conning tower was showing out of the water. To the left was a house. No light was showing from it. We looked it over through the glasses. There was no sign of movement. Then another lorry came down the road, and was overtaken by a private car. One could see all this quite plain. Two dogs were sporting together and their howling sounded like the crying of a little child.

"Now," I whispered.

The commander nodded.

"One moment," he replied. "First we will train our artillery and machine guns on to the shore. If you are surprised jump into the water and swim back to us. I'll give them something to think about on shore meanwhile."

The inflatable rubber dinghy was fetched, its bottom still limp. It could not be pumped up until after it was taken on deck as it would not pass through the narrow tower hatch inflated.

"We'll wait twenty minutes after you've landed," said the commander. "If nothing happens then, we'll start on our way back. We can arrange our next meeting place tomorrow or in a few days' time. You can always reach us with your transmitter."

"If I once get over the landing I'll get through," I replied.

As we pulled the rubber dinghy through the hatch a beam of light came towards us, ever nearer. At night one always has the feeling that one is standing directly in the beam of a headlamp even if it is a mile away.

The rubber dinghy was thrown back and we waited motionless. It was a private car. We held it in our telescope. It was now on the spot at which the road ran closest to the coast. Soon the light would move away again. Another second, another two seconds. We already knew how the road curved from having watched the lorries go by.

But the light did not move away, it came nearer and nearer. It was quite uncanny. A car was drawing aside from the road. Why? How was it possible? We looked at each other. We followed the car with our glasses. It must now be 100, 150, 200 yards to the side of the road.

And then the mist came again, and once more we were blind for a while. Had the car something to do with the coast guards, or was it a navy shore patrol car? We knew exactly how the American coast defences were organised. Destroyers sailed up and down on the three mile limit, naval aircraft kept the coast under constant observation, while the shore was covered by the shore patrols of the coast guards according to a carefully worked out plan. The coast roads were covered by Army jeeps. The American coast defences formed a net five to six layers thick.

"Just look at that!" said the commander.

The mist had parted once again and the moon was now more clearly visible. I pressed the glass to my eye and saw the car. Was it a dream? A figment of the imagination? A man was sitting at the wheel with a woman beside him. He had put his arm round her and their faces were pressed close together. What was this? A tryst in a motorcar? That was something that could be seen on any road in the States. The Americans stay put in their cars whether they are going to attend divine service or see a Wild West film, so why should they get out of their cars to kiss and make love? And for that matter how often had I driven along such a stretch of coast road myself with a girl beside me? I had done it in Lima with Evelyn Texter, and wherever you go there is always an Evelyn Texter. There is always the need for her too when you have had too much to drink and not enough love. And there are plenty of Lovers' Lanes in America. You can suddenly turn off the main road, drive over a stretch of waste ground or over a field to a lane and here you can be alone. Alone to whisper, to kiss and swear eternal love.

But you usually turn off the inside lights of the car, a thing which our pair of lovers had evidently forgotten to do. We observed them through the telescope. Could we be mistaken? Were they what they appeared to be?

I stared at the car, but the longer I looked at it the more blurred the picture became. We stood there observing the couple for twenty minutes and were just thinking that we should have to postpone our landing operation when the car started up again and drove back into the night.

At just about the same moment snow began to fall in thick, wet flakes.

"Now!" I said to Billy.

The dinghy was brought up again, the compressed air tube attached to it, and in a few seconds it was inflated. Two hefty sailors stood ready. To deaden the sound of their paddles they had wrapped them round with rags. The commander shook hands.

"Good luck," he said. "You'll need it. I'll come back at once if you call me."

I nodded. My movements had become purely mechanical. I pulled Billy after me. He was stiff with fear, and was staring at the coast with terrified eyes.

"We'll soon be on shore," I said.

The dinghy was lowered carefully on to the water and we got in.

The snow was driving out from land and we could not see a thing. The water was slightly choppy. We sat in the dinghy, the two sailors paddling strongly and rhythmically. . . . Five yards away from U-1230, then ten yards, then fifteen, then twenty.

It would take us two minutes to reach the shore. Maybe three, maybe four. We sat there like two drones. In moments of danger one often tries desperately to think of something pleasant. We were now halfway there. We had 120–130 yards still to go.

Once more the headlamps of a lorry appeared on the horizon and we could hear the motor.

It's in third gear, I thought. No danger. It's going on. If the driver had been going to stop he would have changed down by now.

Another eighty yards. I had two revolvers in my pocket, both with the safety catches off. What would I have done if I had been on shore and had seen an enemy submarine? What indeed! If I had been alone, I would probably have done absolutely nothing. Or I might have gone to get help. Or I might have kept observation. There is no knowing if the night has eyes.

Another fifty yards.

"Remember the Dasch case," Colonel M. had said. "Don't be a fool. Have you still got the facts of his landing well in mind?"

"Yes," I had replied.

"Dasch was surprised by a coast guard, a dull-witted old man. And he stood there palavering with him instead of shooting him. Don't you make the same stupid mistake. Shoot, man! Remember your life is at stake!"

He had paused for a while and lit a cigarette. "And your mission too," he had added.

What should I do if the person who discovered me happened to be a woman, or a child or an old man? I had had to do many things that I had hated and despised, but I was certain that I could never bring myself to fire on women and children. I had agreed with Hilbig that I would try to take a prisoner and get him on board the U-boat. Throughout the voyage my mind had been filled with this idea. I had imagined how astonished everyone in Kiel would be when U-1230 arrived back with a prisoner on board, a prisoner straight from the American mainland.

With a slight creak the dinghy made contact with the bank. We were there. The two sailors remained seated. They looked as if they were about to say something.

I motioned them to be silent and gave them my hand.

I put one revolver in my left pocket. The other I held in my hand. We had packed the contents of the kit-bag into two suitcases. I gave Billy a gentle kick. He did not want to leave the dinghy.

We went on shore, each of us carrying a suitcase and a revolver. The ground was soft and mossy and squelched with every step, but after ten to fifteen yards it felt firmer. The snow was still falling and the branches of the trees brushed into our faces. We could not help making some noise.

The dinghy now moved off again. The two sailors had waited a few minutes although their orders were to row back to the U-boat at once. We could still see U-1230 with our naked eyes. Hilbig was waiting, his artillery trained upon the road.

We were now through the undergrowth and had reached the woods.

"The worst is over," I said. "Billy, if someone speaks to us, you answer."

I felt suddenly as if I could not trust my English. It was stagefright. I tried to think of various English words but my mind was a blank.

I had a minute luminous compass attached to my watch and had worked out even before I left Germany what direction I would have to take when I was once in the woods. The nearest sizeable place was Ellsworth, a small town two to three miles away, and this we wanted to avoid, for strangers always attract attention in a small town.

It was hard going in the woods; we tripped over tree roots, fell down and picked ourselves up again. And oh, those damned suitcases! There was no point in going on like that. We would have to get onto the road, whatever the consequences.

So we marched along the roadside, I on the left, Billy on the right. The first car approached and the light of the headlamps raked us from head to foot. The car came nearer, the light got brighter. We felt naked, caught, trapped. Billy made as if he wanted to take a dive back into the woods, but I held him back.

"Stay where you are, you idiot," I hissed at him. "If you go rushing off now you'll make yourself look much more suspicious than if you just carry on walking."

It seemed an eternity as we waited for the thing to overtake us.

It drove right past us; it was a lorry. On the hoarding at the roadside we read: "Melas Potato Chips. The best in

Boston." And on the other side: "Drive carefully. Death is so permanent."

"There you are," I said to Billy. "It's quite simple, and it's far better on the road than in the woods."

He nodded. He suddenly seemed to be in possession of himself again. Yes, I thought, it's a good thing I brought him with me.

How close we were to arrest at this hour on the Ellsworth to Boston road we learned only later. The whole of America had, of course, been warned by the Department of Psychological Warfare of the danger of spies and saboteurs, and the country had at first fallen a willing prey to Fifth Column psychosis. You can convince the Americans of anything if only you spend enough money on propaganda. But only for a limited time. The rabid enthusiasm with which they had first embraced the idea was not maintained, and when, after six months, then a year and then two years nothing much happened, no one took spy warnings seriously any more. No one, that is, but the children.

Half an hour after our landing a Boy Scout had cycled past us. He had been taking part in an evening singsong. He was fifteen years old, had close-cropped fair hair, blue eyes, a vivid imagination and a propensity for logical deduction. I got to know him in court much later, and there I learned his story.

He still believed in spies. We were carrying suitcases and no one in America carries a suitcase, at any rate not on a remote country road. We had no hats, and everyone in America, at any rate when he is out walking, wears a hat. We were wearing trench coats, while an American, at any rate in a heavy snowstorm, would have been wearing a thick winter overcoat.

To the fifteen-year-old boy we immediately became objects of suspicion, but he was not content with that. The American Boy Scouts cherish a unique romanticism which is something between practical neighbourly love and a game of Red Indians. The boy searched for footprints and found them in the soft snow. He took his torch and examined them. He applied himself diligently to his task and followed them right back to the shore. He was therefore convinced that we must have come from a ship, and he knew that there were two of us.

That same evening the Boy Scout reported his findings to the nearest police station. A fat sergeant roared with laughter and advised him to go home and get some sleep so as to be fresh for his lessons in the morning. But the boy would not give up so easily. He got in touch with the local branch of the F.B.I. At first they tried to throw him out, but when they saw that he was not to be diverted from his purpose they listened rather unwillingly to his story. He described his observations, presented his conclusions and reported the direction we had taken.

"You're a very good lad," he was told. "Carry on like this and you'll make a fine soldier one day. The only trouble is, the war will be over by that time. Oh no, there haven't been any spies here for a long time. It's only the Boy Scouts who still find spies. At the rate of fifty a day . . ."

We knew nothing of all this, of course, as we trudged along the road, tired, bad-tempered and already a little apathetic when we were not actually in the beam of a headlamp. Our hair was plastered down onto our perspiring brows, our feet ached, our arms were numb from carrying the heavy cases. I no longer had any illusions about our appearance. At best we looked like a pair of criminals. Even the most dimwitted policeman could not fail to notice us and the least he would want to do would be to examine our cases. And then that would be that. Or else I would shoot him as Colonel M. had instructed. Then perhaps I should be hanged four weeks sooner. . . . Once more a car approached us. The glare hurt our eyes. The fellow at the wheel did not dip his lights, but slowed down. As he changed gear there was a slight scraping sound. Something obviously was not quite in order. I thrust my hand into my pocket and put my finger on the trigger.

The car approached us slowly and stopped. The driver wound the window down.

"Hallo, boys!" he called over the road. Billy made as if to run away but I grabbed hold of him.

"Come on," I told him, "let's go over."

The man in the car was alone. We breathed again. He was perhaps fifty, had a chubby face and spoke with a Northeastern accent.

"What *do* you two look like?" he greeted us. "Where do you want to go?"

I had primed Billy as to what he should say. Now this was his moment. An opportunity like this would never occur again. He threw me a helpless look but I glared at him so fiercely that he finally realised that it was now up to him.

"We've had a bit of bad luck," he said. "A goddam awful business. My friend," he said, indicating me, "is that mad he can't even bring himself to say anything. I drove his car into a ditch: you can just imagine what I feel like."

"Have you got any money?"

"Sure."

"And where do you want to get to?"

"We've got to get to Bangor."

"You're in luck's way," said chubby-face. "This happens to be a taxi. It's out of service just now, but even so, it doesn't mind earning a dollar or two."

We got in. Billy sat in front on the right next to the driver. I sat behind, my hand still in my pocket, my finger still on the trigger of the Colt. Just as in some ridiculous crime novel. So far I had never killed a man. How would it be, I thought, if I were forced to do so now? Supposing, for instance, I had to kill the man who was sitting two yards away from me, talking to Billy? Talking about his eight-year-old daughter who wanted a pedal-car for Christmas. It had to be a red pedal-car, but it wasn't going to be a new one. He was getting a secondhand one. Even in America there were people who had to look at every dollar before they spent it.

"What are you going to do about your car?" asked the driver.

"Oh, we're not worrying our heads about that," said

Billy, laughing. "It's only an old bone-shaker. We'll have it hauled out of the ditch tomorrow. We may even let it stay there."

The driver laughed.

"I wondered first of all if I would even stop. You didn't look any great shakes, the pair of you. . . . But then I thought, well, you might have had some sort of accident. Whoever would be walking about in weather like this, carrying a suitcase, if he wasn't obliged to?"

"How far is it now?" asked Billy.

"Oh, another ten minutes or so. Would you like me to drive a bit faster?"

"No," answered Billy, "it's all right. There's not all that hurry."

I did not say a word. I sat slumped down on the back seat with the suitcases beside me. I hoped everything would be all right. But in any case my mind was made up. I knew that I should not shrink from the worst if anything should go wrong; if the man were to get difficult, or if he drove us out of our way. It was the night of the 29th–30th November. We had come on shore at two minutes past eleven. We had taken eight minutes to reach the road. We had walked for twelve minutes along the road before the taxi driver met us. We had now been six minutes in the taxi. It must now be about half-past eleven, if my calculations were correct.

I looked at my watch, an American one of course, procured in Germany with great difficulty; I was seven and a half minutes out. I listened to the conversation in front and wondered whether we would still be able to catch the train coming in from Canada in Bangor. We might just manage it. I sat there repeating to myself:

"My name is Edward Green. I am thirty-three years old. Honourably discharged from the American Navy on grounds of ill health. With the rank of Captain. I was born in Bridgeport, Connecticut. . . . My name is Edward Green. I am thirty-three years old. Thirty-three years and two months. I have been discharged from the American Navy on grounds of ill health. Honourably discharged . . ."

"There are the lights of Bangor already," said the taxi driver. "Where shall I put you down?"

"At the station," answered Billy.

That was of course thoughtless, but not without justification, for the silliest thing of all would have been to spend any longer in the neighbourhood of our landing place. Billy paid six dollars. I still said not a word. I had both the cases. I tried to walk to the waiting room in a matter-of-fact sort of way. Billy was already standing at the ticket office. He took two tickets to Portland. The train was due in four minutes. We had made it. That was something which we could not have expected beforehand.

We sat in a typical American day-coach in which everyone could see everyone else and hear everyone else's conversation. The arrangement of the compartment was similar to that of a German local train. In one corner sat five noisy G.I.'s. They had a bottle of whisky half-full and were telling some wild stories about a certain Elizabeth. Next to them sat a priest, his lips constantly moving as if in prayer. Two country women were discussing poultry farming. The train travelled smoothly and rapidly through the night.

Billy and I said not a word to each other. Our two cases were stowed away on the luggage rack, and I tried to keep my eyes away from them as much as possible.

Another twenty minutes, another sixteen minutes, then ten and then four. Then came the lights of Portland. We would still have to pass the barrier. Then we would be another step forward.

The G.I.'s were making an awful row on the platform. An officer looked at them disapprovingly, and they moved on a few steps, grumbling about the 'damned officers.' Then they threw the empty whisky bottle down on to the lines. Everyone who was about at the time, and it was one hour after midnight, was diverted by the G.I.'s. Everyone was laughing, or grumbling, about the soldiers and did not notice that we weren't wearing proper winter overcoats and were walking bareheaded through the driving snow.

Excitement makes you hungry. We handed our cases in at the luggage office and the whole future of Operation

Elster hung upon a yellow ticket, with which plus twenty cents I could reclaim my transmitter, invisible ink, diamonds, dollars and firearms.

We left the station and went along one or two main streets. They were more lively than German streets normally were in 1944. Santa Claus was already to be seen in the shop windows, wearing a white cotton-wool beard and a red coat as ever and always. He had long since fled from Germany.

Neon lighting was the order of the night. There was no blackout. Everything in the shop windows was still illuminated, gold watches, fountain pens, wallets, food, wines and spirits. At the worst money was tight.

It had stopped snowing. We went back to the station. We still had an hour and a half and then we would go on to Boston. If our landing had indeed been observed, no one would imagine that we could be in Boston on the following morning. There was only one snag about Boston. It was the birthplace of Billy Colepaugh. We could not avoid Boston but it was quite clear to me that I would not be able to let my companion out of my sight there for one instant. He had relatives and friends in the big city, and he was getting more and more jumpy the nearer we approached it.

We found a buffet on the station. A man in a white apron asked us what he could get for us.

"Ham and eggs," I replied. They were the first words of English I had spoken since we had landed.

"What bread would you like?" asked the man.

This was my first blunder. What bread? Were there various kinds of bread then? I faltered. The man repeated his question:

"What bread would you like with your ham and eggs?"

"Oh, anything," I replied.

He looked at me astonished.

"Well, would you like toast?"

"Yes," I replied, "toast will be fine."

I ate as quickly as I could and disappeared. The fact that in America people ate five different kinds of bread had caught me out.

There could be no doubt that the man had been surprised.

We took our seats in the Portland to Boston train. My blunder at the buffet had made me unsure of myself again. I had prepared myself so carefully in Germany, but I had not known about the five different kinds of bread.

I ran through my knowledge of America once again, asking myself how long was the Mississippi, how high was the Empire State Building, what were the names of the last ten American Presidents, who was leading in baseball?

I can't remember how long the journey was but anyhow the day was dawning as we stepped out of the train.

We now had to find a hotel and chose one near the station, the Essex. In America there is no compulsion to register at hotels and as a matter of fact no one carries any identity papers. You give your name, stay there, pay your bill and go. The man in the reception desk wrote our names in a black book without even looking at us and I felt pretty sure he could not have described us afterwards.

We took a double bedroom and slept until midday. It would have been better to have stayed in different hotels, but I had to take care that Billy didn't do anything foolish in Boston.

We ate in a cheap popular restaurant, and after that went to a department store near the station. I lost no time in buying myself two hats and we also got thick winter overcoats. I wore my trench coat only once more and that was in New York. I had gone into a shop to buy myself a tie and the salesman pointed to my coat:

"That coat wasn't bought in the States," he said.

"What do you mean?" I countered.

"I could see it at once from the cloth and the cut."

"You're right," I declared. "As a matter of fact I got it in Spain."

That day I finally parted from the trench coat.

We went back to the Essex and lay down on our beds with our hats and coats on to banish the too-new look of our American clothes. I had once read that Anthony Eden, at that time British Foreign Secretary, always adopted this method of removing the vulgarity of pristine newness from his suits. The tip now stood me in good stead.

We intended next day to travel on to New York. But we felt safer in Boston at night than on a railway train. At ten o'clock in the evening we were still in our room, which was not one of the best, with the wallpaper grinning at us. I did not want to go out, but I knew it was wrong to isolate myself. I had to get used to speaking to people. I must conquer my inhibitions. My English had a slight accent, not a German accent but rather a Scandinavian one, but how many Americans are there who speak English entirely without accent?

I would have to go where I would be least expected, if I was expected at all. I decided on the nightclub known as The Carousel.

True to its name, this was a sort of roundabout. The bar with bar stools and the guests seated upon them turned on its own axis, and only the waiters in the middle remained stationary. There was real Scotch whisky to be had. Doubtless it had crossed the Atlantic more safely than I had in U-1230. A five-piece orchestra was playing hot or sweet, according to taste, and without extra charge.

As we drank, I felt the tension ease, but every time the door opened and someone else came in I felt it there again. Could we be sure that we wouldn't meet any of Billy's friends? It was true that Colepaugh had not been in Boston for five years, but is not the life of a secret agent a constant battle with fatal chance?

A platinum blonde singer was performing in a ghastly mauve evening dress. She smoked as she sang, through an enormous cigarette holder. Billy made straight for her without the slightest hesitation, and she came back and sat between us at the bar.

"You don't belong here?" she asked.

"No," replied Billy.

"And who's this?" she said, pointing at me.

"A friend."

"You've got some very silent friends."

She turned to me.

"What's your name?"

"Edward."

"I've heard nicer names, but I like you. Shall we dance?"

"But nobody's dancing here," I said.

"Ah, dancing's in the next room," she replied.

The music was relayed by loudspeaker. Elly pressed herself close to me. She understood every word I said. She asked no more questions about where I came from and she did not ask where I was going to.

We drank champagne. We clinked glasses. It sounded gay and happy.

The champagne was paid for by Reich Security, but nevertheless it tasted good. I looked at my watch. I still had a few hours in hand. My train went at two minutes past nine in the morning, the train that was to take me to New York, the city where I was to carry out my first instruction.

But the bottle of Pomeroy was still half full. . . .

CHAPTER 9

Tricked by Billy in New York

NEW York received us with all the casualness of a great metropolis. It was swarming with soldiers due to go overseas within the next few days and meeting their dear ones for the last time before sailing. For this reason finding a hotel room was a major problem. Billy and I arrived at Grand Central Station. We left our luggage in the cloakroom and went to try our luck. After two hours' search we found a modest double bedroom in the Kenmore Hall Hotel on 33rd Street in Manhattan. I strolled past the skyscrapers with studied nonchalance although I had never seen them from close to before and was terribly impressed with them. I dare not stand gaping at them and give myself away as a stranger.

We had now been in America for three days, and I was beginning to feel more secure. I was speaking fluently now and letting the devil take care of my accent. Billy was enjoying the whisky, the generous supply of pocket money five thousand dollars, in fact, which I had given him soon after landing), and the willing attentions of the sort of girls whom one can buy anywhere in the world for round about two and a half dollars.

My immediate task lay in reading dozens of newspapers,

visiting the cinema four times a day, making friends with chambermaids, taxi drivers and waiters, in the interests of achieving complete acclimatisation. As far as America was concerned at this period, the war was taking place mainly in the newspaper headlines and the New Yorker was ignoring it in a way which made the hopelessness of my mission only too obvious. But it was not for me to have private doubts; I had to carry out my instructions.

Now, on my third day in the States, I was able to approach a policeman without a thumping heart, I could look a military patrolman smilingly in the face, I could deal with officials and was no longer embarrassed when I was asked what sort of bread I wanted with my hamburgers.

"It's killing," said Billy, "to discover that the F.B.I. are so sound asleep. They should have caught us long ago."

"Yes," I replied, "they should have!"

"Nothing can happen to us now. We're well in. The worst part was the landing."

"It certainly was—apart from our mission," I replied.

But he didn't want to hear anything about that. He strutted about town distributing tips, the size of which made my blood run cold. But I needed him desperately and I wanted to keep him in a good mood. New York was offering him more than bomb-damaged Berlin had been able to offer him a few weeks earlier.

I got busy assembling my transmitter. There were two possible methods for sending my news back to Germany. I had a note, written of course in invisible ink, of some cover addresses in Spain and Portugal. But to have written there would have been so obvious that the dumbest official in the Censorship Department would have become suspicious. It would have been better to use the names and addresses of certain American prisoners in Germany. We had made a close study of their family connections and respective habits and I could have sent a fabricated letter which would have given the impression of being utterly genuine, but between the lines, invisible to the censor, would have been the real text. The International Red Cross could have been made the unsuspecting go-between for my reports and the letters, which would have been directed to certain real names and addresses, would have been opened by M.I. and decoded. But even this course did not commend itself, for it would have been weeks before my reports reached the right quarter, that is to say, Amt VI.

I assembled my transmitter. The good old shortwave, I decided, was as ever the spy's best friend. There were in America, even during the war, many amateur transmitters. Conditions were by no means as strict as they were in Germany. If my set were to be seen—which of course I would try to prevent with every means in my power—I could still be taken for an amateur. The important thing was that all parts of the apparatus should be of American origin. Shortwave amateurs were not in the habit of working with German transmitters. . . .

I bought the various parts for my set from several different New York radio shops. I wanted to have as little to do with radio dealers as possible, and therefore took a very close look at their window displays before I went in so that I should not invite special attention by asking for something they had not got in stock.

I was standing in front of a shop window on 33rd Street wondering whether I could get a 6-L-6 tube there. For the last hundred yards a massive city cop had been walking behind me. He had been strolling along close to the pavement edge, wearing a sky-blue uniform with an outsize badge on his cap. Like all New York policemen he carried a light baton, and this he was swinging round and round from his finger by a cord.

He was walking quite slowly and keeping close to me. Gradually a feeling of suspicion, excitement, horror, crept up my spine. I looked straight in front of me at the shop window. He was perhaps now one yard away from me. I wondered if one of the radio dealers into whose shops I had been had become suspicious and sent the man after me. He had a good-humoured, rather bloated face and did not look in the least like a crafty captor of secret agents. But it had happened often enough in the past, that through some odd chance the most dimwitted policeman had caught the most accomplished spy.

He came to a halt beside me. At his right side he carried an enormous Colt revolver, the weight of which dragged his belt down. He pushed his cap slightly to the back of his head, pointed with his stick to a radio receiver and said:

"That's a nice job, isn't it?"

"Yes," I replied, "very nice."

"I wonder if it's any good?" he continued.

"You can never tell just from looking at the outside," I replied.

He pulled his cap forward again and placed it once more at the regulation angle.

"Perhaps I'll treat myself to it for Christmas," he said, and wandered slowly off. "I'll have to see what the wife says about it."

My nerves were jangling, but I waited until he was out of sight and then I took a taxi. There were still one or two surprises in store for me that day. I changed from 12th Avenue into 50th Street. At Pier No. 88 lay that luxurious ocean-going giant, the *Normandie*, half submerged. In 1942 the ship had been set on fire by German saboteurs.

We drove on. It's no fun driving through New York. You have to stop every hundred yards or so. I had had enough and had just made up my mind to ask the taxi driver to stop, when it happened.

At a road junction, at the top of 28th Street, I think, the lights changed to green. The driver, a short, stout man of about fifty, put his foot down and drove off with a jerk. At the same moment, a woman pedestrian who had not paid attention to the traffic lights ran straight into the car. The driver jammed on his brakes and did a quick turn to the left. But he hit the woman with his right mud-guard. He put his foot down on the the foot-brake; there was a screech and the car came to a halt horizontally across the road. The woman had been thrown against the pavement with the force of the impact and lay there unconscious. It all looked terrible.

The driver was nearly green with excitement. He turned round to me and said in a shaking voice:

"You saw it, sir, didn't you? It wasn't my fault, was it? The woman stepped straight in front of the car. I did everything I possibly could to avoid hitting her."

"Yes," I replied.

A crowd began to form. The driver pulled up by the pavement on the right. More and more people came rushing up to the scene of the accident. A young man took his jacket off and laid it under the woman's head. Two policemen arrived on the scene. The street was sealed off. The crowd was getting bigger every second.

"Clear off!" I said to myself. The slightest hesitation on my part and the police would register me as a witness. They would check up on my papers and all my personal details. They would notice my foreign accent, and would ask questions, dangerous questions. I went the first few yards slowly and when I had got free of the crowd of onlookers I ran as fast as I could. A woman was the first to notice me; she took me for the driver, and assumed that I wanted to run away.

"There he is," she called shrilly. "Catch him!"

Police whistles sounded behind me; passers-by called out; a man barred my path and I elbowed him out of the way.

I was now four to five hundred yards from the scene of the accident. I turned into a side street, ran to the left, then to the right, then once more to the left. I took a taxi and drove for two minutes. I got out, rode for three stations on the underground, got on a bus, took a taxi, got out of the taxi, went into a department store, bought some lemons, a wristwatch and a new hat and ate some steak.

No one was following me. Once more I had got away. . . .

Cautiously I returned to my hotel. Billy was not there. There was a note on my bed:

"Just gone to have a drink. Hope you don't mind. Back in two hours."

I lay on my bed. I had already put my radio parts together. I sat up and decoded the address of a New York businessman who was to put me in touch with people in the atom industry. I learned the address by heart and burned the note. I paced up and down the room. I ordered a whisky, but it did nothing to still my disquiet.

Obliquely opposite my hotel was a cinema. I went in. It was frightful. For an hour and a half I sat through a film which purported to show how German soldiers were mishandling Russian civilians. A Russian woman who had given shelter to a partisan lay on a dung heap and gave birth to a child. Meanwhile German soldiers stood around making jokes. Then came the heroine. A blonde Russian put her arm round her lover, who was a captain in the German Army, and indicated who should be shot. This piece of trash could hardly have been surpassed for lack of taste and for the hatred it tried to inspire. It was the American counterpart of Veit Harlan's *Jew Suss*. I went back to the hotel, drank a few more double whiskies and went to bed.

Suddenly I was awake. I looked at the clock. It was three o'clock. The other bed was still empty. Billy was missing. I was immediately wide awake. I sat up and dressed without turning on the light.

Had he been arrested? Would he have betrayed me intentionally, or unintentionally? What methods did the F.B.I. have of getting a man to talk?

I left the hotel. No one noticed me, at least I hoped not. I walked over to the other side of the street. There was a house which was not locked up. I stepped inside and observed from the passageway what was happening in front of my hotel, wondering what the F.B.I. would do if . . .

Perhaps they would send Billy back to me alone. Perhaps detectives would come and search the hotel. Perhaps they had men posted on the other side to keep an eye on me from close quarters. I smoked one cigarette after another, holding the lighted end to my palm to conceal the glow.

My cases were in the hotel room. I had with me only a small wallet containing some money and a revolver. My observation post was by no means ideal. At any minute someone might come out of the house or enter the house, and a strange man, who at three in the morning stands in the unlit passageway of a house, is already half arrested.

Half-past three. Four o'clock. The night seemed to stretch itself endlessly. There was no sign of Billy. In my imagination I could already see him being put under pressure by the police. I could see his face quite close to me, white with sweat, uneasy, tormented. Then I visualised him sitting in a bar with a blonde woman on his lap and stuffing five-dollar bills down her dress. What was true and what was false in these workings of my imagination? Five o'clock. A mist descended over New York. I wondered whether I should leave my hiding place and walk up and down the street. But I told myself that that would certainly be a mistake. The whole street, not only the occupants of the houses, would notice me then. The seconds passed slowly by; sixty seconds one minute, sixty minutes one hour. You can't have any conception of how long an hour can be if you have never stood motionless and fearful on one spot, waiting, waiting, smoking, staring into the night until your eyes burned, until you've seen movements that were not there and experienced things which existed only in the imagination.

Half-past five. The mist was lifting slowly. Traffic on the road was becoming more dense. Soon the early risers would be getting up. I had now been in America for four days. I stood there waiting, hoping, trembling with my eyes fixed on the entrance of the Kenmore Hall Hotel. I realised that I could remain in my observation post for only a few minutes more. The patches of mist had disappeared, and it was growing lighter with every minute. I would have to leave this entrance and I had to make up my mind either to leave my suitcases where they were or wait in the hotel room for Billy and thereby risk arrest. I looked at my watch. "I'll stay another three minutes," I said to myself. Then two minutes were left. Then only one minute remained.

Traffic was increasing; workers on early shift were passing along the street. I gave myself another two minutes, and then another four. I was just about to leave the house when I heard Billy. I heard him before I saw him. He was not alone and he was not sober. He was laughing uproari-

ously as he staggered slowly nearer. I could see him now.
Whisky was written all over his bleary face. He was prop-
ping himself up against a woman who was also drunk. The
two of them had their arms around each other supporting
each other and were laughing and giggling.

Was it a trap?

I remained in the background. In the shadow of a house.
Billy and his companion came nearer. If they were putting
on an act for my benefit on instructions from the F.B.I.
they were brilliant performers. But no, it was genuine. It
must be genuine.

They stood in the hotel doorway, he clutching on to her.
She had trailing peroxide-blonde hair which fell in untidy
locks over her shoulders, a face that had once been pretty
and a figure that was still good to look at.

"Come along up with me," said Billy.

"You alone?"

"No," he replied, "a friend's with me."

She muttered something to herself. Then I thought I
heard her say: "Why don't you move out?"

"That's just what I will do," replied Billy. "Just wait and
see."

"And then come on to me," she said. "Why don't you
come with me straightaway?"

He was standing twenty yards away from me hanging
on to the wall. I wanted to step forward and jerk him back
to his senses, but I did not want his girlfriend to see me.

"No," answered Billy. "Not until tomorrow . . . but tomorrow I'll come, baby. You can depend on that."

She went on her way alone, staggering along the street.
I shadowed her. I wanted to see if she still staggered when
she was out of sight of Kenmore Hall. I followed her for
ten minutes and no longer had any doubt that she was really
drunk.

Billy had already undressed when I got back. There was
no point in trying to talk to him there and then. I would
wait a few hours. In fact, I could now take a few hours'
sleep myself.

I woke up at nine o'clock, pulled Billy out of bed,

dragged him to the washbasin and held his head under the cold water tap.

"Leave me alone!" he cried.

"The devil I won't," I replied. "I've just about had enough of your nonsense. You stay with me now and stop drinking."

"I'll damn well do what I like," he answered.

He sat crouched in front of me looking as if he'd have liked to hit me.

"Six weeks on that damned U-boat," he went on, "then that hell of a landing with the rope nearly round your neck . . . and then when we get here you start lecturing me like a bloody schoolmaster."

His jacket was thrown over a chair. I took the wallet out. He still had three thousand five hundred dollars. In three days Billy had spent one thousand five hundred dollars. Anyone who goes around town spending money like that attracts attention and for us to attract attention to ourselves was as good as the end.

What was I to do? I needed him, but I could not chain him to myself with handcuffs. Later, some weeks after this episode, an official of the F.B.I. was to say to me:

"You made only one mistake . . . you should have given Billy a shot between the eyes as soon as you landed. . . ."

Billy and I sat at breakfast. I had scrambled eggs and ham. He had soda water and headache powder. He looked pale.

"I don't want to make trouble for you," he said, "but you don't understand. After what we've been through a chap must have a bit of pleasure."

"I've nothing against that," I replied, "but you can't go around giving twenty dollar tips for a couple of steaks and a bottle of wine."

"And why not?" he asked. "Do you know New York, or do I? Either I'm the pilot on this trip or not. In New York it's the small tips that send the eyebrows up, not the big ones."

I let him go on talking and he soon stopped on his own accord.

Everything was now ready. The transmitter was working and Billy was halfway towards becoming a reasonable human being. For the moment we had only temporary accommodation. For the following day we had new quarters in view, an apartment, not a hotel. At last I could conduct myself with some degree of confidence. I had deciphered the New York addresses. The first was the address of a Mr. Brown of 41st Street. It was a business house. Mr. Brown had apparently made himself useful to Germany a few years previously on matters of espionage. I decided to call on him in the afternoon.

Billy wanted to stay in bed and I had nothing against it. I could not do with him around when I went to make my call.

I took a taxi and went the last six hundred yards on foot. Mr. Brown ran a stockbroker's office on the eighth floor. I went up in the lift. The business occupied only two offices, a reception room and the boss's room. A red-haired secretary received me.

"What can I do for you?" she asked.

"I want to see Mr. Brown."

"And what is your name?"

"Kenneth W. Smith."

"And what do you want to see him about?"

"I want to see him on business."

"He's not in," she replied, "but you can have a word with his wife if it's important."

"It's not as important as that," I replied. "When is he expected back?"

"Tomorrow."

She lit herself a cigarette and opened the window.

"You can stay in the cinema until then if you like, or don't you need any tips on how to kill time in New York?"

"No, thank you, I don't," I replied. "I know my way around."

She looked charming and I should have liked to have invited her to have a meal with me, but it was not a good thing to have a girlfriend who was the secretary of a 'business friend.'

In Amt VI they swore by this Mr. Brown, but they had

sworn by a good many people in Amt VI to no good purpose.

I bought myself a few papers and went slowly back to my hotel. I covered the first stretch on foot. The fresh air did me good. Once I had been able to get in touch with Mr. Brown on the following day everything would be in order. I would now go and have something to eat with Billy, then we would go to a cinema and then perhaps I'd go to a nightclub for two or three hours.

I covered the last stretch to the hotel in a taxi. I walked slowly across the foyer. The doorman looked up.

"Have you forgotten something?" he asked.

"What do you mean?"

"Well, you've already moved out, haven't you?"

"I don't understand," I replied.

"But the bill has been paid. Your friend saw to everything. He said you'd already gone away. That was why I was surprised when I saw you walk in again."

I tried to conceal my consternation as well as I could. Billy had disappeared. Billy had flown.

"Is something wrong?" asked the porter.

"No," I replied. "Everything's fine."

I walked on a few yards and then turned round once more.

"What did he do with the luggage?" I asked.

"He took it with him."

"Both suitcases?"

"Yes. Both of them. I was going to call a taxi but he said it wasn't necessary; he hadn't far to go. He seemed to be in a great hurry."

I gave the man a few cents and went out into the street. The situation I now found myself in was indescribable. The transmitter, the revolvers, the diamonds, the dollars. All gone. All gone with William Colepaugh.

There I stood with my mission hardly begun and with about three hundred dollars in my pocket. Everything swam before my eyes. With three hundred dollars I had somehow to find Billy somewhere in America. If I did not find him within the next few hours it would be all up with me.

CHAPTER 10

I Work Out My Own Salvation

THE trail of a man who walks through New York in broad daylight carrying two large suitcases is not all that difficult to follow. The doorman at the Kenmore Hall Hotel on 33rd Street knew the direction Billy had taken. A newspaper man had seen him, and a shoe-shine boy had seen him too. I followed the trail. I had to take care not to make myself conspicuous by asking questions that were too pointed.

Billy had evidently been thinking only of the money and the diamonds. The cases had extra strong locks, and the keys were in my trousers pocket. It would be impossible for Billy to break the cases open without the help of an expert. He would first have to take his booty to some safe place and think up a story with which he could later approach a locksmith.

Another point to be borne in mind was that Billy was wanted all over America as a deserter and in that way he was in a more difficult position than I was. I had already been taken into American custody in 1942 and had been the subject of an exchange repatriation. But I knew for certain that on that occasion the F.B.I. had neither photographed me nor taken my fingerprints. I had in fact been only an internee, and internees were not worried overmuch, at least not in the opening stages of the war.

"What would you do," I kept asking myself, "if you were in Billy's place?" Leave New York! That was quite clear. As quickly as possible, and preferably by train. That way would arouse the least attention. In one of the long-distance expresses. Change trains once or twice on the way. And where should I get in? At the nearest station of course!

Which station was the nearest? I went into a snack bar and consulted a street map of New York.

"Are you looking for something special?" asked the bar-tender.

"No," I replied. "I'm just wandering around New York. I only wanted to see where I was."

"Is this your first visit here?"

"No, I've been once before," I replied. "But I didn't have time then to take a good look at the town."

I drank some coffee and ate doughnuts, swallowing down the haste, the anxiety, the horror, forcing myself to keep calm. I knew that I should have to go after Billy with my head rather than my legs. He had acted upon impulse; that much was quite clear to me. Billy was the sort of man to do a thing first and think about it afterwards.

I had a sudden flash of inspiration. Of course, Billy would have gone to Grand Central Station. If he had not found a train at once he would wait somewhere nearby. For two or three hours perhaps. He would not stand on the platform with the suitcases. He would hand them in at the left luggage office as we had done when we first arrived in New York.

I went to Grand Central Station. There was not a sign of Billy. I confirmed from the timetable that no long-distance train had left the station in the period immediately preceding. I wandered through the restaurants and bars, walked over the platforms and into the lavatories. No sign of him. There was just one chance that remained. The left luggage counter.

"Check your baggage." The words stood on all four sides of the left luggage office, which was placed right in

the middle of the station so that one could walk right round
it. It was half-past five in the afternoon. The place was
swarming with tired rush-hour crowds. Queues were forming at the quick service buffets. Newsboys were striding up
and down the main concourse shouting the headlines.

"Body in the Hudson identified . . ."

"Unhappy love affair drove her to the river!"

"If Bill had kissed her yesterday, she would still be alive
today!"

I let myself be carried by the crowd as near to the left
luggage counter as possible. I was obsessed with one fixed
idea. "Your cases are here," I told myself. Hundreds of
cases were standing close together and piled on top of each
other. The two top-most rows of shelves were still empty.
If luggage was left for a considerable time it was always
put up high. Only when those racks which were easily ac-
cessible from all sides were full, would the officials use the
full depth of the shelves, and stack the cases one behind
another. I could only see the luggage from the outside, but
if Billy, when he handed the luggage in, had said he would
be back for it in an hour or two, it would just be left on
the ground.

Twenty times, thirty times I walked round the left luggage place. Driven and impelled by one thought: It is here;
it must be here; here is your last chance, your only chance.
I bought a newspaper, went back into the crowd and stood
there reading. Again and again I forced myself to look at
the cases. I changed sides; I heard comments on the war
situation, listened to background details about the love
drama in the Hudson river, learned the advantages of a new
nail varnish and the disadvantages of a secondhand car.

I went round to the second side. That was where lost
luggage was claimed. Still less hope of success. And perhaps I had only half an hour, ten minutes or perhaps only
five minutes to do what I had to do.

I posted myself on the opposite side of the luggage
place, pushed this way and that in the stream of humanity,
looking at the cases, walking and walked upon. Two policemen were pushing their way through the crowd with a

determined air. Were they after me already? No, they passed me by.

And just at that moment I saw them. I saw my cases! Three or four yards from the ramp, standing there solidly and indifferently, side by side. Two harmless pieces of luggage in company with a hatbox, an umbrella and a hold-all. There was no doubt about it; they were my cases. There was the property of Amt VI, stolen by my colleague. There was Germany's last desperate attempt at espionage during the Second World War. Favoured by luck, whipped on by desperate hope, I had found my cases again in the biggest city in the world!

It was a quarter to six. I stood there and pondered. Any moment Billy might arrive. He would sneak up to the counter and of course he would see me. That could not be avoided. But what would he do then? Would he come up to me or would he run away?

I knew him and I believed that he was now more frightened of me than he was of the F.B.I. But would he go to the American authorities and try to save his own head by forfeiting mine? That he would not do. He knew precisely what Americans did with traitors, even if they had done them a service. They would accept his information, interrogate him, hold him under arrest and put him before a court-martial, just as they would do with me. In that way they would be consistent. We should both get the death sentence. In the case of the traitor Dasch, at least on the occasion of Operation Pastorius, it had been like that. It might be that after the trial Billy's sentence would be commuted to life imprisonment, and I alone would be put to death, as in the case of Dasch. . . .

Ten to six. Six persons, four men and two women were standing at the counter. The handing out of the luggage was going quickly and smoothly as I watched. The officials looked at the numbers only superficially, the people pointed to their cases, and had them handed out to them a few seconds later. I got nearer to the ramp. Six yards separated me from my cases. I could not simply take them. There were too many people around for that, but I must have them. There were three clerks at the counter. I wondered when they would be relieved. I had been hanging about the place for so long that I felt they might have noticed me. If I had aroused suspicion then it would be hopeless to try to get my property back in the conventional way.

When, a few days previously, Billy and I had handed in our luggage at Grand Central Station and the whole future of Operation Elster had hung upon a number on a ten-cent ticket, I had asked Billy in fun:

"What should we do if we lost the ticket?"

"Oh, it wouldn't matter that much. If you can show that you've got the keys they'll always give you the cases. They're not so punctilious in America, and it's not often anything is stolen. No one's going to get himself sent to prison for the sake of a suitcase. If a man is a criminal he'll concentrate on something more profitable."

Was he right? Should I try it? I had to try it. But not until the present three clerks had been relieved.

I must move away from the ramp and wait in the background. I must keep my eye on the entrances. I must look out for Billy and at the same time watch the left luggage counter.

Two minutes to six. When would they be relieved? Could I enquire about this? No. No one takes any interest in the working hours of luggage clerks. I bought myself a paper. The corpse in the Hudson River had had further repercussions. "Was it murder?" ran a subheading. Americans had had enough of the war. What a refreshing change it was to have a murder, so long as you'd had nothing to do with it yourself.

Three men in uniform caps went up to the counter. Was this the relief? It was! The men exchanged a few words, nothing of any importance, I could see. Oh God, how long were they going to hang about? Why didn't the other guys go home? It was time. They ought to be glad to get off. Their wives would be waiting with a meal for them and the children would be looking forward to seeing their fathers. Dammit all, men, get moving!

They went off in leisurely fashion, obviously in no

hurry. What could they know of me, my fears, my hopeless situation, my mission? They walked past me. One of them looked me in the face, but I didn't think he was at all suspicious. There were two people at the counter. Now there was only one. I went up to the ramp. Would my English be all right? Of course it would! Enough of all these anxieties! I hurried the last steps and was quite out of breath; at least I pretended I was. One of the three clerks came over to me at once and said: "You're in a hurry, aren't you?" and laughed good-naturedly.

"I've got to catch a train," I replied.

"Your ticket, please?"

I searched my pockets. My left overcoat pocket, the right one, my ticket pocket, my trousers pocket. I got more and more flustered and more and more desperate.

"Take your time, sir," said the clerk. "You'd better lose your train than lose your luggage."

"But I can't lose the train!" I blurted out.

"Where are your cases?" asked the man.

"There they are."

"Well now, just look for your ticket quietly," he recommended.

The game began again. Was my act convincing? One or two people were looking at me. Supposing Billy were to come now, or a policeman were to tap me on the shoulder, or a detective of the F.B.I.?

I looked at the man at the counter. I remember thinking to myself that he was about fifty, five feet six tall, and would weigh about twelve and a half stones. He was at least ten pounds overweight, was married and wore a wedding ring. He might already have been a grandfather. In three years he would be bald. He already had no hair at all in front, and was very sparse at the temples. Just above the left corner of his mouth he had a wart. I'd get rid of it if it were mine, I thought. I'd either lance it or use nitrate of silver.

"It's ridiculous," I said. "I've lost the ticket. What am I going to do now?"

"You can go into the office," he said. "You may be

lucky, but there are bound to be some complications. I think you'd do best to go home and look for the ticket. You'll have lost the train by now in any case."

"Where's the office?"

"Here. Behind the glass partition."

It was odd how all the luggage clerks looked the same. The man in the office had his cap on. Perhaps that was one of the rules. He was sitting down with his legs stretched out, talking to two women. One of the two women was very young and pretty, but I had no time for pretty young women.

"In 'Latest News'," said the elder of the two, "it says quite clearly that he murdered her."

"Nonsense," said the clerk. "That's only what the reporters write. In the morning they'll say that the police made a mistake. They always do it like that."

"He's a handsome fellow, the murderer," continued the woman. "Did you see his photograph?"

"He wouldn't be to my taste," said the young one. "His cheekbones stick out too much and his nose is too squat. He looks to me like a prizefighter."

"Lily's got extravagant tastes," said the older woman. "Anyhow it doesn't really matter. He's not in the running now."

"Can I help you?" At last the clerk took notice of me, looking towards me without any particular interest.

I told him my story about the lost luggage ticket. The two women listened. They made no attempt to leave the room. The younger one had bright blue eyes and a high vaulted brow, but I still had no eyes for feminine beauty. She stared at me openly, at the same time managing to look as if she were gazing past me.

"I can't let you have your cases," replied the clerk. "We have to abide by the rules."

"But there must be some solution," I replied. "It must sometimes happen that someone loses his ticket. What do you do then?"

"You take a form," he replied, "and describe the contents. Then you wait three months. If no one else has been to claim the luggage in the meantime the cases are then opened. If the contents tally with your description they are then returned to you."

I took the keys from my pocket.

"Here are the keys," I said. "Look at the lock. It's a very heavy one. I can tell you exactly what's in these cases, but I can't wait three months. I've got to get to Chicago today."

The clerk nodded.

"What I should like to know," said the older woman, "is how he did it. He can't have strangled her in the water. But if she was already dead when he threw her in the water, the police would have found the marks of strangulation on her throat yesterday."

"You ought to have joined the police force," said the young woman.

"Well, let's take a shortcut," said the head clerk of the left luggage office.

"What a good thing we're not in Germany now," I thought.

"What's in the cases?"

"Shirts, socks, two suits, a suit of pyjamas."

"You must give more precise details than that," said the clerk. "That description would fit any suitcase."

"Two white, one green, one pink shirt. And a camera, a very valuable one, a Leica."

There were so many Leicas in America that the German make would not seem particularly strange.

"One moment," said the clerk. "Show me the cases."

I held them in my hand! But only for a few seconds. I carried them into the office. The clerk opened them. The left lock jammed. I helped him. The case had a false bottom. In the false bottom were radio parts, two revolvers, a bag of diamonds, a wallet with about 55,000 dollars. . . . If the man were to take a good look he would find everything. A telephone was at his elbow. He could call the station police. A flick of the finger would be enough and I would be arrested.

The clerk took the Leica in his hand.

"That's a fine camera," he said. "Set you back a bit, didn't it?"

"Yes," I replied, "at least 450 dollars. It's a German make."

"Damn the Germans," he said, laughing.

He put the Leica back in the case, locked it up again, opened the second one and examined it equally superficially.

"Well, you can have your cases," he said, "but you must first let me have your signature."

The man seated himself at the typewriter and typed an inventory with two fingers. He took a terribly long time over it. Or perhaps he only appeared to. Time always seems interminable when you are standing on hot coals. . . .

At last he had finished. I offered him a dollar tip but he thanked me and declined it.

"Give it to the guys outside," he said. "They need it more than I do."

Now away! I heaved a sigh of relief, but I had to be careful not to move too hastily. I must go in the direction of the platform as the clerks at the left luggage counter would certainly be looking after me. And then I must double back. A train was just coming in and I was able to mingle with the people who were leaving it. I had done it again! There was still no sign of Billy. I looked at the clock, it was 6:31. I had to cover another fifty yards to reach the main exit. Now twenty, now ten. I was carried out of the station with the crowd.

"Taxi?" a driver asked me.

"Yes," I replied. I hesitated for a second and looked round once more.

It had been a million to one chance!

What luck I had had again!

But oh, my nerves!

"Hello, Erich!" a voice called behind me.

I swung round. Oh, the devil take it, my name was Edward! But who could be completely master of himself in such a situation!

"Erich, Erich, it can't be true!" the voice continued. Fall-

ing over me, embracing me and kissing me with all the
demonstrativeness of the South American was Paolo Santi,
an old friend from Peru. . . .

The people around me were standing still, either amused
or annoyed by this touching scene. I took Paolo on to one
side.

"Have you got half an hour to spare?" he asked me.

"Yes, have you?"

"Oh, I'll let my train go hang," he replied. "I'll take the
next one. I'm on holiday so I needn't worry."

He smiled at me.

"You've got thinner," he said.

"Yes," I replied.

We took a taxi and went to a restaurant. I handed in my
cases at the cloakroom. Santi had sent his luggage on ahead.

"Now tell me," he said, "how on earth d'you happen to
be in New York?"

I rapidly improvised a story. Actually I had no idea what
Paolo Santi could be doing. In Lima we had gone to dances
together, played poker and pursued the girls. Then I had
been arrested. . . .

"You know, don't you," I said, "that I was deported
from Peru? All because of this damned silly war. Now I've
come to North America. They locked me up for a time,
then they offered me my release if I would stay in the States
and work. I didn't have much choice, and I'm quite sure
Germany will lose the war perfectly well without my assistance; so I'm staying on here. Up to now I've been doing
my own job in Boston."

"And what's happening now?"

"A silly business. My boss has a very young and pretty
wife. You can guess the rest. At the moment I'm out of a
job. I've only just arrived here. Tomorrow I'm going to
start looking for something."

He roared with laughter at my story.

"Still the same old Erich," he said, and gave me a hefty
thump on the back.

"What are you up to?" I asked him. "Married yet?"

"I've been married twice," he replied. "And the day after

tomorrow I'm getting married for the third time. I've found the right one at last. D'you know, only the third American ever clicks. And so far I've only married Yankees."

Now it was my turn to roar with laughter.

"Have you settled down in the States for good then?"

"Yes," he said. "I have to pay my alimony in dollars."

"And you're living in New York?"

"Yes, I've been living here all the time," he replied. "I've got a nice bachelor apartment. It was very pleasant in between the two marriages. Now it looks as if I've got to give it up again."

I was on this in a flash.

"So your apartment is vacant now?"

He grasped the situation immediately.

"Of course," he said. "Fancy my not thinking of that before!" He thrust his hand in his pocket, dragged out a bunch of keys, and put them on the table.

"Here you are," he said. "Help yourself. It's on 44th Street. Number twenty, eleventh floor. The small key is for the lift. As far as the others are concerned you'll have to try them all until you find the right one."

I could hardly believe my eyes and ears. Paolo was beaming at me as if he would have liked to drown me in his smiles.

"Happy now?"

"Yes," I replied. "But you must let me pay you something for it."

"Nonsense. When I get back it will cost you a bottle of whisky, which we'll polish off together."

We took our leave and I let him go back to Grand Central Station alone. He looked put out for a moment. With South Americans you can do anything, but you must never be discourteous. I told him that I had a bad headache and was able to reconcile him to my apparent discourtesy.

I collected my cases and took a taxi. I changed taxis twice. The neon light advertisements were shining brightly, and there was a Santa Claus in every shop window. I felt so grateful for my good fortune that I wanted to raise my hat to him. I covered the last three hundred yards on foot.

I found the lift key at once. I met no one—a further stroke of luck on this exciting day. Eleventh floor. The third key I tried fitted. I turned on the light.

It was a wonderful apartment with bedroom, living-room, study, kitchen and bathroom. It had every comfort, which was unusual during the war even by New York standards. And there I was, quite alone with three rooms and a kitchen and bathroom. I wished Paolo every success in his third marriage.

At the same moment as I was moving into Paolo's apart-ment, a thin, dark-haired young man arrived at the left lug-gage counter on Grand Central Station with a perfectly valid ticket and requested his two cases. He appeared timid and excited but not so timid and excited that it would have struck the luggage clerks if they had not later been inter-rogated by the F.B.I.

"My cases," he said.

"One moment, sir."

The luggage clerk searched, shook his head and went on looking. He went to his colleagues, showed them the ticket, and the three of them started to look. They looked, of course, in vain.

What happened now was recorded in the report prepared by the F.B.I. a few days later.

"We're very sorry, sir," said one of the men. "We can't find your luggage. Would you please come to the Chief Clerk. We must take full details."

"I handed the cases in just three hours ago," said the young man, Billy Colepaugh. "They must be here."

Passengers who wanted to get their cases out were piling up behind him, already getting impatient. Billy stood on the ramp not knowing what to do next. Completely thrown off balance, he let himself be taken to the chief clerk. He had still not tumbled to the fact that I had outwitted him.

"Your cases were collected twenty minutes ago," said the clerk, "by a Mr. Green, Mr. Edward Green. The man told us he had lost his ticket. He was in possession of the keys and gave us an exact description of what was in the cases. I'm very sorry, sir. Perhaps in this case we were not quite careful enough, but I must say we did act correctly. How was it that the man had your keys?"

Horrified, struck dumb and at his wits' end, Billy stood there, incapable of moving, incapable of speaking.

"I'll call the police," said the chief clerk.

"Please don't," said Billy. "I don't want to make a charge. The matter will clear itself up."

"Well, I must say it's a strange business. But just as you please."

"It's some piece of tomfoolery," replied Billy.

He went back into the town, into the metropolis of New York, alone, abandoned, without money, without friends, without colleagues, without a single human being with whom he could speak.

When he had stolen the cases from me my fate was sealed, and now that I had got them back he was hoisted by his own petard. For six hours he wandered through the city, mad with anxiety, rigid with fear, trembling with horror and looking for some person to whom he could tell his story. A man whom he knew, a friend . . .

Meanwhile I was lying on the broad sofa in my new apartment, in a pleasantly central-heated atmosphere, well-fed, contented and happy, reading in peace the Hudson River murder story. The radio was providing some sentimental dance music—I think it was Glenn Miller. The lights were giving a pleasant indirect glow which did my eyes and my nerves good. I had drawn the curtains. I was alone and I was glad to be alone.

I pictured Billy's story to myself in every detail. I felt sorry about him. He could not go to the police. But how long would he be able to hold out before they caught him? He probably had three thousand dollars with him still. If he had been a careful sort of chap he might have gone underground with that, but I knew he was not. Until they caught him I could work in peace, but once he was caught everything was finished. I had no doubts on that score whatsoever. He would hold out for two or three days, perhaps.

That was if he did not act in anger at my turning the tables on him over the suitcases, and put the police on my trail at once. . . .

In that moment Edward Green died. I stood up, took my papers from my wallet, went into the kitchen and burned them. I still had plenty of other names and professions.

The next day I would go to Mr. Brown, the contact man of the German M.I. The next day or the day after that I would perhaps already be in contact with the atomic people. If only Billy had not been caught by that time. I wondered if I should look for Billy? If I found him I would have to shoot him, I thought to myself. There would be no depending upon him and he had sentenced me to death first. If I caught him I could show him no mercy. And any court-martial in the world would uphold my judgement. . . .

I thrust the idea from my mind. I had been reading too many crime novels. I selected a book from the bookcase and then put it down again. I found a bottle of whisky and poured myself a drink.

I lay down luxuriantly on the couch once more, content that my working day was over. The music had come to an end and it was now news time. There were reports from the various theatres of war. Things were going badly in Germany, but there was no doubt that the reports were highly coloured. I simply would not believe that the war was already lost although the whole world, including me, knew it was really. At last the news was over.

"One hour in Paris," said the voice from the ether. A light orchestra was playing. I enjoyed the music as I was enjoying the warmth, the feeling of well-being, the apartment and the whisky.

Suddenly my feeling of well-being deserted me. Was it nerves? Were my senses deceiving me? No. There were sounds, footsteps, footsteps approaching the door. A key in the lock! I jumped up. I snatched the revolver from its holster and released the catch. With one bound I put myself in such a position that I would see whoever entered the apartment before he saw me. What if there were more than one?

The steps came nearer. The second joint of my index finger curled round the trigger. The door opened. I stood there as if frozen to the spot. It was a woman, young and fair. She stood there, frightened at first, then she laughed.

She was tall and was wearing a voluminous coat, which was held in at the waist with a belt. American women often have uncannily strong nerves. She did not call for help. She did not run away. She just stood there and smiled at me.

"Playing Indians?" she said.

I was on the threshold of the most ridiculous experience of my life.

CHAPTER 11

Billy Betrays Me to the F.B.I.

I took in every detail of her face, the high vaulted brow, the slender nose, the delicate, made-up lips, the unaffected, almost invisible smile, the long hair lying casually just as it fell. I stared at her, pondering at the same time how the outsize revolver I was holding could be made inconspicuously to disappear.

"How did you get here?" I asked.

"I could ask you the same thing," she countered.

She closed the door and came a few steps nearer. She walked on her high heels with such assurance and such gracefulness that she might have come into the world wearing them.

"I am a friend of Paolo's," I explained.

"And I am a friend of his too," she said.

I had at length succeeded in shoving the revolver back into my pocket where it was making an ugly bulge. On the radio a jazz drummer was demonstrating his skill in a passage which lasted a full minute. I felt as if my head was being used as the drum.

"Paolo has gone away," I continued, "and has placed his apartment at my disposal for a few days."

"That's not bad," said the girl. "He must have several

keys. He gave me one too. I've got the decorators in my own flat; the place reeks of paint and that's one thing I can't stand."

I decided to introduce myself. "My name is Edward Green."

"I'm Joan Kenneth," she said.

"In the circumstances I'll move out, of course," I said. "You must have priority."

"Well, well, so there are still a few gentlemen left in the world. But actually there's no need for you to go; after all there are several rooms, aren't there?"

I nodded and stood there feeling rather embarrassed. Evidently she liked my reserve. She had no idea, of course, that I was less concerned with her reputation than with my mission.

"Well, isn't there anything to drink here?" she asked.

"The whisky's over there. If you'd have arrived half an hour later you'd have had to drink milk."

"Oh, I always appear at the right moment."

She took off her coat, went into the bathroom for a minute or two and then reappeared.

"I'll take the bedroom," she said. "You can stay in the living room. Turn the wireless on a bit louder. It's Tommy Dorsey, isn't it? Do you like him?"

"Sure, I do."

"We'll make ourselves comfortable. Or do you still want to move out?"

"Not necessarily."

"There you are, you see," she said. "And now come with me into the kitchen and give me a hand. Or aren't you hungry?"

"I'm not hungry but I've got an appetite," I replied.

We made hamburgers and they tasted heavenly. We found two bottles of beer and drank up the rest of the whisky. We listened to Tommy Dorsey, Glenn Miller and Louis Armstrong. Now and again the band stopped playing and a voice from the ether told us how many tons of explosive had been unloaded over the various cities of Germany.

"The war will soon be over," said Joan, "thank God."

"Yes," I replied.

"Have you been in the services?"

"Yes, I was a naval officer."

"My brother was, too. He was killed . . . at Pearl Harbour, right at the beginning."

"To hell with the Japanese," I said.

We each lit a cigarette.

"It's nice here," said Joan. "I hate sitting around in restaurants in the evening but I also hate being alone."

"I'm just the same myself."

"You're not an American, are you?"

I felt my heart turn over. Suddenly all the warmth and comfort of the evening was dispelled. The alarm had sounded. Was she an agent of the F.B.I.? Was she but a charming trap? Was she a precursor of the hangman?

"Why do you say that?" I asked.

"You speak like a European, like a Scandinavian."

"My parents were Norwegians," I answered.

"Why are you so tense about it?" she asked. "I wouldn't mind a scrap if my parents had been Norwegian. Oh, Europe! Paris, Vienna, Budapest, Rome. . . . Oh, damn this war!"

She picked up her handbag, turned to me and said:

"Good night. I hope I won't disturb you getting up early. I have a little dress shop and I have to be first in."

"Good night," I said.

I listened to the radio for another hour. Joan had been to the bathroom and had then gone back into the bedroom. If the F.B.I. were already on my trail why should they post a woman agent here to watch me all night? Why didn't they come at once and arrest me? Claptrap, I told myself. But then it occurred to me how very little notice Joan had taken of my revolver and how few questions she had asked me.

I thought and thought whether I should stay or go. There was a good deal of support for either course of action. If I were to go, Joan, even if she were quite harmless, would become suspicious. If I remained and Joan were not harmless I should be right in the soup. But in that case the house would certainly be surrounded and I should not have been able to leave it anyhow.

I went to bed with the last drop of whisky. I woke up five or six times. By four or five o'clock in the morning I had reached the point where I was indifferent to everything, and in that state of mind I settled down to five hours sleep.

When I awoke Joan had already gone. So as not to waken me she had had her breakfast in the kitchen; her cup was still on the table, a tiny trace of lipstick on the rim. I washed the cup, took a shower, ate two hamburgers left over from the night before and went on my way to Mr. Brown on 41st Street, 8th floor, to talk with him on a matter of atomic espionage. . . .

I turned the corner three times and made sure I was not being followed, thinking meanwhile how lovely it would be to sit by the Christmas tree with Joan instead of chasing off after the Manhattan Project, to celebrate the festival of love and peace instead of working in the service of war.

Here it was. 41st Street. I took the lift up to the 8th floor. The red-haired secretary considered for a moment whether she would attend to her finger-nails or take notice of me. She finally decided for me.

"You're in luck today," she said. "Mr. Brown is in. Actually you meant to come yesterday, didn't you?"

"I intended to," I replied, "but it's never too late to see you, or is it?"

"Oh, oh," she countered. "There's a boxing match on this evening. If you'd care to get some tickets, I'll come with you."

"I'd rather go to a theatre," I replied.

"We'll talk it over when you come out," she said.

She put her nail varnish down, went into Mr. Brown's room and reappeared in a minute or two.

Brown was a small man with a somewhat agitated manner. He got up from his chair and greeted me with outstretched arms.

"What can I do for you?" he asked.

"First make the walls and doors soundproof," I said.

He seemed taken aback for a few seconds.

"I don't do any secret business here," he said.

"You might," I said, "just a bit."

He sat down and offered me a cigar, which I refused.

"From 1938 to 1942 you worked for the German Secret Service," I began. "For your services you received in all 64,293 dollars and 40 cents. You were supposed to have paid your subagents with the money. You were the only man who escaped the wave of arrests that went on at that time. I am here now to see that you give value for money."

He looked as if his limbs had turned to water. His eyes opened wide like the eyes of a rabbit about to be devoured by a snake.

"Who are you?" he asked.

"As far as you are concerned my name is Kenneth W. Smith," I replied. I paused for a while and looked out of the window wondering whether the red-haired secretary could hear our conversation, then I continued:

"I am from Germany, from Berlin. If you will give me your assistance nothing will happen to you . . . you did some very good work on the previous occasion."

"You must be crazy," he said. "Things were different then. Now Germany has lost the war." He stood up and paced the room, throwing his arms about and muttering inarticulately. He paused by the telephone.

"What if I called up the F.B.I.?" he asked.

"They'd hang you," I replied, "and me as well, of course. They don't pull their punches. Anyone who has once worked against America can expect no mercy, and you don't need me to tell you that."

He nodded.

"I have a family," he said. "I have built up some sort of life for myself. The war is lost for Germany, but by God I'd have liked to see her win it. I hate America! For ten, fifteen years I washed dishes and was pushed around by every street-corner cop. Had to put up with every Tom, Dick and Harry calling me a dirty bastard."

"But now you have a flourishing business," I replied,

"and a pretty secretary. And you got it all with the money that came from Berlin."

I went to the window, looked down into the street and turned round to face Brown again.

"I'm giving you a fair deal," I said. "I will trouble you only once more if you will tell me what I want to know. Introduce me to the people I want to get in touch with and you will be free. As far as we are concerned you will be dead, regardless of what may happen afterwards."

I felt sorry for the man. My visit must have been a terrible shock for him, but I dared not take pity on him. Who felt any pity for me? Once you've walked on the devil's highway you have to go on walking there whether you want to or not.

"What do you want to know?" asked Brown.

"All there is to know about the Manhattan Project," I replied.

This obviously wasn't the first he'd heard of it. He grasped the situation immediately.

"Tomorrow," he said. "And then it's the end."

"Then it's the end," I assured him. I was on the point of leaving when he said:

"Have you any money?"

"Yes, I've got a whole heap of money."

"Will you take a bit of good advice?"

"Yes, I can always do with that."

"Listen then," he said. "Take yourself off to South America as fast as your legs will carry you. You're running into disaster with your eyes open. Still to be working for Germany . . . It's sheer madness."

"That's just what we are, fools, you and I," I replied. "And for the moment you must accept the situation."

The redhead had disappeared, which suited me down to the ground. I absented myself with the utmost caution. I was not afraid of Mr. Brown. It was quite obvious that he was afraid of me. He had got old and obese and secret agents who are old and obese are not much use for the dirty work. But at least they know the rules of the game. He would keep his mouth shut. He would buy his freedom by passing on fresh information to me.

Needless to say, the American War Department had done everything humanly possible to keep the atom project secret, but that was impossible. It was, strange to say, child-ishly simple to get into contact with the Hiroshima bomb. I knew that to produce this weapon of destruction they needed uranium, and uranium was to be found in northern Canada. Getting it was a laborious business involving many hundreds and thousands of specialists, and a thing like that could never be kept secret. To an experienced agent like Mr. Brown—I never got to know his real name—there would be no difficulty in getting at any rate some general information.

For the moment I had nothing more to do than wait. There was still no sign of Billy. Strangely enough the air was still clear. I re-doubled my vigilance and the more trouble-free my environment appeared to be, the more as-siduously I studied it.

There was no F.B.I. agent on my tail but Santa Claus seemed to be following my every movement. There he was, on loudspeakers, on the radio, in neon lights and in every kind of advertisement. To the Americans, the coming of Father Christmas meant peace, but in Germany at the same time the festival of the Prince of Peace was being celebrated without joy; that year the German Christmas tree was bare.

I thought of Margarete and drowned my melancholy in whisky, feeling like an octogenarian meditating in his bath-chair on what he would do if he could live his life over again. . . .

The next few days passed without special incident. Joan, my cotenant in Santi's apartment, supplied me with other preoccupations. I had already become expert in drying dishes. What a sensation it would be: "Germany's last se-cret agent wears apron in kitchen, helping enemy girl to polish off Allied food supplies." That would be the sort of thing the newspapers would run if I were caught. Fortu-nately I did not realise how near to arrest I was. I did not learn until later what had happened in the interim, how my fate was catching up on me, and how the American M.I. was coming upon the scent. The sequence of events was retailed to me later by the F.B.I. officials in generous detail.

After his abortive attempt to recover my cases at Grand Central Station, Billy had gone on drinking for two days without pause. And when the drink went to Billy's head he was soft, soft as a jelly.

Some years before he had had a friend in New York and this friend might well have been fighting at Okinawa or Aachen. The chance of his being in New York was a very slim one indeed, but in fact that was just where he was. He had been twice wounded, had become a much-decorated war hero and was now occupying an important position in the American armament industry.

Billy found him. He thought up a story and his friend, Tom S. Warrens, believed him. At any rate he believed him at first. Although the two friends were so different there was one thing they had in common and that was their liking for whisky. Billy still had some money and so they went from bar to bar. They put their arms around the girls' naked shoulders and stuffed money into their garters. They treated the assembled company and sang and danced. They went on like this for days on end. Tom failed to report at his place of work and reported sick. And he was sick, from too much alcohol.

Billy got a thick head. One day at four in the morning he got an attack of the miseries. I was familiar with this mood of his; I had witnessed it once or twice when I had been with him. The friend wallowed in misery with him, at any rate at first, but he was a little more sober than Billy, just a trifle, a fatal trifle.

Billy rambled on incoherently with the crazy logic of the inebriated. He babbled, he stammered, he talked of U-1230. Tom had just laughed at him. He laughed at him for one long day and one short night, but Billy went on and on with the same story. He was now sobering up as his money was running short. His friend went on listening and the apparently inconsequential chatter began to take reasonable shape.

What was to be done? Tom S. Warrens was, like every other American, a patriot; he had been twice wounded in the war and had been discharged from the Army with honour; but he was also a loyal friend. To report the matter to the F.B.I. would be a breach of faith with Billy. And who would contact the secret service on the strength of the ramblings of a drunken man? Yet it all seemed to hang together. Supposing Billy really was working against his own country? Tom sought the counsel of other friends and their advice was clear and unequivocal: "Go to the F.B.I."

The friends recalled the Dasch case, when fathers and mothers were sentenced to death because they had held their sons in their arms and had not at once gone to the police to order the hangman for their own sons. There were no extenuating circumstances, not in wartime. As it happened, the sentences were not carried out, but twenty years' imprisonment was bad enough.

So the F.B.I. was informed and its officers took Billy in charge without any special enthusiasm. They waited until he was sober. He was then interrogated and at once broke down; his sole concern was to save his own neck, but it was already in the noose and the rope was already being drawn tight.

"I want to inform you," said Billy, "that a German agent is at large. He is called Edward Green. He's very dangerous. He is the most dangerous man of the German Reich Security. I crossed the Atlantic with him."

"You say you are an American," an official interrupted him, "and yet you admit that you smuggled a German spy into your own country?"

"I only did it as a means of getting back to America myself, so as I could place myself at the disposal of the Army authorities and hand the German spy over to you. I'm an American and want to remain an American."

The F.B.I. men still could not make up their minds whether they were dealing with a madman or a spy. Spies who spoke as freely as Billy were rare, and hardly worth taking seriously.

Billy's files were produced; they established that he was a deserter and that his sympathies for National Socialism had excluded him from taking a commission in the Navy.

Alarm! Special alarm! The most urgent alarm the F.B.I. had known in New York in the whole course of the war.

"Speak, you swine, or I'll push your face in." Billy was not being handled with delicacy. No, no country of the world deals gently with its own traitors. I, on the other hand, was to be cross-examined with singular fairness, but more of that later. Billy sat there, a small, cowardly figure, trembling with fear.

"What does he look like? Come on, talk! Tell us again! First you said he was not very tall, then you said he *was* very tall. Which is it? Come on, speak up, you swine!"

Billy was too frightened to utter a word. He asked for a cigarette which was given him with bad grace, and then he started babbling. He gave a full description of me. The officials were frightening him to try him out and see if he was lying. But why should he lie? He saw a tiny ray of hope; he hoped that if I were caught he might secure a pardon on the strength of the information he had given against me. The hope was a slim one, but when all reasonable hope has gone you can always dream up something.

"Come on! Don't be so dumb!" said a small, stout F.B.I. man. "Open your mouth, Billy. So he's about five feet ten, is he, your friend? Come along then, just keep on talking. What does he like to eat? What does he drink? Is he left-handed? Has he got a good digestion? Is he colour-blind? Does he go to church? Does he go to nightclubs? Has he got corns on his feet?"

"I don't know any of those things," said Billy.

"Well, what do you know?"

"Well, he's not left-handed," replied Billy. "I know that. His digestion's all right. Grilled steak is his favourite dish and he drinks whisky. He drinks plenty but he can stand it."

"Come on!"

"He's got an English accent."

"We know that already. We're trying to find out something we don't know."

The lamp was shining straight into Billy's face and his interrogators were standing in the dark. They were relieved every twenty minutes. It went on like this for hours and was to continue like it for days. There was no pity, no sympathy for Billy or me. The chase was on, but so far the press knew nothing of it. . . .

"Desperate German Christmas offensive in the Ardennes." Such was the headline of the moment. New York, sure of victory, almost tired of victory already, trembled for a space, the space of a few days, haunted once more by fear of the Nazis, fear that the war could still drag on, fear that the invasion had been in vain.

And the Department for Psychological Warfare worked on. If a German spy should chance to fall into enemy hands at this time of all times, then he'd be especially unlucky.

"I've told you everything," Billy repeated again and again. "There's nothing more I know."

"Haven't you ever noticed anything about him, some little mannerism that's a bit unusual?"

"No."

"Think again, or we'll help you do your thinking."

"I don't know anything more."

The interrogating officer went close up to Billy and stared him straight in the eyes. His face had become gaunt and the eyes were lying deep in their sockets. The light was blinding and Billy wanted to close his eyes but he could not. Again and again the F.B.I. men forced him to look at them, to look into the light, to answer their questions. Always the same questions, put sometimes gently, sometimes quietly, sometimes angrily, sometimes indifferently.

"There's one thing that occurs to me," said Billy. He seemed now almost relieved. He thought perhaps there'd be an end to the questioning if he said something.

"One thing occurs to me," he began. "I have noticed an odd habit. When he pays for something and gets change, he always puts it into his left breast pocket."

One of the officers nodded to his colleagues, and a new identification sign for the German spy was broadcast to all police stations. Attention! Attention!

The search was on for Edward Green alias Erich Gimpel, the German spy. Top secret! The American civil population must not be made to feel uneasy. Every F.B.I. man available must be thrown into the task of finding Erich Gimpel.

They laid their traps to catch me and laid them on an American scale without regard for money, time or men.

BUT I still knew nothing of all this.

I had arranged to meet Mr. Brown in a snack bar on 31st Street. He arrived punctually, and alone. He had every reason to play straight.

"My car is outside," he said.

We got into an old Packard and drove this way and that through New York.

"I've a whole heap of information," he said. "Can I depend on it that this is our last interview?"

"If I find the information satisfactory, yes."

The traffic lights turned to green. Brown put his foot on the accelerator.

"The atomic bomb will be ready for use within a few months."

"How many months?"

"Five or six at the most."

"How do you know?"

"I'll tell you afterwards. My information is a hundred per cent reliable."

"And how are the bombs dropped?"

"They're still experimenting on that. The bomb is terribly heavy. It has to be flown in a special machine. The trials are being made in California. An air force captain has been practising starting and landing with excessive loading there for weeks."

I made a note of name and place. It would be easy to check up on this information.

"They reckon," said Brown, "that they can bring the war to an end with one or two bombs. The effect of the bomb is terrific."

"And how many bombs have they?"

"Only two or three," replied Brown. "But that will be plenty."

"And where are the works?"

"That I cannot say exactly, but mark this name: Mr. Griffiths. He's a physicist. He lives in a hotel on 24th Street. You may care to get in touch with him. But if you do, it'll mean the end for you. You realise that, don't you?"

"That's not your affair," I replied.

He gave me a mass of technical details. I repeated them over to myself until I could carry them in my memory. I wondered how much truth there was in what Brown had told me. I didn't know yet what his information was worth. . . .

"And the bombs will be used?"

"You can depend on that," answered Brown. "America regards the atomic bomb as the only thing to bring the war to an end. There's only one thing that would prevent them using it and that would be if Germany or Japan had the atomic bomb too. You see what I mean?"

"Yes," I replied.

"And now will you take a piece of advice from me?"

"Why not?"

"Make yourself scarce," he said.

He stopped. I got out of the car. Our leave-taking was short and cool.

"Think of my family," he said.

"Give my love to the redhead," I replied.

I wanted to pass my report on to Germany that same day. I walked on for a few blocks. Fortunately I did not know how many of the passersby were keeping an eye on me. Billy's description fitted me, of course, but there were thousands of men in New York whom it would have fitted equally well. Actually I did not think that Billy had already been caught, but I had no illusions about the fact that the days of his freedom and by the same token the days of my freedom too, were numbered.

Now for Griffiths! Whether I could approach this man without drawing attention to myself was another question. If there was a Mr. Griffiths and if he was living in the hotel

which had been named to me, then it would prove that
Brown had not invented his information. In any case my
next task was to establish the reliability of Brown's information.

I found the hotel; it was a second-class establishment,
neither good nor bad, and with the usual, obtrusive cleanliness. I passed into the small foyer. The porter was not
there, but a black book lay upon his desk, the hotel register.

I stood there for a few moments drumming my fingers
on the desk. Two women were sitting on a sofa in the
corner and like all Americans at the time were discussing
the Ardennes offensive. A man was sitting in an armchair.
I could not see his face, which was hidden behind a newspaper.

Was he really reading? In a flash I was on my guard. I
knew that trick. I had learned it myself. I noticed at once
how the newspaper was lowered a trifle, how the eyes
moved to the edge apparently nonchalantly, how the newspaper was raised again and how the manoeuvre was repeated two or three times.

The man who held the newspaper in his hand had had
the same training as I had had. That's the F.B.I., I told
myself.

I turned my back on him. I opened the register and immediately hit upon the name Griffiths, but I turned on further, ran my finger down the page, stopped at a name and
made a note of it. I could not see my shadower but I could
feel him behind me. I felt instinctively that he was waiting
for me, that he had recognised me, and that he was now
about to act. In the next second perhaps. I straightened myself. The porter came back.

"What can I do for you?" he asked.

"A relative of mine was coming here," I replied. "Mr.
James H. Miller."

"He's not here," said the porter. "I'm sorry, sir."

I stood about hesitantly for a few seconds more. My
shadower was once more camouflaging himself behind the
newspaper. His hands were quite still. The paper with the

giant headlines was not shaking. What would he do? How had the F.B.I. been instructed?

While I was playing the part of a disappointed caller who couldn't make up his mind, I was doing some rapid thinking. The F.B.I. have a strict rule that no arrest may be made unless two men are present. My man was alone. Perhaps his colleague had gone to the lavatory. Or perhaps he would have to get reinforcements before he could act. Perhaps the second man had just gone to get some cigarettes.

"Is there a toilet around here?" I asked the porter.

"Back there, to the left," replied the man.

I gave him twenty cents and went slowly off. I did not quicken my steps; even when I was out of sight I could still be heard.

I stopped. From where I was standing I could still see the porter's desk. If my nerves were not playing tricks with me the man with the newspaper would now get up, go to the desk and try to find out what name I had made a note of.

Right! There he stood, bending over the book.

I walked past the lavatory and past the kitchen. A staircase led upwards, but if I went upstairs I should land myself in the cart. If I went back I should be arrested. I might shoot, but I wouldn't get very far in a busy street. There wouldn't be much sense in that.

Quickly, quickly! I told myself, realising at the same time that I must flee with my head rather than with my legs.

I saw the words "Tradesmen's Exit" on a door. Oh god, if only it's not locked! There was my chance, one last small chance. I put my hand upon the latch. . . .

CHAPTER 12

Love—And Then Arrest

ALL was quiet behind me. The F.B.I. man was still standing at the reception desk and the two ladies were still discussing the Ardennes offensive. The sound of their voices carried to where I was moving and I could make out a word here and there. The porter left his desk again and went upstairs. Somewhere a radio was on quietly. The sun suddenly burst out and shone clear and strong through the window. A white-capped chef was making his way along the narrow corridor and I had to step aside to allow him to pass.

"Thank you, sir," he said and raised his hand to his cap.

The door responded to my touch. The tradesmen's entrance was open. This was pure chance, due perhaps to the negligence of some member of the staff. I tried to shake off my nervousness.

"Keep calm," I admonished myself.

Slowly, with the utmost caution, I opened the door, afraid that the hinges might squeak. But they had evidently been recently oiled.

The F.B.I. man could not see me from where he was standing, but he must have been expecting me to reappear at any moment. He would be getting suspicious. I wondered why he had not acted already. Why hadn't he simply put his hand to his revolver and said: "Edward Green! You are under arrest. I warn you that from this moment anything you say may be used in evidence against you."

I was standing in the yard. It was in the form of a small quadrangle with a drive-in for the delivery vans. This stood open. To the left against the wall of the hotel two men were working on a lorry. One was lying underneath it and the other was standing in the cab. They took no notice of me.

I walked slowly, very slowly. I had closed the door behind me. Surely the F.B.I. man must have noticed something by now; I was still twenty yards from the drive-in. A private car was standing in my path, a sky-blue Chevrolet of the latest type. The owner must have known all the right people. During the war there were plenty of jeeps being made but not many Chevrolets.

The two mechanics were shouting to each other but I could not understand what they were saying. I went up to the Chevrolet. Another five yards. Now I was level with it, and I saw something which made me catch my breath. The ignition key was in its place. I pulled myself together, glanced round at the two mechanics and looked back at the door I had come through. I sized up the way out. Everything was quiet. Everything was the same. Everything seemed to be going along as usual.

Now for it. The door was ajar. I seated myself at the steering wheel and pressed the starter. The engine started up straightaway. Now down on the accelerator, slowly release the clutch. Turn left. Look in the mirror. A little more acceleration. Change to second gear. Now one more look in the mirror. Turn to the right. Accelerate again, third gear. . . .

Now away! I took the first two curves so sharply that the back wheels scraped along the curbstones. Right, left, straight ahead. The red light. Amber. The green light. Accelerate. Turn to the left. Straight ahead. Across the main road. Now slowly. Drive slowly. Take care not to arouse attention.

I looked at my wristwatch. I'll use the car for five

minutes, I thought. The two mechanics must have noticed the theft at once. They would report the number to the traffic police, and the police had wireless cars. Everything would move forward at a great pace. If you want to steal a car it's just as well not to do it in America.

I crossed Times Square, did a few more zigzags, making sure that in my excitement I was not driving round in circles.

I found a parking place. Turn right, and now out!

For the first twenty yards, I walked quite slowly, then I crossed over to the other side of the street, took a left turn, increased my pace, then jumped into a taxi.

"Quickly now," I said to the driver, naming a railway station. "If you can make it in ten minutes, I'll just catch my train."

"Depends on the traffic," replied the driver shaking his head. "People are always in a hurry and yet I often have to stand around for hours waiting for a fare."

I replied in the same strain, meanwhile taking an occasional look behind me. The taxi was not being followed. How many F.B.I. men might there be after me now? The officer in the hotel would have given his first alarm. They would have found the car by now but I was still a couple of jumps ahead. I leapt out of the taxi, paid off the driver and gave him a dollar tip. I ran into the station, up to the platform, bought myself a newspaper, changed on to another platform and came out again.

The taxi driver had obviously driven on at once.

I continued on foot. How lovely New York was at this hour. The people seemed so gay, the Christmas bells were ringing joyously and the sound of fun and laughter could be heard everywhere. The passersby were carrying bulky parcels, last minute purchases, and excited children were running along at their heels.

"Merry Christmas," resounded from every loudspeaker. "Merry Christmas, Merry Christmas, Merry Christmas."

"Flowers," I said to myself. "A handkerchief, a few pleasant little trifles." I got everything I wanted, took a taxi, changed taxis, went a stretch on foot and eventually arrived at the door of the apartment house. I pressed the lift button and was carried up to the 11th floor.

I could not find my key and rang the bell. For a few seconds my nerves nearly failed me again. Suppose they were waiting for me here? Suppose the F.B.I. were behind that door? Suppose they were armed?

Yes, someone was waiting for me. Joan. . . .

She smiled at me.

"Darling, you look exhausted," she said.

"Yes," I replied. "New York's a strenuous place."

"You've come at just the right moment," she went on. "I've put up the Christmas tree and the turkey's in the oven. Now you can make yourself useful."

We hung the bright baubles on the tree together.

"We'll decorate it the European way," she said. "I'll like it better like that. I intend that my first Christmas after the war shall be spent in Europe."

"Plans . . . dreams . . . they're the best things there are," I said.

"But I believe in them." She turned to me and smiled. "You are an old pessimist," she said. "After all, you've still got the best years of your life in front of you, haven't you?"

"Yes," I said.

We had finished decorating the Christmas tree. The wireless was on and the music sounded sweet, soothing, alluring. It was as if the spirit of the festival of peace was flowing from the instrument and drawing us ever more into its embrace. We sat together quietly; there was no need to talk.

The meaning of Christmas and how it should be celebrated is something you'll never find in a textbook for secret agents. The previous year I had been in Spain for Christmas. There were plenty of good things to eat. When the faithful were setting out for Midnight Mass we were lying about on the floor. When they were getting ready to go to Matins we were trying to clear our thick heads with more alcohol. Two years previously I had spent Christmas in Holland. On the day before Christmas Eve two German agents had been shot. Two days later an English agent lay in his grave.

Christmas! What was Christmas? Flickering candlelight, the mild, lovable fragrance of scorched pine branches, the excited, exuberant joy of children.

As I sat there at Joan's side beneath the Christmas tree I felt something creep up my spine and catch me by the throat. Something said to me: "It's Christmas for everyone else, but not for you!"

Swiftly, clearly, my memory swung back over the years, over the decades. I saw my father, my mother, my teacher before me. Once before when I was only eight or nine I had experienced this same heaviness of spirit. My friend's father, a bank cashier, had shot himself on Christmas Eve. Twelve thousand marks were missing. That year the spirit of Christmas passed me by, excluded me as it was excluding me now.

I swallowed two glasses of whisky. Smiling, Joan removed the bottle from my reach.

"Not before you've eaten," she said.

We went into the kitchen to see how things were getting along. Everything was in order. We left the turkey to look after itself while we looked after ourselves.

And then came the radio news. They couldn't leave us in peace even on Christmas Eve. The Ardennes offensive had been crushed. Decisively. I wondered whether it was propaganda, and whether the Department for Psychological Warfare had cut the offensive short more quickly than General Eisenhower.

I was the war's last fool, holding out on an outpost that was already lost.

"This would be a good time for a transmission," I thought. Actually all the separate components for my set had been ready for some time and were in a suitcase which was lying underneath a couch in this very room, the room which housed our Christmas tree. No one would be paying any special attention to radio communications on Christmas Eve, but my reports were not ready. The information I had had from Brown had first of all to be checked and then followed up. There were still some difficult days and weeks in front of me. . . . I only hoped that Billy had not yet been caught. I wondered where he might be at that moment.

"You look like a general after a lost battle," said Joan.

"Have you ever seen a general?" I asked.

"Only on the screen," she replied, laughing. "But on the screen they're always victorious."

"That's why they are always much nicer in the cinema than in real life," I replied.

We took the turkey out of the oven, carved it and served it. It was beautifully tender and crisp. We sat facing each other, smiling, eating with enjoyment, toasting each other, going over to the radio now and again to see what programmes we could get. We drank Rhine wine. You could still get it in New York.

"It goes well with the food," I said.

"Yes," said Joan. "Today every American soldier gets a turkey from the Army."

"Yes," I replied, "and there are still three hundred thousand turkeys to spare. That's the number of men the war has cost us so far."

"Three hundred thousand Americans," she went on. "And how many English, French, German and Italian?"

"Let's talk about something else."

Joan stood up, walked over to the light switches, turned the ceiling light off and the wall light on.

"There are two G.I.'s I knew who will never eat turkey again," she said. "One was my brother."

I nodded. Suddenly all the magic of the evening was gone.

"Don't you want to know who the other one was?" she said.

"I can imagine."

"It was Bob," she continued. "He was tall and slim like you, and he had your fair hair. I was going to marry him. I had known him for three years. He was a lieutenant. This time last year Bob and I were celebrating together. Do you see now why I didn't want to go back to my own flat? I didn't want to be alone there."

I said nothing, but got to my feet and paced up and down in the room.

"I'm a fool," she said. "Now I've gone and spoiled everything. But on an evening like this you just can't help thinking. . . . He was killed in March. In the Pacific. Landing on one of those damned coral islands that aren't worth a cent. And after that they gave him a medal."

"They always give them a medal afterwards," I replied. "Oh, there's no sense in going over it all."

She smiled at me. Her eyes were shining. She went up to the Christmas tree and lit the first candle. Then she turned towards me and said:

"You must light the second candle."

"If you light them all," I said, "they'll burn all the more brightly."

"You're a flatterer," she said, "but it does me good. Do you know, I thought this evening was going to be awful, and look how differently it's turned out. I rather reproach myself that I can forget so quickly, that I can suddenly feel so gay at being with you. I feel I shouldn't be enjoying myself like this."

I put my arm round her. Then I went and fetched my little parcel.

"I've probably chosen all wrong," I said.

"I put your flowers in a vase ages ago."

"I'm sure you won't like the handbag; I've no experience with these things."

"It's lovely," she replied. "And if you were more experienced in these things I shouldn't like you nearly so much. But what nonsense. Of course you are experienced, but it doesn't matter."

She took a tiny box from her handbag.

"There," she said, "this is for you."

It was a pair of gold cuff links. I still wear them.

The flickering candlelight caressed her face, illumining eyes, nose, brow. I could not take my eyes off her. I went on staring at her, and she liked it. She was not embarrassed, she was not coquettish. She was just herself. Just Joan.

We sat together on the couch. The music had come on again, and the magic had returned. It was as if there had never been a war, as if there would be no more fighting, as if never again would a mother tremble for her son and a wife tremble for her husband. It was quite simply as if even the most evil, the most unenlightened, the most dangerous of politicians had suddenly heard and understood the message of Bethlehem. For us there was no battlefield. There was only that sitting room on the 11th floor. I was not a German and she was not an American, and we loved each other and we did not need the banalities of speech to tell each other so.

We knew it.

I do not know how long we sat there, silent, relaxed, happy. The candles burned down to tiny stumps, and we had to snuff them out. Their flickering light no longer played over Joan's face but the fragrance and the magic of Joan were there in the dark.

"It's strange," she said. "Actually we know nothing about each other. It's even more strange that we've never asked each other who we are, what we do and where we come from. But I feel that's how it should be."

She frowned fleetingly.

"I feel as if I've always known you."

"I feel just that way myself," I replied.

We kissed, and I forgot all the things that I should have remembered. The time, the place, my mission and the fact that I was a hunted man. Agent 146 of the German M.I., the human machine, the man who went through with every mission that was entrusted to him without question—that man died for a few hours. I sensed, I felt, I realised that I was a human being with his hopes and longings like every other, a human being with a heart which had certain rights that no power nor state on earth could deny it. I realised all this that Christmas Eve in New York. In New York, the biggest city in the world, where the F.B.I. were after me like a pack of bloodhounds. I realised it all as I lay in Joan's arms.

"Will you stay with me always?" asked Joan.

"I don't know," I replied.

"Will you just forget me?"

"No," I said, "that I can promise you; I shall never forget you."

"It's strange," she continued. "I always seem to know just what you are going to say."

It was midnight now. The bells were ringing on the radio and the carol-singers were proclaiming Christmas Day.

We drew closer together. I was happy that things had turned out like this, that I was holding Joan in my arms instead of hunting British agents in Holland or lying with a heap of drunken men in Spain. The night enfolded us in its embrace. A clock was ticking. The sound was painful to me. If only there were no clocks. . . . The feeling of happiness to which I had surrendered became ever more poignant.

Joan had fallen asleep. She was smiling. She lay quite still, her face turned towards me. I had opened the window, and the cool night air was wafting into the room. I covered her with a rug so that she would not feel the cold.

And then once more the secret agent in me gained the upper hand. Uncompromisingly he reported for duty. For an hour, two hours I struggled desperately against the dictates of my conscience.

Life has not dealt gently with me. I have witnessed the death of friends. I have felt the clammy hands of the hangman measuring my neck. I have known the silent despair of a prison cell, the inevitability of the passage of time measuring out life slowly, day by day, hour by hour. In all these situations my role was a passive one, the inevitable result of circumstances beyond my control.

Now, however, I had to anticipate the grim drama. I had to leave Joan, sleeping, smiling Joan who would be looking forward to a joyous awakening at my side. I had to cast behind me all the joy of this evening, all the spirit of Christmas, all recognition of our mutual love. I had to pick up my bag and baggage and step out into the chill of the metropolis, into the heart of the enemy. I was an enemy of the people who were now celebrating Christmas; I was a spy, a spy for a country which had already lost the war.

I would have to wake Joan and explain everything. I was sure she would never denounce me. But therein lay her own undoing. She would be charged with having harboured a German spy. The law of warfare knows no love, no pity. She would be executed. Militant, uncompromising patriotism, that monster produced by war, would make no concessions.

No, I could not do it. No, not as long as a glimmering of understanding was left to me. Not so long as I had any sense of responsibility. No, not so long as I loved her.

She turned in her sleep and what light there was enabled me to study her face in every detail. I imprinted her features upon my memory. I would never see her again, and I would never be able to explain to her why I had slipped away. It was my lot to wound her. Perhaps she would never understand. She might weep, she might be embittered, she might curse the fate that had brought us together. She might hate the happiness that had united us for a few hours.

No, I could never do that! I crept quietly up to her. I would have to wake her. I would have to stay, I would have to risk everything to guard our happiness. The war was already as good as over. I would tell her what my part in it had been. She would understand and would say no more about it. I had money, I could speak Spanish, I knew my way around South America. I knew where I could go and not arouse attention. I knew the places where no one would think of looking for me. She would come with me. There would be two or three days' uncertainty before our getaway was finally accomplished, before we would be safe. We would travel separately. For Joan anyhow there would be no risk, and I knew how to go about it, how to cross frontiers and keep my nerves under control. For once in my life my training would be of some real service to me.

She knew nothing of the inner battle I had to fight, the despair I had to endure. She did not know that her problematical future was already my past.

I got up and packed my belongings. I pulled my case out from under the couch on which she was sleeping. A light sleeper would have been disturbed. I hoped she would wake. I hoped that the terrible, fateful decision would not be left to me alone.

But Joan went on sleeping. Scraps of white mist floated in through the open window. I closed it and again it was not possible to avoid making a slight noise. I carried my bag to the corridor. "At least you can leave a note for her," one half of me said. But the agent remained obdurate. I made my way to the door. I turned once more and looked behind me. . . .

I ignored the most elementary requirements of caution. It was all a matter of indifference to me now and I acted entirely without thought or consideration.

I summoned a taxi and drove straight to a hotel. As far as I was concerned the whole of the F.B.I. could be waiting for me at the reception desk. For all I cared they could have caught me there and then. All I wanted was to be free of the whole business.

I left my bag at the reception desk. They needed only to open it and they would have all the proof they wanted against me. Then I bought myself a bottle of whisky and took it to bed with me. On the following day I did the same thing. That was how I somehow managed to live through Christmas Day. That day and during the days which followed, I forgot everything I had learned at the school for secret agents. Perhaps I could never have done what I eventually did if I had conducted myself like an expert.

The information from Brown gave me a pointer and I carried on without thought or care for the consequences. Not once did I look round to see if I was being followed. It was as if life had put blinkers on me. I visited libraries and reading rooms, I spoke with engineers and workmen and I posed my questions without any inhibitions.

Needless to say, the Manhattan Project was absolutely confidential, but no country could keep an atomic bomb entirely secret. The route of the uranium ore that came from northern Canada—some of it also came from the Belgian Congo—could be precisely traced.

For the cooling of an atomic pile it is necessary to have vast quantities of water. I observed that a section of the

Columbia River had been diverted. It also did not escape my notice that in Oak Ridge in the State of Tennessee a six-storey works building had sprung up within the space of a few months.

I also investigated the matter of test flights. Two distinguished air force officers, specialists in B29, the greatest American long-distance bomber of its time, had been drafted from the Pacific zone. They were now engaged in the seemingly pointless occupation of flying an exceptionally heavy mock bomb backwards and forwards in Arizona. The pilots themselves had no idea of the significance of what they were doing when I reported everything to Germany.

I gritted my teeth and again became more cautious. My report must get through. Perhaps a terrible disaster could be prevented if the German government could be warned in time, and if they took my warning seriously. If . . .

I assembled my transmitter. I had some difficulty in getting it to go at first, but I finally succeeded. At five in the afternoon, American time, all was ready. I formulated my message. It was too long. I shortened it and found I was able to save about fifty words. I coded the text, learned it by heart, then wrote it down once again and found I could cut another sentence. I would need eight to ten minutes. I seated myself at the keyboard, wondering if I would be located in New York, wondering if they still imagined that a German spy could possibly be transmitting a message from their very midst.

I tapped the keys. After a short time I received a reply. I was now quite calm. I was, so to speak, once more in my own element. My transmission took no longer than I had calculated. Reception had been clear; I received confirmation from the ether.

The first part of my mission had been completed. What would they think of my report in Berlin? I wondered whether they would simply throw it into the wastepaper basket as they had done with other important messages which they had not dared to place before Hitler. Or would they simply not believe what I had said? Would they think that I had fallen prey to pacifist feelings? Or would they think I had reported what I had reported just to make myself look important? Anything was possible. I realised all of this. When the war was over I was to know a good deal more besides. . . .

The second part of my mission was—sabotage. I was to marshal together a group of men who would carry out explosive attacks on the main works buildings of the American atomic industry. Men and money for this purpose were ready and waiting for me in South America. The only question was, to what extent were they dependable? It was quite within the bounds of possibility that both were counterfeit.

"What is the point of it all?" I asked myself again and again during this period. Was it all worthwhile? Was it still my duty to go on? Why didn't I just throw the whole thing up? Why didn't I just go undercover for a while? My colleagues and indeed my superiors were not to prove to be such sticklers for duty.

The arrangement was that I should get in touch with contact men in Peru by inserting an advertisement in a South American newspaper. Through the medium of a few innocuous words which I have since forgotten, I was to inform them that they were to come to New York as quickly as possible.

The advertisement appeared. The next step was for the contact men to confirm through an advertisement in the same newspaper that everything was proceeding according to plan. I had therefore to buy this particular paper every day. It was obtainable only at the larger newspaper stands in New York, and unknown to me that was where my fate lurked in wait for me. . . .

The last day of 1944 began for me like any other day. My room was overheated, the wallpaper was grim. I shaved and had some coffee in a snack bar. I was in a bad mood, but I had been in a bad mood ever since I had left Joan. All the time I longed to go back to her. I wondered what she was doing, and what she was thinking of me. I wondered if she had somehow got over the ghastly surprise of the morning when she awoke to find I had disappeared.

I knew the little dress shop in New York that she ran. I had walked past it a few times. I wanted to see her once again. I hadn't even a photograph of her; it would indeed have been wrong of me to have had a photograph of her. I saw her face, her eyes, always before me. It was enough to drive me crazy. Meanwhile I was acting as errand boy for an idiotic war. . . .

I lunched at one o'clock on a double portion of steak and the usual *pommes frites*. I was suddenly terribly hungry. Then I bought myself a few newspapers. Passing over the war reports, I read a speech of Roosevelt's. I couldn't stand the man. Then I turned to a murder case.

There was a cinema close to the restaurant and I went in. The film was a Western of the worst kind and I left the cinema after half an hour of it. I had once again accustomed myself to take a good look around me. I was sure no one was following me. New York was busy preparing to celebrate New Year's Eve. I would have to celebrate alone; I still had no idea where I should go. I walked on towards Times Square. It was a dreary afternoon. There were hundreds of people hanging about in the square, people actively wanting to enjoy themselves, people who were bored or people who were out on business. On the right side of the square was a newspaper stand which carried the paper I had to see.

I walked past the stand first. I always did this when I was buying newspapers. There were a good number of people about, always three or four at the stand putting their cents in a dish and picking up the paper they wanted. A few people were standing about nearby but that's something you always see by a newspaper stand. Some people just can't wait to satisfy their curiosity and stand and look at their papers in the most unsuitable places.

I walked past the stand once more. There were two teenagers behind me giggling over something that had happened at a dancing class. In front of me a wounded man in uniform was walking along on crutches. The people coming towards him looked pained and embarrassed. Cars were driving across the square in a continuous stream. A woman dropped a parcel and I picked it up for her. She thanked me with a smile. I went up to the stand. A glance to the left, and one to the right. It looked as if the coast was clear. Nowhere near could I see two men together; two men together spelled danger for me.

I had to wait a few seconds and looked meanwhile at various magazines as if I were undecided which to take. I bought two and then asked for the South American paper. The man hesitated for a moment then nodded knowingly.

"One moment, sir," he said. He riffled through a stack of papers. Then he found it.

"I don't get asked for this very often," he explained. "If you need it regularly, let me know and I'll put it on one side for you."

"I'm only a visitor here," I replied, "but thanks all the same."

I gave him a dollar.

"Haven't you anything smaller?" he asked.

"Sorry, I haven't," I replied.

He gave me twenty-five cents change, counting it out to me carefully. I unbuttoned my overcoat and dropped the change into the left breast pocket of my jacket. It was an odd habit of mine; my mother had in fact often taken me to task about it when I was a boy at home.

I put the papers in my overcoat pocket, the South American one wrapped round by the two magazines so that it could not be seen. I strolled on a few paces further. A man near me lit a cigarette. His eyes were on the match. Then he approached nearer. The crowd tossed up a group of young soldiers who passed by three abreast, making a great deal of noise.

"One moment, sir," said the man with the cigarette. In the same second another man appeared at his side as if he had been conjured out of a hat.

"Edward Green, I believe?"

"No," I said, "my name's Frank Miller."

"Well, whatever your name is," replied one of the two men, "you are under arrest."

CHAPTER 13

Grilled by the F.B.I.

THEY certainly knew their job and I found myself so wedged in between them that any attempt to escape would have been suicidal; at the same time everything was done so unobtrusively that not one of the thousands who at that time were crossing Times Square could possibly have imagined that anything at all out of the ordinary was going on.

"My name is Nelson," said one of the two men. He was short and stocky, with a round head and lively eyes. He showed me his badge.

"This isn't a very good place to talk," he went on. "Come along with us."

The newspaper stand which had spelled my doom had behind it a small room. We went inside.

"I would now like to know what you want with me," I began.

"I'll tell you that straightaway," replied Nelson. He lit a cigarette, smiled and indicated his colleague.

"May I introduce to you Mr. Gillies, Mr. Green."

"I told you my name is not Green."

"Show me your papers."

I produced a document bearing the name Frank Miller.

"They certainly know how to forge papers in Germany," he replied.

I realised now that I was in for it and the only thing that surprised me was that the F.B.I. did not push me into a car and drive me off for interrogation at once.

"Well, Mr. Miller," said Nelson, "where do you live?"

"I come from Chicago."

"And where do you live in Chicago?"

I gave him an address which I had learned by heart. He made a note of it.

"And how long have you been in New York?"

"Ten days," I replied.

"And what are you doing here?"

"I am on business."

"Mm, mm," he said, "just think of that. Well, I've got a little message for you."

"For me?"

"From William Curtis Colepaugh, otherwise known as Billy. He's been waiting a fortnight for you already."

"I don't know him."

Gillies went to the telephone and dialled a number. He cursed quietly on finding it engaged. At the second attempt he got through.

"We've got him," he said. "Come along over. . . . No, you can be quite sure, there's absolutely no doubt about it." Then he hung up.

Nelson went on with his interrogation.

"I'll tell you something. About five weeks ago you landed in Frenchman Bay. The two of you. Then by a roundabout route you travelled to Boston. From Boston you came to New York. In New York your friend stole the suitcases. You recovered them at Grand Central Station—that was marvellous, the way you did that. You've got a quantity of money and diamonds with you and a wireless transmitter. And I'll wager that you've already sent a report through to Germany.

"Yes," he continued. "We've waited a long time for you. You've certainly held out a good while. Longer than all your colleagues; and you didn't make any mistakes." He toyed with his revolver. It was a Smith & Wesson, the latest model. He took hold of it and aimed out of the window.

"To be precise, you made one solitary mistake. As soon as you landed, you should have taken your revolver and shot Billy between the eyes. No American would have held that against you."

"I'll take your advice next time," I replied.

I knew now that there was no point in pursuing the role of the indignant, wrongfully arrested American. They had Billy, and Billy had given me away. There was no doubt about that. There was no harm in admitting to what they already knew about me, but I must at all costs keep quiet about what they did not know.

I thought of Joan, of Santi, of Brown, of my contact men in South America. All of them would be in the greatest possible danger if I did not keep my mouth shut.

"Where are you staying in New York?"

I hesitated for a moment.

"If you don't tell us, your picture will appear in every New York newspaper tomorrow morning, and I'll bet you anything that we'll have your address by seven o'clock at the latest. Do you believe me?"

"All right," I replied. "I'm staying at the Pennsylvania Hotel, room 1559."

"I'm glad you've decided to be sensible. Now I'm afraid I must search you. Would you please empty your pockets?"

I put everything on the table. A comb, a knife, two handkerchiefs, a wallet and several bundles of banknotes. Gillies counted the money. There was more than 10,000 dollars.

"You certainly carry plenty of money around with you."

"It's an old habit of mine."

"Just have another look in your pockets and make sure you've forgotten nothing," said Nelson, "otherwise I shall get into trouble afterwards."

"I've still got my wristwatch."

"Give it to me, please."

The door opened and a man of medium height with an intelligent face, lively eyes and a small dashing moustache came in.

"Here's the boss," explained Nelson. "Mr. Connelly, deputy head of the F.B.I."

"I'm delighted to make your acquaintance," I said.

"Me too," he replied, and smiled.

"It's a good thing you've managed to keep your sense of humour. You'll certainly need it."

He had a pleasant voice. It was a voice I was to hear for days and weeks on end. The questions he put to me became ever more unpleasant, but the tone in which they were put remained always friendly.

Nelson was in a corner of the room taking notes. Connelly came up to me.

"I've one request," he said. "I'd like to take a look at your hotel room."

"Go ahead," I replied.

"Not without your express permission."

"I don't understand," I replied. "If I don't give you permission you will have it searched just the same."

His smile broadened.

"Tomorrow, yes, but not today. I shan't be able to get a search warrant today."

This punctiliousness seemed so strange to me that I was at a loss to understand it. In the last year of the war the F.B.I. could still afford to abide by the strict letter of the law in respect of an enemy, a spy, a saboteur.

"Go along by all means," I said. "You'll be thrilled with what you find there."

"I've no doubt about that."

Connelly went to the telephone and gave instructions for the room to be searched.

"That's fine," he said. "I'll go on ahead now. We'll question you in my office." He nodded to me and to his two officers.

"I hate to do it," said Nelson, "but I must ask you for your arm."

I stretched out my arm and he handcuffed me to Gillies. "We have our instructions," he said by way of apology.

We got into a car. The noise and bustle on Times Square had increased. New Year's Eve! Confetti was flying above our heads. People were laughing and shouting and joking with each other. A new year was beginning, a year which was certain to bring peace. The Americans were celebrating this in advance. They clapped us on the back, smiled at us and utterly failed to notice that I was handcuffed. They were on the threshold of peace. I was at the gates of death.

Nelson drove and I sat with Gillies at the back of the car.

"It's time we had a drink," I said.

"I could do with one myself," replied Nelson.

"Well then, might I invite you two gentlemen to take a drink with me?"

"But you wouldn't want to go and have a drink like this, would you?" laughed Nelson.

"Well, you could take the handcuffs off. I certainly shan't run away from you."

"I quite believe you," answered Nelson. "But perhaps we'll find a bottle of something in my office."

Connelly was waiting for us. He was wearing a dark suit with a bright tie. He looked full of energy and enterprise.

"Welcome!" he said. It sounded facetious but not malicious.

"The whole of American rejoices at this moment," he said. "You've no idea what a job we've had to catch you. Next time don't put your change in your breast pocket. That's what gave you away."

"I'll make a note of that, Mr. Connelly," I said.

He clapped me on the back.

"He's a nice chap," he said, "our friend Gimpel." So he already knew my real name.

"Where's Billy?" I asked.

"In the next room. Are you impatient to see him?"

"By no means."

"I like you," said Connelly. "But I don't want to have anything to do with your friend. You might have saved us the trouble, but now we've got to hang him."

Connelly brought me a glass of whisky.

"Drink up," he said, "it will do you good. You've got a long night in front of you and a long day. We've got to cross-question you now, but we'll make it as pleasant as we can."

I answered in the same strain.

"Interrogations are always pleasant," I said. "They make the time pass so quickly."

Two officers returned from the Pennsylvania Hotel bringing with them my whole espionage equipment, money, diamonds, photographic apparatus, invisible ink, revolver and parts of my transmitter.

"You've got a nice collection there," said Connelly. He seated himself at his desk. Behind him hung a portrait of Roosevelt, almost life-size, in a silver frame. The picture was slightly hazy which made it look as if the President were perspiring. I gazed at him searchingly and imagined I saw him wink at me with his left eye.

Connelly turned round to the portrait and smiled.

"The President knows all about it already," he said. "He was informed half an hour ago by Mr. Hoover. Mr. Hoover is the Supreme Head of the F.B.I. You know that, of course." He offered me a cigarette and lit it for me. "You certainly cannot complain of lack of attention. Actually no German agent has ever before got as far as you did." He rose from his chair and paced up and down the room.

"Would you like another glass of whisky?" he asked.

I nodded.

"Are you hungry?"

"Yes."

"Tell me what you would like and you shall have it. Not only today either. You're in the best hands. When you've had something to eat we'll continue our conversation," he said. He motioned to an officer who led me out into another room which had been set up as a sort of provisional cell.

"I'll have some grilled steak and *pommes frites*. After that ice cream and a glass of bourbon. Perhaps you can also bring me some sweets and couple of packets of cigarettes."

"It shall be done," answered the officer and carefully locked the door behind him.

I sat on the bunk and listened as two men conversed

sotto voce just outside the door. It was night. On the horizon I could see some improvised fireworks going off. Jumping crackers, rockets and Catherine wheels. The new year was on the way.

"Here's to the New Year," I said to myself and beat my fists upon my forehead. As I waited for my steak I felt only a mixture of scorn and pity for myself.

In the last analysis it was all the same to me whether I was executed with courtesy or without it. However correct the proceedings might be, the outcome was inevitable. Death is the penalty for espionage in wartime the world over. Every secret agent knows that and every secret agent has only one defence against it—not to get caught.

The *pommes frites* smelled tempting. The steak was tender and underdone as I liked it, but every mouthful stuck in my throat. Perhaps now the third degree was about to begin. That horribly cruel method of interrogation attributed to the F.B.I. . . . I ate slowly to kill time. They certainly allowed me plenty.

An officer poked his head around the door.

"All right?" he asked.

"First class," I replied.

I was now on the ice cream. I was thinking of Joan and could see her before me. Her eyes, her lips, her brow. She had moist eyes, red-rimmed. She could not understand what I had done to her. She knew nothing of the work of a spy; thank God, she knew nothing of that. I must concentrate on shielding her at all costs. She and Santi, Brown and the contact men in South America who were probably at this moment trying to cross the frontier.

It was all over. I had been caught. I was lost, betrayed. Operation Elster had come to an end, but half-completed, on Times Square, right in the heart of New York. On the busiest spot of that vast metropolis.

Mr. Connelly, deputy head of the F.B.I. would probably allow me another five minutes. I lit a cigarette. . . .

Damn and blast Times Square! It had a bad name in the files of the German M.I. and it had got me now! Of the serious losses the German Secret Service had sustained on this spot I thought of the Osten case. At any rate it helped me to forget my own troubles for a while. . . .

In 1941, Major von der Osten, one of the shrewdest officers of the German M.I. was commissioned to reorganise the network of German secret agents in the U.S.A. It was a few months before Pearl Harbour, and America had not yet entered the war. The major travelled with a Spanish passport, calling himself Lido, and reached the States via Honolulu and San Francisco. His papers were as expert as his experience, and he aroused no suspicion. He got as far as New York without the American Secret Service becoming aware of his presence in the country.

New York was the centre of the German espionage which was under the direction of a German-American whose name began with L. The results it had so far achieved were meagre and that was why the Major had been sent to New York; he was to inject some life into the proceedings. Von der Osten was tall and slim. He spoke English with an irreproachable American accent and could drink and swear with the best of them.

Von der Osten looked up L. who gave him maps, plans and a list of all the contact men, and von der Osten put the documents in a briefcase. L. and the Major took a taxi and drove through New York.

At Times Square the lights showed red, the taxi stopped and the two men took the opportunity to get out. They paid off the driver, L. stepped out on to the street and von der Osten followed. The lights changed and the traffic moved forward. A sports car, the driver of which was drunk, shot forward like lightning straight at von der Osten. The major leapt to one side and landed right in the path of a Cadillac.

There was a crash, a scream, and a crowd began to form.

L. acted swiftly. He took the briefcase out of the hand of the seriously injured man and disappeared into the crowd. One or two people noticed him and informed the police.

They took the Major to hospital, but he died on the way. They inspected his passport and became suspicious. . . .

This grim accident in Times Square in 1941 cost the

German M.I. fourteen trained agents. The F.B.I. had L.'s description, they went after him and they found him.

L. broke down under interrogation and the F.B.I. made its swoop. One motorcar in Times Square had played a decisive part in the course of the war. It should have been a warning to me. . . .

"If you're ready. . . ." An F.B.I. official came for me. "Mr. Connelly would like to see you in his office."

"Yes, I'm ready," I replied.

I only had to go down a short passageway. Three officials were waiting for me.

"Make yourself comfortable," said Connelly. "It's going to be a long job."

I sat down and put a cigarette in my mouth. The officer threw a box of matches across the table to me; they had taken my lighter away. I had also been relieved of my braces, and my shoelaces had been removed from my shoes; my tie had likewise found its way into the property room. Precautions against suicide are the same the world over.

"You are a German?" asked Connelly.

"Yes."

"You have been going under the name of Edward Green?"

"Yes."

"You have also used the name of Frank Miller here?"

"Yes."

"You made an illegal entry into the United States five weeks ago?"

"Yes."

"By means of a German U-boat?"

"Yes."

"What was the name of the U-boat commander?"

"I don't know."

Connelly nodded.

"Do you not know or do you not wish to tell me?"

"I don't know," I replied.

Nelson laughed.

"You don't expect us to believe that, of course."

"You can do what you like with it," I replied.

"That's fine," replied Connelly.

"You are an agent of the German M.I., are you not?"

"Yes."

"You were trained for the work at the German schools?"

"Yes."

"At which schools?"

"I'm not going to tell you."

"Just as you like."

Connelly got to his feet and paced up and down in the room.

Then he said: "My job is to investigate the case, nothing more. You'll be handled decently here, you'll discover that. We're not the Gestapo. I even have a certain understanding of the fact that you should wish to shield your associates. . . . But don't get me wrong. I mean I have a certain human understanding for it; as an officer of the F.B.I. I must do my duty."

He sat down and lit a cigarette.

"I just had to make my little speech," he said. "You know, of course, that we Americans like making speeches."

"Well, I've nothing against it."

"What were your instructions in America?"

I remained silent.

"Do you deny that you intended to gather information about the American armament industry?"

"No," I replied.

"You know, of course, that that is called espionage."

"Yes."

"Therefore you don't deny that you are a spy?"

"No."

"But you will not tell us what you have been spying upon."

"Have you ever met a spy who'd tell you that?" I asked.

"Oh," said Connelly with a smile, "we've had a whole host of amateurs here."

"Well, I'm no amateur, I can tell you that."

He roared with laughter.

"I haven't much to tell you," I said. "My own story isn't

of much interest to you or to me. . . . I came to America
with a citizen of the States—that's no news to you. There's
no one apart from him who had anything to do with this
undertaking. I just had to find out what I could about the
capacity of the American armament industry. I tried but I
did not succeed. . . . Any questions you may care to ask me
which concern me personally I will answer willingly. You
know, of course, that a secret agent is only one small cog
in a great machine, and that he himself is kept in the dark
as far as possible about the picture as a whole."

Connelly nodded.

"But you're no ordinary secret agent," he replied. "You
were working for Germany when you were in Peru. You
were a layman then, of course, but after that you received
your training. You served under Canaris and you did so
well that you were transferred to Reich Security, a department of the S.S. There you developed into one of Germany's most dangerous spies. Then I could tell you a few
things from your time in Spain. . . . Oh no, when they send
a man like you across the Atlantic they know what they're
doing."

We conversed politely enough but continued to talk past
rather than to each other. We told each other only what we
knew already. The interrogation was being conducted in an
almost leisurely manner, but it was just therein that the
danger lay. The F.B.I. was first of all applying the 'soft'
method; when would they bring the 'hard' into play? When
would they start using noise, loud music, floodlights, shouts
and blows? When would they come at me with an outstretched revolver and threaten to shoot me? When would
they promise me my freedom? When would they describe
the execution? When would they try the sexual methods?
When would they use the lever of religion? When would
they get brutal?

It had to come. Perhaps not today, but certainly tomorrow. Then it would start. They would hold a photograph of
my mother before my eyes and threaten reprisals against
my family. I knew exactly how everything would be done

and I knew that there was small chance of my surviving these methods of torture and keeping quiet.

The officials were relieved every ten minutes. New faces appeared, new names cropped up. Some of the men looked rough and brutal but they spoke gently and courteously. No, I certainly would not fall for the 'soft' methods. . . .

They brought me coffee. I was chain-smoking and my fingers were getting quite brown. The morning mist descended on New York and I could hear the bells ringing in the New Year. The city awoke, milk churns clattered and newspaper men called out the headlines upon the morning air. The people shouted New Year greetings to each other. The postman got his tip, and those who clung to their beliefs went to church. Those who had drunk too much the night before were taking headache powders, and anyone who had a day off from work would certainly go on sleeping.

"What were the names of your contact men in America?"

"Don't lie."

"What were you doing with so much money?"

"Just tell us the names of the people with whom you had dealings and then you can sleep for two days."

They brought me ham and eggs and wonderful coffee. There were cigarettes on the tray. Nothing was spared.

Another crop of new faces. It was hot. I took my jacket off and unbuttoned my shirt. My beard was growing and my face was irritated. I passed my hand over the stubble once or twice.

"Oh, would you like to have a wash?" said one of the officers, interrupting the interrogation. "I'm so sorry. We'll pause for half an hour."

I was taken back into my cell.

"What's the time?" I asked.

"Nine o'clock," answered an official.

The interrogation had already gone on for eleven hours. That was quite enough for me but it was to continue.

At twelve o'clock Connelly appeared again.

"Just tell us what you'd like to eat, and we'll order it from the hotel. You can have whatever you like. You must be tired. I wish I could leave you in peace but you understand I have my duty. . . ."

If this consideration, this attitude of human understanding were false, Connelly must have been the best actor I had ever known. But I believe it was genuine. All the officials, whether they seemed detached or interested, whether they had any private conversation with me or declined to talk to me personally, regarded me with a look that was a mixture of shyness, pity and horror. I was to be the object of this look for weeks on end and I was finally able to define it. It was the look one gives a man who in measurable time is going to be led out to the gallows.

And so the interrogation went on. The same questions again and again, and again the same answers. When evening came we had not progressed one step. The sweat was running off my forehead, my legs were swelling and my mouth was parched although I was drinking coffee and Coca-Cola all the time. Night fell and Connelly went home for a short time.

What was happening in the background meanwhile I learned only later. On my account a special conference was called at the White House and the decision was taken to strengthen the coastal defences. The fact that a German U-boat had been able to break through the defensive ring had caused painful surprise in many quarters, and those responsible were to be summoned to appear before a court-martial. They reconstructed the landing, followed the route we had taken and interrogated all the people we had spoken with, however trifling the conversation might have been. The F.B.I. had been put on its mettle. . . .

Connelly returned. He had food sent up. We ate together and discussed the proper way to grill a steak. We discovered we had the same taste. We had the wireless on while we were eating and let Harry James blow a trumpet solo at us.

"Any complaints?" asked Connelly.

"Actually, no," I replied.

"Let's have another cigarette in peace," he said when we

had finished our meal. He stood up and turned the radio off. "I'll have a doctor sent in to you, if you like."

"Thank you, but I'm as sound as a bell."

"Well," he said, "that's worth a good deal. My wife is in hospital. She suddenly contracted diphtheria. Diphtheria at twenty-four. My children are with their grandparents."

"So you've children too?"

"Two," he said, "a boy and a girl."

He stubbed out his cigarette. At the same moment the door opened and two officials entered the room. The interrogation proceeded. Connelly sat in the background. He put his feet on his desk and brandished an outsize ruler in the air. Now and again I looked over in his direction, but he appeared not to notice it. He was doing everything he could to appear indifferent to what was taking place.

It was midnight and once more the men were relieved.

"Ah well," said Connelly, "we still don't know any more than we knew at the start. You're very uncommunicative, my friend."

"Speech is silver, silence is golden."

"Is that a German saying?"

"Yes."

"You could make things much easier for yourself and for us too. You've only to name the men who are backing you up."

"There are none."

He shrugged.

"Then we shall have to institute a change in the proceedings," he said.

Once more a door opened.

Half pulled, half shoved, Billy appeared on the scene, pale, unshaven, his face swollen.

"Now come along," said Nelson, giving him a push forward, "shake hands with your friend."

Billy remained as if rooted to the spot. You could have heard a pin drop. I lit a cigarette. Billy was incapable of speaking and could not look me in the face. He presented a picture of such complete stupidity that for one moment I had to struggle with a feeling of pity for him. It was, however, soon dispelled.

"Come on," said Connelly. "Say something, Billy. Tell us again what you know about him."

Billy was silent.

"Come along, talk!"

The official shoved him nearer to me. He had a bruise on his head. He certainly had not been handled gently, that was obvious.

"Have you lost your tongue?" asked Connelly.

"You know everything already," said Billy. He still had his eyes on the floor.

"He was with the S.S. He was quite a big shot."

"Go on, Billy," said Connelly, "what else do you know?"

"He intended to blow up some factories here."

"Which factories?"

Billy was silent.

He stood there pale, hangdog, like one paralysed. His long, apelike arms hung limply down. His hair fell into his eyes. He looked sickly and was shaking from head to foot.

"Billy," said Connelly, "you're a swine. Get back into your cell again." He turned to me.

"You didn't pick a very good companion for your trip."

"One learns by one's mistakes, but it's always too late then," I replied.

The interrogation went on. There were days and weeks of it. The court-martial was set up. Counsel were appointed. They did their best to separate the proceedings against Colepaugh from my own case, arguing that I had been a soldier while Colepaugh was a traitor. But they did not succeed. The opening day of the trial loomed ahead. I was approaching my end with uncanny speed.

CHAPTER 14

In the Shadow of the Scaffold

IN my prison cell in Fort Jay, New York State, to which I had been moved after the F.B.I. interrogations had been brought to a close, I became acquainted with the dull, crushing monotony of prison life and the feeling of inward rebellion against it. My cell was a sort of wire cage through the mesh of which it was just possible to push a cigarette. It was kept immaculately clean and was big enough to enable me to walk six steps forward and six steps backwards. It was lit by a 200-watt lamp which burned throughout the day and night. A camp bed provided a minimum degree of comfort for sleeping.

I had now become a captive of the American Army. My fellow prisoners in Fort Jay, whom I saw only rarely, were American soldiers serving sentences for insubordination, cowardice and similar military delinquencies. The guards were men of the military police. The warders wore military uniform and had military rank. One of them, Corporal Kelly, used to push cigarettes through the cage for me and would stand guard so that I should not be caught enjoying my forbidden smoke.

"My brother," he explained, "is a prisoner-of-war in

Germany, and I only hope he's got a warder who can carry on like a human being."

I hoped so too. I had got out of the way of recoiling at the harshness of war, but was very much affected whenever in the midst of it all I came across a man who thought and acted in a human way.

I was the pride of Fort Jay and was visited every day by high-ranking service officers. Three or four times a day the door would be opened, the sentry would call "Attention!" and I would grasp my trousers (my belt having been taken away just as my shoelaces had been removed as a suicide precaution), and stagger towards the staff officers.

They were, without exception, friendly and chivalrous towards me. They enquired searchingly as to how I was treated, whether the quality of the food was to my satisfaction and if I had any requests. These were unfailingly granted so far as lay within their power.

It took me some time to get accustomed to this treatment. I simply could not understand why they should treat an enemy so fairly. The treatment meted out to me was quite different from that which fell to the lot of my Judas friend, Billy Colepaugh. I had already noticed with the F.B.I. that they were particularly nice to me whenever Billy was around. It went something like this:

"Is there anything you want, Mr. Gimpel?" from the warder.

"No, thank you."

"Have you any complaints?"

"No complaints either."

"Unfortunately I may not bring you whisky, but perhaps we can offer you some other form of refreshment?"

"Bring me a Coca-Cola."

Once a colonel visited me.

"How far do you walk each day?" he asked.

I looked at him uncomprehendingly.

"They do allow you exercise, don't they, Mr. Gimpel?"

"I do all my walking in my cell," I replied.

His face coloured up, and he had the officer-of-the-guard called.

"Every prisoner has the right to fresh air," he barked at him. "Can you explain why you have not allowed Mr. Gimpel to leave his cell?"

"How can I, sir?" answered the captain. "I have strict instructions not to allow him any contact with the other prisoners."

"Then just lock the others up for the required length of time," said the colonel.

He offered me a cigarette, lit it for me and added:

"It won't do these fellows any harm."

After that, every day at dusk I was allowed to take a turn in the enormous courtyard of Fort Jay. The guards watched me at my exercise. Once they clapped as I passed them, and the cook asked me if the food he prepared was to my liking. I was, as I have said, the pride of Fort Jay. Another prisoner was the former trumpet soloist of Benny Goodman's orchestra. He performed every evening to the delight of guards and prisoners and instead of the Last Post played "Good Night, Baby." He had been sentenced on account of some military misdeed, and was soon to be released. His warders granted his every wish. They all enjoyed his music. . . .

I had been about three weeks in Fort Jay when things took a serious turn. I was told that Major Charles E. Reagin and Major John E. Haigney had come to see me. I was taken to the visitors' room. Both men were middle-aged, slim and very personable. They were extremely nice to me and introduced themselves with such perfect courtesy that we might have been meeting at the Waldorf Hotel for a business conference.

"If you are agreeable," they began, "we are prepared to take on your defence."

"I am most grateful to you," I replied. "Of course I am agreeable."

"We are familiar with your evidence," said Reagin. "From the legal point of view your case is quite clear."

"Yes," I said.

We sat down and cigarettes were handed round.

"We will conduct your defence with every means at our

disposal, that we can promise you. We can also assure you that the court will in no way limit your defence. As a matter of fact, the court has just recently assembled. President Roosevelt directed the matter personally."

"And what do you think my chances are?" I asked.

The major looked me calmly in the eye.

"Legally speaking," he replied, "they're nil. You must know that as well as I do. I think it would be foolish to have any illusions on that score."

I nodded.

"However, in spite of that I do not regard your case as hopeless," continued Reagin. "If Germany capitulates, that will probably save your life, but if the war goes on, you'll be hanged. It's really a race between your life and the end of the war. It can't go on much longer. The Russians are at the Oder and our troops are in the Ruhr."

"You've certainly brought me some good news," I said.

"We must drag out the proceedings as long as we possibly can," Reagin went on. "And I'll tell you this: We will use every trick we can think up; we'll make things as difficult for the prosecution as we possibly can. In the first place we'll delay the start of the case. We've not yet completed our study of the documents. That will dispose of a week. And now listen carefully to what I have to say."

The major got to his feet and paced up and down the room. He had a fresh, healthy complexion. On his left breast he wore a row of medal ribbons. He spoke with emphasis but without raising his voice, and underlined his words with economical, unobtrusive gestures.

"They will call you into the witness box. They will ask you if you are guilty or not guilty. If you say you are guilty you are as good as dead already. Don't worry about the depositions you have already made to the F.B.I. That counts for nothing in a court of law. Just stand up there and think and do what you like—as far as I am concerned you can scratch your backside if you want to—but whatever else you do, say as loudly as you can, 'Not guilty!' "

The two majors shook hands with me and departed. Both had a fine reputation in the Army. They were the best counsel I could have had and they went all out for me in such a way that it was hard to imagine that they belonged to a people against whom I had been sent to spy.

"It was bad luck," Major Haigney had said to me at our first meeting, "that you were caught, but you're fortunate in that you will appear before an American court. Just think what it would have been like if you'd been on the other side and had fallen into the hands of Reich Security, for instance."

The distractions which the warders did their best to provide for me, the chivalrous treatment and the businesslike conversations with my counsel could not close my eyes to the one ghastly certainty that my days were numbered.

Any court-martial in the world would sentence me to death. That was beyond all possible doubt, and there could be no appeal against this judgment. It was unalterable. I could present a plea for pardon to the American President but it would only be a waste of paper.

When you have perhaps only three or four more weeks of life in front of you, the tendency is to thrust aside all thought of the final hour. But at the end of each day the thought that you're one day nearer the grave comes home with added force. You can think of death in a manly way when you've not been sentenced to death, but heroics die a natural death of their own in the shadow of the scaffold. Before you meet your own death, the phrase 'Death for the Fatherland' dies. Those who preached it, did not, alas, die that way.

The anxiety, the fear, the horror, came ever closer and I became their prey. I counted the meshes in my wire cage—once I got to ten thousand—but while I tried to divert myself by some mechanical means, fear clawed at my back, dried up my mouth and caused the sweat to stream from my pores. Sometimes I tore up and down like a madman, racking my brains day and night for some possibility of escape from prison or some legal loophole to escape the hangman.

During this period, in the course of which my mind and my nerves were approaching breaking point, I received another visit from some senior American officers. A colonel and two majors had me called to the Interrogation Room. The colonel was tall and broad shouldered and looked like an overfed physical training instructor. One of his companions was short and frail looking and had a pale, pointed face with a somewhat fanatical expression; the other one wore an ash blond moustache on a completely expressionless face. I always took a good look at any visitors I had as I was glad of any break in the monotony, however meaningless.

"How do you do?" said the colonel. "Do sit down. Can I offer you a cigarette?"

"Thank you."

He pushed a whole packet of Camels across the table to me.

"We've come straight from Washington," he began. "It was a long journey, but let's hope it will prove worthwhile for you."

I listened carefully.

"You know what lies in front of you?"

"I'm being reminded of it half a dozen times every day," I replied.

He stood up and walked round the table. He held a long cigar between his fat fingers and puffed quick little clouds of blue smoke into the air.

"We are from the O.S.S.," he said, "the Office of Strategic Service. You know, of course, what that is."

"Of course," I replied. "I've already met some of your agents somewhere."

The O.S.S. was the military espionage organisation of the United States. The German M.I. had sparred with it with varying degrees of skill.

"We have a proposition to put to you. . . . You don't have to make up your mind at once, but in any case, listen carefully."

He remained standing.

"Who do you think is going to win the war?" he asked.

I remained silent.

"Come, come," he said jovially. "Let's leave hopes and

fears on one side for the moment. You've got a good head—use it! Have you really any doubt that we are going to win the war?"

"No."

"Good," he said. "Germany hasn't a chance now."

"That may be so."

"It is so."

The thin major with the fanatical expression now took a hand in the conversation.

"I'll be delighted to give you details," he said. "Yesterday there was a particularly heavy air attack on Berlin. Field-Marshal Model has shot himself in the Ruhr. Eleven Gauleiters have deserted. If you like, I'll give you the names. . . . The German people, or at any rate those who have taken no part in the war crimes, want only one thing, peace. Every day by which the war is shortened means less bloodshed. And it's mostly German blood that's being shed now."

"That's true," I said.

"I'm glad you're amenable to reason," said the major. "I think we're going to get along well together."

"What actually do you want with me?"

"You are going to be hanged," said the colonel.

"Thanks to your readiness to give information, that fact is already abundantly clear to me."

There was a pause, and I looked from one officer to the other. The massive colonel appeared to be quite indifferent. The major with the fanatical expression was staring out of the window. The third officer was carefully studying his well-kept fingernails. There was plenty of time, time for everyone, except me. For me, time had run out, or hadn't it?

"You could work for us," said the colonel.

I remained silent.

"You can, for example, sit down at your Morse keyboard and make a few transmissions to Germany which interest us."

"So you want to turn me into a double-crosser?"

"Put it that way if you must," replied the colonel.

"It would be treason."

"No," interrupted the colonel. "I believe that in present circumstances it would be the greatest service you could do your country."

"You would be preventing more bloodshed," said one major.

"And you would save your own head," put in the other. "I imagine that is an argument you won't want to dismiss out of hand."

There was another pause. My mind worked feverishly. The offer was certainly attractive. As I considered it a terrible weariness came over me. What I should most of all have liked to do at that moment was to lie down and go to sleep. Temptation, soft, insidious, temptation! Freedom! Release from the prison cage! Release from the cell, from fear of the judge, from the threat of the gallows! Back perhaps to Joan, to Joan of whom I thought day and night, whom I saw constantly before my eyes, near enough to touch, and who disappeared as soon as I stretched out my hands towards her.

The war was as good as over. Lost. Everything had been in vain. The blood that was shed in Russia, the losses in Africa, the suffering in France, all for nothing. All for a system of government that had deserved its collapse a hundred, thousandfold. The continuance of hostilities now was pointless except for the purpose of gaining a few more months for the ruling clique before they were overtaken by their inevitable doom. During the past weeks I had had opportunity enough to ponder well on many things which formerly I had obstinately thrust away from me. It had become clear to me that in this war one could not serve Germany without at the same time becoming a tool of Hitler.

But I had realised this too late. I might have considered turning against Hitler, but against Germany—never.

"No," I answered the colonel, "I can't do it. Just think for a moment if you were in captivity in Germany and it was suggested to you that you should work against America, what would your answer be?"

He remained silent.

"We could force you," interrupted one of the two majors.

"You might shoot me but you could never force me."

There was a painful silence. After a while the colonel took up the conversation again.

"There is no need for you to reach a decision today. We will call again tomorrow. I have this proposition to make to you, that you enter our service. I am not sure yet how we can make use of you. Perhaps you can broadcast to the German people. You have seen now what things look like in America, and you have yourself admitted that Germany will lose the war. You are the only man who could make this clear to your fellow countrymen. When the war is over they will thank you. If you accept this proposition you are a free man, with certain conditions, of course. When the war is over you may leave America or remain here, as you wish. The decision on that rests entirely with you. You will not have to appear before a court-martial. The American newspapers know absolutely nothing about you. Do I make myself clear? There simply would be no German spy Gimpel. There would just be a German reader for Allied broadcasts to Germany for whom we should have to think up a name and a background story."

He stopped speaking, remained standing and looked me fixedly in the eyes. The two majors also looked hard at me. A few seconds passed. The electric fan was humming softly. It was warm in the room. The Americans have the unfortunate habit of overdoing the central heating. In front of the window a whistle sounded; the guard was being changed. Then I heard my fellow prisoner from Benny Goodman's orchestra play a few bars on his trumpet. Then came laughter, and footsteps sounded outside the door. A man stopped in the corridor and then walked slowly away again. . . .

The officers were still staring at me. Once again I felt that dry feeling in my mouth. I passed my tongue over my lips a few times. They were parched. I wanted to say something but no word came. It didn't matter anyhow. What I wanted to say I could not say and what I had to say they knew already.

"It's damned hot in here," said one of the two majors. He opened a window and looked out for a moment into the yard.

I took a cigarette from the packet of Camels the colonel had produced. He gave me a light and put his hand on my shoulder.

"You can let us have your decision tomorrow morning at ten. Your fate is in your own hands. You can be your own hangman, of course, if you want it that way."

I went back into my cage, and threw myself down on the bed. I felt a mixture of hate, fear, defiance and self-pity well up in me. What I should really have liked to do at that moment was to shriek and at the same time weep. Senselessly I beat my hands against the wire mesh.

"O.K., boy," a warder called out laughing. "I know what you want." He pushed a cigarette through for me.

My two counsel came to see me. I told them of the offer I had received from the O.S.S. They shrugged their shoulders and made no attempt to influence me, but later Major Reagin said:

"I never expected you'd do any differently, and I must say I wouldn't have been too keen on defending you if at that juncture you had wavered in your attitude. To me, you are a soldier, nothing more, nothing less. I am a soldier too. Actually the only thing that distinguishes us is the colour of our uniform, and our language, of course."

Meanwhile my counsel's manoeuvre had come off and the case was postponed for a week.

"As I see it," said Reagin, "the war will come to an end in May 1945. We are short of four weeks. How we can get over the difficulty I don't quite know. The case begins on the 6th February and will last at least a week. Sentence will be executed about four weeks after its pronouncement, that is to say, roughly in the second week in April. I reckon that the war will come to an end in the second week of May but those damned four weeks may cost you your life."

I was certainly in a strange situation. My sole chance of

survival lay in the immediate capitulation of my Fatherland.
It was a terrible position to be in. The annihilation of Germany was the condition for my continuing in the land of
the living. I could, I should, I must speculate on total surrender. Meanwhile my brother had fallen at Stalingrad, my
father had been wounded in the First World War, my closest friends had fallen in the north, the east and the west,
millions had fallen for Führer and Fatherland, and the architect of all this misery was at the last moment to desert
by suicide. . . .

My warders did all they could to cheer me up, but I was
my own worst enemy. Strangely enough, my appetite for
life increased and day and night I plagued myself with
thoughts of all the things I had missed. My mind was full
of fantasies which would have been good material for a
psychiatrist. I drove in Cadillacs, bathed at Miami, kissed
tall, slim, beautiful women, ordered expensive made-to-
measure suits, ate lobster mayonnaise and counted out thousand dollar bills. I bought jewellery and drank champagne,
and ate pounds of caviare which I had never actually cared
for.

Then my father was there again.

I saw his drawn, lined face. I felt his hunger, his fear of
the bombs, his anxiety for me—after all, I was all he had
now, and he would probably have me for only three more
weeks. He had no idea where I was and he could have no
conception of the situation in which I now found myself.

My superiors in Berlin must of course be aware of what
was happening, but they would take great care not to give
away any details. When Dr. S. of Reich Security learned
that I had been caught, he swore vigorously to himself.

A conference of colleagues was called and they discussed whether I would be likely to hold my tongue under
F.B.I. interrogation. Most of them believed I would, and
not without justification. I did, in fact, succeed in keeping
secret the names of our men who were working in America
or who had worked for us there, but it must be admitted
that I owe my steadfastness largely to the fair treatment I

received at the hands of the F.B.I. who made no serious attempt to coerce me.

My fate was naturally of no special concern to my colleagues at Reich Security. They were all very much concerned with their own affairs, preparing their getaway. Most of them were trying to find some way of slipping out to Spain. One of them started a new life for himself with the proceeds from my gold watch and other personal valuables which I had been obliged to leave behind in the safe of the Reich Security Central Office in Berlin.

My case was still being kept a close secret and I still cannot imagine how the F.B.I. and the Army authorities succeeded in keeping the high-pressure American journalists away from me. But still no Gimpel story appeared in the press. The repercussions of the landing of U-1230 in Frenchman Bay were, however, felt in innermost government circles and President Roosevelt himself ordered the convening of the court-martial which was to try me. I must say that they did one-time Agent 146 of the German M.I. every honour.

The Army order for the opening of the trial was signed by General T. A. Terry. At the judge's table sat Colonels Clinton J. Harrold, Lathrop R. Bullens and John B. Grier and in addition, one lieutenant-colonel and three majors sat with the jury. The case for the prosecution was conducted by Major Robert Carey and First-Lieutenant Kenneth F. Graf. The leading Public Prosecutor of the U.S.A.—he was entitled to be referred to as Your Honour—attended as observer and adviser. Next to him sat the leading Public Prosecutor for the State of New York.

The case was heard in a government building on Governor's Island. The general commanding the Second Army Corps also had his headquarters there. I was taken there in a closed car in handcuffs. Billy travelled in a second car. The Army had taken enormous trouble to see that we were kept apart, but in any case we had no desire for contact.

It was at this point that I saw the first reporters. They had no idea what was going on but the preparations for the court-martial had not escaped their notice and they had stationed themselves with flashlight apparatus and newsreel cameras at the entrance to the court. They were waging a desperate battle with the military police, and needless to say the military police won.

As soon as I entered the building my handcuffs were removed. I was to appear before the judges as a free man. The corridors reeked of cleanliness. It was a modern building with a pleasant atmosphere. The room in which the case was to be heard was on the ground floor. It was not very big and was filled to capacity.

Nearly all the people there were either Navy or Army officers. In the background of my own case, the Navy and the Army were conducting a private battle, trying to push the blame for my successful landing onto each other. The domestic arguments had in fact become very heated and neither arm of the American forces was disposed to spare the other. Among the many witnesses who had been summoned were several high-ranking officers who were responsible for the coastal defences of the State of Maine. They all left the witness box with red faces.

On the 6th February at 9 a.m. sharp I was led into the room. To the left and right of me walked members of the military police. Much decorated war heroes had been selected to be my guards, and everything had been done to make a good spectacle and achieve the maximum effect. On the President's table which was draped with the Stars and Stripes lay an enormous wooden gavel. An outsize portrait head of Roosevelt stared at me with icy indifference from out its wooden frame.

Everyone stared at me. I sat down between the two majors who were my counsel and they nodded to me encouragingly. One minute later Billy was brought in and one could positively feel the wave of animosity that greeted his arrival. There was much hissing and whispering.

Before the proceedings began, everyone had to stand; members of the jury, counsel for the prosecution, counsel for the defence, the court personnel and everyone present had to take the oath that they would preserve secrecy on all details of the case.

The President, Colonel Clinton J. Harrold (like all other members of the court, he was in uniform), took his wooden gavel and brought it down ceremoniously three times on the table. Harrold was tall, slim, grey-haired and fresh-complexioned. He spoke slowly and very distinctly, weighing every word. He was so soigné in both manner and appearance that he might have been a candidate for the American Presidency appearing before the television cameras.

"The session has begun," he said.

CHAPTER 15

Sentenced to Death

MAJOR Carey, counsel for the prosecution, rose briskly from his seat. He was small and wiry, had black hair, a pale, austere face and dark, staring eyes. He spoke very distinctly and very convincingly. Naturally the Army had put forward its best prosecutor.

That morning, my warder had said to me:

"Go carefully with Carey. That man's darned dangerous."

I had already met the major. The law demanded that he must serve the indictment on me personally and at the same time formally acquaint me of the fact that I was to stand trial. This formal pronouncement had to be made while I was a free citizen and that was why the handcuffs were removed.

While the major was reeling off his little speech I had noticed that he was holding his right arm bent behind his back. I thought at first that he must have been wounded in the war and had got into the habit of holding his injured hand out of the way, but I learned later that he had been holding a loaded revolver. He was so utterly convinced of the truth of his indictment, which described me as the most dangerous German spy, that he had regarded the loaded revolver as a necessary precaution.

"With the Court's permission," Carey began now—he spoke slowly in a deep voice, and mouthed his words with an almost coquettish precision—"I will open the case for the prosecution. The United States of America against Erich Gimpel and William Curtis Colepaugh."

"Please begin," said the President.

Major Carey struck a pose. His voice took on a brighter ring and he seemed to become more personally involved in what he was doing. All the same it was obvious that to him it was all a matter of routine. He had done the same thing hundreds of times before. I, on the other hand, was appearing in a court of law for the first time in my life. If there was anything which I feared as much as the sentence it was the trial itself.

I took a look at the members of the court commission, and as I glanced from one to the other I felt that there was an impenetrable veil between us.

"The prisoners, Erich Gimpel and William Curtis Colepaugh," continued Carey, "enemies of the United States, in the month of November 1944, secretly and in civilian dress and acting upon the instructions of the German Reich, an enemy nation at war, passed through the coast and land defences of the United States with the intention of carrying out espionage and other hostile activities. The prosecution is prepared to present evidence of this in the course of these proceedings."

Carey seated himself slowly. He leaned back, riffled through the files in front of him and assumed an attitude of cool boredom. The President of the court, Colonel Clinton J. Harrold, threw a glance in Carey's direction. The prosecutor rose to his feet again, walked a few paces towards me, looked me in the face and then raised his voice:

"I now ask the accused, Erich Gimpel, if he admits his guilt within the terms of the prosecution."

I stood up, but Major Haigney, one of my counsel, forestalled me.

"Before we proceed with the case," he said, addressing himself to the President, "may I, as counsel for Mr. Gimpel, make a submission?"

"Please proceed," said the President.

Haigney paused for effect.

"This court," began the major, "is trying two men, one of whom is a German and the other an American citizen. Germany and America are at war with one another. They are declared enemies. Counsel for the defence is of the opinion that it is not fitting to try a traitor, as Colepaugh is, together with a German patriot, even if he is an enemy of this country. I do not wish to anticipate events, but everyone present knows that the other prisoner, Colepaugh, is the lowest type of American ever to stand trial, and counsel for the defence is of the opinion that the justifiable indignation of the American people at what Colepaugh has done will automatically be transferred to my client, whose actions according to the evidence are to be judged by quite different standards."

The President interrupted him.

"You submit, in fact, that there should be two cases?"

"That is exactly what I wish to submit," said Haigney.

Carey was on the spot at once. He tried to nullify Haigney's proposal with legal arguments. The court evidently was undecided and there developed a vigorous legal duologue which went on over two hours, the greater part of which was beyond my comprehension. All I gathered was that my counsel maintained that the proceedings would be simplified by separating the Colepaugh and Gimpel cases, whereas counsel for the prosecution held the opposite view. The court withdrew for an hour to discuss the point. Then once again the President banged his gavel on the table.

"The submission put forward by counsel for the defence has been rejected by the court," he announced. He then turned to Major Carey.

"Please proceed," he said.

Once more the major came up to me.

"I ask the accused, Gimpel, to answer the charge, guilty, or not guilty."

I stood up. It is a strange experience to be suddenly the cynosure of several hundred eyes. I had now to follow the advice of my counsel. I knew little of the juristic background of the case. I thought only that it would sound strange when I now protested my innocence after having admitted in the course of the interrogation which preceded the case that I had come to America with the express intention of spying. I tried to conceal the uncertainty in my voice and looked straight ahead of me as I said, as I had been bidden:

"Not guilty."

The same question was now put to Colepaugh, and he too declared that he was not guilty.

The prosecutor now began to build up his case point by point, disclosing some exceptionally fine work on the part of the F.B.I. who had succeeded in tracing back practically every step we had taken on American soil. He also revealed that the American Secret Service knew details about our past lives which we found positively astonishing. Billy's strange route from Boston to Berlin was accurately reproduced in all its stages. Major Carey even knew the names of the German officials who had been in touch with him. He produced Billy's reports from the naval academy, and drew attention to the collaboration of the former American sea cadet with German diplomatic missions.

As far as my own past was concerned, Major Carey's account was a bright nosegay of the true and the false, of exaggerations and wrong imputations. Nevertheless, it was amazing with what care the F.B.I. had X-rayed my past.

The break for luncheon was not made until after midday and the President then allowed only an hour. The case for the prosecution was then resumed. It was about four in the afternoon. Carey remained noticeably detached and unmoved. He now seemed something like an overpedantic schoolmaster lecturing about the Thirty Years' War in an institute of adult education. I could not imagine why I had been told that he was particularly fanatic and aggressive, but I was soon to learn.

At the end of our respective biographies, Carey said:

"I have shown how the two accused arrived in the United States by enemy U-boat to work against us. I have today reconstructed their route from Frenchman Bay via Portland and Boston to New York, and I have narrated their activities in New York. A whole crowd of witnesses is waiting outside, and we can start cross-examining them straightaway. But before we pass on to that I should like to introduce an entirely new point into the case."

His apparent boredom, his weary indifference, his pedantic matter-of-factness suddenly fell from him. He stood there now, quiet, cynical, obviously feeling his power. He straightened himself, his voice became penetrating, his gaze wandered from one to the other, over us the accused, the defence, the court, and back to the spectators.

"It is now my duty to present proof that the two accused have in fact caused infinite suffering. The matter does not rest with the mission which they failed to fulfil." He paused. Then his voice became louder, more penetrating. His whole countenance seemed to be aflame and his eyes had a fanatical glint.

"I maintain no more and no less," he said with infuriating slowness, "than that forty-seven gallant American sailors paid with their lifeblood for the entry of these men into our country. I put it to you that the grain steamer s.s. *Cornwallis* was betrayed through shortwave transmission by Gimpel to U-boat 1230, and that this act of betrayal cost the lives of forty-seven men, citizens of this country."

"I protest," called my counsel, Major Haigney, in a loud voice. "This occurrence has nothing whatever to do with the substance of the prosecution."

"We will see about that," answered Carey with vigour.

"Protest rejected," said the President. He leaned back and added *sotto voce*: "The court commission has no more intention of limiting the rights of the prosecution than of limiting the rights of the defence. Please proceed, Major Carey."

A fleeting smile passed across Carey's face. He was in his element. He leaned slightly forward. At that moment he looked alarmingly small and frail, but from that moment he was to drive the proceedings forward, blow for blow, re-morselessly, without respite.

"I request the court to call First-Lieutenant Frank C. Gordon of the American Navy as witness."

The colonel nodded.

The man who stepped into the witness box looked the typical American officer. He was of medium height, pow-erfully built and suntanned. He gave his replies loudly, with precision and without looking to the right or left.

Carey began his examination.

"Where are you stationed, Lieutenant?"

"In East Atlantic Coast Headquarters."

"What do you do there?"

"I am responsible for the area."

"Would you please explain your function more pre-cisely?"

"I am responsible for seeing that all sections of the coast are evenly covered by air and sea patrols in accordance with a precisely laid plan."

"So you work in collaboration with the Air Force?"

"Yes, sir, we complement each other's function."

"And what are your terms of reference from the military point of view?"

"Our instructions are to attack and destroy the enemy, to protect our own ocean traffic and to keep the sea lanes open."

The lieutenant gave his reply smartly and automatically. It was obvious that he had repeated the words over and over again in dozens of instruction sessions.

I had no idea what Major Carey could be driving at. Actually at that moment I knew nothing of the disaster which had taken place on the high seas on the 3rd Decem-ber, 1944. It was the only point in the indictment on which I was completely innocent, but the prosecutor made it his business to see that the occurrence should redound very much to my discredit, at any rate from the psychological point of view.

"So the matter of defence against U-boats is also in your sphere," continued Carey.

"Of course, sir," replied Lieutenant Gordon.

"When did you record the last U-boat attack?"

"I protest," called one of my counsel. "This question has nothing to do with the matter under discussion."

"I would ask you to leave the matter of how I conduct the prosecution to me," replied Carey with severity.

The President took no part in this battle of words. The argument went this way and that till finally he put in the decisive word.

"The court considers that the question as to the date of the last U-boat attack is justified. The objection cannot be allowed. Please continue, Major."

Carey passed his tongue over his lips. He held out a document to the lieutenant.

"I have here a report from the few survivors of the grain steamer s.s. *Cornwallis*. Do you recognize the signature?"

"Yes, sir. It is the signature of Admiral Felix Gygax, Commander of North Group Navy."

The major turned quickly to the President, and laid the document on his table.

"I present this document as evidence."

"I protest in the strongest possible terms," called Haigney.

"Why?" asked the President.

"The prosecution is making no attempt to keep to the facts of the case. The sinking of the grain ship has nothing whatever to do with the terms of the indictment already presented. The prosecution is obviously attempting with the help of the forty-seven dead of s.s. *Cornwallis* to influence the court against my client. It is an attempt to whip up emotion and animosity which is unworthy of an American court of law."

"This document," interrupted Major Carey, "is signed by an admiral. I have selected this report from a whole pile of documents because it presents in the clearest and most concise way possible the essential facts of the case. . . . It is clear proof that a German U-boat—and we know that this U-boat was U-1230—torpedoed a grain ship which was sailing with lights on, without any previous warning. I strongly protest that the official report of an American admiral should be described as an unworthy attempt to whip up feeling."

The atmosphere of the courtroom was at fever pitch. Major Carey's dramatic revelation had not failed to gain its effect. It had still not been decided whether the document could be allowed as evidence or not, but in the course of the heated discussion which followed, the prosecutor succeeded in introducing, not without a certain relish, the most gruesome details of the death of the forty-seven sailors.

"I uphold my protest," said Haigney. "I consider it out of order to admit this document as evidence."

The President addressed him sharply:

"I should be obliged if you would leave it to the court to decide what is admissible and what is not."

Then my second counsel took a hand.

"I should like to put a few questions to the witness," said Major Reagin. "You are carrying a briefcase, Lieutenant, and I assume that it contains all the documents relevant to the sinking of s.s. *Cornwallis*."

"That's right," replied the officer.

"Please open your briefcase," said Reagin, "and take out the documents. Now, have you also got the official report of the sinking of s.s. *Cornwallis* in front of you?"

"Yes, sir."

"Will you please look at it," said Reagin, "and tell us what is given there as the reason for sinking."

"It is stated that the ship was in all probability destroyed by an enemy U-boat."

"And what is the meaning of 'in all probability'?"

"It means that the authorities can imagine no other cause."

"But that does not mean," Major Reagin continued sternly, "that there could be no other cause."

"No, of course not."

It was plain that Reagin felt a sense of achievement.

"What other reason could you suggest?"

"A mine, sir."

"But you cannot say with certainty that it was a mine?"

"No, certainly not."

"I would like to point out," said Carey, "that in this operational zone there are no enemy mines."

In his eagerness he had for the first time run straight into the trap set by my defence.

"Who said," interrupted Reagin with delight, "that it might have been an enemy mine? I ask you, Lieutenant," and he turned now to the witness, "whether in this area mines are laid for coastal defence?"

"Yes, they are," answered Gordon reluctantly.

"It would therefore be quite possible that s.s. *Cornwallis* ran into an American mine?"

"That possibility cannot be excluded."

"Thank you," said Reagin.

He turned with a bow to the President and smiled.

"I leave it to the court," he said, "to draw its own conclusions from this piece of evidence. And I should like to repeat that I consider that the way in which the prosecutor has attempted to use an unhappy accident of war which we all regret to trip up the accused, to be unfair and un-American. I request that the matter of s.s. *Cornwallis* be excluded from the case."

The President nodded.

"The court will have to decide upon that when they are considering their verdict. The court is now adjourned until tomorrow."

THE case proceeded with nerve-racking slowness. The court investigated everything so thoroughly that I could no longer be in any doubt as to the outcome of the case. For hours on end my counsel battled with Major Carey. Victory and defeat followed on one another in tantalising sequence, but my counsel were really defending a hopeless case, and displaying their forensic skill on a dead horse.

My case had by now appeared in the press, without comment. On the first day of the proceedings a press photographer had caught me and my picture had appeared with the caption 'An Enemy Spy.'

The newspapers did not know the details of the case, and I cannot say that the photograph they reproduced was particularly flattering. Anyhow I attached no special importance to it at the time. But this photograph was to bring about a situation which—I think it was on the fifth day of the case—was to leave me shattered and helpless.

The President opened the session as usual with cool, gentlemanly detachment.

I think it was the thirtieth witness who was being cross-examined. Everyone who in any way had come in contact with me, the first taxi driver, the sausage salesman, the man at the newspaper stand, the hotel porters, even the char-women, all were questioned.

The President, consulting a small scrap of paper in his hand, announced:

"Another witness has reported. She is waiting outside. We could hear her now."

"I attach no importance to her," Carey said at once.

"The defence is of the opinion that no possibility of establishing the true facts should be excluded," said Reagin.

"Then the court will hear her," said the colonel. He motioned to the bullet-headed sergeant at the door. The man went out. For just a minute subdued conversation could be heard in the courtroom. Then the door opened slowly. I did not at once look in that direction. It was only when everyone else had turned round that I took a look at the witness.

I got the shock of my life. I wanted to jump up, run towards her and rush her away. I wanted to scream, to implore, to threaten, but I remained seated in my chair as if rooted to the spot.

"Your name?" asked the President.

She walked up to him confidently. She was tall, slim and lovely. She looked straight ahead. Only as she passed me did she throw a quick glance in my direction. It was a sad, an infinitely sad look.

"My name is Joan Kenneth," she said. "I am an American citizen. I live in New York and run a small fashion shop."

She gave her personal details.

"You know the accused?"

"Yes," she replied.

"Where did you meet him?"

"In the apartment of a mutual friend."

"When?"

"Six weeks ago."

"Did you know," asked Major Carey, "that the accused was a German spy?"

"No," answered Joan quietly.

Carey turned to the President. "I cannot see how this witness is relevant to the case," he said.

The President hesitated for a moment.

"But I can!" Reagin broke in before I could stop him. "I should like to put a few questions to you, Miss Kenneth, with the court's permission."

"Allowed," said Colonel Harrold.

Joan turned towards me. She looked at me. Her face was pale, she tried to smile at me but somehow the smile went astray. She made a helpless gesture with her hand as if she wanted to come to me and comfort me. She ignored all the men who were staring at her, the strained surprise on the faces of the court, the lurking hatred of the prosecutor.

"Why have you offered yourself as a witness?" asked Major Reagin with caution.

"Because I have a close relationship with the accused."

"What am I to understand by that?"

"I love him," said Joan simply.

For a few seconds there was a complete silence in the courtroom.

"You may be surprised to hear me say that," continued Joan, "in view of the fact that the accused is an enemy of our country. I do not know if the work he did here was bad or harmful . . . the war is to blame for everything, and everyone who is in the service of war is also its victim. I am a woman and a woman knows a man far better than men can ever know him, and as a woman there is something I must tell you."

She paused for a while. The words came with difficulty.

She swallowed. No one but Reagin attempted to meet her halfway, but it seemed she did not need this.

I could not take my eyes off her. Until this moment I had followed the case with a sort of numb indifference. Now I felt worked up. Pain, excitement, and a feeling of suffocation came over me. I felt like shouting: "Leave her alone. Tell her she must be quiet. All this is our affair, ours alone. It's nothing to do with anyone else, the court, the defence or the prosecution. Hang me, hang me if you like, but leave her alone!"

I forgot time and place. I saw and heard nothing more. Everything was spinning in front of my eyes. Faster, louder, faster, faster! It was suddenly as if a roundabout was there, with figures with human faces, evil, mocking faces. And in the midst of them stood Joan, and everything was dancing around her. They all wanted to get hold of her, to drag her into the mud. But she smiled and looked through the round-about at me, looked me straight in the face, and once more I was standing beside her just as I had stood on Christmas Eve. . . .

We had opened the window because the room was too hot. We were standing close together and I put my arm round her. The cool night air fanned our faces. We stood there without saying a word. We already knew all there was to say to each other. I drew her to me more closely and we kissed. Our nearness took on a new beauty as time, war, fear, everything fell away from us. The future and the past fused into the present, into this one hour which was ours alone. No power in the world, no state, no country, no war, no court of justice could rob us of our golden hour.

"It's just as if I had always known you," said Joan. "I've been waiting for you always, only for you, and I've always known what you would be like."

I forgot everything, I looked into her eyes and we kissed again. To me it was a painful happiness . . .

And then came the end, the morning, flight. It was all over. It had to be all over, for Joan's sake. And Joan would always hate me.

But she didn't! She understood! She understood the incomprehensible. She knew why I had left her. If I had not left her I would have gone away with her, fled into happiness, happiness that knew no frontiers, no tears, no wars. If only I had put everything behind me. What a fool I had been. . . .

"THE accused is a man, a human being," Joan said quietly. "He feels as a man, he thinks as a man, he lives as a man. I do not know in what light he has been presented here, but if this man has done anything which is punishable by law I must ask you to remember that you are not sitting in judgment on a barbarian but on a man who is loved by a woman, a woman who is a citizen of this country."

The courtroom was silent. No one said a word. All eyes were on Joan, on her dear face, her lovely hair, her graceful figure, her elegant fur coat. The President turned to Major Carey.

"Do you wish to cross-examine the witness?"

"No, thank you," said the prosecutor.

"Does the defence wish to put any questions?" asked the colonel.

"No, thank you," said Reagin quickly.

He looked round the room. Joan had really had no evidence to give, but no one had remained unaffected by what she had said, and in an American court feeling counts for a good deal. The dead of the *Cornwallis* were being weighed against the love of a young American woman.

"You are dismissed," the President told Joan.

For a second she hesitated, and once more she turned to me. We looked at each other, our lips tightly compressed. Then she tightened her grip on her handbag and walked calmly and confidently to the door. Each one of her retreating footsteps was like a pain in my heart. The wound had been torn wide open, for I had glimpsed once more the happiness which was to be denied to me forever.

Joan was an important psychological factor in my defence, but what had the matter of my defence to do with our love?

*   *   *

THE case went on, endlessly, relentlessly. I followed it
with something akin to apathy, as witness followed witness,
gave evidence, took the oath and went. The arraignment of
the officers of the American coastal defences was a nice
little titbit of military scandal for those who could extract
any enjoyment from the situation. They certainly got a severe handling. The witnesses entered the courtroom as pale
as if they had been the accused. Every bit of negligence
and carelessness was censured in the harshest terms. My
judges were all military men who were very much at home
on matters of defence.

When the fifteen-year old scout, Johnny Miller, stepped
into the witness box, the lamentable spectacle reached its
climax. The boy, a bright lad who seemed much older than
his years, described how he had discovered our footprints
but had tried in vain to apprise the American authorities of
our arrival. Perhaps it was only my impression, but it
seemed to me that both the prosecution and the President
cross-examined Miller with special thoroughness. Finally,
Colonel Harrold said:

"You have shown courage and foresight, my boy, and I
feel it is my duty on behalf of the American people to thank
you for your action. You have demonstrated a greater feeling of responsibility than many a grown man and indeed
many an officer who was explicitly entrusted with the task
of guarding his homeland."

The hearing of the evidence was concluded. For six
whole days there had been a tug-of-war between prosecution and defence and there was no doubt that the prosecution was winning. But that went without saying. Anyhow,
the rope they were tugging at was to become a rope for my
neck . . .

The seventh day brought the final pleadings. This, of
course, produced nothing new, but Major Carey, the prosecutor, who at the start of the proceedings had so firmly
refused to recognise any distinction between my case and
Billy's, suddenly changed his tactics. He could see which

way the wind was blowing and he did it for effect. He abandoned the attitude of contempt and constant accusation and became almost chivalrous. He knew he had led me up to the noose and thought it superfluous to dance about on the corpse.

Mr. Tom C. Clark, the Chief Public Prosecutor, who so far had functioned only as an observer, spoke at the end:

"I have not a great deal to say about Gimpel, the accused. He stood before us and told us that he had nothing to say. I am sure he realised what lay in store for him when he left his homeland. He will see his own situation as the American national hero, Nathan Hale, saw his when he said before his execution: 'I regret that I have only one life to lay down for my country.'

"The case of Colepaugh is quite different. He is a traitor, a liar and a deserter. In the first place he betrayed his country, then he betrayed Germany and then he betrayed his comrade Gimpel. There is only one thing for him, the rope."

The court withdrew to consider its verdict. Another forty-eight hours passed. Then they took me back into the courtroom. There was a deathly silence. Everyone knew what was coming. The court commission entered the room, and we stood up. The President called my name and I walked up to the judge's table.

"Erich Gimpel, as President of this Court it is my duty to inform you of the sentence which has been passed upon you. You have been found guilty on all charges . . ."

The judge stood up. He did not look at me as he spoke the words which I shall never forget. ". . . to be hanged by the neck until dead."

CHAPTER 16

Sized Up by the Hangman

IN four days, the rope, thirteen times knotted in accordance with the grim rules of hanging, would encircle my neck. I had ninety-six hours left in which to think and breathe, and then the horror of the night, the waiting in the cell, the choking sensation in the throat, all that would be over.

I paced my wire cage at Fort Jay like a madman. The hours, the minutes lay upon me heavily as lead, now oppressing me, now rushing away from me, now standing still, now stretching themselves like some grim accompaniment to my fear of imminent death.

My forehead streamed with sweat, my tongue was as dry as a piece of old leather. I drank indiscriminately everything I was given, and I was given everything I asked for. The prison officials viewed me either with timid sidelong glances or with grinning embarrassment. They nearly all felt sorry for me, but with Americans sympathy often shows itself in strange guises.

I was an exhibition piece. Everyone was brought to see me before I was hanged, everyone, that is, who was on good terms with Fort Jay and its commandant, everyone who counted for something in the Army. I was seldom alone. Nearly all my visitors shook me feelingly by the hand, told me things which I did not understand and wanted me to tell them things which I did not know. They asked me how I was and it sounded facetious, but it was worse than that, it was just a habit.

The sun rose as on every other day, the hour had sixty minutes and the minutes had sixty seconds. The children played, the mothers laughed and the men went to work as they always did. The typists arrived at their offices just as usual and told each other about their little adventures of the previous night. The lift boys said their 'good mornings,' and the recruits were marched up and down on the barrack squares. The world went its normal way, but for me everything was abnormal. In four days' time I would know no more.

The verdict had been given just five weeks before. The judgment was clear. There could be no appeal. My counsel shook hands with me. Major Reagin said:

"It was a privilege to represent you, Mr. Gimpel."

He gave me a cigarette and offered me a light. My hands were already in chains. Just twenty seconds after the verdict had been made known a military policeman had clapped the handcuffs on me. It appeared that they were to accompany me through the days which still remained to me.

"You made a good impression in court," continued Reagin. "If there's one thing I can't stand it's an abject defendant. You can't imagine some of the cases I've had to handle."

I nodded.

"Keep your chin up," said Reagin, "at any rate while you can. The verdict will now go to the Supreme Court and will be examined to see if there have been any faults in the procedure, but I'm afraid they won't find anything."

"And then?" I asked.

"There's still the possibility of a petition to the President."

"But there wouldn't be much point in that?"

"As good as none at all," replied Reagin, "at any rate while the war's still on. But a petition has at least one advantage—

it shows you're not a dyed-in-the-wool Nazi. . . . Many men who've been sentenced could perhaps have saved their lives if they had not been too proud to petition the President."

"Would you please prepare the petition?" I asked. I tried to smile but I don't know if I succeeded.

"I'll keep in touch with you," said Reagin, "and let you know what's happening. I'll visit you every week. Let me know if you have any complaints about the way you are treated. I can always have anything like that put right at once."

We shook hands.

"I should have liked to spare you the handcuffs," he said, "but I'm afraid that's not possible. That's a rule that can't be changed."

A week passed, then a second week, then a third and a fourth. I had now reached the point when an official came to me for the address of my next-of-kin in Germany. I knew what that meant. The chef enquired what I wished to eat during the next few days. I knew what that meant. The Army chaplain enquired whether he could visit me, and I knew what that meant, too. . . .

When I gave them my father's address I had to pause for a few seconds to remember where my father was living. How far, how long, how hopelessly all my past life seemed to lie behind me.

I called to mind the man whose face, bearing, eyes and nose I had inherited, together with a liking for forbidden things. When I was three years old I had stood beside my mother's coffin, still too young to realise what was happening, and I had grown up at Father's side, in that silent, matter-of-fact comradeship which is often brought into being between father and son by the early death of the mother. As a boy I had done all the things I ought not to have done. Once when I was playing football in the street I scored a goal and the ball went right through a café window. I quickly retrieved my ball from the heap of broken glass before the proprietress shooed me off with her broom. I was two hours late getting home, and was full of the darkest forebodings. But when I arrived back, my father had already paid for the damage.

"You're not frightened, are you?" he asked.

"Yes," I admitted in a small voice.

"Don't be silly," continued Father. "Do you imagine I never did anything like that when I was a boy?"

What would he be doing now? Would he be thinking about me? He had never questioned me about my work.

"I just don't want to know," he said once. "You know what you're doing and there's only one thing I want. When the war is over I want you back, sound and healthy."

When the war is over. . . .

Johnny, my warder, arrived and pushed a lighted cigarette through the wire mesh.

"Hurry," he said. "With you, you never know who might be coming along."

"Edward," he called after a while—all the men called me by my assumed name—"things aren't nearly so bad as you imagine."

"I'm sure they're not," I replied.

"I read a book recently," continued Johnny, "written by a schoolmaster. It was about the American War of Independence."

"Very interesting," I replied.

"But listen," said Johnny. "A man was condemned to death and they hung him on a tree. He was already strung up when the pardon came through. They cut him off the rope again."

"Do you think that's what might happen with me?"

"I must admit it's improbable," answered Johnny, "but I'm telling you about it for this reason: afterwards the man wrote a book on what it felt like to be hanged. He said that you feel terribly afraid at first and then suddenly you don't feel anything more. Suddenly everything becomes soft and gentle and easy and you feel you're already in another world and that the last moments of your life are far more beautiful than you've ever imagined . . . Only," continued Johnny, "when they cut him off the rope and tried artificial respiration on him he suffered the most terrible pain."

I tried not to listen to any more. Johnny was a fool, but he was harmless and good natured. He really was trying to comfort me, but his comfort was horrifying. He had a frank, youthful face. One finger of his left hand was paralysed through an injury which had got him his cushy job at Fort Jay. He wrote letters to all his friends and relatives, telling them about me. I was the adventure of his life. But the adventure was to come to an end in ninety-six hours.

I felt I would go mad at the thought of it.

A sergeant entered my cell. I had never seen him before. He was a frail-looking fellow with a sharp little face and a certain nonchalance about his dress that you could almost call slovenliness. He shook hands with me, at the same time looking past me out of the window. He had small, dark eyes which could not keep still. He came just about up to my shoulder.

"Is there anything you want, Mr. Gimpel?" he asked.

"No," I replied.

"Is the food to your liking?"

"Yes."

"Would you like a cigarette?"

"Yes."

I took it. The man observed me from the side. He looked at me in a sort of businesslike way, carefully sizing me up. I took one or two quick draws at the cigarette, wishing the fellow would go to the devil. "He's had his look at me now," I thought. "And he's had a word with me. Now he can go and write his postcard to his girlfriend."

But he stayed on and walked all round me. When I took my eyes off him his stealthy sideways glance was there again. I felt instinctively that he wanted something of me, something uncanny, something horrible, something shudderingly frightful.

"Unfortunately I'm not allowed to give you anything to read," he said. "That's a very strict rule here. That is, nothing but the Bible."

"I have the Bible already."

"Well, so long," he said. He shook hands with me, looked past me once again and walked off.

"Hi, you!" called Johnny. "Do you know who that was?"

"Of course I don't."

Johnny was all excitement.

"That was the hangman," he said. "He came to get an idea of your weight and measurements so that he'll know what he's got to do. He's taken your measurements for sure. Didn't you notice him? Didn't you know that everyone in here gets a new rope? Money's no object here."

He laughed. He just couldn't keep his mouth shut. He kept pushing cigarettes through the wire to me, just blabbing out whatever came into his mind. He was a fool, such a fool, but an honest, well-meaning fellow.

"Johnny," I said. "How much longer have I got to live?"

"I don't know," he replied. "You never know the exact time until one night before, but I think they're coming for you on April 15th. I heard something of the sort."

At eleven o'clock they called me to the commandant. For a moment I was relieved of my handcuffs.

"Mr. Gimpel," he said. "I have something to tell you. The President has rejected your petition for pardon. That means that the death sentence can now be carried out. You will be told twelve hours before execution when it is to be."

He had a small mouth, a straight nose and a round head. I kept repeating this description to myself so as not to lose my grip.

"So far you have borne yourself like a man. Keep it up. Good morning."

I was back in my cell again, alone once more. Once more a prey to time and idle chatter.

What was my life? Would it not be all to the good for it to be brought to an end? A saying came to my mind and I kept repeating it aloud to myself:

"Better an end with fear than a fear without end."

It would soon be all over. They would carry me out in a simple wooden coffin and my body would be used for purposes of anatomical research.

"Here, gentlemen, you see the liver, the spleen and the gallbladder," the professor would lecture. "The heart was quite sound. How does one reach that conclusion, Mr. Miller?"

Never again would I see the cherry trees in bloom, never again would I hold a woman in my arms, never again would I sit at the wheel of a car, never again would I hear the trumpet of Louis Armstrong or the trombone of Tommy Dorsey. Never again . . . never again . . . never again. . . .

The women in my life passed through my mind. I stood at the rail of the *Drottningholm*—it was 1940—and at my side stood the blonde Swedish girl, Karen S., in a wispy summer dress, the wind playing with her hair.

"Come with me. I know my father will like you. He likes your type. We can get married. I'm not badly off and the war will then be over for you. If you love me, come with me."

"I do love you," I replied.

"You don't love me."

I kissed her.

Later I said: "When the war's over."

When the war's over. What nonsense. . . .

And then I saw Margarete, my pert little Berliner.

"Don't be crazy," she said. "Stay here. Don't go to America. Everyone says you'll never come back. You're mad to go. Just look at this Billy, look at his apelike arms, look at his shifty eyes. He'll give you away, you can be sure of that. A woman feels these things. Stay here in Germany, stay with me."

How many of fate's warning lights had I ignored!

And then Joan; Joan, tall, slim, graceful.

"It's odd," she said, "I've a feeling that we've known each other for such a long time. . . . I always seem to know in advance what you're going to say and what you're thinking. Men like you always say what they think and they think straight."

She put her arms round me and I looked into her eyes. Time stood still. Dare I kiss her? Dare I love her? Dare I bind her life to the curse that clung to my life as a spy? Heart and head were at variance. We laughed, we whispered, we kissed. Then in a few hours it was all over and I had to leave her.

Was an hour then the same length as an hour now? Now, as I waited for the sergeant with the sharp little face who was expertly to tie the thirteen knots about my neck? I threw myself onto my cell bed only to jerk myself up again in the same moment.

Once again I was bathed in sweat, once more there was the dryness in my mouth, my tongue like a piece of leather. "No, don't think about it! Keep away from it!" I told myself. "Think of something else! Think of the good things of life! Keep off this thrice-damned war! Keep off your own accursed end! Best of all, make your mind a blank!"

And then I saw the motto of Reich Security in front of me and heard one of my chiefs say:

"Leave thinking to horses; they've got bigger heads."

It was now ten o'clock and Johnny was relieved. He'd be back again at twelve. His colleague immediately offered me a cigarette. It was odd how at Fort Jay all the regulations were punctiliously observed except that concerning smoking. All the prison officers made an exception of smoking.

A G.I. from the kitchen brought me a midmorning snack, coffee, rolls, butter and marmalade.

"Now eat up today," he said, putting the food on the small cell table. "You can't go on like this, you know. You left half your food yesterday. Take a cue from the others, they eat like horses."

"I don't want anything."

"You're only making matters worse," he said. "Keep your stomach full and the world takes on a different look."

He grinned.

"You need a good square meal," he said.

"Oh, shut up!" I said.

We weren't exactly refined at Fort Jay but we understood each other.

"The chef wants to know what you'd like to eat tomorrow," continued the soldier from the kitchen. "He says he knows how to do a goose in the European way with chestnut puree. He'll roast one for you, if you like."

"No, thank you," I said. "It doesn't appeal to me at all. All I want is to be left in peace. Now shut the door from the outside, will you?"

"Right you are," he replied, and went on: "I don't know, the others always seem to be in better spirits when I visit them."

"Well, the others aren't going to be hanged the day after tomorrow."

"True enough," he agreed, and finally took himself off.

For a quarter of an hour everything was quiet. I lay on the bed and tried to sleep, but of course it was hopeless.

There was still today. And tomorrow. And the next day. Then, I told myself for the hundredth time, it would be all over. They would come for me at five o'clock in the morning. They would offer me a last cigarette. The death sentence would once more be read out to me. It was short enough and it would not take long. Then they would put me in a black jacket, with a hood, and I would have to put the hood on my head. Then they would take me to the place of execution. It was a little outside Fort Jay. As a rule no one was executed in Fort Jay. Fort Jay was military territory, and the military was not the competent body for executions, not at any rate in the ordinary course of events. Prisoners under sentence of death were sent to Sing Sing in New York State and there put in the electric chair.

But I had been expressly sentenced to death by hanging and Sing Sing was not the place for that. Therefore the matter of execution had been left within the province of Fort Jay. That was why there had been all the excitement, the constant visits, the care for me personally. It was only the attraction of something novel—my execution was something out of the ordinary for Fort Jay.

Until now I had never thought much about death. Who does think of death when he's young and healthy? To me dying had always been something that lay a long time off. When I was seventy or eighty perhaps, or even later. When you're old and tired, when you've lost all interest in food, when your eyesight's failing and your hands are shaking, then you might perhaps give a thought to the eternal sleep, and in those circumstances the thought may not be unpleasant. Then one day you close your eyes for good and people say:

"Well, well, poor old Erich. He lived to a good old age; it was time for him to pop off."

But I wasn't old, damn it, I didn't want to die. Damn it again, I wanted to live, to live like everyone else who was young and healthy.

I looked in the mirror. I was certainly rather paler and thinner than I had been, but apart from that I looked just about the same. And yet I was to be in the land of the living for only a few more days, a few more days, another ninety-four hours and a few minutes and then a notice would be posted at the gate of Fort Jay:

"For espionage, sabotage and conspiracy against the United States of America, the German citizen Erich Gimpel, alias Edward Green, was hanged by the rope this morning at 5:13. According to the results of the medical examination, death occurred seventy seconds after execution. Gimpel was found guilty by court-martial. The Supreme Court of the United States confirmed the death sentence. A petition from the German spy for mercy was refused by the President."

It was now twelve o'clock and Johnny had come back.

"Here I am again," he called.

"So I see," I replied.

This time I was glad he was on duty again. His chatter was preferable to my own thoughts. But I could not stop my thoughts from straying constantly to the grim scene in the half-light of dawn. I could not help thinking of the unthinkable. Years before I had seen a film about Mata Hari. It was a piece of sentimental trash with a tragic end. Practically everyone in the cinema was in tears, but I was laughing. I think Margarete was with me and she too had tears in her eyes. The woman spy wore a dark dress and had a face well suited to the tragedy of execution. She wore a silver cross round her neck, and this she kissed and presented to her wardress. The wardress wept. A soldier in a steel helmet entered, his face twitching. He was a young French lieutenant.

"My duty, madam," he said.

Any who had so far restrained themselves now finally gave way to tears, but I laughed even louder. The lieutenant's voice sounded hoarse.

"I can't think why she's being executed if she's so noble," I said to my companion.

A woman behind me told me angrily to keep quiet.

Mata Hari was led down a seemingly endless corridor. One saw her from the front, the back, the side. Above all one saw her face. From every angle it looked equally beautiful and noble and sad and lost.

Then at last the corridor came to an end and she stepped out into the open air. There was a dense mist. Suddenly a group of soldiers appeared. They were all wearing a funereal expression for the occasion. "Wonderful," I thought. "Soldiers can usually think of something better to do with a beautiful woman than shoot her." Then the salvo was heard and Mata Hari died slowly and photogenically.

How would I die? Would I call out? Would I try to tear myself free? Would I scream for help? What's left of the photogenic, heroic approach to death when the hangman is close upon one's heels?

"Hi, Edward!" called Johnny. "Would you like to have a word with the chaplain?"

"No," I replied.

"Don't be a fool," he said. "He's a nice chap. I can thoroughly recommend him."

The parson wore the uniform of an Army captain. He was tall, slim and broad shouldered, and somehow combined the figure of a baseball player with the nobility of a gentleman rider. And he didn't seem a bit pious. That was why I took to him immediately.

"This is a terrible business," he began. He walked up and down. "We can speak about it quite openly. It's easier to talk about death than to die. That's where you've got the advantage of me straightaway."

"Well said, Captain," I replied.

He smiled.

"I am only a captain as a sideline," he said. "You know of course that I'm a priest. The uniform is just camouflage."

"There's no need for you to camouflage yourself," I replied.

We shook hands. For the first time in days I felt relaxed. For the first time I forgot what lay in front of me.

"I don't want to get on your nerves," said the priest, "and don't worry, I'm not going to preach a sermon to you. Unfortunately, everything that's coming is your own affair. Somehow you've got to come to terms with it yourself. I only wish I could help you a little." He looked at his fingernails. "Easy to talk, isn't it?"

"But you talk well, Captain."

We then went on to talk about baseball and gangster films. After half an hour he made to go but I asked him to stay. The soldier from the kitchen brought my midday meal.

"I could eat a second portion," I said smiling.

"Well, look now, at last he's seeing reason," he said.

We ate together. The priest told me his name and where he came from. He had in fact been a baseball player at the university and was a well-known member of the team. He had wanted to become an engineer.

"And why did you become a priest?"

"That's a long story," he said, "and you probably won't understand it. I was not what you might call a friend of the Church.

"What happened?"

"I became a priest in spite of that. My young sister died. How shall I explain it to you? I loved her more than anything else in the world. I used to cut lectures and go for walks with her. At five she was a real little lady. She had real charm. I just don't know how to explain it to you. You can't imagine how sweet she was."

"And then?"

"She was run over by a lorry. Seven years ago. I think I lost my reason for a while. My parents had been dead a long time and I had been alone in the world with my sister. There was no consolation for me. Not a glimmer of understanding. To this day I don't know how I survived that period. It took me months, years even, to get over it."

I had kept my eyes averted and now I looked at his face. Every word he spoke was genuine, direct, convincing. He got to his feet and paced up and down. His face, which for a few moments had looked rigid, became animated again.

"Then you see," he said, "I became a priest. For just that reason, really. Just to be able to stand by people who have to get through something like I had been through, to help them keep their grip."

"Yes," I replied.

"You see," he continued, "you're one of those who've somehow got to get through a spot like that."

"I think I'll manage," I replied. "And even if I don't, it won't do anyone else any harm."

He was quiet. We smoked away, sitting together on the bed, so closely that our shoulders touched.

"Have you ever prayed?" he asked me.

"Yes, of course. But it's a long time ago now, when I was a child. When I grew up I forgot how to pray."

"That's how it is with so many people," he said. "They just forget. But it often comes back to them again." He stood up.

"I'll come again tomorrow. That is, if it's all right with you. I'll come any time you want to see me."

We shook hands.

Prayer. . . . Could I pray? Should I pray? Ought I to pray?

I tried to remember how it had been when I was a child, the organ playing in church and the parson giving the blessing. I was wearing my first dark blue suit with long trousers, and the burning candles were giving off that holy fragrance which all my life I had avoided. . . .

I tried to remember the words of the prayer, but it was a long time before I could recall them, and then I could not get them past my lips. All the same, I determined I would try to pray.

"Our Father," I said to myself, "which art in Heaven."

I said it again and again, mechanically, dully, until it began to take on some meaning.

Who had thought of prayer in the terrible time just past? Reich Security had abolished all such things—God, Heaven, the work of Christ. There was only one thing which it was unable to abolish: death, dying, the end. Death took no account of Reich Security.

It was now two o'clock in the afternoon. Once more Johnny was relieved. There was a good deal of scurrying about in the cell block of Fort Jay today and I could hear the soft thudding of rubber boots in the corridor all the time. My new warder was very correct. I wanted to smoke, but I had no matches. I called him. He did not answer. Perhaps he was afraid of reprimand.

At about three o'clock in the afternoon the officer-of-the-guard came to see me.

"Everything all right?" he asked.

"Yes, so far," I said.

"Good."

"I could do with a glass of whisky," I said.

"Apart from your freedom that's the only thing I can't give you, but," he reflected for a moment, "perhaps we can just go along to my office for one. I know what it's like without a drink." He sat down on my bed. "Have you had a word with the chaplain?"

"Yes."

"I'm glad."

A G.I. ran excitedly along the corridor. Suddenly I heard shouts. I strained to hear what was happening but I couldn't gather what it was all about.

The Captain got up with a sigh. A G.I., red in the face, rushed into the cell. He was just about to blurt out something but the officer motioned to him and they withdrew into a corner.

I had got into the way of lip-reading, and I kept my eyes on the mouths of the soldier and the officer as they spoke. Something quite extraordinary must have happened, something which had cut right across the normal routine of Fort Jay.

I watched the G.I.'s lips and I thought I had grasped what he was saying. Yes, I did understand, but surely . . . it couldn't be true!

The G.I. had said: "Roosevelt is dead."

The whole of America heard this same piece of news at that moment . . . Roosevelt is dead. The man in the White House had died, from a haemorrhage of the brain. Roosevelt was dead. . . .

The officer came up to me and put his hand on my shoulder.

"This is a bit of luck for you," he said.

"Why?" I asked.

"The President is dead. That means that there will be four weeks' state mourning."

"And what's the use of that to me?" I asked.

"During the period of state mourning no death sentences will be carried out."

The officer left. I could hardly believe my ears. Franklin Delano Roosevelt had done me a good turn. . . .

CHAPTER 17

Germany's Capitulation Saves
My Life

THE truth of what the officer had said was confirmed on the morning appointed for my execution. It did not take place. A few hours later, relayed by all American radio stations, the ceremonial obsequies for Franklin Delano Roosevelt began. I listened to everything and understood nothing. I had to get used to the idea that I was still alive, I had to thank pure chance that I was not already hanged, and adjustment to the new situation came slowly. The congratulations of my warders were almost overwhelming. They all wanted to shake me by the hand. A sergeant said laughingly:

"We'd rather have you alive than dead."

"That goes for me too," I replied. No one took it amiss that I preferred Roosevelt's death to my own.

Four weeks' postponement! What an eternity it seemed, and at the same time how short a respite! The war in Europe was approaching its end by leaps and bounds. You could almost work it out on your fingers when the last bomb would be dropped. Capitulation was imminent. But how imminent? Days? Weeks? My counsel were confident. All America was confident. I wanted to be confident too, but one day I ran into my hangman in the yard at Fort Jay, and once more I became anxious and unsettled. . . .

Germany's capitulation happened, so to speak, with the utmost punctuality, and once more I received congratulations from every side. I waited impatiently for my final pardon, but it did not come. Still, there was no talk about hanging. It seemed as if they had simply forgotten all about me.

Then I was moved. In American style. I was dragged through half of America in handcuffs, the handcuffs being required by the regulations, for which my escorts apologised at least three times a day. There were some remarkable scenes: people stared at me, schoolboys ran after me, and shoppers in the streets stood to watch me go by.

My journey took me by long-distance express train through the States of New York, via Pennsylvania, Ohio, Indiana and Illinois to Missouri. At St. Louis we had to leave our comfortable train for a six-hour wait. My escorting officer said:

"I want to look up some friends here, and I can't take you around with me, so I'll put you in the city gaol for a few hours."

"All right," I said.

"I don't know what the food's like there," he continued, "so I think we'd better eat out."

We stayed in the station restaurant and never in my life have I eaten in such strange circumstances. There was a private dining room there, but this was occupied by a choral society, so we had to go into the main part of the restaurant.

My handcuffs were now removed, but my guard was not going to miss an opportunity for a piece of real American showmanship and he placed four tall military policemen around the table with their machine guns trained straight on to my plate. They looked very warlike standing with their arms at the ready while I ate my steak.

The table next to us was occupied by some members of the American Women's Army Corps, the WACS, and they kept looking over at me. They evidently thought that I was an American soldier who was being punished for some military misdeed and kept making rude noises at my guards and sticking their tongues out. One of them, a tall, slim blonde, went up to the officer in charge and said:

"Don't make such heavy weather of it, boys, or are you afraid of him?"

The officer kept a straight face and the girls went on making fun of him.

I ate my ice cream and then they took me to the city gaol in a jeep.

"You'll survive a few hours here," said my escort.

I was taken in charge by a tough-looking warder. While the formalities of introduction were taking their course I had to put my hands on the table as everything was taken out of my pockets and listed. This did not amount to a great deal. Above the desk of the guard on duty I read in large letters:

"If you don't like it, tell us. If you do like it, tell your friends."

I had to laugh out loud.

"There's no need to put you in a cell," said the warder, who was much nicer after my guard had withdrawn. "You look such a good boy. What have you been up to? Are you hungry?"

"No," I replied.

"You'll soon get used to eating," he replied. "None of them are hungry when they first come in, but when they go they're all eating like horses."

I was put in a cell for a few hours, after all, and then I was fetched. My journey continued by car right across Missouri to Kansas. I was then delivered to Leavenworth prison and my escorts took friendly leave of me.

I was put into the Fort at the outset. I was later to be transferred to the civilian penitentiary, but during those first few days I came into contact with death in the most horrible way.

Five German soldiers were executed. It was all quite senseless. Just because they had declined to petition the American President for pardon.

They had been prisoners-of-war. Two opposing factions

had come into being in their camp, one of which cooperated with the Americans, the other working against them. Certain denunciations had been made and men were continually being betrayed to the camp authorities.

The prisoner responsible for these betrayals lost a letter and this led to his being found out. There was a skirmish and in the course of it he was lynched. In the heat of the moment the camp authorities grabbed five men as scapegoats. Whether they were in any way guilty in fact no one knew, but they were sentenced to death for murder. The sentence would immediately have been set aside if they had agreed to present a petition for pardon, but one of the five, a fanatical Nazi, declared:

"As a German soldier I refuse to petition an American President."

The five condemned men remained obdurate to all pleas, threats or arguments and just let themselves be hanged in Fort Leavenworth. I saw them a few hours before their end, their faces pale and distorted with hatred. They were the war's last fanatics. . . .

THE Leavenworth penitentiary houses more than 2,400 prisoners. I was given number 62008. I was now among the men who were to be my constant companions for the next ten years of my life—murderers, procurers, thieves and bank robbers. They all had their criminal records and were proud of them. Prisons have their own quite rigid hierarchy. At the top of the tree are the bank robbers, but murderers are outsiders. Petty thieves rank as small-fry while burglars and housebreakers are well regarded. As for the procurers, no one can abide them.

Spies occupied no clearly defined place in the criminal hierarchy. They were assessed according to the way in which they conducted themselves in captivity. The same applied to the élite of the American communists who were my fellow prisoners for a while. They and I succeeded in achieving good rank and high prestige.

But I am anticipating. First I entered the quarantine

block where I had to stay for four weeks. Quarantine must have been an invention of the devil. Everyone concerned seemed to take a positive delight in my discomfiture. I, for my part, thought it would be a matter of taking certain hygienic measures but it was in fact a sort of novitiate training to accustom the prisoner to the discipline, the drill and the changeover to a new way of life with a number and striped clothing.

The warders wore uniform. Some of them were men, some were machines, and I was to have some interesting experiences with them, to say the least. I did not at all like the man who received me at the quarantine block. He had a coarse, florid face, shouted louder than was necessary and used insulting and offensive forms of expression to tease and torment me. It was just as well that he did only six hours duty at a time and was then relieved. The man who took over from him was more tolerable, but even he was by no means as good-natured as he looked.

"Oh, ho," he said, "so your name's Gimpel. Funny name. Now what have you been up to? Oh, espionage! Well, you should have left that alone. You'll realise that. You'll have plenty of time to think about it."

The prisoners called him the Pumpkin. All the warders had nicknames. All their peculiarities, their habits, their gestures were very keenly observed by the prisoners, and many of them were almost completely in the prisoners' hands. The Pumpkin pursued a middle path. Working in the quarantine block he had an easier time than his colleagues outside. After all, he was occupied with beginners and could always fall back on having the regulations tightened up.

There were twenty of us and we were isolated. Our course of instruction was to begin on the following morning, in the lecture room to start with. The inspector appeared in person.

"Smoking is not allowed," he said. "Anyone found smoking will be sent to the 'house.' "

The 'house.' That was solitary, close confinement with bread and water and no exercise.

"We want no laughing here. No walking; everything at the double. If a warder speaks to you, you must stand to attention at once and answer 'yes' or 'no.' If there is any answering back you will be sent to the 'house.' The same applies for any rudeness, or carelessness."

He went on barking out his lecture. He had given it every month for twenty years. His face was grey and drawn. He had trouble with his stomach, and dyspeptic prison overseers are never very popular.

"You may go to church if you wish every Sunday. You may have your hair cut once a month. You may take a shower twice a week. If you behave yourselves you can go to the cinema once a week, but there won't be any crime films or love films. You already know how criminals carry on and you don't need love in here. If you work you get paid and you can buy chocolate, biscuits, sweets, shaving soap and cigarettes in the canteen. You can have two packets of cigarettes a week, that's enough for you." He ran his eyes over us. Then he continued.

"Anyone who won't listen to instructions must take the consequences. Anyone who doesn't shave will be sent to the 'house'. Likewise anyone who leaves his jacket buttons undone. The 'house' is always ready for you. Remember that. We've plenty of single cells."

Some of us laughed while he was delivering his lecture, but laughter was soon to desert us. At bedmaking, for instance. The edges of the pillows had to be damped so that they did not slip. There were the most trifling regulations. An American prison has a devilish resemblance to a German barracks.

We had to learn our rights and duties by heart.

"What are you allowed?" I was asked.

"Two razor blades a week."

"A month, you fool."

"And what else?"

"Earphones for the radio."

"How long for?"

"Till nine at night, sir."

The Pumpkin grinned.

"When you get outside again you can listen longer," he remarked. "But for the present you're staying here. And don't forget the 'house.' It's lonely there. Not at all nice. You'll see."

Every day we were taken last into the dining hall. We had to sit down without speaking and take our soup in silence. Once we had to get under the tables because of disobedience. Our tin plates were overturned and the meat fell on the floor. It was not replaced. After that I made a practice of eating my meat first and have retained the habit to this day.

At first my fellow convicts were very reserved in their attitude towards me. I was an outsider. It was true that I had the distinction of a life sentence, but the deeds of a spy were appraised with some discrimination in the penitentiary.

One day, however, I succeeded in gaining the full acclaim of my fellow prisoners. For twenty-four hours on end I was the sole topic of conversation in Leavenworth and was thereafter received into the society of old lags.

We were sitting in the dining hall as on every other day. Everyone had his own place at table. The chef, himself a prisoner, came along and ladled out the food. He spoke German. He bent over me.

"There are two packets of Camels under the table," he whispered. "Don't forget to take them with you."

I thought he was joking. The tables had no drawers and their undersurfaces were quite flat. Surreptitiously I felt about underneath and discovered that the chef had cleverly wedged a fork there and had impaled the cigarettes onto the fork. I pushed them into my pocket, feeling not too happy about the situation, for fellow prisoners at the same table must have noticed something and the warders always noticed any disturbance, however slight.

"Right!" shouted the 'Rat,' the most unpopular of our overseers, when the meal was over. "Stand up!"

We all jumped up from our chairs like automatons and the march out of the room proceeded in precise order. In due course it was the turn of our table to file out. We went silently, one after the other.

"Halt!" called the Rat. Then: "Hands up!"

Our pockets were searched as we left the dining hall. It all went very rapidly as prisoner after prisoner left the room.

I flung my arms up. I had the two packets of cigarettes wedged between my fingers. The Rat stood in front of me, small, puny, suspicious. If he had pulled himself to his full height, his head would just have reached to my shoulder. He tapped my pockets, got impatient and then thrust both hands into them. Meanwhile the other prisoners were standing around. He found nothing. His face turned scarlet. He had made a fool of himself. The prisoners were all grinning now.

I went on standing there with my hands in the air, the cigarettes between my fingers. Everyone could see them except the Rat.

"Get on, back to your work!" he shouted. Then he barked at me: "Be off with you! What are you hanging about for?"

I let my hands drop and shoved the cigarettes into my pocket as quickly as I could. Then I ran off as fast as my legs would carry me. My trick had won me my spurs.

I managed to get through the four weeks quarantine period without a visit to the 'house.' I was promoted to the rank of a 'proper' convict, was moved to the main section of the prison and became eligible for the usual privileges.

I was amazed at how many Germans there were among my fellow convicts. Most of them had been sentenced as recalcitrant prisoners-of-war or as associates of the German M.I. I met Hermann Lang, said to have been responsible for the leakage of information to Germany about a bomb-directing device. I also got to know an American of German descent who had been a prison guard and had allowed German prisoners-of-war to escape. I found myself in contact with some remarkable types and learned some extraordinary histories.

The cell I occupied was the one in which Cook, the self-styled North Pole explorer, had done remission for his ludicrous imposture. Cook had declared that he had reached the North Pole and his success had been acclaimed all over the world until it was revealed that he had never been there. America never forgave him for having made a fool of his country and he remained in prison until he died.

My fate remained uncertain. Technically I was still under sentence of death. My counsel had presented a second petition to Mr. Truman. Actually this was unconstitutional as the decision to reject it had already been made by Truman's predecessor.

The war in Europe had now been over for several months, and I had become an accomplished coal-heaver. I had to shift forty tons each day, with no Sundays off. I could not manage this formidable quota alone, and was assisted by two hefty negroes. In other respects, and inside the prison, coloured men and whites were strictly segregated, but in regard to the most despised form of labour, coal-heaving, no race distinction was observed. I had to thank the governor of Leavenworth for this edifying job. He detested me. Contrary to all regulations, he had neither been present to receive me nor was he to appear to take leave of me. However, my departure was to take place a few years later in strange circumstances. . . .

My fellow convicts, and particularly the Germans among them, were most friendly towards me. Immediately upon my arrival there, a former prisoner-of-war presented me with a packet containing sweets, soap and cigarettes to the value of ten dollars. To a prisoner this represented a veritable fortune. They all worked together to help to make things bearable for me. At first, when I returned to my cell from my coal-heaving activities, I fell literally flat with exhaustion; gradually, however, my biceps developed until I had muscles like a prizefighter. Once I got into an argument with an ex-housebreaker and knocked him out. From that moment I became a member of the ruling class of Leavenworth.

One September evening in 1945, I was listening to my favourite band (Tommy Dorsey) on the radio. The pro-

gramme came to an end at eight o'clock and the news followed on. I felt like tugging the earphones off with
annoyance, but for some reason left them there.

There were political reports from all over the world and
I listened desultorily to the account of some sort of dis-
agreement with the Russians. Then came the news from
Washington. Suddenly I sprang from my bed as if electri-
fied. I had heard my own name quite plainly, without a
shadow of doubt. The newsreader went on slowly and carefully. He could not know, of course, what his words meant
to me:

"President Truman has today commuted the death sentence of the German spy, Erich Gimpel, to one of life imprisonment. Gimpel made an illegal entry into the United
States at the end of last year on board a German U-boat,
to spy out atomic secrets. The F.B.I. succeeded in catching
him. An American court-martial sentenced him to death by
hanging. Execution was postponed indefinitely after the
sudden death of Mr. Roosevelt."

My companions congratulated me excitedly. A warder
came, stuck his head in the window and said:

"Did you hear, Gimpel? So you can keep your head.
Some people are lucky."

The American President had held a press conference at
the White House that afternoon and the time had been taken
up with political questions. The session had already lasted
nearly two and a half hours when Mr. Truman read out my
pardon. About a hundred American journalists were present. I got the details from the newspaper the following day.

"Why have you pardoned Gimpel?" President Truman
was asked.

"Gimpel was a spy," replied Truman, "and a spy is a
man who fights for his country. No country in the world
fights a war without spies. We, of course, had our own spies
in Germany. It is customary to hang spies during a war,
but it is also customary to pardon them when the war is
over."

The President had smiled woodenly into the flashlights
of the press cameras.

"For that reason I decided to commute the death sentence to one of life imprisonment."

I was to feel the influence of the invisible governor of Leavenworth for some time yet. I heaved coal for four years. The monotony of the work at first dulled all thought, but later my anxieties became ever more insistent.

Was my father still alive? What was it like in Germany now? Would I ever leave prison? Would this eternal waiting, this unchanging hopelessness, this life in which a few cigarettes or a bit of chocolate could be of paramount importance, would this ever come to an end? Would I ever again speak with men who neither boasted about crime nor protested innocence? Would I ever again hold a woman in my arms? Would I ever again enter a restaurant as a free man and choose what I wanted to eat?

One day I was taken off coal-heaving and drafted to some excavation work. At first I could not imagine why. Then suddenly I realised. I took a closer look at the man who was digging opposite me and I recognised him.

It was Dasch.

Dasch the traitor, the murderer of his comrades, the man who was responsible for the fact that the six German agents who had regarded him as a colleague, had died on the electric chair.

He shovelled away slowly. No one talked to him. He was despised by all prisoners alike, whether German or American. He looked deliberately right past me. Very rarely did he make any attempt to talk, for he knew well enough that no one would answer him.

Out of the twenty-four hundred men in Leavenworth who between them had broken all the Ten Commandments, the traitors alone were singled out for ostracism. Even among this company of pimps, robbers and murderers, a traitor was always an outsider.

We were exactly facing each other, separated only by a ridiculously shallow ditch about six feet wide. The prison governor had seen to it that we were placed like this. Each of us had a spade handy, a good, solid American spade. I would only have to give him a blow. No doubt that is what everyone in Leavenworth was waiting for. But they waited in vain. The man who worked facing me was a prisoner of his own thoughts. He was on the martyr's pile of his own conscience, pilloried by his own crime. He had been a Judas-friend, and he knew it.

I got used to Dasch. I looked past him as he looked past me. Later I mastered myself sufficiently to exchange a few trifling words with him. He was small and seedy-looking. He was obviously frightened, and looked as if he never had enough sleep. Perhaps the last desperate cries of his victims still sounded in his ears. Perhaps he could see them before him, dying with a curse on their lips, one slowly, another quickly, according to how their bodies reacted to the electric charge. Perhaps he saw before him the simple, cheap wooden coffins in which the bodies of his comrades were taken away for medical dissection. I didn't know and I couldn't worry my head about him. Our respective backgrounds were known in Leavenworth and the men were surprised that my spade didn't someday, somehow slip out of my hand. . . .

"Of course you know what's the matter with Dasch, don't you?" a fellow prisoner asked me one day.

"Of course," I replied.

"You know, don't you, that he's got your pals on his conscience?"

"What are you getting at?"

"Fellows like him deserve to be rubbed out," he went on. "They've no right to go on living."

I nodded.

He grinned.

"If you'd like to give me ten packets of cigarettes I'll see to it that Dasch quits the land of the living."

"How do you propose to do it?"

"Quite simple," he replied. "A slight accident, you know. I'm working up there on the scaffolding. Tomorrow when Dasch passes by I'll let a two hundredweight girder drop on his head. See?"

"Yes," I replied.

He stretched out his hand.

"That's a bargain then. Ten packets of cigarettes. You needn't give them all to me at once."

"I haven't got any," I said, and left him standing.

Dasch is still alive today. He was pardoned long before me and sent back to Germany.

One thought, one project, one fixed idea now became rooted in my mind. Day and night I thought of only one thing—escape! I wanted to try it, however hopeless it seemed, and slowly, patiently, surreptitiously I went about my preparations.

I was now able to move much more freely within the prison walls and I knew my way about. It was clear to me that on three sides escape was quite impossible. On the fourth side the cell block formed a natural wall which was supplemented a few feet away by a fence of steel mesh. There were watchtowers all round, occupied by guards armed with machine guns; the guards, however, often took a nap. The wire fence was illuminated at night, and no escape that way had been attempted for years. There were, after all, plenty of other opportunities, in the course of the day's work outside, for instance, which was where the privileged prisoners, among others, made their attempts to get away. Two or three times a month the Leavenworth sirens would wail, giving the alarm that a convict had escaped. The farmers in the neighbourhood would then band together and take part in the hunt. For every escaped convict they intercepted they got a reward of fifty dollars. Some of them had made it into quite a profitable sideline and were highly skilled in the technique of pursuit.

I wanted to try another method. Anyhow, I was not allowed to work outside. The governor saw to that too. Once the coal elevator in the engine room went wrong and the whole heating system threatened to break down. A crisis seemed imminent, for in Kansas the winters are extremely cold. The chief engineer of the prison tried desperately to put things right but was unsuccessful. Then he remembered me and the two of us managed it together. But the governor was not to know that I had helped. . . .

After that the engineer suggested that I would be useful

to him as an assistant and he made a great deal of my expert knowledge to the governor. But no luck. I went on digging, dreaming day and night of escape.

My first task was to discover how I could get out of the cell block, which at night was locked up. To this end I made a tool with which the iron bars could be prised apart so that I could slip through them. "Necessity can break iron bars. . . ."

I told no one of my plans.

Then one day all was ready.

I waited until midnight. Then I put my levering tool to work and was successful at the first attempt. I jumped out of the cell block into the open—the narrow no-man's-land between the cell block and the wire fence. I could still keep in the shadow of the main building. Now I had to make a quick leap across the brightly lit space between. If I was seen I wouldn't have a chance. It was just a matter of luck. Once I reached the wire fence the first step would have been completed, and the second, and more difficult, would begin. Perhaps the machine guns of the guards would be trained upon just that spot at which I intended to work my way through the wire.

I flattened myself against the wall of the cell block. Then I crouched, ready to spring. "Now," I said to myself, "keep calm." Then I bounded forward.

CHAPTER 18

My Years in Alcatraz

IN the same moment the beam of a searchlight swept the wall of the cell block. It moved about slowly, and rather casually, two or three yards away from me. Then it moved further away; then came nearer. And nearer. I flung myself to the ground; the beam passed over me and then was lowered, capturing me in its cone of light. And there I was, as exposed as if I had been in broad daylight. Within the next second, the first warning shots were heard. I jumped from the ground, raised my arms and waited. I had been caught.

On the following morning I appeared before the vice-governor of Leavenworth for questioning.

"Do you admit that you attempted to escape?" he asked me.

"I have no alternative but to admit it."

He nodded.

"Perhaps in your place I would have done the same," he said, "but you realise, don't you, that you must pay the penalty. I sentence you to fourteen days close arrest with bread and water." He nodded again. "Well, that's all, thank you."

I got through those fourteen days pretty well. When you know that the punishment will come to an end on a definite date, it is not so bad, and I had meanwhile become a hardened prison inmate, well able to stand up to such passing afflictions.

But there was a fly in the ointment, and that was the governor himself, who, as I have said, could not stand me. When I had got through the period of close arrest with bread and water, I was put into solitary confinement for eight months 'on silence,' that is to say, I was forbidden to speak. Every day before lunch, in accordance with the terms of my punishment, prison service cadets appeared, in front of whom I had to strip completely. This burdensome performance, which was designed ostensibly to prevent any further attempt at escape, was only another means of causing me annoyance. Fresh air and any chance of exercise outside the few square feet of my cell were denied me. When I was taken out into the corridor for the daily roll-call I occasionally succeeded in communicating with my fellow sufferers by means of sign language.

It is a terrible thing not to hear the sound of your own voice for eight months, to see no ray of sunshine, to breathe no fresh air and have no idea of what is happening in the world outside. Time stands still, and memories come crowding in, memories of things long ago and far away; things that can never come again. Among these memories was Joan, whom I could see standing before me smiling and talking, only to disappear when I put out my hand to touch her.

I don't know how I managed to get through this period. Many prisoners before and after me have taken their own lives during spells of solitary confinement. I actually never entertained the idea, although it did seem as if all hope had departed from my life.

When, after eight months, I was allowed to leave the cell, I was unable to walk. I should have fallen downstairs if the warder who escorted me had not seized me by the arm.

"Don't be in such a hurry, old chap," he said. "You've got to learn to walk again. It's the same with all of them when they first come out. You've got to get your balance back."

My days in Leavenworth were numbered. My attempt at escape had been reported to Washington, and the supreme authorities thereupon took a decision which made my blood run cold.

I was to be transferred to Alcatraz, the Devil's Island in the Bay of San Francisco, the safest prison in the world, the gaol of living corpses, the penitentiary which only the dead or dying had been known to leave.

Two of us in handcuffs and ankle chains were rushed across America in a prison car. The man who was attached to me like a Siamese twin was called W. Kingdom de Norman, and was the right-hand man of the celebrated gangster king, Dutch Schultz, who had been shot in the street by the machine gun of a rival gang. The nature of his past was indicated by half a dozen bullet scars. He was a nice fellow with a touch of gaiety about him and he had pleasant manners. We behaved like gentlemen, as befitted the circumstances, for we had to stay together even when we ate or went to the lavatory. The honour of ranking as an intrepid gaolbreaker had to be paid for by many discomforts.

After several days' driving, we landed in Alcatraz, having sailed from San Francisco in a motorboat belonging to the prison. In Alcatraz, which is a rock two miles from the mainland, there is a warder to every prisoner. There are never more than two thousand prisoners on this Devil's Island. I was the smallest fry among them. With only one sentence of life imprisonment I had to display a certain diffidence. One of my fellow prisoners had been sentenced to six hundred years' imprisonment, many had sentences of life imprisonment plus one day, and many more one hundred ninety-nine years. Others had had three life imprisonments plus one day. It was here that Al Capone, one of the most famous of American gangsters, had spent the last years of his life. The most celebrated inhabitant of my time was Machine Gun Kelly, so called because he could shoot his name on a wall with a machine gun. It was estimated that he had thirty murders on his conscience. A prisoner by the name of Straub had started prison life at the age of seventeen, and had celebrated his fiftieth year in prison in

Alcatraz. Straub's hair was snow white, and his face had an unnatural ruddy colour.

I was received by the captain of the prison guards. In Alcatraz there are only single cells, but they are so arranged that one can talk with one's neighbours. They are iron cages running the length of a long corridor. One can also see one's neighbours if one uses a mirror, and every inmate was well-equipped with mirrors which were used mostly to keep an eye on the movements of the guards. The man in the next cell to me was a Negro. He grinned at me in a friendly way and gave me a newspaper as a welcoming present. The light was very bad and I could hardly read. A man wearing civilian clothes surprised me while I was peering busily at the paper.

"You'll ruin your eyes," he remarked.

"I'm sure you're right," I replied.

"I'll see that you get a light," he said.

My first thought was that I was going to be punished again with bread and water, but five minutes later the electric bulb in my cell was actually turned on. The man who had ordered this was called Edward B. Swope, governor of the prison island.

Strangely enough, Alcatraz represented an improvement for me. The island is one of the sights of America and nearly every week senators, foreign journalists and police experts come to view it and admire the model way in which it is run. It is, among other things, the only prison in the world from which a convict has never escaped. Four prisoners were once successful in breaking out over the rocks but they were shot in the water.

In fine weather, excursion boats circled our rocks and we could hear the voice of the guide coming over the ship's loudspeakers:

"Ladies and gentlemen, at the top, left of the long building you see the cell which Al Capone occupied until his death from a tumour on the brain. If you look lower down and a little further to the right you can see the cell of Machine Gun Kelly. So far it has proved impossible to convict him of the thirty murders he has committed. If he had a machine gun now he could pick each one of you off even from this distance."

The guide related in full detail the crimes that the inmates of Alcatraz had committed. On one occasion my name was mentioned too; the wind carried a few words into my cell:

"Gimpel, that's the man whom the death of President Roosevelt saved from the hangman's rope."

Sometimes the excursion ships came too near to the island and our warders fired warning shots into the air while the prisoners glued themselves to the tiny spy holes to get a look out into the world. They saw pretty women and ugly women, slim women and fat women clad in light, summer clothes, and well-groomed men who enjoyed their coffee while they were regaled with hair-raising stories about Devil's Island. When the weather was fine, and if one had good eyes, one could pick out every detail on the ships. One could see how the holiday-makers had themselves photographed with Alcatraz as a background. One could see women indulging in the rather poor joke of blowing kisses to the invisible prisoners, while the cruel rock of the island was constantly being committed to the tourists' ciné-cameras.

At dusk the ships would sail back, their passengers having got a little nervous titillation for the price of a few dollars. In the evening we could see the lights of San Francisco and the Golden Gate Bridge, the longest suspension bridge in the world. With hungry eyes we would cling to the neon light advertisements, while the wind would blow scraps of dance music into our cells as the members of the various golf clubs and yachting clubs took their evening's pleasure.

The prisoner in Alcatraz is written off for good. The utter hopelessness of the situation led to a bloody revolt in 1946, in which five men died and fifteen were seriously wounded.

The rising began on the 2nd May, 1946, and it lasted forty-eight hours. The warders were helpless, for the prisoners had armed themselves to the teeth. The American

Marines landed on the island in force. . . . The American public did not learn what had happened on Alcatraz until some days later.

Two convicts had attacked and overcome a warder, taken his bunch of keys from him and locked him in the 'bloody cell,' that is, cell 403. The two prisoners then succeeded in reaching the armaments gallery. A second warder was relieved of his revolver. The other prisoners were then freed and shouted as one man:

"Now Alcatraz is ours. Let's clear out."

But this first, fine careless rapture did not last long.

The rebels did not have the keys to the massive steel doors which shut off the cell blocks from the outside world. A few prisoners returned voluntarily to their cells but three officers who were trying to restore the prisoners to a reasonable frame of mind, were overpowered and locked into cell 403. The rebels also shot at the watchtowers.

"Keep your heads!" called Captain Weinhold from cell 403. "You won't be able to hold out like this for long and you'll have to pay dearly."

One of the prisoners replied:

"If someone's got to die, you can be first!"

The sirens wailed. Alarm! In a sudden access of rage Convict Kretzer fired his gun into cell 403. The governor of Alcatraz had to summon help from outside. The rebels barricaded themselves into the armament gallery. It was like a Wild West film. The battle lasted two days. The Marines worked their way up as far as the ventilators, then they dropped gas grenades, but even then the revolt was not crushed. The soldiers took off the roof and threw hand grenades into the armament gallery. The last prisoners to hold out barricaded themselves in a tunnel below the cell block and they died fighting. . . .

Alcatraz was almost completely destroyed and had to be rebuilt. I was convict number 866 in this gaol with the bloody past.

Although every form of organisation was officially prohibited, prisoners were nowhere so closely organised as in Alcatraz. The bank robbers and kidnappers were the ringleaders. While rope-making was supposed to be in progress, alcoholic liquor was being brewed from sugar, yeast and raisins stolen from the kitchens. Specialists in the art brewed a mixture of high alcohol percentage and this was distributed among those prisoners whom the 'leaders' favoured. For a long time I was quite ignorant about all this, but one day one of the prisoners called over to me:

"Hey, Dutch, come over here! You can have some too."

I drank a whole mug of the stuff and couldn't walk straight afterwards. From then onwards I received my daily ration. Alcohol makes everything more tolerable. Our supplies of liquor were discovered and confiscated, but we retained our primitive distillery. The warders, of course, observed that we were drinking, but there was a sort of tacit agreement that it should not be ruled out entirely.

One fellow convict, Kenny Palmer, drank too much one day and lay on the ground in a state of semiconsciousness. When we had finished our day's work and were ready to be taken back to our cells, he, to our horror, staggered over to the captain of the prison guards and blurted out:

"You're really not a bad bloke, Captain, but I don't know how I'm going to get up those stairs."

The captain put his arm round him and dragged him into his cell.

"Have a good sleep," he said. "You're not well. See that you soon get better again."

He did not report the matter, a fact which put him right on top in the prisoners' estimation. Since the bloody uprising of 1946, prisoners and guards had learned a good deal from each other.

Although Alcatraz is known as the toughest of American gaols it also has its pleasant aspects; the dining hall, for instance, which was so appetising and almost comfortable, that you might easily have imagined yourself in a hotel. The tables were of walnut, and we sat in groups as we wished. The menus were well balanced and the food tastily prepared. Of all the American prisons in which I have been obliged to spend nearly eleven years of my life, Devil's Island had the best cuisine.

That was typical of the spirit of the penal system: as

none of the prisoners had any chance of ever being free again, the authorities tried to mitigate the desperate monotony of their existence by allowing certain essential reliefs within the framework of the otherwise severe routine. Here too, I was allowed to go to the cinema twice a month. Once a year, each prisoner appeared before a disciplinary commission of which the captain of the prison guards, the governor of the prison, the block warders and the prison chaplain were members. Although this commission was competent to grant only trifling privileges, the fact that one could appeal to them was in itself of great psychological importance.

For instance, one official said to me:

"Actually, Gimpel, I have no idea why you are still here. After all, you are a prisoner-of-war. I will see if anything can be done for you."

And the governor said:

"Your conduct is excellent, and apart from that you work voluntarily, which is another very good point in your favour. Of all the prisoners here I like you best."

The hope that I might someday be allowed to leave Alcatraz was naturally nourished by these words, although after what I had already been through, it was really foolish of me to cherish any hopes at all.

My sixth year of imprisonment had meanwhile come round. I knew nothing of what was going on in the world outside apart from what I could gather now and then from newspapers which were smuggled into the prison. Every link with my homeland had been broken. I received no letters, and when a warder came to me one day and said: "There's a visitor for you, Gimpel. Get yourself ready," I thought I must have been confused with another prisoner.

But no, he was right.

I was taken into the visitors' room, one of the most remarkable affairs in Alcatraz. Visitors and 'hosts' were separated from each other by a wall in which were spyholes of thick glass. You could see the other person but you couldn't hear what he was saying, so telephones had been installed on either side of the wall, and you talked to your visitor by telephone. A warder was there to listen to what was said, and if the conversation took a turn which was considered unsuitable for some reason, he pressed a button and cut off all communication.

I entered the visitors' room like a sleepwalker. My escort showed me a spy-hole and I looked through it. On the other side stood a middle-aged man in a well-cut suit. He smiled at me and I picked up the receiver.

"Good morning, Herr Gimpel," he said in German. "You will be surprised to receive a visit. I have been wanting to come to see you for a long time, but I have only just been given permission. I am the German Consul-General in San Francisco, Dr. Schönbach."

"I am delighted to meet you," I stammered.

"I just wanted to tell you that we have not forgotten you. We are doing everything we can to get you out of here. You will understand that we have to proceed carefully. You must have patience and yet more patience."

"I'm quite used to being patient," I replied. "Thank you very much, Consul. You can have no idea what it means to me to be able to speak to someone other than a warder or a convict."

"That I can imagine. I should like to offer you some comfort, but it's easy to talk. I have not come alone," he added. "I have brought with me the chaplain of the German colony in San Francisco." He smiled at me again and a man wearing the typical dress of a pastor stood before the spy-hole. We talked for twenty minutes. Both men promised me that they would come again, and they kept their word. On the second visit, the governor made a quite unusual concession. I was allowed to meet my visitors in an ordinary room, that is to say, without spy-hole and telephone.

During this time when I began once more to have hope, I was involved, quite without meaning to be, in a small-scale convict revolt. We had come into the dininghall as on every other day. The menu was spaghetti with meat sauce, that is to say, the prisoners' dinner was much more frugal than usual. While we were eating there was an un-natural quiet in the room; not a word was exchanged at any table. Evidently something had been arranged, something I knew nothing about. Then it started. As if at a word of command, the prisoners jumped from their chairs, threw the tables over and smashed everything within reach.

"Meat! Meat!" they roared. "Where's the meat? We don't want your filthy sauces, we want meat!"

The guards' machine guns were thrust through the dining hall windows and we flung ourselves to the ground. The shooting might start at any moment now. After the bloody uprising of 1946, the guards were in no mood to trifle and the prisoners of Alcatraz were not regarded as men to be reasoned or reckoned with; some of them were, in fact, nothing more or less than beasts.

The captain entered the dining hall and the men whistled at him. Then the governor appeared in person, and the room was suddenly as quiet as it had been before the outbreak.

"What's the matter?" he asked. "Have you all gone mad?" No answer. "I request you to leave the dining hall singly, do you understand? Anyone who does not obey my instructions will be treated as a mutineer. Just remember that."

No one moved.

"I will give you another sixty seconds," continued Mr. Swope, "another fifty-five, another fifty, another forty-five. . . ."

A prisoner stood up hesitantly, looking neither to the left nor to the right. The others whistled at him. But some more men followed him. Most of us were more afraid of the instigators of the revolt than of any punitive measures the governor might take. It was a tricky thing to decide when it might be too soon to leave the room or too late to stay there. Then one of the prisoners stood up and said:

"If we don't get any meat tomorrow, it will happen again. We have every right to have meat, we need meat as part of our diet."

"I will have the matter investigated," said the governor.

The speaker, Pinszky, was, as ringleader, removed to Block D, the silent block, for his punishment. He stuck it out for six months, then he committed suicide—on Christmas Eve. He had somehow managed to get hold of a razor blade and severed his main artery. How he succeeded in doing this was never explained, for on Alcatraz the distribution of razor blades was attended by great ceremony. Twice a week, a privileged prisoner appeared with a tray on which were arrayed a number of razor blades, spaced according to a precise layout. Each prisoner was allowed to use a blade for three minutes and had then to replace it on the tray. The blades were changed every week. The prison authorities were anxious to prevent other prisoners going the same way as Mr. Pinszky.

The safety system on Alcatraz worked with all the latest technical refinements. Anyone who had reported for work, had on leaving and entering the cell block, to walk past a device which registered the tiniest piece of metal. If the apparatus buzzed the prisoner had to strip completely and submit to a thorough search. It was therefore quite impossible to smuggle any sort of escape tool into one's cell.

In contrast to other prisons work was not compulsory in Alcatraz. Nor could one buy anything with the few dollars one earned. The so-called 'canteen goods' were not sold but distributed. Everyone got three packets of cigarettes a week. Shaving soap was free, also fruit. A certain amount of chocolate was also distributed.

I was three and a half years in Alcatraz and came into contact there with the most incredible men with the most incredible histories. I was there when an oil millionaire struggled in vain for the freedom of the man who had kidnapped him. And practically every day I met Machine Gun Kelly, who had extracted 200,000 dollars from another oil magnate. He died in Alcatraz on his fifty-ninth birthday from a heart attack.

I had acquired a certain dexterity with rope-making and a few hundred dollars with which I could do nothing stood to my credit. I had gained the confidence both of my fellow convicts and of the prison authorities. I went to work every day and lay every evening disconsolately in bed. I had become a part of the barren monotony of prison life.

Then one night I was suddenly awakened. I looked at the clock. It was three in the morning.

"Has something happened?" I enquired sleepily.

"Yes," replied the warder, "something has happened. Come on, guess what!"

"I know nothing about it," I answered surlily. "Leave me to my sleep or I'll complain in the morning. You've no right to come and disturb me."

"Pack your things, you dolt," said the warder. "Would you believe that a chap could sleep away his own release?"

"Release?" I asked.

"I'll come back for you in five minutes. You've been transferred to Atlanta, Georgia."

I thought I was dreaming. A miracle had happened! I was to leave the Devil's Island of Alcatraz alive and well. It was a sensation which was to appear in all the newspapers, a piece of news which seemed incredible. Transferred to Atlanta! That might be the anteroom to freedom.

CHAPTER 19

Promoted from Convict to Mister

MY hopes soared, but the American legal machine moved slowly. The Atlanta penitentiary to which I was transferred was in the State of Georgia on the east coast of America, that is to say, exactly at the opposite side of the States from Alcatraz. I entered the prison feeling strangely detached from all that was going on around me. But I was once more to learn the meaning of waiting—hopeful, stupid, resigned waiting.

For the second time my sentence had been reduced. I was now to serve thirty years' detention. A good conduct prisoner can, according to American usage, apply for release within the framework of 'parole procedure' when he has served a third of his sentence. Prisoners who are released on these terms must report every day to a certain police station, they must also be indoors at a certain time, and they may drink no alcohol. They have, in fact, still one foot in prison.

I applied for 'release on parole' and was allocated to a parole officer, Mr. Boone, a coloured man. He was tall, slim and sported a little moustache, and he proved that a prison overseer can conduct himself with all the considerate good manners of a gentleman. He was a human being and I owe it to him that I am today a free man.

My first application for parole was rejected. I was in despair, hope alternating with apathy. I ate hardly anything, could not sleep and lapsed into a state of dull resentment.

A prisoner could appear before the parole panel only once a year. I had therefore to spend another three hundred and sixty-five days in Atlanta before my case could be reconsidered. Mr. Boone did all he could to banish my mood of resignation. On his advice I took up weaving on the prison looms and became expert at the work. There is no doubt that work does distract one. It was at this time that I completed my first decade in prison, blown with the wind to Atlanta, the scene of the famous novel, *Gone with the Wind*. Ten years among crooks and murderers, in the company of hate-filled prisoners and indifferent overseers, ten years with a number on my arm, three thousand six hundred and fifty nights in a prison cell, nights full of longing, full of hope, full of unshed tears, full of imagined kisses, full of angry curses.

I may have been coal-heaving on the day my father died. I didn't know, I didn't know anything. I didn't want to know anything. East-West relations, the war in Korea, the conflict in Indo-China, none of these things interested me in the slightest.

Nothing but eating, sleeping and once a week the cinema. Then I was joined in my cell by the man who had murdered his wife. It was strange how good-looking a murderer could be. He was young, fair and handsome. He laughed heartily and had a pleasant manner. Apart from the fact that he had killed his wife there was nothing about him to which I could take exception. He had been in Germany, in Munich. He had got to know his girlfriend in the street, and then the thing had happened. The psychiatrist had saved him from the gallows. They sent him from Munich to Atlanta under a life sentence. He told stories of Germany, and as I listened I nearly choked with revulsion.

There were six of us in the cell, including another German, also a spy.

"You can have any woman in Germany," said the murderer. "Sometimes I had to give ten cigarettes, sometimes twenty, occasionally a bar of chocolate as well perhaps."

"Keep your mouth shut," I said.

"But I'm serious," the murderer continued. "They're easier to get than French women."

"Don't be an ass," said my German coprisoner. "You could get an American woman and a packet of cigarettes thrown in."

I felt sick and walked over to the window. It was of course shut. Nothing all day but dry, stale prison air, coarse talk, the old jokes, hideous laughter and the morose faces of the overseers.

Once again I was called away from my work. Mr. Boone, the coloured parole officer, took me on one side.

"Now pull yourself together," he said. "I have arranged that you are to appear again today before the parole judge. Ahead of your time. See that you leave him with a good impression."

The man at the judge's table looked pleasant enough, the typical American petit-bourgeois. He was neither indifferent nor sympathetic. He was simply the mouthpiece of the Washington bureaucracy. He could hardly be aware that he held the fate of men in his hands.

"So you are Gimpel?"

"Yes, sir."

He pushed his spectacles up onto his forehead. I hadn't even had time to wash my hands, my clothes were grubby and I felt awkward and inhibited.

"Now what have you got to say to me?" asked the judge encouragingly.

I couldn't get a word out.

"Is there something you wanted to ask me?" he continued.

"I want my freedom, sir."

He fiddled about with his pencil.

"Well?"

Mr. Boone now took a hand.

"The prisoner has just come straight from his work, sir.

He had no idea that he was going to be called before the parole panel today. I would ask you to take that into consideration."

The judge hesitated for a moment, then he became just a shade more friendly.

"I know that your conduct here has been good, but . . . but"—he cleared his throat a few times—"espionage against the United States. That's no trifle, you know." He paused for a while, then he said: "If we sent you back to Germany, would you go to East Germany or West Germany?" He looked at me expectantly.

"To West Germany, sir."

He nodded, satisfied.

"Well, I'll see what I can do for you."

I went back to my work. I heard no more from him for weeks, and months, not a word. Once more Mr. Boone talked to me and tried to keep my spirits up, but prison psychosis, attacks of which I had so far happily escaped, finally got a grip on me and I vacillated all the time between complete numbness and intense excitability. The crisis was reached when I was transferred to another cell.

They were an unappetising lot of men with whom I found myself now, and I wanted to have nothing to do with them. When I had finished my work, I spoke to my warder.

"I'm not going back into that cell anymore," I said.

"That's insubordination, and you know what the penalty for that is."

"I don't care."

"I shall have to report you," he said.

I was put into solitary confinement. That was nothing new for me. Bread and water again. By the tenth day I had lost forty pounds and was as thin as a rake. I never answered when I was spoken to and the prison authorities began to get worried about me.

One day I was summoned to the presence of the deputy-governor. The man who took me to him was called Mr. Lowe. He was a human being too.

"Pull yourself together," he said. "Don't be so obstinate.

They're all quite well-disposed towards you here, but you mustn't kick against the regulations."

I made no reply.

The vice-governor looked me over from head to foot.

"Well, Gimpel," he began, "are you still obdurate?"

"Yes, sir."

"I will give you one minute to reconsider your answer," he said. He got to his feet and paced up and down the room. "You're not a child, you know. Think well what you are saying."

He remained standing.

"Are you going back into your cell?"

"No, sir."

"Take him away," said the vice-governor reluctantly.

Mr. Lowe walked by my side. He stopped in the corridor.

"Listen," he said. "You know me, don't you?"

"Yes."

"You know, don't you, that I don't wish you any harm?"

"Yes."

"Well then, just go back to the governor, and tell him that you will obey orders. I dare not tell you what is at stake, but I beg you to go back to him. If you don't, you'll bitterly regret it."

My obstinacy knew no bounds, but I had a high regard for Mr. Lowe and I liked him. He was an elderly man and often talked to me about his family. So I turned back just to please him. Beaming with pleasure, he told the vice-governor that I wished to speak to him again.

"Have you thought it over again?" he asked.

"Yes, sir."

"You realise that you acted wrongly?"

"Yes, sir."

"Very well, you will be released tomorrow morning. Your parole has been granted."

I could hardly believe my ears. I had waited for my freedom for nearly eleven years and when it was granted me I could not realise what it meant. I looked into the beaming face of Mr. Lowe.

"You see now what I meant, don't you?" he asked.

"Yes."

"I couldn't tell you, but if you hadn't gone back just now your pardon would have been withdrawn because of insubordination. It's a good thing I was there to advise you."

I grasped his hand and pressed myself against the wall. I was on the point of breaking down.

Things moved forward at great speed. I chose a suit and a shirt. I received personal documents and a cheque for a few hundred dollars. I was just able to shake hands with a few of the men and then I was taken out of the prison. I was free. I was wearing ordinary clothes. I was a man among men. A person with a name and without a number. I was accompanied by an official of the emigration authority, a nice chap.

We drove off at high speed to the Atlanta airfield. The *Italia*, the ship which was to take me back to Germany, was leaving New York harbour the following day.

Then there I was at the airport, with my ticket in my pocket. I laughed, I breathed and looked at everybody and all the everyday happenings around me with radiant eyes. And still I could not fully realise what was happening. I walked over the runway to the four-engined machine. A stewardess in a smart blue costume was standing on the steps of the aircraft. She was slim, blonde and beautiful, and she was smiling. For a few seconds I stood there as if rooted to the spot, staring at her and trying to smile, but the smile failed to come off. My escort gave me a friendly thump on the shoulder.

"Go on," he said.

I sat down, took a piece of chewing gum and tightened my belt. 3,000 feet. 4,500 feet. One hour, two hours. We landed in Washington and then flew on to New York. I was met at the airport by a coloured police official.

"Are you Gimpel?"

My escort answered for me.

The Negro nonchalantly produced some handcuffs from his pocket and clasped them onto me.

"Are you crazy?" said my escort. "He's free."

"I've got my instructions," replied the Negro coldly and in front of all the aircraft passengers he led me away as if I were a criminal. The pretty blonde stewardess looked at me dumbfounded. The emigration authority official apologised to me for his colleague and went away shaking his head.

We drove through New York, the city in which I had been hunted down, the city in which I had loved and left Joan. Joan . . . the memory was like a pain in my heart, even after ten years.

In the city prison I was torn out of my melancholy dreams and became the convict once more, to be photographed and registered.

"Come on, don't fool about," said the warder. "Stick your paws in the ink."

For the last time my fingerprints were taken.

I could not sleep a wink. In a few hours my ship would be leaving harbour; without me perhaps. Perhaps it had all been a misunderstanding. Perhaps they had heard about my insubordination and had withdrawn the parole. Theoretically I was free. But when a free man is locked up on his last night in the country with murderers, thieves and robbers, and is himself treated as if he were a thief or a robber, then something must be wrong somewhere.

At a quarter to six there was a shaking on my cell door. "Get dressed!" The words were bawled at me harshly. Then a cup of coffee and two slices of white bread were pushed through the cell window.

I was taken to the interrogation room.

Then the procedure of the previous day began for the second time. Photographing, registration, fingerprints, handcuffs. A car drove up.

The official who had the day before fetched me from the airport seated himself beside me. He looked out of the window and didn't say a word. I suppose he was thinking of his instructions.

The *Italia* was to leave within the hour and friends and relatives of the passengers were standing at the pier, laughing and joking, some with tears in their eyes. It was hot, oppressively hot and the women were wearing light summer dresses.

The curious among them formed a lane for me as, still in handcuffs, I crossed the gangway and was taken on board. The press photographers were on the spot and I was 'shot' from every angle.

It seemed as if my escort must have delivered prisoners on to the *Italia* many times before, for he certainly knew the ropes. Without asking anyone he piloted me towards the children's playroom. Then he removed my handcuffs, threw my papers on to a table and shoved a piece of chewing gum into his mouth.

"Sit down," he said. It was the first time he had said anything at all. He looked at his watch. Evidently he was in a hurry.

I looked round at the gay murals of Snow White and the Seven Dwarfs.

My guardian consulted his watch once more and then stood up.

"O.K.," he said, and casually raised his index finger to his cap. That was my leave-taking from America.

He locked the door from the outside and exchanged a few words with one of the stewards. The ship left harbour, for Germany, my homeland, and freedom. I was sailing into the greatest adventure of my life.

When we had passed beyond the three-mile zone, the steward came and unlocked the playroom.

"It's all a lot of red tape," he said. "Just a lot of nonsense."

He showed me the printed passenger list. My name was right at the bottom, added at the last moment.

"Mr. Erich Gimpel," I read.

Mister.

I looked at this word again and again. Promoted from Convict to Mister!

It took me days, weeks, months to understand the miracle of freedom. It was a long time before I could look people in the face without embarrassment, before I could eat just what I liked once more, before my palate learned again to distinguish a Moselle from a Rhine wine. It was a long time before I shook off the habit of avoiding women, before I dared to make enquiries about my relations. . . .

I was now forty-five years, seven months and six days old and had 424 dollars and 24 cents in my pocket. I had been free for six days. Released from prison, expelled from the U.S.A. On parole. I still owed the U.S.A. more than nineteen years detention. To the American authorities I was a spy; to the German a late repatriate. I should in fact have been dead nine years and eleven days.

I avoided going on deck until it was dark. I had forgotten how to speak to people. I had first to get used to the world again. To time. To fresh air. To money. To laughter.

In the long, dreary years of captivity I had become unsure of myself and had to force myself to go to the bar. I ordered a whisky and it came. Whisky's cheap when you're free. The bartender smiled. The people near me were talking about me and made no attempt to hide their curiosity. Rumour is the quickest, cheapest and most irresponsible newspaper in the world. A woman was sitting next to me at the bar. I had no idea what she looked like. I had accustomed myself not to look at women anymore. She spoke to me, but I did not grasp what she was saying; I was much too agitated. I would never have dared to start a conversation with a woman myself. Women are dead to you when you're living in a cell.

We went on deck together. The *Italia* was now on the high seas. A light breeze blew up and the clouds slowly blew away and revealed the stars. The crests of the little waves danced in changing colours in the moonlight. The ship's engines were working almost silently. The wind was playing with my companion's hair, and as we stood there in the dark, I dared for the first time to look at her. She was good to look at. I was actually standing in the company of a woman at the ship's rail. I was seeing the stars. A fresh breeze was blowing. Suddenly, everything was changed. It was as if all the old imaginings and anxieties had been blown away. For minutes, for hours, I forgot the unforget-

table. I forgot that I had been measured by the hangman. I
ceased to see the face of the judge as he murmured quietly:
"Death by hanging"; I no longer remembered how my two
counsel, having done their best for me, shook me silently
by the hand and, embarrassed, quickly turned away. I no
longer felt I was Agent 146 who had sailed for forty-six
days with U-1230 through depth charges and air attack to
land in Frenchman Bay, North America, and carry out the
most fantastic task the war could command.

"You look ill," said my companion.

"I am ill," I answered.

"Is it serious?"

"I hope not."

"I noticed at once that there was something wrong with
you," she continued. "I think you must be very lonely."

"Yes," I said.

We went back to the bar. My companion was wearing
a red cocktail dress and she had thrown a mink wrap round
her shoulders. She looked fresh, young and well-off. She
smiled. How lovely it was to see a woman smile. A woman
who looked young and pretty and rich. That same morning
I had still been in the hands of the New York Criminal
Investigation Department together with thieves, murderers
and pimps; that evening I realised for the first time all it
meant to be free. Free! And alive! And going home! Home
to Germany.

"Do you dance?" asked the lady.

"No," I answered. I wanted to tell her why but I couldn't
bring myself to it.

"Just as I thought," she said.

We sat together for another half hour, then I went to my
cabin. I could not sleep, although I knew I wouldn't be
wakened here every two hours for roll call.

In the morning I realised that I wasn't a convict anymore. I forced myself to stay in bed. Free men don't get
up at a quarter to six. I tried to fix my tie, but I couldn't
manage it and had to appear at breakfast with an open-neck
shirt. My companion of the previous evening was waiting
for me. Red seemed to be her favourite colour. She was

wearing a woollen dress. She stretched out her hand to me as I approached her.

"I didn't know who you were yesterday, but I do now. Do forgive my tactless questions."

"I was only too happy to have you talking to me," I replied. I wanted to tell her how helpless I still felt but I couldn't find the right words. People were still staring at me. The papers had got quickly to work and were after the Gimpel story like a pack of hounds. So long as I was in captivity no one knew anything about me, but now . . . A hundred and fifty American reporters had waited at the wrong gangway at New York docks. The cables were piling up now. Offers were coming in from all over the world. I had had no experience with newspapers and publishers, and although I didn't know what to do with myself, I wanted to be left in peace.

"Shall we go on deck?" asked the lady whose name I still did not know.

"Yes," I answered.

I doubt if she could possibly have realised what it meant for me to walk on deck with a woman, to talk with her, to see her smile, to breathe her fragrance, to feel the pressure of her hand. That morning I had looked in the mirror. I had grown old. My hair was snow-white. My face was pale, the skin was taut and leathern. According to my birth certificate, I was forty-five but the mirror told a different story.

"ARE you Mr. Gimpel?" An officer of the *Italia* had come up to me. "We're putting into Plymouth this afternoon. The English newspapers are bombarding us for an interview with you. Are you willing?"

"Must I?" I asked.

He shrugged his shoulders.

"All right," I said.

There was not much prospect of my being able to avoid the reporters for long.

I met them in the smoking room. The officers of the *Italia* didn't at all mind these press conferences. It would be reported that I had travelled back to Europe in their ship. The United States government had paid for my passage—tourist class. I had first of all been placed in a cabin with people who were a bit too noisy for me. I had gone to the purser to ask him if I could change quarters. I had made a slip of the tongue, and said: "Would it be possible for you to give me a different cell, sir?"

He had smiled.

"We haven't any cells, but perhaps a cabin will suit you." We shook hands and had a drink together.

The British reporters were not so persistent as their American colleagues.

"Have you had a good journey?"

"Oh yes," I replied.

"Have you been in England before?"

"Oh yes."

"What do you think of England?"

"It's a very lovely country."

"What do you think of English people?"

"They are very nice people."

"Do you hate America?"

"No, by no means."

I didn't want to say more than a few commonplace courtesies. I still didn't know whether I should keep silence or whether I should speak, and so long as I was unsure the cleverest reporter would not have got anything out of me. But now the German pressmen were after me. One who had flown to Plymouth to meet me was observing my every movement. I was constantly being called into the wireless room to talk on the radio-telephone. This was a foretaste of what was to await me in Hamburg.

"Did you enjoy being a spy?"

"No, not at all."

"Were you a member of the Party?"

"No."

"Did you know Hitler well?"

I had to smile. What ideas these people did have about spies! I had been a soldier like any other man, but on a specially tricky sector. I had not volunteered for it anymore than ordinary soldiers volunteered for any special posting. We were the servants of the most unyielding master the world has ever known. War.

"Have you parents waiting for you at home?"

"No."

"No wife?"

"No."

"Where will you go?"

"I don't know."

"All the best," said the reporters.

"All the best," I replied.

I was now only a few hours from Hamburg. I wished to leave the ship unrecognized and to this end secured the cooperation of the ship's officers and the German Red Cross. They asked a German exchange student if she would care to be Frau Gimpel for ten minutes and with her I left the *Italia* through a side exit, just above the waterline. We made a somewhat ill-assorted married couple but excited no attention. One woman photographer penetrated the ruse and released her shutter, but I escaped the main hustle and bustle. I climbed into a Red Cross car and was taken to the Friedland camp. I was home again. I was given a gratuity and a late repatriate's passport, and so that I could remain undisturbed for a while they sent me to the Black Forest for a few weeks, to the Marxzell Convalescent Home for Mothers.

It was late summer and the sun smiled on me. I went for walks in the woods at six in the morning. People greeted me in friendly fashion. In the evenings I sat in the Marxzeller Mühle eating trout and drinking Moselle. My digestion was not proving as resilient as my tongue. There was peace here and quiet. Most of the summer visitors had already gone. There was a lady from Karlsruhe recovering from an operation; a hotel-keeper and a master hairdresser from Bonn were taking a few days' holiday; a builders' foreman was killing time between contracts. I was with human beings, gradually getting used to human society. It was peacetime. The war was over. Over. The War. . . .

Then I suddenly knew that I must write my story. I knew

that I must draw the veil from an aspect of the war which no one knew about. I must tell of the silent war which I had fought for years and which became my murderer. I wanted to place on record what it had been like. How mean. How cold. How merciless. Over here as over there, in the east as in the west, how men had suffered and died and how men had been tortured to death.

I have spent a few months writing my reminiscences. I have tried to present them in a deliberately unsentimental way and I have not glossed anything over. There is not, there was not and there never will be any glamour in the metier of spy. The silent battle the secret agent fights is a dirty battle, merciless and cold. It is the dirtiest side of war.

And I hate war. And I hate the job of a spy—I always shall. . . .

Agent 146 is a man named **ERICH GIMPEL** who was recruited by the Third Reich to spy on America. He was caught in New York in January 1945, sentenced to hang, but then given a last-minute pardon. Erich Gimpel returned home to Germany in 1947.

THE LAST OF THE MOHICANS

THE LAST OF THE MOHICANS

James Fenimore Cooper

Supplementary materials written by Michelle Lee
Series edited by Cynthia Brantley Johnson

POCKET BOOKS
NEW YORK LONDON TORONTO SYDNEY

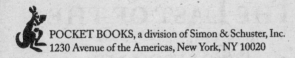

POCKET BOOKS, a division of Simon & Schuster, Inc.
1230 Avenue of the Americas, New York, NY 10020

This book is a work of fiction. Names, characters, places, and incidents either are products of the author's imagination or are used fictitiously. Any resemblance to actual events or locales or persons living or dead is entirely coincidental.

Supplementary materials copyright © 2008 by Simon & Schuster, Inc.

First Pocket Books paperback edition May 2008

POCKET and colophon are registered trademarks of Simon & Schuster, Inc.

For information about special discounts for bulk purchases, please contact Simon & Schuster Special Sales at 1-800-456-6798 or business@simonandschuster.com.

Front cover illustration by Tim O'Brien

Manufactured in the United States of America

10 9 8 7 6 5 4 3 2 1

ISBN-13: 978-1-4165-6144-6
ISBN-10:   1-4165-6144-7

CONTENTS

INTRODUCTION

The Last of the Mohicans:
THE SAVAGERY, SENTIMENTALITY, AND SUSPENSE OF A CLASSIC

In more ways than one, James Fenimore Cooper sets the stage for *The Last of the Mohicans* (1826) in the second paragraph of the novel: "Perhaps no district throughout the wide extent of the intermediate frontiers can furnish a livelier picture of the cruelty and fierceness of the savage warfare of those periods than the country which lies between the head waters of the Hudson and the adjacent lakes." With this passage, Cooper suggests to the reader that the setting—this parcel of frontier in upstate New York between the Hudson River and "the adjacent lakes"—will play a vital role in telling this story about the violent clash of cultures coming to a head during the French and Indian War. This tale, the second in Cooper's *Leatherstocking* series, provides an account of the "savage warfare" experienced by two British colonial sisters, Cora and Alice Munro, and their traveling party as they make their way through the wilderness toward the safety of their father, a colonel holding down Fort William Henry.

Cooper's "savage warfare" does not simply refer to tactics used by the Native Americans; the phrase refers to the brutality exhibited by both sides in the conflict. Cooper's novel is unusual for its insistence on calling into question the reader's ideas of the difference between "civilization" and "wilderness" or "savage" and "gentleman." Characters such as Uncas, a young Mohican warrior with integrity and intelligence, helped alter the nineteenth-century perception of Native Americans as bloodthirsty brutes. Characters such as Hawkeye, a rugged woodsman who has chosen to leave his "white" heritage behind, and Cora, a woman who is still admired despite her "mixed" heritage, also prompted reconsiderations of common categories of race and gender.

Cooper's work, though extremely popular in the United States and around the world for its blend of Gothic, romantic, and suspenseful adventure elements, was not without its critics. Mark Twain famously blasted Cooper for his overly sentimental style, excessive use of clichés, and blatant inaccuracies. Even today, some readers and critics agree with many of Twain's opinions, finding Cooper's work a bit convoluted, melodramatic, and confusing.

Nevertheless, generations of readers have judged *The Last of the Mohicans,* along with the other books in *The Leatherstocking Tales,* as more than just a fine piece of historical fiction. The novel reopens the door to both the eighteenth- and nineteenth-century American frontiers, reminding us how the pioneer, individualist spirit in this country started. The novel also triggers our inherent desire for adventure, our need for good to triumph over evil, and our search for identity in a world where cultures still struggle for supremacy. Often called America's first novelist, Cooper could be considered the pioneer of the frontier adventure genre.

The Life and Work of James Fenimore Cooper

Born in 1789, the year the new Constitution went into effect, James Fenimore Cooper first encountered the wilderness when his family moved to the area surrounding Otsego Lake, New York, a year after his birth. He was educated in Albany and New Haven and also attended Yale, though his time there was cut short when he was expelled for playing a schoolboy prank on a classmate. His interest in the sea, which would inspire future novels, began three years later, in 1808, when he joined the United States Navy at the age of nineteen. At first, he worked out of a merchant vessel heading for England and Spain, but ultimately he was assigned to a position in Oswego, New York, where he oversaw the production of America's first warship. His time on the water increased his desire for more compelling sea duty, but after meeting the wealthy Susan De Lancey, he exchanged his naval ambition for marriage in 1811. Cooper turned to the country life, where his writing career began to develop.

After the death of his father, William Cooper, a judge, congressman, and the founder of Cooperstown, New York, the younger Cooper inherited his father's estate—and his debts. Under pressure from creditors, Cooper started writing on a dare from his wife about whether he could pen a book better than the one he was reading (Cooper biographers offer different versions of how the incident actually occurred). Unfortunately, his first novel, *Precaution* (1820), a domestic comedy set in England, was a critical failure. But Cooper was not discouraged and quickly wrote a second book, *The Spy* (1821), based on the *Waverly* series of the popular Scottish author Sir Walter Scott and set during the American Revolution. This novel, whose protagonist, Harvey Birch, secretly is a spy for George Washington, was Cooper's first writing success, read widely in both the United States and in Europe.

Cooper's third book, *The Pioneers* (1823), was the first of what would come to be called the *Leatherstocking Tales*. In it, readers meet an elderly frontier hero named Natty Bumppo and the Mohican sage Chingachgook. Cooper drew on his own childhood experiences near Lake Otsego in crafting the book, and with it he established a theme that carries through the entire *Leatherstocking* series: How should humans treat the environment?

Cooper's next book, *The Pilot* (1823), was also inspired by his frustration with a book he was reading, this time *The Pirate* by Sir Walter Scott (whom Cooper would meet during his travels to Paris in 1826). Finding Scott's imagery unrealistic, Cooper set out to write a novel that could capture his own experiences of the sea. With a protagonist based on American naval hero John Paul Jones and a backdrop of the Revolutionary War, Cooper spins a nautical adventure located off the English coast, establishing the popular maritime adventure genre. Writers such as Herman Melville and Joseph Conrad acknowledged that Cooper laid the foundation for their own work set on the seas. Conrad once said that Cooper "looked at [the sea] with consummate understanding. In his sea tales the sea inter-penetrates with life. . . . His descriptions have the magisterial ampleness of a gesture indicating the sweep of a vast horizon. They embrace the colours of sunset, the peace of starlight, the aspects of calm and storm, the great loneliness of the waters, the stillness of silent coasts, and the alert readiness which marks men who live face to face with the promise and the menace of the sea."

Cooper's passion for the sea is evident not only in his novels but also in his historical nonfiction work. Susan Fenimore Cooper tells of her father giving his children "lessons in naval architecture, object lessons, with the different craft passing in the narrow channel between the Sunswick Bank and Blackwell's Island as models." Cooper's knowledge of watercraft and naval history are evident in his two-volume work *History of the Navy of the United States of America* (1839), a comprehensive chronicle from the Revolutionary War to the War of 1812. Although the book was updated after Cooper's death and was subsequently used as a reliable source for decades, the publication did generate controversy among the descendants of Commodore Oliver Perry, who disagreed with Cooper's portrayal of Perry's second in command. Cooper sued over the matter; an arbitration tribunal heard his case and ruled that Cooper's version of the facts could stand.

Cooper's distinction as an author of nonfiction extends beyond maritime histories. From 1826 to 1833, his position as a U.S. consul living in Lyons, France, inspired political writings that challenged the ideals of American democracy. Some of these essays are collected in the two-volume account of his family's experience in France called *A Residence in France: With an Excursion up the Rhine, and a Second Visit to Switzerland* (1836), framed in the context of personal correspondence. This journal

includes Cooper's encounters with—and opinions of—
royalty, his record of a cholera epidemic, his observations of Americans on foreign soil, and his view of
customs and habit in both Europe and America.

Although James Fenimore Cooper is often given the
distinction of being the first true American novelist, he
was, at his core, a gregarious man who enjoyed sharing a
tale by the fire. His daughter Susan once wrote that
"[w]hen, in the course of reading, any thing of this nature
came in his way, he was never satisfied unless it was
shared with others; very frequently the laughable passage was carried immediately into the family circle, and
read by him with infinite zest, and with a singularly
hearty laugh—tears of merriment, meanwhile, rolling
down his cheeks." Cooper may not be commonly identified as a humorist, but a storyteller he was, entertaining
his readers with tales of adventure, exploration, danger,
and courage. When readers slip into the lush pine forests
of *The Last of the Mohicans* or senses the ominous threat
lurking just beneath the ocean's peaceful tide in *The
Pilot,* they fall into the imagination of a boy "whose veins
would thrill with a strange delight" as he roamed the
woods and sailed the lake near his home, as one of
Cooper's closest friends, George Washington Greene,
recounted fondly in 1852. Cooper died the day before
his sixty-second birthday.

Historical and Literary Context of
The Last of the Mohicans

*The French and Indian War: Nine Years of the Seven
Years' War*

From 1756 to 1763, the Seven Years' War in Europe, pit-
ting Austria, France, Spain, Russia, and Sweden against
Prussia, Great Britain, and Hanover, was rooted in two
conflicts: a territorial battle for supremacy between Austria and Prussia and a struggle over colonial empire between Britain and France. This Anglo-French battle
over territory was ignited across the sea in North America, as both countries staked their claims to the "Ohio
Country," a vast area stretching from the Appalachian
Mountains to the Mississippi River, from the Great
Lakes to the Gulf of Mexico.

Although war was not officially declared until 1756,
the first engagement occurred in 1753, when the British
attempted to gain control of the fur trade in Ohio. General George Washington and a small party of men, including an interpreter and a Mingo chief, hand-delivered
a letter from the governor of Virginia requesting that the
French leave the territory. Needless to say, the French
declined, choosing instead to advance further into the
country. Washington was ordered to prevent further invasion and established a camp where a large number of
troops and arms could be called. Realizing that the
French were scouting his troops' movements, Washington retaliated by ambushing a group of French soldiers
and ultimately sparking the combat that initiated a war
that lasted longer than its counterpart in Europe. Although the war unofficially ended in 1760 with the fall of

Montreal to the British, the Treaty of Paris, in which France surrendered its territories in North America, was not signed until 1763.

Although Cooper fictionalizes the war in *The Last of the Mohicans*, he captures the economic, political, and social upheaval of the period in representing characters on all sides of the conflict. His main characters, from Chingachgook to Alice Munro, show the varied outlook among the Indian allies; the role of women in a world where men fought over territory and claimed what they deemed was theirs, both honorably and dishonorably; and how men defined morality, humanity, and civility. Although scholars still argue about how accurate Cooper's tale really is and where he acquired his research, Cooper succeeds in weaving these characters into a history of actual events and real people. The French and Indian War is not simply a backdrop for the novel; it is a world in which Cooper immerses his reader, assuming that the reader will become part of the story itself, someone for whom the history is alive and at hand.

Indian Removal

At the time Cooper wrote *The Last of the Mohicans*, many of the political and social issues stirred up by the French and Indian War were still unsettled, particularly with regard to the Native American people. Two years before the publication of *The Last of the Mohicans*, the Bureau of Indian Affairs was established; however, Native Americans were still being pushed from their native land onto reserved tracts in the West and were widely considered "savages" by the white population, despite efforts from people such as Elias Boudinot (1804–1839), a Cherokee activist for Native American rights. In 1826, the same year Cooper published *The Last of the Mohicans,* Boudinot produced a pamphlet called "An Address to the Whites," in which he asked his readers to redefine their perception of the Native Americans and suggested that they held the fate of that race in their hands: "I ask you, shall red men live, or shall they be swept from the earth? With you and this public at large, the decision chiefly rests. Must they perish? Must they all, like the unfortunate Creeks, (victims of the unchristian policy of certain persons) go down in sorrow to their grave?"

Four years later, President Andrew Jackson signed the Indian Removal Act, pushing many Indian tribes westward into Oklahoma in a brutal forced relocation that came to be known as the Trail of Tears. Jackson considered the Native American tribes an obstacle to his economic development of the United States, especially since they often occupied fertile land that could be cultivated into crops and profit. In *Notions of the Americans* (1828), Cooper supported a plan reported by the Indian Office that gave Native Americans a formal U.S. territory west of the Mississippi, as well as the right to send delegates to Congress. He wrote, "If the plan can be effected there is reason to think that the constant diminution of the numbers of the Indians will be checked, and that a race about whom there is so much that is poetic and fine in recollection will be preserved. . . . There is just ground to hope that the dangerous point of communication has been passed, and that they may continue to advance in civilization to maturity."

The struggle between savagery and civilization, between man and land, between races and cultures, was not passé but rather a firsthand experience for Cooper's

readers. As Americans went west to claim their own
space, the Native Americans were displaced, denied
basic rights, and denigrated.

The Romantic Savagery of the Frontier Adventure Genre

In the early nineteenth century, Americans were as yet
unsure how to view the vast, unsettled lands to their
west. As a dark, forbidding land of savages? As a challenge to be met and mastered? As a source of fabled
riches and unheard-of opportunity? Cooper used his fiction to blend all these ideas into a genre that became
known as frontier adventure. Although his *Leatherstocking Tales* were set in the days of the French and Indian
War, Cooper appealed to his readership by fictionalizing
the early days of exploration, a time when men were just
beginning to experience the romance and adventure of
the land.

Of course, before Cooper's genre invention, the public had read about frontier experiences through captivity
narratives (firsthand accounts of whites kidnapped by
Native Americans), personal correspondence, journalis-
tic accounts, poetry, and histories published in magazines and newspapers. One of the most famous stories, *A
Narrative of the Captivity and Restauration of Mrs.
Mary Rowlandson,* was published in 1682. It discussed
the capture of Mary Rowlandson and her children from
the frontier settlement of Lancaster, Massachusetts. Her
tale perpetuated the myth that Indians were "roaring
lions and savage bears" and begins with her account of
the Indian attack and the murder of her friends and their
children. Rowlandson describes the horror as a man

"running along was shot and wounded, and fell down; he begged of them his life, promising them Money (as they told me) but they would not hearken to him but knockt him in the head, and stript him naked, and split open his Bowels." Rowlandson's honest, straightforward depiction of her harrowing experience generated fear in the public but also made for a compelling and entertaining read.

Certain common elements of these firsthand reports and biographical sketches carry over into Cooper's work: the pagan wilderness, the demonic savage, the noble savage, the individualist hero, the theme of the New World as a lost paradise, the struggle between man and nature, the triumph of good over evil. For Cooper, the frontier adventure genre combined the adventurous and dangerous aspects of the dramatic public narratives with the sublime, organic, and individualistic aspects of Romanticism, a philosophical, political, and artistic movement of the early to mid-nineteenth century in Europe and America. Cooper, like other writers of the period including Emily Dickinson, Herman Melville, and Ralph Waldo Emerson, held to the Romantic philosophy that civilization corrupted humanity. In their writing, nature became a symbol for growth, renewal, revelation, and renovation.

In *The Epic of America* (1931), James Truslow Adams describes the wild frontier: "Because the frontiersmen had developed the right combination of qualities to conquer the wilderness, they began to believe quite naturally that they knew best, so to say, how to conquer the world, to solve its problems, and that their own qualities were the only ones worth a man's having." Cooper's frontier adventure was a precursor to those dime-store novels and Western epics that epitomized the can-do spirit, tracked the long, arduous paths of wagon trains, and announced a new sheriff in town. Cooper's style carved a path out of the literary wilderness for future writers such as A. B. Guthrie, Jr., whose six-book epic series *The Big Sky* (1946) follows the journey of a mountain man from St. Louis to the Rockies; Walter Van Tilburg Clark, whose *The Ox-Bow Incident* (1940) focuses on the moral questions of mob violence in the Wild West; and Wallace Stegner, whose book *Angle of Repose* (1972) frames a story of traveling westward with a contemporary tale of learning about the past.

CHRONOLOGY OF JAMES FENIMORE COOPER'S LIFE AND WORK

1789: James Cooper is born on September 15, the twelfth of thirteen children to Elizabeth and William Cooper in Burlington, New Jersey.

1790: The Cooper family relocates to Otsego Lake in upstate New York.

1803: Cooper enters Yale College in New Haven, Connecticut. He is expelled two years later.

1808: Cooper joins the U.S. Navy.

1809: His father, William Cooper, judge, congressman, and founder of Cooperstown, New York, dies.

1811: Cooper marries Susan Augusta De Lancey and resigns his commission in the navy.

1820: Cooper writes his first novel, a comedy of manners called *Precaution*.

1821: After the failure of *Precaution*, Cooper tries a second novel, *The Spy*, an adventure tale set during the American Revolution.

1823: Cooper publishes the first novel in his *Leatherstocking* series, *The Pioneers: or The Sources of the Susquehanna.* In this same year, Cooper also writes *The Pilot.*

1826: *The Last of the Mohicans,* second novel of *The Leatherstocking Tales,* is released. Cooper legally adds "Fenimore"—his mother's maiden name—to his name. This same year, Cooper travels to Europe with his family, where he lives for six years and serves as U.S. consul to France.

1827: Cooper publishes the third *Leatherstocking* book, *The Prairie.*

1830: "A Letter to General Lafayette" is published, a 50-page essay in which Cooper expresses his opinions about the French domestic budget through the context of the economic plan used by the American government.

1834: Cooper presents his opinion about the danger regarding America's limited constitutional powers in "A Letter to His Countrymen."

1836: Cooper's record of his family's experience in Europe during his tenure as U.S. consul appears as the travelogue/journal/autobiography *A Residence in France.*

1837: Upon returning to the United States and his boyhood home in Otsego, Cooper orders the public to stop trespassing on a spit of land at the lake. The citizens protest the demand and resolve to remove Cooper's books from the local library, while newspaper editors report the conflict and side with the public. Cooper sues three of the editors, but the incident does not go to trial. Instead, Cooper writes a book loosely based on the incident, *Home As Found,* published the next year. Libel suits related to this incident continue for the next eight years.

1838: Inspired by his notion that the American political system is complacent, tyrannical, and determined by both emotional rhetoric and propaganda, Cooper published *The American Democrat*.

1839: Cooper's knowledge and experiences in the navy, as well as his love of the sea, lead him to write *The History of the Navy of the United States of America*.

1841: *The Deerslayer,* fourth book in the *Leatherstocking* series, is published.

1846: Borrowing on the success of his historical chronicle of the navy, Cooper publishes *Lives of Distinguished American Naval Officers,* each biography having been previously printed in *Graham's Magazine*.

1848: The sea novel *Jack Tier,* first released as a serial in *Graham's Magazine*, is published in its entirety.

1851: Cooper dies on September 14. The last book he is writing is left unfinished, *New York: Or the Towns of Manhattan*.

HISTORICAL CONTEXT OF
The Last of the Mohicans

1789: George Washington is elected first president of United States. James Cooper is born.

1791: Washington, D.C., becomes the U.S. capital.

1800: The Library of Congress is established.

1803: Meriwether Lewis and William Clark embark on a three-year expedition from Pittsburgh to the Pacific.

1808: James N. Barker writes *The Indian Princess, or La Belle Sauvage*, a play about Pocahontas. *The Indian Princess* is the first play to have Native American life as its subject.

1811: In the Battle of Tippecanoe, William Henry Harrison and U.S. troops fight against Tecumseh's confederation of Shawnee and Creek forces, who are led by Tecumseh's younger brother Tenskwatawa, also known as the Prophet.

1812: The War of 1812 between the Americans and the British begins. America declares war against England to stop the seizure of thousands of American sailors who are forced to join the British navy,

British restrictions on neutral trade while it warred with France, and British support to Indians in their fight against white settlement of the West.

1814: Francis Scott Key pens "The Star-Spangled Banner." British forces invade Washington and burn the White House.

1819: Washington Irving's "Rip Van Winkle" appears in *The Sketch Book*.

1824: Washington Irving publishes *Tales of a Traveller*. The Bureau of Indian Affairs is established to manage Native Americans and their land.

1825: Indian Chief William McIntosh signs a treaty ceding Creek lands to the United States. He is murdered by his own people for the act.

1826: James Fenimore Cooper publishes *The Last of the Mohicans*.

1827: Edgar Allan Poe publishes *Tamerlane and Other Poems*.

1830: Emily Dickinson is born. President Andrew Jackson signs the Indian Removal Act, authorizing displacement of Indians westward.

1831: Alexis de Tocqueville spends nine months touring America, inspiring his *Democracy in America* (1835).

1836: Ralph Waldo Emerson publishes his essay *Nature*.

1845: Henry David Thoreau begins living at Walden Pond. In 1854, he publishes *Walden (or Life in the Woods)*.

1849: The California gold rush begins.

1850: Nathaniel Hawthorne publishes *The Scarlet Letter*.

1851 Herman Melville publishes *Moby-Dick*. James Fenimore Cooper dies on September 14.

The Last of the Mohicans

I

"Mine ear is open, and my heart prepared:
The worst is worldly loss thou canst unfold:
Say, is my kingdom lost?"
Richard II[1]

impervious—unable to be affected by

IT WAS A FEATURE peculiar to the colonial wars of North America, that the toils and dangers of the wilderness were to be encountered before the adverse hosts could meet. A wide and apparently an <u>impervious</u> boundary of forests severed the possessions of the <u>hostile provinces of France and England.</u> The hardy colonist, and the trained European who fought at his side, frequently expended months in struggling against the rapids of the streams, or in effecting the rugged passes of the mountains, in quest of an opportunity to exhibit their courage in a more martial conflict. But, <u>emulating</u> the patience and self-denial of the practised native warriors, they learned to overcome every difficulty; and it would seem that, in time, there was no recess of the woods so dark, nor any secret place so lovely, that it might claim exemption from the inroads of those who had pledged their blood to satiate their vengeance, or to uphold the cold and selfish policy of the distant monarchs of Europe.

Perhaps no district throughout the wide extent of the

emulate—match or surpass
satiate—to satisfy to the full 3

intermediate frontiers can furnish a livelier picture of the cruelty and fierceness of the savage warfare of those periods than the country which lies between the head waters of the Hudson and the adjacent lakes.

The facilities which nature had there offered to the march of the combatants were too obvious to be neglected. The lengthened sheet of the Champlain stretched from the frontiers of Canada, deep within the borders of the neighboring province of New York, forming a natural passage across half the distance that the French were compelled to master in order to strike their enemies. Near its southern termination, it received the contributions of another lake, whose waters were so limpid as to have been exclusively selected by the Jesuit missionaries to perform the typical purification of baptism, and to obtain for it the title of lake "du Saint Sacrement." The less zealous English thought they conferred a sufficient honor on its unsullied fountains, when they bestowed the name of their reigning prince, the second of the house of Hanover. The two united to rob the untutored possessors of its wooded scenery of their native right to perpetuate its original appellation of "Horican."

Winding its way among countless islands, and imbedded in mountains, the "holy lake" extended a dozen leagues still farther to the south. With the high plain that there interposed itself to the further passage of the water, commenced a portage of as many miles, which conducted the adventurer to the banks of the Hudson, at a point where, with the usual obstructions of the rapids, or rifts, as they were then termed in the language of the country, the river became navigable to the tide.

While, in the pursuit of their daring plans of annoyance, the restless enterprise of the French even at-

tempted the distant and difficult gorges of the Allegheny,
it may easily be imagined that their proverbial acuteness
would not overlook the natural advantages of the district
we have just described. It became, emphatically, the
bloody arena, in which most of the battles for the mastery
of the colonies were contested. Forts were erected at the
different points that commanded the facilities of the
route, and were taken and retaken, razed and rebuilt, as
victory alighted on the hostile banners. While the _hus-_
bandman[2] shrank back from the dangerous passes,
within the safer boundaries of the more ancient settlements, armies larger than those that had often disposed
of the sceptres of the mother countries, were seen to bury
themselves in these forests, whence they rarely returned
but in skeleton bands, that were haggard with care, or dejected by defeat. Though the arts of peace were unknown
to this fatal region, its forests were alive with men; its
shades and glens rang with the sounds of martial music,
and the echoes of its mountains threw back the laugh, or
repeated the wanton cry, of many a gallant and reckless
youth, as he hurried by them, in the noontide of his spirits, to slumber in a long night of forgetfulness.

It was in this scene of strife and bloodshed that the incidents we shall attempt to relate occurred, during the
third year of the war which England and France last
waged for the possession of a country that neither was
destined to retain.

The imbecility of her military leaders abroad, and the
fatal want of energy in her councils at home, had lowered
the character of Great Britain from the proud elevation
on which it had been placed by the talents and enterprise
of her former warriors and statesmen. No longer
dreaded by her enemies, her servants were fast losing

the confidence of self-respect. In this mortifying abasement, the colonists, though innocent of her imbecility, and too humble to be the agents of her blunders, were but the natural participators.

They had recently seen a chosen army from that country, which, reverencing as a mother, they had blindly believed invincible—an army led by a chief who had been selected from a crowd of trained warriors, for his rare military endowments, disgracefully routed by a handful of French and Indians, and only saved from annihilation by the coolness and spirit of a Virginian boy, whose riper fame has since diffused itself, with the steady influence of moral truth, to the uttermost confines of Christendom. A wide frontier had been laid naked by this unexpected disaster, and more substantial evils were preceded by a thousand fanciful and imaginary dangers. The alarmed colonists believed that the yells of the savages mingled with every fitful gust of wind that issued from the interminable forests of the west. The terrific character of their merciless enemies increased immeasurably the natural horrors of warfare. Numberless recent massacres were still vivid in their recollections; nor was there any ear in the provinces so deaf as not to have drunk in with avidity the narrative of some fearful tale of midnight murder, in which the natives of the forest were the prinicipal and barbarous actors. As the credulous and excited traveller related the hazardous chances of the wilderness, the blood of the timid curdled with terror, and mothers cast anxious glances even at those children which slumbered within the security of the largest towns. In short, the magnifying influence of fear began to set at naught the calculations of reason, and to render those who should have remembered their manhood, the slaves of the basest of passions.

Even the most confident and the stoutest hearts began to think the issue of the contest was becoming doubtful; and the abject class was hourly increasing in numbers, who thought they foresaw all the possessions of the English crown in America subdued by their Christian foes, or laid waste by the inroads of their relentless allies.

When, therefore, intelligence was received at the fort, which covered the southern termination of the portage between the Hudson and the lakes, that Montcalm[3] had been seen moving up the Champlain, with an army "numerous as the leaves on the trees,"[4] its truth was admitted with more of the craven reluctance of fear than with the stern joy that a warrior should feel, in finding an enemy within reach of his blow. The news had been brought, towards the decline of a day in midsummer, by an Indian runner, who also bore an urgent request from Munro,[5] the commander of a work on the shore of the "holy lake," for a speedy and powerful reinforcement. It has already been mentioned that the distance between these two posts was less than five leagues.[6] The rude path, which originally formed their line of communication, had been widened for the passage of wagons; so that the distance which had been travelled by the son of the forest in two hours, might easily be effected by a detachment of troops, with their necessary baggage, between the rising and setting of a summer sun. The loyal servants of the British crown had given to one of these forest fastnesses the name of William Henry, and to the other that of Fort Edward; calling each after a favorite prince of the reigning family. The veteran Scotchman just named held the first, with a regiment of regulars and a few provincials; a force really by far too small to make head against the formidable power that Montcalm was

leading to the foot of his earthen mounds. At the latter,
however, lay General Webb, who commanded the
armies of the king in the northern provinces, with a body
of more than five thousand men. By uniting the several
detachments of his command, this officer might have arrayed nearly double that number of combatants against
the enterprising Frenchman, who had ventured so far
from his reinforcements, with an army but little superior
in numbers.

But under the influence of their degraded fortunes,
both officers and men appeared better disposed to await
the approach of their formidable antagonists, within
their works, than to resist the progress of their march, by
emulating the successful example of the French at Fort
du Quesne, and striking a blow on their advance.

After the first surprise of the intelligence had a little
abated, a rumor was spread through the entrenched
camp, which stretched along the margin of the Hudson,
forming a chain of outworks to the body of the fort itself,
that a chosen detachment of fifteen hundred men was to
depart, with the dawn, for William Henry, the post at the
northern extremity of the portage. That which at first
was only rumor, soon became certainty, as orders passed
from the quarters of the commander-in-chief to the several corps he had selected for this service, to prepare for
their speedy departure. All doubt as to the intention of
Webb now vanished, and an hour or two of hurried footsteps and anxious faces succeeded. The novice in the
military art flew from point to point, retarding his own
preparations by the excess of his violent and somewhat
distempered zeal; while the more practised veteran
made his arrangements with a deliberation that scorned
every appearance of haste; though his sober lineaments

and anxious eye sufficiently betrayed that he had no very strong professional relish for the as yet untried and dreaded warfare of the wilderness. At length the sun set in a flood of glory, behind the distant western hills, and as darkness drew its veil around the secluded spot the sounds of preparation diminished; the last light finally disappeared from the log cabin of some officer; the trees cast their deeper shadows over the mounds and the rippling stream, and a silence soon pervaded the camp, as deep as that which reigned in the vast forest by which it was environed.

According to the orders of the preceding night, the heavy sleep of the army was broken by the rolling of the warning drums, whose rattling echoes were heard issuing, on the damp morning air, out of every vista of the woods, just as day began to draw the shaggy outlines of some tall pines of the vicinity, on the opening brightness of a soft and cloudless eastern sky. In an instant the whole camp was in motion; the meanest soldier arousing from his lair to witness the departure of his comrades, and to share in the excitement and incidents of the hour. The simple array of the chosen band was soon completed. While the regular and trained hirelings of the king marched with haughtiness to the right of the line, the less pretending colonists took their humbler position on its left, with a docility that long practice had rendered easy. The scouts departed; strong guards preceded and followed the lumbering vehicles that bore the baggage; and before the gray light of the morning was mellowed by the rays of the sun, the main body of the combatants wheeled into column, and left the encampment with a show of high military bearing, that served to drown the slumbering apprehensions of many a novice, who was now about to make his first essay in arms. While in view of their admiring comrades, the same proud front and ordered array was observed, until the notes of their fifes growing fainter in distance, the forest at length appeared to swallow up the living mass which had slowly entered its bosom.

The deepest sounds of the retiring and invisible column had ceased to be borne on the breeze to the listeners, and the latest straggler had already disappeared in pursuit; but there still remained the signs of another departure, before a log cabin of unusual size and accommodations, in front of which those sentinels paced their rounds, who were known to guard the person of the English general. At this spot were gathered some half dozen horses, caparisoned in a manner which showed that two, at least, were destined to bear the persons of females, of a rank that it was not usual to meet so far in the wilds of the country. A third wore the trappings and arms of an officer of the staff; while the rest, from the plainness of the housings, and the travelling mails with which they were encumbered, were evidently fitted for the reception of as many menials, who were, seemingly, already awaiting the pleasure of those they served. At a respectful distance from this unusual show were gathered divers groups of curious idlers; some admiring the blood and bone of the high-mettled military charger, and others gazing at the preparations, with dull wonder of vulgar curiosity. There was one man, however, who, by his countenance and actions, formed a marked exception to those who composed the latter class of spectators, being neither idle, nor seemingly very ignorant.

The person of this individual was to the last degree ungainly, without being in any particular manner deformed. He had all the bones and joints of other men,

without any of their proportions. Erect, his stature surpassed that of his fellows; seated, he appeared reduced
within the ordinary limits of the race. The same contrar-
ity in his members seemed to exist throughout the whole
man. His head was large; his shoulders narrow; his arms
long and dangling; while his hands were small, if not delicate. His legs and thighs were thin, nearly to emaciation,
but of extraordinary length; and his knees would have
been considered tremendous, had they not been outdone by the broader foundations on which this false su-
perstructure of the blended human orders was so
profanely reared. The ill-assorted and injudicious attire
of the individual only served to render his awkwardness
more conspicuous. A sky-blue coat, with short and broad
skirts and low cape, exposed a long thin neck, and longer
and thinner legs, to the worst animadversions of the evil
disposed. His nether garment was of yellow nankeen,[7]
closely fitted to the shape, and tied at his bunches of
knees by large knots of white ribbon, a good deal sullied
by use. Clouded cotton stockings, and shoes, on one of
the latter of which was a plated spur, completed the costume of the lower extremity of this figure, no curve or
angle of which was concealed, but, on the other hand,
studiously exhibited, through the vanity or simplicity of
its owner. From beneath the flap of an enormous pocket
of a soiled vest of embossed silk, heavily ornamented
with tarnished silver lace, projected an instrument,
which, from being seen in such martial company, might
have been easily mistaken for some mischievous and unknown implement of war. Small as it was, this uncommon engine had excited the curiosity of most of the
Europeans in the camp, though several of the provincials
were seen to handle it, not only without fear, but with the

utmost familiarity. A large, civil cocked hat, like those worn by clergymen within the last thirty years, surmounted the whole, furnishing dignity to a good-natured and somewhat vacant countenance, that apparently needed such artificial aid, to support the gravity of some high and extraordinary trust.

While the common herd stood aloof, in deference to the quarters of Webb, the figure we have described stalked into the centre of the domestics, freely expressing his censures or commendations on the merits of the horses, as by chance they displeased or satisfied his judgment.

"This beast, I rather conclude, friend, is not of home raising, but is from foreign lands, or perhaps from the little island itself over the blue water?" he said, in a voice as remarkable for the softness and sweetness of its tones, as was his person for its rare proportions: "I may speak of these things, and be no braggart; for I have been down at both havens;[8] that which is situate at the mouth of Thames, and is named after the capital of Old England, and that which is called 'Haven,' with the addition of the word 'New'; and have seen the scows and brigantines collecting their droves, like the gathering to the ark, being outward bound to the Island of Jamaica, for the purpose of barter and traffic in four-footed animals; but never before have I beheld a beast which verified the true Scripture war-horse like this: 'He paweth in the valley, and rejoiceth in his strength: he goeth on to meet the armed men. He saith among the trumpets, Ha, ha; and he smelleth the battle afar off, the thunder of the captains, and the shouting.' It would seem that the stock of the horse of Israel has descended to our own time; would it not, friend?"

Receiving no reply to this extraordinary appeal, which in truth, as it was delivered with the vigor of full and sonorous tones, merited some sort of notice, he who had thus sung forth the language of the Holy Book turned to the silent figure to whom he had unwittingly addressed himself, and found a new and more powerful subject of admiration in the object that encountered his gaze. His eyes fell on the still, upright, and rigid form of the "Indian runner," who had borne to the camp the unwelcome tidings of the preceding evening. Although in a state of perfect repose, and apparently disregarding, with characteristic stoicism, the excitement and bustle around him, there was a sullen fierceness mingled with the quiet of the savage, that was likely to arrest the attention of much more experienced eyes than those which now scanned him, in unconcealed amazement. The native bore both the tomahawk and knife of his tribe; and yet his appearance was not altogether that of a warrior. On the contrary, there was an air of neglect about his person, like that which might have proceeded from great and recent exertion, which he had not yet found leisure to repair. The colors of the war-paint had blended in dark confusion about his fierce countenance, and rendered his swarthy lineaments still more savage and repulsive than if art had attempted an effect which had been thus produced by chance. His eye, alone, which glistened like a fiery star amid lowering clouds, was to be seen in its state of native wildness. For a single instant, his searching and yet wary glance met the wondering look of the other, and then changing its direction, partly in cunning, and partly in disdain, it remained fixed, as if penetrating the distant air.

It is impossible to say what unlooked-for remark this

short and silent communication, between two such singular men, might have elicited from the white man, had not his active curiosity been again drawn to other objects. A general movement among the domestics, and a low sound of gentle voices, announced the approach of those whose presence alone was wanted to enable the cavalcade to move. The simple admirer of the war-horse instantly fell back to a low, gaunt, switch-tailed mare, that was unconsciously gleaning the faded herbage of the camp nigh by; where, leaning with one elbow on the blanket that concealed an apology for a saddle, he became a spectator of the departure, while a foal was quietly making its morning repast, on the opposite side of the same animal.

A young man, in the dress of an officer, conducted to their steeds two females, who, as it was apparent by their dresses, were prepared to encounter the fatigues of a journey in the woods. One, and she was the most juvenile in her appearance, though both were young, permitted glimpses of her dazzling complexion, fair golden hair, and bright blue eyes, to be caught, as she artlessly suffered the morning air to blow aside the green veil which descended low from her beaver. The flush which still lingered above the pines in the western sky was not more bright nor delicate than the bloom on her cheek; nor was the opening day more cheering than the animated smile which she bestowed on the youth, as he assisted her into the saddle. The other, who appeared to share equally in the attentions of the young officer, concealed her charms from the gaze of the soldiery, with a care that seemed better fitted to the experience of four or five additional years. It could be seen, however, that her person, though moulded with the same exquisite proportions, of which none of the graces were lost by the travelling dress she wore, was rather fuller and more mature than that of her companion.

No sooner were these females seated, than their attendant sprang lightly into the saddle of the war-horse, when the whole three bowed to Webb, who, in courtesy, awaited their parting on the threshold of his cabin, and turning their horses' heads, they proceeded at a slow amble, followed by their train, towards the northern entrance of the encampment. As they traversed that short distance, not a voice was heard amongst them; but a slight exclamation proceeded from the younger of the females, as the Indian runner glided by her, unexpectedly, and led the way along the military road in her front. Though this sudden and startling movement of the Indian produced no sound from the other, in the surprise her veil also was allowed to open its folds, and betrayed an indescribable look of pity, admiration, and horror, as her dark eye followed the easy motions of the savage. The tresses of this lady were shining and black, like the plumage of the raven. Her complexion was not brown, but it rather appeared charged with the color of the rich blood, that seemed ready to burst its bounds. And yet there was neither coarseness nor want of shadowing in a countenance that was exquisitely regular and dignified, and surpassingly beautiful. She smiled, as if in pity at her own momentary forgetfulness, discovering by the act a row of teeth that would have shamed the purest ivory; when, replacing the veil, she bowed her face, and rode in silence, like one whose thoughts were abstracted from the scene around her.

Montcalm (French) to take Fort William Henry. Magua tells British Webb. Tells Heyward to escort Alice + Cora (Munros daughters. Alice intrigued by Magua

II

"Sola, sola, wo, ha, ho, sola!"
The Merchant of Venice[1]

WHILE ONE of the lovely beings we have so cursorily presented to the reader was thus lost in thought, the other quickly recovered from the alarm which induced the exclamation, and, laughing at her own weakness, she inquired of the youth who rode by her side,—

"Are such spectres frequent in the woods, Heyward, or is this sight an especial entertainment on our behalf? If the latter, gratitude must close our mouths; but if the former, both Cora and I shall have need to draw largely on that stock of hereditary courage which we boast, even before we are made to encounter the redoubtable Montcalm."

"Yon Indian is a 'runner' of the army; and, after the fashion of his people, he may be accounted a hero," returned the officer. "He has volunteered to guide us to the lake, by a path but little known, sooner than if we followed the tardy movements of the column: and, by consequence, more agreeably."

"I like him not," said the lady, shuddering, partly in assumed, yet more in real terror. "You know him, Duncan, or you would not trust yourself so freely to his keeping?"

"Say, rather, Alice, that I would not trust you. I do know him, or he would not have my confidence, and least of all at this moment. He is said to be a Canadian, too; and yet he served with our friends the Mohawks, who, as you know, are one of the six allied nations. He was brought among us, as I have heard, by some strange accident in which your father was interested, and in which the savage was rigidly dealt by—but I forgot the idle tale; it is enough, that he is now our friend."

"If he has been my father's enemy, I like him still less!" exclaimed the now really anxious girl. "Will you not speak to him, Major Heyward, that I may hear his tones? Foolish though it may be, you have often heard me avow my faith in the tones of the human voice!"

"It would be in vain; and answered, most probably, by an ejaculation. Though he may understand it, he affects, like most of his people, to be ignorant of the English; and least of all will he condescend to speak it, now that war demands the utmost exercise of his dignity. But he stops; the private path by which we are to journey is, doubtless, at hand."

The conjecture of Major Heyward was true. When they reached the spot where the Indian stood, pointing into the thicket that fringed the military road, a narrow and blind path, which might, with some little inconvenience, receive one person at a time, became visible.

"Here, then, lies our way," said the young man, in a low voice. "Manifest no distrust, or you may invite the danger you appear to apprehend."

"Cora, what think you?" asked the reluctant fair one. "If we journey with the troops, though we may find their presence irksome, shall we not feel better assurance of our safety?"

"Being little accustomed to the practices of the savages, Alice, you mistake the place of real danger," said Heyward. "If enemies have reached the portage at all, a thing by no means probable, as our scouts are abroad, they will surely be found skirting the column where scalps abound the most. The route of the detachment is known, while ours, having been determined within the hour, must still be secret."

"Should we distrust the man because his manners are not our manners, and that his skin is dark?" coldly asked Cora.

Alice hesitated no longer; but giving her Narragansett[2] a smart cut of the whip, she was the first to dash aside the slight branches of the bushes, and to follow the runner along the dark and tangled pathway. The young man regarded the last speaker in open admiration, and even permitted her fairer though certainly not more beautiful companion to proceed unattended, while he sedulously opened the way himself for the passage of her who has been called Cora. It would seem that the domestics had been previously instructed; for, instead of penetrating the thicket, they followed the route of the column; a measure which Heyward stated had been dictated by the sagacity of their guide, in order to diminish the marks of their trail, if, haply, the Canadian savages should be lurking so far in advance of their army. For many minutes the intricacy of the route admitted of no further dialogue; after which they emerged from the broad border of underbrush which grew along the line of the highway, and entered under the high but dark arches of the forest. Here their progress was less interrupted, and the instant the guide perceived that the females could command their steeds, he moved on, at a pace between a trot and a walk, and at a rate which kept the sure-footed and peculiar animals they rode, at a fast yet easy amble. The youth had turned to speak to the dark-eyed Cora, when the distant sound of horses' hoofs, clattering over the roots of the broken way in his rear, caused him to check his charger; and, as his companions drew their reins at the same instant, the whole party came to a halt, in order to obtain an explanation of the unlooked-for interruption.

In a few moments a colt was seen gliding, like a fallow-deer, among the straight trunks of the pines; and, in another instant, the person of the ungainly man described in the preceding chapter, came into view, with as much rapidity as he could excite his meagre beast to endure without coming to an open rupture. Until now this personage had escaped the observation of the travellers. If he possessed the power to arrest any wandering eye when exhibiting the glories of his altitude on foot, his equestrian graces were still more likely to attract attention. Notwithstanding a constant application of his one armed heel to the flanks of the mare, the most confirmed gait that he could establish was a Canterbury gallop with the hind legs, in which those more forward assisted for doubtful moments, though generally content to maintain a loping trot. Perhaps the rapidity of the changes from one of these paces to the other created an optical illusion, which might thus magnify the powers of the beast; for it is certain that Heyward, who possessed a true eye for the merits of a horse, was unable, with his utmost ingenuity, to decide by what sort of movement his pursuer worked his sinuous way on his footsteps with such persevering hardihood.

The industry and movements of the rider were not less remarkable than those of the ridden. At each change in the evolutions of the latter, the former raised his tall person in the stirrups; producing, in this manner, by the undue elongation of his legs, such sudden growths and diminishings of the stature, as baffled every conjecture that might be made as to his dimensions. If to this be added the fact that, in consequence of the *ex parte* application of the spur, one side of the mare appeared to journey faster than the other; and that the aggrieved flank was resolutely indicated by unremitted flourishes of a bushy tail, we finish the picture of both horse and man.

. The frown which had gathered around the handsome, open, and manly brow of Heyward, gradually relaxed, and his lips curled into a slight smile, as he regarded the stranger. Alice made no very powerful effort to control her merriment; and even the dark, thoughtful eye of Cora lighted with a humor that, it would seem, the habit, rather than the nature of its mistress repressed.

"Seek you any here?" demanded Heyward, when the other had arrived sufficiently nigh to abate his speed; "I trust you are no messenger of evil tidings?"

"Even so," replied the stranger, making diligent use of his triangular castor,[3] to produce a circulation in the close air of the woods, and leaving his hearers in doubt to which of the young man's questions he responded; when, however, he had cooled his face, and recovered his breath, he continued, "I hear you are riding to William Henry; as I am journeying thitherward myself, I concluded good company would seem consistent to the wishes of both parties."

"You appear to possess the privilege of a casting vote," returned Heyward; "we are three, whilst you have consulted no one but yourself."

"Even so. The first point to be obtained is to know

one's own mind. Once sure of that, and where women are concerned it is not easy, the next is, to act up to the decision. I have endeavored to do both, and here I am."

"If you journey to the lake, you have mistaken your route," said Heyward, haughtily; "the highway thither is at least half a mile behind you."

"Even so," returned the stranger, nothing daunted by this cold reception; "I have tarried at 'Edward' a week, and I should be dumb not to have inquired the road I was to journey; and if dumb there would be an end to my calling." After simpering in a small way, like one whose modesty prohibited a more open expression of his admiration of a witticism that was perfectly unintelligible to his hearers, he continued: "It is not prudent for any one of my profession to be too familiar with those he is to instruct; for which reason I follow not the line of the army; besides which, I conclude that a gentleman of your character has the best judgment in matters of wayfaring; I have therefore decided to join company, in order that the ride may be made agreeable, and partake of social communion."

"A most arbitrary, if not a hasty decision!" exclaimed Heyward, undecided whether to give vent to his growing anger, or to laugh in the other's face. "But you speak of instruction, and of a profession; are you an adjunct to the provincial corps, as a master of the noble science of defence and offence; or, perhaps, you are one who draws lines and angles, under the pretence of expounding the mathematics?"

The stranger regarded his interrogator a moment, in wonder; and then, losing every mark of self-satisfaction in an expression of solemn humility, he answered:—

"Of offence, I hope there is none, to either party; of defence, I make none—by God's good mercy, having committed no palpable sin since last entreating His pardoning grace. I understand not your allusions about lines and angles; and I leave expounding to those who have been called and set apart for that holy office. I lay claim to no higher gift than a small insight into the glorious art of petitioning and thanksgiving, as practised in psalmody."[4]

"The man is, most manifestly, a disciple of Apollo," cried the amused Alice, "and I take him under my own especial protection. Nay, throw aside that frown, Heyward, and in pity to my longing ears, suffer him to journey in our train. Besides," she added, in a low and hurried voice, casting a glance at the distant Cora, who slowly followed the footsteps of their silent but sullen guide, "it may be a friend added to our strength, in time of need."

"Think you, Alice, that I would trust those I love by this secret path, did I imagine such need could happen?"

"Nay, nay, I think not of it now; but this strange man amuses me; and if he 'hath music in his soul,'[5] let us not churlishly reject his company." She pointed persuasively along the path with her riding-whip, while their eyes met in a look which the young man lingered a moment to prolong; then yielding to her gentle influence, he clapped his spurs into his charger, and in a few bounds was again at the side of Cora.

"I am glad to encounter thee, friend," continued the maiden, waving her hand to the stranger to proceed, as she urged her Narragansett to renew its amble. "Partial relatives have almost persuaded me that I am not entirely worthless in a duet myself; and we may enliven our wayfaring by indulging in our favorite pursuit. It might be of signal advantage to one, ignorant as I, to hear the opinions and experience of a master in the art."

"It is refreshing both to the spirits and to the body to

indulge in psalmody, in befitting seasons," returned the master of song, unhesitatingly complying with her intimation to follow; "and nothing would relieve the mind more than such a consoling communion. But four parts are altogether necessary to the perfection of melody. You have all the manifestations of a soft and rich treble; I can, by especial aid, carry a full tenor to the highest letter; but we lack counter and bass! Yon officer of the king, who hesitated to admit me to his company, might fill the latter, if one may judge from the intonations of his voice in common dialogue."

"Judge not too rashly from hasty and deceptive appearances," said the lady, smiling; "though Major Heyward can assume such deep notes on occasion, believe me, his natural tones are better fitted for a mellow tenor than the bass you heard."

"Is he, then, much practised in the art of psalmody?" demanded her simple companion.

Alice felt disposed to laugh, though she succeeded in suppressing her merriment, ere she answered,—

"I apprehend that he is rather addicted to profane song. The chances of a soldier's life are but little fitted for the encouragement of more sober inclinations."

"Man's voice is given to him, like other talents, to be used, and not to be abused. None can say they have ever known me neglect my gifts! I am thankful that, though my boyhood may be said to have been set apart, like the youth of the royal David, for the purposes of music, no syllable of rude verse has ever profaned my lips."

"You have, then, limited your efforts to sacred song?"

"Even so. As the psalms of David exceed all other language, so does the psalmody that has been fitted to them by the divines and sages of the land, surpass all vain poetry. Happily, I may say that I utter nothing but the thoughts and the wishes of the King of Israel himself; for though the times may call for some slight changes, yet does this version which we use in the colonies of New England, so much exceed all other versions, that, by its richness, its exactness, and its spiritual simplicity, it approacheth, as near as may be, to the great work of the inspired writer. I never abide in any place, sleeping or waking, without an example of this gifted work. 'Tis the six-and-twentieth edition, promulgated at Boston, Anno Domini 1744; and is entitled, *The Psalms, Hymns, and Spiritual Songs of the Old and New Testaments; faithfully translated into English Metre, for the Use, Edification, and Comfort of the Saints, in Public and Private, especially in New England.*"[6]

During this eulogium on the rare production of his native poets, the stranger had drawn the book from his pocket, and, fitting a pair of iron-rimmed spectacles to his nose, opened the volume with a care and veneration suited to its sacred purposes. Then, without circumlocution or apology, first pronouncing the word "Standish," and placing the unknown engine,[7] already described, to his mouth, from which he drew a high, shrill sound, that was followed by an octave below, from his own voice, he commenced singing the following words, in full, sweet, and melodious tones, that set the music, the poetry, and even the uneasy motion of his ill-trained beast at defiance:—

"How good it is, O see,
　　And how it pleaseth well,
Together, e 'en in unity,
　　For brethren so to dwell.

It's like the choice ointment,
  From the head to the beard did go:
Down Aaron's beard, that downward went,
  His garment's skirts unto."

The delivery of these skilful rhymes was accompanied, on the part of the stranger, by a regular rise and fall of his right hand, which terminated at the descent, by suffering the fingers to dwell a moment on the leaves of the little volume; and on the ascent, by such a flourish of the member as none but the initiated may ever hope to imitate. It would seem that long practice had rendered this manual accompaniment necessary; for it did not cease until the preposition which the poet had selected for the close of his verse, had been duly delivered like a word of two syllables.

Such an innovation on the silence and retirement of the forest could not fail to enlist the ears of those who journeyed at so short a distance in advance. The Indian muttered a few words in broken English to Heyward, who, in his turn, spoke to the stranger; at once interrupting, and, for the time, closing his musical efforts.

"Though we are not in danger, common prudence would teach us to journey through this wilderness in as quiet a manner as possible. You will, then, pardon me, Alice, should I diminish your enjoyments, by requesting this gentleman to postpone his chant until a safer opportunity."

"You will diminish them, indeed," returned the arch girl, "for never did I hear a more unworthy conjunction of execution and language, than that to which I have been listening; and I was far gone in a learned inquiry into the causes of such an unfitness between sound and

sense, when you broke the charm of my musings by that
bass of yours, Duncan!"

"I know not what you call my bass," said Heyward,
piqued at her remark, "but I know that your safety, and
that of Cora, is far dearer to me than could be any orchestra of Handel's music." He paused and turned his
head quickly towards a thicket, and then bent his eyes
suspiciously on their guide, who continued his steady
pace, in undisturbed gravity. The young man smiled to
himself, for he believed he had mistaken some shiny
berry of the woods for the glistening eyeballs of a prowling savage, and he rode forward, continuing the conversation which had been interrupted by the passing
thought.

Major Heyward was mistaken only in suffering his
youthful and generous pride to suppress his active
watchfulness. The cavalcade had not long passed, before
the branches of the bushes that formed the thicket were
cautiously moved asunder, and a human visage, as
fiercely wild as savage art and unbridled passions could
make it, peered out on the retiring footsteps of the travellers. A gleam of exultation shot across the darkly
painted lineaments of the inhabitant of the forest, as he
traced the route of his intended victims, who rode unconsciously onward; the light and graceful forms of the
females waving among the trees, in the curvatures of
their path, followed at each bend by the manly figure of
Heyward, until, finally, the shapeless person of the
singing-master was concealed behind the numberless
trunks of trees, that rose, in dark lines, in the intermediate space.

*Magua leads them, find David Gamut singer
sermon (stranger)*

III

"Before these fields were shorn and tilled,
    Full to the brim our rivers flowed;
The melody of waters filled
    The fresh and boundless wood;
And torrents dashed, and rivulets played,
    And fountains spouted in the shade."
        William Culler Bryant,
"Indian at the Burial Place of His Fathers"[1]

LEAVING THE UNSUSPECTING Heyward and his confiding companions to penetrate still deeper into a forest that contained such treacherous inmates, we must use an author's privilege, and shift the scene a few miles to the westward of the place where we have last seen them.

On that day, two men were lingering on the banks of a small but rapid stream, within an hour's journey of the encampment of Webb, like those who awaited the appearance of an absent person, or the approach of some expected event. The vast canopy of woods spread itself to the margin of the river overhanging the water, and shadowing its dark current with a deeper hue. The rays of the sun were beginning to grow less fierce, and the intense heat of the day was lessened, as the cooler vapors of the

springs and fountains rose above their leafy beds, and
rested in the atmosphere. Still that breathing silence,
which marks the drowsy sultriness of an American landscape in July, pervaded the secluded spot, interrupted
only by the low voices of the men, the occasional and lazy
tap of a woodpecker, the discordant cry of some gaudy
jay, or a swelling on the ear, from the dull roar of a distant
waterfall.

These feeble and broken sounds were, however, too
familiar to the foresters, to draw their attention from the
more interesting matter of their dialogue. While one of
these loiterers showed the red skin and wild accoutrements of a native of the woods, the other exhibited,
through the mask of his rude and nearly savage equipments, the brighter, though sunburnt and long-faded
complexion of one who might claim descent from a European parentage. The former was seated on the end of a
mossy log, in a posture that permitted him to heighten
the effect of his earnest language, by the calm but expressive gestures of an Indian engaged in debate. His
body, which was nearly naked, presented a terrific emblem of death, drawn in intermingled colors of white and
black. His closely shaved head, on which no other hair
than the well known and chivalrous scalping tuft was
preserved, was without ornament of any kind, with the
exception of a solitary eagle's plume, that crossed his
crown, and depended over the left shoulder. A tomahawk and scalping-knife, of English manufacture, were
in his girdle; while a short military rifle, of that sort with
which the policy of the whites armed their savage allies,
lay carelessly across his bare and sinewy knee. The expanded chest, full formed limbs, and grave countenance
of this warrior, would denote that he had reached the

vigor of his days, though no symptoms of decay appeared
to have yet weakened his manhood.

The frame of the white man, judging by such parts as
were not concealed by his clothes, was like that of one
who had known hardships and exertion from his earliest
youth. His person, though muscular, was rather attenu-
ated than full; but every nerve and muscle appeared
strung and indurated by unremitted exposure and toil.
He wore a hunting-shirt of forest green, fringed with
faded yellow, and a summer cap of skins which had been
shorn of their fur. He also bore a knife in a girdle of
wampum, like that which confined the scanty garments
of the Indian, but no tomahawk. His moccasins were ornamented after the gay fashion of the natives, while the
only part of his under-dress which appeared below the
hunting-frock, was a pair of buckskin leggings, that laced
at the sides, and which were gartered above the knees
with the sinews of a deer. A pouch and horn completed
his personal accoutrements, though a rifle of great
length, which the theory of the more ingenious whites
had taught them was the most dangerous of all fire-arms,
leaned against a neighboring sapling. The eye of the
hunter, or scout, whichever he might be, was small,
quick, keen, and restless, roving while he spoke, on every
side of him, as if in quest of game, or distrusting the sudden approach of some lurking enemy. Notwithstanding
the symptoms of habitual suspicion, his countenance was
not only without guile, but at the moment at which he is
introduced, it was charged with an expression of sturdy
honesty.

"Even your traditions make the case in my favor,
Chingachgook," he said, speaking in the tongue which
was known to all the natives who formerly inhabited the

country between the Hudson and the Potomac, and of which we shall give a free translation for the benefit of the reader; endeavoring, at the same time, to preserve some of the peculiarities, both of the individual and of the language. "Your fathers came from the setting sun, crossed the big river, fought the people of the country, and took the land; and mine came from the red sky of the morning, over the salt lake, and did their work much after the fashion that had been set them by yours; then let God judge the matter between us, and friends spare their words!"

"My fathers fought with the naked redmen!" returned the Indian sternly, in the same language. "Is there no difference, Hawkeye, between the stone-headed arrow of the warrior, and the leaden bullet with which you kill?"

"There is reason in an Indian, though nature has made him with a red skin!" said the white man, shaking his head like one on whom such an appeal to his justice was not thrown away. For a moment he appeared to be conscious of having the worst of the argument, then, rallying again, he answered the objection of his antagonist in the best manner his limited information would allow: "I am no scholar, and I care not who knows it; but judging from what I have seen, at deer chases and squirrel hunts, of the sparks below, I should think a rifle in the hands of their grandfathers was not so dangerous as a hickory bow and a good flint-head might be, if drawn with Indian judgment, and sent by an Indian eye."

"You have the story told by your fathers," returned the other, coldly waving his hand. "What say your old men? Do they tell the young warriors, that the pale faces met the redmen, painted for war and armed with the stone hatchet and wooden gun?"

"I am not a prejudiced man, nor one who vaunts himself on his natural privileges, though the worst enemy I have on earth, and he is an Iroquois, daren't deny that I am genuine white," the scout replied, surveying, with secret satisfaction, the faded color of his bony and sinewy hand; "and I am willing to own that my people have many ways, of which, as an honest man, I can't approve. It is one of their customs to write in books what they have done and seen, instead of telling them in their villages, where the lie can be given to the face of a cowardly boaster, and the brave soldier can call on his comrades to witness for the truth of his words. In consequence of this bad fashion, a man who is too conscientious to misspend his days among the women, in learning the names of black marks, may never hear of the deeds of his fathers, nor feel a pride in striving to outdo them. For myself, I conclude the Bumppos could shoot, for I have a natural turn with a rifle, which must have been handed down from generation to generation, as, our holy commandments tell us, all good and evil gifts are bestowed; though I should be loth to answer for other people in such a matter. But every story has its two sides; so I ask you, Chingachgook, what passed, according to the traditions of the redmen, when our fathers first met?"

A silence of a minute succeeded, during which the Indian sat mute; then, full of the dignity of his office, he commenced his brief tale, with a solemnity that served to heighten its appearance of truth.

"Listen, Hawkeye, and your ear shall drink no lie. 'Tis what my fathers have said, and what the Mohicans have done." He hesitated a single instant, and bending a cautious glance toward his companion, he continued, in a manner that was divided between interrogation and assertion, "Does not this stream at our feet run towards the summer, until its waters grow salt, and the current flows upward?"

"It can't be denied that your traditions tell you true in both these matters," said the white man; "for I have been there, and have seen them; though, why water, which is so sweet in the shade, should become bitter in the sun, is an alteration for which I have never been able to account."

"And the current!" demanded the Indian, who expected his reply with that sort of interest that a man feels in the confirmation of testimony, at which he marvels even while he respects it; "the fathers of Chingachgook have not lied!"

"The Holy Bible is not more true, and that is the truest thing in nature. They call this up-stream current the tide, which is a thing soon explained, and clear enough. Six hours the waters run in, and six hours they run out, and the reason is this: when there is higher water in the sea than in the river, they run in, until the river gets to be highest, and then it runs out again."

"The waters in the woods, and on the great lakes, run downward until they lie like my hand," said the Indian, stretching the limb horizontally before him, "and then they run no more."

"No honest man will deny it," said the scout, a little nettled at the implied distrust of his explanation of the mystery of the tides; "and I grant that it is true on the small scale, and where the land is level. But everything depends on what scale you look at things. Now, on the small scale, the 'arth is level; but on the large scale it is round. In this manner, pools and ponds, and even the great fresh-water lake, may be stagnant, as you and I both know they are, having seen them; but when you come to spread water over a great tract, like the sea, where the earth is round, how in reason can the water be quiet? You might as well expect the river to lie still on the brink of those black rocks a mile above us, though your own ears tell you that it is tumbling over them at this very moment!"

If unsatisfied by the philosophy of his companion, the Indian was far too dignified to betray his unbelief. He listened like one who was convinced, and resumed his narrative in his former solemn manner.

"We came from the place where the sun is hid at night, over great plains where the buffaloes live, until we reached the big river. There we fought the Alligewi, till the ground was red with their blood. From the banks of the big river to the shores of the salt lake, there was none to meet us. The Maquas[2] followed at a distance. We said the country should be ours from the place where the water runs up no longer on this stream, to a river twenty suns' journey toward the summer. The land we had taken like warriors, we kept like men. We drove the Maquas into the woods with the bears. They only tasted salt at the licks; they drew no fish from the great lake; we threw them the bones."

"All this I have heard and believe," said the white man, observing that the Indian paused; "but it was long before the English came into the country."

"A pine grew then where this chestnut now stands. The first pale-faces who came among us spoke no English. They came in a large canoe, when my fathers had buried the tomahawk with the redmen around them. Then, Hawkeye," he continued, betraying his deep emotion only by permitting his voice to fall to those low, guttural tones, which rendered his language, as spoken at times, so very musical; "then, Hawkeye, we were one people, and we were happy. The salt lake gave us its fish, the wood its deer, and the air its birds. We took wives who bore us children; we worshipped the Great Spirit; and we kept the Maquas beyond the sound of our songs of triumph!"

"Know you anything of your own family at that time?" demanded the white. "But you are a just man, for an Indian! and, as I suppose you hold their gifts, your fathers must have been brave warriors, and wise men at the council fire."

"My tribe is the grandfather of nations, but I am an unmixed man. The blood of chiefs is in my veins, where it must stay forever. The Dutch[3] landed, and gave my people the fire-water; they drank until the heavens and the earth seemed to meet, and they foolishly thought they had found the Great Spirit. Then they parted with their land. Foot by foot, they were driven back from the shores, until I, that am a chief and a sagamore,[4] have never seen the sun shine but through the trees, and have never visited the graves of my fathers!"

"Graves bring solemn feelings over the mind," returned the scout, a good deal touched at the calm suffering of his companion; "and they often aid a man in his good intentions; though, for myself, I expect to leave my own bones unburied, to bleach in the woods, or to be torn asunder by the wolves. But where are to be found those of your race who came to their kin in the Delaware country, so many summers since?"

"Where are the blossoms of those summers!—fallen, one by one: so all of my family departed, each in his turn, to the land of spirits. I am on the hill-top, and must go down into the valley; and when Uncas follows in my foot-steps, there will no longer be any of the blood of the sag-amores, for my boy is the last of the Mohicans."

"Uncas is here!" said another voice, in the same soft, guttural tones, near his elbow; "who speaks to Uncas?"

The white man loosened his knife in his leathern sheath, and made an involuntary movement of the hand towards his rifle, at this sudden interruption; but the In-dian sat composed, and without turning his head at the unexpected sounds.

At the next instant, a youthful warrior passed between them, with a noiseless step, and seated himself on the bank of the rapid stream. No exclamation of surprise es-caped the father, nor was any question asked, or reply given, for several minutes; each appearing to await the moment when he might speak, without betraying wom-anish curiosity or childish impatience. The white man seemed to take counsel from their customs, and, relin-quishing his grasp of the rifle, he also remained silent and reserved. At length Chingachgook turned his eyes slowly towards his son, and demanded,—

"Do the Maquas dare to leave the print of their moc-casins in these woods?"

"I have been on their trail," replied the young Indian, "and know that they number as many as the fingers of my two hands; but they lie hid, like cowards."

"The thieves are outlying for scalps and plunder!" said the white man, whom we shall call Hawkeye, after the manner of his companions. "That bushy Frenchman, Montcalm, will send his spies into our very camp, but he will know what road we travel!"

" 'Tis enough!" returned the father, glancing his eye towards the setting sun; "they shall be driven like deer from their bushes. Hawkeye, let us eat to-night, and show the Maquas that we are men to-morrow."

"I am as ready to do the one as the other; but to fight the Iroquois 'tis necessary to find the skulkers; and to eat, 'tis necessary to get the game—talk of the devil and he will come; there is a pair of the biggest antlers I have seen this season, moving the bushes below the hill! Now, Uncas," he continued in a half whisper, and laughing with a kind of inward sound, like one who had learnt to be watchful, "I will bet my charger three times full of powder, against a foot of wampum, that I take him atwixt the eyes, and nearer to the right than to the left."

"It cannot be!" said the young Indian, springing to his feet with youthful eagerness; "all but the tips of his horns are hid!"

"He's a boy!" said the white man, shaking his head while he spoke, and addressing the father. "Does he think when a hunter sees a part of the creatur', he can't tell where the rest of him should be!"

Adjusting his rifle, he was about to make an exhibition of that skill, on which he so much valued himself, when the warrior struck up the piece with his hand, saying—

"Hawkeye! will you fight the Maquas?"

"These Indians know the nature of the woods, as it might be by instinct!" returned the scout, dropping his rifle, and turning away like a man who was convinced of his error. "I must leave the buck to your arrow, Uncas, or we may kill a deer for them thieves, the Iroquois, to eat."

The instant the father seconded this intimation by an expressive gesture of the hand, Uncas threw himself on the ground, and approached the animal with wary movements. When within a few yards of the cover, he fitted an arrow to his bow with the utmost care, while the antlers moved, as if their owner snuffed an enemy in the tainted air. In another moment the twang of the cord was heard, a white streak was seen glancing into the bushes, and the wounded buck plunged from the cover, to the very feet of his hidden enemy. Avoiding the horns of the infuriated animal, Uncas darted to his side, and passed his knife across the throat, when bounding to the edge of the river it fell, dyeing the waters with its blood.

" 'Twas done with Indian skill," said the scout, laughing inwardly, but with vast satisfaction; "and 'twas a pretty sight to behold! Though an arrow is a near shot, and needs a knife to finish the work."

"Hugh!" ejaculated his companion, turning quickly, like a hound who scented game.

"By the Lord, there is a drove of them!" exclaimed the scout, whose eyes began to glisten with the ardor of his usual occupation; "if they come within range of a bullet I will drop one, though the whole Six Nations should be lurking within sound! What do you hear, Chingachgook? for to my ears the woods are dumb."

"There is but one deer, and he is dead," said the Indian, bending his body till his ear nearly touched the earth. "I hear the sounds of feet!"

"Perhaps the wolves have driven the buck to shelter, and are following on his trail."

"No. The horses of white men are coming!" returned the other, raising himself with dignity, and resuming his seat on the log with his former composure. "Hawkeye, they are your brothers; speak to them."

"That will I, and in English that the king needn't be ashamed to answer," returned the hunter, speaking in the language of which he boasted; "but I see nothing, nor do I hear the sounds of man or beast; 'tis strange that an

Indian should understand white sounds better than a man who, his very enemies will own, has no cross in his blood, although he may have lived with the redskins long enough to be suspected! Ha! there goes something like the cracking of a dry stick, too—now I hear the bushes move—yes, yes, there is a trampling that I mistook for the falls—and—but here they come themselves; God keep them from the Iroquois!"

Hawkeye, white. Chingachgook, mohican. Uncas, chingachgooks son. Iraquois enemies close

IV

"Well, go thy way: thou shalt not from this grove
Till I torment thee for this injury."
A Midsummer night's Dream[1]

THE WORDS WERE STILL in the mouth of the scout, when the leader of the party, whose approaching footsteps had caught the vigilant ear of the Indian, came openly into view. A beaten path, such as those made by the periodical passage of the deer, wound through a little glen at no great distance, and struck the river at the point where the white man and his red companions had posted themselves. Along this track the travellers, who had produced a surprise so unusual in the depths of the forest, advanced slowly towards the hunter, who was in front of his associates, in readiness to receive them.

"Who comes?" demanded the scout, throwing his rifle carelessly across his left arm, and keeping the forefinger of his right hand on the trigger, though he avoided all appearance of menace in the act, "Who comes hither, among the beasts and dangers of the wilderness?"

"Believers in religion, and friends to the law and to the king," returned he who rode foremost. "Men who have journeyed since the rising sun, in the shades of this

39

forest, without nourishment, and are sadly tired of their wayfaring."

"You are, then, lost," interrupted the hunter, "and have found how helpless 'tis not to know whether to take the right hand or the left?"

"Even so; sucking babes are not more dependent on those who guide them than we who are of larger growth, and who may now be said to possess the stature without the knowledge of men. Know you the distance to a post of the crown called William Henry?"

"Hoot!" shouted the scout, who did not spare his open laughter, though, instantly checking the dangerous sounds, he indulged his merriment at less risk of being overheard by any lurking enemies. "You are as much off the scent as a hound would be, with Horican atwixt him and the deer! William Henry, man! if you are friends to the king, and have business with the army, your better way would be to follow the river down to Edward, and lay the matter before Webb; who tarries there, instead of pushing into the defiles, and driving this saucy Frenchman back across Champlain, into his den again."

Before the stranger could make any reply to this unexpected proposition, another horseman dashed the bushes aside, and leaped his charger into the pathway, in front of his companion.

"What, then, may be our distance from Fort Edward?" demanded a new speaker; "the place you advise us to seek we left this morning, and our destination is the head of the lake."

"Then you must have lost your eyesight afore losing your way, for the road across the portage is cut to a good two rods, and is as grand a path, I calculate, as any that runs into London, or even before the palace of the king himself."

"We will not dispute concerning the excellence of the passage," returned Heyward, smiling; for, as the reader has anticipated, it was he. "It is enough, for the present, that we trusted to an Indian guide to take us by a nearer, though blinder path, and that we are deceived in his knowledge. In plain words, we know not where we are."

"An Indian lost in the woods!" said the scout, shaking his head doubtingly; "when the sun is scorching the tree-tops, and the water-courses are full; when the moss on every beech he sees, will tell him in which quarter the north star will shine at night! The woods are full of deer paths which run to the streams and licks, places well known to everybody; nor have the geese done their flight to the Canada waters altogether! 'Tis strange that an Indian should be lost atwixt Horican and the bend in the river. Is he a Mohawk?"

"Not by birth, though adopted in that tribe; I think his birthplace was farther north, and he is one of those you call a Huron."

"Hugh!" exclaimed the two companions of the scout, who had continued, until this part of the dialogue, seated immovable, and apparently indifferent to what passed, but who now sprang to their feet with an activity and interest that had evidently got the better of their reserve, by surprise.

"A Huron!" repeated the sturdy scout, once more shaking his head in open distrust; "they are a thievish race, nor do I care by whom they are adopted; you can never make anything of them but skulks and vagabonds. Since you trusted yourself to the care of one of that nation, I only wonder that you have not fallen in with more."

"Of that there is little danger, since William Henry is so many miles in our front. You forget that I have told you our guide is now a Mohawk, and that he serves with our forces as a friend."

"And I tell you that he who is born a Mingo[2] will die a Mingo," returned the other, positively. "A Mohawk! No, give me a Delaware or a Mohican for honesty; and when they will fight, which they won't all do, having suffered their cunning enemies, the Maquas, to make them women—but when they will fight at all, look to a Delaware, or a Mohican, for a warrior!"

"Enough of this," said Heyward, impatiently; "I wish not to inquire into the character of a man that I know, and to whom you must be a stranger. You have not yet answered my question: what is our distance from the main army at Edward?"

"It seems that may depend on who is your guide. One would think such a horse as that might get over a good deal of ground atwixt sun-up and sun-down."

"I wish no contention of idle words with you, friend," said Heyward, curbing his dissatisfied manner, and speaking in a more gentle voice; "if you will tell me the distance to Fort Edward, and conduct me thither, your labor shall not go without its reward."

"And in so doing, how know I that I don't guide an enemy, and a spy of Montcalm, to the works of the army? It is not every man who can speak the English tongue that is an honest subject."

"If you serve with the troops, of whom I judge you to be a scout, you should know of such a regiment of the king as the 60th."

"The 60th! you can tell me little of the Royal Americans that I don't know, though I do wear a hunting-shirt instead of a scarlet jacket."

"Well, then, among the other things, you may know the name of its major?"

"Its major!" interrupted the hunter, elevating his body like one who was proud of his trust. "If there is a man in the country who knows Major Effingham, he stands before you."

"It is a corps which has many majors; the gentleman you name is the senior, but I speak of the junior of them all; he who commands the companies in garrison at William Henry."

"Yes, yes, I have heard that a young gentleman of vast riches, from one of the provinces far south, has got the place. He is over young, too, to hold such rank, and to be put above men whose heads are beginning to bleach; and yet they say he is a soldier in his knowledge, and a gallant gentleman!"

"Whatever he may be, or however he may be qualified for his rank, he now speaks to you, and of course can be no enemy to dread."

The scout regarded Heyward in surprise, and then lifting his cap, he answered, in a tone less confident than before, though still expressing doubt,—

"I have heard a party was to leave the encampment this morning, for the lake shore."

"You have heard the truth; but I preferred a nearer route, trusting to the knowledge of the Indian I mentioned."

"And he deceived you, and then deserted?"

"Neither, as I believe; certainly not the latter, for he is to be found in the rear."

"I should like to look at the creatur'; if it is a true Iroquois I can tell him by his knavish look, and by his paint," said the scout, stepping past the charger of Heyward, and entering the path behind the mare of the singing-master, whose foal had taken advantage of the halt to exact the maternal contribution. After shoving aside the bushes, and proceeding a few paces, he encountered the females, who awaited the result of the conference with anxiety, and not entirely without apprehension. Behind these, the runner leaned against a tree, where he stood the close examination of the scout with an air unmoved, though with a look so dark and savage, that it might in itself excite fear. Satisfied with his scrutiny, the hunter soon left him. As he repassed the females, he paused a moment to gaze upon their beauty, answering to the smile and nod of Alice with a look of open pleasure. Thence he went to the side of the motherly animal, and spending a minute in a fruitless inquiry into the character of her rider, he shook his head and returned to Heyward.

"A Mingo is a Mingo, and God having made him so, neither the Mohawks nor any other tribe can alter him," he said, when he had regained his former position. "If we were alone, and you would leave that noble horse at the mercy of the wolves tonight, I could show you the way to Edward, myself, within an hour, for it lies only about an hour's journey hence; but with such ladies in your company 'tis impossible!"

"And why? they are fatigued, but they are quite equal to a ride of a few more miles."

"'Tis a natural impossibility!" repeated the scout; "I wouldn't walk a mile in these woods after night gets into them, in company with that runner, for the best rifle in the colonies. They are full of outlying Iroquois, and your mongrel Mohawk knows where to find them too well, to be my companion."

"Think you so?" said Heyward, leaning forward in the saddle, and dropping his voice nearly to a whisper; "I confess I have not been without my own suspicions, though I have endeavored to conceal them, and affected a confidence I have not always felt, on account of my companions. It was because I suspected him that I would follow no longer; making him, as you see, follow me."

"I knew he was one of the cheats as soon as I laid eyes on him!" returned the scout, placing a finger on his nose, in sign of caution. "The thief is leaning against the foot of the sugar sapling, that you can see over them bushes; his right leg is in a line with the bark of the tree, and," tapping his rifle, "I can take him from where I stand, between the ankle and the knee, with a single shot, putting an end to his tramping through the woods, for at least a month to come. If I should go back to him, the cunning varmint would suspect something, and be dodging through the trees like a frightened deer."

"It will not do. He may be innocent, and I dislike the act. Though, if I felt confident of his treachery—"

" 'Tis a safe thing to calculate on the knavery of an Iroquois," said the scout, throwing his rifle forward, by a sort of instinctive movement.

"Hold!" interrupted Heyward, "it will not do—we must think of some other scheme; and yet, I have much reason to believe the rascal has deceived me."

The hunter, who had already abandoned his intention of maiming the runner, mused a moment, and then made a gesture, which instantly brought his two red companions to his side. They spoke together earnestly in the Delaware language, though in an undertone; and by the gestures of the white man, which were frequently directed towards the top of the sapling, it was evident he pointed out the situation of their hidden enemy. His companions were not long in comprehending his wishes, and laying aside their fire-arms, they parted, taking opposite sides of the path, and burying themselves in the thicket, with such cautious movements, that their steps were inaudible.

"Now, go you back," said the hunter, speaking again to Heyward, "and hold the imp in talk; these Mohicans here will take him without breaking his paint."

"Nay," said Heyward, proudly, "I will seize him myself."

"Hist! what could you do, mounted, against an Indian in the bushes?"

"I will dismount."

"And, think you, when he saw one of your feet out of the stirrup, he would wait for the other to be free? Whoever comes into the woods to deal with the natives, must use Indian fashions, if he would wish to prosper in his undertakings. Go, then, talk openly to the miscreant, and seem to believe him the truest friend you have on 'arth."

Heyward prepared to comply, though with strong disgust at the nature of the office he was compelled to execute. Each moment, however, pressed upon him a conviction of the critical situation in which he had suffered his invaluable trust to be involved through his own confidence. The sun had already disappeared, and the woods, suddenly deprived of his light, were assuming a dusky hue, which keenly reminded him that the hour the savage usually chose for his most barbarous and remorseless acts of vengeance or hostility, was speedily drawing near. Stimulated by apprehension, he left the

scout, who immediately entered into a loud conversation
with the stranger that had so unceremoniously enlisted
himself in the party of travellers that morning. In passing
his gentler companions Heyward uttered a few words of
encouragement, and was pleased to find that, though fatigued with the exercise of the day, they appeared to entertain no suspicion that their present embarrassment
was other than the result of accident. Giving them reason to believe he was merely employed in a consultation
concerning the future route, he spurred his charger, and
drew the reins again, when the animal had carried him
within a few yards of the place where the sullen runner
still stood, leaning against the tree.

"You may see, Magua," he said, endeavoring to assume an air of freedom and confidence, "that the night is
closing around us, and yet we are no nearer to William
Henry than when we left the encampment of Webb with
the rising sun. You have missed the way, nor have I been
more fortunate. But, happily we have fallen in with a
hunter, he whom you hear talking to the singer, that is acquainted with the deer-paths and by-ways of the woods,
and who promises to lead us to a place where we may
rest securely till the morning."

The Indian riveted his glowing eyes on Heyward as he
asked, in his imperfect English, "Is he alone?"

"Alone!" hesitatingly answered Heyward to whom deception was too new to be assumed without embarrassment. "O! not alone, surely, Magua, for you know that we
are with him."

"Then Le Renard Subtil will go," returned the runner,
coolly raising his little wallet from the place where it had
lain at his feet; "and the pale-faces will see none but their
own color."

"Go! Whom call you Le Renard?"

" 'Tis the name his Canada fathers have given to Magua," returned the runner, with an air that manifested his pride at the distinction. "Night is the same as day to Le Subtil, when Munro waits for him."

"And what account will Le Renard give the chief of William Henry concerning his daughters? Will he dare to tell the hot-blooded Scotsman that his children are left without a guide, though Magua promised to be one?"

"Though the gray head has a loud voice, and a long arm, Le Renard will not hear him, or feel him, in the woods."

"But what will the Mohawks say? They will make him petticoats, and bid him stay in the wigwam with the women, for he is no longer to be trusted with the business of a man."

"Le Subtil knows the path to the great lakes, and he can find the bones of his fathers," was the answer of the unmoved runner.

"Enough, Magua," said Heyward; "are we not friends? Why should there be bitter words between us? Munro has promised you a gift for your services when performed, and I shall be your debtor for another. Rest your weary limbs, then, and open your wallet to eat. We have a few moments to spare; let us not waste them in talk like wrangling women. When the ladies are refreshed we will proceed."

"The pale-faces make themselves dogs to their women," muttered the Indian, in his native language, "and when they want to eat, their warriors must lay aside the tomahawk to feed their laziness."

"What say you, Renard?"

"Le Subtil says it is good."

The Indian then fastened his eyes keenly on the open countenance of Heyward, but meeting his glance, he turned them quickly away, and seating himself deliberately on the ground, he drew forth the remnant of some former repast, and began to eat, though not without first bending his looks slowly and cautiously around him.

"This is well," continued Heyward; "and Le Renard will have strength and sight to find the path in the morning"; he paused, for sounds like the snapping of a dried stick, and the rustling of leaves, rose from the adjacent bushes, but recollecting himself instantly, he continued,—"we must be moving before the sun is seen, or Montcalm may lie in our path, and shut us out from the fortress."

The hand of Magua dropped from his mouth to his side, and though his eyes were fastened on the ground, his head was turned aside, his nostrils expanded, and his ears seemed even to stand more erect than usual, giving to him the appearance of a statue that was made to represent intense attention.

Heyward, who watched his movements with a vigilant eye, carelessly extricated one of his feet from the stirrup, while he passed a hand towards the bear-skin covering of his holsters. Every effort to detect the point most regarded by the runner was completely frustrated by the tremulous glances of his organs, which seemed not to rest a single instant on any particular object, and which, at the same time, could be hardly said to move. While he hesitated how to proceed, Le Subtil cautiously raised himself to his feet, though with a motion so slow and guarded, that not the slightest noise was produced by the change. Heyward felt it had now become incumbent on him to act. Throwing his leg over the saddle, he dismounted, with a determination to advance and seize his treacherous companion, trusting the result to his own manhood. In order, however, to prevent unnecessary alarm, he still preserved an air of calmness and friendship.

"Le Renard Subtil does not eat," he said, using the appellation he had found most flattering to the vanity of the Indian. "His corn is not well parched, and it seems dry. Let me examine; perhaps something may be found among my own provisions that will help his appetite."

Magua held out the wallet to the proffer of the other. He even suffered their hands to meet, without betraying the least emotion, or varying his riveted attitude of attention. But when he felt the fingers of Heyward moving gently along his own naked arm, he struck up the limb of the young man, and uttering a piercing cry as he darted beneath it, plunged, at a single bound, into the opposite thicket. At the next instant the form of Chingachgook appeared from the bushes, looking like a spectre in its paint, and glided across the path in swift pursuit. Next followed the shout of Uncas, when the woods were lighted by a sudden flash, that was accompanied by the sharp report of the hunter's rifle.

Hawkeye + Heyward meet. Don't trust mangua. Mangua is a huron (untrustworthy tribe) Delaware is a good tribe. Mangua to be called Le Renard Subtil. Mangua runs away. Hawkeye shoots

V

"In such a night
Did Thisbe fearfully o'ertrip the dew;
And saw the lion's shadow ere himself."
The Merchant of Venice[1]

THE SUDDENNESS of the flight of his guide, and the wild cries of the pursuers, caused Heyward to remain fixed, for a few moments, in inactive surprise. Then recollecting the importance of securing the fugitive, he dashed aside the surrounding bushes, and pressed eagerly forward to lend his aid in the chase. Before he had, however, proceeded a hundred yards, he met the three foresters already returning from their unsuccessful pursuit.

"Why so soon disheartened!" he exclaimed; "the scoundrel must be concealed behind some of these trees, and may yet be secured. We are not safe while he goes at large."

"Would you set a cloud to chase the wind?" returned the disappointed scout; "I heard the imp, brushing over the dry leaves, like a black snake, and blinking a glimpse of him, just over ag'in yon big pine, I pulled as it might be on the scent; but 'twouldn't do! and yet for a reasoning aim, if anybody but myself had touched the trigger, I

should call it a quick sight; and I may be accounted to
have experience in these matters, and one who ought to
know. Look at this sumach; its leaves are red, though
everybody knows the fruit is in the yellow blossom, in the
month of July!"

" 'Tis the blood of Le Subtil! he is hurt, and may yet
fall!"

"No, no," returned the scout, in decided disapprobation of this opinion, "I rubbed the bark off a limb, perhaps, but the creature leaped the longer for it. A
rifle-bullet acts on a running animal, when it barks him,
much the same as one of your spurs on a horse; that is, it
quickens motion, and puts life into the flesh, instead of
taking it away. But when it cuts the ragged hole, after a
bound or two, there is, commonly, a stagnation of further
leaping, be it Indian or be it deer!"

"We are four able bodies, to one wounded man!"

"Is life grievous to you?" interrupted the scout. "Yonder red devil would draw you within swing of the tomahawks of his comrades, before you were heated in the
chase. It was an unthoughtful act in a man who has so
often slept with the war-whoop ringing in the air, to let
off his piece within sound of an ambushment! But then it
was a natural temptation! 'twas very natural! Come,
friends, let us move our station, and in such a fashion,
too, as will throw the cunning of a Mingo on a wrong
scent, or our scalps will be drying in the wind in front of
Montcalm's marquee, ag'in this hour to-morrow."

This appalling declaration, which the scout uttered
with the cool assurance of a man who fully comprehended, while he did not fear to face the danger, served
to remind Heyward of the importance of the charge with
which he himself had been intrusted. Glancing his eyes

around, with a vain effort to pierce the gloom that was thickening beneath the leafy arches of the forest, he felt as if, cut off from human aid, his unresisting companions would soon lie at the entire mercy of those barbarous enemies, who, like beasts of prey, only waited till the gathering darkness might render their blows more fatally certain. His awakened imagination, deluded by the deceptive light, converted each waving bush, or the fragment of some fallen tree, into human forms, and twenty times he fancied he could distinguish the horrid visages of his lurking foes, peering from their hiding-places, in never-ceasing watchfulness of the movements of his party. Looking upward, he found that the thin fleecy clouds, which evening had painted on the blue sky, were already losing their faintest tints of rose-color, while the imbedded stream, which glided past the spot where he stood, was to be traced only by the dark boundary of its wooded banks.

"What is to be done?" he said, feeling the utter helplessness of doubt in such a pressing strait; "desert me not, for God's sake! remain to defend those I escort, and freely name your own reward!"

His companions, who conversed apart in the language of their tribe, heeded not this sudden and earnest appeal. Though their dialogue was maintained in low and cautious sounds, but little above a whisper, Heyward, who now approached, could easily distinguish the earnest tones of the younger warrior from the more deliberate speeches of his seniors. It was evident that they debated on the propriety of some measure that nearly concerned the welfare of the travellers. Yielding to his powerful interest in the subject, and impatient of a delay that seemed fraught with so much additional danger,

Heyward drew still nigher to the dusky group, with an intention of making his offers of compensation more definite, when the white man, motioning with his hand, as if he conceded the disputed point, turned away, saying in a sort of soliloquy, and in the English tongue,—

"Uncas is right! it would not be the act of men to leave such harmless things to their fate, even though it breaks up the harboring place forever. If you would save these tender blossoms from the fangs of the worst of sarpents, gentleman, you have neither time to lose nor resolution to throw away!"

"How can such a wish be doubted! have I not already offered—"

"Offer your prayers to Him who can give us wisdom to circumvent the cunning of the devils who fill these woods," calmly interrupted the scout, "but spare your offers of money, which neither you may live to realize, nor I to profit by. These Mohicans and I will do what man's thoughts can invent, to keep such flowers, which, though so sweet, were never made for the wilderness, from harm, and that without hope of any other recompense but such as God always gives to upright dealings. First, you must promise two things, both in your own name and for your friends, or without serving you, we shall only injure ourselves!"

"Name them."

"The one is, to be still as these sleeping woods, let what will happen; and the other is, to keep the place where we shall take you, forever a secret from all mortal men."

"I will do my utmost to see both these conditions fulfilled."

"Then follow, for we are losing moments that are as precious as the heart's blood to a stricken deer!"

Heyward could distinguish the impatient gesture of the scout, through the increasing shadows of the evening, and he moved in his footsteps, swiftly, towards the place where he had left the remainder of his party. When they rejoined the expecting and anxious females, he briefly acquainted them with the conditions of their new guide, and with the necessity that existed for their hushing every apprehension, in instant and serious exertions. Although his alarming communication was not received without much secret terror by the listeners, his earnest and impressive manner, aided perhaps by the nature of the danger, succeeded in bracing their nerves to undergo some unlooked-for and unusual trial. Silently, and without a moment's delay, they permitted him to assist them from their saddles, when they descended quickly to the water's edge, where the scout had collected the rest of the party, more by the agency of expressive gestures than by any use of words.

"What to do with these dumb creatures!" muttered the white man, on whom the sole control of their future movements appeared to devolve; "it would be time lost to cut their throats, and cast them into the river; and to leave them here, would be to tell the Mingos that they have not far to seek to find their owners!"

"Then give them their bridles, and let them range the woods," Heyward ventured to suggest.

"No; it would be better to mislead the imps, and make them believe they must equal a horse's speed to run down their chase. Ay, ay, that will blind their fire-balls of eyes! Chingach—Hist? what stirs the bush?"

"The colt."

"That colt, at least, must die," muttered the scout, grasping the mane of the nimble beast, which easily eluded his hand; "Uncas, your arrows!"

"Hold!" exclaimed the proprietor of the condemned animal, aloud, without regard to the whispering tones used by the others; "spare the foal of Miriam! it is the comely offspring of a faithful dam, and would willingly injure naught."

"When men struggle for the single life God has given them," said the scout sternly, "even their own kind seem no more than the beasts of the wood. If you speak again, I shall leave you to the mercy of the Maquas! Draw to your arrow's head, Uncas; we have no time for second blows."

The low, muttering sounds of his threatening voice were still audible, when the wounded foal, first rearing on its hinder legs, plunged forward to its knees. It was met by Chingachgook, whose knife passed across its throat quicker than thought, and then precipitating the motions of the struggling victim, he dashed it into the river, down whose stream it glided away, gasping audibly for breath with its ebbing life. This deed of apparent cruelty, but of real necessity, fell upon the spirits of the travellers like a terrific warning of the peril in which they stood, heightened as it was by the calm though steady resolution of the actors in the scene. The sisters shuddered and clung closer to each other, while Heyward instinctively laid his hand on one of the pistols he had just drawn from their holsters, as he placed himself between his charge and those dense shadows that seemed to draw an impenetrable veil before the bosom of the forest.

The Indians, however, hesitated not a moment, but

taking the bridles, they led the frightened and reluctant horses into the bed of the river.

At a short distance from the shore they turned, and were soon concealed by the projection of the bank, under the brow of which they moved, in a direction opposite to the course of the waters. In the meantime, the scout drew a canoe of bark from its place of concealment beneath some low bushes, whose branches were waving with the eddies of the current, into which he silently motioned for the females to enter. They complied without hesitation, though many a fearful and anxious glance was thrown behind them towards the thickening gloom which now lay like a dark barrier along the margin of the stream.

So soon as Cora and Alice were seated, the scout, without regarding the element, directed Heyward to support one side of the frail vessel, and posting himself at the other, they bore it up against the stream, followed by the dejected owner of the dead foal. In this manner they proceeded, for many rods, in a silence that was only interrupted by the rippling of the water, as its eddies played around them, or the low dash made by their own cautious footsteps. Heyward yielded the guidance of the canoe implicitly to the scout, who approached or receded from the shore, to avoid the fragments of rocks, or deeper parts of the river, with a readiness that showed his knowledge of the route they held. Occasionally he would stop; and in the midst of a breathing stillness, that the dull but increasing roar of the waterfall only served to render more impressive, he would listen with painful intenseness, to catch any sounds that might arise from the slumbering forest. When assured that all was still, and unable to detect, even by the aid of his practised

senses, any sign of his approaching foes, he would deliberately resume his slow and unguarded progress. At
length they reached a point in the river, where the roving
eye of Heyward became riveted on a cluster of black objects, collected at a spot where the high bank threw a
deeper shadow than usual on the dark waters. Hesitating
to advance, he pointed out the place to the attention of
his companion.

"Ay," returned the composed scout, "the Indians have
hid the beasts with the judgment of natives! Water leaves
no trail, and an owl's eyes would be blinded by the darkness of such a hole."

The whole party was soon reunited, and another consultation was held between the scout and his new comrades, during which, they whose fates depended on the
faith and ingenuity of these unknown foresters, had a little leisure to observe their situation more minutely.

The river was confined between high and cragged
rocks, one of which impended above the spot where the
canoe rested. As these, again, were surmounted by tall
trees, which appeared to totter on the brows of the
precipice, it gave the stream the appearance of running
through a deep and narrow dell. All beneath the fantastic
limbs and ragged tree-tops, which were, here and there,
dimly painted against the starry zenith, lay alike in shadowed obscurity. Behind them, the curvature of the banks
soon bounded the view, by the same dark and wooded
outline; but in front, and apparently at no great distance,
the water seemed piled against the heavens, whence it
tumbled into caverns, out of which issued those sullen
sounds that had loaded the evening atmosphere. It
seemed, in truth, to be a spot devoted to seclusion, and
the sisters imbibed a soothing impression of security, as

they gazed upon its romantic, though not unappalling beauties. A general movement among their conductors, however, soon recalled them from a contemplation of the wild charms that night had assisted to lend the place, to a painful sense of their real peril.

The horses had been secured to some scattered shrubs that grew in the fissures of the rocks, where, standing in the water, they were left to pass the night. The scout directed Heyward and his disconsolate fellow-travellers to seat themselves in the forward end of the canoe, and took possession of the other himself, as erect and steady as if he floated in a vessel of much firmer materials. The Indians warily retraced their steps towards the place they had left, when the scout, placing his pole against a rock, by a powerful shove, sent his frail bark directly into the centre of the turbulent stream. For many minutes the struggle between the light bubble in which they floated, and the swift current, was severe and doubtful. Forbidden to stir even a hand, and almost afraid to breathe, lest they should expose the frail fabric to the fury of the stream, the passengers watched the glancing waters in feverish suspense. Twenty times they thought the whirling eddies were sweeping them to destruction, when the master-hand of their pilot would bring the bows of the canoe to stem the rapid. A long, a vigorous, and, as it appeared to the females, a desperate effort, closed the struggle. Just as Alice veiled her eyes in horror, under the impression that they were about to be swept within the vortex at the foot of the cataract, the canoe floated, stationary, at the side of a flat rock, that lay on a level with the water.

"Where are we? and what is next to be done?" demanded Heyward, perceiving that the exertions of the scout had ceased.

"You are at the foot of Glenn's,"[2] returned the other, speaking aloud, without fear of consequences, within the roar of the cataract; "and the next thing is to make a steady landing, lest the canoe upset, and you should go down again the hard road we have travelled, faster than you came up; 'tis a hard rift to stem, when the river is a little swelled; and five is an unnatural number to keep dry, in the hurry-skurry, with a little birchen bark and gum. There, go you all on the rock, and I will bring up the Mohicans with the venison. A man had better sleep without his scalp, than famish in the midst of plenty."

His passengers gladly complied with these directions. As the last foot touched the rock, the canoe whirled from its station, when the tall form of the scout was seen, for an instant, gliding above the waters, before it disappeared in the impenetrable darkness that rested on the bed of the river. Left by their guide, the travellers remained a few minutes in helpless ignorance, afraid even to move along the broken rocks, lest a false step should precipitate them down some one of the many deep and roaring caverns, into which the water seemed to tumble, on every side of them. Their suspense, however, was soon relieved; for aided by the skill of the natives, the canoe shot back into the eddy, and floated again at the side of the low rock before they thought the scout had even time to rejoin his companions.

"We are now fortified, garrisoned, and provisioned," cried Heyward, cheerfully, "and may set Montcalm and his allies at defiance. How, now, my vigilant sentinel, can you see anything of those you call the Iroquois, on the mainland?"

"I call them Iroquois, because to me every native, who speaks a foreign tongue, is accounted an enemy, though he may pretend to serve the king! If Webb wants faith and honesty in an Indian, let him bring out the tribes of the Delawares, and send these greedy and lying Mohawks and Oneidas, with their six nations of varlets, where in nature they belong, among the French!"

"We should then exchange a warlike for a useless friend! I have heard that the Delawares have laid aside the hatchet, and are content to be called women!"

"Ay, shame on the Hollanders and Iroquois, who circumvented them by their deviltries, into such a treaty! But I have known them for twenty years, and I call him liar, that says cowardly blood runs in the veins of a Delaware. You have driven their tribes from the seashore, and would now believe what their enemies say, that you may sleep at night upon an easy pillow. No, no; to me, every Indian who speaks a foreign tongue is an Iroquois, whether the castle of his tribe be in Canada, or be in New York."

Heyward, perceiving that the stubborn adherence of the scout to the cause of his friends the Delawares or Mohicans, for they were branches of the same numerous people, was likely to prolong a useless discussion, changed the subject.

"Treaty or no treaty, I know full well, that your two companions are brave and cautious warriors! have they heard or seen anything of our enemies?"

"An Indian is a mortal to be felt afore he is seen," returned the scout, ascending the rock, and throwing the deer carelessly down. "I trust to other signs than such as come in at the eye, when I am outlying on the trail of the Mingos."

"Do your ears tell you that they have traced our retreat?"

"I should be sorry to think they had, though this is a spot that stout courage might hold for a smart skrimmage. I will not deny, however, but the horses cowered when I passed them, as though they scented the wolves; and a wolf is a beast that is apt to hover about an Indian ambushment, craving the offals of the deer the savages kill."

"You forget the buck at your feet! or, may we not owe their visit to the dead colt? Ha! what noise is that?"

"Poor Miriam!" murmured the stranger; "thy foal was fore-ordained to become a prey to ravenous beasts!" Then, suddenly lifting up his voice, amid the eternal din of the waters, he sang aloud,—

"First born of Egypt, smite did He,
Of mankind, and of beast also;
O, Egypt! wonders sent 'midst thee,
On Pharaoh and his servants too!"

"The death of the colt sits heavy on the heart of its owner," said the scout; "but it's a good sign to see a man account upon his dumb friends. He has the religion of the matter, in believing what is to happen will happen; and with such a consolation, it won't be long afore he submits to the rationality of killing a four-footed beast, to save the lives of human men. It may be as you say," he continued, reverting to the purport of Heyward's last remark; "and the greater the reason why we should cut our steaks, and let the carcass drive down the stream, or we shall have the pack howling along the cliffs, begrudging every mouthful we swallow. Besides, though the Delaware tongue is the same as a book to the Iroquois, the cunning varlets are quick enough at understanding the reason of a wolf's howl."

The scout, whilst making his remarks, was busied in collecting certain necessary implements; as he concluded, he moved silently by the group of travellers, accompanied by the Mohicans, who seemed to comprehend his intentions with instinctive readiness, when the whole three disappeared in succession, seeming to vanish against the dark face of a perpendicular rock, that rose to the height of a few yards within as many feet of the water's edge.

Mangua gone. Hawk finds blood on a tree (Mangua shot but not killed), decide not to chase after him go to Mohicans secret hideout. Kill Gumats colt (too loud) hide the other horses, canoe upstream. Smell wolves which mans indiuns near. Hawk + 2 mohicans are gone.

VI

"Those strains that once did sweet in Zion glide;
He wales a portion with judicious care;
And 'Let us worship God,' he says, with solemn air."
Robert Burns, "The Cotters Saturday Night"[1]

HEYWARD, AND his female companions, witnessed this mysterious movement with secret uneasiness; for, though the conduct of the white man had hitherto been above reproach, his rude equipments, blunt address, and strong antipathies, together with the character of his silent associates, were all causes for exciting distrust in minds that had been so recently alarmed by Indian treachery.

The stranger alone disregarded the passing incidents. He seated himself on a projection of the rocks, whence he gave no other signs of consciousness than by the struggles of his spirit, as manifested in frequent and heavy sighs. Smothered voices were next heard, as though men called to each other in the bowels of the earth, when a sudden light flashed upon those without, and laid bare the much-prized secret of the place.

At the farther extremity of a narrow, deep cavern in the rock, whose length appeared much extended by the perspective and the nature of the light by which it was seen, was seated the scout, holding a blazing knot of pine. The strong glare of the fire fell full upon his sturdy, weatherbeaten countenance and forest attire, lending an air of romantic wildness to the aspect of an individual, who, seen by the sober light of day, would have exhibited the peculiarities of a man remarkable for the strangeness of his dress, the iron-like inflexibility of his frame, and the singular compound of quick, vigilant sagacity, and of exquisite simplicity, that by turns usurped the possession of his muscular features. At a little distance in advance stood Uncas, his whole person thrown powerfully into view. The travellers anxiously regarded the upright, flexible figure of the young Mohican, graceful and unrestrained in the attitudes and movements of nature. Though his person was more than usually screened by a green and fringed hunting-shirt, like that of the white man, there was no concealment to his dark, glancing, fearless eye, alike terrible and calm; the bold outline of his high, haughty features, pure in their native red; or to the dignified elevation of his receding forehead, together with all the finest proportions of a noble head, bared to the generous scalping tuft. It was the first opportunity possessed by Duncan and his companions, to view the marked lineaments of either of their Indian attendants, and each individual of the party felt relieved from a burden of doubt, as the proud and determined, though wild expression of the features of the young warrior forced itself on their notice. They felt it might be a being partially benighted in the vale of ignorance, but it could not be one who would willingly devote his rich natural gifts to the purposes of wanton treachery. The ingenuous Alice gazed at his free air and proud carriage, as she would have looked upon some precious relic of the

Grecian chisel, to which life had been imparted by the intervention of a miracle; while Heyward, though accustomed to see the perfection of form which abounds among the uncorrupted natives, openly expressed his admiration at such an unblemished specimen of the noblest proportions of man. ↓ *Alice feelings for unchs?*

"I could sleep in peace," whispered Alice, in reply, "with such a fearless and generous-looking youth for my sentinel. Surely, Duncan, those cruel murders, those terrific scenes of torture, of which we read and hear so much, are never acted in the presence of such as he!"

"This, certainly, is a rare and brilliant instance of those natural qualities, in which these peculiar people are said to excel," he answered. "I agree with you, Alice, in thinking that such a front and eye were formed rather to intimidate than to deceive; but let us not practise a deception upon ourselves, by expecting any other exhibition of what we esteem virtue than according to the fashion of a savage. As bright examples of great qualities are but too uncommon among Christians, so are they singular and solitary with the Indians; though, for the honor of our common nature, neither are incapable of producing them. Let us then hope that this Mohican may not disappoint our wishes, but prove, what his looks assert him to be, a brave and constant friend."

"Now Major Heyward speaks as Major Heyward should," said Cora; "who, that looks at this creature of nature, remembers the shade of his skin!"

A short, and apparently an embarrassed silence succeeded this remark, which was interrupted by the scout calling to them, aloud, to enter.

"This fire begins to show too bright a flame," he continued, as they complied, "and might light the Mingos to our undoing. Uncas, drop the blanket, and show the knaves its dark side. This is not such a supper as a major of the Royal Americans has a right to expect, but I've known stout detachments of the corps glad to eat their venison raw, and without a relish too. Here, you see, we have plenty of salt, and can make a quick broil. There's fresh sassafras boughs for the ladies to sit on, which may not be as proud as their my-hog-guinea chairs, but which sends up a sweeter flavor than the skin of any hog can do, be it of Guinea, or be it of any other land. Come, friend, don't be mournful for the colt; 'twas an innocent thing, and had not seen much hardship. Its death will save the creature many a sore back and weary foot!"

Uncas did as the other had directed, and when the voice of Hawkeye ceased, the roar of the cataract sounded like the rumbling of distant thunder.

"Are we quite safe in this cavern?" demanded Heyward. "Is there no danger of surprise? A single armed man, at its entrance, would hold us at his mercy."

A spectral-looking figure stalked from out the darkness behind the scout, and seizing a blazing brand, held it towards the farther extremity of their place of retreat. Alice uttered a faint shriek, and even Cora rose to her feet, as this appalling object moved into the light; but a single word from Heyward calmed them, with the assurance it was only their attendant, Chingachgook, who, lifting another blanket, discovered that the cavern had two outlets. Then, holding the brand, he crossed a deep, narrow chasm in the rocks, which ran at right angles with the passage they were in, but which, unlike that, was open to the heavens, and entered another cave, answering to the description of the first, in every essential particular.

"Such old foxes as Chingachgook and myself are not often caught in a burrow with one hole," said Hawkeye, laughing; "you can easily see the cunning of the place—the rock is black limestone, which everybody knows is soft; it makes no uncomfortable pillow, where brush and pine wood is scarce; well, the fall was once a few yards below us, and I dare to say was, in its time, as regular and as handsome a sheet of water as any along the Hudson. But old age is a great injury to good looks, as these sweet young ladies have yet to l'arn! The place is sadly changed! These rocks are full of cracks, and in some places they are softer than at othersome, and the water has worked out deep hollows for itself, until it has fallen back, ay, some hundred feet, breaking here and wearing there, until the falls have neither shape nor consistency."

"In what part of them are we?" asked Heyward.

"Why, we are nigh the spot that Providence first placed them at, but where, it seems, they were too rebellious to stay. The rock proved softer on each side of us, and so they left the centre of the river bare and dry, first working out these two little holes for us to hide in."

"We are then on an island?"

"Ay! there are the falls on two sides of us, and the river above and below. If you had daylight, it would be worth the trouble to step up on the height of this rock, and look at the perversity of the water. It falls by no rule at all; sometimes it leaps, sometimes it tumbles; there, it skips; here, it shoots; in one place 'tis white as snow, and in another 'tis green as grass; hereabouts, it pitches into deep hollows, that rumble and quake the 'arth; and hereaway, it ripples and sings like a brook, fashioning whirlpools and gulleys in the old stone, as if 'twas no harder than trodden clay. The whole design of the river seems disconcerted. First it runs smoothly, as if meaning to go down the descent as things were ordered; then it angles about and faces the shores; nor are there places wanting where it looks backward, as if unwilling to leave the wilderness, to mingle with the salt! Ay, lady, the fine cobweb-looking cloth you wear at your throat, is coarse, and like a fish-net, to little spots I can show you, where the river fabricates all sorts of images, as if, having broke loose from order, it would try its hand at everything. And yet what does it amount to! After the water has been suffered to have its will, for a time, like a headstrong man, it is gathered together by the hand that made it, and a few rods below you may see it all, flowing on steadily towards the sea, as was foreordained from the first foundation of the 'arth!"

While his auditors received a cheering assurance of the security of their place of concealment, from this untutored description of Glenn's they were much inclined to judge differently from Hawkeye, of its wild beauties. But they were not in a situation to suffer their thoughts to dwell on the charms of natural objects; and, as the scout had not found it necessary to cease his culinary labors while he spoke, unless to point out, with a broken fork, the direction of some particularly obnoxious point in the rebellious stream, they now suffered their attention to be drawn to the necessary, though more vulgar consideration of their supper.

The repast, which was greatly aided by the addition of a few delicacies that Heyward had the precaution to bring with him when they left their horses, was exceedingly refreshing to the wearied party. Uncas acted as attendant to the females, performing all the little offices within his power, with a mixture of dignity and anxious grace, that served to amuse Heyward, who well knew that it was an utter innovation on the Indian customs, which forbid their warriors to descend to any menial employment, especially in favor of their women. As the rites of hospitality were, however, considered sacred among them, this little departure from the dignity of manhood excited no audible comment. Had there been one there sufficiently disengaged to become a close observer, he might have fancied that the services of the young chief were not entirely impartial. That while he tendered to Alice the gourd of sweet water and the venison in a trencher, neatly carved from the knot of the pepperidge, with sufficient courtesy, in performing the same offices to her sister, his dark eye lingered on her rich, speaking countenance. Once or twice he was compelled to speak, to command the attention of those he served. In such cases, he made use of English, broken and imperfect, but sufficiently intelligible, and which he rendered so mild and musical, by his deep, guttural voice, that it never failed to cause both ladies to look up in admiration and astonishment. In the course of these civilities, a few sentences were exchanged, that served to establish the appearance of an amicable intercourse between the parties.

In the meanwhile, the gravity of Chingachgook remained immovable. He had seated himself more within the circle of light, where the frequent uneasy glances of his guests were better enabled to separate the natural expression of his face from the artificial terrors of the warpaint. They found a strong resemblance between father and son, with the difference that might be expected from age and hardships. The fierceness of his countenance now seemed to slumber, and in its place was to be seen the quiet, vacant composure, which distinguishes an Indian warrior, when his faculties are not required for any of the greater purposes of his existence. It was, however, easy to be seen, by the occasional gleams that shot across his swarthy visage, that it was only necessary to arouse his passions, in order to give full effect to the terrific device which he had adopted to intimidate his enemies. On the other hand, the quick, roving eye of the scout seldom rested. He ate and drank with an appetite that no sense of danger could disturb, but his vigilance seemed never to desert him. Twenty times the gourd or the venison was suspended before his lips, while his head was turned aside, as though he listened to some distant and distrusted sounds—a movement that never failed to recall his guests from regarding the novelties of their situation, to a recollection of the alarming reasons that had driven them to seek it. As these frequent pauses were never followed by any remark, the momentary uneasiness they created quickly passed away, and for a time was forgotten.

"Come, friend," said Hawkeye, drawing out a keg from beneath a cover of leaves, towards the close of the repast, and addressing the stranger who sat at his elbow, doing great justice to his culinary skill, "try a little spruce; 'twill wash away all thoughts of the colt, and quicken the life in your bosom. I drink to our better friendship, hoping that a little horse-flesh may leave no heartburnings atween us. How do you name yourself?"

"Gamut—David Gamut," returned the singing-master, preparing to wash down his sorrows in a powerful draught of the woodman's high-flavored and well-laced compound.

"A very good name, and, I dare say, handed down

from honest forefathers. I'm an admirator of names, though the Christian fashions fall far below savage customs in this particular. The biggest coward I ever knew was called Lyon; and his wife, Patience, would scold you out of hearing in less time than a hunted deer would run a rod. With an Indian 'tis a matter of conscience; what he calls himself, he generally is—not that Chingachgook, which signifies Big Sarpent, is really a snake, big or little; but that he understands the windings and turnings of human natur', and is silent, and strikes his enemies when they least expect him. What may be your calling?"

"I am an unworthy instructor in the art of psalmody."

"Anan!"

"I teach singing to the youths of the Connecticut levy."[2]

"You might be better employed. The young hounds go laughing and singing too much already through the woods, when they ought not to breathe louder than a fox in his cover. Can you use the smooth bore, or handle the rifle?"

"Praised be God, I have never had occasion to meddle with murderous implements!"

"Perhaps you understand the compass, and lay down the water-courses and mountains of the wilderness on paper, in order that they who follow may find places by their given names?"

"I practise no such employment."

"You have a pair of legs that might make a long path seem short! you journey sometimes, I fancy, with tidings for the general."

"Never; I follow no other than my own high vocation, which is instruction in sacred music!"

" 'Tis a strange calling!" muttered Hawkeye, with an

inward laugh, "to go through life, like a catbird, mocking all the ups and downs that may happen to come out of other men's throats. Well, friend, I suppose it is your gift, and mustn't be denied any more than if 'twas shooting, or some other better inclination. Let us hear what you can do in that way; 'twill be a friendly manner of saying good-night, for 'tis time that these ladies should be getting strength for a hard and a long push, in the pride of the morning, afore the Maquas are stirring!"

"With joyful pleasure do I consent," said David, adjusting his iron-rimmed spectacles, and producing his beloved little volume, which he immediately tendered to Alice. "What can be more fitting and consolatory, than to offer up evening praise, after a day of such exceeding jeopardy!"

Alice smiled; but regarding Heyward, she blushed and hesitated.

"Indulge yourself," he whispered: "ought not the suggestion of the worthy namesake of the Psalmist to have its weight at such a moment?"

Encouraged by his opinion, Alice did what her pious inclinations and her keen relish for gentle sounds, had before so strongly urged. The book was open at a hymn not ill adapted to their situation, and in which the poet, no longer goaded by his desire to excel the inspired king of Israel, had discovered some chastened and respectable powers. Cora betrayed a disposition to support her sister, and the sacred song proceeded, after the indispensable preliminaries of the pitch-pipe and the tune had been duly attended to by the methodical David.

The air was solemn and slow. At times it rose to the fullest compass of the rich voices of the females, who hung over their little book in holy excitement, and again it sank so low, that the rushing of the waters ran through their melody, like a hollow accompaniment. The natural taste and true ear of David governed and modified the sounds to suit the confined cavern, every crevice and cranny of which was filled with the thrilling notes of their flexible voices. The Indians riveted their eyes on the rocks, and listened with an attention that seemed to turn them into stone. But the scout, who had placed his chin in his hand, with an expression of cold indifference, gradually suffered his rigid features to relax, until, as verse succeeded verse, he felt his iron nature subdued, while his recollection was carried back to boyhood, when his ears had been accustomed to listen to similar sounds of praise, in the settlements of the colony. His roving eyes began to moisten, and before the hymn was ended, scalding tears rolled out of fountains that had long seemed dry, and followed each other down those cheeks, that had oftener felt the storms of heaven than any testimonials of weakness. The singers were dwelling on one of those low, dying chords, which the ear devours with such greedy rapture, as if conscious that it is about to lose them, when a cry, that seemed neither human nor earthly, rose in the outward air, penetrating not only the recesses of the cavern, but to the inmost hearts of all who heard it. It was followed by a stillness apparently as deep as if the waters had been checked in their furious progress, at such a horrid and unusual interruption.

"What is it?" murmured Alice, after a few moments of terrible suspense.

"What is it?" repeated Heyward aloud.

Neither Hawkeye nor the Indians made any reply. They listened, as if expecting the sound would be repeated, with a manner that expressed their own astonishment. At length they spoke together earnestly, in the Delaware language, when Uncas, passing by the inner and most concealed aperture, cautiously left the cavern. When he had gone, the scout first spoke in English.

"What it is, or what it is not, none here can tell; though two of us have ranged the woods for more than thirty years! I did believe there was no cry that Indians or beast could make, that my ears had not heard; but this has proved that I was only a vain and conceited mortal!"

"Was it not, then, the shout the warriors make when they wish to intimidate their enemies?" asked Cora, who stood drawing her veil about her person, with a calmness to which her agitated sister was a stranger.

"No, no; this was bad, and shocking, and had a sort of unhuman sound; but when you once hear the war-whoop, you will never mistake it for anything else! Well, Uncas!" speaking in Delaware to the young chief as he re-entered, "what see you? do our lights shine through the blankets?"

The answer was short, and apparently decided, being given in the same tongue.

"There is nothing to be seen without," continued Hawkeye, shaking his head in discontent; "and our hiding-place is still in darkness! Pass into the other cave, you that need it, and seek for sleep; we must be afoot long before the sun, and make the most of our time to get to Edward, while the Mingos are taking their morning nap."

Cora set the example of compliance, with a steadiness that taught the more timid Alice the necessity of obedience. Before leaving the place, however, she whispered a request to Duncan that he would follow. Uncas raised the blanket for their passage, and as the sisters turned to thank him for this act of attention, they saw the scout seated again before the dying embers, with his face resting on his hands in a manner which showed how deeply he brooded on the unaccountable interruption which had broken up their evening devotions.

Heyward took with him a blazing knot, which threw a dim light through the narrow vista of their new apartment. Placing it in a favorable position, he joined the females, who now found themselves alone with him for the first time since they had left the friendly ramparts of Fort Edward.

"Leave us not, Duncan," said Alice; "we cannot sleep in such a place as this, with that horrid cry still ringing in our ears!"

"First let us examine into the security of your fortress," he answered, "and then we will speak of rest."

He approached the farther end of the cavern, to an outlet, which, like the others, was concealed by blankets, and removing the thick screen, breathed the fresh and reviving air from the cataract. One arm of the river flowed through a deep, narrow ravine, which its current had worn in the soft rock, directly beneath his feet, forming an effectual defence, as he believed, against any danger from that quarter; the water, a few rods above them, plunging, glancing, and sweeping along, in its most violent and broken manner.

"Nature has made an impenetrable barrier on this side," he continued, pointing down the perpendicular declivity into the dark current, before he dropped the blanket; "and as you know that good men and true are on guard in front, I see no reason why the advice of our honest host should be disregarded. 1 am certain Cora will join me in saying that sleep is necessary to you both."

"Cora may submit to the justice of your opinion, though she cannot put it in practise," returned the elder sister, who had placed herself by the side of Alice, on a couch of sassafras; "there would be other causes to chase away sleep, though we had been spared the shock of this mysterious noise. Ask yourself, Heyward, can daughters forget the anxiety a father must endure, whose children lodge, he knows not where or how, in such a wilderness, and in the midst of so many perils?"

"He is a soldier, and knows how to estimate the chances of the woods."

"He is a father, and cannot deny his nature."

"How kind has he ever been to all my follies! how tender and indulgent to all my wishes!" sobbed Alice. "We have been selfish, sister, in urging our visit at such hazard!"

"I may have been rash in pressing his consent in a moment of much embarrassment, but I would have proved to him, that however others might neglect him in his strait, his children at least were faithful!"

"When he heard of your arrival at Edward," said Heyward, kindly, "there was a powerful struggle in his bosom between fear and love; though the latter, heightened, if possible, by so long a separation, quickly prevailed. 'It is the spirit of my noble-minded Cora that leads them, Duncan,' he said, 'and I will not balk it. Would to God, that he who holds the honor of our royal master in his guardianship, would show but half her firmness!' "

"And did he not speak of me, Heyward?" demanded Alice, with jealous affection. "Surely, he forgot not altogether his little Elsie?"

"That was impossible," returned the young man; "he called you by a thousand endearing epithets, that I may not presume to use, but to the justice of which I can warmly testify. Once, indeed, he said—"

Duncan ceased speaking; for while his eyes were riveted on those of Alice, who had turned towards him with the eagerness of filial affection, to catch his words, the same strong horrid cry, as before, filled the air, and rendered him mute. A long, breathless silence succeeded, during which each looked at the others in fearful expectation of hearing the sound repeated. At length the blanket was slowly raised, and the scout stood in the aperture with a countenance whose firmness evidently began to give way, before a mystery that seemed to threaten some danger, against which all his cunning and experience might prove of no avail.

Found hawk + mohicans in cave. Uncas shows
intrest in Cora. Gamut talks + sings. Hawkeye
remembers his white childhood. Loud cry
outside, Uncas investigates, finds nothing.
Heyward Cora + Alice go to sleep in safe cavern,
Cora wishes they hadn't come. Loud cry,
Hawk investigates, comes back w/ mystification
on his face

VII

"They do not sleep.
On yonder cliffs, a grisly band,
I see them sit."
Thomas Gray, "The Bard"[1]

"Twould be neglecting a warning that is given for our good, to lie hid any longer," said Hawkeye, "when such sounds are raised in the forest! The gentle ones may keep close, but the Mohicans and I will watch upon the rock, where I suppose a major of the 60th would wish to keep us company."

"Is then our danger so pressing?" asked Cora.

"He who makes strange sounds, and gives them out for man's information, alone knows our danger. I should think myself wicked, unto rebellion against his will, was I to burrow with such warnings in the air! Even the weak soul who passes his days in singing, is stirred by the cry, and, as he says, is 'ready to go forth to the battle.' If 'twere only a battle, it would be a thing understood by us all, and easily managed; but I have heard that when such shrieks are atween heaven and 'arth, it betokens another sort of warfare!"

"If all our reasons for fear, my friend, are confined to such as proceed from supernatural causes, we have but little occasion to be alarmed," continued the undisturbed Cora; "are you certain that our enemies have not invented some new and ingenious method to strike us with terror, that their conquest may become more easy?"

"Lady," returned the scout, solemnly, "I have listened to all the sounds of the woods for thirty years, as a man will listen, whose life and death depend on the quickness of his ears. There is no whine of the panther, no whistle of the catbird, nor any invention of the devilish Mingos, that can cheat me! I have heard the forest moan like mortal men in their affliction; often, and again, have I listened to the wind playing its music in the branches of the girdled trees; and I have heard the lightning cracking in the air, like the snapping of blazing brush, as it spitted forth sparks and forked flames; but never have I thought that I heard more than the pleasure of Him who sported with the things of his hand. But neither the Mohicans, nor I, who am a white man without a cross, can explain the cry just heard. We, therefore, believe it a sign given for our good."

"It is extraordinary!" said Heyward, taking his pistols from the place where he had laid them on entering; "be it a sign of peace or a signal of war, it must be looked to. Lead the way, my friend; I follow."

On issuing from their place of confinement, the whole party instantly experienced a grateful renovation of spirits, by exchanging the pent air of the hiding-place for the cool and invigorating atmosphere, which played around the whirlpools and pitches of the cataract. A heavy evening breeze swept along the surface of the river, and seemed to drive the roar of the falls into the recesses of their own caverns, whence it issued heavily and constant, like thunder rumbling beyond the distant hills. The moon had risen, and its light was already glancing here and there on the waters above them; but the extremity of the rock where they stood still lay in shadow. With the exception of the sounds produced by the rushing waters, and an occasional breathing of the air, as it murmured past them in fitful currents, the scene was as still as night and solitude could make it. In vain were the eyes of each individual bent along the opposite shores, in quest of some signs of life, that might explain the nature of the interruption they had heard. Their anxious and eager looks were baffled by the deceptive light, or rested only on naked rocks, and straight and immovable trees.

"There is nothing to be seen but the gloom and quiet of a lovely evening," whispered Duncan: "how much should we prize such a scene, and all this breathing solitude, at any other moment, Cora! Fancy yourselves in security and what now, perhaps, increases your terror, may be made conducive to enjoyment—"

"Listen!" interrupted Alice.

The caution was unnecessary. Once more the same sound arose, as if from the bed of the river, and having broken out of the narrow bounds of the cliffs, was heard undulating through the forest, in distant and dying cadences.

"Can any here give a name to such a cry?" demanded Hawkeye, when the last echo was lost in the woods; "if so, let him speak; for myself, I judge it not to belong to 'arth!"

"Here, then, is one who can undeceive you," said Duncan; "I know the sound full well, for often have I heard it on the field of battle, and in situations which are frequent in a soldier's life. 'Tis the horrid shriek that a horse will give in his agony; oftener drawn from him in pain, though sometimes in terror. My charger is either a prey to the beasts of the forest, or he sees his danger without the power to avoid it. The sound might deceive me in the cavern, but in the open air I know it too well to be wrong."

The scout and his companions listened to this simple explanation with the interest of men who imbibe new ideas, at the same time that they get rid of old ones, which had proved disagreeable inmates. The two latter uttered their usual and expressive exclamation, "Hugh!" as the truth first glanced upon their minds, while the former, after a short musing pause, took upon himself to reply.

"I cannot deny your words," he said; "for I am little skilled in horses, though born where they abound. The wolves must be hovering above their heads on the bank, and the timorsome creatures are calling on man for help, in the best manner they are able. Uncas,"—he spoke in Delaware—"Uncas, drop down in the canoe, and whirl a brand among the pack; or fear may do what the wolves can't get at to perform, and leave us without horses in the morning, when we shall have so much need to journey swiftly!"

The young native had already descended to the water, to comply, when a long howl was raised on the edge of the river, and was borne swiftly off into the depths of the forest, as though the beasts, of their own accord, were abandoning their prey in sudden terror. Uncas, with instinctive quickness, receded, and the three foresters held another of their low, earnest conferences.

"We have been like hunters who have lost the points of the heavens, and from whom the sun has been hid for days," said Hawkeye, turning away from his companions; "now we begin again to know the signs of our course, and the paths are cleared from briers! Seat yourselves in the shade which the moon throws from yonder beech—'tis thicker than that of the pines—and let us wait for that which the Lord may choose to send next. Let all your conversation be in whispers; though it would be better, and perhaps, in the end, wiser, if each one held discourse with his own thoughts, for a time."

The manner of the scout was seriously impressive, though no longer distinguished by any signs of unmanly apprehension. It was evident that his momentary weakness had vanished with the explanation of a mystery which his own experience had not served to fathom; and though he now felt all the realities of their actual condition, that he was prepared to meet them with the energy of his hardy nature. This feeling seemed also common to the natives, who placed themselves in positions which commanded a full view of both shores, while their own persons were effectually concealed from observation. In such circumstances, common prudence dictated that Heyward and his companions should imitate a caution that proceeded from so intelligent a source. The young man drew a pile of the sassafras from the cave, and placing it in the chasm which separated the two caverns, it was occupied by the sisters, who were thus protected by the rocks from any missiles, while their anxiety was relieved by the assurance that no danger could approach without a warning. Heyward himself was posted at hand, so near that he might communicate with his companions without raising his voice to a dangerous elevation, while David, in imitation of the woodsmen, bestowed his person in such a manner among the fissures of the rocks, that his ungainly limbs were no longer offensive to the eye.

In this manner, hours passed by without further interruption. The moon reached the zenith, and shed its mild light perpendicularly on the lovely sight of the sisters slumbering peacefully in each other's arms. Duncan cast the wide shawl of Cora before a spectacle he so much loved to contemplate, and then suffered his own head to seek a pillow on the rock. David began to utter sounds that would have shocked his delicate organs in more wakeful moments; in short, all but Hawkeye and the Mohicans lost every idea of consciousness, in uncontrollable drowsiness. But the watchfulness of these vigilant protectors neither tired nor slumbered. Immovable as that rock, of which each appeared to form a part, they lay, with their eyes roving, without intermission, along the dark margin of trees that bounded the adjacent shores of the narrow stream. Not a sound escaped them; the most subtle examination could not have told they breathed. It was evident that this excess of caution proceeded from an experience that no subtlety on the part of their enemies could deceive. It was, however, continued without any apparent consequences, until the moon had set, and a pale streak above the tree-tops, at the bend of the river a little below, announced the approach of day.

Then, for the first time, Hawkeye was seen to stir. He crawled along the rock, and shook Duncan from his heavy slumbers.

"Now is the time to journey," he whispered; "awake the gentle ones, and be ready to get into the canoe when I bring it to the landing-place."

"Have you had a quiet night?" said Heyward; "for myself, I believe sleep has got the better of my vigilance."

"All is yet still as midnight. Be silent, but be quick."

By this time Duncan was thoroughly awake, and he immediately lifted the shawl from the sleeping females.

The motion caused Cora to raise her hand as if to repulse him, while Alice murmured in her soft, gentle voice, "No, no, dear father, we were not deserted; Duncan was with us!"

"Yes, sweet innocence," whispered the youth; "Duncan is here, and while life continues or danger remains, he will never quit thee. Cora! Alice! awake! The hour has come to move!"

A loud shriek from the younger of the sisters, and the form of the other standing upright before him, in bewildered horror, was the unexpected answer he received. While the words were still on the lips of Heyward, there had arisen such a tumult of yells and cries as served to drive the swift currents of his own blood back from its bounding course into the fountains of his heart. It seemed, for near a minute, as if demons of hell had possessed themselves of the air about them, and were venting their savage humors in barbarous sounds. The cries came from no particular direction, though it was evident they filled the woods, and as the appalled listeners easily imagined, the caverns of the falls, the rocks, the bed of the river, and the upper air. David raised his tall person in the midst of the infernal din, with a hand on either ear, exclaiming—

"Whence comes this discord! Has hell broke loose, that man should utter sounds like these!"

The bright flashes and the quick reports of a dozen rifles, from the opposite banks of the stream, followed this incautious exposure of his person, and left the unfortunate singing-master senseless on that rock where he had been so long slumbering. The Mohicans boldly sent back the intimidating yell of their enemies, who raised a shout of savage triumph at the fall of Gamut. The flash of rifles was then quick and close between them, but either party was too well skilled to leave even a limb exposed to the hostile aim. Duncan listened with intense anxiety for the strokes of the paddle, believing that flight was now their only refuge. The river glanced by with its ordinary velocity, but the canoe was nowhere to be seen on its dark waters. He had just fancied they were cruelly deserted by the scout, as a stream of flame issued from the rock beneath him, and a fierce yell, blended with a shriek of agony, announced that the messenger of death, sent from the fatal weapon of Hawkeye, had found a victim. At this slight repulse the assailants instantly withdrew, and gradually the place became as still as before the sudden tumult.

Duncan seized the favorable moment to spring to the body of Gamut, which he bore within the shelter of the narrow chasm that protected the sisters. In another minute the whole party was collected in this spot of comparative safety.

"The poor fellow has saved his scalp," said Hawkeye, coolly passing his hand over the head of David; "but he is a proof that a man may be born with too long a tongue! 'Twas downright madness to show six feet of flesh and blood, on a naked rock, to the raging savages. I only wonder he has escaped with life."

"Is he not dead?" demanded Cora, in a voice whose husky tones showed how powerfully natural horror struggled with her assumed firmness. "Can we do aught to assist the wretched man?"

"No, no! the life is in his heart yet, and after he has slept awhile he will come to himself, and be a wiser man for it, till the hour of his real time shall come," returned Hawkeye, casting another oblique glance at the insensible body, while he filled his charger with admirable nicety. "Carry him in, Uncas, and lay him on the sassafras. The longer his nap lasts the better it will be for him, as I doubt whether he can find a proper cover for such a shape on these rocks; and singing won't do any good with the Iroquois."

"You believe, then, the attack will be renewed?" asked Heyward.

"Do I expect a hungry wolf will satisfy his craving with a mouthful! They have lost a man, and 'tis their fashion, when they meet a loss, and fail in the surprise, to fall back; but we shall have them on again; with new expedients to circumvent us, and master our scalps. Our main hope," he continued, raising his rugged countenance, across which a shade of anxiety just then passed like a darkening cloud, "will be to keep the rock until Munro can send a party to our help! God send it may be soon, and under a leader that knows the Indian customs!"

"You hear our probable fortunes, Cora," said Duncan, "and you know we have everything to hope from the anxiety and experience of your father. Come, then, with Alice, into this cavern, where you, at least, will be safe from the murderous rifles of our enemies and where you may bestow a care suited to your gentle natures on our unfortunate comrade."

The sisters followed him into the outer cave, where David was beginning, by his sighs, to give symptoms of returning consciousness; and then commending the wounded man to their attention, he immediately prepared to leave them.

"Duncan!" said the tremulous voice of Cora, when he had reached the mouth of the cavern. He turned, and beheld the speaker, whose color had changed to a deadly paleness, and whose lip quivered, gazing after him, with an expression of interest which immediately recalled him to her side. "Remember, Duncan, how necessary your safety is to our own—how you bear a father's sacred trust—how much depends on your discretion and care—in short," she added, while the tell-tale blood stole over her features, crimsoning her very temples, "how very deservedly dear you are to all of the name of Munro."

"If anything could add to my own base love of life," said Heyward, suffering his unconscious eyes to wander to the youthful form of the silent Alice, "it would be so kind an assurance. As major of the 60th, our honest host will tell you I must take my share of the fray; but our task will be easy; it is merely to keep these blood-hounds at bay for a few hours."

Without waiting for reply, he tore himself from the presence of the sisters, and joined the scout and his companions, who still lay within the protection of the little chasm between the two caves.

"I tell you, Uncas," said the former, as Heyward joined them, "you are wasteful of your powder, and the kick of the rifle disconcerts your aim! Little powder, light lead, and a long arm, seldom fail of bringing the death screech from a Mingo! At least, such has been my experience with the creatur's. Come, friends; let us to our covers, for no man can tell when or where a Maqua will strike his blow."

The Indians silently repaired to their appointed stations, which were fissures in the rocks, whence they could command the approaches to the foot of the falls. In the centre of the little island, a few short and stunted pines had found root, forming a thicket, into which Hawkeye darted with the swiftness of a deer, followed by

the active Duncan. Here they secured themselves, as
well as circumstances would permit, among the shrubs
and fragments of stone that were scattered about the
place. Above them was a bare, rounded rock, on each
side of which the water played its gambols, and plunged
into the abysses beneath, in the manner already described. As the day had now dawned, the opposite shores
no longer presented a confused outline, but they were
able to look into the woods, and distinguish objects beneath the canopy of gloomy pines.

A long and anxious watch succeeded, but without any
further evidences of a renewed attack; and Duncan
began to hope that their fire had proved more fatal than
was supposed, and that their enemies had been effectually repulsed. When he ventured to utter this impression
to his companion, it was met by Hawkeye with an incredulous shake of the head.

"You know not the nature of a Maqua, if you think he
is so easily beaten back without a scalp!" he answered. "If
there was one of the imps yelling this morning, there
were forty! and they know our number and quality too
well to give up the chase so soon. Hist! look into the
water above, just where it breaks over the rocks. I am no
mortal, if the risky devils haven't swam down upon the
very pitch, and, as bad luck would have it, they have hit
the head of the island. Hist! man, keep close! or the hair
will be off your crown in the turning of a knife!"

Heyward lifted his head from the cover, and beheld
what he justly considered a prodigy of rashness and skill.
The river had worn away the edge of the soft rock in such
a manner, as to render its first pitch less abrupt and perpendicular than is usual at waterfalls. With no other
guide than the ripple of the stream where it met the head

of the island, a party of their insatiable foes had ventured into the current, and swam down upon this point, knowing the ready access it would give, if successful, to their intended victims. As Hawkeye ceased speaking, four human heads could be seen peering above a few logs of drift-wood that had lodged on these naked rocks, and which had probably suggested the idea of the practicability of the hazardous undertaking. At the next moment, a fifth form was seen floating over the green edge of the fall, a little from the line of the island. The savage struggled powerfully to gain the point of safety, and, favored by the glancing water, he was already stretching forth an arm to meet the grasp of his companions, when he shot away again with the whirling current, appeared to rise into the air, with uplifted arms and starting eyeballs, and fell, with a sullen plunge, into that deep and yawning abyss over which he hovered. A single, wild, despairing shriek rose from the cavern, and all was hushed again, as the grave.

The first generous impulse of Duncan was to rush to the rescue of the hapless wretch; but he felt himself bound to the spot by the iron grasp of the immovable scout.

"Would ye bring certain death upon us, by telling the Mingos where we lie?" demanded Hawkeye, sternly; " 'tis a charge of powder saved, and ammunition is as precious now as breath to a worried deer! Freshen the priming of your pistols—the mist of the falls is apt to dampen the brimstone—and stand firm for a close struggle, while I fire on their rush."

He placed his finger in his mouth, and drew a long, shrill whistle, which was answered from the rocks that were guarded by the Mohicans. Duncan caught glimpses of heads above the scattered drift-wood, as this signal rose on the air, but they disappeared again as suddenly as they had glanced upon his sight. A low, rustling sound next drew his attention behind him, and turning his head, he beheld Uncas within a few feet, creeping to his side. Hawkeye spoke to him in Delaware, when the young chief took his position with singular caution and undisturbed coolness. To Heyward this was a moment of feverish and impatient suspense; though the scout saw fit to select it as a fit occasion to read a lecture to his more youthful associates on the art of using fire-arms with discretion.

"Of all we'pons," he commenced, "the long-barrelled, true-grooved, soft-metalled rifle is the most dangerous in skilful hands, though it wants a strong arm, a quick eye, and great judgment in charging, to put forth all its beauties. The gunsmiths can have but little insight into their trade, when they make their fowling-pieces and short horsemen's—"

He was interrupted by the low but expressive "Hugh!" of Uncas.

"I see them, boy, I see them!" continued Hawkeye; "they are gathering for the rush, or they would keep their dingy backs below the logs. Well, let them," he added, examining his flint; "the leading man certainly comes on to his death, though it should be Montcalm himself!"

At that moment the woods were filled with another burst of cries, and at the signal four savages sprang from the cover of the drift-wood. Heyward felt a burning desire to rush forward to meet them, so intense was the delirious anxiety of the moment; but he was restrained by the deliberate examples of the scout and Uncas. When their foes who leaped over the black rock that divided them, with long bounds, uttering the wildest yells, were within a few rods, the rifle of Hawkeye slowly rose among the shrubs, and poured out its fatal contents. The foremost Indian bounded like a stricken deer, and fell headlong among the clefts of the island.

"Now, Uncas!" cried the scout, drawing his long knife, while his quick eyes began to flash with ardor, "take the last of the screeching imps; of the other two we are sartain!"

He was obeyed; and but two enemies remained to be overcome. Heyward had given one of his pistols to Hawkeye, and together they rushed down a little declivity towards their foes; they discharged their weapons at the same instant, and equally without success.

"I know'd it! and I said it!" muttered the scout, whirling the despised little implement over the falls with bitter disdain. "Come on, ye bloody minded hell-hounds! ye meet a man without a cross!"

The words were barely uttered, when he encountered a savage of gigantic stature, and of the fiercest mien. At the same moment, Duncan found himself engaged with the other, in a similar contest of hand to hand. With ready skill, Hawkeye and his antagonist each grasped that uplifted arm of the other which held the dangerous knife. For near a minute they stood looking one another in the eye, and gradually exerting the power of their muscles for the mastery. At length, the toughened sinews of the white man prevailed over the less practised limbs of the native. The arm of the latter slowly gave way before the increasing force of the scout, who suddenly wresting his armed hand from the grasp of the foe, drove the sharp weapon through his naked bosom to the heart. In the meantime Heyward had been pressed in a more deadly struggle. His slight sword was snapped in the first encounter. As he was destitute of any other means of defence, his safety now depended entirely on bodily strength and resolution. Though deficient in neither of these qualities, he had met an enemy every way his equal. Happily, he soon succeeded in disarming his adversary, whose knife fell on the rock at their feet; and from this moment it became a fierce struggle, who should cast the other over the dizzy height into a neighboring cavern of the falls. Every successive struggle brought them nearer to the verge, where Duncan perceived the final and conquering effort must be made. Each of the combatants threw all his energies into that effort, and the result was, that both tottered on the brink of the precipice. Heyward felt the grasp of the other at his throat, and saw the grim smile the savage gave, under the revengeful hope that he hurried his enemy to a fate similar to his own, as he felt his body slowly yielding to a resistless power, and the young man experienced the passing agony of such a moment in all its horrors. At that instant of extreme danger, a dark hand and glancing knife appeared before him; the Indian released his hold, as the blood flowed freely from around the severed tendons of the wrist; and while Duncan was drawn backward by the saving arm of Uncas, his charmed eyes were still riveted on the fierce and disappointed countenance of his foe, who fell sullenly and disappointed down the irrecoverable precipice.

"To cover! to cover!" cried Hawkeye, who just then had despatched the enemy; "to cover, for your lives! the work is but half ended!"

The young Mohican gave a shout of triumph, and, followed by Duncan, he glided up the acclivity they had descended to the combat, and sought the friendly shelter of the rocks and shrubs. *Figure out the cry is a horse scared of a wolf. Hears wolves, then the wolves leave as if scared off by a tribe. Hide + fall asleep (except Hawk + Mohicans)*

VIII

"They linger yet,
Avengers of their native land."
Thomas Gray, "The Bard"[1]

THE WARNING CALL of the scout was not uttered without occasion. During the occurrence of the deadly encounter just related, the roar of the falls was unbroken by any human sound whatever. It would seem that interest in the result had kept the natives on the opposite shores in breathless suspense, while the quick evolutions and swift changes in the position of the combatants, effectually prevented a fire that might prove dangerous alike to friend and enemy. But the moment the struggle was decided, a yell arose as fierce and savage as wild and revengeful passions could throw into the air. It was followed by the swift flashes of the rifles, which sent their leaden messengers across the rock in volleys, as though the assailants would pour out their impotent fury on the insensible scene of the fatal contest.

A steady, though deliberate return was made from the rifle of Chingachgook, who had maintained his post throughout the fray with unmoved resolution. When the triumphant shout of Uncas was borne to his ears, the gratified father raised his voice in a single responsive cry, after which his busy piece alone proved that he still guarded his pass with unwearied diligence. In this manner many minutes flew by with the swiftness of thought: the rifles of the assailants speaking, at times, in rattling volleys, and at others, in occasional, scattering shots. Though the rock, the trees, and the shrubs, were cut and torn in a hundred places around the besieged, their cover was so close, and so rigidly maintained, that, as yet, David had been the only sufferer in their little band.

"Let them burn their powder," said the deliberate scout, while bullet after bullet whizzed by the place where he securely lay; "there will be a fine gathering of lead when it is over, and I fancy the imps will tire of the sport, afore these old stones cry out for mercy! Uncas, boy, you waste the kernels by overcharging: and a kicking rifle never carries a true bullet. I told you to take that loping miscreant under the line of white paint; now, if your bullet went a hair's breadth, it went two inches above it. The life lies low in a Mingo, and humanity teaches us to make a quick end of the sarpents."

A quiet smile lighted the haughty features of the young Mohican, betraying his knowledge of the English language, as well as of the other's meaning; but he suffered it to pass away without vindication or reply.

"I cannot permit you to accuse Uncas of want of judgment or of skill," said Duncan; "he saved my life in the coolest and readiest manner, and he has made a friend who never will require to be reminded of the debt he owes."

Uncas partly raised his body, and offered his hand to the grasp of Heyward. During this act of friendship, the two young men exchanged looks of intelligence which caused Duncan to forget the character and condition of his wild associate. In the meanwhile, Hawkeye, who looked on this burst of youthful feeling with a cool but kind regard, made the following reply:—

"Life is an obligation which friends often owe each other in the wilderness. I dare say I may have served Uncas some such turn myself before now; and I very well remember that he has stood between me and death five different times: three times from the Mingos, once in crossing Horican, and—"

"That bullet was better aimed than common!" exclaimed Duncan, involuntarily shrinking from a shot which struck the rock at his side with a smart rebound.

Hawkeye laid his hand on the shapeless metal, and shook his head as he examined it, saying, "Falling lead is never flattened! had it come from the clouds this might have happened!"

But the rifle of Uncas was deliberately raised towards the heavens, directing his companions to a point, where the mystery was immediately explained. A ragged oak grew on the right bank of the river, nearly opposite to their position, which, seeking the freedom of the open space, had inclined so far forward, that its upper branches overhung that arm of the stream which flowed nearest to its own shore. Among the topmost leaves, which scantily concealed the gnarled and stunted limbs, a savage was nestled, partly concealed by the trunk of the tree, and partly exposed, as though looking down upon them to ascertain the effect produced by his treacherous aim.

"These devils will scale heaven to circumvent us to our ruin," said Hawkeye; "keep him in play, boy, until I can bring 'Killdeer' to bear, when we will try his metal on each side of the tree at once."

Uncas delayed his fire until the scout uttered the word. The rifles flashed, the leaves and the bark of the oak flew into the air, and were scattered by the wind, but the Indian answered their assault by a taunting laugh, sending down upon them another bullet in return, that struck the cap of Hawkeye from his head. Once more the savage yells burst out of the woods, and the leaden hail whistled above the heads of the besieged, as if to confine them to a place where they might become easy victims to the enterprise of the warrior who had mounted the tree.

"This must be looked to!" said the scout, glancing about him with an anxious eye. "Uncas, call up your father; we have need of all our we'pons to bring the cunning varmint from his roost."

The signal was instantly given; and, before Hawkeye had reloaded his rifle, they were joined by Chingachgook. When his son pointed out to the experienced warrior the situation of their dangerous enemy, the usual exclamatory "Hugh!" burst from his lips; after which, no further expression of surprise or alarm was suffered to escape him. Hawkeye and the Mohicans conversed earnestly together in Delaware for a few moments, when each quietly took his post, in order to execute the plan they had speedily devised.

The warrior in the oak had maintained a quick, though ineffectual fire, from the moment of his discovery. But his aim was interrupted by the vigilance of his enemies, whose rifles instantaneously bore on any part of his person that was left exposed. Still his bullets fell in the centre of the crouching party. The clothes of Heyward, which rendered him peculiarly conspicuous, were repeatedly cut, and once blood was drawn from a slight wound in his arm.

At length, emboldened by the long and patient watchfulness of his enemies, the Huron attempted a better and more fatal aim. The quick eye of the Mohicans caught the dark line of his lower limbs incautiously exposed through the thin foliage, a few inches from the trunk of the tree. Their rifles made a common report, when, sinking on his wounded limb, part of the body of the savage came into view. Swift as thought, Hawkeye seized the advantage and discharged his fatal weapon into the top of the oak. The leaves were unusually agitated; the dangerous rifle fell from its commanding elevation, and after a few moments of vain struggling, the form of the savage was seen swinging in the wind, while he still grasped a ragged and naked branch of the tree, with hands clenched in desperation.

"Give him, in pity give him—the contents of another rifle!" cried Duncan, turning away his eyes in horror from the spectacle of a fellow-creature in such awful jeopardy.

"Not a karnel!" exclaimed the obdurate Hawkeye; "his death is certain, and we have no powder to spare, for Indian fights sometimes last for days; 'tis their scalps or ours!—and God, who made us, has put into our natures the craving to keep the skin on the head!"

Against this stern and unyielding morality, supported as it was by such visible policy, there was no appeal. From that moment the yells in the forest once more ceased, the fire was suffered to decline, and all eyes, those of friends as well as enemies, became fixed on the hopeless condition of the wretch who was dangling between heaven and earth. The body yielded to the currents of air, and though no murmur or groan escaped the victim, there were instants when he grimly faced his foes, and the anguish of cold despair might be traced, through the intervening distance, in possession of his swarthy lineaments. Three several times the scout raised his piece in mercy, and as often prudence getting the better of his intention, it was again silently lowered. At length one hand of the Huron lost its hold, and dropped exhausted to his side. A desperate and fruitless struggle to recover the branch succeeded, and then the savage was seen for a fleeting instant, grasping wildly at the empty air. The lightning is not quicker than was the flame from the rifle of Hawkeye; the limbs of the victim trembled and contracted, the head fell to the bosom, and the body parted the foaming waters like lead, when the element closed above it, in its ceaseless velocity, and every vestige of the unhappy Huron was lost forever.

No shout of triumph succeeded this important advantage, but even the Mohicans gazed at each other in silent horror. A single yell burst from the woods, and all was again still. Hawkeye, who alone appeared to reason on the occasion, shook his head at his own momentary weakness, even uttering his self-disapprobation aloud.

" 'Twas the last charge in my horn, and the last bullet in my pouch, and 'twas the act of a boy!" he said; "what mattered it whether he struck the rock living or dead! feeling would soon be over. Uncas, lad, go down to the canoe, and bring up the big horn; it is all the powder we have left, and we shall need it to the last grain, or I am ignorant of the Mingo nature."

The young Mohican complied, leaving the scout turning over the useless contents of his pouch, and shaking the empty horn with renewed discontent. From this unsatisfactory examination, however, he was soon called by a loud and piercing exclamation from Uncas, that sounded, even to the unpractised ears of Duncan, as the signal of some new and unexpected calamity. Every thought filled with apprehension for the precious treasure he had concealed in the cavern, the young man started to his feet, totally regardless of the hazard he incurred by such an exposure. As if actuated by a common impulse, his movement was imitated by his companions, and, together, they rushed down the pass to the friendly chasm, with a rapidity that rendered the scattering fire of their enemies perfectly harmless. The unwonted cry had brought the sisters, together with the wounded David, from their place of refuge; and the whole party, at a single glance, was made acquainted with the nature of the disaster that had disturbed even the practised stoicism of their youthful Indian protector.

At a short distance from the rock, their little bark was to be seen floating across the eddy, towards the swift current of the river, in a manner which proved that its course was directed by some hidden agent. The instant this unwelcome sight caught the eye of the scout, his rifle was levelled as by instinct, but the barrel gave no answer to the bright sparks of the flint.

" 'Tis too late, 'tis too late!" Hawkeye exclaimed, dropping the useless piece in bitter disappointment; "the miscreant has struck the rapid; and had we powder, it could hardly send the lead swifter than he now goes!"

The adventurous Huron raised his head above the shelter of the canoe, and while it glided swiftly down the stream, he waved his hand, and gave forth the shout, which was the known signal of success. His cry was answered by a yell and a laugh from the woods, as tauntingly exulting as if fifty demons were uttering their blasphemies at the fall of some Christian soul.

"Well may you laugh, ye children of the devil!" said the scout, seating himself on a projection of the rock, and suffering his gun to fall neglected at his feet, "for the three quickest and surest rifles in these woods are no better than so many stalks of mullein, or the last year's horns of a buck!"

"What is to be done?" demanded Duncan, losing the first feeling of disappointment in a more manly desire for exertion; "what will become of us?"

Hawkeye made no other reply than by passing his finger around the crown of his head, in a manner so significant, that none who witnessed the action could mistake its meaning.

"Surely, surely, our case is not so desperate!" exclaimed the youth; "the Hurons are not here; we may make good the caverns; we may oppose their landing."

"With what?" coolly demanded the scout. "The arrows of Uncas, or such tears as women shed! No, no; you are young, and rich, and have friends, and at such an age I know it is hard to die! But," glancing eyes at the Mohicans, "let us remember we are men without a cross, and let us teach these natives of the forest that white blood can run as freely as red, when the appointed hour is come."

Duncan turned quickly in the direction indicated by the other's eyes, and read a confirmation of his worst apprehensions in the conduct of the Indians. Chingachgook, placing himself in a dignified posture on another fragment of the rock, had already laid aside his knife and tomahawk, and was in the act of taking the eagle's plume from his head, and smoothing the solitary tuft of hair in readiness to perform its last and revolting office. His countenance was composed, though thoughtful, while his dark gleaming eyes were gradually losing the fierceness of the combat in an expression better suited to the change he expected momentarily to undergo.

"Our case is not, cannot be so hopeless!" said Duncan; "even at this moment succor may be at hand. I see no enemies! they have sickened of a struggle in which they risk so much with so little prospect of gain!"

"It may be a minute, or it may be an hour, afore the wily sarpents steal upon us, and it is quite in natur' for them to be lying within hearing at this very moment," said Hawkeye; "but come they will, and in such a fashion as will leave us nothing to hope! Chingachgook"—he spoke in Delaware—"my brother, we have fought our last battle together, and the Maquas will triumph in the death of the sage man of the Mohicans, and of the paleface, whose eyes can make night as day, and level the clouds to the mists of the springs!"

"Let the Mingo women go weep over their slain!" returned the Indian, with characteristic pride and unmoved firmness; "the Great Snake of the Mohicans has coiled himself in their wigwams, and has poisoned their triumph with the wailings of children whose fathers have not returned! Eleven warriors lie hid from the graves of their tribes since the snows have melted, and none will tell where to find them when the tongue of Chingachgook shall be silent! Let them draw the sharpest knife, and whirl the swiftest tomahawk, for their bitterest enemy is in their hands. Uncas, topmost branch of a noble trunk, call on the cowards to hasten or their hearts will soften, and they will change to women!"

"They look among the fishes for their dead!" returned the low, soft voice of the youthful chieftain; "the Hurons float with the slimy eels! They drop from the oaks like fruit that is ready to be eaten! and the Delawares laugh!"

"Ay, ay," muttered the scout, who had listened to this peculiar burst of the natives with deep attention; "they have warmed their Indian feelings and they'll soon provoke the Maquas to give them a speedy end. As for me, who am of the whole blood of the whites, it is befitting that I should die as becomes my color, with no words of scoffing in my mouth, and without bitterness at the heart!"

"Why die at all!" said Cora, advancing from the place where natural horror had, until this moment, held her riveted to the rock; "the path is open on every side; fly, then, to the woods, and call on God for succor. Go, brave men, we owe you too much already; let us no longer involve you in our hapless fortunes!"

"You but little know the craft of the Iroquois, lady, if you judge they have left the path open to the woods!" returned Hawkeye, who, however, immediately added in his simplicity, "the down stream current, it is certain, might soon sweep us beyond the reach of their rifles or the sounds of their voices."

"Then try the river. Why linger to add to the number of the victims of our merciless enemies?"

"Why," repeated the scout, looking about him proudly, "because it is better for a man to die at peace with himself than to live haunted by an evil conscience! What answer could we give Munro, when he asked us where and how we left his children?"

"Go to him and say, that you left them with a message to hasten to their aid," returned Cora, advancing nigher to the scout, in her generous ardor; "that the Hurons bear them into the northern wilds, but that by vigilance and speed they may yet be rescued; and if, after all, it should please heaven that his assistance come too late, bear to him," she continued, her voice gradually lowering, until it seemed nearly choked, "the love, the blessings, the final prayers of his daughters, and bid him not mourn their early fate, but to look forward with humble confidence to the Christian's goal to meet his children."

The hard, weather-beaten features of the scout began to work, and when she had ended, he dropped his chin to his hand, like a man musing profoundly on the nature of the proposal.

"There is reason in her words!" at length broke from his compressed and trembling lips; "ay, and they bear the spirit of Christianity; what might be right and proper in a redskin, may be sinful in a man who has not even a cross in blood to plead for his ignorance. Chingachgook! Uncas! hear you the talk of the dark-eyed woman!"

He now spoke in Delaware to his companions, and his address, though calm and deliberate, seemed very decided. The elder Mohican heard him with deep gravity, and appeared to ponder on his words, as though he felt the importance of their import. After a moment of hesitation, he waved his hand in assent, and uttered the English word "Good!" with the peculiar emphasis of his people. Then, replacing his knife and tomahawk in his girdle, the warrior moved silently to the edge of the rock which was most concealed from the banks of the river. Here he paused a moment, pointed significantly to the woods below, and saying a few words in his own language, as if indicating his intended route, he dropped into the water, and sank from before the eyes of the witnesses of his movements.

The scout delayed his departure to speak to the generous girl, whose breathing became lighter as she saw the success of her remonstrance.

"Wisdom is sometimes given to the young, as well as to the old," he said; "and what you have spoken is wise, not to call it by a better word. If you are led into the woods, that is such of you as may be spared for a while, break the twigs on the bushes as you pass, and make the marks of your trail as broad as you can, when, if mortal eyes can see them, depend on having a friend who will follow to the ends of 'arth afore he desarts you."

He gave Cora an affectionate shake of the hand, lifted his rifle, and after regarding it a moment with melancholy solicitude, laid it carefully aside, and descended to the place where Chingachgook had just disappeared. For an instant he hung suspended by the rock; and looking about him, with a countenance of peculiar care, he added, bitterly, "Had the powder held out, this disgrace could never have befallen!" then, loosening his hold, the water closed above his head, and he also became lost to view.

All eyes were now turned on Uncas, who stood leaning against the ragged rock, in immovable composure. After waiting a short time, Cora pointed down the river, and said:—

"Your friends have not been seen, and are now, most probably, in safety; is it not time for you to follow?"

"Uncas will stay," the young Mohican calmly answered in English.

"To increase the horror of our capture, and to diminish the chances of our release! Go, generous young man," Cora continued, lowering her eyes under the gaze of the Mohican, and, perhaps, with an intuitive consciousness of her power; "go to my father, as I have said, and be the most confidential of my messengers. Tell him to trust you with the means to buy the freedom of his daughters. Go! 'tis my wish, 'tis my prayer, that you will go!"

The settled, calm look of the young chief changed to an expression of gloom, but he no longer hesitated. With a noiseless step he crossed the rock, and dropped into the troubled stream. Hardly a breath was drawn by those he left behind, until they caught a glimpse of his head emerging for air, far down the current, when he again sank, and was seen no more.

These sudden and apparently successful experiments had all taken place in a few minutes of that time which had now become so precious. After the last look at Uncas, Cora turned, and, with a quivering lip, addressed herself to Heyward:—

"I have heard of your boasted skill in the water, too, Duncan," she said; "follow, then, the wise example set you by these simple and faithful beings."

"Is such the faith that Cora Munro would exact from her protector?" said the young man, smiling mournfully, but with bitterness.

"This is not a time for idle subtleties and false opinions," she answered; "but a moment when every duty should be equally considered. To us you can be of no further service here, but your precious life may be saved for other and nearer friends."

He made no reply, though his eyes fell wistfully on the beautiful form of Alice, who was clinging to his arm with the dependency of an infant.

"Consider," continued Cora, after a pause, during which she seemed to struggle with a pang even more acute than any that her fears had excited, "that the worst to us can be but death; a tribute that all must pay at the good time of God's appointment."

"There are evils worse than death," said Duncan, speaking hoarsely, and as if fretful at her importunity, "but which the presence of one who would die in your behalf may avert."

Cora ceased her entreaties; and, veiling her face in her shawl, drew the nearly insensible Alice after her into the deepest recess of the inner cavern.

Iraqvois attack, Gamut wounded, Heyward, Alice, cora + Gamut hide in cave, Hawk fights + wants to wait for Munro to send reinforcements. Fighting stops, silently watch. Hawk + Hey hide + watch. Hawk sees 4 indians swimming close. Uncas comes + another fight. Hey wounded, Hawk wounds indian, Iraqvois stole their ammunition. Cora tells men to leave down river + come save she + Alice later. Says indians won't kill women. Uncas refuses but Cora tells him to be her personal messenger to her father, so he leaves. Hey says he has to stay + protect the girls.

IX

"Be gay securely;
Dispel, my fair, with smiles, the tim'rous clouds,
That hang on thy clear brow."
Thomas Gray, *Agrippina*[1]

THE SUDDEN and almost magical change, from the
stirring incidents of the combat to the stillness that
now reigned around him, acted on the heated imagination of Heyward like some exciting dream. While all the
images and events he had witnessed remained deeply
impressed on his memory, he felt a difficulty in persuad-
ing himself of their truth. Still ignorant of the fate of
those who had trusted to the aid of the swift current, he
at first listened intently to any signal, or sounds of alarm,
which might announce the good or evil fortune of their
hazardous undertaking. His attention was, however, bestowed in vain; for, with the disappearance of Uncas,
every sign of the adventurers had been lost, leaving him
in total uncertainty of their fate.

In a moment of such painful doubt, Duncan did not
hesitate to look about him, without consulting that protection from the rocks which just before had been so
necessary to his safety. Every effort, however, to detect
the least evidence of the approach of their hidden ene-

mies, was as fruitless as the inquiry after his late companions. The wooded banks of the rivers seemed again deserted by everything possessing animal life. The uproar which had so lately echoed through the vaults of the forest was gone, leaving the rush of the waters to swell and sink on the currents of the air, in the unmingled sweetness of nature. A fish-hawk, which, secure on the topmost branches of a dead pine, had been a distant spectator of the fray, now stooped from his high and ragged perch, and soared, in wide sweeps, above his prey; while a jay, whose noisy voice had been stilled by the hoarser cries of the savages, ventured again to open his discordant throat, as though once more in undisturbed possession of his wild domains. Duncan caught from these natural accompaniments of the solitary scene a glimmering of hope; and he began to rally his faculties to renewed exertions, with something like a reviving confidence of success.

"The Hurons are not to be seen," he said, addressing David, who had by no means recovered from the effects of the stunning blow he had received; "let us conceal ourselves in the cavern, and trust the rest to Providence."

"I remember to have united with two comely maidens, in lifting up our voices in praise and thanksgiving," returned the bewildered singing-master; "since which time I have been visited by a heavy judgment for my sins. I have been mocked with the likeness of sleep, while sounds of discord have rent my ears, such as might manifest the fulness of time, and that nature had forgotten her harmony."

"Poor fellow! thine own period was, in truth, near its accomplishment! But arouse, and come with me; I will lead you where all other sounds but those of your own psalmody shall be excluded."

"There is melody in the fall of the cataract, and the rushing of many waters is sweet to the senses!" said David, pressing his hand confusedly on his brow. "Is not the air yet filled with shrieks and cries, as though the departed spirits of the damned—"

"Not now, not now," interrupted the impatient Heyward, "they have ceased, and they who raised them, I trust in God, they are gone too! everything but the water is still and at peace; in, then, where you may create those sounds you love so well to hear."

David smiled sadly, though not without a momentary gleam of pleasure, at this allusion to his beloved vocation. He no longer hesitated to be led to a spot which promised such unalloyed gratification to his wearied senses; and, leaning on the arm of his companion, he entered the narrow mouth of the cave. Duncan seized a pile of the sassafras, which he drew before the passage, studiously concealing every appearance of an aperture. Within this fragile barrier he arranged the blankets abandoned by the foresters, darkening the inner extremity of the cavern, while its outer received a chastened light from the narrow ravine, through which one arm of the river rushed, to form the junction with its sister branch, a few rods below.

"I like not that principle of the natives, which teaches them to submit without a struggle, in emergencies that appear desperate," he said, while busied in this employment; "our own maxim, which says, 'while life remains there is hope,' is more consoling, and better suited to a soldier's temperament. To you, Cora, I will urge no words of idle encouragement; your own fortitude and undisturbed reason will teach you all that may become your sex; but cannot we dry the tears of that trembling weeper on your bosom?"

"I am calmer, Duncan," said Alice, raising herself from the arms of her sister, and forcing an appearance of composure through her tears; "much calmer, now. Surely, in this hidden spot we are safe, we are secret, free from injury; we will hope everything from those generous men who have risked so much already in our behalf."

"Now does our gentle Alice speak like a daughter of Munro!" said Heyward, pausing to press her hand as he passed towards the outer entrance of the cavern. "With two such examples of courage before him, a man would be ashamed to prove other than a hero." He then seated himself in the centre of the cavern, grasping his remaining pistol with a hand convulsively clenched, while his contracted and frowning eye announced the sullen desperation of his purpose. "The Hurons, if they come, may not gain our position so easily as they think," he lowly muttered; and dropping his head back against the rock, he seemed to await the result in patience, though his gaze was unceasingly bent on the open avenue to their place of retreat.

With the last sound of his voice, a deep, a long, and almost breathless silence succeeded. The fresh air of the morning had penetrated the recess, and its influence was gradually felt on the spirits of its inmates. As minute after minute passed by, leaving them in undisturbed security, the insinuating feeling of hope was gradually gaining possession of every bosom, though each one felt reluctant to give utterance to expectations that the next moment might so fearfully destroy.

David alone formed an exception to these varying

emotions. A gleam of light from the opening crossed his wan countenance, and fell upon the pages of the little volume, whose leaves he was again occupied in turning, as if searching for some song more fitted to their condition than any that had yet met his eye. He was, most probably, acting all this time under a confused recollection of the promised consolation of Duncan. At length, it would seem, his patient industry found its reward; for, without explanation or apology, he pronounced aloud the words "Isle of Wight," drew a long, sweet sound from his pitch-pipe, and then ran through the preliminary modulations of the air, whose name he had just mentioned with the sweeter tones of his own musical voice.

"May not this prove dangerous?" asked Cora, glancing her dark eye at Major Heyward.

"Poor fellow! his voice is too feeble to be heard amid the din of the falls," was the answer; "besides, the cavern will prove his friend. Let him indulge his passion, since it may be done without hazard."

"Isle of Wight!" repeated David, looking about him with that dignity with which he had long been wont to silence the whispering echoes of his school; " 'tis a brave tune, and set to solemn words; let it be sung with meet respect!"

After allowing a moment of stillness to enforce his discipline, the voice of the singer was heard, in low, murmuring syllables, gradually stealing on the ear, until it filled the narrow vault with sounds rendered trebly thrilling by the feeble and tremulous utterance produced by his debility. The melody, which no weakness could destroy, gradually wrought its sweet influence on the senses of those who heard it. It even prevailed over the miserable travesty of the song of David which the singer had selected from a volume of similar effusions, and caused the sense to be forgotten in the insinuating harmony of the sounds. Alice unconsciously dried her tears, and bent her melting eyes on the pallid features of Gamut with an expression of chastened delight that she neither affected nor wished to conceal. Cora bestowed an approving smile on the pious efforts of the namesake of the Jewish prince, and Heyward soon turned his steady stern look from the outlet of the cavern, to fasten it, with a milder character, on the face of David, or to meet the wandering beams which at moments strayed from the humid eyes of Alice. The open sympathy of the listeners stirred the spirit of the votary of music, whose voice regained its richness and volume, without losing that touching softness which proved its secret charm. Exerting his renovated powers to their utmost, he was yet filling the arches of the cave with long and full tones, when a yell burst into the air without, that instantly stilled his pious strains, choking his voice suddenly, as though his heart had literally bounded into the passage of his throat.

"We are lost!" exclaimed Alice, throwing herself into the arms of Cora.

"Not yet, not yet," returned the agitated but undaunted Heyward; "the sound came from the centre of the island, and it has been produced by the sight of their dead companions. We are not yet discovered, and there is still hope."

Faint and almost despairing as was the prospect of escape, the words of Duncan were not thrown away, for it awakened the powers of the sisters in such a manner that they awaited the result in silence. A second yell soon followed the first, when a rush of voices was heard pouring down the island, from its upper to its lower extremity, until they reached the naked rock above the caverns, where, after a shout of savage triumph, the air continued full of horrible cries and screams, such as man alone can utter, and he only when in a state of the fiercest barbarity.

The sounds quickly spread around them in every direction. Some called to their fellows from the water's edge, and were answered from the heights above. Cries were heard in the startling vicinity of the chasm between the two caves, which mingled with hoarser yells that arose out of the abyss of the deep ravine. In short, so rapidly had the savage sounds diffused themselves over the barren rock, that it was not difficult for the anxious listeners to imagine they could be heard beneath, as in truth they were above and on every side of them.

In the midst of this tumult, a triumphant yell was raised within a few yards of the hidden entrance to the cave. Heyward abandoned every hope, with the belief it was the signal that they were discovered. Again the impression passed away, as he heard the voices collect near the spot where the white man had so reluctantly abandoned his rifle. Amid the jargon of the Indian dialects that he now plainly heard, it was easy to distinguish not only words, but sentences, in the *patois*[2] of the Canadas. A burst of voices had shouted simultaneously, "La Longue Carabine!" causing the opposite woods to re-echo with a name which, Heyward well remembered, had been given by his enemies to a celebrated hunter and scout of the English camp, and who, he now learnt for the first time, had been his late companion.

"La Longue Carabine! La Longue Carabine!" passed from mouth to mouth, until the whole band appeared to be collected around a trophy which would seem to an-

nounce the death of its formidable owner. After a vocif-
erous consultation, which was, at times, deafened by
bursts of savage joy, they again separated, filling the air
with the name of a foe, whose body, Heyward could collect from their expressions, they hoped to find concealed
in some crevice of the island.

"Now," he whispered to the trembling sisters, "now is
the moment of uncertainty! if our place of retreat escape
this scrutiny, we are still safe! In every event, we are assured, by what has fallen from our enemies, that our
friends have escaped, and in two short hours we may
look for succor from Webb."

There were now a few minutes of fearful stillness,
during which Heyward well knew that the savages conducted their search with greater vigilance and method.
More than once he could distinguish their footsteps, as
they brushed the sassafras, causing the faded leaves to
rustle, and the branches to snap. At length, the pile
yielded a little, a corner of the blanket fell, and a faint ray
of light gleamed into the inner part of the cave. Cora
folded Alice to her bosom in agony, and Duncan sprang
to his feet. A shout was at that moment heard, as if issuing from the centre of the rock, announcing that the
neighboring cavern had at length been entered. In a
minute, the number and loudness of the voices indicated
that the whole party was collected in and around that secret place.

As the inner passages to the two caves were so close to
each other, Duncan, believing that escape was no longer
possible, passed David and the sisters, to place himself
between the latter and the first onset of the terrible
meeting. Grown desperate by his situation, he drew nigh
the slight barrier which separated him only by a few feet

from his relentless pursuers, and placing his face to the casual opening, he even looked out, with a sort of desperate indifference, on their movements.

Within reach of his arm was the brawny shoulder of a gigantic Indian, whose deep and authoritative voice appeared to give directions to the proceedings of his fellows. Beyond him again, Duncan could look into the vault opposite, which was filled with savages, upturning and rifling the humble furniture of the scout. The wound of David had dyed the leaves of sassafras with a color that the natives well knew was anticipating the season. Over this sign of their success, they set up a howl, like an opening from so many hounds who had recovered a lost trail. After this yell of victory, they tore up the fragrant bed of the cavern, and bore the branches into the chasm, scattering the boughs, as if they suspected them of concealing the person of the man they had so long hated and feared. One fierce and wild-looking warrior approached the chief bearing a load of the brush, and pointing, exultingly, to the deep red stains with which it was sprinkled, uttered his joy in Indian yells, whose meaning Heyward was only enabled to comprehend by the frequent repetition of the name of "La Longue Carabine!" When his triumph had ceased, he cast the brush on the slight heap that Duncan had made before the entrance of the second cavern, and closed the view. His example was followed by others, who, as they drew the branches from the cave of the scout, threw them into one pile, adding, unconsciously, to the security of those they sought. The very slightness of the defence was its chief merit, for no one thought of disturbing a mass of brush, which all of them believed, in that moment of hurry and confusion, had been accidentally raised by the hands of their own party.

As the blankets yielded before the outward pressure, and the branches settled in the fissure of the rock by their own weight, forming a compact body, Duncan once more breathed freely. With a light step, and lighter heart, he returned to the centre of the cave, and took the place he had left, where he could command a view of the opening next the river. While he was in the act of making this movement, the Indians, as if changing their purpose by a common impulse, broke away from the cavern in a body, and were heard rushing up the island again, towards the point whence they had originally descended. Here another wailing cry betrayed that they were again collected around the bodies of their dead comrades.

Duncan now ventured to look at his companions; for, during the most critical moments of their danger, he had been apprehensive that the anxiety of his countenance might communicate some additional alarm to those who were so little able to sustain it.

"They are gone, Cora!" he whispered; "Alice, they are returned whence they came, and we are saved! To Heaven, that has alone delivered us from the grasp of so merciless an enemy, be all the praise!"

"Then to Heaven will I return my thanks!" exclaimed the younger sister, rising from the encircling arms of Cora, and casting herself with enthusiastic gratitude on the naked rock; "to that Heaven who has spared the tears of a gray-headed father; has saved the lives of those I so much love—"

Both Heyward, and the more tempered Cora, witnessed the act of involuntary emotion with powerful sympathy, the former secretly believing that piety had never worn a form so lovely as it had now assumed in the youthful person of Alice. Her eyes radiant with the glow of grateful feelings; the flush of her beauty was again seated on her cheeks, and her whole soul seemed ready and anxious to pour out its thanksgivings, through the medium of her eloquent features. But when her lips moved, the words they should have uttered appeared frozen by some new and sudden chill. Her bloom gave place to the paleness of death; her soft and melting eyes grew hard, and seemed contracting with horror; while those hands which she had raised, clasped in each other, towards heaven, dropped in horizontal lines before her, the fingers pointed forward in convulsed motion. Heyward turned, the instant she gave a direction to his suspicions, and, peering just above the ledge which formed the threshold of the open outlet of the cavern, he beheld the malignant, fierce, and savage features of Le Renard Subtil.

In that moment of surprise, the self-possession of Heyward did not desert him. He observed by the vacant expression of the Indian's countenance, that his eye, accustomed to the open air, had not yet been able to penetrate the dusky light which pervaded the depth of the cavern. He had even thought of retreating beyond a curvature in the natural wall, which might still conceal him and his companions, when, by the sudden gleam of intelligence that shot across the features of the savage, he saw it was too late, and that they were betrayed.

The look of exultation and brutal triumph which announced this terrible truth was irresistibly irritating. Forgetful of everything but the impulses of his hot blood, Duncan levelled his pistol and fired. The report of the weapon made the cavern bellow like an eruption from a volcano; and when the smoke it vomited had been driven away before the current of air which issued from the ravine, the place so lately occupied by the features of his treacherous guide was vacant. Rushing to the outlet, Heyward caught a glimpse of his dark figure, stealing around a low and narrow ledge, which soon hid him entirely from sight.

Among the savages, a frightful stillness succeeded the explosion, which had just been heard bursting from the bowels of the rock. But when Le Renard raised his voice in a long and intelligible whoop, it was answered by a spontaneous yell from the mouth of every Indian within hearing of the sound. The clamorous noises again rushed down the island; and before Duncan had time to recover from the shock, his feeble barrier of brush was scattered to the winds, the cavern was entered at both its extremities, and he and his companions were dragged from their shelter and borne into the day, where they stood surrounded by the whole band of the triumphant Hurons.

Heyward, Cora, Alice + Gamut hide in cave. Hear indians. Figure out Hawkeye is famous hunter/scout. Indians don't find them, frustrated their men are dead + not english dead. suddenly Magua finds them, hey tries to shoot + misses, taken prisoner

X

"I fear we shall outsleep the coming morn
As much as we this night have overwatched!"
A Midsummer Night's Dream[1]

THE INSTANT THE SHOCK of this sudden misfortune
had abated, Duncan began to make his observations
on the appearance and proceedings of their captors.
Contrary to the usages of the natives in the wantonness
of their success, they had respected, not only the persons of the trembling sisters, but his own. The rich ornaments of his military attire had indeed been repeatedly
handled by different individuals of the tribe with eyes
expressing a savage longing to possess the baubles; but
before the customary violence could be resorted to, a
mandate in the authoritative voice of the large warrior
already mentioned, stayed the uplifted hand, and convinced Heyward that they were to be reserved for some
object of particular moment.

While, however, these manifestations of weakness
were exhibited by the young and vain of the party, the
more experienced warriors continued their search
throughout both caverns, with an activity that denoted
they were far from being satisfied with those fruits of
their conquest which had already been brought to light.

Unable to discover any new victim, these diligent workers of vengeance soon approached their male prisoners,
pronouncing the name of "La Longue Carabine," with a
fierceness that could not easily be mistaken. Duncan affected not to comprehend the meaning of their repeated
and violent interrogatories, while his companion was
spared the effort of a similar deception by his ignorance
of French. Wearied, at length, by their importunities,
and apprehensive of irritating his captors by too stubborn a silence, the former looked about him in quest of
Magua; who might interpret his answers to questions
which were at each moment becoming more earnest and
threatening.

The conduct of this savage had formed a solitary exception to that of all his fellows. While the others were
busily occupied in seeking to gratify their childish passion for finery, by plundering even the miserable effects
of the scout, or had been searching, with such bloodthirsty vengeance in their looks, for their absent owner,
Le Renard had stood at a little distance from the prisoners, with a demeanor so quiet and satisfied, as to betray
that he had already effected the grand purpose of this
treachery. When the eyes of Heyward first met those of
his recent guide, he turned them away in horror at the
sinister though calm look he encountered. Conquering
his disgust, however, he was able, with an averted face, to
address his successful enemy.

"Le Renard Subtil is too much of a warrior," said the
reluctant Heyward, "to refuse telling an unarmed man
what his conquerors say."

"They ask for the hunter who knows the paths
through the woods," returned Magua, in his broken English, laying his hand, at the same time, with a ferocious

smile, on the bundle of leaves with which a wound on his own shoulder was bandaged. "La Longue Carabine! his rifle is good, and his eye never shut; but, like the short gun of the white chief, it is nothing against the life of Le Subtil!"

"Le Renard is too brave to remember the hurts received in war, or the hands that gave them!"

"Was it war, when the tired Indian rested at the sugar-tree to taste his corn! who filled the bushes with creeping enemies! who drew the knife! whose tongue was peace, while his heart was colored with blood! Did Magua say that the hatchet was out of the ground, and that his hand had dug it up?"

As Duncan dared not retort upon his accuser by reminding him of his own premeditated treachery, and disdained to deprecate his resentment by any words of apology, he remained silent. Magua seemed also content to rest the controversy as well as all further communication there, for he resumed the leaning attitude against the rock, from which, in momentary energy, he had arisen. But the cry of "La Longue Carabine" was renewed the instant the impatient savages perceived that the short dialogue was ended.

"You hear," said Magua, with stubborn indifference; "the red Hurons call for the life of 'The Long Rifle,' or they will have the blood of them that keep him hid!"

"He is gone—escaped; he is far beyond their reach."

Renard smiled with cold contempt, as he answered,—

"When the white man dies, he thinks he is at peace; but the redmen know how to torture even the ghosts of their enemies. Where is his body? Let the Hurons see his scalp!"

"He is not dead, but escaped."

Magua shook his head incredulously.

"Is he a bird, to spread his wings; or is he a fish, to swim without air! The white chief reads in his books, and he believes the Hurons are fools!"

"Though no fish, The Long Rifle can swim. He floated down the stream when the powder was all burnt, and when the eyes of the Hurons were behind a cloud."

"And why did the white chief stay?" demanded the still incredulous Indian. "Is he a stone that goes to the bottom, or does the scalp burn his head?"

"That I am not a stone, your dead comrade, who fell into the falls, might answer, were the life still in him," said the provoked young man, using, in his anger, that boastful language which was most likely to excite the admiration of an Indian. "The white man thinks none but cowards desert their women."

Magua muttered a few words, inaudibly, between his teeth, before he continued, aloud,—

"Can the Delawares swim, too, as well as crawl in the bushes? Where is Le Gros Serpent?"

Duncan, who perceived by the use of these Canadian appellations, that his late companions were much better known to his enemies than to himself, answered, reluctantly, "He also is gone down with the water."

"Le Cerf Agile is not here?"

"I know not whom you call 'The Nimble Deer,'" said Duncan, gladly profiting by any excuse to create delay.

"Uncas," returned Magua, pronouncing the Delaware name with even greater difficulty than he spoke his English words. "'Bounding Elk' is what the white man says, when he calls to the young Mohican."

"Here is some confusion in names between us, Le Renard," said Duncan, hoping to provoke a discussion.

"*Daim* is the French for deer, and *cerf* for stag; *élan* is the true term, when one would speak of an elk."

"Yes," muttered the Indian, in his native tongue; "the pale-faces are prattling women! they have two words for each thing, while a redskin will make the sound of his voice speak for him." Then changing his language, he continued, adhering to the imperfect nomenclature of his provincial instructors, "The deer is swift, but weak; the elk is swift, but strong; and the son of Le Serpent is Le Cerf Agile. Has he leaped the river to the woods?"

"If you mean the younger Delaware, he too is gone down with the water."

As there was nothing improbable to an Indian in the manner of the escape, Magua admitted the truth of what he had heard, with a readiness that afforded additional evidence how little he would prize such worthless captives. With his companions, however, the feeling was manifestly different.

The Hurons had awaited the result of this short dialogue with characteristic patience, and with a silence that increased until there was a general stillness in the band. When Heyward ceased to speak, they turned their eyes, as one man, on Magua, demanding, in this expressive manner, an explanation of what had been said. Their interpreter pointed to the river, and made them acquainted with the result, as much by the action as by the few words he uttered. When the fact was generally understood, the savages raised a frightful yell, which declared the extent of their disappointment. Some ran furiously to the water's edge, beating the air with frantic gestures, while others spat upon the element, to resent the supposed treason it had committed against their acknowledged rights as conquerors. A few, and they not the least powerful and terrific of the band, threw lowering looks, in which the fiercest passion was only tempered by habitual self-command, at those captives who still remained in their power; while one or two even gave vent to their malignant feelings by the most menacing gestures, against which neither the sex nor the beauty of the sisters was any protection. The young soldier made a desperate, but fruitless effort, to spring to the side of Alice, when he saw the dark hand of a savage twisted in the rich tresses which were flowing in volumes over her shoulders, while a knife was passed around the head from which they fell, as if to denote the horrid manner in which it was about to be robbed of its beautiful ornament. But his hands were bound; and at the first movement he made, he felt the grasp of the powerful Indian who directed the band, pressing his shoulder like a vise. Immediately conscious how unavailing any struggle against such an overwhelming force must prove, he submitted to his fate, encouraging his gentle companions by a few low and tender assurances that the natives seldom failed to threaten more than they performed.

But, while Duncan resorted to these words of consolation to quiet the apprehensions of the sisters, he was not so weak as to deceive himself. He well knew that the authority of an Indian chief was so little conventional, that it was oftener maintained by physical superiority than by any moral supremacy he might possess. The danger was, therefore, magnified exactly in proportion to the number of the savage spirits by which they were surrounded. The most positive mandate from him who seemed the acknowledged leader, was liable to be violated at each moment, by any rash hand that might choose to sacrifice a victim to the *manes*[2] of some dead friend or relative. While, therefore, he sustained an outward appearance of calmness and fortitude, his heart leaped into his throat whenever any of their fierce captors drew nearer than common to the helpless sisters, or fastened one of their sullen wandering looks on those fragile forms which were so little able to resist the slightest assault.

His apprehensions were, however, greatly relieved, when he saw that the leader had summoned his warriors to himself in council. Their deliberations were short, and it would seem, by the silence of most of the party, the decision unanimous. By the frequency with which the few speakers pointed in the direction of the encampment of Webb, it was apparent they dreaded the approach of danger from that quarter. This consideration probably hastened their determination, and quickened the subsequent movements.

During this short conference, Heyward, finding a respite from his greatest fears, had leisure to admire the cautious manner in which the Hurons had made their approaches, even after hostilities had ceased.

It has already been stated, that the upper half of the island was a naked rock, and destitute of any other defences than a few scattered logs of drift-wood. They had selected this point to make their descent, having borne the canoe through the wood around the cataract for that purpose. Placing their arms in the little vessel, a dozen men clinging to its sides had trusted themselves to the direction of the canoe, which was controlled by two of the most skilful warriors, in attitudes that enabled them to command a view of the dangerous passage. Favored by this arrangement, they touched the head of the island at that point which had proved so fatal to their first adventures, but with the advantages of superior numbers, and the possession of firearms. That such had been the manner of their descent was rendered quite apparent to Duncan; for they now bore the light bark from the upper end of the rock, and placed it in the water, near the mouth of the outer cavern. As soon as this change was made, the leader made signs to the prisoners to descend and enter.

As resistance was impossible, and remonstrance useless, Heyward set the example of submission, by leading the way into the canoe, where he was soon seated with the sisters, and the still wondering David. Notwithstanding the Hurons were necessarily ignorant of the little channels among the eddies and rapids of the stream, they knew the common signs of such a navigation too well to commit any material blunder. When the pilot chosen for the task of guiding the canoe had taken his station, the whole band plunged again into the river, the vessel glided down the current, and in a few moments the captives found themselves on the south bank of the stream, nearly opposite to the point where they had struck it the preceding evening.

Here was held another short but earnest consultation, during which the horses, to whose panic their owners ascribed their heaviest misfortune, were led from the cover of the woods, and brought to the sheltered spot. The band now divided. The great chief so often mentioned, mounting the charger of Heyward, led the way directly across the river, followed by most of his people, and disappeared in the woods, leaving the prisoners in charge of six savages, at whose head was Le Renard Subtil. Duncan witnessed all their movements with renewed uneasiness.

He had been fond of believing, from the uncommon forbearance of the savages, that he was reserved as a prisoner to be delivered to Montcalm. As the thoughts of those who are in misery seldom slumber, and the invention is never more lively than when it is stimulated by hope, however feeble and remote, he had even imagined that the parental feelings of Munro were to be made instrumental in seducing him from his duty to the king. For though the French commander bore a high character for courage and enterprise, he was also thought to be expert in those political practices, which do not always respect the nicer obligations of morality, and which so generally disgraced the European diplomacy of that period.

All those busy and ingenious speculations were now annihilated by the conduct of his captors. That portion of the band who had followed the huge warrior took the route towards the foot of the Horican, and no other expectation was left for himself and companions, than that they were to be retained as hopeless captives by their savage conquerors. Anxious to know the worst, and willing, in such an emergency, to try the potency of gold, he overcame his reluctance to speak to Magua. Addressing himself to his former guide, who had now assumed the authority and manner of one who was to direct the future movements of the party, he said, in tones as friendly and confiding as he could assume,—

"I would speak to Magua, what is fit only for so great a chief to hear."

The Indian turned his eyes on the young soldier scornfully, as he answered,—

"Speak; trees have no ears!"

"But the red Hurons are not deaf; and counsel that is

fit for the great men of a nation would make the young warriors drunk. If Magua will not listen, the officer of the king knows how to be silent."

The savage spoke carelessly to his comrades, who were busied, after their awkward manner, in preparing the horses for the reception of the sisters, and moved a little to one side, whither, by a cautious gesture, he induced Heyward to follow.

"Now speak," he said; "if the words are such as Magua should hear."

"Le Renard Subtil has proved himself worthy of the honorable name given to him by his Canada fathers," commenced Heyward; "I see his wisdom, and all that he has done for us, and shall remember it, when the hour to reward him arrives. Yes! Renard has proved that he is not only a great chief in council, but one who knows how to deceive his enemies!"

"What has Renard done?" coldly demanded the Indian.

"What! has he not seen that the woods were filled with outlying parties of the enemies, and that the Serpent could not steal through them without being seen? Then, did he not lose his path to blind the eyes of the Hurons? Did he not pretend to go back to his tribe, who had treated him ill, and driven him from their wigwams like a dog? And, when we saw what he wished to do, did we not aid him, by making a false face, that the Hurons might think the white man believed that his friend was his enemy? Is not all this true? And when Le Subtil had shut the eyes and stopped the ears of his nation by his wisdom, did they not forget that they had once done him wrong, and forced him to flee to the Mohawks? And did they not leave him on the south side of the river, with their prisoners, while they have gone foolishly on the north? Does not Renard mean to turn like a fox on his footsteps, and to carry to the rich and gray-headed Scotchman his daughters? Yes, Magua, I see it all, and I have already been thinking how so much wisdom and honesty should be repaid. First, the chief of William Henry will give as a great chief should for such a service. The medal of Magua will no longer be of tin, but of beaten gold; his horn will run over with powder; dollars will be as plenty in his pouch as pebbles on the shore of Horican; and the deer will lick his hand, for they will know it to be vain to fly from the rifle he will carry! As for myself, I know not how to exceed the gratitude of the Scotchman, but I—yes, I will—"

"What will the young chief who comes from towards the sun, give?" demanded the Huron, observing that Heyward hesitated in his desire to end the enumeration of benefits with that which might form the climax of an Indian's wishes.

"He will make the fire-water from the Islands in the salt lake flow before the wigwam of Magua, until the heart of the Indian shall be lighter than the feathers of the humming-bird, and his breath sweeter than the wild honeysuckle."

Le Renard had listened gravely as Heyward slowly proceeded in his subtle speech. When the young man mentioned the artifice he supposed the Indian to have practised on his own nation, the countenance of the listener was veiled in an expression of cautious gravity. At the allusion to the injury which Duncan affected to believe had driven the Huron from his native tribe, a gleam of such ungovernable ferocity flashed from the other's eyes, as induced the adventurous speaker to believe he had struck the proper chord. And by the time he reached the part where he so artfully blended the thirst of vengeance with the desire of gain, he had, at least, obtained a command of the deepest attention of the savage. The question put by Le Renard had been calm, and with all the dignity of an Indian; but it was quite apparent, by the thoughtful expression of the listener's countenance, that the answer was most cunningly devised. The Huron mused a few moments, and then laying his hand on the rude bandages of his wounded shoulder, he said, with some energy,—

"Do friends make such remarks?"

"Would La Longue Carabine cut one so light on an enemy?"

"Do the Delawares crawl upon those they love, like snakes, twisting themselves to strike?"

"Would Le Gros Serpent have been heard by the ears of one he wished to be deaf?"

"Does the white chief burn his powder in the faces of his brothers?"

"Does he ever miss his aim, when seriously bent to kill?" returned Duncan, smiling with well acted sincerity.

Another long and deliberate pause succeeded these sententious questions and ready replies. Duncan saw that the Indian hesitated. In order to complete his victory, he was in the act of recommencing the enumeration of the rewards, when Magua made an expressive gesture and said—

"Enough; Le Renard is a wise chief, and what he does will be seen. Go, and keep the mouth shut. When Magua speaks, it will be the time to answer."

Heyward, perceiving that the eyes of his companion were warily fastened on the rest of the band, fell back immediately, in order to avoid the appearance of any suspicious confederacy with their leader. Magua approached the horses, and affected to be well pleased with the diligence and ingenuity of his comrades. He then signed to Heyward to assist the sisters into the saddles, for he seldom deigned to use the English tongue, unless urged by some motive of more than usual moment.

There was no longer any plausible pretext for delay; and Duncan was obliged, however reluctantly, to comply. As he performed this office, he whispered his reviving hopes in the ears of the trembling females, who, through dread of encountering the savage countenances of their captors, seldom raised their eyes from the ground. The mare of David had been taken with the followers of the large chief; in consequence, its owner, as well as Duncan, was compelled to journey on foot. The latter did not, however, so much regret this circumstance, as it might enable him to retard the speed of the party; for he still turned his longing looks in the direction of Fort Edward, in the vain expectation of catching some sound from that quarter of the forest, which might denote the approach of succor.

When all were prepared, Magua made the signal to proceed, advancing in front to lead the party in person. Next followed David, who was gradually coming to a true sense of his condition, as the effects of the wound became less and less apparent. The sisters rode in his rear, with Heyward at their side, while the Indians flanked the party, and brought up the close of the march, with a caution that seemed never to tire.

In this manner they proceeded in uninterrupted silence, except when Heyward addressed some solitary word of comfort to the females, or David gave vent to the moanings of his spirit in piteous exclamations, which he intended should express the humility of resignation. Their direction lay towards the south, and in a course nearly opposite to the road to William Henry. Notwithstanding this apparent adherence in Magua to the original determination of his conquerors, Heyward could not believe his tempting bait was so soon forgotten; and he knew the windings of an Indian path too well, to suppose that its apparent course led directly to its object, when artifice was at all necessary. Mile after mile was, however, passed through the boundless woods, in this painful manner, without any prospect of a termination to their journey. Heyward watched the sun, as he darted his meridian rays through the branches of the trees, and pined for the moment when the policy of Magua should change their route to one more favorable to his hopes. Sometimes he fancied the wary savage, despairing of passing the arm of Montcalm in safety, was holding his way towards a well-known border settlement, where a distinguished officer of the crown, and a favored friend of the Six Nations, held his large possessions, as well as his usual residence. To be delivered into the hands of Sir William Johnson[3] was far preferable to being led into the wilds of Canada; but in order to effect even the former, it would be necessary to traverse the forest for many weary leagues, each step of which was carrying him farther from the scene of the war, and, consequently, from the post, not only of honor, but of duty.

Cora alone remembered the parting injunctions of the scout, and whenever an opportunity offered, she stretched forth her arm to bend aside the twigs that met her hands. But the vigilance of the Indians rendered this act of precaution both difficult and dangerous. She was often defeated in her purpose, by encountering their watchful eyes, when it became necessary to feign an alarm she did not feel, and occupy the limb by some gesture of feminine apprehension. Once, and once only, was she completely successful; when she broke down the bough of a large sumach, and, by a sudden thought, let her glove fall at the same instant. This sign, intended for those that might follow, was observed by one of her conductors, who restored the glove, broke the remaining branches of the bush in such a manner that it appeared to proceed from the struggling of some beast in its branches, and then laid his hand on his tomahawk, with a look so significant, that it put an effectual end to these stolen memorials of their passage.

As there were horses, to leave the prints of their footsteps, in both bands of the Indians, this interruption cut off any probable hopes of assistance being conveyed through the means of their trail.

Heyward would have ventured a remonstrance, had there been anything encouraging in the gloomy reserve of Magua. But the savage, during all this time, seldom turned to look at his followers, and never spoke. With the sun for his only guide, or aided by such blind marks as are only known to the sagacity of a native, he held his way along the barrens of pine, through occasional little fertile vales, across brooks and rivulets, and over undulating hills, with the accuracy of instinct, and nearly with the directness of a bird. He never seemed to hesitate. Whether the path was hardly distinguishable, whether it disappeared, or whether it lay beaten and plain before him, made no sensible difference in his speed or certainty. It seemed as if fatigue could not affect him. Whenever the eyes of the wearied travellers rose from the decayed leaves over which they trod, his dark form was to be seen glancing among the stems of the trees in front, his head immovably fastened in a forward position, with the light plume on his crest fluttering in a current of air, made solely by the swiftness of his own motion.

But all this diligence and speed were not without an object. After crossing a low vale, through which a gushing brook meandered, he suddenly ascended a hill, so steep and difficult of ascent, that the sisters were compelled to alight, in order to follow. When the summit was gained, they found themselves on a level spot, but thinly covered with trees, under one of which Magua had thrown his dark form, as if willing and ready to seek that rest which was so much needed by the whole party.

Hurons threaten to kill hey but save him to question, hey convinces Hurons that Hawk+andicans escaped. Furious, the indians almost kill Alice but then cheif decides to ~~move~~ have tribal councilt move to south bank of river. Hey ~~says~~ tells Magua that he thinks Magua wants to decieve Hurons for personal gain. Magua neither denies nor admits. Cora tries leave trail, but indians catch on + threaten her. Magua leads to steep hill (perfect for defense+attack)

XI

"Cursed by my tribe
If I forgive him."
The Merchant of Venice[1]

THE INDIAN HAD SELECTED, for this desirable purpose, one of those steep, pyramidal hills, which bear
a strong resemblance to artificial mounds, and which so
frequently occur in the valleys of America. The one in
question was high and precipitous; its top flattened, as
usual; but with one of its sides more than ordinarily irregular. It possessed no other apparent advantage for a
resting-place than in its elevation and form, which might
render defence easy, and surprise nearly impossible. As
Heyward, however, no longer expected that rescue
which time and distance now rendered so improbable,
he regarded these little peculiarities with an eye devoid
of interest, devoting himself entirely to the comfort and
condolence of his feebler companions. The Narragansetts were suffered to browse on the branches of the
trees and shrubs that were thinly scattered over the summit of the hill, while the remains of their provisions were
spread under the shade of a beech, that stretched its horizontal limbs like a canopy above them.

Notwithstanding the swiftness of their flight, one of

the Indians had found an opportunity to strike a straggling fawn with an arrow, and had borne the more
preferable fragments of the victim patiently on his shoulders, to the stopping-place. Without any aid from the science of cookery, he was immediately employed, in
common with his fellows, in gorging himself with this di-
gestible sustenance. Magua alone sat apart, without participation in the revolting meal, and apparently buried in
the deepest thought.

This abstinence, so remarkable in an Indian, when he
possessed the means of satisfying hunger, at length attracted the notice of Heyward. The young man willingly
believed that the Huron deliberated on the most eligible
manner of eluding the vigilance of his associates. With a
view to assist his plans, by any suggestion of his own, and
to strengthen the temptation, he left the beech, and
straggled as if without an object, to the spot where Le
Renard was seated.

"Has not Magua kept the sun in his face long enough
to escape all danger from the Canadians?" he asked, as
though no longer doubtful of the good intelligence established between them; "and will not the chief of
William Henry be better pleased to see his daughters before another night may have hardened his heart to their
loss, to make him less liberal in his reward?"

"Do the pale-faces love their children less in the
morning than at night?" asked the Indian, coldly.

"By no means," returned Heyward, anxious to recall
his error, if he had made one; "the white man may, and
does often, forget the burial-place of his fathers; he
sometimes ceases to remember those he should love and
has promised to cherish; but the affection of a parent for
his child is never permitted to die."

"And is the heart of the white-headed chief soft, and will he think of the babes that his squaws have given him? He is hard to his warriors, and his eyes are made of stone!"

"He is severe to the idle and wicked, but to the sober and deserving he is a leader, but just and humane. I have known many fond and tender parents, but never have I seen a man whose heart was softer towards his child. You have seen the gray-head in front of his warriors, Magua; but I have seen his eyes swimming in water, when he spoke of those children who are now in your power!"

Heyward paused, for he knew not how to construe the remarkable expression that gleamed across the swarthy features of the attentive Indian. At first it seemed as if the remembrance of the promised reward grew vivid in his mind, while he listened to the sources of parental feeling which were to assure its possession; but as Duncan proceeded, the expression of joy became so fiercely malignant, that it was impossible not to apprehend it proceeded from some passion more sinister than avarice.

"Go," said the Huron, suppressing the alarming exhibition in an instant, in a death-like calmness of countenance; "go to the dark-haired daughter, and say, Magua waits to speak. The father will remember what the child promises."

Duncan, who interpreted this speech to express a wish for some additional pledge that the promised gifts should not be withheld, slowly and reluctantly repaired to the place where the sisters were now resting from their fatigue, to communicate its purport to Cora.

"You understand the nature of an Indian's wishes," he concluded, as he led her towards the place where she was expected, "and must be prodigal of your offers of powder and blankets. Ardent spirits are, however, the most prized by such as he; nor would it be amiss to add some boon from your own hand, with that grace you so well know how to practise. Remember, Cora, that on your presence of mind and ingenuity even your life, as well as that of Alice, may in some measure depend."

"Heyward, and yours!"

"Mine is of little moment; it is already sold to my king, and is a prize to be seized by any enemy who may possess the power. I have no father to expect me, and but few friends to lament a fate which I have courted with the insatiable longings of youth after distinction. But hush! we approach the Indian. Magua, the lady with whom you wish to speak is here."

The Indian rose slowly from his seat, and stood for near a minute silent and motionless. He then signed with his hand for Heyward to retire, saying coldly,—

"When the Huron talks to the women, his tribe shut their ears."

Duncan, still lingering, as if refusing to comply, Cora said, with a calm smile—

"You hear, Heyward, and delicacy at least should urge you to retire. Go to Alice, and comfort her with our reviving prospects."

She waited until he had departed, and then turning to the native, with the dignity of her sex in her voice and manner, she added, "What would Le Renard say to the daughter of Munro?"

"Listen," said the Indian, laying his hand firmly upon her arm, as if willing to draw her utmost attention to his words; a movement that Cora as firmly but quietly repulsed, by extricating the limb from his grasp: "Magua was born a chief and a warrior among the red Hurons of the lakes; he saw the suns of twenty summers make the snows of twenty winters run off in the streams, before he saw a pale-face; and he was happy! Then, his Canada fathers came into the woods, and taught him to drink the fire-water, and he became a rascal. The Hurons drove him from the graves of his fathers, as they would chase the hunted buffalo. He ran down the shores of the lakes, and followed their outlet to the 'city of cannon.'² There he hunted and fished, till the people chased him again through the woods into the arms of his enemies. The chief, who was born a Huron, was at last a warrior among the Mohawks!"

"Something like this I had heard before," said Cora, observing that he paused to suppress those passions which began to burn with too bright a flame, as he recalled the recollection of his supposed injuries.

"Was it the fault of Le Renard that his head was not made of rock? Who gave him the fire-water? who made him a villain? 'Twas the pale-faces, the people of your own color."

"And am I answerable that thoughtless and unprincipled men exist, whose shades of countenance may resemble mine?" Cora calmly demanded of the excited savage.

"No; Magua is a man, and not a fool; such as you never open their lips to the burning stream: the Great Spirit has given you wisdom!"

"What then have I to do, or say, in the matter of your misfortunes, not to say of your errors?"

"Listen," repeated the Indian, resuming his earnest attitude; "when his English and French fathers dug up the hatchet, Le Renard struck the war-post of the Mohawks, and went out against his own nation. The pale-faces have driven the redskins from their hunting-grounds, and now when they fight, a white man leads the way. The old chief at Horican, your father, was the great captain of our war-party. He said to the Mohawks do this, and do that, and he was minded. He made a law, that if an Indian swallowed the fire-water, and came into the cloth wigwams of his warriors, it should not be forgotten. Magua foolishly opened his mouth, and the hot liquor led him into the cabin of Munro. What did the gray-head? let his daughter say."

"He forgot not his words, and did justice by punishing the offender," said the undaunted daughter.

"Justice!" repeated the Indian, casting an oblique glance of the most ferocious expression at her unyielding countenance; "is it justice to make evil, and then punish for it? Magua was not himself; it was the fire-water that spoke and acted for him! but Munro did not believe it. The Huron chief was tied up before all the pale-faced warriors, and whipped like a dog."

Cora remained silent, for she knew not how to palliate this imprudent severity on the part of her father, in a manner to suit the comprehension of an Indian.

"See!" continued Magua, tearing aside the slight cal-ico that very imperfectly concealed his painted breast; "here are scars given by knives and bullets—of these a warrior may boast before his nation; but the gray-head has left marks on the back of the Huron chief, that he must hide, like a squaw, under this painted cloth of the whites."

"I had thought," resumed Cora, "that an Indian war-rior was patient, and that his spirit felt not, and knew not, the pain his body suffered."

"When the Chippewas tied Magua to the stake, and cut this gash," said the other, laying his finger on a deep scar, "the Huron laughed in their faces, and told them, Women struck so light! His spirit was then in the clouds! But when he felt the blows of Munro, his spirit lay under the birch. The spirit of a Huron is never drunk; it remembers forever!"

"But it may be appeased. If my father has done you this injustice, show him how an Indian can forgive an injury, and take back his daughters. You have heard from Major Heyward—"

Magua shook his head, forbidding the repetition of offers he so much despised.

"What would you have?" continued Cora, after a most painful pause, while the conviction forced itself on her mind that the too sanguine and generous Duncan had been cruelly deceived by the cunning of the savage.

"What a Huron loves—good for good; bad for bad!"

"You would then revenge the injury inflicted by Munro on his helpless daughters. Would it not be more like a man to go before his face, and take the satisfaction of a warrior?"

"The arms of the pale-faces are long, and their knives sharp!" returned the savage, with a malignant laugh: "why would Le Renard go among the muskets of his warriors, when he holds the spirit of the gray-head in his hand?"

"Name your intention, Magua," said Cora, struggling with herself to speak with steady calmness. "Is it to lead us prisoners to the woods, or do you contemplate even some greater evil? Is there no reward, no means of palliating the injury, and of softening your heart? At least, release my gentle sister, and pour out all your malice on me. Purchase wealth by her safety, and satisfy your revenge with a single victim. The loss of both of his daughters might bring the aged man to his grave, and where would then be the satisfaction of Le Renard?"

"Listen," said the Indian again. "The light eyes can go back to the Horican, and tell the old chief what has been done, if the dark-haired woman will swear by the Great Spirit of her fathers to tell no lie."

"What must I promise?" demanded Cora, still maintaining a secret ascendency over the fierce native, by the collected and feminine dignity of her presence.

"When Magua left his people, his wife was given to another chief; he has now made friends with the Hurons, and will go back to the graves of his tribe, on the shores of the great lake.[3] Let the daughter of the English chief follow, and live in his wigwam forever."

However revolting a proposal of such a character might prove to Cora, she retained, notwithstanding her powerful disgust, sufficient self-command to reply, without betraying the weakness.

"And what pleasure would Magua find in sharing his cabin with a wife he did not love; one who would be of a nation and color different from his own? It would be better to take the gold of Munro, and buy the heart of some Huron maid with his gifts."

The Indian made no reply for near a minute, but bent his fierce looks on the countenance of Cora, in such wavering glances, that her eyes sank with shame, under an impression that, for the first time, they had encountered an expression that no chaste female might endure. While she was shrinking within herself, in dread of having her ears wounded by some proposal still more shocking than the last, the voice of Magua answered, in its tones of deepest malignancy—

"When the blows scorched the back of the Huron, he would know where to find a woman to feel the smart. The daughter of Munro would draw his water, hoe his corn, and cook his venison. The body of the gray-head would sleep among his cannon, but his heart would lie within reach of the knife of Le Subtil."

"Monster! well dost thou deserve thy treacherous name!" cried Cora, in an ungovernable burst of filial indignation. "None but a fiend could meditate such a vengeance! But thou overratest thy power! You shall find it is, in truth, the heart of Munro you hold, and that it will defy your utmost malice!"

The Indian answered this bold defiance by a ghastly smile, that showed an unaltered purpose, while he motioned her away, as if to close the conference forever. Cora, already regretting her precipitation, was obliged to comply, for Magua instantly left the spot, and approached his gluttonous comrades. Heyward flew to the side of the agitated female, and demanded the result of a dialogue that he had watched at a distance with so much interest. But unwilling to alarm the fears of Alice, she evaded a direct reply, betraying only by her countenance her utter want of success, and keeping her anxious looks fastened on the slightest movements of their captors. To the reiterated and earnest questions of her sister, concerning their probable destination, she made no other answer than by pointing towards the dark group, with an agitation she could not control, and murmuring, as she folded Alice to her bosom—

"There, there; read our fortunes in their faces; we shall see; we shall see!"

The action, and the choked utterance of Cora, spoke more impressively than any words, and quickly drew the attention of her companions on that spot where her own was riveted with an intenseness that nothing but the importance of the stake could create.

When Magua reached the cluster of lolling savages, who, gorged with their disgusting meal, lay stretched on the earth in brutal indulgence, he commenced speaking with the dignity of an Indian chief. The first syllables he uttered had the effect to cause his listeners to raise themselves in attitudes of respectful attention. As the Huron used his native language, the prisoners, notwithstanding the caution of the natives had kept them within the swing of their tomahawks, could only conjecture the substance of his harangue, from the nature of those significant gestures with which an Indian always illustrates his eloquence.

At first, the language, as well as the action of Magua, appeared calm and deliberate. When he had succeeded in sufficiently awakening the attention of his comrades, Heyward fancied, by his pointing so frequently towards the direction of the great lakes, that he spoke of the land of their fathers, and of their distant tribe. Frequent indications of applause escaped the listeners, who, as they uttered the expressive "Hugh!" looked at each other in commendation of the speaker. Le Renard was too skilful to neglect his advantage. He now spoke of the long and painful route by which they had left those spacious grounds and happy villages, to come and battle against the enemies of their Canadian fathers. He enumerated the warriors of the party; their several merits; their frequent services to the nation; their wounds, and the number of the scalps they had taken. Whenever he alluded to any present (and the subtle Indian neglected none), the dark countenance of the flattered individual gleamed with exultation, nor did he even hesitate to assert the truth of the words, by gestures of applause and confirmation. Then the voice of the speaker fell, and lost the loud, animated tones of triumph with which he had enumerated their deeds of success and victory. He described the cataract of Glenn's; the impregnable position of its rocky island, with its caverns, and its numerous rapids and whirlpools; he named the name of La Longue Carabine, and paused until the forest beneath them had sent up the last echo of a loud and long yell, with which the hated appellation was received. He pointed towards the youthful military captive, and described the death of a favorite warrior, who had been precipitated into the deep ravine by his hand. He not only mentioned the fate of him who, hanging between heaven and earth, had presented such a spectacle of horror to the whole band, but he acted anew the terrors of his situation, his resolution and his death, on the branches of a sapling; and, finally, he rapidly recounted the manner in which each of their friends had fallen, never failing to touch upon their courage, and their most acknowledged virtues. When this recital of events was ended, his voice once more changed, and became plaintive, and even musical, in its low guttural sounds. He now spoke of the wives and children of the slain; their destitution; their misery, both physical and moral; their distance; and, at last, of their unavenged wrongs. Then suddenly lifting his voice to a pitch of terrific energy, he concluded by demanding,—

"Are the Hurons dogs to bear this? Who shall say to the wife of Menowgua that the fishes have his scalp, and that his nation have not taken revenge! Who will dare meet the mother of Wassawattimie, that scornful woman, with his hands clean! What shall be said to the old men when they ask us for scalps, and we have not a hair from a white head to give them! The women will point their fingers at us. There is a dark spot on the names of the Hurons, and it must be hid in blood!"

His voice was no longer audible in the burst of rage which now broke into the air, as if the wood, instead of containing so small a band, was filled with the nation. During the foregoing address the progress of the speaker was too plainly read by those most interested in his success, through the medium of the countenances of the men he addressed. They had answered his melancholy and mourning by sympathy and sorrow; his assertions, by gestures of confirmation; and his boastings, with the exultation of savages. When he spoke of courage, their looks were firm and responsive; when he alluded to their injuries, their eyes kindled with fury; when he mentioned the taunts of the women, they dropped their heads in shame; but when he pointed out their means of vengeance, he struck a chord which never failed to thrill in the breast of an Indian. With the first intimation that it was within their reach, the whole band sprang upon their feet as one man; giving utterance to their rage in the most frantic cries, they rushed upon their prisoners in a body with drawn knives and uplifted tomahawks. Heyward threw himself between the sisters and the foremost, whom he grappled with a desperate strength that for a moment checked his violence. This unexpected resistance gave Magua time to interpose, and with rapid enunciation and animated gesture, he drew the attention of the band again to himself. In that language he knew so well how to assume, he diverted his comrades from their instant purpose, and invited them to prolong the misery of their victims. His proposal was received with acclamations, and executed with the swiftness of thought.

Two powerful warriors cast themselves on Heyward, while another was occupied in securing the less active singing-master. Neither of the captives, however, submitted without a desperate though fruitless struggle. Even David hurled his assailant to the earth; nor was Heyward secured until the victory over his companion enabled the Indians to direct their united force to that object. He was then bound and fastened to the body of the sapling, on whose branches Magua had acted the pantomime of the falling Huron. When the young soldier regained his recollection, he had the painful certainty before his eyes that a common fate was intended for the whole party. On his right was Cora, in a durance similar to his own, pale and agitated, but with an eye whose steady look still read the proceedings of their enemies. On his left, the withes [4] which bound her to a pine, performed that office for Alice which her trembling limbs refused, and alone kept her fragile form from sinking. Her hands were clasped before her in prayer, but instead of looking upwards towards that power which alone could rescue them, her unconscious looks wandered to the countenance of Duncan with infantile dependency. David had contended, and the novelty of the circumstance held him silent, in deliberation on the propriety of the unusual occurrence.

The vengeance of the Hurons had now taken a new direction, and they prepared to execute it with that barbarous ingenuity with which they were familiarized by the practice of centuries. Some sought knots, to raise the blazing pile; one was riving[5] the splinters of pine, in order to pierce the flesh of their captives with the burning fragments; and others bent the tops of two saplings to the earth, in order to suspend Heyward by the arms between the recoiling branches. But the vengeance of Magua sought a deeper and a more malignant enjoyment.

While the less refined monsters of the band prepared, before the eyes of those who were to suffer, these well known and vulgar means of torture, he approached Cora, and pointed out, with the most malign expression of countenance, the speedy fate that awaited her:—

"Ha!" he added, "what says the daughter of Munro? Her head is too good to find a pillow in the wigwam of Le Renard; will she like it better when it rolls about this hill a plaything for the wolves? Her bosom cannot nurse the children of a Huron; she will see it spit upon by Indians!"

"What means the monster!" demanded the astonished Heyward.

"Nothing!" was the firm reply. "He is a savage, a barbarous and ignorant savage, and knows not what he does. Let us find leisure, with our dying breath, to ask for him penitence and pardon."

"Pardon!" echoed the fierce Huron, mistaking, in his anger, the meaning of her words; "the memory of an Indian is longer than the arm of the pale-faces; his mercy shorter than their justice! Say; shall I send the yellow hair to her father, and will you follow Magua to the great lakes, to carry his water, and feed him with corn?"

Cora beckoned him away, with an emotion of disgust she could not control.

"Leave me," she said, with a solemnity that for a moment checked the barbarity of the Indian; "you mingle bitterness in my prayers; you stand between me and my God!"

The slight impression produced on the savage was, however, soon forgotten, and he continued pointing, with taunting irony, towards Alice.

"Look! the child weeps! She is young to die! Send her to Munro, to comb his gray hairs, and keep life in the heart of the old man."

Cora could not resist the desire to look upon her youthful sister, in whose eyes she met an imploring glance, that betrayed the longings of nature.

"What says he, dearest Cora?" asked the trembling voice of Alice. "Did he speak of sending me to our father?"

For many moments the elder sister looked upon the younger, with a countenance that wavered with powerful and contending emotions. At length she spoke, though her tones had lost their rich and calm fulness, in an expression of tenderness that seemed maternal.

"Alice," she said, "the Huron offers us both life, nay, more than both; he offers to restore Duncan, our invaluable Duncan, as well as you, to our friends—to our father—to our heart-stricken, childless father, if I will bow down this rebellious, stubborn pride of mine, and consent—"

Her voice became choked, and clasping her hands, she looked upward, as if seeking, in her agony, intelligence from a wisdom that was infinite.

"Say on," cried Alice; "to what, dearest Cora? O, that the proffer were made to me! to save you, to cheer our aged father, to restore Duncan, how cheerfully could I die!"

"Die!" repeated Cora, with a calmer and a firmer voice, "that were easy! Perhaps the alternative may not be less so. He would have me," she continued, her accents sinking under a deep consciousness of the degradation of the proposal, "follow him to the wilderness; go to the habitations of the Hurons; to remain there; in short to become his wife! Speak, then, Alice; child of my affections! sister of my love! And you, too, Major Heyward, aid my weak reason with your counsel. Is life to be purchased by such a sacrifice? Will you, Alice, receive it at my hands at such a price? And *you*, Duncan, guide me; control me between you; for I am wholly yours."

"Would I!" echoed the indignant and astonished youth. "Cora! Cora! you jest with our misery! Name not the horrid alternative again; the thought itself is worse than a thousand deaths."

"That such would be *your* answer, I well knew!" exclaimed Cora, her cheeks flushing, and her dark eyes once more sparkling with the lingering emotions of a woman. "What says my Alice? for her will I submit without another murmur."

Although both Heyward and Cora listened with painful suspense and the deepest attention, no sounds were heard in reply. It appeared as if the delicate and sensitive form of Alice would shrink into itself, as she listened to this proposal. Her arms had fallen lengthwise before her, the fingers moving in slight convulsions; her head dropped upon her bosom, and her whole person seemed suspended against the tree, looking like some beautiful emblem of the wounded delicacy of her sex, devoid of animation, and yet keenly conscious. In a few moments, however, her head began to move slowly, in a sign of deep, unconquerable disapprobation.

"No, no, no; better that we die as we have lived, together!"

"Then die!" shouted Magua, hurling his tomahawk with violence at the unresisting speaker, and gnashing his teeth with a rage that could no longer be bridled, at this sudden exhibition of firmness in the one he believed the weakest of the party. The axe cleaved the air in front of Heyward, and cutting some of the flowing ringlets of Alice, quivered in the tree above her head. The sight maddened Duncan to desperation. Collecting all his energies in one effort, he snapped the twigs which bound him and rushed upon another savage who was preparing with loud yells, and a more deliberate aim, to repeat the blow. They encountered, grappled, and fell to the earth together. The naked body of his antagonist afforded Heyward no means of holding his adversary, who glided from his grasp, and rose again with one knee on his chest, pressing him down with the weight of a giant. Duncan already saw the knife gleaming in the air, when a whistling sound swept past him, and was rather accompanied, than followed, by the sharp crack of a rifle. He felt his breast relieved from the load it had endured; he saw the savage expression of his adversary's countenance change to a look of vacant wildness, when the Indian fell dead on the faded leaves by his side.

Hey tries to convince Magua to save girls. Mag demands caucus w/ Cora + says this is revenge on Monro. Says he used to be chief, but tribe ditched when he learned to drink firewater, came to camp drunk + Monro whipped him, so he wants to marry Cora for revenge. Says Alice free if Cora marry. Cora refuses, Magua says to torture prisoners. Tied to stakes, Mag cuts some of Alices curls, Hey attacks, rifle shot. Heys attacker dead

XII

"Clo.—I am gone, sir,
And anon, sir,
I'll be with you again."
Twelfth Night[1]

THE HURONS STOOD AGHAST at this sudden visitation
of death on one of their band. But, as they regarded
the fatal accuracy of an aim which had dared to immolate
an enemy at so much hazard to a friend, the name of "La
Longue Carabine" burst simultaneously from every lip,
and was succeeded by a wild and a sort of plaintive howl.
The cry was answered by a loud shout from a little
thicket, where the incautious party had piled their arms;
and at the next moment, Hawkeye, too eager to load the
rifle he had regained, was seen advancing upon them,
brandishing the clubbed weapon, and cutting the air
with wide and powerful sweeps. Bold and rapid as was
the progress of the scout, it was exceeded by that of a
light and vigorous form which, bounding past him,
leaped, with incredible activity and daring, into the very
centre of the Hurons, where it stood, whirling a tomahawk, and flourishing a glittering knife, with fearful
menaces, in front of Cora. Quicker than the thoughts
could follow these unexpected and audacious move-

ments, an image, armed in the emblematic panoply of death, glided before their eyes, and assumed a threatening attitude at the other's side. The savage tormentors recoiled before these warlike intruders, and uttered as they appeared in such quick succession, the often repeated and peculiar exclamation of surprise, followed by the well known and dreaded appellations of—

"Le Cerf Agile! Le Gros Serpent!"

But the wary and vigilant leader of the Hurons was not so easily disconcerted. Casting his keen eyes around the little plain, he comprehended the nature of the assault at a glance, and encouraging his followers by his voice as well as by his example, he unsheathed his long and dangerous knife, and rushed with a loud whoop upon the expecting Chingachgook. It was the signal for a general combat. Neither party had fire-arms, and the contest was to be decided in the deadliest manner; hand to hand, with weapons of offence, and none of defence.

Uncas answered the whoop, and leaping on an enemy, with a single, well directed blow of his tomahawk, cleft him to the brain. Heyward tore the weapon of Magua from the sapling, and rushed eagerly towards the fray. As the combatants were now equal in number, each singled an opponent from the adverse band. The rush and blows passed with the fury of a whirlwind, and the swiftness of lightning. Hawkeye soon got another enemy within reach of his arm, and with one sweep of his formidable weapon he beat down the slight and inartificial defences of his antagonist, crushing him to the earth with the blow. Heyward ventured to hurl the tomahawk he had seized, too ardent to await the moment of closing. It struck the Indian he had selected on the forehead, and checked for an instant his onward rush. Encouraged by this slight advantage, the impetuous young man continued his onset, and sprang upon his enemy with naked hands. A single instant was enough to assure him of the rashness of the measure, for he immediately found himself fully engaged, with all his activity and courage, in endeavoring to ward the desperate thrusts made with the knife of the Huron. Unable longer to foil an enemy so alert and vigilant, he threw his arms about him, and succeeded in pinning the limbs of the other to his side, with an iron grasp, but one that was far too exhausting to himself to continue long. In this extremity he heard a voice near him, shouting—

"Exterminate the varlets! no quarter to an accursed Mingo!"

At the next moment, the breech of Hawkeye's rifle fell on the naked head of his adversary, whose muscles appeared to wither under the shock, as he sank from the arms of Duncan, flexible and motionless.

When Uncas had brained his first antagonist, he turned, like a hungry lion, to seek another. The fifth and only Huron disengaged at the first onset had paused a moment, and then seeing that all around him were employed in the deadly strife, he sought, with hellish vengeance, to complete the baffled work of revenge. Raising a shout of triumph, he sprang towards the defenceless Cora, sending his keen axe, as the dreadful precursor of his approach. The tomahawk grazed her shoulder, and cutting the withes which bound her to the tree, left the maiden at liberty to fly. She eluded the grasp of the savage, and reckless of her own safety, threw herself on the bosom of Alice, striving with convulsed and ill-directed fingers, to tear asunder the twigs which confined the person of her sister. Any other than a monster would have relented at such an act of generous devotion to the best and purest affection; but the breast of the Huron was a stranger to sympathy. Seizing Cora by the rich tresses which fell in confusion about her form, he tore her from her frantic hold, and bowed her down with brutal violence to her knees. The savage drew the flowing curls through his hand, and raising them on high with an outstretched arm, he passed the knife around the exquisitely moulded head of his victim, with a taunting and exulting laugh. But he purchased this moment of fierce gratification with the loss of the fatal opportunity. It was just then the sight caught the eye of Uncas. Bounding from his footsteps he appeared for an instant darting through the air, and descending in a ball he fell on the chest of his enemy, driving him many yards from the spot, headlong and prostrate. The violence of the exertion cast the young Mohican at his side. They arose together, fought, and bled, each in his turn. But the conflict was soon decided; the tomahawk of Heyward and the rifle of Hawkeye descended on the skull of the Huron, at the same moment that the knife of Uncas reached his heart.

The battle was now entirely terminated, with the exception of the protracted struggle between Le Renard Subtil and Le Gros Serpent. Well did these barbarous warriors prove that they deserved those significant names which had been bestowed for deeds in former wars. When they engaged, some little time was lost in eluding the quick and vigorous thrusts which had been aimed at their lives. Suddenly darting on each other, they closed, and came to the earth, twisted together like twining serpents, in pliant and subtle folds. At the moment

when the victors found themselves unoccupied, the spot
where these experienced and desperate combatants lay,
could only be distinguished by a cloud of dust and leaves
which moved from the centre of the little plain towards
its boundary, as if raised by the passage of a whirlwind.
Urged by the different motives of filial affection, friendship, and gratitude, Heyward and his companions
rushed with one accord to the place, encircling the little
canopy of dust which hung above the warriors. In vain
did Uncas dart around the cloud, with a wish to strike his
knife into the heart of his father's foe; the threatening
rifle of Hawkeye was raised and suspended in vain, while
Duncan endeavored to seize the limbs of the Huron with
hands that appeared to have lost their power. Covered,
as they were, with dust and blood, the swift evolutions of
the combatants seemed to incorporate their bodies into
one. The death-like looking figure of the Mohican, and
the dark form of the Huron, gleamed before their eyes in
such quick and confused succession, that the friends of
the former knew not where nor when to plant the suc-
coring blow. It is true there were short and fleeting moments, when the fiery eyes of Magua were seen
glittering, like the fabled organs of the basilisk, through
the dusty wreath by which he was enveloped, and he
read by those short and deadly glances the fate of the
combat in the presence of his enemies; ere, however, any
hostile hand could descend on his devoted head, its
place was filled by the scowling visage of Chingachgook.
In this manner the scene of the combat was removed
from the centre of the little plain to its verge. The Mohican now found an opportunity to make a powerful thrust
with his knife; Magua suddenly relinquished his grasp,

and fell backward without motion, and seemingly without life. His adversary leaped on his feet, making the arches of the forest ring with the sounds of triumph.

"Well done for the Delawares! victory to the Mohican!" cried Hawkeye, once more elevating the butt of the long and fatal rifle; "a finishing blow from a man without a cross will never tell against his honor, nor rob him of his right to the scalp."

But, at the very moment when the dangerous weapon was in the act of descending, the subtle Huron rolled swiftly from beneath the danger, over the edge of the precipice, and falling on his feet, was seen leaping, with a single bound, into the centre of a thicket of low bushes, which clung along its sides. The Delawares who had believed their enemy dead, uttered their exclamation of surprise, and were following with speed and clamor, like hounds in open view of the deer, when a shrill and peculiar cry from the scout instantly changed their purpose, and recalled them to the summit of the hill.

" 'Twas like himself," cried the inveterate forester, whose prejudices contributed so largely to veil his natural sense of justice in all matters which concerned the Mingos; "a lying and deceitful varlet as he is. An honest Delaware now, being fairly vanquished, would have lain still, and been knocked on the head, but these knavish Maquas cling to life like so many cats-o'-the-mountain. Let him go—let him go; 'tis but one man, and he without rifle or bow, many a long mile from his French commerades; and, like a rattler that has lost his fangs, he can do no further mischief, until such time as he, and we too, may leave the prints of our moccasins over a long reach of sandy plain. See, Uncas," he added, in Delaware, "your father is flaying the scalps already. It may be well to go round and feel the vagabonds that are left, or we may have another of them loping through the woods, and screeching like a jay that has been winged."

So saying, the honest, but implacable scout, made the circuit of the dead, into whose senseless bosoms he thrust his long knife, with as much coolness as though they had been so many brute carcasses. He had, however, been anticipated by the elder Mohican, who had already torn the emblems of victory from the unresisting heads of the slain.

But Uncas, denying his habits, we had almost said his nature, flew with instinctive delicacy, accompanied by Heyward, to the assistance of the females, and quickly releasing Alice, placed her in the arms of Cora. We shall not attempt to describe the gratitude to the Almighty Disposer of events which glowed in the bosoms of the sisters, who were thus unexpectedly restored to life and to each other. Their thanksgivings were deep and silent; the offerings of their gentle spirits, burning brightest and purest on the secret altars of their hearts; and their renovated and more earthly feelings exhibiting themselves in long and fervent, though speechless caresses. As Alice rose from her knees, where she had sunk by the side of Cora, she threw herself on the bosom of the latter, and sobbed aloud the name of their aged father, while her soft, dove-like eyes sparkled with the rays of hope.

"We are saved! we are saved!" she murmured; "to return to the arms of our dear, dear father, and his heart will not be broken with grief. And you too, Cora, my sister; my more than sister, my mother; you too are spared. And Duncan," she added, looking round upon the youth with a smile of ineffable innocence, "even our own brave and noble Duncan has escaped without a hurt."

To these ardent and nearly incoherent words Cora made no other answer than by straining the youthful speaker to her heart, as she bent over her, in melting tenderness. The manhood of Heyward felt no shame in dropping tears over this spectacle of affectionate rapture; and Uncas stood, fresh and blood-stained from the combat, a calm and, apparently, an unmoved looker-on, it is true, but with eyes that had already lost their fierceness, and were beaming with a sympathy that elevated him far above the intelligence, and advanced him probably centuries before the practices of his nation.

During this display of emotions so natural in their situation, Hawkeye, whose vigilant distrust had satisfied itself that the Hurons, who disfigured the heavenly scene, no longer possessed the power to interrupt its harmony, approached David, and liberated him from the bonds he had, until that moment, endured with the most exemplary patience.

"There," exclaimed the scout, casting the last withe behind him, "you are once more master of your own limbs, though you seem not to use them with greater judgment than that in which they were first fashioned. If advice from one who is not older than yourself, but who having lived most of his time in the wilderness, may be said to have experience beyond his years, will give no offence, you are welcome to my thoughts; and these are, to part with the little tooting instrument in your jacket to the first fool you meet with, and buy some useful we'pon with the money, if it be only the barrel of a horseman's pistol. By industry and care, you might thus come to some prefarment; for by this time, I should think, your eyes would plainly tell you that a carrion crow is a better bird than a mocking thresher. The one will, at least, remove foul sights from before the face of man, while the other is only good to brew disturbances in the woods, by cheating the ears of all that hear them."

"Arms and the clarion for the battle, but the song of thanksgiving to the victory!" answered the liberated David. "Friend," he added, thrusting forth his lean, delicate hand towards Hawkeye, in kindness, while his eyes twinkled and grew moist, "I thank thee that the hairs of my head still grow where they were first rooted by Providence; for, though those of other men may be more glossy and curling, I have ever found mine own well suited to the brain they shelter. That I did not join myself to the battle, was less owing to disinclination, than to the bonds of the heathen. Valiant and skilful hast thou proved thyself in the conflict, and I hereby thank thee, before proceeding to discharge other and more important duties, because thou hast proved thyself well worthy of a Christian's praise."

"The thing is but a trifle, and what you may often see, if you tarry long among us," returned the scout, a good deal softened towards the man of song, by this unequivocal expression of gratitude. "I have got back my old companion, 'Killdeer,'" he added, striking his hand on the breech of his rifle; "and that in itself is a victory. These Iroquois are cunning, but they outwitted themselves when they placed their fire-arms out of reach; and had Uncas or his father been gifted with only their common Indian patience, we should have come in upon the knaves with three bullets instead of one, and that would have made a finish of the whole pack; yon loping varlet, as well as his commerades. But 'twas all foreordered, and for the best."

"Thou sayest well," returned David, "and hast caught

the true spirit of Christianity. He that is to be saved will be saved, and he that is predestined to be damned will be damned. This is the doctrine of truth, and most consoling and refreshing it is to the true believer."

The scout, who by this time was seated, examining into the state of his rifle with a species of parental assiduity, now looked up at the other in a displeasure that he did not affect to conceal, roughly interrupting further speech.

"Doctrine, or no doctrine," said the sturdy woodsman, " 'tis the belief of knaves, and the curse of an honest man. I can credit that yonder Huron was to fall by my hand, for with my own eyes I have seen it; but nothing short of being a witness will cause me to think he had met with any reward, or that Chingachgook, there, will be condemned at the final day."

"You have no warranty for such an audacious doctrine, nor any covenant to support it," cried David, who was deeply tinctured with the subtle distinctions which, in his time, and more especially in his province, had been drawn around the beautiful simplicity of revelation, by endeavoring to penetrate the awful mystery of the divine nature, supplying faith by self-sufficiency, and by consequence, involving those who reasoned from such human dogmas in absurdities and doubt; "your temple is reared on the sands, and the first tempest will wash away its foundation. I demand your authorities for such an uncharitable assertion (like other advocates of a system, David was not always accurate in his use of terms). Name chapter and verse; in which of the holy books do you find language to support you?"

"Book!" repeated Hawkeye, with singular and ill-concealed disdain; "do you take me for a whimpering boy

at the apron-string of one of your old gals; and this good
rifle on my knee for the feather of a goose's wing, my ox's
horn for a bottle of ink, and my leathern pouch for a cross-
barred handkercher to carry my dinner? Book! what have
such as I, who am a warrior of the wilderness, though a
man without a cross, to do with books? I never read but in
one, and the words that are written there are too simple
and too plain to need much schooling; though I may boast
that of forty long and hard-working years."

"What call you the volume?" said David, misconceiv-
ing the other's meaning.

" 'Tis open before your eyes," returned the scout;
"and he who owns it is not a niggard of its use. I have
heard it said that there are men who read in books to
convince themselves there is a God. I know not but man
may so deform his works in the settlement, as to leave
that which is so clear in the wilderness a matter of doubt
among traders and priests. If any such there be, and he
will follow me from sun to sun, through the windings of
the forest, he shall see enough to teach him that he is a
fool, and that the greatest of his folly lies in striving to
rise to the level of One he can never equal, be it in good-
ness, or be it in power."

The instant David discovered that he battled with a
disputant who imbibed his faith from the lights of nature, eschewing all subtleties of doctrine, he willingly
abandoned a controversy from which he believed neither profit nor credit was to be derived. While the scout
was speaking, he had also seated himself, and producing
the ready little volume and the iron-rimmed spectacles;
he prepared to discharge a duty, which nothing but the
unexpected assault he had received in his orthodoxy
could have so long suspended. He was, in truth, a min-

strel of the western continent—of a much later day, certainly, than those gifted bards, who formerly sang the profane renown of baron and prince, but after the spirit of his own age and country; and he was now prepared to exercise the cunning of his craft, in celebration of, or rather in thanksgiving for, the recent victory. He waited patiently for Hawkeye to cease, then lifting his eyes, together with his voice, he said, aloud,—

"I invite you, friends, to join in praise for this signal deliverance from the hands of barbarians and infidels, to the comfortable and solemn tones of the tune, called 'Northampton.'"

He next named the page and verse where the rhymes selected were to be found, and applied the pitch-pipe to his lips, with the decent gravity that he had been wont to use in the temple. This time he was, however, without any accompaniment, for the sisters were just then pouring out those tender effusions of affection which have been already alluded to. Nothing deterred by the smallness of his audience, which, in truth, consisted only of the discontented scout, he raised his voice, commencing and ending the sacred song without accident or interruption of any kind.

Hawkeye listened, while he coolly adjusted his flint and reloaded his rifle; but the sounds, wanting the extraneous assistance of scene and sympathy, failed to awaken his slumbering emotions. Never minstrel, or by whatever more suitable name David should be known, drew upon his talents in the presence of more insensible auditors; though considering the singleness and sincerity of his motive, it is probable that no bard of profane song ever uttered notes that ascended so near to that throne where all homage and praise is due. The scout shook his head, and muttering some unintelligible words, among which "throat" and "Iroquois," were alone audible, he walked away, to collect, and to examine into, the state of the captured arsenal of the Hurons. In this office he was now joined by Chingachgook, who found his own, as well as the rifle of his son, among the arms. Even Heyward and David were furnished with weapons; nor was ammunition wanting to render them all effectual.

When the foresters had made their selection, and distributed their prizes, the scout announced that the hour had arrived when it was necessary to move. By this time the song of Gamut had ceased, and the sisters had learned to still the exhibition of their emotions. Aided by Duncan and the younger Mohican, the two latter descended the precipitous sides of that hill which they had so lately ascended under so very different auspices, and whose summit had so nearly proved the scene of their massacre. At the foot, they found the Narragansetts browsing the herbage of the bushes; and having mounted, they followed the movements of a guide, who, in the most deadly straits, had so often proved himself their friend. The journey was, however, short. Hawkeye, leaving the blind path that the Hurons had followed, turned short to his right, and entering the thicket, he crossed a babbling brook, and halted in a narrow dell, under the shade of a few water elms. Their distance from the base of the fatal hill was but a few rods, and the steeds had been serviceable only in crossing the shallow stream.

The scout and the Indians appeared to be familiar with the sequestered place where they now were; for, leaning their rifles against the trees, they commenced throwing aside the dried leaves, and opening the blue clay, out of which a clear and sparkling spring of bright, glancing water, quickly bubbled. The white man then looked about him, as though seeking for some object, which was not to be found as readily as he expected:—

"Them careless imps, the Mohawks, with their Tuscarora and Onondaga brethren, have been here slaking their thirst," he muttered, "and the vagabonds have thrown away the gourd! This is the way with benefits, when they are bestowed on such disremembering hounds! Here has the Lord laid his hand, in the midst of the howling wilderness, for their good, and raised a fountain of water from the bowels of the 'arth, that might laugh at the richest shop of apothecary's ware in all the colonies; and see! the knaves have trodden in the clay, and deformed the cleanliness of the place, as though they were brute beasts, instead of human men."

Uncas silently extended towards him the desired gourd, which the spleen of Hawkeye had hitherto prevented him from observing, on a branch of an elm. Filling it with water, he retired a short distance, to a place where the ground was more firm and dry; here he coolly seated himself, and after taking a long and, apparently, a grateful draught, he commenced a very strict examination of the fragments of food left by the Hurons, which had hung in a wallet on his arm.

"Thank you, lad!" he continued, returning the empty gourd to Uncas; "now we will see how these rampaging Hurons lived, when outlying in ambushments. Look at this! The varlets know the better pieces of the deer; and one would think they might carve and roast a saddle, equal to the best cook in the land! But everything is raw, for the Iroquois are thorough savages. Uncas, take my steel, and kindle a fire; a mouthful of a tender broil will give natur' a helping hand, after so long a trail."

Heyward, perceiving that their guides now set about their repast in sober earnest, assisted the ladies to alight, and placed himself at their side, not unwilling to enjoy a few moments of grateful rest, after the bloody scene he had just gone through. While the culinary process was in hand, curiosity induced him to inquire into the circumstances which had led to their timely and unexpected rescue:—

"How is it that we see you so soon, my generous friend," he asked, "and without aid from the garrison of Edward?"

"Had we gone to the bend in the river, we might have been in time to rake the leaves over your bodies, but too late to have saved your scalps," coolly answered the scout. "No, no; instead of throwing away strength and opportunity by crossing to the fort, we lay by, under the bank of the Hudson, waiting to watch the movements of the Hurons."

"You were, then, witnesses of all that passed?"

"Not of all; for Indian sight is too keen to be easily cheated, and we kept close. A difficult matter it was, too, to keep this Mohican boy snug in the ambushment. Ah! Uncas, Uncas, your behavior was more like that of a curious woman than of a warrior on his scent."

Uncas permitted his eyes to turn for an instant on the sturdy countenance of the speaker, but he neither spoke nor gave any indication of repentance. On the contrary, Heyward thought the manner of the young Mohican was disdainful, if not a little fierce, and that he suppressed passions that were ready to explode, as much in compliment to the listeners, as from the deference he usually paid to his white associate.

"You saw our capture?" Heyward next demanded.

"We heard it," was the significant answer. "An Indian yell is plain language to men who have passed their days in the woods. But when you landed, we were driven to crawl, like sarpents, beneath the leaves; and then we lost sight of you entirely, until we placed eyes on you again, trussed to the trees, and ready bound for an Indian massacre."

"Our rescue was the deed of Providence. It was nearly a miracle that you did not mistake the path, for the Hurons divided, and each band had its horses."

"Ay! there we were thrown off the scent, and might, indeed, have lost the trail, had it not been for Uncas; we took the path, however, that led into the wilderness; for we judged, and judged rightly, that the savages would hold that course with their prisoners. But when we had followed it for many miles, without finding a single twig broken, as I had advised, my mind misgave me; especially as all the footsteps had the prints of moccasins."

"Our captors had the precaution to see us shod like themselves," said Duncan, raising a foot, and exhibiting the buckskin he wore.

"Ay, 'twas judgmatical, and like themselves; though we were too expart to be thrown from a trail by so common an invention."

"To what, then, are we indebted for our safety?"

"To what, as a white man who has no taint of Indian blood, I should be ashamed to own; to the judgment of the young Mohican, in matters which I should know better than he, but which I can now hardly believe to be true, though my own eyes tell me it is so."

" 'Tis extraordinary! will you not name the reason?"

"Uncas was bold enough to say, that the beasts ridden by the gentle ones," continued Hawkeye, glancing his eyes, not without curious interest, on the fillies of the ladies, "planted the legs of one side on the ground at the same time, which is contrary to the movements of all trotting four-footed animals of my knowledge, except the bear. And yet here are horses that always journey in this manner, as my own eyes have seen, and as their trail has shown for twenty long miles."

" 'Tis the merit of the animal! They come from the shores of Narragansett Bay, in the small province of Providence Plantations, and are celebrated for their hardihood, and the ease of this peculiar movement; though other horses are not unfrequently trained to the same."

"It may be—it may be," said Hawkeye, who had listened with singular attention to this explanation; "though I am a man who has the full blood of the whites, my judgment in deer and beaver is greater than in beasts of burden. Major Effingham[2] has many noble chargers, but I have never seen one travel after such a sideling gait."

"True; for he would value the animals for very different properties. Still is this a breed highly esteemed, and as you witness, much honored with the burdens it is often destined to bear."

The Mohicans had suspended their operations about the glimmering fire, to listen; and when Duncan had done, they looked at each other significantly, the father uttering the never-failing exclamation of surprise. The scout ruminated, like a man digesting his newly acquired knowledge, and once more stole a curious glance at the horses.

"I dare to say there are even stranger sights to be seen in the settlements!" he said, at length; "natur' is sadly abused by man, when he once gets the mastery. But, go sideling or go straight, Uncas had seen the movement, and their trail led us on to the broken bush. The outer branch, near the prints of one of the horses, was bent upward, as a lady breaks a flower from its stem, but all the rest were ragged and broken down, as if the strong hand of a man had been tearing them! So I concluded that the cunning varmints had seen the twig bent, and had torn the rest, to make us believe a buck had been feeling the boughs with his antlers."

"I do believe your sagacity did not deceive you; for some such thing occurred!"

"That was easy to see," added the scout, in no degree conscious of having exhibited any extraordinary sagacity; "and a very different matter it was from a waddling horse! It then struck me the Mingos would push for this spring, for the knaves well know the vartue of its waters!"

"Is it, then, so famous?" demanded Heyward, examining, with a more curious eye, the secluded dell, with its bubbling fountain, surrounded, as it was, by earth of a deep dingy brown.

"Few redskins, who travel south and east of the great lakes, but have heard of its qualities. Will you taste for yourself?"

Heyward took the gourd, and after swallowing a little of the water, threw it aside with grimaces of discontent. The scout laughed in his silent, but heartfelt manner, and shook his head with vast satisfaction.

"Ah! you want the flavor that one gets by habit; the time was when I liked it as little as yourself; but I have come to my taste, and I now crave it, as a deer does the licks. Your high spiced wines are not better liked than a redskin relishes this water; especially when his natur' is ailing. But Uncas has made his fire, and it is time we think of eating, for our journey is long, and all before us."

Interrupting the dialogue by this abrupt transition, the scout had instant recourse to the fragments of food which had escaped the voracity of the Hurons. A very summary process completed the simple cookery, when he and the Mohicans commenced their humble meal, with the silence and characteristic diligence of men who ate in order to enable themselves to endure great and unremitting toil.

When this necessary, and, happily, grateful duty had been performed, each of the foresters stooped and took a long and parting draught at that solitary and silent spring around which and its sister fountains, within fifty years, the wealth, beauty, and talents of a hemisphere were to assemble in throngs, in pursuit of health and pleasure. Then Hawkeye announced his determination to proceed. The sisters resumed their saddles; Duncan and David grasped their rifles, and followed on their footsteps; the scout leading the advance, and the Mohicans bringing up the rear. The whole party moved swiftly through the narrow path, towards the north, leaving the healing waters to mingle unheeded with the adjacent brook, and the bodies of the dead to fester on the neighboring mount, without the rites of sepulture; a fate but too common to the warriors of the woods to excite either commiseration or comment.

Fight, Uncas saves Cora, Chingachgook + Magua 1-oh-1, Magua runs away. Whites win. Hawk + Gamut argue about efficacy of prayer song. Travel northward towards Fort William Henry. Hawk says they had tracked Hurons for 20 mi.

XIII

"I'll seek a readier path."
Thomas Parnell, "A Night Piece on Death"[1]

THE ROUTE TAKEN by Hawkeye lay across those sandy plains, relieved by occasional valleys and swells of land, which had been traversed by their party on the morning of the same day, with the baffled Magua for their guide. The sun had now fallen low towards the distant mountains; and as their journey lay through the interminable forest, the heat was no longer oppressive. Their progress, in consequence, was proportionate; and long before the twilight gathered about them, they had made good many toilsome miles on their return.

The hunter, like the savage whose place he filled, seemed to select among the blind signs of their wild route, with a species of instinct, seldom abating his speed, and never pausing to deliberate. A rapid and oblique glance at the moss on the trees, with an occasional upward gaze towards the setting sun, or a steady but passing look at the direction of the numerous watercourses, through which he waded, were sufficient to determine his path, and remove his greatest difficulties. In the meantime, the forest began to change its hues, losing that lively green which had embellished its arches, in the graver light which is the usual precursor of the close of day.

While the eyes of the sisters were endeavoring to catch glimpses through the trees, of the flood of golden glory which formed a glittering halo around the sun, tinging here and there with ruby streaks, or bordering with narrow edgings of shining yellow, a mass of clouds that lay piled at no great distance above the western hills, Hawkeye turned suddenly, and, pointing upwards towards the gorgeous heavens, he spoke:—

"Yonder is the signal given to a man to seek his food and natural rest," he said: "better and wiser would it be, if he could understand the signs of nature, and take a lesson from the fowls of the air and the beasts of the fields! Our night, however, will soon be over; for, with the moon, we must be up and moving again. I remember to have fou't the Maquas, hereaways, in the first war in which I ever drew blood from man; and we threw up a work of blocks, to keep the ravenous varmints from handling our scalps. If my marks do not fail me, we shall find the place a few rods farther to our left."

Without waiting for an assent, or, indeed, for any reply, the sturdy hunter moved boldly into a dense thicket of young chestnuts, shoving aside the branches of the exuberant shoots which nearly covered the ground, like a man who expected, at each step, to discover some object he had formerly known. The recollection of the scout did not deceive him. After penetrating through the brush, matted as it was with briers, for a few hundred feet he entered an open space, that surrounded a low, green hillock, which was crowned by the decayed blockhouse in question. This rude and neglected building was one of those deserted works, which, having been thrown up on an emergency, had been abandoned with the disappearance of danger, and was now quietly crumbling in the solitude of the forest, neglected, and nearly forgotten, like the circumstances which had caused it to be reared. Such memorials of the passage and struggles of man are yet frequent throughout the broad barrier of wilderness which once separated the hostile provinces, and form a species of ruins that are intimately associated with the recollections of colonial history, and which are in appropriate keeping with the gloomy character of the surrounding scenery. The roof of bark had long since fallen, and mingled with the soil; but the huge logs of pine, which had been hastily thrown together, still preserved their relative positions, though one angle of the work had given way under the pressure, and threatened a speedy downfall to the remainder of the rustic edifice. While Heyward and his companions hesitated to approach a building so decayed, Hawkeye and the Indians entered within the low walls, not only without fear, but with obvious interest. While the former surveyed the ruins, both internally and externally, with the curiosity of one whose recollections were reviving at each moment, Chingachgook related to his son, in the language of the Delawares, and with the pride of a conqueror, the brief history of the skirmish which had been fought, in his youth, in that secluded spot. A strain of melancholy, however, blended with his triumph, rendering his voice, as usual, soft and musical.

In the meantime, the sisters gladly dismounted, and prepared to enjoy their halt in the coolness of the evening, and in a security which they believed nothing but the beasts of the forest could invade.

"Would not our resting-place have been more retired,

my worthy friend," demanded the more vigilant Duncan, perceiving that the scout had already finished his short survey, "had we chosen a spot less known, and one more rarely visited than this?"

"Few live who know the block-house was ever raised," was the slow and musing answer; " 'tis not often that books are made, and narratives written, of such a scrimmage as was here fou't atween the Mohicans and the Mohawks, in a war of their own waging.[2] I was then a younker, and went out with the Delawares, because I know'd they were a scandalized and wronged race. Forty days and forty nights did the imps crave our blood around this pile of logs, which I designed and partly reared, being, as you'll remember, no Indian myself, but a man without a cross. The Delawares lent themselves to the work, and we made it good, ten to twenty, until our numbers were nearly equal, and then we sallied out upon the hounds, and not a man of them ever got back to tell the fate of his party. Yes, yes; I was then young, and new to the sight of blood; and not relishing the thought that creatures who had spirits like myself should lay on the naked ground, to be torn asunder by beasts, or to bleach in the rains, I buried the dead with my own hands, under that very little hillock where you have placed yourselves; and no bad seat does it make neither, though it be raised by the bones of mortal men."

Heyward and the sisters arose, on the instant, from the grassy sepulchre; nor could the two latter, notwithstanding the terrific scenes they had so recently passed through, entirely suppress an emotion of natural horror, when they found themselves in such familiar contact with the grave of the dead Mohawks. The gray light, the gloomy little area of dark grass, surrounded by its border

of brush, beyond which the pines rose, in breathing silence, apparently, into the very clouds, and the deathlike
stillness of the vast forest, were all in unison to deepen
such a sensation.

"They are gone, and they are harmless," continued
Hawkeye, waving his hand, with a melancholy smile, at
their manifest alarm: "they'll never shout the war-whoop
nor strike a blow with the tomahawk again! And of all
those who aided in placing them where they lie, Chingachgook and I only are living! The brothers and family
of the Mohican formed our war-party; and you see before you all that are now left of his race."

The eyes of the listeners involuntarily sought the
forms of the Indians, with a compassionate interest in
their desolate fortune. The dark persons were still to be
seen within the shadows of the block-house, the son listening to the relation of his father with that sort of intenseness which would be created by a narrative that
redounded so much to the honor of those whose names
he had long revered for their courage and savage virtues.

"I had thought the Delawares a pacific people," said
Duncan, "and that they never waged war in person;
trusting the defence of their lands to those very Mohawks that you slew!"

" 'Tis true in part," returned the scout, "and yet, at the
bottom, 'tis a wicked lie. Such a treaty was made in ages
gone by, through the deviltries of the Dutchers, who
wished to disarm the natives that had the best right to the
country where they had settled themselves. The Mohicans, though a part of the same nation, having to deal
with the English, never entered into the silly bargain, but
kept to their manhood; as in truth did the Delawares,
when their eyes were opened to their folly. You see be-

fore you a chief of the great Mohican Sagamores! Once
his family could chase their deer over tracts of country
wider than that which belongs to the Albany Patteroon,[3]
without crossing brook or hill that was not their own; but
what is left to their descendant! He may find his six feet
of earth when God chooses, and keep it in peace, perhaps, if he has a friend who will take the pains to sink his
head so low that the ploughshares cannot reach it!"

"Enough!" said Heyward, apprehensive that the subject might lead to a discussion that would interrupt the
harmony so necessary to the preservation of his fair companions: "we have journeyed far, and few among us are
blessed with forms like that of yours, which seems to
know neither fatigue nor weakness."

"The sinews and bones of a man carry me through it
all," said the hunter, surveying his muscular limbs with a
simplicity that betrayed the honest pleasure the compliment afforded him: "there are larger and heavier men to
be found in the settlements, but you might travel many
days in a city before you could meet one able to walk fifty
miles without stopping to take breath, or who has kept
the hounds within hearing during a chase of hours. However, as flesh and blood are not always the same, it is
quite reasonable to suppose that the gentle ones are willing to rest, after all they have seen and done this day.
Uncas, clear out the spring, while your father and I make
a cover for their tender heads of these chestnut shoots,
and a bed of grass and leaves."

The dialogue ceased, while the hunter and his companions busied themselves in preparations for the comfort and protection of those they guided. A spring, which
many long years before had induced the natives to select
the place for their temporary fortification, was soon

cleared of leaves, and a fountain of crystal gushed from the bed, diffusing its waters over the verdant hillock. A corner of the building was then roofed in such a manner as to exclude the heavy dew of the climate, and piles of sweet shrubs and dried leaves were laid beneath it for the sisters to repose on.

While the diligent woodsmen were employed in this manner, Cora and Alice partook of that refreshment which duty required much more than inclination prompted them to accept. They then retired within the walls, and first offering up their thanksgivings for past mercies, and petitioning for a continuance of the divine favor throughout the coming night, they laid their tender forms on the fragrant couch, and in spite of recollections and forebodings, soon sank into those slumbers which nature so imperiously demanded, and which were sweetened by hopes for the morrow. Duncan had prepared himself to pass the night in watchfulness near them, just without the ruin, but the scout, perceiving his intention, pointed towards Chingachgook as he coolly disposed his own person on the grass, and said—

"The eyes of a white man are too heavy and too blind for such a watch as this! The Mohican will be our sentinel, therefore let us sleep."

"I proved myself a sluggard on my post during the past night," said Heyward, "and have less need of repose than you, who did more credit to the character of a soldier. Let all the party seek their rest, then, while I hold guard."

"If we lay among the white tents of the 60th, and in front of an enemy like the French, I could not ask for a better watchman," returned the scout; "but in the darkness and among the signs of the wilderness your judgment would be like the folly of a child, and your vigilance thrown away. Do then, like Uncas and myself, sleep, and sleep in safety."

Heyward perceived, in truth, that the younger Indian had thrown his form on the side of the hillock while they were talking, like one who sought to make the most of the time allotted to rest, and that his example had been followed by David, whose voice literally "clove to his jaws," with the fever of his wound, heightened, as it was, by their toilsome march.

Unwilling to prolong a useless discussion, the young man affected to comply, by posting his back against the logs of the block-house, in a half-recumbent posture, though resolutely determined, in his own mind, not to close an eye until he had delivered his precious charge into the arms of Munro himself. Hawkeye, believing he had prevailed, soon fell asleep, and a silence as deep as the solitude in which they had found it, pervaded the retired spot.

For many minutes Duncan succeeded in keeping his senses on the alert, and alive to every moaning sound that arose from the forest. His vision became more acute as the shades of evening settled on the place; and even after the stars were glimmering above his head, he was able to distinguish the recumbent forms of his companions, as they lay stretched on the grass, and to note the person of Chingachgook, who sat upright and motionless as one of the trees which formed the dark barrier on every side. He still heard the gentle breathings of the sisters, who lay within a few feet of him, and not a leaf was ruffled by the passing air, of which his ear did not detect the whispering sound. At length, however, the mournful notes of a whippoorwill became blended with the moan-

ings of an owl; his heavy eyes occasionally sought the
bright rays of the stars, and then he fancied he saw them
through the fallen lids. At instants of momentary wake-
fulness he mistook a bush for his associate sentinel; his
head next sank upon his shoulder, which, in its turn,
sought the support of the ground; and, finally, his whole
person became relaxed and pliant, and the young man
sank into a deep sleep, dreaming that he was a knight of
ancient chivalry, holding his midnight vigils before the
tent of a recaptured princess, whose favor he did not despair of gaining, by such a proof of devotion and watchfulness.

How long the tired Duncan lay in this insensible state
he never knew himself, but his slumbering visions had
been long lost in total forgetfulness, when he was awakened by a light tap on the shoulder. Aroused by this signal, slight as it was, he sprang upon his feet with a
confused recollection of the self-imposed duty he had
assumed with the commencement of the night.

"Who comes?" he demanded, feeling for his sword at
the place where it was usually suspended. "Speak! friend
or enemy?"

"Friend," replied the low voice of Chingachgook;
who, pointing upwards at the luminary which was shedding its mild light through the opening in the trees, directly in their bivouac,[4] immediately added, in his rude
English, "moon comes, and white man's fort far—far off;
time to move, when sleep shuts both eyes of the Frenchman!"

"You say true! call up your friends, and bridle the
horses, while I prepare my own companions for the
march!"

"We are awake, Duncan," said the soft, silvery tones of Alice within the building, "and ready to travel very fast after so refreshing a sleep; but you have watched through the tedious night in our behalf, after having endured so much fatigue the livelong day!"

"Say, rather, I would have watched, but my treacherous eyes betrayed me; twice have I proved myself unfit for the trust I bear."

"Nay, Duncan, deny it not," interrupted the smiling Alice, issuing from the shadows of the building into the light of the moon, in all the loveliness of her freshened beauty; "I know you to be a heedless one, when self is the object of your care, and but too vigilant in favor of others. Can we not tarry here a little longer, while you find the rest you need? Cheerfully, most cheerfully, will Cora and I keep the vigils, while you, and all these brave men, endeavor to snatch a little sleep!"

"If shame could cure me of my drowsiness, I should never close an eye again," said the uneasy youth, gazing at the ingenuous countenance of Alice, where, however, in its sweet solicitude, he read nothing to confirm his half-awakened suspicion. "It is but too true, that after leading you into danger by my heedlessness, I have not even the merit of guarding your pillows as should become a soldier."

"No one but Duncan himself should accuse Duncan of such a weakness. Go, then, and sleep; believe me, neither of us, weak girls as we are, will betray our watch."

The young man was relieved from the awkwardness of making any further protestations of his own demerits, by an exclamation from Chingachgook, and the attitude of riveted attention assumed by his son.

"The Mohicans hear an enemy!" whispered Hawkeye, who, by this time, in common with the whole party, was awake and stirring. "They scent danger in the wind!"

"God forbid!" exclaimed Heyward. "Surely we have had enough of bloodshed!"

While he spoke, however, the young soldier seized his rifle, and advancing towards the front, prepared to atone for his venial remissness, by freely exposing his life in defence of those he attended.

" 'Tis some creature of the forest prowling around us in quest of food," he said, in a whisper, as soon as the low, and apparently distant sounds, which had startled the Mohicans, reached his own ears.

"Hist!" returned the attentive scout; " 'tis man; even I can now tell his tread, poor as my senses are when compared to an Indian's! That scampering Huron has fallen in with one of Montcalm's outlying parties, and they have struck upon our trail. I shouldn't like, myself, to spill more human blood in this spot," he added, looking around with anxiety in his features, at the dim objects by which he was surrounded; "but what must be, must! Lead the horses into the block-house, Uncas; and, friends, do you follow to the same shelter. Poor and old as it is, it offers a cover, and has rung with the crack of a rifle afore tonight!"

He was instantly obeyed, the Mohicans leading the Narragansetts within the ruin, whither the whole party repaired with the most guarded silence.

The sounds of approaching footsteps were now too distinctly audible to leave any doubts as to the nature of the interruption. They were soon mingled with voices calling to each other in an Indian dialect, which the hunter, in a whisper, affirmed to Heyward was the language of the Hurons. When the party reached the point where the horses had entered the thicket which surrounded the block-house, they were evidently at fault, having lost those marks which, until that moment, had directed their pursuit.

It would seem by the voices that twenty men were soon collected at that one spot, mingling their different opinions and advice in noisy clamor.

"The knaves know our weakness," whispered Hawkeye, who stood by the side of Heyward, in deep shade, looking through an opening in the logs, "or they wouldn't indulge their idleness in such a squaw's march. Listen to the reptiles! each man among them seems to have two tongues, and but a single leg."

Duncan, brave as he was in the combat, could not, in such a moment of painful suspense, make any reply to the cool and characteristic remark of the scout. He only grasped his rifle more firmly, and fastened his eyes upon the narrow opening, through which he gazed upon the moonlight view with increasing anxiety. The deeper tones of one who spoke as having authority were next heard, amid a silence that denoted the respect with which his orders, or rather advice, was received. After which, by the rustling of leaves, and cracking of dried twigs, it was apparent the savages were separating in pursuit of the lost trail. Fortunately for the pursued, the light of the moon, while it shed a flood of mild lustre upon the little area around the ruin, was not sufficiently strong to penetrate the deep arches of the forest, where the objects still lay in deceptive shadow. The search proved fruitless; for so short and sudden had been the passage from the faint path the travellers had journeyed into the thicket, that every trace of their footsteps was lost in the obscurity of the woods.

It was not long, however, before the restless savages were heard beating the brush, and gradually approaching the inner edge of that dense border of young chestnuts which encircled the little area.

"They are coming," muttered Heyward, endeavoring to thrust his rifle through the chink in the logs; "let us fire on their approach."

"Keep everything in the shade," returned the scout; "the snapping of a flint, or even the smell of a single karnel of the brimstone, would bring the hungry varlets upon us in a body. Should it please God that we must give battle for the scalps, trust to the experience of men who know the ways of the savages, and who are not often backward when the war-whoop is howled."

Duncan cast his eyes behind him, and saw that the trembling sisters were cowering in the far corner of the building, while the Mohicans stood in the shadow, like two upright posts, ready, and apparently willing, to strike when the blow should be needed. Curbing his impatience, he again looked out upon the area, and awaited the result in silence. At that instant the thicket opened, and a tall and armed Huron advanced a few paces into the open space. As he gazed upon the silent block-house, the moon fell upon his swarthy countenance, and betrayed its surprise and curiosity. He made the exclamation which usually accompanies the former emotion in an Indian, and, calling in a low voice, soon drew a companion to his side.

These children of the woods stood together for several moments pointing at the crumbling edifice, and conversing in the unintelligible language of their tribe. They then approached, though with slow and cautious steps, pausing every instant to look at the building, like startled deer, whose curiosity struggled powerfully with their awakened apprehensions for the mastery. The foot of one of them suddenly rested on the mound, and he stooped to examine its nature. At this moment, Heyward observed that the scout loosened his knife in his sheath, and lowered the muzzle of his rifle. Imitating these movements, the young man prepared himself for the struggle, which now seemed inevitable.

The savages were so near, that the least motion in one of the horses, or even a breath louder than common, would have betrayed the fugitives. But, in discovering the character of the mound, the attention of the Hurons appeared directed to a different object. They spoke together, and the sounds of their voices were low and solemn, as if influenced by a reverence that was deeply blended with awe. Then they drew warily back, keeping their eyes riveted on the ruin, as if they expected to see the apparitions of the dead issue from its silent walls, until having reached the boundary of the area, they moved slowly into the thicket, and disappeared.

Hawkeye dropped the breech of his rifle to the earth, and drawing a long, free breath, exclaimed, in an audible whisper,—

"Ay! they respect the dead, and it has this time saved their own lives, and, it may be, the lives of better men too."

Heyward lent his attention for a single moment to his companion, but without replying, he again turned towards those who just then interested him more. He heard the two Hurons leave the bushes, and it was soon plain that all the pursuers were gathered about them, in deep attention to their report. After a few minutes of earnest and solemn dialogue, altogether different from the noisy clamor with which they had first collected about the spot, the sounds grew fainter and more distant, and finally were lost in the depths of the forest.

Hawkeye waited until a signal from the listening Chingachgook assured him that every sound from the retiring party was completely swallowed by the distance, when he motioned to Heyward to lead forth the horses, and to assist the sisters into their saddles. The instant this was done, they issued through the broken gateway, and stealing out by a direction opposite to the one by which they had entered, they quitted the spot, the sisters casting furtive glances at the silent grave and crumbling ruin, as they left the soft light of the moon, to bury themselves in the gloom of the woods.

To a blockhouse where Hawk + Ching once won a battle. Hawk says Ching + Uncas are last of the mohicans. All but Ching sleep. Hear enemies. Sound is lost Hurons 2 indians approach but respect for the site keeps them away.

XIV

"Guard.—Qui est là?
Puc.—Paisans, pauvres gens de France."
Henry vi, Part I[1]

D URING THE RAPID MOVEMENT from the block-
house, and until the party was deeply buried in the
forest, each individual was too much interested in the escape to hazard a word even in whispers. The scout resumed his post in the advance, though his steps, after he
had thrown a safe distance between himself and his enemies, were more deliberate than in their previous
march, in consequence of his utter ignorance of the localities of the surrounding woods. More than once he
halted to consult with his confederates, the Mohicans,
pointing upwards at the moon, and examining the barks
of the trees with care. In these brief pauses, Heyward
and the sisters listened, with senses rendered doubly
acute by the danger, to detect any symptoms which
might announce the proximity of their foes. At such moments, it seemed as if a vast range of country lay buried
in eternal sleep; not the least sound arising from the forest, unless it was the distant and scarcely audible rippling
of a water-course. Birds, beasts, and man, appeared to
slumber alike, if, indeed, any of the latter were to be

found in that wide tract of wilderness. But the sounds of the rivulet, feeble and murmuring as they were, relieved the guides at once from no trifling embarrassment, and towards it they immediately held their way.

When the banks of the little stream were gained, Hawkeye made another halt; and, taking the moccasins from his feet, he invited Heyward and Gamut to follow his example. He then entered the water, and for near an hour they travelled in the bed of the brook, leaving no trail. The moon had already sunk into an immense pile of black clouds, which lay impending above the western horizon, when they issued from the low and devious water-course to rise again to the light and level of the sandy but wooded plain. Here the scout seemed to be once more at home, for he held on his way with the certainty and diligence of a man who moved in the security of his own knowledge. The path soon became more uneven, and the travellers could plainly perceive that the mountains drew nigher to them on each hand, and that they were, in truth, about entering one of their gorges. Suddenly, Hawkeye made a pause, and waiting until he was joined by the whole party, he spoke, though in tones so low and cautious, that they added to the solemnity of his words, in the quiet and darkness of the place.

"It is easy to know the pathways, and to find the licks[2] and water-courses of the wilderness," he said; "but who that saw this spot could venture to say, that a mighty army was at rest among yonder silent trees and barren mountains?"

"We are then at no great distance from William Henry?" said Heyward, advancing nigher to the scout.

"It is yet a long and weary path, and when and where

to strike it, is now our greatest difficulty. See," he said, pointing through the trees towards a spot where a little basin of water reflected the stars from its placid bosom, "here is the 'bloody pond'; and I am on the ground that I have not only often travelled, but over which I have fou't the enemy, from the rising to the setting sun."

"Ha! that sheet of dull and dreary water, then, is the sepulchre of the brave men who fell in the contest. I have heard it named, but never have I stood on its banks before."

"Three battles did we make with the Dutch-Frenchman in a day," continued Hawkeye, pursuing the train of his own thoughts, rather than replying to the remark of Duncan. "He met us hard by, in our outward march to ambush his advance, and scattered us, like driven deer, through the defile, to the shores of Horican. Then we rallied behind our fallen trees, and made head against him, under Sir William—who was made Sir William for that very deed; and well did we pay him for the disgrace of the morning! Hundreds of Frenchmen saw the sun that day for the last time; and even the leader, Dieskau[3] himself, fell into our hands so cut and torn with the lead, that he has gone back to his own country, unfit for further acts in war."

" 'Twas a noble repulse!" exclaimed Heyward, in the heat of his youthful ardor; "the fame of it reached us early, in our southern army."

"Ay! but it did not end there. I was sent by Major Effingham, at Sir William's own bidding, to outflank the French, and carry the tidings of their disaster across the portage, to the fort on the Hudson. Just hereaway, where you see the trees rise into a mountain swell, I met a party coming down to our aid, and I led them where the enemy were taking their meal, little dreaming that they had not finished the bloody work of the day."

"And you surprised them?"

"If death can be a surprise to men who are thinking only of the cravings of their appetites. We gave them but little breathing time, for they had borne hard upon us in the fight of the morning, and there were few in our party who had not lost friend or relative by their hands. When all was over, the dead, and some say the dying, were cast into that little pond.[4] These eyes have seen its waters colored with blood, as natural water never yet flowed from the bowels of the 'arth."

"It was a convenient, and, I trust, will prove a peaceful grave for a soldier. You have, then, seen much service on this frontier?"

"I!" said the scout, erecting his tall person with an air of military pride; "there are not many echoes among these hills that haven't rung with the crack of my rifle, nor is there the space of a square mile atwixt Horican and the river, that 'Killdeer' hasn't dropped a living body on, be it an enemy or be it a brute beast. As for the grave, there, being as quiet as you mention, it is another matter. There are them in the camp who say and think, man, to lie still, should not be buried while the breath is in the body; and certain it is that in the hurry of that evening, the doctors had but little time to say who was living and who was dead. Hist! see you nothing walking on the shore of the pond?"

" 'Tis not probable that any are as houseless as ourselves, in this dreary forest."

"Such as he may care but little for house or shelter, and night dew can never wet a body that passes its days in the water," returned the scout, grasping the shoulder of Heyward with such convulsive strength as to make the young soldier painfully sensible how much superstitious terror had got the mastery of a man usually so dauntless.

"By heaven! there is a human form, and it approaches! Stand to your arms, my friends; for we know not whom we encounter."

"Qui vive?"[5] demanded a stern, quick voice, which sounded like a challenge from another world, issuing out of that solitary and solemn place.

"What says it?" whispered the scout; "it speaks neither Indian nor English!"

"Qui vive?" repeated the same voice, which was quickly followed by the rattling of arms, and a menacing attitude.

"France!" cried Heyward, advancing from the shadow of the trees to the shore of the pond, within a few yards of the sentinel.

"D'où venez-vous—où allez-vous, d'aussi bonne heure?"[6] demanded the grenadier, in the language and with the accent of a man from old France.

"Je viens de la découverte, et je vais me coucher."[7]

"Etes-vous officier du roi?"[8]

"Sans doute, mon camarade; me prends-tu pour un provincial! Je suis capitaine de chasseurs (Heyward well knew that the other was of a regiment in the line); j'ai ici, avec moi, les filles du commandant de la fortification. Aha! tu en as entendu parler! je les ai fait prisonnières près de l'autre fort, et je les conduis au général."[9]

"Ma foi! mesdames; j'en suis fâché pour vous," exclaimed the young soldier, touching his cap with grace; "mais—fortune de guerre! vous trouverez notre général un brave homme, et bien poli avec les dames."[10]

"C'est le caractère des gens de guerre," said Cora, with admirable self-possession. "Adieu, mon ami; je vous souhaiterais un devoir plus agréable à remplir." [11]

The soldier made a low and humble acknowledgment for her civility; and Heyward adding a "Bonne nuit, mon camarade," [12] they moved deliberately forward, leaving the sentinel pacing the banks of the silent pond, little suspecting an enemy of so much effrontery, and humming to himself those words, which were recalled to his mind by the sight of women, and perhaps by recollections of his own distant and beautiful France—

"*Vive le vin, l'amour,*" etc., etc. [13]

" 'Tis well you understood the knave!" whispered the scout, when they had gained a little distance from the place, and letting his rifle fall into the hollow of his arm again; "I soon saw that he was one of them uneasy Frenchers; and well for him it was that his speech was friendly and his wishes kind, or a place might have been found for his bones among those of his countrymen."

He was interrupted by a long and heavy groan which arose from the little basin, as though, in truth, the spirits of the departed lingered about their watery sepulchre.

"Surely it was of flesh!" continued the scout; "no spirit could handle its arms so steadily!"

"It *was* of flesh; but whether the poor fellow still belongs to this world may well be doubted," said Heyward, glancing his eyes around him, and missing Chingachgook from their little band. Another groan more faint than the former, was succeeded by a heavy and sullen plunge into the water, and all was as still again as if the borders of the dreary pool had never been awakened from the silence of creation. While they yet hesitated in uncertainty, the form of the Indian was seen gliding out of the thicket. As the chief rejoined them, with one hand he attached the reeking scalp of the unfortunate young Frenchman to his girdle, and with the other he replaced the knife and tomahawk that had drunk his blood. He then took his wonted station, with the air of a man who believed he had done a deed of merit.

The scout dropped one end of his rifle to the earth, and leaning his hands on the other, he stood musing in profound silence. Then shaking his head in a mournful manner, he muttered,—

" 'Twould have been a cruel and an unhuman act for a white-skin; but 'tis the gift and natur' of an Indian, and I suppose it should not be denied. I could wish, though, it had befallen an accursed Mingo, rather than that gay young boy from the old countries."

"Enough!" said Heyward, apprehensive the unconscious sisters might comprehend the nature of the detention, and conquering his disgust by a train of reflections very much like that of the hunter; " 'tis done; and though better it were left undone, cannot be amended. You see we are, too obviously, within the sentinels of the enemy; what course do you propose to follow?"

"Yes," said Hawkeye, rousing himself again, " 'tis as you say, too late to harbor further thoughts about it. Ay, the French have gathered around the fort in good earnest, and we have a delicate needle to thread in passing them."

"And but little time to do it in," added Heyward, glancing his eyes upward, toward the bank of vapor that concealed the setting moon.

"And little time to do it in!" repeated the scout. "The thing may be done in two fashions, by the help of Providence, without which it may not be done at all."

"Name them quickly, for time presses."

"One would be to dismount the gentle ones, and let their beasts range the plain; by sending the Mohicans in front, we might then cut a lane through their sentries, and enter the fort over the dead bodies."

"It will not do—it will not do!" interrupted the generous Heyward; "a soldier might force his way in this manner, but never with such a convoy."

" 'Twould be, indeed, a bloody path for tender feet to wade in," returned the equally reluctant scout; "but I thought it befitting my manhood to name it. We must then turn on our trail and get without the line of their look-outs, when we will bend short to the west, and enter the mountains; where I can hide you, so that all the devil's hounds in Montcalm's pay would be thrown off the scent, for months to come."

"Let it be done, and that instantly."

Further words were unnecessary; for Hawkeye, merely uttering the mandate to "follow," moved along the route by which they had just entered their present critical and even dangerous situation. Their progress, like their late dialogue, was guarded, and without noise; for none knew at what moment a passing patrol, or a crouching picket of the enemy, might rise upon their path. As they held their silent way along the margin of the pond, again Heyward and the scout stole furtive glances at its appalling dreariness. They looked in vain for the form they had so recently seen stalking along its silent shores, while a low and regular wash of the little waves, by announcing that the waters were not yet subsided, furnished a frightful memorial of the deed of blood they had just witnessed. Like all that passing and gloomy scene, the low basin, however, quickly melted in the darkness, and became blended with the mass of black objects in the rear of the travellers.

Hawkeye soon deviated from the line of their retreat, and striking off towards the mountains which form the western boundary of the narrow plain, he led his followers, with swift steps, deep within the shadows that were cast from their high and broken summits. The route was now painful; lying over ground ragged with rocks, and intersected with ravines, and their progress proportionately slow. Bleak and black hills lay on every side of them, compensating in some degree for the additional toil of the march, by the sense of security they imparted. At length the party began slowly to climb a steep and rugged ascent by a path that curiously wound among rocks and trees, avoiding the one, and supported by the other, in a manner that showed it had been devised by men long practised in the arts of the wilderness. As they gradually rose from the level of the valleys, the thick darkness which usually precedes the approach of day began to disperse, and objects were seen in the plain and palpable colors with which they had been gifted by nature. When they issued from the stunted woods which clung to the barren sides of the mountain, upon a flat and mossy rock that formed its summit, they met the morning, as it came blushing above the green pines of a hill that lay on the opposite side of the valley of the Horican.

The scout now told the sisters to dismount; and taking the bridles from the mouths, and the saddles off the backs of the jaded beasts, he turned them loose, to glean a scanty subsistence among the shrubs and meagre herbage of that elevated region.

"Go," he said, "and seek your food where natur' gives it you; and beware that you become not food to ravenous wolves yourselves, among these hills."

"Have we no further need of them?" demanded Heyward.

"See, and judge with your own eyes," said the scout, advancing towards the eastern brow of the mountain, whither he beckoned for the whole party to follow; "if it was as easy to look into the heart of man as it is to spy out the nakedness of Montcalm's camp from this spot, hypocrites would grow scarce, and the cunning of a Mingo might prove a losing game, compared to the honesty of a Delaware."

When the travellers reached the verge of the precipice, they saw, at a glance, the truth of the scout's declaration, and the admirable foresight with which he had led them to their commanding station.

The mountain on which they stood, elevated perhaps a thousand feet in the air, was a high cone that rose a little in advance of that range which stretches for miles along the western shores of the lake, until meeting its sister piles, beyond the water, it ran off towards the Canadas, in confused and broken masses of rock, thinly sprinkled with evergreens. Immediately at the feet of the party, the southern shore of the Horican swept in a broad semicircle, from mountain to mountain, marking a wide strand, that soon rose into an uneven and somewhat elevated plain. To the north stretched the limpid, and, as it appeared from that dizzy height, the narrow sheet of the "holy lake," indented with numberless bays, embellished by fantastic headlands, and dotted with countless islands. At the distance of a few leagues, the bed of the waters became lost among mountains, or was wrapped in the masses of vapor that came slowly rolling along their bosom, before a light morning air. But a narrow opening between the crests of the hills pointed out the passage by which they found their way still farther north, to spread their pure and ample sheets again, before pouring out their tribute into the distant Champlain. To the south stretched the defile, or rather broken plain, so often mentioned. For several miles in this direction, the mountains appeared reluctant to yield their dominion, but within reach of the eye they diverged, and finally melted into the level and sandy lands, across which we have accompanied our adventurers in their double journey. Along both ranges of hills, which bounded the opposite sides of the lake and valley, clouds of light vapor were rising in spiral wreaths from the uninhabited woods, looking like the smokes of hidden cottages; or rolled lazily down the declivities, to mingle with the fogs of the lower land. A single, solitary, snow-white cloud floated above the valley, and marked the spot beneath which lay the silent pool of the "bloody pond."

Directly on the shore of the lake, and nearer to its western than to its eastern margin, lay the extensive earthen ramparts and low buildings of William Henry. Two of the sweeping bastions appeared to rest on the water which washed their bases, while a deep ditch and extensive morasses guarded its other sides and angles. The land had been cleared of wood for a reasonable distance around the work, but every other part of the scene lay in the green livery of nature, except where the limpid water mellowed the view, or the bold rocks thrust their black and naked heads above the undulating outline of the mountain ranges. In its front might be seen the scattered sentinels, who held a weary watch against their numerous foes; and within the walls themselves, the travellers looked down upon men still drowsy with a night of vigilance. Towards the southeast, but in immediate contact with the fort, was an entrenched camp, posted on a rocky eminence, that would have been far more eligible for the work itself, in which Hawkeye pointed out the presence of those auxiliary regiments that had so recently left the Hudson in their company. From the woods, a little farther to the south, rose numerous dark and lurid smokes, that were easily to be distinguished from the purer exhalations of the springs, and which the scout also showed to Heyward, as evidences that the enemy lay in force in that direction.

But the spectacle which most concerned the young soldier was on the western bank of the lake, though quite near to its southern termination. On a strip of land, which appeared, from his stand, too narrow to contain such an army, but which, in truth, extended many hundreds of yards from the shores of the Horican to the base of the mountain, were to be seen the white tents and military engines of an encampment of ten thousand men. Batteries were already thrown up in their front, and even while the spectators above them were looking down, with such different emotions, on a scene which lay like a map beneath their feet, the roar of artillery rose from the valley, and passed off in thundering echoes, along the eastern hills.

"Morning is just touching them below," said the deliberate and musing scout, "and the watchers have a mind to wake up the sleepers by the sound of cannon. We are a few hours too late! Montcalm has already filled the woods with his accursed Iroquois."

"The place is, indeed, invested," returned Duncan, "but is there no expedient by which we may enter? capture in the works would be far preferable to falling again into the hands of roving Indians."

"See!" exclaimed the scout, unconsciously directing the attention of Cora to the quarters of her own father, "how that shot has made the stones fly from the side of the commandant's house! Ay! these Frenchers will pull it to pieces faster than it was put together, solid and thick though it be."

"Heyward, I sicken at the sight of danger that I cannot share," said the undaunted, but anxious daughter. "Let us go to Montcalm, and demand admission: he dare not deny a child the boon."

"You would scarce find the tent of the Frenchman with the hair on your head," said the blunt scout. "If I had but one of the thousand boats which lie empty along that shore, it might be done. Ha! here will soon be an end of the firing, for yonder comes a fog that will turn day to night, and make an Indian arrow more dangerous than a moulded cannon. Now, if you are equal to the work, and will follow, I will make a push; for I long to get down into that camp, if it be only to scatter some Mingo dogs that I see lurking in the skirts of yonder thicket of birch."

"We are equal," said Cora, firmly: "on such an errand we will follow to any danger."

The scout turned to her with a smile of honest and cordial approbation as he answered,—

"I would I had a thousand men, of brawny limbs and quick eyes, that feared death as little as you! I'd send them jabbering Frenchers back into their den again, afore the week was ended, howling like so many fettered hounds or hungry wolves. But stir," he added, turning from her to the rest of the party, "the fog comes rolling down so fast, we shall have but just the time to meet it on the plain, and use it as a cover. Remember, if any accident should befall me, to keep the air blowing on your left cheeks—or rather, follow the Mohicans; they'd scent their way, be it in day or be it at night."

He then waved his hand for them to follow, and threw himself down the steep declivity, with free, but careful footsteps. Heyward assisted the sisters to descend, and in a few minutes they were all far down a mountain whose sides they had climbed with so much toil and pain.

The direction taken by Hawkeye soon brought the travellers to the level of the plain, nearly opposite to a sally-port in the western curtain of the fort, which lay, itself, at the distance of about half a mile from the point where he halted to allow Duncan to come up with his charge. In their eagerness, and favored by the nature of the ground, they had anticipated the fog, which was rolling heavily down the lake, and it became necessary to pause, until the mists had wrapped the camp of the enemy in their fleecy mantle. The Mohicans profited by the delay, to steal out of the woods, and to make a survey of surrounding objects. They were followed at a little distance by the scout, with a view to profit early by their report, and to obtain some faint knowledge for himself of the more immediate localities.

In a very few moments he returned, his face reddened with vexation, while he muttered his disappointment in words of no very gentle import.

"Here has the cunning Frenchman been posting a picket directly in our path," he said; "redskins and whites; and we shall be as likely to fall into their midst as to pass them in the fog!"

"Cannot we make a circuit to avoid the danger," asked Heyward, "and come into our path again when it is passed?"

"Who that once bends from the line of his march in a fog can tell when or how to turn to find it again! The mists of Horican are not like the curls from a peace-pipe, or the smoke which settles above a mosquito fire."

He was yet speaking, when a crashing sound was heard, and a cannon-ball entered the thicket, striking the body of a sapling, and rebounding to the earth, its force being much expended by previous resistance. The Indians followed instantly like busy attendants on the terrible messenger, and Uncas commenced speaking earnestly and with much action, in the Delaware tongue.

"It may be so, lad," muttered the scout, when he had ended; "for desperate fevers are not to be treated like a toothache. Come, then, the fog is shutting in."

"Stop!" cried Heyward; "first explain your expectations."

" 'Tis soon done, and a small hope it is; but it is better than nothing. This shot that you see," added the scout, kicking the harmless iron with his foot, "has ploughed the 'arth in its road from the fort, and we shall hunt for the furrow it has made, when all other signs may fail. No more words, but follow, or the fog may leave us in the middle of our path, a mark for both armies to shoot at."

Heyward perceiving that, in fact, a crisis had arrived when acts were more required than words, placed himself between the sisters, and drew them swiftly forward, keeping the dim figure of their leader in his eye. It was soon apparent that Hawkeye had not magnified the power of the fog, for before they had proceeded twenty yards, it was difficult for the different individuals of the party to distinguish each other, in the vapor.

They had made their little circuit to the left, and were already inclining again towards the right, having, as Heyward thought, got over nearly half the distance to the friendly works, when his ears were saluted with the fierce summons, apparently within twenty feet of them, of—

"Qui va là?" [14]

"Push on!" whispered the scout, once more bending to the left.

"Push on!" repeated Heyward; when the summons was renewed by a dozen voices, each of which seemed charged with menace.

"C'est moi," [15] cried Duncan, dragging rather than leading those he supported, swiftly onward.

"Bête!—qui?—moi!" [16]

"Ami de la France." [17]

"Tu m'as plus l'air d'un *ennemi* de la France; arrête! ou pardieu je te ferai ami du diable. Non! feu, camarades, feu!" [18]

The order was instantly obeyed, and the fog was stirred by the explosion of fifty muskets. Happily, the aim was bad, and the bullets cut the air in a direction a little different from that taken by the fugitives; though still so nigh them, that to the unpractised ears of David and the two females, it appeared as if they whistled within a few inches of the organs. The outcry was renewed, and the order, not only to fire again, but to pursue, was too plainly audible. When Heyward briefly explained the meaning of the words they heard, Hawkeye halted, and spoke with quick decision and great firmness.

"Let us deliver our fire," he said; "they will believe it a

sortie, and give way, or they will wait for reinforcements."

The scheme was well conceived, but failed in its effect. The instant the French heard the pieces, it seemed as if the plain was alive with men, muskets rattling along its whole extent, from the shores of the lake to the farthest boundary of the woods.

"We shall draw their entire army upon us, and bring on a general assault," said Duncan: "lead on, my friend, for your own life, and ours."

The scout seemed willing to comply; but, in the hurry of the moment, and in the change of position, he had lost the direction. In vain he turned either cheek towards the light air; they felt equally cool. In this dilemma, Uncas lighted on the furrow of the cannon-ball, where it had cut the ground in three adjacent ant-hills.

"Give me the range!" said Hawkeye, bending to catch a glimpse of the direction, and then instantly moving onward.

Cries, oaths, voices calling to each other, and the reports of muskets, were now quick and incessant, and, apparently, on every side of them. Suddenly, a strong glare of light flashed across the scene, the fog rolled upwards in thick wreaths, and several cannon belched across the plain, and the roar was thrown heavily back from the bellowing echoes of the mountain.

" 'Tis from the fort!" exclaimed Hawkeye, turning short on his tracks; "and we, like stricken fools, were rushing to the woods, under the very knives of the Maquas."

The instant their mistake was rectified, the whole party retraced the error with the utmost diligence. Duncan willingly relinquished the support of Cora to the arm of Uncas, and Cora as readily accepted the welcome assistance. Men, hot and angry in pursuit, were evidently on their footsteps, and each instant threatened their capture, if not their destruction.

"Point de quartier aux coquins!"[19] cried an eager pursuer, who seemed to direct the operations of the enemy.

"Stand firm, and be ready, my gallant 60ths!" suddenly exclaimed a voice above them; "wait to see the enemy,—fire low, and sweep the glacis."[20]

"Father! father!" exclaimed a piercing cry from out the mist; "it is I! Alice! thy own Elsie! spare, O! save your daughters!"

"Hold!" shouted the former speaker, in the awful tones of parental agony, the sound reaching even to the woods, and rolling back in solemn echo. " 'Tis she! God has restored me my children! Throw open the sally-port;[21] to the field, 60ths, to the field; pull not a trigger, lest ye kill my lambs! Drive off these dogs of France with your steel."

Duncan heard the grating of the rusty hinges, and darting to the spot, directed by the sound, he met a long line of dark red warriors, passing swiftly towards the glacis. He knew them for his own battalion of the royal Americans, and flying to their head, soon swept every trace of his pursuers from before the works.

For an instant, Cora and Alice had stood trembling and bewildered by this unexpected desertion; but, before either had leisure for speech, or even thought, an officer of gigantic frame whose locks were bleached with years and service, but whose air of military grandeur had been rather softened than destroyed by time, rushed out of the body of the mist, and folded them to his bosom, while large scalding tears rolled down his pale and wrinkled cheeks, and he exclaimed, in the peculiar accent of Scotland,—

"For this I thank thee, Lord! Let danger come as it will, thy servant is now prepared!"

Go through a river, by a pond that Hawk says is filled w/ dead French soldiers. encounter a french sentinel. Hey talk in French to him while ching sneaks, kills, + scalps him. English troops + French start fighting. Hidden by fog, they find their way, french follow but get to fort safe. Munro weeps for joy to see his daughters.

XV

"Then go we in, to know his embassy;
Which I could, with ready guess, declare
Before the Frenchman speak a word of it."
Henry v[1]

A FEW SUCCEEDING DAYS were passed amid the privations, the uproar, and the dangers of the siege,
which was vigorously pressed by a power against whose
approaches Munro possessed no competent means of
resistance. It appeared as if Webb, with his army, which
lay slumbering on the banks of the Hudson, had utterly
forgotten the strait to which his countrymen were reduced. Montcalm had filled the woods of the portage
with his savages, every yell and whoop from whom rang
through the British encampment, chilling the hearts of
men who were already but too much disposed to magnify the danger.

Not so, however, with the besieged. Animated by the
words, and stimulated by the examples, of their leaders,
they had found their courage, and maintained their ancient reputation, with zeal that did justice to the stern
character of their commander. As if satisfied with the toil
of marching through the wilderness to encounter his
enemy, the French general, though of approved skill,

had neglected to seize the adjacent mountains; whence the besieged might have been exterminated with impunity, and which, in the more modern warfare of the country, would not have been neglected for a single hour. This sort of contempt for eminences, or rather dread of the labor of ascending them, might have been termed the besetting weakness of the warfare of the period. It originated in the simplicity of the Indian contests, in which, from the nature of the combats, and the density of the forests, fortresses were rare, and artillery next to useless. The carelessness engendered by these usages descended even to the war of the Revolution, and lost the States the important fortress of Ticonderoga,[2] opening a way for the army of Burgoyne into what was then the bosom of the country. We look back at this ignorance, or infatuation, whichever it may be called, with wonder, knowing that the neglect of an eminence, whose difficulties, like those of Mount Defiance, have been so greatly exaggerated, would, at the present time, prove fatal to the reputation of the engineer who had planned the works at their base, or to that of the general whose lot it was to defend them.

The tourist, the valetudinarian, or the amateur of the beauties of nature, who, in the train of his four-in-hand, now rolls through the scenes we have attempted to describe, in quest of information, health, or pleasure, or floats steadily towards his object on those artificial waters[3] which have sprung up under the administration of a statesman who has dared to stake his political character on the hazardous issue, is not to suppose that his ancestors traversed those hills, or struggled with the same currents with equal facility. The transportation of a single heavy gun was often considered equal to a victory

gained; if, happily, the difficulties of the passage had not
so far separated it from its necessary concomitant, the
ammunition, as to render it no more than a useless tube
of unwieldy iron.

The evils of this state of things pressed heavily on the
fortunes of the resolute Scotsman who now defended
William Henry. Though his adversary neglected the hills,
he had planted his batteries with judgment on the plain,
and caused them to be served with vigor and skill. Against
this assault, the besieged could only oppose the imperfect and hasty preparations of a fortress in the wilderness.

It was in the afternoon of the fifth day of the siege, and
the fourth of his own service in it, that Major Heyward
profited by a parley that had just been beaten, by repair-
ing to the ramparts of one of the water bastions, to
breathe the cool air from the lake, and to take a survey of
the progress of the siege. He was alone, if the solitary
sentinel who paced the mound be excepted; for the ar-
tillerists had hastened also to profit by the temporary
suspension of their arduous duties. The evening was de-
lightfully calm, and the light air from the limpid water
fresh and soothing. It seemed as if, with the termination
to the roar of artillery and the plunging of shot, nature
had also seized the moment to assume her mildest and
most captivating form. The sun poured down his parting
glory on the scene, without the oppression of those fierce
rays that belong to the climate and the season. The
mountains looked green and fresh and lovely; tempered
with the milder light, or softened in shadow, as thin vapors floated between them and the sun. The numerous
islands rested on the bosom of the Horican, some low
and sunken, as if imbedded in the waters, and others appearing to hover above the element, in little hillocks of

green velvet; among which the fishermen of the belea-
guering army peacefully rowed their skiffs, or floated at
rest on the glassy mirror, in quiet pursuit of their employment.

The scene was at once animated and still. All that pertained to nature was sweet, or simply grand; while those
parts which depended on the temper and movements of
man were lively and playful.

Two little spotless flags were abroad, the one on a
salient angle of the fort, and the other on the advanced
battery of the besiegers; emblems of the truce which existed, not only to the acts, but it would seem, also, to the
enmity of the combatants.

Behind these, again, swung, heavily opening and closing in silken folds, the rival standards of England and
France.

A hundred gay and thoughtless young Frenchmen
were drawing a net to the pebbly beach, within dangerous proximity to the sullen but silent cannon of the fort,
while the eastern mountain was sending back the loud
shouts and gay merriment that attended their sport.
Some were rushing eagerly to enjoy the aquatic games of
the lake, and others were already toiling their way up the
neighboring hills, with the restless curiosity of their nation. To all these sports and pursuits, those of the enemy
who watched the besieged, and the besieged themselves, were, however, merely the idle, though sympa-
thizing spectators. Here and there a picket had, indeed,
raised a song, or mingled in a dance, which had drawn
the dusky savages around them, from their lairs in the
forest. In short, everything wore rather the appearance
of a day of pleasure, than of an hour stolen from the dangers and toil of a bloody and vindictive warfare.

Duncan had stood in a musing attitude, contemplating this scene a few minutes, when his eyes were directed to the glacis in front of the sally-port already mentioned, by the sounds of approaching footsteps. He walked to an angle of the bastion, and beheld the scout advancing, under the custody of a French officer, to the body of the fort. The countenance of Hawkeye was haggard and careworn, and his air dejected, as though he felt the deepest degradation at having fallen into the power of his enemies. He was without his favorite weapon, and his arms were even bound behind him with thongs, made of the skin of a deer. The arrival of flags, to cover the messengers of summons, had occurred so often of late, that when Heyward first threw his careless glance on this group, he expected to see another of the officers of the enemy, charged with a similar office; but the instant he recognized the tall person, and still sturdy, though downcast features of his friend the woodsman, he started with surprise, and turned to descend from the bastion into the bosom of the work.

The sounds of other voices, however, caught his attention, and for a moment caused him to forget his purpose. At the inner angle of the mound he met the sisters, walking along the parapet in search, like himself, of air and relief from confinement. They had not met from that painful moment when he deserted them on the plain, only to assure their safety. He had parted from them worn with care, and jaded with fatigue; he now saw them refreshed and blooming, though timid and anxious. Under such an inducement, it will cause no surprise that the young man lost sight, for a time, of other objects in order to address them. He was, however, anticipated by the voice of the ingenuous and youthful Alice.

"Ah! thou truant! thou recreant knight! he who abandons his damsels in the very lists!" she cried; "here have we been days, nay, ages, expecting you at our feet, imploring mercy and forgetfulness of your craven backsliding, or, I should rather say, backrunning—for verily you fled in a manner that no stricken deer, as our worthy friend the scout would say, could equal!"

"You know that Alice means our thanks and our blessings," added the graver and more thoughtful Cora. "In truth, we have a little wondered why you should so rigidly absent yourself from a place where the gratitude of the daughters might receive the support of a parent's thanks."

"Your father himself could tell you, that though absent from your presence, I have not been altogether forgetful of your safety," returned the young man; "the mastery of yonder village of huts," pointing to the neighboring entrenched camp, "has been keenly disputed; and he who holds it is sure to be possessed of this fort, and that which it contains. My days and my nights have all been passed there since we separated, because I thought that duty called me thither. But," he added with an air of chagrin, which he endeavored, though unsuccessfully, to conceal, "had I been aware that what I then believed a soldier's conduct could so be construed, shame would have been added to the list of reasons."

"Heyward!—Duncan!" exclaimed Alice, bending forward to read his half-averted countenance, until a lock of her golden hair rested on her flushed cheek, and nearly concealed the tear that had started to her eye; "did I think this idle tongue of mine had pained you, I would silence it forever. Cora can say, if Cora would, how justly we have prized your services, and how deep—I had almost said, how fervent—is our gratitude."

"And will Cora attest the truth of this?" cried Duncan, suffering the cloud to be chased from his countenance by a smile of open pleasure. "What says our graver sister? Will she find an excuse for the neglect of the knight in the duty of a soldier?"

Cora made no immediate answer, but turned her face towards the water, as if looking on the sheet of the Horican. When she did bend her dark eyes on the young man, they were yet filled with an expression of anguish that at once drove every thought but that of kind solicitude from his mind.

"You are not well, dearest Miss Munro!" he exclaimed; "we have trifled while you are in suffering."

" 'Tis nothing," she answered, refusing his offered support with feminine reserve. "That I cannot see the sunny side of the picture of life, like this artless but ardent enthusiast," she added, laying her hand lightly, but affectionately, on the arm of her sister, "is the penalty of experience, and, perhaps, the misfortune of my nature. See," she continued, as if determined to shake off infirmity, in a sense of duty; "look around you, Major Heyward, and tell me what a prospect is this for the daughter of a soldier whose greatest happiness is his honor and his military renown."

"Neither ought nor shall be tarnished by circumstances over which he has had no control," Duncan warmly replied. "But your words recall me to my own duty. I go now to your gallant father, to hear his determination in matters of the last moment to the defence. God bless you in every fortune, noble—Cora—I may and must call you." She frankly gave him her hand, though her lip quivered, and her cheeks gradually became of an ashy paleness. "In every fortune, I know you will be an ornament and honor to your sex. Alice, adieu"—his tone changed from admiration to tenderness—"adieu, Alice; we shall soon meet again; as conquerors, I trust, and amid rejoicings!"

Without waiting for an answer from either, the young man threw himself down the grassy steps of the bastion, and moving rapidly across the parade, he was quickly in the presence of their father. Munro was pacing his narrow apartment with a disturbed air and gigantic strides as Duncan entered.

"You have anticipated my wishes, Major Heyward," he said; "I was about to request this favor."

"I am sorry to see, sir, that the messenger I so warmly recommended has returned in custody of the French! I hope there is no reason to distrust his fidelity?"

"The fidelity of 'The Long Rifle' is well known to me," returned Munro, "and is above suspicion; though his usual good fortune seems, at last, to have failed. Montcalm has got him, and with the accursed politeness of his nation, he has sent him in with a doleful tale, of 'knowing how I valued the fellow, he could not think of retaining him.' A jesuitical way, that, Major Duncan Heyward, of telling a man of his misfortunes!"

"But the general and his succor?"

"Did ye look to the south as ye entered, and could ye not see them?" said the old soldier, laughing bitterly. "Hoot! hoot! you're an impatient boy, sir, and cannot give the gentlemen leisure for their march!"

"They are coming, then? The scout has said as much?"

"When? and by what path? for the dunce has omitted to tell me this. There is a letter, it would seem, too; and that is the only agreeable part of the matter. For the customary attentions of your Marquis of Montcalm—I warrant me, Duncan, that he of Lothian [4] would buy a dozen such marquisates—but, if the news of the letter were bad, the gentility of this French monsieur would certainly compel him to let us know it."

"He keeps the letter, then, while he releases the messenger!"

"Ay, that does he, and all for the sake of what you call your 'bonhommie.' I would venture, if the truth was known, the fellow's grandfather taught the noble science of dancing."

"But what says the scout? he has eyes and ears, and a tongue: what verbal report does he make?"

"O! sir, he is not wanting in natural organs, and he is free to tell all that he has seen and heard. The whole amount is this: there is a fort of his majesty's on the banks of the Hudson, called Edward, in honor of his gracious highness of York, you'll know; and it is well filled with armed men, as such a work should be."

"But was there no movement, no signs of any intention to advance to our relief?"

"There were the morning and evening parades; and when one of the provincial loons—you'll know, Duncan, you're half a Scotsman yourself—when one of them dropped his powder over his porretch, if it touched the coals, it just burnt!" Then suddenly changing his bitter, ironical manner, to one more grave and thoughtful, he continued; "and yet there might, and must be, something in that letter which it would be well to know!"

"Our decision should be speedy," said Duncan, gladly availing himself of this change of humor, to press the more important objects of their interview; "I cannot conceal from you, sir, that the camp will not be much longer tenable; and I am sorry to add, that things appear no better in the fort; more than half the guns are bursted."

"And how should it be otherwise? Some were fished from the bottom of the lake; some have been rusting in the woods since the discovery of the country; and some were never guns at all—mere privateersmen's playthings! Do you think, sir, you can have Woolwich Warren[5] in the midst of a wilderness, three thousand miles from Great Britain!"

"The walls are crumbling about our ears, and provisions begin to fail us," continued Heyward, without regarding this new burst of indignation; "even the men show signs of discontent and alarm."

"Major Heyward," said Munro, turning to his youthful associate with the dignity of his years and superior rank; "I should have served his majesty for half a century, and earned these gray hairs, in vain, were I ignorant of all you say, and of the pressing nature of our circumstances; still, there is everything due to the honor of the king's arms and something to ourselves. While there is hope of succor, this fortress will I defend, though it be to be done with pebbles gathered on the lake shore. It is a sight of the letter, therefore, that we want, that we may know the intentions of the man the Earl of Loudon[6] has left among us as his substitute."

"And can I be of service in the matter?"

"Sir, you can; the Marquis of Montcalm has, in addition to his other civilities, invited me to a personal interview between the works and his own camp; in order, as he says, to impart some additional information. Now, I think it would not be wise to show any undue solicitude to meet him, and I would employ you, an officer of rank, as my substitute; for it would but ill comport with the honor of Scotland to let it be said one of her gentlemen was outdone in civility by a native of any other country on earth."

Without assuming the supererogatory task of entering into a discussion of the comparative merits of national courtesy, Duncan cheerfully assented to supply the place of the veteran in the approaching interview. A long and confidential communication now succeeded, during which the young man received some additional insight into his duty, from the experience and native acuteness of his commander, and then the former took his leave.

As Duncan could only act as the representative of the commandant of the fort, the ceremonies which should have accompanied a meeting between the heads of the adverse forces were of course dispensed with. The truce still existed, and with a roll and beat of the drum, and covered by a little white flag, Duncan left the sally-port, within ten minutes after his instructions were ended. He was received by the French officer in advance with the usual formalities, and immediately accompanied to a distant marquee[7] of the renowned soldier who led the forces of France.

The general of the enemy received the youthful messenger, surrounded by his principal officers, and by a swarthy band of the native chiefs, who had followed him to the field, with the warriors of their several tribes. Heyward paused short, when, in glancing his eyes rapidly over the dark group of the latter, he beheld the malignant countenance of Magua, regarding him with the calm but sullen attention which marked the expression of that subtle savage. A slight exclamation of surprise even burst from the lips of the young man; but instantly recollecting his errand, and the presence in which he stood, he suppressed every appearance of emotion, and turned to the hostile leader, who had already advanced a step to receive him.

The Marquis of Montcalm was, at the period of which we write, in the flower of his age, and, it may be added, in the zenith of his fortunes. But, even in that enviable situation, he was affable, and distinguished as much for his attention to the forms of courtesy, as for that chivalrous courage which, only two short years afterwards, induced him to throw away his life on the plains of Abraham.[8] Duncan, in turning his eyes from the malign expression of Magua, suffered them to rest with pleasure on the smiling and polished features, and the noble military air, of the French general.

"Monsieur," said the latter, "j'ai beaucoup de plaisir à—bah!—où est cet interprète?"[9]

"Je crois, monsieur, qu'il ne sera pas nécessaire," Heyward modestly replied; "je parle un peu Français."[10]

"Ah! j'en suis bien aise," said Montcalm, taking Duncan familiarly by the arm, and leading him deep into the marquee, a little out of ear-shot; "je déteste ces fripons-la; on ne sait jamais sur quel pié on est avec eux. Eh, bien! monsieur,"[11] he continued, still speaking in French; "though I should have been proud of receiving your commandant, I am very happy that he has seen proper to employ an officer so distinguished, and who, I am sure, is so amiable, as yourself."

Duncan bowed low, pleased with the compliment, in spite of a most heroic determination to suffer no artifice to allure him into forgetfulness of the interest of his prince; and Montcalm, after a pause of a moment, as if to recollect his thoughts, proceeded,—

"Your commandant is a brave man, and well qualified

to repel my assault. Mais, monsieur, is it not time to begin to take more counsel of humanity, and less of your courage? The one as strongly characterizes the hero as the other."

"We consider the qualities as inseparable," returned Duncan, smiling; "but while we find in the vigor of your excellency every motive to stimulate the one, we can, as yet, see no particular call for the exercise of the other."

Montcalm, in his turn, slightly bowed, but it was with the air of a man too practised to remember the language of flattery. After musing a moment, he added,—

"It is possible my glasses have deceived me, and that your works resist our cannon better than I had supposed. You know our force?"

"Our accounts vary," said Duncan, carelessly; "the highest, however, has not exceeded twenty thousand men."

The Frenchman bit his lip, and fastened his eyes keenly on the other as if to read his thoughts; then, with a readiness peculiar to himself, he continued, as if assenting to the truth of an enumeration which quite doubled his army,—

"It is a poor compliment to the vigilance of us soldiers, monsieur, that, do what we will, we never can conceal our numbers. If it were to be done at all, one would believe it might succeed in these woods. Though you think it too soon to listen to the calls of humanity," he added, smiling archly, "I may be permitted to believe that gallantry is not forgotten by one so young as yourself. The daughters of the commandant, I learn, have passed into the fort since it was invested?"

"It is true, monsieur; but, so far from weakening our efforts, they set us an example of courage in their own fortitude. Were nothing but resolution necessary to repel so accomplished a soldier as M. de Montcalm, I would gladly trust the defence of William Henry to the elder of those ladies."

"We have a wise ordinance in our Salique laws,[12] which says, 'The crown of France shall never degrade the lance to the distaff,' " said Montcalm, dryly, and with a little hauteur; but instantly adding, with his former frank and easy air, "as all the nobler qualities are hereditary, I can easily credit you; though, as I said before, courage has its limits, and humanity must not be forgotten. I trust, monsieur, you come authorized to treat for the surrender of the place?"

"Has your excellency found our defence so feeble as to believe the measure necessary?"

"I should be sorry to have the defence protracted in such a manner as to irritate my red friends there," continued Montcalm, glancing his eyes at the group of grave and attentive Indians, without attending to the other's question; "I find it difficult, even now, to limit them to the usages of war."

Heyward was silent; for a painful recollection of the dangers he had so recently escaped came over his mind, and recalled the images of those defenceless beings who had shared in all his sufferings.

"Ces messieurs-là," said Montcalm, following up the advantage which he conceived he had gained, "are most formidable when baffled: and it is unnecessary to tell you with what difficulty they are restrained in their anger. Eh bien, monsieur! shall we speak of the terms?"

"I fear your excellency has been deceived as to the strength of William Henry, and the resources of its garrison!"

"I have not sat down before Quebec, but an earthen

work, that is defended by twenty-three hundred gallant men," was the laconic reply.

"Our mounds are earthen, certainly—nor are they seated on the rocks of Cape Diamond; but they stand on that shore which proved so destructive to Dieskau and his army. There is also a powerful force within a few hours' march of us, which we account upon as part of our means."

"Some six or eight thousand men," returned Montcalm, with much apparent indifference, "whom their leader wisely judges to be safer in their works than in the field."

It was now Heyward's turn to bite his lip with vexation, as the other so coolly alluded to a force which the young man knew to be overrated. Both mused a little while in silence, when Montcalm renewed the conversation, in a way that showed he believed the visit of his guest was solely to propose terms of capitulation. On the other hand, Heyward began to throw sundry inducements in the way of the French general, to betray the discoveries he had made through the intercepted letter. The artifice of neither, however, succeeded; and after a protracted and fruitless interview, Duncan took his leave, favorably impressed with an opinion of the courtesy and talents of the enemy's captain, but as ignorant of what he came to learn as when he arrived. Montcalm followed him as far as the entrance of the marquee, renewing his invitations to the commandant of the fort to give him an immediate meeting in the open ground, between the two armies.

There they separated, and Duncan returned to the advanced post of the French, accompanied as before; whence he instantly proceeded to the fort, and to the quarters of his own commander.

French captured Hawk, French realease Hawk. Montcalm (french)
keeps letter from Webb to Hawk, Mont urges hey to
surrender

XVI

"Edg.—Before you fight the battle, ope this letter."
King Lear[1]

M AJOR HEYWARD FOUND Munro attended only by his
daughters. Alice sat upon his knee, parting the
gray hairs on the forehead of the old man with her delicate fingers; and, whenever he affected to frown on her
trifling, appeasing his assumed anger by pressing her
ruby lips fondly on his wrinkled brow. Cora was seated
nigh them, a calm and amused looker-on; regarding the
wayward movements of her more youthful sister, with
that species of maternal fondness which characterized
her love for Alice. Not only the dangers through which
they had passed, but those which still impended above
them, appeared to be momentarily forgotten, in the
soothing indulgence of such a family meeting. It seemed
as if they had profited by the short truce, to devote an instant to the purest and best affections; the daughters for-
getting their fears, and the veteran his cares, in the
security of the moment. Of this scene, Duncan, who in
his eagerness to report his arrival had entered unan-
nounced, stood many moments an unobserved and a delighted spectator. But the quick and dancing eyes of
Alice soon caught a glimpse of his figure reflected from a

glass, and she sprang blushing from her father's knee, exclaiming aloud,—

"Major Heyward!"

"What of the lad?" demanded the father; "I have sent him to crack a little with the Frenchman. Ha! sir, you are young, and you're nimble! Away with you, ye baggage; as if there were not troubles enough for a soldier, without having his camp filled with such prattling hussies as yourself!"

Alice laughingly followed her sister, who instantly led the way from an apartment where she perceived their presence was no longer desirable. Munro, instead of demanding the result of the young man's mission, paced the room for a few moments, with his hands behind his back, and his head inclined towards the floor, like a man lost in thought. At length he raised his eyes, glistening with a father's fondness, and exclaimed,—

"They are a pair of excellent girls, Heyward, and such as any one may boast of."

"You are not now to learn my opinion of your daughters, Colonel Munro."

"True, lad, true," interrupted the impatient old man; "you were about opening your mind more fully on that matter the day you got in; but I did not think it becoming in an old soldier to be talking of nuptial blessings and wedding jokes when the enemies of his king were likely to be unbidden guests at the feast! But I was wrong, Duncan, boy, I was wrong there; and I am now ready to hear what you have to say."

"Notwithstanding the pleasure your assurance gives me, dear sir, I have just now a message from Montcalm—"

"Let the Frenchman and all his host go to the devil, sir!" exclaimed the hasty veteran. "He is not yet master of William Henry, nor shall he ever be, provided Webb proves himself the man he should. No, sir! thank Heaven, we are not yet in such a strait that it can be said Munro is too much pressed to discharge the little domestic duties of his own family. Your mother was the only child of my bosom friend, Duncan; and I'll just give you a hearing, though all the knights of St. Louis were in a body at the sally-port, with the French saint at their head, craving to speak a word under favor. A pretty degree of knighthood, sir, is that which can be bought with sugar-hogsheads![2] and then your two-penny marquisates! The thistle[3] is the order for dignity and antiquity; the veritable *nemo me impune lacessit*[4] of chivalry! Ye had ancestors in that degree, Duncan, and they were an ornament to the nobles of Scotland."

Heyward, who perceived that his superior took a malicious pleasure in exhibiting his contempt for the message of the French general, was fain to humor a spleen that he knew would be short-lived; he therefore replied with as much indifference as he could assume on such a subject,—

"My request, as you know, sir, went so far as to presume to the honor of being your son."

"Ay, boy, you found words to make yourself very plainly comprehended. But, let me ask ye, sir, have you been as intelligible to the girl?"

"On my honor, no," exclaimed Duncan, warmly; "there would have been an abuse of a confided trust, had I taken advantage of my situation for such a purpose."

"Your notions are those of a gentleman, Major Heyward, and well enough in their place. But Cora Munro is a maiden too discreet, and of a mind too elevated and improved, to need the guardianship even of a father."

"Cora!"

"Ay—Cora! we are talking of your pretensions to Miss Munro, are we not, sir?"

"I—I—I was not conscious of having mentioned her name," said Duncan, stammering.

"And to marry whom, then, did you wish my consent, Major Heyward?" demanded the old soldier, erecting himself in the dignity of offended feeling.

"You have another, and not less lovely child."

"Alice!" exclaimed the father, in an astonishment equal to that with which Duncan had just repeated the name of her sister.

"Such was the direction of my wishes, sir."

The young man awaited in silence the result of the extraordinary effect produced by a communication which, as it now appeared, was so unexpected. For several minutes Munro paced the chamber with long and rapid strides, his rigid features working convulsively, and every faculty seemingly absorbed in the musings of his own mind. At length, he paused directly in front of Heyward, and riveting his eyes upon those of the other, he said, with a lip that quivered violently,—

"Duncan Heyward, I have loved you for the sake of him whose blood is in your veins; I have loved you for your own good qualities; and I have loved you, because I thought you would contribute to the happiness of my child. But all this love would turn to hatred, were I assured that what I so much apprehend is true."

"God forbid that any act or thought of mine should lead to such a change!" exclaimed the young man, whose

eye never quailed under the penetrating look it encountered. Without adverting the impossibility of the other's
comprehending those feelings which were hid in his own
bosom, Munro suffered himself to be appeased by the
unaltered countenance he met, and with a voice sensibly
softened, he continued,—

"You would be my son, Duncan, and you're ignorant
of the history of the man you wish to call your father. Sit
ye down, young man, and I will open to you the wounds
of a seared heart, in as few words as may be suitable."

By this time, the message of Montcalm was as much
forgotten by him who bore it as by the man for whose
ears it was intended. Each drew a chair, and while the
veteran communed a few moments with his own
thoughts, apparently in sadness, the youth suppressed
his impatience in a look and attitude of respectful attention. At length the former spoke:—

"You'll know, already, Major Heyward, that my family
was both ancient and honorable," commenced the Scotsman; "though it might not altogether be endowed with
that amount of wealth that should correspond with its
degree. I was, may be, such an one as yourself when I
plighted my faith to Alice Graham, the only child of a
neighboring laird of some estate. But the connection was
disagreeable to her father, on more accounts than my
poverty. I did therefore what an honest man should—restored the maiden her troth, and departed the country in
the service of my king. I had seen many regions, and had
shed much blood in different lands, before duty called
me to the islands of the West Indies. There it was my lot
to form a connection with one who in time became my
wife, and the mother of Cora. She was the daughter of a
gentleman of those isles, by a lady whose misfortune it

was, if you will," said the old man, proudly, "to be descended, remotely, from that unfortunate class who are so basely enslaved to administer to the wants of a luxurious people. Ay, sir, that is a curse entailed on Scotland by her unnatural union with a foreign and trading people. But could I find a man among them who would dare to reflect on my child, he should feel the weight of a father's anger! Ha! Major Heyward, you are yourself born at the south, where these unfortunate beings are considered of a race inferior to your own."

" 'Tis most unfortunately true, sir," said Duncan, unable any longer to prevent his eyes from sinking to the floor in embarrassment.

"And you cast it on my child as a reproach! You scorn to mingle the blood of the Heywards with one so degraded—lovely and virtuous though she be?" fiercely demanded the jealous parent.

"Heaven protect me from a prejudice so unworthy of my reason!" returned Duncan, at the same time conscious of such a feeling, and that as deeply rooted as if it had been ingrafted in his nature. "The sweetness, the beauty, the witchery of your younger daughter, Colonel Munro, might explain my motives, without imputing to me this injustice."

"Ye are right, sir," returned the old man, again changing his tones to those of gentleness, or rather softness; "the girl is the image of what her mother was at her years, and before she had become acquainted with grief. When death deprived me of my wife I returned to Scotland, enriched by the marriage; and would you think it, Duncan! the suffering angel had remained in the heartless state of celibacy twenty long years, and that for the sake of a man who could forget her! She did more, sir; she overlooked my want of faith, and all difficulties being now removed, she took me for her husband."

"And became the mother of Alice?" exclaimed Duncan, with an eagerness that might have proved dangerous at a moment when the thoughts of Munro were less occupied than at present.

"She did, indeed," said the old man, "and dearly did she pay for the blessing she bestowed. But she is a saint in heaven, sir; and it ill becomes one whose foot rests on the grave to mourn a lot so blessed. I had her but a single year, though; a short term of happiness for one who had seen her youth fade in hopeless pining."

There was something so commanding in the distress of the old man, that Heyward did not dare to venture a syllable of consolation. Munro sat utterly unconscious of the other's presence, his features exposed and working with the anguish of his regrets, while heavy tears fell from his eyes, and rolled unheeded from his cheeks to the floor. At length he moved, as if suddenly recovering his recollection; when he arose, and taking a single turn across the room, he approached his companion with an air of military grandeur, and demanded,—

"Have you not, Major Heyward, some communication that I should hear from the Marquis de Montcalm?"

Duncan started, in his turn, and immediately commenced, in an embarrassed voice, the half-forgotten message. It is unnecessary to dwell upon the evasive, though polite manner, with which the French general had eluded every attempt of Heyward to worm from him the purport of the communication he had proposed making, or on the decided, though still polished message, by which he now gave his enemy to understand, that unless he chose to receive it in person, he should not receive it at all. As Munro listened to the detail of Duncan, the excited feelings of the father gradually gave way before the obligations of his station, and when the other was done, he saw before him nothing but the veteran, swelling with the wounded feelings of a soldier.

"You have said enough, Major Heyward!" exclaimed the angry old man: "enough to make a volume of commentary on French civility. Here has this gentleman invited me to a conference, and when I send him a capable substitute, for ye're all that, Duncan, though your years are but few, he answers me with a riddle."

"He may have thought less favorably of the substitute, my dear sir; and you will remember that the invitation, which he now repeats, was to the commandant of the works, and not to his second."

"Well, sir, is not a substitute clothed with all the power and dignity of him who grants the commission? He wishes to confer with Munro! Faith, sir, I have much inclination to indulge the man, if it should only be to let him behold the firm countenance we maintain in spite of his numbers and his summons. There might be no bad policy in such a stroke, young man."

Duncan, who believed it of the last importance that they should speedily come at the contents of the letter borne by the scout, gladly encouraged this idea.

"Without doubt, he could gather no confidence by witnessing our indifference," he said.

"You never said truer word. I could wish, sir, that he would visit the works in open day, and in the form of a storming party: that is the least failing method of proving the countenance of an enemy, and would be far preferable to the battering system he has chosen. The beauty and manliness of warfare has been much deformed,

Major Heyward, by the arts of your Monsieur Vauban.[5] Our ancestors were far above such scientific cowardice!"

"It may be very true, sir; but we are now obliged to repel art by art. What is your pleasure in the matter of the interview?"

"I will meet the Frenchman, and that without fear or delay; promptly, sir, as becomes a servant of my royal master. Go, Major Heyward, and give them a flourish of the music; and send out a messenger to let them know who is coming. We will follow with a small guard, for such respect is due to one who holds the honor of his king in keeping; and harkee, Duncan," he added, in a half whisper, though they were alone, "it may be prudent to have some aid at hand, in case there should be treachery at the bottom of it all."

The young man availed himself of this order to quit the apartment; and, as the day was fast coming to a close, he hastened, without delay, to make the necessary arrangements. A very few minutes only were necessary to parade a few files, and to despatch an orderly with a flag to announce the approach of the commandant of the fort. When Duncan had done both these, he led the guard to the sally-port, near which he found his superior ready, waiting his appearance. As soon as the usual ceremonials of a military departure were observed, the veteran and his more youthful companion left the fortress, attended by the escort.

They had proceeded only a hundred yards from the works, when the little array which attended the French general to the conference, was seen issuing from the hollow way, which formed the bed of a brook that ran between the batteries of the besiegers and the fort. From the moment that Munro left his own works to appear in front of his enemies, his air had been grand, and his step and countenance highly military. The instant he caught a glimpse of the white plume that waved in the hat of Montcalm, his eye lighted, and age no longer appeared to possess any influence over his vast and still muscular person.

"Speak to the boys to be watchful, sir," he said, in an undertone, to Duncan; "and to look well to their flints and steel, for one is never safe with a servant of these Louises; at the same time, we will show them the front of men in deep security. Ye'll understand me, Major Heyward!"

He was interrupted by the clamor of a drum from the approaching Frenchmen, which was immediately answered, when each party pushed an orderly in advance, bearing a white flag, and the wary Scotsman halted, with his guard close at his back. As soon as this slight salutation had passed, Montcalm moved towards them with a quick but graceful step, baring his head to the veteran, and dropping his spotless plume nearly to the earth in courtesy. If the air of Munro was more commanding and manly, it wanted both the ease and insinuating polish of that of the Frenchman. Neither spoke for a few moments, each regarding the other with curious and interested eyes. Then, as became his superior rank and the nature of the interview, Montcalm broke the silence. After uttering the usual words of greeting, he turned to Duncan, and continued with a smile of recognition, speaking always in French,—

"I am rejoiced, monsieur, that you have given us the pleasure of your company on this occasion. There will be no necessity to employ an ordinary interpreter; for, in your hands, I feel the same security as if I spoke your language myself."

Duncan acknowledged the compliment, when Montcalm, turning to his guard, which, in imitation of that of their enemies, pressed close upon him, continued,—

"En arrière, mes enfants—il fait chaud; retirez-vous un peu."[6]

Before Major Heyward would imitate this proof of confidence, he glanced his eyes around the plain, and beheld with uneasiness the numerous dusky groups of savages, who looked out from the margin of the surrounding woods, curious spectators of the interview.

"Monsieur de Montcalm will readily acknowledge the difference in our situation," he said, with some embarrassment, pointing at the same time towards those dangerous foes, who were to be seen in almost every direction. "Were we to dismiss our guard, we should stand here at the mercy of our enemies."

"Monsieur, you have the plighted faith of *un gentilhomme Français*, for your safety," returned Montcalm, laying his hand impressively on his heart; "it should suffice."

"It shall. Fall back," Duncan added to the officer who led the escort; "fall back, sir, beyond hearing, and wait for orders."

Munro witnessed this movement with manifest uneasiness; nor did he fail to demand an instant explanation.

"Is it not our interest, sir, to betray no distrust?" retorted Duncan. "Monsieur de Montcalm pledges his word for our safety, and I have ordered the men to withdraw a little, in order to prove how much we depend on his assurance."

"It may be all right, sir, but I have no overweening reliance on the faith of these marquesses, or marquis, as they call themselves. Their patents of nobility are too common to be certain that they bear the seal of true honor."

"You forget, dear sir, that we confer with an officer distinguished alike in Europe and America for his deeds. From a soldier of his reputation we can have nothing to apprehend."

The old man made a gesture of resignation, though his rigid features still betrayed his obstinate adherence to a distrust, which he derived from a sort of hereditary contempt of his enemy, rather than from any present signs which might warrant so uncharitable a feeling. Montcalm waited patiently until this little dialogue in demi-voice was ended, when he drew nigher, and opened the subject of their conference.

"I have solicited this interview from your superior, monsieur," he said, "because I believe he will allow himself to be persuaded that he has already done everything which is necessary for the honor of his prince, and will not listen to the admonitions of humanity. I will forever bear testimony that his resistance has been gallant, and was continued as long as there was hope."

When this opening was translated to Munro, he answered with dignity, but with sufficient courtesy,—

"However I may prize such testimony from Monsieur Montcalm, it will be more valuable when it shall be better merited."

The French general smiled, as Duncan gave him the purport of this reply, and observed,—

"What is now so freely accorded to approved courage, may be refused to useless obstinacy. Monsieur would wish to see my camp, and witness, for himself, our numbers, and the impossibility of his resisting them, with success?"

"I know that the king of France is well served," returned the unmoved Scotsman, as soon as Duncan ended his translation; "but my own royal master has as many and as faithful troops."

"Though not at hand, fortunately for us," said Montcalm, without waiting, in his ardor, for the interpreter. "There is a destiny in war, to which a brave man knows how to submit, with the same courage that he faces his foes."

"Had I been conscious that Monsieur Montcalm was master of the English, I should have spared myself the trouble of so awkward a translation," said the vexed Duncan, dryly; remembering instantly his recent by-play with Munro.

"Your pardon, monsieur," rejoined the Frenchman, suffering a slight color to appear on his dark cheek. "There is a vast difference between understanding and speaking a foreign tongue; you will, therefore, please to assist me still." Then after a short pause, he added, "These hills afford us every opportunity of reconnoitering your works, messieurs, and I am possibly as well acquainted with their weak condition as you can be yourselves."

"Ask the French general if his glasses can reach to the Hudson," said Munro, proudly; "and if he knows when and where to expect the army of Webb."

"Let General Webb be his own interpreter," returned the politic Montcalm, suddenly extending an open letter towards Munro, as he spoke; "you will there learn, monsieur, that his movements are not likely to prove embarrassing to my army."

The veteran seized the offered paper, without waiting for Duncan to translate the speech, and with an eagerness that betrayed how important he deemed its contents. As his eye passed hastily over the words, his countenance changed from its look of military pride to one of deep chagrin: his lip began to quiver; and, suffering the paper to fall from his hand, his head dropped upon his chest, like that of a man whose hopes were withered at a single blow. Duncan caught the letter from the ground, and without apology for the liberty he took, he read at a glance its cruel purport. Their common superior, so far from encouraging them to resist, advised a speedy surrender, urging in the plainest language as a reason, the utter impossibility of his sending a single man to their rescue.

"Here is no deception!" exclaimed Duncan, examining the billet both inside and out; "this is the signature of Webb, and must be the captured letter."

"The man has betrayed me!" Munro at length bitterly exclaimed; "he has brought dishonor to the door of one where disgrace was never before known to dwell, and shame has he heaped heavily on my gray hairs."

"Say not so," cried Duncan; "we are yet masters of the fort, and of our honor. Let us then sell our lives at such a rate as shall make our enemies believe the purchase too dear."

"Boy, I thank thee," exclaimed the old man, rousing himself from his stupor; "you have, for once, reminded Munro of his duty. We will go back, and dig our graves behind those ramparts."

"Messieurs," said Montcalm, advancing towards them a step, in generous interest, "you little know Louis de St.

Véran, if you believe him capable of profiting by this letter to humble brave men, or to build up a dishonest reputation for himself. Listen to my terms before you leave me."

"What says the Frenchman?" demanded the veteran, sternly; "does he make a merit of having captured a scout, with a note from headquarters? Sir, he had better raise this siege, to go and sit down before Edward if he wishes to frighten his enemy with words."

Duncan explained the other's meaning.

"Monsieur de Montcalm, we will hear you," the veteran added, more calmly, as Duncan ended.

"To retain the fort is now impossible," said his liberal enemy; "it is necessary to the interests of my master that it should be destroyed; but, as for yourselves, and your brave comrades, there is no privilege dear to a soldier that shall be denied."

"Our colors?" demanded Heyward.

"Carry them to England, and show them to your king."

"Our arms?"

"Keep them; none can use them better."

"Our march; the surrender of the place?"

"Shall all be done in a way most honorable to yourselves."

Duncan now turned to explain these proposals to his commander, who heard him with amazement, and a sensibility that was deeply touched by such unusual and unexpected generosity.

"Go you, Duncan," he said; "go with this marquess, as indeed marquess he should be; go to his marquee and arrange it all. I have lived to see two things in my old age, that never did I expect to behold. An Englishman afraid to support a friend, and a Frenchman too honest to profit by his advantage."

So saying, the veteran again dropped his head to his chest, and returned slowly towards the fort, exhibiting, by the dejection of his air, to the anxious garrison, a harbinger of evil tidings.

From the shock of this unexpected blow the haughty feelings of Munro never recovered; but from that moment there commenced a change in his determined character, which accompanied him to a speedy grave. Duncan remained to settle the terms of the capitulation. He was seen to re-enter the works during the first watches of the night, and immediately after a private conference with the commandant, to leave them again. It was then openly announced, that hostilities must cease—Munro having signed a treaty, by which the place was to be yielded to the enemy, with the morning; the garrison to retain their arms, their colors, and their baggage, and consequently, according to military opinion, their honor.

Hey tells Munro Monts message, Munro uninterested. Munro calls hey racist for choosing Alice over Cora. Munro says they have different moms. Coras mom, from west indies, part negroe. Alice, munros kid sweety, scotish. Hey denies he thinks less of cora, but admits his racism. Munro + Hey to Mont. Mont gives letter, says if surrender they can keep arms bags + colors + no indian attacks. Munro accepts.

XVII

"Weave we the woof. The thread is spun.
The web is wove. The work is done."
Thomas Gray, "The Bard" [1]

THE HOSTILE ARMIES, which lay in the wilds of the
Horican, passed the night of the 9th of August,
1757, much in the manner they would had they encountered on the fairest fields of Europe. While the conquered were still, sullen, and dejected, the victors
triumphed. But there are limits alike to grief and joy; and
long before the watches of the morning came, the stillness of those boundless woods was only broken by a gay
call from some exulting young Frenchman of the advanced pickets, or a menacing challenge from the fort,
which sternly forbade the approach of any hostile footsteps before the stipulated moment. Even these occasional threatening sounds ceased to be heard in that dull
hour which precedes the day, at which period a listener
might have sought in vain any evidence of the presence
of those armed powers that then slumbered on the
shores of the "holy lake."

It was during these moments of deep silence, that the
canvas which concealed the entrance to a spacious marquee in the French encampment was shoved aside, and a

man issued from beneath the drapery into the open air.
He was enveloped in a cloak that might have been intended as a protection from the chilling damps of the
woods, but which served equally well as a mantle, to conceal his person. He was permitted to pass the grenadier,
who watched over the slumbers of the French commander, without interruption, the man making the usual
salute which betokens military deference, as the other
passed swiftly through the little city of tents, in the direction of William Henry. Whenever this unknown individual encountered one of the numberless sentinels who
crossed his path, his answer was prompt, and as it appeared satisfactory; for he was uniformly allowed to proceed, without further interrogation.

With the exception of such repeated, but brief interruptions, he had moved, silently, from the centre of the
camp, to its most advanced outposts, when he drew nigh
the soldier who held his watch nearest to the works of the
enemy. As he approached he was received with the usual
challenge,—

"Qui vive?"

"France," was the reply.

"Le mot d'ordre?"[2]

"La victoire,"[3] said the other, drawing so nigh as to be
heard in a loud whisper.

"C'est bien," returned the sentinel, throwing his
musket from the charge to his shoulder; "vous vous
promenez bien matin, monsieur!"[4]

"Il est nécessaire d'être vigilant, mon enfant,"[5] the
other observed, dropping a fold of his cloak, and looking
the soldier close in the face, as he passed him, still continuing his way towards the British fortification. The
man started; his arms rattled heavily, as he threw them

forward, in the lowest and most respectful salute; and
when he had again recovered his piece, he turned to
walk his post, muttering between his teeth,—

"Il faut être vigilant, en vérité! je crois que nous avons
là, un caporal qui ne dort jamais!"[6]

The officer proceeded, without affecting to hear the
words which escaped the sentinel in his surprise; nor did
he again pause until he had reached the low strand, and
in a somewhat dangerous vicinity to the western water
bastion of the fort. The light of an obscure moon was just
sufficient to render objects, though dim, perceptible in
their outlines. He, therefore, took the precaution to
place himself against the trunk of a tree, where he leaned
for many minutes, and seemed to contemplate the dark
and silent mounds of the English works in profound attention. His gaze at the ramparts was not that of a curious or idle spectator; but his looks wandered from point
to point, denoting his knowledge of military usages, and
betraying that his search was not unaccompanied by distrust. At length he appeared satisfied; and having cast his
eyes impatiently upwards towards the summit of the
eastern mountain, as if anticipating the approach of the
morning, he was in the act of turning on his footsteps,
when a light sound on the nearest angle of the bastion
caught his ear, and induced him to remain.

Just then a figure was seen to approach the edge of the
rampart, where it stood, apparently contemplating in its
turn the distant tents of the French encampment. Its
head was then turned towards the east, as though equally
anxious for the appearance of light, when the form
leaned against the mound, and seemed to gaze upon the
glassy expanse of the waters, which, like a submarine firmament, glittered with its thousand mimic stars. The

melancholy air, the hour, together with the vast frame of the man who thus leaned, in musing, against the English ramparts, left no doubt as to his person, in the mind of his observant spectator. Delicacy, no less than prudence, now urged him to retire; and he had moved cautiously round the body of the tree for that purpose, when another sound drew his attention, and once more arrested his footsteps. It was a low and almost inaudible movement of the water, and was succeeded by a grating of pebbles one against the other. In a moment he saw a dark form rise, as it were out of the lake, and steal without further noise to the land, within a few feet of the place where he himself stood. A rifle next slowly rose between his eyes and the watery mirror; but before it could be discharged his own hand was on the lock.

"Hugh!" exclaimed the savage, whose treacherous aim was so singularly and so unexpectedly interrupted.

Without making any reply, the French officer laid his hand on the shoulder of the Indian, and led him in profound silence to a distance from the spot, where their subsequent dialogue might have proved dangerous, and where it seemed that one of them, at least, sought a victim. Then, throwing open his cloak, so as to expose his uniform and the cross of St. Louis[7] which was suspended at his breast, Montcalm sternly demanded,—

"What means this! Does not my son know that the hatchet is buried between the English and his Canadian Father?"

"What can the Hurons do?" returned the savage, speaking also, though imperfectly, in the French language. "Not a warrior has a scalp, and the pale-faces make friends!"

"Ha! Le Renard Subtil! Methinks this is an excess of

zeal for a friend who was so late an enemy! How many suns have set since Le Renard struck the war-post of the English?"

"Where is that sun!" demanded the sullen savage. "Behind the hill; and it is dark and cold. But when he comes again, it will be bright and warm. Le Subtil is the sun of his tribe. There have been clouds, and many mountains between him and his nation; but now he shines, and it is a clear sky!"

"That Le Renard has power with his people, I well know," said Montcalm; "for yesterday he hunted for their scalps, and to-day they hear him at the council-fire."

"Magua is a great chief."

"Let him prove it, by teaching his nation how to conduct itself towards our new friends."

"Why did the chief of the Canadas bring his young men into the woods, and fire his cannon at the earthen house?" demanded the subtle Indian.

"To subdue it. My master owns the land, and your father has been ordered to drive off these English squatters. They have consented to go, and now he calls them enemies no longer."

" 'Tis well. Magua took the hatchet to color it with blood. It is now bright; when it is red, it shall be buried."

"But Magua is pledged not to sully the lilies of France. The enemies of the great king across the salt lake are his enemies; his friend, the friends of the Hurons."

"Friends!" repeated the Indian, in scorn. "Let his father give Magua a hand."

Montcalm, who felt that his influence over the warlike tribes he had gathered was to be maintained by concession rather than by power, complied reluctantly with the other's request. The savage placed the finger of the

French commander on a deep scar in his bosom, and then exultingly demanded,—

"Does my father know that?"

"What warrior does not? 'tis where a leaden bullet has cut."

"And this?" continued the Indian, who had turned his naked back to the other, his body being without its usual calico mantle.

"This!—my son has been sadly injured, here; who has done this?"

"Magua slept hard in the English wigwams, and the sticks have left their mark," returned the savage, with a hollow laugh, which did not conceal the fierce temper that nearly choked him. Then recollecting himself, with sudden and native dignity, he added, "Go; teach your young men, it is peace. Le Renard Subtil knows how to speak to a Huron warrior."

Without deigning to bestow further words, or to wait for any answer, the savage cast his rifle into the hollow of his arm, and moved silently through the encampment towards the woods where his own tribe was known to lie. Every few yards as he proceeded he was challenged by the sentinels; but he stalked sullenly onward, utterly disregarding the summons of the soldiers, who only spared his life because they knew the air and tread no less than the obstinate daring of an Indian.

Montcalm lingered long and melancholy on the strand, where he had been left by his companion, brooding deeply on the temper which his ungovernable ally had just discovered. Already had his fair fame been tarnished by one horrid scene, and in circumstances fearfully resembling those under which he now found himself. As he mused he became keenly sensible of the deep responsibility they assume who disregard the means to attain their end, and of all the danger of setting in motion an engine which it exceeds human power to control. Then shaking off a train of reflections that he accounted a weakness in such a moment of triumph, he retraced his steps towards his tent, giving the order as he passed, to make the signal that should arouse the army from its slumbers.

The first tap of the French drums was echoed from the bosom of the fort, and presently the valley was filled with the strains of martial music, rising long, thrilling, and lively above the rattling accompaniment. The horns of the victors sounded merry and cheerful flourishes, until the last laggard of the camp was at his post; but the instant the British fifes had blown their shrill signal, they became mute. In the meantime the day had dawned, and when the line of the French army was ready to receive its general, the rays of a brilliant sun were glancing along the glittering array. Then that success, which was already so well known, was officially announced; the favored band who were selected to guard the gates of the fort were detailed, and defiled before their chief; the signal of their approach was given, and all the usual preparations for a change of masters were ordered and executed directly under the guns of the contested works.

A very different scene presented itself within the lines of the Anglo-American army. As soon as the warning signal was given, it exhibited all the signs of a hurried and forced departure. The sullen soldiers shouldered their empty tubes and fell into their places, like men whose blood had been heated by the past contest, and who only desired the opportunity to revenge an indignity which was still wounding to their pride, concealed as it was under all the observances of military etiquette. Women and children ran from place to place, some bearing the scanty remnants of their baggage, and others searching in the ranks for those countenances they looked up to for protection.

Munro appeared among his silent troops firm but dejected. It was evident that the unexpected blow had struck deep into his heart, though he struggled to sustain his misfortune with the port of man.

Duncan was touched at the quiet and impressive exhibition of his grief. He had discharged his own duty, and he now pressed to the side of the old man, to know in what particular he might serve him.

"My daughters," was the brief but expressive reply.

"Good heavens! are not arrangements already made for their convenience?"

"To-day I am only a soldier, Major Heyward," said the veteran. "All that you see here, claim alike to be my children."

Duncan had heard enough. Without losing one of those moments which had now become so precious, he flew towards the quarters of Munro, in quest of the sisters. He found them on the threshold of the low edifice, already prepared to depart, and surrounded by a clamorous and weeping assemblage of their own sex, that had gathered about the place, with a sort of instinctive consciousness that it was the point most likely to be protected. Though the cheeks of Cora were pale, and her countenance anxious, she had lost none of her firmness; but the eyes of Alice were inflamed, and betrayed how long and bitterly she had wept. They both, however, received the young man with undisguised pleasure; the former, for a novelty, being the first to speak.

"The fort is lost," she said, with a melancholy smile; "though our good name, I trust, remains."

" 'Tis brighter than ever. But, dearest Miss Munro, it is time to think less of others, and to make some provision for yourself. Military usage,—pride,—that pride on which you so much value yourself, demands that your father and I should for a little while continue with the troops. Then where to seek a proper protector for you against the confusion and chances of such a scene?"

"None is necessary," returned Cora; "who will dare to injure or insult the daughter of such a father, at a time like this?"

"I would not leave you alone," continued the youth, looking about him in a hurried manner, "for the command of the best regiment in the pay of the king. Remember, our Alice is not gifted with all your firmness, and God only knows the terror she might endure."

"You may be right," Cora replied, smiling again, but far more sadly than before. "Listen! chance has already sent us a friend when he is most needed."

Duncan did listen, and on the instant comprehended her meaning. The low and serious sounds of the sacred music, so well known to the eastern provinces, caught his ear, and instantly drew him to an apartment in an adjacent building, which had already been deserted by its customary tenants. There he found David, pouring out his pious feelings, through the only medium in which he ever indulged. Duncan waited, until, by the cessation of the movement of the hand, he believed the strain was ended, when, by touching his shoulder, he drew the attention of the other to himself, and in a few words explained his wishes.

"Even so," replied the single-minded disciple of the

King of Israel, when the young man had ended; "I have found much that is comely and melodious in the maidens, and it is fitting that we who have consorted in so much peril, should abide together in peace. I will attend them, when I have completed my morning praise, to which nothing is now wanting but the doxology. Wilt thou bear a part, friend? The metre is common, and the tune, 'Southwell.' "

Then, extending the little volume, and giving the pitch of the air anew with considerate attention, David recommenced and finished his strains, with a fixedness of manner that it was not easy to interrupt. Heyward was fain to wait until the verse was ended; when, seeing David relieving himself from the spectacles, and replacing the book, he continued,—

"It will be your duty to see that none dare to approach the ladies with any rude intention, or to offer insult or taunt at the misfortune of their brave father. In this task you will be seconded by the domestics of their household."

"Even so."

"It is possible that the Indians and stragglers of the enemy may intrude, in which case you will remind them of the terms of the capitulation, and threaten to report their conduct to Montcalm. A word will suffice."

"If not, I have that here which shall," returned David, exhibiting his book, with an air in which meekness and confidence were singularly blended. "Here are words which, uttered, or rather thundered, with proper emphasis, and in measured time, shall quiet the most unruly temper:—

" 'Why rage the heathen furiously!' "—[8]

"Enough," said Heyward, interrupting the burst of his musical invocation: "we understand each other; it is time that we should now assume our respective duties."

Gamut cheerfully assented, and together they sought the females. Cora received her new, and somewhat extraordinary protector, courteously at least; and even the pallid features of Alice lighted again with some of their native archness as she thanked Heyward for his care. Duncan took occasion to assure them he had done the best that circumstances permitted, and, as he believed, quite enough for the security of their feelings; of danger there was none. He then spoke gladly of his intention to rejoin them the moment he had led the advance a few miles towards the Hudson, and immediately took his leave.

By this time the signal of departure had been given, and the head of the English column was in motion. The sisters started at the sound, and glancing their eyes around, they saw the white uniforms of the French grenadiers, who had already taken possession of the gates of the fort. At that moment, an enormous cloud seemed to pass suddenly above their heads, and looking upward, they discovered that they stood beneath the wide folds of the standard of France.

"Let us go," said Cora; "this is no longer a fit place for the children of an English officer."

Alice clung to the arm of her sister, and together they left the parade, accompanied by the moving throng that surrounded them.

As they passed the gates, the French officers, who had learned their rank, bowed often and low, forbearing, however, to intrude those attentions which they saw, with peculiar tact, might not be agreeable. As every vehicle and each beast of burden was occupied by the sick and wounded,[9] Cora had decided to endure the fatigues of a foot march, rather than interfere with their comforts. Indeed, many a maimed and feeble soldier was compelled to drag his exhausted limbs in the rear of the columns, for the want of the necessary means of conveyance, in that wilderness. The whole, however, was in motion; the weak and wounded, groaning, and in suffering; their comrades, silent and sullen; and the women and children in terror, they knew not of what.

As the confused and timid throng left the protecting mounds of the fort, and issued on the open plain, the whole scene was at once presented to their eyes. At a little distance on the right, and somewhat in the rear, the French army stood to their arms, Montcalm having collected his parties, so soon as his guards had possession of the works. They were attentive but silent observers of the proceedings of the vanquished, failing in none of the stipulated military honors, and offering no taunt or insult, in their success, to their less fortunate foes. Living masses of the English, to the amount in the whole of near three thousand, were moving slowly across the plain, towards the common centre, and gradually approached each other, as they converged to the point of their march, a vista cut through the lofty trees, where the road to the Hudson entered the forest. Along the sweeping borders of the woods, hung a dark cloud of savages, eyeing the passage of their enemies, and hovering, at a distance, like vultures, who were only kept from swooping on their prey, by the presence and restraint of a superior army. A few had straggled among the conquered columns, where they stalked in sullen discontent; attentive, though, as yet, passive observers of the moving multitude.

The advance, with Heyward at its head, had already reached the defile, and was slowly disappearing, when the attention of Cora was drawn to a collection of stragglers, by the sounds of contention. A truant provincial was paying the forfeit of his disobedience, by being plundered of those very effects which had caused him to desert his place in the ranks. The man was of powerful frame, and too avaricious to part with his goods without a struggle. Individuals from either party interfered; the one side to prevent, and the other to aid in the robbery. Voices grew loud and angry, and a hundred savages appeared, as it were by magic, where a dozen only had been seen a minute before. It was then that Cora saw the form of Magua gliding among his countrymen, and speaking with his fatal and artful eloquence. The mass of women and children stopped, and hovered together like alarmed and fluttering birds. But the cupidity of the Indian was soon gratified, and the different bodies again moved slowly onward.

The savages now fell back, and seemed content to let their enemies advance without further molestation. But as the female crowd approached them, the gaudy colors of a shawl attracted the eyes of a wild and untutored Huron. He advanced to seize it, without the least hesitation. The woman, more in terror than through love of the ornament, wrapped her child in the coveted article, and folded both more closely to her bosom. Cora was in the act of speaking, with an intent to advise the woman to abandon the trifle, when the savage relinquished his hold of the shawl, and tore the screaming infant from her arms. Abandoning everything to the greedy grasp of those around her, the mother darted, with distraction in her mien, to reclaim her child. The Indian smiled grimly,

and extended one hand, in sign of a willingness to exchange, while with the other, he flourished the babe over
his head, holding it by the feet as if to enhance the value
of the ransom.

"Here—here—there—all—any—everything!" exclaimed the breathless woman; tearing the lighter articles of dress from her person, with ill-directed and
trembling fingers; "take all, but give me my babe!"

The savage spurned the worthless rags, and perceiving that the shawl had already become a prize to another,
his bantering but sullen smile changing to a gleam of ferocity, he dashed the head of the infant against a rock,
and cast its quivering remains to her very feet.[10] For an
instant, the mother stood, like a statue of despair, looking
wildly down at the unseemly object, which had so lately
nestled in her bosom and smiled in her face; and then
she raised her eyes and countenance towards heaven, as
if calling on God to curse the perpetrator of the foul
deed. She was spared the sin of such a prayer; for, maddened at his disappointment, and excited at the sight of
blood, the Huron mercifully drove his tomahawk into
her own brain. The mother sank under the blow, and fell,
grasping at her child, in death, with the same engrossing
love that had caused her to cherish it when living.

At that dangerous moment Magua placed his hands to
his mouth, and raised the fatal and appalling whoop. The
scattered Indians started at the well-known cry, as coursers bound at the signal to quit the goal; and, directly,
there arose such a yell along the plain, and through the
arches of the wood, as seldom burst from human lips before. They who heard it listened with a curdling horror at
the heart, little inferior to that dread which may be expected to attend the blasts of the final summons.

More than two thousand raving savages broke from the forest at the signal, and threw themselves across the fatal plain with instinctive alacrity. We shall not dwell on the revolting horrors that succeeded. Death was everywhere, and in his most terrific and disgusting aspects. Resistance only served to inflame the murderers, who inflicted their furious blows long after their victims were beyond the power of their resentment. The flow of blood might be likened to the outbreaking of a torrent; and, as the natives became heated and maddened by the sight, many among them even kneeled to the earth, and drank freely, exultingly, hellishly, of the crimson tide.

The trained bodies of the troops threw themselves quickly into solid masses, endeavoring to awe their assailants by the imposing appearance of a military front. The experiment in some measure succeeded, though far too many suffered their unloaded muskets to be torn from their hands, in the vain hope of appeasing the savages.

In such a scene none had leisure to note the fleeting moments. It might have been ten minutes (it seemed an age), that the sisters had stood riveted to one spot, horror-stricken, and nearly helpless. When the first blow was struck, their screaming companions had pressed upon them in a body, rendering flight impossible; and now that fear or death had scattered most, if not all, from around them, they saw no avenue open, but such as conducted to the tomahawks of their foes. On every side arose shrieks, groans, exhortations, and curses. At this moment Alice caught a glimpse of the vast form of her father, moving rapidly across the plain, in the direction of the French army. He was, in truth, proceeding to Montcalm, fearless of every danger, to claim the tardy escort for which he had before conditioned. Fifty glittering axes and barbed spears were offered unheeded at his life, but the savages respected his rank and calmness, even in their fury. The dangerous weapons were brushed aside by the still nervous arm of the veteran, or fell of themselves, after menacing an act that it would seem no one had courage to perform. Fortunately, the vindictive Magua was searching for his victim in the very band the veteran had just quitted.

"Father—father—we are here!" shrieked Alice, as he passed, at no great distance, without appearing to heed them. "Come to us, father, or we die!"

The cry was repeated, and in terms and tones that might have melted a heart of stone, but it was unanswered. Once, indeed, the old man appeared to catch the sounds, for he paused and listened; but Alice had dropped senseless on the earth, and Cora had sunk at her side, hovering in untiring tenderness over her lifeless form. Munro shook his head in disappointment, and proceeded, bent on the high duty of his station.

"Lady," said Gamut, who, helpless and useless as he was, had not yet dreamed of deserting his trust, "it is the jubilee of the devils, and this is not a meet place for Christians to tarry in. Let us up and fly."

"Go," said Cora, still gazing at her unconscious sister; "save thyself. To me thou canst not be of further use."

David comprehended the unyielding character of her resolution, by the simple but expressive gesture that accompanied her words. He gazed, for a moment, at the dusky forms that were acting their hellish rites on every side of him, and his tall person grew more erect, while his chest heaved, and every feature swelled, and seemed to speak with the power of the feelings by which he was governed.

"If the Jewish boy might tame the evil spirit of Saul by the sound of his harp, and the words of sacred song, it may not be amiss," he said, "to try the potency of music here."

Then raising his voice to its highest tones, he poured out a strain so powerful as to be heard even amid the din of that bloody field. More than one savage rushed towards them, thinking to rifle the unprotected sisters of their attire, and bear away their scalps; but when they found this strange and unmoved figure riveted to his post, they paused to listen. Astonishment soon changed to admiration, and they passed on to other and less courageous victims, openly expressing their satisfaction at the firmness with which the white warrior sang his death song. Encouraged and deluded by his success, David exerted all his powers to extend what he believed so holy an influence. The unwonted sounds caught the ears of a distant savage, who flew raging from group to group, like one who, scorning to touch the vulgar herd, hunted for some victim more worthy of his renown. It was Magua, who uttered a yell of pleasure when he beheld his ancient prisoners again at his mercy.

"Come," he said, laying his soiled hands on the dress of Cora, "the wigwam of the Huron is still open. Is it not better than this place?"

"Away!" cried Cora, veiling her eyes from his revolting aspect.

The Indian laughed tauntingly, as he held up his reeking hand, and answered,—"It is red, but it comes from white veins!"

"Monster! there is blood, oceans of blood, upon thy soul; thy spirit has moved this scene."

"Magua is a great chief!" returned the exulting savage; "will the dark hair go to his tribe?"

"Never! strike, if thou wilt, and complete thy revenge."

He hesitated a moment; and then catching the light and senseless form of Alice in his arms, the subtle Indian moved swiftly across the plain towards the woods.

"Hold!" shrieked Cora, following wildly on his footsteps; "release the child! wretch! what is't you do?"

But Magua was deaf to her voice; or rather he knew his power, and was determined to maintain it.

"Stay—lady—stay," called Gamut, after the unconscious Cora. "The holy charm is beginning to be felt, and soon shalt thou see this horrid tumult stilled."

Perceiving that, in his turn, he was unheeded, the faithful David followed the distracted sister, raising his voice again in sacred song, and sweeping the air to the measure, with his long arm, in diligent accompaniment. In this manner they traversed the plain, through the flying, the wounded, and the dead. The fierce Huron was, at any time, sufficient for himself and the victim that he bore; though Cora would have fallen, more than once, under the blows of her savage enemies, but for the extraordinary being who stalked in her rear, and who now appeared to the astonished natives gifted with the protecting spirit of madness.

Magua, who knew how to avoid the more pressing dangers, and also to elude pursuit, entered the woods through a low ravine, where he quickly found the Narragansetts, which the travellers had abandoned so shortly before, awaiting his appearance, in custody of a savage as fierce and as malign in his expression as himself. Laying Alice on one of the horses, he made a sign to Cora to mount the other.

Notwithstanding the horror excited by the presence of her captor, there was a present relief in escaping from the bloody scene enacting on the plain, to which Cora could not be altogether insensible. She took her seat, and held forth her arms for her sister, with an air of entreaty and love that even the Huron could not deny. Placing Alice, then, on the same animal with Cora, he seized the bridle, and commenced his route by plunging deeper into the forest. David, perceiving that he was left alone, utterly disregarded, as a subject too worthless even to destroy, threw his long limb across the saddle of the beast they had deserted, and made such progress in the pursuit as the difficulties of the path permitted.

They soon began to ascend, but as the motion had a tendency to revive the dormant faculties of her sister, the attention of Cora was too much divided between the tenderest solicitude in her behalf, and in listening to the cries which were still too audible on the plain, to note the direction in which they journeyed. When, however, they gained the flattened surface of the mountain-top, and approached the eastern precipice, she recognized the spot to which she had once before been led under the more friendly auspices of the scout. Here Magua suffered them to dismount; and, notwithstanding their own captivity, the curiosity which seems inseparable from horror, induced them to gaze at the sickening sight below.

The cruel work was still unchecked. On every side the captured were flying before their relentless persecutors, while the armed columns of the Christian king stood fast in an apathy which has never been explained, and which has left an unmovable blot on the otherwise fair escutcheon of their leader. Nor was the sword of death stayed until cupidity got the mastery of revenge. Then, indeed, the shrieks of the wounded and the yells of their murderers grew less frequent, until, finally, the cries of horror were lost to their ear, or were drowned in the loud, long, and piercing whoops of the triumphant savages.

English leave, indian steals english wowgams shawl, she takes it back, he takes her baby + smashes it against rock, stabs mom, Magua yells, indians attack english, kill + drink their blood. Magua takes Alice + runs away, Cora follows, Gamut follows.

XVIII

"Why, anything:
An honorable murderer, if you will:
For naught I did in hate, but all in honor."
Othello[1]

THE BLOODY AND inhuman scene rather incidentally mentioned than described in the preceding chapter, is conspicuous in the pages of colonial history, by the merited title of "The Massacre of William Henry." It so far deepened the stain which a previous and very similar event had left upon the reputation of the French commander, that it was not entirely erased by his early and glorious death. It is now becoming obscured by time; and thousands, who know that Montcalm died like a hero on the plains of Abraham, have yet to learn how much he was deficient in that moral courage without which no man can be truly great. Pages might be written to prove, from this illustrious example, the defects of human excellence; to show how easy it is for generous sentiments, high courtesy, and chivalrous courage, to lose their influence beneath the chilling blight of selfishness, and to exhibit to the world a man who was great in all the minor attributes of character, but who was found wanting when it became necessary to prove how much principle is superior to policy. But the task would exceed our prerogatives; and, as history, like love, is so apt to surround her heroes with an atmosphere of imaginary brightness, it is probable that Louis de Saint Véran will be viewed by posterity only as the gallant defender of his country, while his cruel apathy on the shores of the Oswego and of the Horican will be forgotten. Deeply regretting this weakness on the part of a sister muse, we shall at once retire from her sacred precincts, within the proper limits of our own humble vocation.

The third day from the capture of the fort was drawing to a close, but the business of the narrative must still detain the reader on the shores of the "holy lake." When last seen, the environs of the works were filled with violence and uproar. They were now possessed by stillness and death. The blood-stained conquerers had departed; and their camp, which had so lately rung with the merry rejoicings of a victorious army, lay a silent and deserted city of huts. The fortress was a smouldering ruin; charred rafters, fragments of exploded artillery, and rent masonwork, covering its earthen mounds in confused disorder.

A frightful change had also occurred in the season. The sun had hid its warmth behind an impenetrable mass of vapor, and hundreds of human forms, which had blackened beneath the fierce heats of August, were stiffening in their deformity, before the blasts of a premature November. The curling and spotless mists, which had been seen sailing above the hills towards the north, were now returning in an interminable dusky sheet, that was urged along by the fury of a tempest. The crowded mirror of the Horican was gone; and, in its place, the green and angry waters lashed the shores, as if indignantly casting back its impurities to the polluted strand. Still the clear fountain retained a portion of its charmed influence, but it reflected only the sombre gloom that fell from the impending heavens. That humid and congenial atmosphere which commonly adorned the view, veiling its harshness, and softening its asperities, had disappeared, and the northern air poured across the waste of water so harsh and unmingled, that nothing was left to be conjectured by the eye, or fashioned by the fancy.

The fiercer element had cropped the verdure of the plain, which looked as though it were scathed by the consuming lightning. But, here and there, a dark green tuft rose in the midst of the desolation; the earliest fruits of a soil that had been fattened with human blood. The whole landscape, which, seen by a favoring light, and in a genial temperature, had been found so lovely, appeared now like some pictured allegory of life, in which objects were arrayed in their harshest but truest colors, and without the relief of any shadowing.

The solitary and arid blades of grass arose from the passing gusts fearfully perceptible; the bold and rocky mountains were too distinct in their barrenness, and the eye even sought relief, in vain, by attempting to pierce the illimitable void of heaven, which was shut to its gaze by the dusky sheet of ragged and driving vapor.

The wind blew unequally; sometimes sweeping heavily along the ground, seeming to whisper its moanings in the cold ears of the dead, then rising in a shrill and mournful whistling, it entered the forest with a rush that filled the air with the leaves and branches it scattered in its path. Amid the unnatural shower, a few hungry ravens struggled with the gale; but no sooner was the green ocean of woods, which stretched beneath them, passed, than they gladly stopped, at random, to their hideous banquet.

In short, it was the scene of wildness and desolation; and it appeared as if all who had profanely entered it had been stricken, at a blow, by the relentless arm of death. But the prohibition had ceased; and for the first time since the perpetrators of those foul deeds which had assisted to disfigure the scene were gone, living human beings had now presumed to approach the place.

About an hour before the setting of the sun, on the day already mentioned, the forms of five men might have been seen issuing from the narrow vista of trees, where the path to the Hudson entered the forest, and advancing in the direction of the ruined works. At first their progress was slow and guarded, as though they entered with reluctance amid the horrors of the spot, or dreaded the renewal of its frightful incidents. A light figure preceded the rest of the party, with the caution and activity of a native; ascending every hillock to reconnoitre, and indicating, by gestures, to his companions, the route he deemed it most prudent to pursue. Nor were those in the rear wanting in every caution and foresight known to forest warfare. One among them, he also was an Indian, moved a little on one flank, and watched the margin of the woods, with eyes long accustomed to read the smallest sign of danger. The remaining three were white, though clad in vestments adapted, both in quality and color, to their present hazardous pursuit,—that of hanging on the skirts of a retiring army in the wilderness.

The effects produced by the appalling sights that constantly arose in their path to the lake shore, were as different as the characters of the respective individuals who composed the party. The youth in front threw serious but furtive glances at the mangled victims, as he stepped lightly across the plain, afraid to exhibit his feelings, and yet too inexperienced to quell entirely their sudden and powerful influence. His red associate, however, was superior to such a weakness. He passed the groups of dead with a steadiness of purpose, and an eye so calm, that nothing but long and inveterate practice could enable him to maintain. The sensations produced in the minds of even the white men were different, though uniformly sorrowful. One, whose gray locks, and furrowed lineaments, blending with a martial air and tread, betrayed, in spite of the disguise of a woodsman's dress, a man long experienced in scenes of war, was not ashamed to groan aloud, whenever a spectacle of more than usual horror came under his view. The young man at his elbow shuddered, but seemed to suppress his feelings in tenderness to his companion. Of them all, the straggler who brought up the rear appeared alone to betray his real thoughts, without fear of observation or dread of consequences. He gazed at the most appalling sight with eyes and muscles that knew not how to waver, but with execrations so bitter and deep as to denote how much he denounced the crime of his enemies.

The reader will perceive at once, in these respective characters, the Mohicans, and their white friend, the scout; together with Munro and Heyward. It was, in truth, the father in quest of his children, attended by the youth who felt so deep a stake in their happiness, and those brave and trusty foresters, who had already proved their skill and fidelity through the trying scenes related.

When Uncas, who moved in front, had reached the centre of the plain, he raised a cry that drew his compan-

ions in a body to the spot. The young warrior had halted
over a group of females who lay in a cluster, a confused
mass of dead. Notwithstanding the revolting horror of
the exhibition, Munro and Heyward flew towards the
festering heap, endeavoring, with a love that no unseem-
liness could extinguish, to discover whether any vestiges
of those they sought were to be seen among the tattered
and many-colored garments. The father and lover found
instant relief in the search; though each was condemned
again to experience the misery of an uncertainty that was
hardly less insupportable than the most revolting truth.
They were standing, silent and thoughtful, around the
melancholy pile, when the scout approached. Eyeing the
sad spectacle with an angry countenance, the sturdy
woodsman, for the first time since his entering the plain,
spoke intelligibly and aloud:—

"I have been on many a shocking field, and have followed a trail of blood for many miles," he said, "but never
have I found the hand of the devil so plain as it is here to
be seen! Revenge is an Indian feeling, and all who know
me know that there is no cross in my veins; but this
much will I say—here, in the face of heaven, and
with the power of the Lord so manifest in this howling
wilderness,—that should these Frenchers ever trust
themselves again within the range of a ragged bullet,
there is one rifle shall play its part, so long as flint will
fire or powder burn! I leave the tomahawk and knife to
such as have a natural gift to use them. What say you,
Chingachgook," he added in Delaware; "shall the
Hurons boast of this to their women when the deep
snows come?"

A gleam of resentment flashed across the dark lineaments of the Mohican chief: he loosened his knife in its

sheath; and then turning calmly from the sight, his countenance settled into a repose as deep as if he never knew
the instigation of passion.

"Montcalm! Montcalm!" continued the deeply resentful and less self-restrained scout; "they say a time
must come, when all the deeds done in the flesh will be
seen at a single look; and that by eyes cleared from mortal infirmities. Woe betide the wretch who is born to behold this plain, with the judgment hanging about his
soul! Ha—as I am a man of white blood, yonder lies a
redskin, without the hair of his head where nature
rooted it! Look at him, Delaware; it may be one of your
missing people; and he should have burial like a stout
warrior. I see it in your eye, Sagamore: a Huron pays for
this, afore the fall winds have blown away the scent of the
blood!"

Chingachgook approached the mutilated form, and
turning it over, he found the distinguishing marks of one
of those six allied tribes, or nations, as they were called,
who, while they fought in the English ranks, were so
deadly hostile to his own people. Spurning the loathsome object with his foot, he turned from it with the
same indifference he would have quitted a brute carcass.
The scout comprehended the action, and very deliberately pursued his own way, continuing, however, his denunciations against the French commander in the same
resentful strain.

"Nothing but vast wisdom and unlimited power
should dare to sweep off men in multitudes," he added;
"for it is only the one that can know the necessity of the
judgment; and what is there, short of the other, that can
replace the creatures of the Lord? I hold it a sin to kill the
second buck afore the first is eaten, unless a march in the

front, or an ambushment, be contemplated. It is a different matter with a few warriors in open and rugged fight, for 'tis their gift to die with the rifle or the tomahawk in hand; according as their natures may happen to be, white or red. Uncas, come this way, lad, and let the ravens settle upon the Mingo. I know, from often seeing it, that they have a craving for the flesh of an Oneida; and it is as well to let the bird follow the gift of its natural appetite."

"Hugh!" exclaimed the young Mohican, rising on the extremities of his feet, and gazing intently in his front, frightening the raven to some other prey, by the sound and the action.

"What is it, boy?" whispered the scout, lowering his tall form into a crouching attitude, like a panther about to take his leap; "God send it be a tardy Frencher, skulking for plunder. I do believe 'Killdeer' would take an uncommon range today!"

Uncas, without making any reply, bounded away from the spot, and in the next instant he was seen tearing from a bush, and waving in triumph a fragment of the green riding-veil of Cora. The movement, the exhibition, and the cry, which again burst from the lips of the young Mohican, instantly drew the whole party about him.

"My child!" said Munro, speaking quick and wildly; "give me my child!"

"Uncas will try," was the short and touching answer.

The simple but meaning assurance was lost on the father, who seized the piece of gauze, and crushed it in his hand, while his eyes roamed fearfully among the bushes, as if he equally dreaded and hoped for the secrets they might reveal.

"Here are no dead," said Heyward; "the storm seems not to have passed this way."

"That's manifest; and clearer than the heavens above our heads," returned the undisturbed scout; "but either she, or they that have robbed her, have passed the bush; for I remember the rag she wore to hide a face that all did love to look upon. Uncas, you are right; the dark-hair has been here, and she has fled like a frightened fawn, to the wood; none who could fly would remain to be murdered. Let us search for the marks she left; for to Indian eyes, I sometimes think even a humming-bird leaves his trail in the air."

The young Mohican darted away at the suggestion, and the scout had hardly done speaking, before the former raised a cry of success from the margin of the forest. On reaching the spot, the anxious party perceived another portion of the veil fluttering on the lower branch of a beech.

"Softly, softly," said the scout, extending his long rifle in front of the eager Heyward; "we now know our work, but the beauty of the trail must not be deformed. A step too soon may give us hours of trouble. We have them, though; that much is beyond denial."

"Bless ye, bless ye, worthy man!" exclaimed Munro; "whither, then, have they fled, and where are my babes?"

"The path they have taken depends on many chances. If they have gone alone, they are quite as likely to move in a circle as straight, and they may be within a dozen miles of us; but if the Hurons, or any of the French Indians, have lain hands on them, 'tis probable they are now near the borders of the Canadas. But what matters that?" continued the deliberate scout, observing the powerful anxiety and disappointment the listeners exhibited; "here are the Mohicans and I on one end of the trail, and, rely on it, we find the other, though they should be a hundred leagues asunder! Gently, gently, Uncas, you are as impatient as a man in the settlements; you forget that light feet leave but faint marks!"

"Hugh!" exclaimed Chingachgook, who had been occupied in examining an opening that had been evidently made through the low underbrush, which skirted the forest; and who now stood erect, as he pointed downwards, in the attitude and with the air of a man who beheld a disgusting serpent.

"Here is the palpable impression of the footstep of a man," cried Heyward, bending over the indicated spot; "he has trod in the margin of this pool, and the mark cannot be mistaken. They are captives."

"Better so than left to starve in the wilderness," returned the scout; "and they will leave a wider trail. I would wager fifty beaver skins against as many flints, that the Mohicans and I enter their wigwams within the month! Stoop to it, Uncas, and try what you can make of the moccasin; for moccasin it plainly is, and no shoe."

The young Mohican bent over the track, and removing the scattered leaves from around the place, he examined it with much of that sort of scrutiny that a money-dealer, in these days of pecuniary doubts, would bestow on a suspected due-bill. At length he arose from his knees, satisfied with the result of the examination.

"Well, boy," demanded the attentive scout, "what does it say? Can you make anything of the tell-tale?"

"Le Renard Subtil!"

"Ha! that rampaging devil again! there never will be an end of his loping, till 'Killdeer' has said a friendly word to him."

Heyward reluctantly admitted the truth of this intelligence, and now expressed rather his hopes than his doubts by saying,—

"One moccasin is so much like another, it is probable there is some mistake."

"One moccasin like another! you may as well say that one foot is like another; though we all know that some are long, and others short; some broad, and others narrow; some with high, and some with low insteps; some in-toed, and some out. One moccasin is no more like another than one book is like another; though they who can read in one are seldom able to tell the marks of the other. Which is all ordered for the best, giving to every man his natural advantages. Let me get down to it, Uncas; neither book nor moccasin is the worse for having two opinions, instead of one." The scout stooped to the task, and instantly added, "You are right, boy; here is the patch we saw so often in the other chase. And the fellow will drink when he can get an opportunity: your drinking Indian always learns to walk with a wider toe than the natural savage, it being the gift of a drunkard to straddle, whether of white or red skin. 'Tis just the length and breadth too! look at it, Sagamore: you measured the prints more than once, when we hunted the varmints from Glenn's to the health-springs."

Chingachgook complied; and after finishing his short examination, he arose, and with a quiet demeanor, he merely pronounced the word—

"Magua!"

"Ay, 'tis a settled thing; here then have passed the dark-hair and Magua."

"And not Alice?" demanded Heyward.

"Of her we have not yet seen the signs," returned the

scout, looking closely around at the trees, the bushes, and the ground. "What have we there? Uncas, bring hither the thing you see dangling from yonder thorn-bush."

When the Indian had complied, the scout received the prize, and holding it on high, he laughed in his silent but heartfelt manner.

" 'Tis the tooting we'pon of the singer! now we shall have a trail a priest might travel," he said. "Uncas, look for the marks of a shoe that is long enough to uphold six feet two of tottering human flesh. I begin to have some hopes of the fellow, since he has given up squalling to follow some better trade."

"At least, he has been faithful to his trust," said Heyward; "and Cora and Alice are not without a friend."

"Yes," said Hawkeye, dropping his rifle, and leaning on it with an air of visible contempt, "he will do their singing. Can he slay a buck for their dinner, journey by the moss on the beeches, or cut the throat of a Huron? If not, the first catbird he meets is the cleverest of the two. Well, boy, any signs of such a foundation?"

"Here is something like the footstep of one who has worn a shoe; can it be that of our friend?"

"Touch the leaves lightly, or you'll disconsart the formation. That! that is the print of a foot, but 'tis the dark-hair's; and small it is, too, for one of such a noble height and grand appearance. The singer would cover it with his heel."

"Where! let me look on the footsteps of my child," said Munro, shoving the bushes aside, and bending fondly over the nearly obliterated impression. Though the tread, which had left the mark, had been light and rapid, it was still plainly visible. The aged soldier examined it with eyes that grew dim as he gazed; nor did he rise from his stooping posture until Heyward saw that he had watered the trace of his daughter's passage with a scalding tear. Willing to divert a distress which threatened each moment to break through the restraint of appearances, by giving the veteran something to do, the young man said to the scout,—

"As we now possess these infallible signs, let us commence our march. A moment, at such a time, will appear an age to the captives."

"It is not the swiftest leaping deer that gives the longest chase," returned Hawkeye, without moving his eyes from the different marks that had come under his view; "we know that the rampaging Huron has passed,—and the dark-hair,—and the singer,—but where is she of the yellow locks and blue eyes? Though little, and far from being as bold as her sister, she is fair to the view, and pleasant in discourse. Has she no friend, that none care for her?"

"God forbid she should ever want hundreds! Are we not now in her pursuit? For one, I will never cease the search till she be found."

"In that case we may have to journey by different paths; for here she has not passed, light and little as her footstep would be."

Heyward drew back, all his ardor to proceed seeming to vanish on the instant. Without attending to this sudden change in the other's humor, the scout, after musing a moment, continued,—

"There is no woman in this wilderness could leave such a print as that, but the dark-hair or her sister. We know that the first has been here, but where are the signs of the other? Let us push deeper on the trail, and if nothing offers, we must go back to the plain and strike another scent. Move on, Uncas, and keep your eyes on the dried leaves. I will watch the bushes, while your father shall run with a low nose to the ground. Move on, friends; the sun is getting behind the hills."

"Is there nothing that I can do?" demanded the anxious Heyward.

"You!" repeated the scout, who, with his red friends, was already advancing in the order he had prescribed; "yes, you can keep in our rear, and be careful not to cross the trail."

Before they had proceeded many rods, the Indians stopped, and appeared to gaze at some signs on the earth, with more than their usual keenness. Both father and son spoke quick and loud, now looking at the object of their mutual admiration, and now regarding each other with the most unequivocal pleasure.

"They have found the little foot!" exclaimed the scout, moving forward, without attending further to his own portion of the duty. "What have we here? An ambushment has been planted in the spot? No, by the truest rifle on the frontiers, here have been them one-sided horses again! Now the whole secret is out, and all is plain as the north star at midnight. Yes, here they have mounted. There the beasts have been bound to a sapling, in waiting; and yonder runs the broad path away to the north, in full sweep for the Canadas."

"But still there are no signs of Alice—of the younger Miss Munro,"—said Duncan.

"Unless the shining bauble Uncas has just lifted from the ground should prove one. Pass it this way, lad, that we may look at it."

Heyward instantly knew it for a trinket that Alice was

fond of wearing, and which he recollected, with the tenacious memory of a lover, to have seen, on the fatal morning of the massacre, dangling from the fair neck of his mistress. He seized the highly prized jewel; and as he proclaimed the fact, it vanished from the eyes of the wondering scout, who in vain looked for it on the ground, long after it was warmly pressed against the beating heart of Duncan.

"Pshaw!" said the disappointed Hawkeye, ceasing to rake the leaves with the breech of his rifle; " 'tis a certain sign of age, when the sight begins to weaken. Such a glittering gewgaw, and not to be seen! Well, well, I can squint along a clouded barrel yet, and that is enough to settle all disputes between me and the Mingos. I should like to find the thing too, if it were only to carry it to the right owner, and that would be bringing the two ends of what I call a long trail together,—for by this time the broad St. Lawrence, or, perhaps, the Great Lakes themselves, are atwixt us."

"So much the more reason why we should not delay our march," returned Heyward; "let us proceed."

"Young blood and hot blood, they say, are much the same thing. We are not about to start on a squirrel hunt, or to drive a deer into the Horican, but to outlie for days and nights, and to stretch across a wilderness where the feet of men seldom go, and where no bookish knowledge would carry you through harmless. An Indian never starts on such an expedition without smoking over his council-fire; and though a man of white blood, I honor their customs in this particular, seeing that they are deliberate and wise. We will, therefore, go back, and light our fire to-night in the ruins of the old fort, and in the morning we shall be fresh, and ready to undertake our work like men, and not like babbling women or eager boys."

Heyward saw, by the manner of the scout, that altercation would be useless. Munro had again sunk into that sort of apathy which had beset him since his late overwhelming misfortunes, and from which he was apparently to be roused only by some new and powerful excitement. Making a merit of necessity, the young man took the veteran by the arm, and followed in the footsteps of the Indians and the scout, who had already begun to retrace the path which conducted them to the plain.

Hawk, munro, the mohicans + hey go back to site of seige. Uncas finds part of coras riding veil, led to the horses, conclude that the missing are in the wilderness. Hey wants to go immediately. hawk insists they plan, Munro depressed

XIX

"Salar.—Why, I am sure, if he forfeit, thou wilt not take
his flesh; what's that good for?"
"Shy.—To bait fish withal: if it will feed nothing else, it
will feed my revenge."
The Merchant of Venice[1]

THE SHADES OF EVENING had come to increase the
dreariness of the place, when the party entered the
ruins of William Henry. The scout and his companions
immediately made their preparations to pass the night
there; but with an earnestness and sobriety of demeanor,
that betrayed how much the unusual horrors they had
just witnessed worked on even their practised feelings. A
few fragments of rafters were reared against a blackened
wall; and when Uncas had covered them slightly with
brush, the temporary accommodations were deemed
sufficient. The young Indian pointed towards his rude
hut, when his labor was ended; and Heyward, who understood the meaning of the silent gesture, gently urged
Munro to enter. Leaving the bereaved old man alone
with his sorrows, Duncan immediately returned to the
open air, too much excited himself to seek the repose he
had recommended to his veteran friend.

While Hawkeye and the Indians lighted their fire, and

took their evening's repast, a frugal meal of dried bear's meat, the young man paid a visit to that curtain of the dilapidated fort which looked out on the sheet of the Horican. The wind had fallen, and the waves were already rolling on the sandy beach beneath him, in a more regular and tempered succession. The clouds, as if tired of their furious chase, were breaking asunder; the heavier volumes, gathering in black masses about the horizon, while the lighter scud still hurried above the water, or eddied among the tops of the mountains, like broken flights of birds, hovering around their roosts. Here and there, a red and fiery star struggled through the drifting vapor, furnishing a lurid gleam of brightness to the dull aspect of the heavens. Within the bosom of the encircling hills, an impenetrable darkness had already settled; and the plain lay like a vast and deserted charnel-house, without omen or whisper to disturb the slumbers of its numerous and hapless tenants.

Of this scene, so chillingly in accordance with the past, Duncan stood for many minutes a rapt observer. His eyes wandered from the bosom of the mound, where the foresters were seated around their glimmering fire, to the fainter light which still lingered in the skies, and then rested long and anxiously on the embodied gloom, which lay like a dreary void on that side of him where the dead reposed. He soon fancied that inexplicable sounds arose from the place, though so indistinct and stolen, as to render not only their nature but even their existence uncertain. Ashamed of his apprehensions, the young man turned towards the water, and strove to divert his attentions to the mimic stars that dimly glimmered on its moving surface. Still, his too conscious ears performed their ungrateful duty, as if to warn him of some lurking danger. At length a swift trampling seemed quite audibly to rush athwart the darkness. Unable any longer to quiet his uneasiness, Duncan spoke in a low voice to the scout, requesting him to ascend the mound to the place where he stood. Hawkeye threw his rifle across an arm, and complied, but with an air so unmoved and calm, as to prove how much he counted on the security of their position.

"Listen!" said Duncan, when the other placed himself deliberately at his elbow: "there are suppressed noises on the plain which may show that Montcalm has not yet entirely deserted his conquest."

"Then ears are better than eyes," said the undisturbed scout, who, having just deposited a portion of bear between his grinders, spoke thick and slow, like one whose mouth was doubly occupied. "I, myself, saw him caged in Ty, with all his host; for your Frenchers, when they have done a clever thing, like to get back, and have a dance, or a merry-making, with the women over their success."

"I know not. An Indian seldom sleeps in war, and plunder may keep a Huron here after his tribe has departed. It would be well to extinguish the fire, and have a watch—listen! you hear the noise I mean!"

"An Indian more rarely lurks about the graves. Though ready to slay, and not over-regardful of the means, he is commonly content with the scalp, unless when blood is hot, and temper up; but after the spirit is once fairly gone, he forgets his enmity, and is willing to let the dead find their natural rest. Speaking of spirits, Major, are you of the opinion that the heaven of a redskin and of us whites will be one and the same?"

"No doubt—no doubt. I thought I heard it again! or was it the rustling of the leaves in the top of the beech?"

"For my own part," continued Hawkeye, turning his face, for a moment, in the direction indicated by Heyward, but with a vacant and careless manner, "I believe that paradise is ordained for happiness; and that men will be indulged in it according to their dispositions and gifts. I therefore judge that a redskin is not far from the truth when he believes he is to find them glorious huntinggrounds of which his traditions tell; nor, for that matter, do I think it would be any disparagement to a man without a cross to pass his time—"

"You hear it again?" interrupted Duncan.

"Ay, ay; when food is scarce, and when food is plenty, a wolf grows bold," said the unmoved scout. "There would be picking, too, among the skins of the devils, if there was light and time for the sport. But, concerning the life that is to come, Major: I have heard preachers say, in the settlements, that heaven was a place of rest. Now men's minds differ as to their ideas of enjoyment. For myself, and I say it with reverence to the ordering of Providence, it would be no great indulgence to be kept shut up in those mansions of which they preach, having a natural longing for motion and the chase."

Duncan, who was now made to understand the nature of the noises he had heard, answered with more attention to the subject which the humor of the scout had chosen for discussion, by saying,—

"It is difficult to account for the feelings that may attend the last great change."

"It would be a change, indeed, for a man who has passed his days in the open air," returned the singleminded scout; "and who has so often broken his fast on the head-waters of the Hudson, to sleep within sound of the roaring Mohawk. But it is a comfort to know we serve a merciful Master, though we do it each after his fashion, and with great tracts of wilderness atween us—what goes there?"

"Is it not the rushing of the wolves you have mentioned?"

Hawkeye slowly shook his head, and beckoned for Duncan to follow him to a spot, to which the glare from the fire did not extend. When he had taken this precaution, the scout placed himself in an attitude of intense attention, and listened long and keenly for a repetition of the low sound that had so unexpectedly startled him. His vigilance, however, seemed exercised in vain; for, after a fruitless pause, he whispered to Duncan,—

"We must give a call to Uncas. The boy has Indian senses, and may hear what is hid from us; for being a white-skin, I will not deny my nature."

The young Mohican, who was conversing in a low voice with his father, started as he heard the moaning of an owl, and springing on his feet he looked towards the black mounds, as if seeking the place whence the sounds proceeded. The scout repeated the call, and in a few moments, Duncan saw the figure of Uncas stealing cautiously along the rampart, to the spot where they stood.

Hawkeye explained his wishes in a very few words, which were spoken in the Delaware tongue. So soon as Uncas was in possession of the reason why he was summoned, he threw himself flat on the turf; where, to the eyes of Duncan, he appeared to lie quiet and motionless. Surprised at the immovable attitude of the young warrior, and curious to observe the manner in which he employed his faculties to obtain the desired information, Heyward advanced a few steps, and bent over the dark object, on which he had kept his eyes riveted. Then it was he discovered that the form of Uncas had vanished, and that he beheld only the dark outline of an inequality in the embankment.

"What has become of the Mohican?" he demanded of the scout, stepping back in amazement; "it was here that I saw him fall, and I could have sworn that here he yet remained."

"Hist! speak lower; for we know not what ears are open, and the Mingos are a quick-witted breed. As for Uncas, he is out on the plain, and the Maquas, if any such are about us, will find their equal."

"You think that Montcalm has not called off all his Indians? Let us give the alarm to our companions, that we may stand to our arms. Here are five of us, who are not unused to meet an enemy."

"Not a word to either, as you value life. Look at the Sagamore, how like a grand Indian chief he sits by the fire. If there are any skulkers out in the darkness, they will never discover by his countenance that we suspect danger at hand."

"But they may discover him, and it will prove his death. His person can be too plainly seen by the light of that fire, and he will become the first and most certain victim."

"It is undeniable that now you speak the truth," returned the scout, betraying more anxiety than was usual; "yet what can be done? A single suspicious look might bring on an attack before we are ready to receive it. He knows, by the call I gave to Uncas, that we have struck a scent: I will tell him that we are on the trail of the Mingos; his Indian nature will teach him how to act."

The scout applied his fingers to his mouth, and raised a low hissing sound, that caused Duncan, at first, to start

aside, believing that he heard a serpent. The head of
Chingachgook was resting on a hand, as he sat musing by
himself; but the moment he heard the warning of the animal whose name he bore, it arose to an upright position
and his dark eyes glanced swiftly and keenly on every
side of him. With this sudden and perhaps involuntary
movement, every appearance of surprise or alarm
ended. His rifle lay untouched, and apparently unnoticed, within reach of his hand. The tomahawk that he
had loosened in his belt for the sake of ease, was even
suffered to fall from its usual situation to the ground, and
his form seemed to sink, like that of a man whose nerves
and sinews were suffered to relax for the purpose of rest.
Cunningly resuming his former position, though with a
change of hands, as if the movement had been made
merely to relieve the limb, the native awaited the result
with a calmness and fortitude that none but an Indian
warrior would have known how to exercise.

But Heyward saw that while to a less instructed eye
the Mohican chief appeared to slumber, his nostrils were
expanded, his head was turned a little to one side, as if to
assist the organs of hearing, and that his quick and rapid
glances ran incessantly over every object within the
power of his vision.

"See the noble fellow!" whispered Hawkeye, pressing
the arm of Heyward; "he knows that a look or a motion
might disconsart our schemes, and put us at the mercy of
them imps—"

He was interrupted by the flash and report of a rifle.
The air was filled with sparks of fire around that spot
where the eyes of Heyward were still fastened with admiration and wonder. A second look told him that Chingachgook had disappeared in the confusion. In the

meantime the scout had thrown forward his rifle, like one prepared for service, and awaited impatiently the moment when an enemy might rise to view. But with the solitary and fruitless attempt made on the life of Chingachgook, the attack appeared to have terminated. Once or twice the listeners thought they could distinguish the distant rustling of bushes, as bodies of some unknown description rushed through them; nor was it long before Hawkeye pointed out the "scampering of the wolves," as they fled precipitately before the passage of some intruder on their proper domains. After an impatient and breathless pause, a plunge was heard in the water, and it was immediately followed by the report of another rifle.

"There goes Uncas!" said the scout; "the boy bears a smart piece! I know its crack, as well as a father knows the language of his child, for I carried the gun myself until a better offered."

"What can this mean?" demanded Duncan; "we are watched, and, as it would seem, marked for destruction."

"Yonder scattered brand can witness that no good was intended, and this Indian will testify that no harm has been done," returned the scout, dropping his rifle across his arm again, and following Chingachgook, who just then reappeared within the circle of light, into the bosom of the works. "How is it, Sagamore? Are the Mingos upon us in earnest, or is it only one of those reptyles who hang upon the skirts of a war-party, to scalp the dead, go in, and make their boast among the squaws of the valiant deeds done on the pale-faces?"

Chingachgook very quietly resumed his seat; nor did he make any reply, until after he had examined the firebrand which had been struck by the bullet that had nearly proved fatal to himself. After which, he was content to reply, holding a single finger up to view, with the English monosyllable,—

"One."

"I thought as much," returned Hawkeye, seating himself; "and as he had got the cover of the lake afore Uncas pulled upon him, it is more than probable the knave will sing his lies about some great ambushment, in which he was outlying on the trail of two Mohicans and a white hunter—for the officers can be considered as little better than idlers in such a scrimmage. Well, let him—let him. There are always some honest men in every nation, though heavens knows, too, that they are scarce among the Maquas, to look down an upstart when he brags ag'in the face of reason. The varlet sent his lead within whistle of your ears, Sagamore."

Chingachgook turned a calm and incurious eye towards the place where the ball had struck, and then resumed his former attitude, with a composure that could not be disturbed by so trifling an incident. Just then Uncas glided into the circle, and seated himself at the fire, with the same appearance of indifference as was maintained by his father.

Of these several movements Heyward was a deeply interested and wondering observer. It appeared to him as though the foresters had some secret means of intelligence, which had escaped the vigilance of his own faculties. In place of that eager and garrulous narration with which a white youth would have endeavored to communicate, and perhaps exaggerate, that which had passed out in the darkness of the plain, the young warrior was seemingly content to let his deeds speak for themselves. It was, in fact, neither the moment nor the occasion for an Indian to boast of his exploits; and it is probable, that had Heyward neglected to inquire, not another syllable would, just then, have been uttered on the subject.

"What has become of our enemy, Uncas?" demanded Duncan: "we heard your rifle, and hoped you had not fired in vain."

The young chief removed a fold of his hunting-shirt, and quietly exposed the fatal tuft of hair, which he bore as the symbol of victory. Chingachgook laid his hand on the scalp, and considered it for a moment with deep attention. Then dropping it, with disgust depicted in his strong features, he ejaculated,—

"Oneida!"

"Oneida!" repeated the scout, who was fast losing his interest in the scene, in an apathy nearly assimilated to that of his red associates, but who now advanced with uncommon earnestness to regard the bloody badge. "By the Lord, if the Oneidas are outlying upon the trail, we shall be flanked by devils on every side of us! Now, to white eyes there is no difference between this bit of skin and that of any other Indian, and yet the Sagamore declares it came from the poll of a Mingo; nay, he even names the tribe of the poor devil with as much ease as if the scalp was the leaf of a book, and each hair a letter. What right have Christian whites to boast of their learning, when a savage can read a language that would prove too much for the wisest of them all! What say *you*, lad; of what people was the knave?"

Uncas raised his eyes to the face of the scout, and answered, in his soft voice,—

"Oneida."

"Oneida, again! when one Indian makes a declaration it is commonly true; but when he is supported by his people, set it down as gospel!"

"The poor fellow has mistaken us for French," said Heyward; "or he would not have attempted the life of a friend."

"He mistake a Mohican in his paint for a Huron! You would be as likely to mistake the white-coated grenadiers of Montcalm for the scarlet jackets of the 'Royal Americans,'" returned the scout. "No, no, the sarpent knew his errand; nor was there any great mistake in the matter, for there is but little love atween a Delaware and a Mingo, let their tribes go out to fight for whom they may, in a white quarrel. For that matter, though the Oneidas do serve his sacred majesty, who is my own sovereign lord and master, I should not have deliberated long about letting off 'Killdeer' at the imp myself, had luck thrown him in my way."

"That would have been an abuse of our treaties, and unworthy of your character."

"When a man consorts much with a people," continued Hawkeye, "if they are honest and he no knave, love will grow up atwixt them. It is true that white cunning has managed to throw the tribes into great confusion as respects friends and enemies; so that the Hurons and the Oneidas, who speak the same tongue, or what may be called the same, take each other's scalps, and the Delawares are divided among themselves; a few hanging about their great council-fire on their own river, and fighting on the same side with the Mingos, while the greater part are in the Canadas, out of natural enmity to the Maquas—thus throwing everything into disorder, and destroying all the harmony of warfare. Yet a red natur' is not likely to alter with every shift of policy; so that the love atwixt a Mohican and a Mingo is much like the regard between a white man and a sarpent."

"I regret to hear it; for I had believed those natives who dwelt within our boundaries had found us too just and liberal, not to identify themselves fully with our quarrels."

"Why, I believe it is natur' to give a preference to one's own quarrels before those of strangers. Now, for myself, I do love justice; and therefore I will not say I hate a Mingo, for that may be unsuitable to my color and my religion, though I will just repeat, it may have been owing to the night that 'Killdeer' had no hand in the death of this skulking Oneida."

Then, as if satisfied with the force of his own reasons, whatever might be their effect on the opinions of the other disputant, the honest but implacable woodsman turned from the fire, content to let the controversy slumber. Heyward withdrew to the rampart, too uneasy and too little accustomed to the warfare of the woods to remain at ease under the possibility of such insidious attacks. Not so, however, with the scout and the Mohicans. Those acute and long practised senses, whose powers so often exceed the limits of all ordinary credulity, after having detected the danger, had enabled them to ascertain its magnitude and duration. Not one of the three appeared in the least to doubt their perfect security, as was indicated by the preparations that were soon made to sit in council over their future proceedings.

The confusion of nations, and even of tribes, to which Hawkeye alluded, existed at that period in the fullest force. The great tie of language, and, of course, of a common origin, was severed in many places; and it was one of its consequences, that the Delaware and the Mingo (as the people of the Six Nations were called) were found fighting in the same ranks, while the latter sought the scalp of the Huron, though believed to be the root of his own stock. The Delawares were even divided among themselves. Though love for the soil which had belonged to his ancestors kept the Sagamore of the Mohicans with a small band of followers who were serving at Edward, under the banners of the English king, by far the largest portion of his nation were known to be in the field as allies of Montcalm. The reader probably knows, if enough has not already been gleaned from this narrative, that the Delaware, or Lenape, claimed to be the progenitors of that numerous people, who once were masters of most of the Eastern and Northern States of America, of whom the community of the Mohicans was an ancient and highly honored member.

It was, of course, with a perfect understanding of the minute and intricate interest which had armed friend against friend, and brought natural enemies to combat by each other's side, that the scout and his companions now disposed of themselves to deliberate on the measures that were to govern their future movements, amid so many jarring and savage races of men. Duncan knew enough of Indian customs to understand the reason that the fire was replenished, and why the warriors, not excepting Hawkeye, took their seats within the curl of its smoke with so much gravity and decorum. Placing himself at an angle of the works, where he might be a spectator of the scene within, while he kept a watchful eye against any danger from without, he awaited the result with as much patience as he could summon.

After a short and impressive pause, Chingachgook lighted a pipe whose bowl was curiously carved in one of the soft stones of the country, and whose stem was a tube of wood, and commenced smoking. When he had in-

haled enough of the fragrance of the soothing weed, he
passed the instrument into the hands of the scout. In this
manner the pipe had made its rounds three several
times, amid the most profound silence, before either of
the party opened his lips. Then the Sagamore, as the oldest and highest in rank, in a few calm and dignified
words, proposed the subject for deliberation. He was answered by the scout; and Chingachgook rejoined, when
the other objected to his opinions. But the youthful
Uncas continued a silent and respectful listener, until
Hawkeye, in complaisance, demanded his opinion. Heyward gathered from the manners of the different speakers, that the father and son espoused one side of a
disputed question, while the white man maintained the
other. The contest gradually grew warmer, until it was
quite evident the feelings of the speakers began to be
somewhat enlisted in the debate.

Notwithstanding the increasing warmth of the amicable contest, the most decorous Christian assembly, not
even excepting those in which its reverend ministers are
collected, might have learned a wholesome lesson of
moderation from the forbearance and courtesy of the
disputants. The words of Uncas were received with the
same deep attention as those which fell from the ma-
turer wisdom of his father; and so far from manifesting
any impatience, neither spoke in reply, until a few moments of silent meditation were, seemingly, bestowed in
deliberating on what had already been said.

The language of the Mohicans was accompanied by
gestures so direct and natural, that Heyward had but little difficulty in following the thread of their argument.
On the other hand, the scout was obscure; because, from
the lingering pride of color, he rather affected the cold

and artificial manner which characterizes all classes of Anglo-Americans, when unexcited. By the frequency with which the Indians described the marks of a forest trail, it was evident they urged a pursuit by land, while the repeated sweep of Hawkeye's arm towards the Horican denoted that he was for a passage across its waters.

The latter was, to every appearance, fast losing ground, and the point was about to be decided against him, when he arose to his feet, and shaking off his apathy, he suddenly assumed the manner of an Indian, and adopted all the arts of native eloquence. Elevating an arm, he pointed out the track of the sun, repeating the gesture for every day that was necessary to accomplish their object. Then he delineated a long and painful path, amid rocks and water-courses. The age and weakness of the slumbering and unconscious Munro were indicated by signs too palpable to be mistaken. Duncan perceived that even his own powers were spoken lightly of, as the scout extended his palm, and mentioned him by appellation of the "Open Hand,"—a name his liberality had purchased of all the friendly tribes. Then came a representation of the light and graceful movements of a canoe, set in forcible contrast to the tottering steps of one enfeebled and tired. He concluded by pointing to the scalp of the Oneida, and apparently urging the necessity of their departing speedily, and in a manner that should leave no trail.

The Mohicans listened gravely, and with countenances that reflected the sentiments of the speaker. Conviction gradually wrought its influence, and towards the close of Hawkeye's speech, his sentences were accompanied by the customary exclamation of commendation. In short, Uncas and his father became converts to his way of thinking, abandoning their own previously expressed opinions with a liberality and candor that, had they been the representatives of some great and civilized people, would have infallibly worked their political ruin, by destroying, forever, their reputation for consistency.

The instant the matter in discussion was decided, the debate, and everything connected with it, except the results, appeared to be forgotten. Hawkeye, without looking round to read his triumph in applauding eyes, very composedly stretched his tall frame before the dying embers, and closed his own organs in sleep.

Left now in a measure to themselves, the Mohicans, whose time had been so much devoted to the interests of others, seized the moment to devote some attention to themselves. Casting off, at once, the grave and austere demeanor of an Indian chief, Chingachgook commenced speaking to his son in the soft and playful tones of affection. Uncas gladly met the familiar air of his father; and before the hard breathing of the scout announced that he slept, a complete change was effected in the manner of his two associates.

It is impossible to describe the music of their language, while thus engaged in laughter and endearments, in such a way as to render it intelligible to those whose ears have never listened to its melody. The compass of their voices, particularly that of the youth, was wonderful,—extending from the deepest bass to tones that were even feminine in softness. The eyes of the father followed the plastic and ingenious movements of the son with open delight, and he never failed to smile in reply to the other's contagious, but low laughter. While under the influence of these gentle and natural feelings, no trace of ferocity was to be seen in the softened features of the

Sagamore. His figured panoply of death looked more like a disguise assumed in mockery, than a fierce annunciation of a desire to carry destruction in his footsteps.

After an hour passed in the indulgence of their better feelings, Chingachgook abruptly announced his desire to sleep, by wrapping his head in his blanket, and stretching his form on the naked earth. The merriment of Uncas instantly ceased; and carefully raking the coals in such a manner that they should impart their warmth to his father's feet, the youth sought his own pillow among the ruins of the place.

Imbibing renewed confidence from the security of these experienced foresters, Heyward soon imitated their example; and long before the night had turned, they who lay in the bosom of the ruined work, seemed to slumber as heavily as the unconscious multitude whose bones were already beginning to bleach on the surrounding plain.

camp fire, bear for dinner, ney hears noises, uncas says wolves nearby. hawk ponders paradise, another sound, uncas investigates, group hears a shot, ching follows son, group hears splash + another shot, ching + uncas come back w/ scalp of an oneida, plan next day, fall asleep

XX

"Land of Albania! let me bend mine eyes
On thee, thou rugged nurse of savage men!"
Lord Byron, "Childe Harold's Pilgrimage"[1]

THE HEAVENS WERE STILL studded with stars, when Hawkeye came to arouse the sleepers. Casting aside their cloaks Munro and Heyward were on their feet while the woodsman was still making his low calls, at the entrance of the rude shelter where they had passed the night. When they issued from beneath its concealment, they found the scout awaiting their appearance nigh by, and the only salutation between them was the significant gesture for silence, made by their sagacious leader.

"Think over your prayers," he whispered, as they approached him; "for He to whom you make them knows all tongues; that of the heart as well as those of the mouth. But speak not a syllable; it is rare for a white voice to pitch itself properly in the woods, as we have seen by the example of that miserable devil, the singer. Come," he continued, turning towards a curtain of the works; "let us get into the ditch on this side, and be regardful to step on the stones and fragments of wood as you go."

His companions complied, though to two of them the

reasons of this extraordinary precaution were yet a mystery. When they were in the low cavity that surrounded the earthen fort on three sides, they found the passage nearly choked by the ruins. With care and patience, however, they succeeded in clambering after the scout, until they reached the sandy shore of the Horican.

"That's a trail that nothing but a nose can follow," said the satisfied scout, looking back along their difficult way; "grass is a treacherous carpet for a flying party to tread on, but wood and stone take no print from a moccasin. Had you worn your armed boots, there might, indeed, have been something to fear; but with the deer-skin suitably prepared, a man may trust himself, generally, on rocks with safety. Shove in the canoe nigher to the land, Uncas; this sand will take a stamp as easily as the butter of the Jarmans on the Mohawk.[2] Softly, lad, softly, it must not touch the beach, or the knaves will know by what road we have left the place."

The young man observed the precaution; and the scout, laying a board from the ruins to the canoe, made a sign for the two officers to enter. When this was done, everything was studiously restored to its former disorder; and then Hawkeye succeeded in reaching his little birchen vessel, without leaving behind him any of those marks which he appeared so much to dread. Heyward was silent, until the Indians had cautiously paddled the canoe some distance from the fort, and within the broad and dark shadow that fell from the eastern mountain on the glassy surface of the lake; then he demanded,—

"What need have we for this stolen and hurried departure?"

"If the blood of an Oneida could stain such a sheet of pure water as this we float on," returned the scout, "your two eyes would answer your own question. Have you forgotten the skulking reptile that Uncas slew?"

"By no means. But he was said to be alone, and dead men give no cause for fear."

"Ay, he was alone in his deviltry! but an Indian whose tribe counts so many warriors, need seldom fear his blood will run, without the death-shriek coming speedily from some of his enemies."

"But our presence—the authority of Colonel Munro—would prove a sufficient protection against the anger of our allies, especially in a case where a wretch so well merited his fate. I trust in Heaven you have not deviated a single foot from the direct line of our course, with so slight a reason!"

"Do you think the bullet of that varlet's rifle would have turned aside, though his majesty the king had stood in its path?" returned the stubborn scout. "Why did not the grand Frencher, he who is captain-general of the Canadas, bury the tomahawks of the Hurons, if a word from a white can work so strongly on the natur' of an Indian?"

The reply of Heyward was interrupted by a groan from Munro; but after he had paused a moment, in deference to the sorrow of his aged friend, he resumed the subject.

"The Marquis of Montcalm can only settle that error with his God," said the young man solemnly.

"Ay, ay; now there is reason in your words, for they are bottomed on religion and honesty. There is a vast difference between throwing a regiment of white coats atwixt the tribes and the prisoners, and coaxing an angry savage to forget he carries a knife and a rifle, with words that must begin with calling him your son. No, no," continued

the scout, looking back at the dim shore of William
Henry, which was now fast receding, and laughing in his
own silent but heartfelt manner; "I have put a trail of
water atween us; and unless the imps can make friends
with the fishes, and hear who has paddled across their
basin, this fine morning, we shall throw the length of the
Horican behind us, before they have made up their
minds which path to take."

"With foes in front, and foes in our rear, our journey is
like to be one of danger."

"Danger!" repeated Hawkeye, calmly; "no, not absolutely of danger; for, with vigilant ears and quick eyes,
we can manage to keep a few hours ahead of the knaves;
or, if we must try the rifle, there are three of us who understand its gifts as well as any you can name on the borders. No, not of danger; but that we shall have what you
may call a brisk push of it is probable; and it may happen,
a brush, a skrimmage, or some such divarsion, but always
where covers are good, and ammunition abundant."

It is possible that Heyward's estimate of danger differed in some degree from that of the scout, for, instead
of replying, he now sat in silence, while the canoe glided
over several miles of water. Just as the day dawned, they
entered the narrows of the lake, and stole swiftly and
cautiously among their numberless little islands. It was
by this road that Montcalm had retired with his army;
and the adventurers knew not but he had left some of his
Indians in ambush, to protect the rear of his forces, and
collect the stragglers. They, therefore, approached the
passage with the customary silence of their guarded
habits.

Chingachgook laid aside his paddle; while Uncas and
the scout urged the light vessel through crooked and in-

tricate channels, where every foot that they advanced exposed them to the danger of some sudden rising on their progress. The eyes of the Sagamore moved warily from islet to islet, and copse to copse, as the canoe proceeded; and when a clearer sheet of water permitted, his keen vision was bent along the bald rocks and impending forests, that frowned upon the narrow strait.

Heyward, who was a doubly interested spectator, as well from the beauties of the place as from the apprehension natural to his situation, was just believing that he had permitted the latter to be excited without sufficient reason, when the paddle ceased moving, in obedience to a signal from Chingachgook.

"Hugh!" exclaimed Uncas, nearly at the moment that the light tap his father had made on the side of the canoe notified them of the vicinity of danger.

"What now?" asked the scout; "the lake is as smooth as if the winds had never blown, and I can see along its sheet for miles; there is not so much as the black head of a loon dotting the water."

The Indian gravely raised his paddle, and pointed in the direction in which his own steady look was riveted. Duncan's eyes followed the motion. A few rods in their front lay another of the low wooded islets, but it appeared as calm and peaceful as if its solitude had never been disturbed by the foot of man.

"I see nothing," he said, "but land and water; and a lovely scene it is."

"Hist!" interrupted the scout. "Ay, Sagamore, there is always a reason for what you do. 'Tis but a shade, and yet it is not natural. You see the mist, major, that is rising above the island; you can't call it a fog for it is more like a streak of thin cloud—"

"It is vapor from the water."

"That a child could tell. But what is the edging of blacker smoke that hangs along its lower side, and which you may trace down into the thicket of hazel! 'Tis from a fire; but one that, in my judgment, has been suffered to burn low."

"Let us then push for the place, and relieve our doubts," said the impatient Duncan; "the party must be small that can lie on such a bit of land."

"If you judge of Indian cunning by the rules you find in books, or by white sagacity, they will lead you astray, if not to your death," returned Hawkeye, examining the signs of the place with that acuteness which distinguished him. "If I may be permitted to speak in this matter, it will be to say, that we have but two things to choose between: the one is, to return, and give up all thoughts of following the Hurons—"

"Never!" exclaimed Heyward, in a voice far too loud for their circumstances.

"Well, well," continued Hawkeye, making a hasty sign to repress his impatience; "I am much of your mind myself; though I thought it becoming my experience to tell the whole. We must then make a push, and if the Indians or Frenchers are in the narrows, run the gauntlet through these toppling mountains. Is there reason in my words, Sagamore?"

The Indian made no other answer than by dropping his paddle into the water, and urging forward the canoe. As he held the office of directing its course, his resolution was sufficiently indicated by the movement. The whole party now plied their paddles vigorously, and in a very few moments they had reached a point whence they might command an entire view of the northern shore of the island, the side that had hitherto been concealed.

"There they are, by all the truth of signs," whispered the scout; "two canoes and a smoke. The knaves haven't yet got their eyes out of the mist, or we should hear the accursed whoop. Together, friend! we are leaving them, and are already nearly out of whistle of a bullet."

The well-known crack of a rifle, whose ball came skipping along the placid surface of the strait, and a shrill yell from the island, interrupted his speech, and announced that their passage was discovered. In another instant several savages were seen rushing into the canoes, which were soon dancing over the water, in pursuit. These fearful precursors of a coming struggle produced no change in the countenances and movements of his three guides, so far as Duncan could discover, except that the strokes of their paddles were longer and more in unison, and caused the little bark to spring forward like a creature possessing life and volition.

"Hold them there, Sagamore," said Hawkeye, looking coolly backward over his left shoulder, while he still plied his paddle; "keep them just there. Them Hurons have never a piece in their nation that will execute at this distance; but 'Killdeer' has a barrel on which a man may calculate."

The scout having ascertained that the Mohicans were sufficient of themselves to maintain the requisite distance, deliberately laid aside his paddle, and raised the fatal rifle. Three several times he brought the piece to his shoulder, and when his companions were expecting its report, he as often lowered it to request the Indians would permit their enemies to approach a little nigher. At length his accurate and fastidious eye seemed satisfied, and throwing out his left arm on the barrel, he was slowly elevating the muzzle, when an exclamation from Uncas, who sat in the bow, once more caused him to suspend the shot.

"What now, lad?" demanded Hawkeye; "you saved a Huron from the death-shriek by that word; have you reason for what you do?"

Uncas pointed towards the rocky shore a little in their front, whence another war canoe was darting directly across their course. It was too obvious now that their situation was imminently perilous to need the aid of language to confirm it. The scout laid aside his rifle, and resumed the paddle, while Chingachgook inclined the bows of the canoe a little towards the western shore, in order to increase the distance between them and this new enemy. In the meantime they were reminded of the presence of those who pressed upon their rear, by wild and exulting shouts. The stirring scene awakened even Munro from his apathy.

"Let us make for the rocks on the main," he said, with the mien of a tired soldier, "and give battle to the savages. God forbid that I, or those attached to me and mine, should ever trust again to the faith of any servant of the Louis's!"

"He who wishes to prosper in Indian warfare," returned the scout, "must not be too proud to learn from the wit of a native. Lay her more along the land, Sagamore; we are doubling on the varlets, and perhaps they may try to strike our trail on the long calculation."

Hawkeye was not mistaken; for when the Hurons found their course was likely to throw them behind their chase, they rendered it less direct, until, by gradually bearing more and more obliquely, the two canoes were

ere long, gliding on parallel lines, within two hundred yards of each other. It now became entirely a trial of speed. So rapid was the progress of the light vessels, that the lake curled in their front, in miniature waves, and their motion became undulating by its own velocity. It was, perhaps, owing to this circumstance, in addition to the necessity of keeping every hand employed at the paddles, that the Hurons had not immediate recourse to their fire-arms. The exertions of the fugitives were too severe to continue long, and the pursuers had the advantage of numbers. Duncan observed, with uneasiness, that the scout began to look anxiously about him, as if searching for some further means of assisting their flight.

"Edge her a little more from the sun, Sagamore," said the stubborn woodsman; "I see the knaves are sparing a man to the rifle. A single broken bone might lose us our scalps. Edge more from the sun and we will put the island between us."

The expedient was not without its use. A long, low island lay at a little distance before them, and as they closed with it, the chasing canoe was compelled to take a side opposite to that on which the pursued passed. The scout and his companions did not neglect this advantage, but the instant they were hid from observation by the bushes, they redoubled efforts that before had seemed prodigious. The two canoes came round the last low point, like two coursers at the top of their speed, the fugitives taking the lead. This change had brought them nigher to each other, however, while it altered their relative positions.

"You showed knowledge in the shaping of birchen bark, Uncas, when you chose this from among the Huron canoes," said the scout, smiling, apparently more in satisfaction at their superiority in the race, than from that prospect of final escape which now began to open a little upon them. "The imps have put all their strength again at the paddles, and we are to struggle for our scalps with bits of flattened wood, instead of clouded barrels and true eyes. A long stroke, and together, friends."

"They are preparing for a shot," said Heyward; "and as we are in a line with them, it can scarcely fail."

"Get you then into the bottom of the canoe," returned the scout; "you and the colonel; it will be so much taken from the size of the mark."

Heyward smiled, as he answered,—

"It would be but an ill example for the highest in rank to dodge, while the warriors were under fire!"

"Lord! Lord! That is now a white man's courage!" exclaimed the scout; "and like too many of his notions, not to be maintained by reason. Do you think the Sagamore, or Uncas, or even I, who am a man without a cross, would deliberate about finding a cover in the skrimmage, when an open body would do no good? For what have the Frenchers reared up their Quebec, if fighting is always to be done in the clearings?"

"All that you say is very true, my friend," replied Heyward; "still, our customs must prevent us from doing as you wish."

A volley from the Hurons interrupted the discourse, and as the bullets whistled about them, Duncan saw the head of Uncas turned, looking back at himself and Munro. Notwithstanding the nearness of the enemy, and his own great personal danger, the countenance of the young warrior expressed no other emotion, as the former was compelled to think, than amazement at finding men willing to encounter so useless an exposure. Chingachgook was probably better acquainted with the notions of white men, for he did not even cast a glance aside from the riveted look his eye maintained on the object by which he governed their course. A ball soon struck the light and polished paddle from the hands of the chief, and drove it through the air, far in the advance. A shout arose from the Hurons, who seized the opportunity to fire another volley. Uncas described an arc in the water with his own blade, and as the canoe passed swiftly on, Chingachgook recovered his paddle, and flourishing it on high, he gave the war-whoop of the Mohicans, and then lent his strength and skill again to the important task.

The clamorous sounds of "Le Gros Serpent!" "La Longue Carabine!" "Le Cerf Agile!" burst at once from the canoes behind, and seemed to give new zeal to the pursuers. The scout seized "Killdeer" in his left hand, and elevating it above his head, he shook it in triumph at his enemies. The savages answered the insult with a yell, and immediately another volley succeeded. The bullets pattered along the lake, and one even pierced the bark of their little vessel. No perceptible emotion could be discovered in the Mohicans during this critical moment, their rigid features expressing neither hope nor alarm; but the scout again turned his head, and laughing in his own silent manner, he said to Heyward,—

"The knaves love to hear the sounds of their pieces; but the eye is not to be found among the Mingos that can calculate a true range in a dancing canoe! You see the dumb devils have taken off a man to charge, and by the smallest measurement that can be allowed, we move three feet to their two!"

Duncan, who was not altogether as easy under this

nice estimate of distances as his companions, was glad to find, however, that owing to their superior dexterity, and the diversion among their enemies, they were very sensibly obtaining the advantage. The Hurons soon fired again, and a bullet struck the blade of Hawkeye's paddle without injury.

"That will do," said the scout, examining the slight indentation with a curious eye; "it would not have cut the skin of an infant, much less of men, who, like us, have been blown upon by the heavens in their anger. Now, major, if you will try to use this piece of flattened wood, I'll let 'Killdeer' take a part in the conversation."

Heyward seized the paddle, and applied himself to the work with an eagerness that supplied the place of skill, while Hawkeye was engaged in inspecting the priming of his rifle. The latter then took a swift aim, and fired. The Huron in the bows of the leading canoe had risen with a similar object, and he now fell backward, suffering his gun to escape from his hands into the water. In an instant, however, he recovered his feet, though his gestures were wild and bewildered. At the same moment his companions suspended their efforts, and the chasing canoes clustered together, and became stationary. Chingachgook and Uncas profited by the interval to regain their wind, though Duncan continued to work with the most persevering industry. The father and son now cast calm but inquiring glances at each other, to learn if either had sustained any injury by the fire; for both well knew that no cry or exclamation would, in such a moment of necessity, have been permitted to betray the accident. A few large drops of blood were trickling down the shoulder of the Sagamore, who, when he perceived that the eyes of Uncas dwelt too long on the sight, raised some water in the hollow of his hand, and washing off the stain, was content to manifest, in this simple manner, the slightness of the injury.

"Softly, softly, major," said the scout, who by this time had reloaded his rifle; "we are a little too far already for a rifle to put forth its beauties, and you see younder imps are holding a council. Let them come up within striking distance—my eye may well be trusted in such a matter—and I will trail the varlets the length of the Horican, guaranteeing that not a shot of theirs shall, at the worst, more than break the skin, while 'Killdeer' shall touch the life twice in three times."

"We forget our errand," returned the diligent Duncan. "For God's sake let us profit by this advantage, and increase our distance from the enemy."

"Give me my children," said Munro hoarsely; "trifle no longer with a father's agony, but restore me my babes."

Long and habitual deference to the mandates of his superiors had taught the scout the virtue of obedience. Throwing a last and lingering glance at the distant canoes, he laid aside his rifle, and relieving the wearied Duncan, resumed the paddle, which he wielded with sinews that never tired. His efforts were seconded by those of the Mohicans, and a very few minutes served to place such a sheet of water between them and their enemies, that Heyward once more breathed freely.

The lake now began to expand, and their route lay along a wide reach, that was lined, as before, by high and ragged mountains. But the islands were few, and easily avoided. The strokes of the paddles grew more measured and regular, while they who plied them continued their labor, after the close and deadly chase from which they had just relieved themselves, with as much coolness as though their speed had been tried in sport, rather than under such pressing, nay, almost desperate circumstances.

Instead of following the western shore, whither their errand led them, the wary Mohican inclined his course more towards those hills behind which Montcalm was known to have led his army into the formidable fortress of Ticonderoga. As the Hurons, to every appearance, had abandoned the pursuit, there was no apparent reason for this excess of caution. It was, however, maintained for hours, until they had reached a bay, nigh the northern termination of the lake. Here the canoe was driven upon the beach, and the whole party landed. Hawkeye and Heyward ascended an adjacent bluff, where the former, after considering the expanse of water beneath him, pointed out to the latter a small black object, hovering under a headland, at the distance of several miles.

"Do you see it?" demanded the scout. "Now, what would you account that spot, were you left alone to white experience to find your way through this wilderness?"

"But for its distance and its magnitude, I should suppose it a bird. Can it be a living object?"

" 'Tis a canoe of good birchen bark, and paddled by fierce and crafty Mingos. Though Providence has lent to those who inhabit the woods eyes that would be needless to men in the settlements, where there are inventions to assist the sight, yet no human organs can see all the dangers which at this moment circumvent us. These varlets pretend to be bent chiefly on their sun-down meal, but the moment it is dark they will be on our trail, as true as hounds on the scent. We must throw them off, or our pursuit of Le Renard Subtil may be given up. These lakes are useful at times, especially when the game takes the water," continued the scout, gazing about him with a countenance of concern; "but they give no cover, except it be to the fishes. God knows what the country would be, if the settlements should ever spread far from the two rivers. Both hunting and war would lose their beauty."

"Let us not delay a moment, without some good and obvious cause."

"I little like that smoke, which you may see worming up along the rock above the canoe," interrupted the abstracted scout. "My life on it, other eyes than ours see it, and know its meaning. Well, words will not mend the matter, and it is time that we were doing."

Hawkeye moved away from the look-out, and descended, musing profoundly, to the shore. He communicated the result of his observations to his companions, in Delaware, and a short and earnest consultation succeeded. When it terminated, the three instantly set about executing their new resolutions.

The canoe was lifted from the water, and borne on the shoulders of the party. They proceeded into the wood, making as broad and obvious a trail as possible. They soon reached a water-course, which they crossed, and continued onward, until they came to an extensive and naked rock. At this point, where their footsteps might be expected to be no longer visible, they retraced their route to the brook, walking backwards, with the utmost care. They now followed the bed of the little stream to the lake, into which they immediately launched their canoe again. A low point concealed them from the headland, and the margin of the lake was fringed for some distance with dense and overhanging bushes. Under the cover of these natural advantages, they toiled their way, with patient industry, until the scout pronounced that he believed it would be safe once more to land.

The halt continued until evening rendered objects indistinct and uncertain to the eye. Then they resumed their route, and, favored by the darkness, pushed silently and vigorously towards the western shore. Although the rugged outline of mountain, to which they were steering, presented no distinctive marks to the eyes of Duncan, the Mohican entered the little haven he had selected with the confidence and accuracy of an experienced pilot.

The boat was again lifted and borne into the woods where it was carefully concealed under a pile of brush. The adventurers assumed their arms and packs, and the scout announced to Munro and Heyward that he and the Indians were at last in readiness to proceed.

Hawk says to head north across lake in canoe, Hurons find them, out paddle Hurons, Hawk wounds an indian, move east to trick enemy canoe on shoulders, obvious trail through woods to ade, follow own footprints to shore + hide on west shore

XXI

"If you find a man there, he shall die a flea's death."
The Merry Wives of Windsor[1]

THE PARTY HAD LANDED on the border of a region that is, even to this day, less known to the inhabitants of the States, than the deserts of Arabia, or the steppes of Tartary. It was the sterile and rugged district which separates the tributaries of Champlain from those of the Hudson, the Mohawk, and the St. Lawrence. Since the period of our tale, the active spirit of the country has surrounded it with a belt of rich and thriving settlements, though none but the hunter or the savage is ever known, even now, to penetrate its wild recesses.

As Hawkeye and the Mohicans had, however, often traversed the mountains and valleys of this vast wilderness, they did not hesitate to plunge into its depths, with the freedom of men accustomed to its privations and difficulties. For many hours the travellers toiled on their laborious way, guided by a star, or following the direction of some water-course, until the scout called a halt, and holding a short consultation with the Indians, they lighted their fire, and made the usual preparations to pass the remainder of the night where they then were.

Imitating the example, and emulating the confidence,

of their more experienced associates, Munro and Duncan slept without fear, if not without uneasiness. The dews were suffered to exhale, and the sun dispersed the mists, and was shedding a strong and clear light in the forest, when the travellers resumed their journey.

After proceeding a few miles, the progress of Hawkeye, who led the advance, became more deliberate and watchful. He often stopped to examine the trees; nor did he cross a rivulet without attentively considering the quantity, the velocity, and the color of its waters. Distrusting his own judgment, his appeals to the opinion of Chingachgook were frequent and earnest. During one of these conferences, Heyward observed that Uncas stood a patient and silent, though, as he imagined, an interested listener. He was strongly tempted to address the young chief, and demand his opinion of their progress; but the calm and dignified demeanor of the native induced him to believe that, like himself, the other was wholly dependent on the sagacity and intelligence of the seniors of the party. At last, the scout spoke in English, and at once explained the embarrassment of their situation.

"When I found that the home path of the Hurons ran north," he said, "it did not need the judgment of many long years to tell that they would follow the valleys, and keep atween the waters of the Hudson and the Horican, until they might strike the springs of the Canada streams, which would lead them into the heart of the country of the Frenchers. Yet here are we, within a short range of the Scaroon, and not a sign of a trail have we crossed! Human natur' is weak, and it is possible we may not have taken the proper scent."

"Heaven protect us from such an error!" exclaimed

Duncan. "Let us retrace our steps, and examine as we go, with keener eyes. Has Uncas no counsel to offer in such a strait?"

The young Mohican cast a glance at his father, but maintaining his quiet and reserved mien, he continued silent. Chingachgook had caught the look, and motioning with his hand, he bade him speak. The moment this permission was accorded, the countenance of Uncas changed from its grave composure to a gleam of intelligence and joy. Bounding forward like a deer, he sprang up the side of a little acclivity, a few rods in advance, and stood exultingly over a spot of fresh earth that looked as though it had been recently upturned by the passage of some heavy animal. The eyes of the whole party followed the unexpected movement, and read their success in the air of triumph that the youth assumed.

" 'Tis the trail!" exclaimed the scout, advancing to the spot: "the lad is quick of sight and keen of wit for his years."

" 'Tis extraordinary that he should have withheld his knowledge so long," muttered Duncan, at his elbow.

"It would have been more wonderful had he spoken without a bidding. No, no; your young white, who gathers his learning from books and can measure what he knows by the page, may conceit that his knowledge, like his legs, outruns that of his father; but where experience is the master, the scholar is made to know the value of years, and respects them accordingly."

"See!" said Uncas, pointing north and south, at the evident marks of the broad trail on either side of him: "the dark-hair has gone towards the frost."

"Hound never ran on a more beautiful scent," responded the scout, dashing forward, at once, on the indicated route; "we are favored, greatly favored, and can follow with high noses. Ay, here are both your waddling beasts: this Huron travels like a white general. The fellow is stricken with a judgment, and is mad! Look sharp for wheels, Sagamore," he continued, looking back, and laughing in his newly awakened satisfaction; "we shall soon have the fool journeying in a coach, and that with three of the best pair of eyes on the borders, in his rear."

The spirits of the scout, and the astonishing success of the chase, in which a circuitous distance of more than forty miles had been passed, did not fail to impart a portion of hope to the whole party. Their advance was rapid; and made with as much confidence as a traveller would proceed along a wide highway. If a rock, or a rivulet, or a bit of earth harder than common, severed the links of the clue they followed, the true eye of the scout recovered them at a distance, and seldom rendered the delay of a single moment necessary. Their progress was much facilitated by the certainty that Magua had found it necessary to journey through the valleys; a circumstance which rendered the general direction of the route sure. Nor had the Huron entirely neglected the arts uniformly practised by the natives when retiring in front of any enemy. False trails, and sudden turnings, were frequent, wherever a brook, or the formation of the ground, rendered them feasible; but his pursuers were rarely deceived, and never failed to detect their error, before they had lost either time or distance on the deceptive track.

By the middle of the afternoon they had passed the Scaroon, and were following the route of the declining sun. After descending an eminence to a low bottom, through which a stream glided, they suddenly came to a place where the party of Le Renard had made a halt. Extinguished brands were lying around a spring, the offals of a deer were scattered about the place, and the trees bore evident marks of having been browsed by the horses. At a little distance, Heyward discovered, and contemplated with tender emotion, the small bower under which he was fain to believe that Cora and Alice had reposed. But while the earth was trodden, and the footsteps of both men and beasts were so plainly visible around the place, the trail appeared to have suddenly ended.

It was easy to follow the track of the Narragansetts, but they seemed only to have wandered without guides, or any other object than the pursuit of food. At length Uncas, who, with his father, had endeavored to trace the route of the horses, came upon a sign of their presence that was quite recent. Before following the clue, he communicated his success to his companions; and while the latter were consulting on the circumstance, the youth reappeared, leading the two fillies, with their saddles broken, and the housings soiled, as though they had been permitted to run at will for several days.

"What should this mean?" said Duncan, turning pale, and glancing his eyes around him, as if he feared the brush and leaves were about to give up some horrid secret.

"That our march is come to a quick end, and that we are in an enemy's country," returned the scout. "Had the knaves been pressed, and the gentle ones wanted horses to keep up with the party, he might have taken their scalps; but without an enemy at his heels, and with such rugged beasts as these, he would not hurt a hair of their heads. I know your thoughts, and shame be it to our color that you have reason for them; but he who thinks that even a Mingo would ill-treat a woman, unless it be to tomahawk her, knows nothing of Indian natur', or the laws of the woods. No, no; I have heard that the French Indians had come into these hills, to hunt the moose, and we are getting within scent of their camp. Why should they not? The morning and evening guns of Ty may be heard any day among these mountains; for the Frenchers are running a new line atween the provinces of the king and the Canadas. It is true that the horses are here, but the Hurons are gone; let us then hunt for the path by which they departed."

Hawkeye and the Mohicans now applied themselves to their task in good earnest. A circle of a few hundred feet in circumference was drawn, and each of the party took a segment for his portion. The examination, however, resulted in no discovery. The impressions of footsteps were numerous, but they all appeared like those of men who had wandered about the spot, without any design to quit it. Again the scout and his companions made the circuit of the halting-place, each slowly following the other, until they assembled in the centre once more, no wiser than when they started.

"Such cunning is not without its deviltry," exclaimed Hawkeye, when he met the disappointed looks of his assistants.

"We must get down to it, Sagamore, beginning at the spring, and going over the ground by inches. The Huron shall never brag in his tribe that he has a foot which leaves no print."

Setting the example himself, the scout engaged in the scrutiny with renewed zeal. Not a leaf was left unturned. The sticks were removed, and the stones lifted; for Indian cunning was known frequently to adopt these objects as covers, laboring with the utmost patience and industry, to conceal each footstep as they proceeded. Still no discovery was made. At length Uncas, whose activity had enabled him to achieve his portion of the task the soonest, raked the earth across the turbid little rill which ran from the spring, and diverted its course into another channel. So soon as its narrow bed below the dam was dry, he stooped over it with keen and curious eyes. A cry of exultation immediately announced the success of the young warrior. The whole party crowded to the spot where Uncas pointed out the impression of a moccasin in the moist alluvion.[2]

"The lad will be an honor to his people," said Hawk-eye, regarding the trail with as much admiration as a naturalist would expend on the tusk of a mammoth or the rib of a mastodon; "ay, and a thorn in the sides of the Hurons. Yet that is not the footstep of an Indian! the weight is too much on the heel, and the toes are squared, as though one of the French dancers had been in, pigeon-winging his tribe! Run back, Uncas, and bring me the size of the singer's foot. You will find a beautiful print of it just opposite yon rock, agin the hillside."

While the youth was engaged in this commission, the scout and Chingachgook were attentively considering the impressions. The measurements agreed, and the former unhesitatingly pronounced that the footstep was that of David, who had once more been made to exchange his shoes for moccasins.

"I can now read the whole of it, as plainly as if I had seen the arts of Le Subtil," he added; "the singer, being a man whose gifts lay chiefly in his throat and feet, was made to go first, and the others have trod in his steps, imitating their formation."

"But," cried Duncan, "I see no signs of—"

"The gentle ones," interrupted the scout; "the varlet has found a way to carry them, until he supposed he had thrown any followers off the scent. My life on it, we see their pretty little feet again, before many rods go by."

The whole party now proceeded, following the course of the rill, keeping anxious eyes on the regular impressions. The water soon flowed into its bed again, but watching the ground on either side, the foresters pursued their way content with knowing that the trail lay beneath. More than half a mile was passed, before the rill rippled close around the base of an extensive and dry rock. Here they paused to make sure that the Hurons had not quitted the water.

It was fortunate they did so. For the quick and active Uncas soon found the impression of a foot on a bunch of moss, where it would seem an Indian had inadvertently trodden. Pursuing the direction given by this discovery, he entered the neighboring thicket, and struck the trail, as fresh and obvious as it had been before they reached the spring. Another shout announced the good fortune of the youth to his companions, and at once terminated the search.

"Ay, it has been planned with Indian judgment," said the scout, when the party was assembled around the place; "and would have blinded white eyes."

"Shall we proceed?" demanded Heyward.

"Softly, softly: we know our path; but it is good to examine the formation of things. This is my schooling, major; and if one neglects the book, there is little chance of learning from the open hand of Providence. All is plain but one thing, which is the manner that the knave contrived to get the gentle ones along the blind trail.

Even a Huron would be too proud to let their tender feet touch the water."

"Will this assist in explaining the difficulty?" said Heyward, pointing towards the fragments of a sort of hand-barrow, that had been rudely constructed of boughs, and bound together with withes, and which now seemed carelessly cast aside as useless.

" 'Tis explained!" cried the delighted Hawkeye. "If them varlets have passed a minute, they have spent hours in striving to fabricate a lying end to their trail! Well, I've known them to waste a day in the same manner, to as little purpose. Here we have three pair of moccasins, and two of little feet. It is amazing that any mortal beings can journey on limbs so small! Pass me the thong of buckskin, Uncas, and let me take the length of this foot. By the Lord, it is no longer than a child's and yet the maidens are tall and comely. That Providence is partial in its gifts, for its own wise reasons, the best and most contented of us must allow."

"The tender limbs of my daughters are unequal to these hardships," said Munro, looking at the light footsteps of his children, with a parent's love: "we shall find their fainting forms in this desert."

"Of that there is little cause of fear," returned the scout, slowly shaking his head; "this is a firm and straight, though a light step, and not over long. See, the heel has hardly touched the ground; and there the dark-hair has made a little jump, from root to root. No, no; my knowledge for it, neither of them was nigh fainting, hereaway. Now, the singer was beginning to be foot-sore and leg-weary as is plain by his trail. There, you see, he slipped; here he has travelled wide, and tottered; and there, again, it looks as though he journeyed on snow-shoes. Ay, ay, a man who uses his throat altogether, can hardly give his legs a proper training."

From such undeniable testimony did the practised woodsman arrive at the truth, with nearly as much certainty and precision as if he had been a witness of all those events which his ingenuity so easily elucidated. Cheered by these assurances, and satisfied by a reasoning that was so obvious, while it was so simple, the party resumed its course, after making a short halt to take a hurried repast.

When the meal was ended, the scout cast a glance upwards at the setting sun, and pushed forward with a rapidity which compelled Heyward and the still vigorous Munro to exert all their muscles to equal. Their route now lay along the bottom which had already been mentioned. As the Hurons had made no further efforts to conceal their footsteps, the progress of the pursuers was no longer delayed by uncertainty. Before an hour had elapsed, however, the speed of Hawkeye sensibly abated, and his head, instead of maintaining its former direct and forward look, began to turn suspiciously from side to side, as if he were conscious of approaching danger. He soon stopped again, and waited for the whole party to come up.

"I scent the Hurons," he said, speaking to the Mohicans; "yonder is open sky, through the tree-tops, and we are getting too nigh their encampment. Sagamore, you will take the hillside, to the right; Uncas will bend along the brook to the left, while I will try the trail. If anything should happen, the call will be three croaks of a crow. I saw one of the birds fanning himself in the air, just beyond the dead oak—another sign that we are touching an encampment."

The Indians departed their several ways without reply, while Hawkeye cautiously proceeded with the two gentlemen. Heyward soon pressed to the side of their guide, eager to catch an early glimpse of those enemies he had pursued with so much toil and anxiety. His companion told him to steal to the edge of the wood, which, as usual, was fringed with a thicket, and wait his coming, for he wished to examine certain suspicious signs a little on one side. Duncan obeyed, and soon found himself in a situation to command a view which he found as extraordinary as it was novel.

The trees of many acres had been felled, and the glow of a mild summer's evening had fallen on the clearing, in beautiful contrast to the gray light of the forest. A short distance from the place where Duncan stood, the stream had seemingly expanded into a little lake, covering most of the low land, from mountain to mountain. The water fell out of this wide basin, in a cataract so regular and gentle, that it appeared rather to be the work of human hands, than fashioned by nature. A hundred earthen dwellings stood on the margin of the lake, and even in its water, as though the latter had overflowed its usual banks. Their rounded roofs, admirably moulded for defence against the weather, denoted more of industry and foresight than the natives were wont to bestow on their regular habitations, much less on those they occupied for the temporary purposes of hunting and war. In short, the whole village or town, whichever it might be termed, possessed more of method and neatness of execution, than the white men had been accustomed to believe belonged, ordinarily, to the Indian habits. It appeared, however, to be deserted. At least, so thought Duncan for many minutes; but, at length, he fancied he discovered several human forms advancing towards him on all fours, and apparently dragging in their train some heavy, and as he was quick to apprehend, some formidable engine. Just then a few dark-looking heads gleamed out of the dwellings, and the place seemed suddenly alive with beings, which, however, glided from cover to cover so swiftly, as to allow no opportunity of examining their humors or pursuits. Alarmed at these suspicious and inexplicable movements, he was about to attempt the signal of the crows, when the rustling of leaves at hand drew his eyes in another direction.

The young man started, and recoiled a few paces instinctively, when he found himself within a hundred yards of a stranger Indian. Recovering his recollection on the instant, instead of sounding an alarm, which might prove fatal to himself, he remained stationary, an attentive observer of the other's motions.

An instant of calm observation served to assure Duncan that he was undiscovered. The native, like himself, seemed occupied in considering the low dwellings of the village, and the stolen movements of its inhabitants. It was impossible to discover the expression of his features, through the grotesque mask of paint under which they were concealed; though Duncan fancied it was rather melancholy than savage. His head was shaved, as usual, with the exception of the crown, from whose tuft three or four faded feathers from a hawk's wing were loosely dangling. A ragged calico mantle half-encircled his body, while his nether garment was composed of an ordinary shirt, the sleeves of which were made to perform the office that is usually executed by a much more commodious arrangement. His legs were bare, and sadly cut and torn by briers. The feet were,

however, covered with a pair of good deer-skin moccasins. Altogether, the appearance of the individual was
forlorn and miserable.

Duncan was still curiously observing the person of his
neighbor, when the scout stole silently and cautiously to
his side.

"You see we have reached their settlement or encampment," whispered the young man; "and here is one
of the savages himself, in a very embarrassing position
for our further movements."

Hawkeye started, and dropped his rifle, when, directed by the finger of his companion, the stranger came
under his view. Then lowering the dangerous muzzle, he
stretched forward his long neck, as if to assist a scrutiny
that was already intensely keen.

"The imp is not a Huron," he said, "nor of any of the
Canada tribes and yet you see, by his clothes, the knave
has been plundering a white. Ay, Montcalm has raked
the woods for his inroad, and a whooping, murdering set
of varlets has he gathered together. Can you see where
he has put his rifle or his bow?"

"He appears to have no arms; nor does he seem to be
viciously inclined. Unless he communicate the alarm to
his fellows, who as you see are dodging about the water,
we have but little to fear from him."

The scout turned to Heyward, and regarded him a
moment with unconcealed amazement. Then opening
wide his mouth, he indulged in unrestrained and heartfelt laughter, though in that silent and peculiar manner
which danger had so long taught him to practise.

Repeating the words, "fellows who are dodging about
the water!" he added, "so much for schooling and passing
a boyhood in the settlements! The knave has long legs,

though, and shall not be trusted. Do you keep him under your rifle while I creep in behind, through the bush, and take him alive. Fire on no account."

Heyward had already permitted his companion to bury part of his person in the thicket, when, stretching forth an arm, he arrested him, in order to ask,—

"If I see you in danger, may I not risk a shot?"

Hawkeye regarded him a moment, like one who knew not how to take the question; then nodding his head, he answered, still laughing, though inaudibly,—

"Fire a whole platoon, major."

In the next moment he was concealed by the leaves. Duncan waited several minutes in feverish impatience, before he caught another glimpse of the scout. Then he reappeared, creeping along the earth, from which his dress was hardly distinguishable, directly in the rear of his intended captive. Having reached within a few yards of the latter, he arose to his feet, silently and slowly. At that instant, several loud blows were struck on the water, and Duncan turned his eyes just in time to perceive that a hundred dark forms were plunging, in a body, into the troubled little sheet. Grasping his rifle, his looks were again bent on the Indian near him. Instead of taking the alarm, the unconscious savage stretched forward his neck, as if he also watched the movements about the gloomy lake, with a sort of silly curiosity. In the meantime, the uplifted hand of Hawkeye was above him. But, without any apparent reason, it was withdrawn, and its owner indulged in another long, though still silent, fit of merriment. When the peculiar and hearty laughter of Hawkeye was ended, instead of grasping his victim by the throat, he tapped him lightly on the shoulder, and exclaimed aloud,—

"How now, friend! have you a mind to teach the beavers to sing?"

"Even so," was the ready answer. "It would seem that the Being that gave them power to improve His gifts so well, would not deny them voices to proclaim His praise."

uncas finds trail follow+hope for women, loose hope, uncas finds a footprint, hawk says Magua must have abandoned horses once in Huron territory. men enter enemy territory past beaver pond whose dams they thinks are indian wigwams, see an indian, hawk almost kills him but sees its gramut dressed as an indian

XXII

"Bot.—Are we all met?
Qui.—Pat—pat; and here's a marvellous
Convenient place for our rehearsal."
A *Midsummer Night's Dream*[1]

THE READER MAY BETTER IMAGINE, than we describe, the surprise of Heyward. His lurking Indians were suddenly converted into four-footed beasts; his lake into a beaver pond; his cataract into a dam, constructed by those industrious and ingenious quadrupeds; and a suspected enemy into his tried friend, David Gamut, the master of psalmody. The presence of the latter created so many unexpected hopes relative to the sisters that, without a moment's hesitation, the young man broke out of his ambush, and sprang forward to join the two principal actors in the scene.

The merriment of Hawkeye was not easily appeased. Without ceremony, and with a rough hand, he twirled the supple Gamut around on his heel, and more than once affirmed that the Hurons had done themselves great credit in the fashion of his costume. Then seizing the hand of the other, he squeezed it with a gripe that brought the tears into the eyes of the placid David, and wished him joy of his new condition.

"You were about opening your throat-practysings among the beavers, were ye?" he said. "The cunning devils know half the trade already, for they beat the time with their tails, as you heard just now; and in good time it was too, or 'Killdeer' might have sounded the first note among them. I have known greater fools, who could read and write, than an experienced old beaver; but as for squalling, the animals are born dumb! What think you of such a song as this?"

David shut his sensitive ears, and even Heyward, apprised as he was of the nature of the cry, looked upwards in quest of the bird, as the cawing of a crow rang in the air about them.

"See!" continued the laughing scout, as he pointed towards the remainder of the party, who, in obedience to the signal, were already approaching: "this is music which has its natural virtues; it brings two good rifles to my elbow, to say nothing of the knives and tomahawks. But we see that you are safe; now tell us what has become of the maidens."

"They are captives to the heathen," said David; "and though greatly troubled in spirit, enjoying comfort and safety in the body."

"Both?" demanded the breathless Heyward.

"Even so. Though our wayfaring has been sore and our sustenance scanty, we have had little other cause for complaint, except the violence done our feelings, by being thus led in captivity into a far land."

"Bless ye for these very words!" exclaimed the trembling Munro; "I shall then receive my babes spotless and angel-like, as I lost them!"

"I know not that their delivery is at hand," returned the doubting David; "the leader of these savages is possessed of an evil spirit that no power short of Omnipotence can tame. I have tried him sleeping and waking, but neither sounds nor language seem to touch his soul."

"Where is the knave?" bluntly interrupted the scout.

"He hunts the moose to-day, with his young men; and tomorrow, as I hear, they pass farther into these forests, and nigher to the borders of Canada. The elder maiden is conveyed to a neighboring people, whose lodges are situate beyond yonder black pinnacle of rock; while the younger is detained among the women of the Hurons, whose dwellings are but two short miles hence, on a table-land, where the fire has done the office of the axe, and prepared the place for their reception."

"Alice, my gentle Alice!" murmured Heyward; "she has lost the consolation of her sister's presence!"

"Even so. But so far as praise and thanksgiving in psalmody can temper the spirit in affliction, she had not suffered."

"Has she then a heart for music?"

"Of the graver and more solemn character; though it must be acknowledged that, in spite of all my endeavors, the maiden weeps oftener than she smiles. At such moments I forbear to press the holy songs; but there are many sweet and comfortable periods of satisfactory communication, when the ears of the savages are astounded with the upliftings of our voices."

"And why are you permitted to go at large, unwatched?"

David composed his features into what he intended should express an air of modest humility, before he meekly replied—

"Little be the praise to such a worm as I. But, though the power of psalmody was suspended in the terrible business of that field of blood through which we passed, it has recovered its influence even over the souls of the heathen, and I am suffered to go and come at will."

The scout laughed, and tapping his own forehead significantly, he perhaps explained the singular indulgence more satisfactorily when he said—

"The Indians never harm a non-composser. But why, when the path lay open before your eyes, did you not strike back on your own trail (it is not so blind as that which a squirrel would make), and bring in the tidings to Edward?"

The scout, remembering only his own sturdy and iron nature, had probably exacted a task that David, under no circumstances, could have performed. But, without entirely losing the meekness of his air, the latter was content to answer—

"Though my soul would rejoice to visit the habitations of Christendom once more, my feet would rather follow the tender spirits intrusted to my keeping, even into the idolatrous province of the Jesuits, than take one step backward, while they pined in captivity and sorrow."

Though the figurative language of David was not very intelligible, the sincere and steady expression of his eye, and the glow on his honest countenance, were not easily mistaken. Uncas pressed closer to his side, and regarded the speaker with a look of commendation, while his father expressed his satisfaction by the ordinary pithy exclamation of approbation. The scout shook his head as he rejoined—

"The Lord never intended that the man should place all his endeavors in his throat, to the neglect of other and better gifts! But he has fallen into the hands of some silly woman, when he should have been gathering his education under a blue sky, among the beauties of the forest. Here, friend; I did intend to kindle a fire with this tooting whistle of thine; but as you value the thing, take it, and blow your best on it!"

Gamut received his pitch-pipe with as strong an expression of pleasure as he believed compatible with the grave functions he exercised. After essaying its virtues repeatedly, in contrast with his own voice, and satisfying himself that none of its melody was lost, he made a very serious demonstration towards achieving a few stanzas of one of the longest effusions in the little volume so often mentioned.

Heyward, however, hastily interrupted his pious purpose, by continuing questions concerning the past and present condition of his fellow-captives, and in a manner more methodical than had been permitted by his feelings in the opening of their interview. David, though he regarded his treasure with longing eyes, was constrained to answer: especially as the venerable father took a part in the interrogatories, with an interest too imposing to be denied. Nor did the scout fail to throw in a pertinent inquiry, whenever a fitting occasion presented. In this manner, though with frequent interruptions, which were filled with certain threatening sounds from the recovered instrument, the pursuers were put in possession of such leading circumstances as were likely to prove useful in accomplishing their great and engrossing object—the recovery of the sisters. The narrative of David was simple, and the facts but few.

Magua had waited on the mountain until a safe moment to retire presented itself, when he had descended, and taken the route along the western side of the Horican, in the direction of the Canadas. As the subtle Huron was familiar with the paths, and well knew there was no immediate danger of pursuit, their progress had been moderate, and far from fatiguing. It appeared from the unembellished statement of David, that his own presence had been rather endured than desired; though even Magua had not been entirely exempt from that veneration with which the Indians regard those whom the Great Spirit has visited in their intellects. At night, the utmost care had been taken of the captives, both to prevent injury from the damps of the woods, and to guard against an escape. At the spring, the horses were turned loose, as has been seen; and notwithstanding the remoteness and length of their trail, the artifices already named were resorted to, in order to cut off every clue to their place of retreat. On their arrival at the encampment of his people, Magua, in obedience to a policy seldom departed from, separated his prisoners. Cora had been sent to a tribe that temporarily occupied an adjacent valley, though David was too ignorant of the customs and history of the natives to be able to declare anything satisfactory concerning their name or character. He only knew that they had not engaged in the late expedition against William Henry; that, like the Hurons themselves, they were allies of Montcalm; and that they maintained an amicable, though a watchful intercourse with the warlike and savage people, whom chance had, for a time, brought in such close and disagreeable contact with themselves.

The Mohicans and the scout listened to his interrupted and imperfect narrative, with an interest that obviously increased as he proceeded; and it was while attempting to explain the pursuits of the community in which Cora was detained, that the latter abruptly demanded—

"Did you see the fashion of their knives? Were they of English or French formation?"

"My thoughts were bent on no such vanities, but rather mingled in consolation with those of the maidens."

"The time may come when you will not consider the knife of a savage such a despisable vanity," returned the scout, with a strong expression of contempt for the other's dullness. "Had they held their corn-feast—or can you say anything of the totems of the tribe?"

"Of corn, we had many and plentiful feasts; for the grain, being in the milk, is both sweet to the mouth and comfortable to the stomach. Of totem, I know not the meaning; but if it appertaineth in any wise to the art of Indian music, it need not be inquired after at their hands. They never join their voices in praise, and it would seem that they are among the profanest of the idolatrous."

"Therein you belie the natur' of an Indian. Even the Mingo adores but the true and living God. 'Tis a wicked fabrication of the whites, and I say it to the shame of my color, that would make the warrior bow down before images of his own creation. It is true, they endeavor to make truces with the wicked one—as who would not with an enemy he cannot conquer!—but they look up for favor and assistance to the Great and Good Spirit only."

"It may be so," said David; "but I have seen strange and fantastic images drawn in their paint, of which their admiration and care savored of spiritual pride; especially one, and that, too, a foul and loathsome object."

"Was it a sarpent?" quickly demanded the scout.

"Much the same. It was in the likeness of an abject and creeping tortoise."

"Hugh!" exclaimed both the attentive Mohicans in a

breath; while the scout shook his head with an air of one
who had made an important, but by no means a pleasing
discovery. Then the father spoke, in the language of the
Delawares, and with a calmness and dignity that instantly arrested the attention even of those to whom his
words were unintelligible. His gestures were impressive,
and at times energetic. Once he lifted his arm on high;
and as it descended, the action threw aside the folds of
his light mantle, a finger resting on his breast, as if he
would enforce his meaning by the attitude. Duncan's
eyes followed the movement, and he perceived that the
animal just mentioned was beautifully, though faintly,
worked in a blue tint, on the swarthy breast of the chief.
All that he had ever heard of the violent separation of the
vast tribes of the Delawares rushed across his mind, and
he awaited the proper moment to speak, with a suspense
that was rendered nearly intolerable, by his interest in
the stake. His wish, however, was anticipated by the
scout, who turned from his red friend, saying—

"We have found that which may be good or evil to us,
as Heaven disposes. The Sagamore is of the high blood
of the Delawares, and is the great chief of their Tortoises! That some of this stock are among the people of
whom the singer tells us, is plain, by his words; and had
he but spent half the breath in prudent questions, that
he has blown away in making a trumpet of his throat, we
might have known how many warriors they numbered. It
is, altogether, a dangerous path we move in; for a friend
whose face is turned from you often bears a bloodier
mind than the enemy who seeks your scalp."

"Explain," said Duncan.

" 'Tis a long and melancholy tradition, and one I little
like to think of; for it is not to be denied, that the evil has

been mainly done by men with white skins. But it has ended in turning the tomahawk of brother against brother, and brought the Mingo and the Delaware to travel in the same path."

"You then suspect it is a portion of that people among whom Cora resides?"

The scout nodded his head in assent, though he seemed anxious to waive the further discussion of a subject that appeared painful. The impatient Duncan now made several hasty and desperate propositions to attempt the release of the sisters. Munro seemed to shake off his apathy, and listened to the wild schemes of the young man with a deference that his gray hairs and reverend years should have denied. But the scout, after suffering the ardor of the lover to expend itself a little, found means to convince him of the folly of precipitation, in a matter that would require their coolest judgment and utmost fortitude.

"It would be well," he added, "to let this man go in again, as usual, and for him to tarry in the lodges, giving notice to the gentle ones of our approach, until we call him out, by signal, to consult. You know the cry of a crow, friend, from the whistle of the whippoorwill?"

" 'Tis a pleasing bird," returned David, "and has a soft and melancholy note! though the time is rather quick and ill-measured."

"He speaks of the wish-ton-wish,"[2] said the scout; "well, since you like his whistle, it shall be your signal. Remember, then, when you hear the whippoorwill's call three times repeated, you are to come into the bushes where the bird might be supposed—"

"Stop," interrupted Heyward; "I will accompany him."

"You!" exclaimed the astonished Hawkeye; "are you tired of seeing the sun rise and set?"

"David is a living proof that the Hurons can be merciful."

"Ay, but David can use his throat, as no man in his senses would pervart the gift."

"I, too, can play the madman, the fool, the hero; in short, any or everything to rescue her I love. Name your objections no longer; I am resolved."

Hawkeye regarded the young man a moment in speechless amazement. But Duncan, who, in deference to the other's skill and services, had hitherto submitted somewhat implicitly to his dictation, now assumed the superior, with a manner that was not easily resisted. He waved his hand, in sign of his dislike to all remonstrance, and then, in more tempered language, he continued—

"You have the means of disguise; change me; paint me, too, if you will; in short, alter me to anything—a fool."

"It is not for one like me to say that he who is already formed by so powerful a hand as Providence, stands in need of a change," muttered the discontented scout. "When you send your parties abroad in war, you find it prudent, at least, to arrange the marks and places of encampment, in order that they who fight on your side may know when and where to expect a friend."

"Listen," interrupted Duncan; "you have heard from this faithful follower of the captives, that the Indians are of two tribes, if not of different nations. With one, whom you think to be a branch of the Delawares, is she you call the 'dark-hair'; the other, and younger of the ladies, is undeniably with our declared enemies, the Hurons. It becomes my youth and rank to attempt the latter adventure. While you, therefore, are negotiating with your friends for the release of one of the sisters, I will effect that of the other, or die."

The awakened spirit of the young soldier gleamed in his eyes, and his form became imposing under its influence. Hawkeye, though too much accustomed to Indian artifices not to foresee the danger of the experiment, knew not well how to combat this sudden resolution.

Perhaps there was something in the proposal that suited his own hardy nature, and that secret love of desperate adventure, which had increased with his experience, until hazard and danger had become, in some measure, necessary to the enjoyment of his existence. Instead of continuing to oppose the scheme of Duncan, his humor suddenly altered, and he lent himself to its execution.

"Come," he said, with a good-humored smile; "the buck that will take to the water must be headed, and not followed. Chingachgook has as many different paints as the engineer officer's wife, who takes down natur' on scraps of paper, making the mountains look like cocks of rusty hay, and placing the blue sky in reach of your hand. The Sagamore can use them, too. Seat yourself on the log; and my life on it, he can soon make a natural fool of you, and that well to your liking."

Duncan complied; and the Mohican, who had been an attentive listener to the discourse, readily undertook the office. Long practised in all the subtle arts of his race, he drew, with great dexterity and quickness, the fantastic shadow that the natives were accustomed to consider as the evidence of a friendly and jocular disposition. Every line that could possibly be interpreted into a secret inclination for war, was carefully avoided; while, on the other hand, he studied those conceits that might be construed into amity.

In short, he entirely sacrificed every appearance of the warrior to the masquerade of a buffoon. Such exhibitions were not uncommon among the Indians; and as Duncan was already sufficiently disguised in his dress, there certainly did exist some reason for believing that, with his knowledge of French, he might pass for a juggler from Ticonderoga, straggling among the allied and friendly tribes.

When he was thought to be sufficiently painted, the scout gave him much friendly advice; concerted signals, and appointed the place where they should meet, in the event of mutual success. The parting between Munro and his young friend was more melancholy; still, the former submitted to the separation with an indifference that his warm and honest nature would never have permitted in a more healthful state of mind. The scout led Heyward aside, and acquainted him with his intention to leave the veteran in some safe encampment, in charge of Chingachgook, while he and Uncas pursued their inquiries among the people they had reason to believe were Delawares. Then renewing his cautions and advice, he concluded by saying, with a solemnity and warmth of feeling, with which Duncan was deeply touched:

"And now God bless you! You have shown a spirit that I like; for it is the gift of youth, more especially one of warm blood and a stout heart. But believe the warning of a man who has reason to know all he says to be true. You will have occasion for your best manhood, and for a sharper wit than what is to be gathered in books, afore you outdo the cunning, or get the better of the courage of a Mingo. God bless you! if the Hurons master your scalp, rely on the promise of one who has two stout warriors to back him. They shall pay for their victory, with a life for every hair it holds. I say, young gentleman, may Providence bless your undertaking, which is altogether for good; and remember, that to outwit the knaves it is lawful to practise things that may not be naturally the gift of a white skin."

Duncan shook his worthy and reluctant associate warmly by the hand, once more recommended his aged friend to his care, and returning his good wishes, he motioned to David to proceed. Hawkeye gazed after the high-spirited and adventurous young man for several moments, in open admiration; then shaking his head doubtingly, he turned, and led his own division of the party into the concealment of the forest.

The route taken by Duncan and David lay directly across the clearing of the beavers, and along the margin of their pond.

When the former found himself alone with one so simple, and so little qualified to render any assistance in desperate emergencies, he first began to be sensible of the difficulties of the task he had undertaken. The fading light increased the gloominess of the bleak and savage wilderness that stretched so far on every side of him; and there was even a fearful character in the stillness of those little huts, that he knew were so abundantly peopled. It struck him, as he gazed at the admirable structures and the wonderful precautions of their sagacious inmates, that even the brutes of these vast wilds were possessed of an instinct nearly commensurate with his own reason; and he could not reflect, without anxiety, on the unequal contest that he had so rashly courted. Then came the glowing image of Alice; her distress; her actual danger;

and all the peril of his situation was forgotten. Cheering David, he moved on with the light and vigorous step of youth and enterprise.

After making nearly a semicircle around the pond, they diverged from the water-course, and began to ascend to the level of a slight elevation in that bottom land, over which they journeyed. Within half an hour they gained the margin of another opening that bore all the signs of having been also made by the beavers, and which those sagacious animals had probably been induced, by some accident, to abandon, for the more eligible position they now occupied. A very natural sensation caused Duncan to hesitate a moment, unwilling to leave the cover of their bushy path, as a man pauses to collect his energies before he essays any hazardous experiment, in which he is secretly conscious they will all be needed. He profited by the halt, to gather such information as might be obtained from his short and hasty glances.

On the opposite side of the clearing, and near the point where the brook tumbled over some rocks, from a still higher level, some fifty or sixty lodges, rudely fabricated of logs, brush, and earth intermingled, were to be discovered. They were arranged without any order, and seemed to be constructed with very little attention to neatness or beauty. Indeed, so very inferior were they in the two latter particulars to the village Duncan had just seen, that he began to expect a second surprise, no less astonishing than the former. This expectation was in no degree diminished, when, by the doubtful twilight, he beheld twenty or thirty forms rising alternately from the cover of the tall, coarse grass, in front of the lodges, and then sinking again from the sight, as it were to burrow in the earth. By the sudden and hasty glimpses that he caught of these figures, they seemed more like dark glancing spectres, or some other unearthly beings, than creatures fashioned with the ordinary and vulgar materials of flesh and blood. A gaunt, naked form was seen, for a single instant, tossing its arms wildly in the air, and then the spot it had filled was vacant; the figure appearing suddenly in some other and distant place, or being succeeded by another, possessing the same mysterious character. David, observing that his companion lingered, pursued the direction of his gaze, and in some measure recalled the recollection of Heyward, by speaking.

"There is much fruitful soil uncultivated here," he said; "and I may add, without the sinful leaven of self-commendation, that since my short sojourn in these heathenish abodes, much good seed has been scattered by the wayside."

"The tribes are fonder of the chase than of the arts of men of labor," returned the unconscious Duncan, still gazing at the objects of his wonder.

"It is rather joy than labor to the spirit, to lift up the voice in praise; but sadly do these boys abuse their gifts. Rarely have I found any of their age, on whom nature has so freely bestowed the elements of psalmody; and surely, surely, there are none who neglect them more. Three nights have I now tarried here, and three several times have I assembled the urchins to join in sacred song; and as often have they responded to my efforts with whoopings and howlings that have chilled my soul!"

"Of whom speak you?"

"Of those children of the devil, who waste the precious moments in yonder idle antics. Ah! the wholesome restraint of discipline is but little known among this self-abandoned people. In a country of birches, a rod is never seen; and it ought not to appear a marvel in my eyes, that the choicest blessings of Providence are wasted in such cries as these."

David closed his ears against the juvenile pack, whose yell just then rang shrilly through the forest; and Duncan, suffering his lip to curl, as in mockery of his own superstition, said firmly:

"We will proceed."

Without removing the safeguards from his ears, the master of song complied, and together they pursued their way towards what David was sometimes wont to call "the tents of the Philistines."

Hawk laughs @ Gamut, Gamut says Mgua
seperated girls, alice to Huron camp + cora to
delaware settlement, Gamut release (thought crazy
for his singing), Gamut + Hey to secretly warn
girls of rescue, Ching dresses Hey as clown
(to be a French juggler from Ticonderoga). Hey + Gamut
to Huron, Uncas + Hawk to Cora. Hey + Gamut
to camp, see strange forms, just kids playing

XXIII

"But though the beast of game
The privilege of chase may claim;
Though space and law the stag we lend
Ere hound we slip, or bow we bend;
Who ever recked, where, how, or when
The prowling fox was trapped or slain?"
Sir Walter Scott, "The Lady of the Lake"[1]

IT IS UNUSUAL to find an encampment of the natives, like those of the more instructed whites, guarded by the presence of armed men. Well informed of the approach of every danger, while it is yet at a distance, the Indian generally rests secure under his knowledge of the signs of the forest, and the long and difficult paths that separate him from those he has most reason to dread. But the enemy who, by any lucky concurrence of accidents, has found means to elude the vigilance of the scouts, will seldom meet with sentinels nearer home to sound the alarm. In addition to this general usage, the tribes friendly to the French knew too well the weight of the blow that had just been struck, to apprehend any immediate danger from the hostile nations that were tributary to the crown of Britain.

When Duncan and David, therefore, found themselves in the centre of the children, who played the antics already mentioned, it was with the least previous intimation of their approach. But so soon as they were observed, the whole of the juvenile pack raised, by common consent, a shrill and warning whoop; and then sank, as it were, by magic, from before the sight of their visitors. The naked, tawny bodies of the crouching urchins blended so nicely, at that hour, with the withered herbage, that at first it seemed as if the earth had, in truth, swallowed up their forms; though when surprise permitted Duncan to bend his look more curiously about the spot, he found it everywhere met by dark, quick, and rolling eyeballs.

Gathering no encouragement from this startling presage of the nature of the scrutiny he was likely to undergo from the more mature judgments of the men, there was an instant when the young soldier would have retreated. It was, however, too late to appear to hesitate. The cry of the children had drawn a dozen warriors to the door of the nearest lodge, where they stood clustered in a dark and savage group, gravely awaiting the nearer approach of those who had unexpectedly come among them.

David, in some measure familiarized to the scene, led the way with a steadiness that no slight obstacle was likely to disconcert, into this very building. It was the principal edifice of the village, though roughly constructed of the bark and branches of trees; being the lodge in which the tribe held its councils and public meetings during their temporary residence on the borders of the English province. Duncan found it difficult to assume the necessary appearance of unconcern, as he brushed the dark and powerful frames of the savages who thronged its threshold; but, conscious that his existence depended on his presence of mind, he trusted to the discretion of his companion, whose footsteps he closely followed, endeavoring, as he proceeded, to rally his thoughts for the occasion. His blood curdled when he found himself in absolute contact with such fierce and implacable enemies; but he so far mastered his feelings as to pursue his way into the centre of the lodge, with an exterior that did not betray the weakness. Imitating the example of the deliberate Gamut, he drew a bundle of fragrant brush from beneath a pile that filled a corner of the hut, and seated himself in silence.

So soon as their visitor had passed, the observant warriors fell back from the entrance, and arranging themselves about him, they seemed patiently to await the moment when it might comport with the dignity of the stranger to speak. By far the greater number stood leaning, in lazy, lounging attitudes, against the upright posts that supported the crazy building, while three or four of the oldest and most distinguished of the chiefs placed themselves on the earth a little more in advance.

A flaring torch was burning in the place, and sent its red glare from face to face and figure to figure, as it waved in the currents of air. Duncan profited by its light to read the probable character of his reception, in the countenances of his hosts. But his ingenuity availed him little, against the cold artifices of the people he had encountered. The chiefs in front scarce cast a glance at his person, keeping their eyes on the ground, with an air that might have been intended for respect, but which it was quite easy to construe into distrust. The men in shadow were less reserved. Duncan soon detected their searching, but stolen looks, which, in truth, scanned his person and attire inch by inch; leaving no emotion of the countenance, no gesture, no line of the·paint, nor even the fashion of a garment, unheeded, and without comment.

At length one whose hair was beginning to be sprinkled with gray, but whose sinewy limbs and firm tread announced that he was still equal to the duties of manhood, advanced out of the gloom of a corner, whither he had probably posted himself to make his observations unseen, and spoke. He used the language of the Wyandots, or Hurons; his words were, consequently, unintelligible to Heyward, though they seemed, by the gestures that accompanied them, to be uttered more in courtesy than anger. The latter shook his head, and made a gesture indicative of his inability to reply.

"Do none of my brothers speak the French or the English?" he said, in the former language, looking about him from countenance to countenance, in hopes of finding a nod of assent.

Though more than one had turned, as if to catch the meaning of his words, they remained unanswered.

"I should be grieved to think," continued Duncan, speaking slowly, and using the simplest French of which he was the master, "to believe, that none of this wise and brave nation understand the language that the 'Grand Monarque' uses when he talks to his children. His heart would be heavy did he believe his red warriors paid him so little respect!"

A long and grave pause succeeded, during which no movement of a limb, nor any expression of an eye, betrayed the impression produced by his remark. Duncan, who knew that silence was a virtue among his hosts, gladly had recourse to the custom, in order to arrange his ideas. At length the same warrior who had before addressed him replied, by dryly demanding, in the language of the Canadas—

"When our Great Father speaks to his people, is it with the tongue of a Huron?"

"He knows no difference in his children, whether the color of the skin be red, or black, or white," returned Duncan, evasively; "though chiefly is he satisfied with the brave Hurons."

"In what manner will he speak," demanded the wary chief, "when the runners count to him the scalps which five nights ago grew on the heads of the Yengeese?"

"They were his enemies," said Duncan, shuddering involuntarily; "and, doubtless, he will say, It is good; my Hurons are very gallant."

"Our Canada father does not think it. Instead of looking forward to reward his Indians, his eyes are turned backward. He sees the dead Yengeese, but no Huron. What can this mean?"

"A great chief, like him, has more thoughts than tongues. He looks to see that no enemies are on his trail."

"The canoe of a dead warrior will not float on the Horican," returned the savage, gloomily. "His ears are open to the Delawares, who are not our friends, and they fill them with lies."

"It cannot be. See; he has bid me, who am a man that knows the art of healing, to go to his children, the red Hurons of the great lakes, and ask if any are sick!"

Another silence succeeded this annunciation of the character Duncan had assumed. Every eye was simultaneously bent on his person, as if to inquire into the truth or falsehood of the declaration, with an intelligence and keenness that caused the subject of their scrutiny to tremble for the result. He was, however, relieved again by the former speaker.

"Do the cunning men of the Canadas paint their skins?" the Huron coldly continued; "we have heard them boast that their faces were pale."

"When an Indian chief comes among his white fathers," returned Duncan, with great steadiness, "he lays aside his buffalo robe, to carry the shirt that is offered him. My brothers have given me paint, and I wear it."

A low murmur of applause announced that the compliment to the tribe was favorably received. The elderly chief made a gesture of commendation, which was answered by most of his companions, who each threw forth a hand, and uttered a brief exclamation of pleasure. Duncan began to breathe more freely, believing that the weight of his examination was past; and as he had already prepared a simple and probable tale to support his pretended occupation, his hopes of ultimate success grew brighter.

After a silence of a few moments, as if adjusting his thoughts, in order to make a suitable answer to the declaration their guest had just given, another warrior arose, and placed himself in an attitude to speak. While his lips were yet in the act of parting, a low but fearful sound arose from the forest, and was immediately succeeded by a high, shrill yell, that was drawn out, until it equalled the longest and most plaintive howl of the wolf. The sudden and terrible interruption caused Duncan to start from his seat, unconscious of everything but the effect produced by so frightful a cry. At the same moment, the warriors glided in a body from the lodge, and the outer air was filled with loud shouts, that nearly drowned those awful sounds, which were still ringing beneath the arches of the woods. Unable to command himself any longer, the youth broke from the place, and presently stood in the centre of a disorderly throng, that included nearly everything having life, within the limits of the encampment. Men, women, and children; the aged, the infirm, the active, and the strong, were alike abroad; some exclaiming aloud, others clapping their hands with a joy that seemed frantic, and all expressing their savage pleasure in some unexpected event. Though astounded, at first, by the uproar, Heyward was soon enabled to find its solution by the scene that followed.

There yet lingered sufficient light in the heavens to exhibit those bright openings among the tree-tops, where different paths left the clearing to enter the depths of the wilderness. Beneath one of them, a line of warriors issued from the woods, and advanced slowly towards the dwellings. One in front bore a short pole, on which, as it afterwards appeared, were suspended several human scalps. The startling sounds that Duncan had heard were what the whites have not inappropriately called the "death-halloo"; and each repetition of the cry was intended to announce to the tribe the fate of an enemy. Thus far the knowledge of Heyward assisted him in the explanation; and as he now knew that the interruption was caused by the unlooked-for return of a successful war-party, every disagreeable sensation was quieted in inward congratulation, for the opportune relief and insignificance it conferred on himself.

When at the distance of a few hundred feet from the lodges, the newly arrived warriors halted. Their plaintive and terrific cry, which was intended to represent equally the wailings of the dead and the triumph of the victors, had entirely ceased. One of their number now called aloud, in words that were far from appalling, though not more intelligible to those for whose ears they were intended, than their expressive yells. It would be difficult to convey a suitable idea of the savage ecstasy with which the news thus imparted was received. The whole encampment, in a moment, became a scene of the most violent bustle and commotion. The warriors drew their knives, and flourishing them, they arranged themselves in two lines, forming a lane that extended from the war-party to the lodges. The squaws seized clubs, axes, or whatever weapon of offence first offered itself to their hands, and rushed eagerly to act their part in the cruel game that was at hand. Even the children would not be excluded; but boys, little able to wield the instruments, tore the tomahawks from the belts of their fathers, and stole into the ranks, apt imitators of the savage traits exhibited by their parents.

Large piles of brush lay scattered about the clearing, and a wary and aged squaw was occupied in firing as many as might serve to light the coming exhibition. As the flame arose, its power exceeded that of the parting day, and assisted to render objects at the same time more distinct and more hideous. The whole scene formed a striking picture, whose frame was composed of the dark and tall border of pines. The warriors just arrived were the most distant figures. A little in advance stood two men, who were apparently selected from the rest, as the principal actors in what was to follow. The light was not strong enough to render their features distinct, though it was quite evident that they were governed by very different emotions. While one stood erect and firm, prepared to meet his fate like a hero, the other bowed his head, as if palsied by terror or stricken with shame. The high-spirited Duncan felt a powerful impulse of admiration and pity towards the former, though no opportunity could offer to exhibit his generous emotions. He watched his slightest movement, however, with eager eyes; and as he traced the fine outline of his admirably proportioned and active frame, he endeavored to persuade himself, that if the powers of man, seconded by such noble resolution, could bear one harmless through so severe a trial, the youthful captive before him might hope for success in the hazardous race he was about to run. Insensibly the young man drew nigher to the swarthy lines of the Hurons, and scarcely breathed, so intense became his interest in the spectacle. Just then the signal yell was given, and the momentary quiet which had preceded it was broken by a burst of cries, that far exceeded any before heard. The most abject of the two victims continued motionless; but the other bounded from the place at the cry, with the activity and swiftness of a deer. Instead of rushing through the hostile lines, as had been expected, he just entered the dangerous defile, and before time was given for a single blow, turned short, and leaping the heads of a row of children, he gained at once the exterior and safer side of the formidable array. The artifice was answered by a hundred voices raised in imprecations; and the whole of the excited multitude broke from their order, and spread themselves about the place in wild confusion.

A dozen blazing piles now shed their lurid brightness on the place, which resembled some unhallowed and supernatural arena, in which malicious demons had assembled to act their bloody and lawless rites. The forms in the background looked like unearthly beings, gliding be-

fore the eye, and cleaving the air with frantic and unmeaning gestures; while the savage passions of such as
passed the flames, were rendered fearfully distinct by
the gleams that shot athwart their inflamed visages.

It will be easily understood, that amid such a concourse of vindictive enemies, no breathing time was allowed the fugitive. There was a single moment when it
seemed as if he would have reached the forest, but the
whole body of his captors threw themselves before him,
and drove him back into the centre of his relentless persecutors. Turning like a headed deer, he shot, with the
swiftness of an arrow, through a pillar of forked flame,
and passing the whole multitude harmless, he appeared
on the opposite side of the clearing. Here too he was met
and turned by a few of the older and more subtle of the
Hurons. Once more he tried the throng, as if seeking
safety in its blindness, and then several moments succeeded, during which Duncan believed the active and
courageous young stranger was lost.

Nothing could be distinguished but a dark mass of
human forms tossed and involved in inexplicable confusion. Arms, gleaming knives, and formidable clubs, appeared above them, but the blows were evidently given
at random. The awful effect was heightened by the
piercing shrieks of the women and the fierce yells of the
warriors. Now and then Duncan caught a glimpse of a
light form cleaving the air in some desperate bound, and
he rather hoped than believed that the captive yet retained the command of his astonishing powers of activity.
Suddenly the multitude rolled backward, and approached the spot where he himself stood. The heavy
body in the rear pressed upon the women and children
in front, and bore them to the earth. The stranger reap-

peared in the confusion. Human power could not, however, much longer endure so severe a trial. Of this the captive seemed conscious. Profiting by the momentary opening, he darted from among the warriors, and made a desperate, and, what seemed to Duncan, a final effort to gain the wood. As if aware that no danger was to be apprehended from the young soldier, the fugitive nearly brushed his person in his flight. A tall and powerful Huron, who had husbanded his forces, pressed close upon his heels, and with an uplifted arm menaced a fatal blow. Duncan thrust forward a foot, and the shock precipitated the eager savage headlong, many feet in advance of his intended victim. Thought itself is not quicker than was the motion with which the latter profited by the advantage; he turned, gleamed like a meteor again before the eyes of Duncan, and at the next moment, when the latter recovered his recollection, and gazed around in quest of the captive, he saw him quietly leaning against a small painted post, which stood before the door of the principal lodge.

Apprehensive that the part he had taken in the escape might prove fatal to himself, Duncan left the place without delay. He followed the crowd, which drew nigh the lodges, gloomy and sullen, like any other multitude that had been disappointed in an execution. Curiosity, or perhaps a better feeling, induced him to approach the stranger. He found him, standing with one arm cast about the protecting post, and breathing thick and hard, after his exertions, but disdaining to permit a single sign of suffering to escape. His person was now protected by immemorial and sacred usage, until the tribe in council had deliberated and determined on his fate. It was not difficult, however, to foretell the result, if any presage could be drawn from the feelings of those who crowded the place.

There was no term of abuse known to the Huron vocabulary that the disappointed women did not lavishly expend on the successful stranger. They flouted at his efforts, and told him, with bitter scoffs, that his feet were better than his hands; and that he merited wings, while he knew not the use of an arrow or a knife. To all this the captive made no reply; but was content to preserve an attitude in which dignity was singularly blended with disdain. Exasperated as much by his composure as by his good-fortune, their words became unintelligible, and were succeeded by shrill, piercing yells. Just then the crafty squaw, who had taken the necessary precaution to fire the piles, made her way through the throng, and cleared a place for herself in front of the captive. The squalid and withered person of this hag might well have obtained for her the character of possessing more than human cunning. Throwing back her light vestment, she stretched forth her long skinny arm, in derision, and using the language of the Lenape, as more intelligible to the subject of her gibes, she commenced aloud—

"Look you, Delaware!" she said, snapping her fingers in his face; "your nation is a race of women, and the hoe is better fitted to your hands than the gun. Your squaws are the mothers of deer; but if a bear, or a wildcat, or a serpent were born among you, ye would flee. The Huron girls shall make you petticoats, and we will find you a husband."

A burst of savage laughter succeeded this attack, during which the soft and musical merriment of the younger females strangely chimed with the cracked voice of their older and more malignant companion. But the stranger was superior to all their efforts. His head was immovable; nor did he betray the slightest consciousness that any were present, except when his haughty eye rolled towards the dusky forms of the warriors, who stalked in the background, silent and sullen observers of the scene.

Infuriated at the self-command of the captive, the woman placed her arms akimbo; and throwing herself into a posture of defiance, she broke out anew, in a torrent of words that no art of ours could commit successfully to paper. Her breath was, however, expended in vain; for, although distinguished in her own nation as a proficient in the art of abuse, she was permitted to work herself into such a fury as actually to foam at the mouth, without causing a muscle to vibrate in the motionless figure of the stranger. The effect of his indifference began to extend itself to the other spectators; and a youngster, who was just quitting the condition of a boy, to enter the state of manhood, attempted to assist the termagant,[2] by flourishing his tomahawk before their victim, and adding his empty boasts to the taunts of the woman. Then, indeed, the captive turned his face towards the light, and looked down on the stripling with an expression that was superior to contempt. At the next moment he resumed his quiet and reclining attitude against the post. But the change of posture had permitted Duncan to exchange glances with the firm and piercing eyes of Uncas.

Breathless with amazement, and heavily oppressed with the critical situation of his friend, Heyward recoiled before the look, trembling lest its meaning might, in some unknown manner, hasten the prisoner's fate. There was not, however, any instant cause for such an apprehension. Just then a warrior forced his way into the exasperated crowd. Motioning the women and children aside with a stern gesture, he took Uncas by the arm, and led him towards the door of the council lodge. Thither all the chiefs, and most of the distinguished warriors, followed; among whom the anxious Heyward found means to enter without attracting any dangerous attention to himself.

A few minutes were consumed in disposing of those present in a manner suitable to their rank and influence in the trible. An order very similar to that adopted in the preceding interview was observed; the aged and superior chiefs occupying the area of the spacious apartment, within the powerful light of a glaring torch, while their juniors and inferiors were arranged in the background, presenting a dark outline of swarthy and marked visages. In the very centre of the lodge, immediately under an opening that admitted the twinkling light of one or two stars, stood Uncas, calm, elevated, and collected. His high and haughty carriage was not lost on his captors, who often bent their looks on his person, with eyes which, while they lost none of their inflexibility of purpose, plainly betrayed their admiration of the stranger's daring.

The case was different with the individual whom Duncan had observed to stand forth with his friend, previously to the desperate trial of speed; and who, instead of joining in the chase, had remained, throughout its turbulent uproar, like a cringing statue, expressive of shame and disgrace. Though not a hand had been extended to greet him, nor yet an eye had condescended to watch his movements, he had also entered the lodge, as though impelled by a fate to whose decrees he submitted, seemingly, without a struggle. Heyward profited by the first opportunity to gaze in his face, secretly apprehensive he might find the features of another acquaintance; but they proved to be those of a stranger, and, what was still more inexplicable, of one who bore all the distinctive marks of a Huron warrior. Instead of mingling with his tribe, however, he sat apart, a solitary being in a multitude, his form shrinking into a crouching and abject attitude, as if anxious to fill as little space as possible. When each individual had taken his proper station, and silence reigned in the place, the gray-haired chief already introduced to the reader, spoke aloud, in the language of the Lenni Lenape.

"Delaware," he said, "though one of a nation of women, you have proved yourself a man. I would give you food; but he who eats with a Huron should become his friend. Rest in peace till the morning sun, when our last words shall be spoken."

"Seven nights, and as many summer days, have I fasted on the trail of the Hurons," Uncas coldly replied; "the children of the Lenape know how to travel the path of the just without lingering to eat."

"Two of my young men are in pursuit of your companion," resumed the other, without appearing to regard the boast of his captive; "when they get back, then will our wise men say to you 'live' or 'die.' "

"Has a Huron no ears?" scornfully exclaimed Uncas; "twice, since he has been your prisoner, has the Delaware heard a gun that he knows. Your young men will never come back!"

A short and sullen pause succeeded this bold assertion. Duncan, who understood the Mohican to allude to the fatal rifle of the scout, bent forward in earnest observation of the effect it might produce on the conquerors; but the chief was content with simply retorting,—

"If the Lenape are so skilful, why is one of their bravest warriors here?"

"He followed in the steps of a flying coward, and fell into a snare. The cunning beaver may be caught."

As Uncas thus replied, he pointed with his finger toward the solitary Huron, but without deigning to bestow any other notice on so unworthy an object. The words of the answer and the air of the speaker produced a strong sensation among his auditors. Every eye rolled sullenly towards the individual indicated by the simple gesture, and a low, threatening murmur passed through the crowd. The ominous sounds reached the outer door, and the women and children pressing into the throng, no gap had been left, between shoulder and shoulder, that was not now filled with the dark lineaments of some eager and curious human countenance.

In the meantime, the more aged chiefs, in the centre, communed with each other in short and broken sentences. Not a word was uttered that did not convey the meaning of the speaker, in the simplest and most energetic form. Again, a long and deeply solemn pause took place. It was known, by all present, to be the grave precursor of a weighty and important judgment. They who composed the outer circle of faces were on tiptoe to gaze; and even the culprit for an instant forgot his shame in a deeper emotion, and exposed his abject features, in order to cast an anxious and troubled glance at the dark assemblage of chiefs. The silence was finally broken by the aged warrior so often named. He arose from the earth, and moving past the immovable form of Uncas, placed himself in a dignified attitude before the offender. At that moment, the withered squaw already mentioned moved into the circle, in a slow, sideling sort of a dance, holding the torch, and muttering the indistinct words of what might have been a species of incantation. Though her presence was altogether an intrusion, it was unheeded.

Approaching Uncas, she held the blazing brand in such a manner as to cast its red glare on his person, and to expose the slightest emotion of his countenance. The Mohican maintained his firm and haughty attitude; and his eye, so far from deigning to meet her inquisitive look, dwelt steadily on the distance, as though it penetrated the obstacles which impeded the view, and looked into futurity. Satisfied with her examination, she left him, with a slight expression of pleasure, and proceeded to practise the same trying experiment on her delinquent countryman.

The young Huron was in his war-paint, and very little of a finely moulded form was concealed by his attire. The light rendered every limb and joint discernible, and Duncan turned away in horror when he saw they were writhing in irrepressible agony. The woman was commencing a low and plaintive howl at the sad and shameful spectacle, when the chief put forth his hand and gently pushed her aside.

"Reed-that-bends," he said, addressing the young culprit by name, and in his proper language, "though the Great Spirit has made you pleasant to the eyes, it would have been better that you had not been born. Your tongue is loud in the village, but in battle it is still. None of my young men strike the tomahawk deeper into the war-post—none of them so lightly on the Yengeese. The enemy know the shape of your back, but they have never seen the color of your eyes. Three times have they called on you to come, and as often did you forget to answer.

Your name will never be mentioned again in your tribe—
it is already forgotten."

As the chief slowly uttered these words, pausing impressively between each sentence, the culprit raised his
face, in deference to the other's rank and years. Shame,
horror, and pride struggled in its lineaments. His eye,
which was contracted with inward anguish, gleamed on
the persons of those whose breath was his fame; and the
latter emotion for an instant predominated. He arose to
his feet, and baring his bosom, looked steadily on the
keen, glittering knife, that was already upheld by his in-
exorable judge. As the weapon passed slowly into his
heart he even smiled, as if in joy at having found death
less dreadful than he had anticipated, and fell heavily on
his face, at the feet of the rigid and unyielding form of
Uncas.

The squaw gave a loud and plaintive yell, dashed the
torch to the earth, and buried everything in darkness.
The whole shuddering group of spectators glided from
the lodge, like troubled sprites; and Duncan thought
that he and the yet throbbing body of the victim of an Indian judgment had now become its only tenants.

Hey acts as French doctor for Hurons
(who think French ditched them), a group of indians
come with prisoner + scalps, prisoner forced to
race warriors to escape, he wins cuz hey trips
nis competitor; the prisoner is uncas, the father
of uncas' capturer stabs his son for cowardice

XXIV

"Thus spoke the sage: the kings without delay
Dissolve the council, and their chief obey."
Alexander Pope, *The Iliad of Homer*[1]

A SINGLE MOMENT SERVED to convince the youth that he was mistaken. A hand was laid, with a powerful pressure, on his arm, and the low voice of Uncas muttered in his ears:

"The Hurons are dogs. The sight of a coward's blood can never make a warrior tremble. The 'Gray Head' and the Sagamore are safe, and the rifle of Hawkeye is not asleep. Go,—Uncas and the 'Open Hand' are now strangers. It is enough."

Heyward would gladly have heard more, but a gentle push from his friend urged him towards the door, and admonished him of the danger that might attend the discovery of their intercourse. Slowly and reluctantly yielding to the necessity, he quitted the place, and mingled with the throng that hovered nigh. The dying fires in the clearing cast a dim and uncertain light on the dusky figures that were silently stalking to and fro; and occasionally a brighter gleam than common glanced into the lodge, and exhibited the figure of Uncas still maintaining its upright attitude near the dead body of the Huron.

A knot of warriors soon entered the place again, and reissuing, they bore the senseless remains into the adjacent woods. After this termination of the scene, Duncan wandered among the lodges, unquestioned and unnoticed, endeavoring to find some trace of her in whose behalf he incurred the risk he ran. In the present temper of the tribe, it would have been easy to have fled and rejoined his companions, had such a wish crossed his mind. But, in addition to the never-ceasing anxiety on account of Alice, a fresher, though feebler interest in the fate of Uncas assisted to chain him to the spot. He continued, therefore, to stray from hut to hut, looking into each only to encounter additional disappointment, until he had made the entire circuit of the village. Abandoning a species of inquiry that proved so fruitless, he retraced his steps to the council lodge, resolved to seek and question David, in order to put an end to his doubts.

On reaching the building which had proved alike the seat of judgment and the place of execution, the young man found that the excitement had already subsided. The warriors had reassembled, and were now calmly smoking, while they conversed gravely on the chief incidents of their recent expedition to the head of the Horican. Though the return of Duncan was likely to remind them of his character, and the suspicious circumstances of his visit, it produced no visible sensation. So far, the terrible scene that had just occurred proved favorable to his views, and he required no other prompter than his own feelings to convince him of the expediency of profiting by so unexpected an advantage.

Without seeming to hesitate, he walked into the lodge, and took his seat with a gravity that accorded admirably with the deportment of his hosts. A hasty but searching glance sufficed to tell him that, though Uncas still remained where he had left him, David had not reappeared. No other restraint was imposed on the former than the watchful looks of a young Huron, who had placed himself at hand; though an armed warrior leaned against the post that formed one side of the narrow doorway. In every other respect, the captive seemed at liberty; still he was excluded from all participation in the discourse, and possessed much more of the air of some finely moulded statue than a man having life and volition.

Heyward had too recently witnessed a frightful instance of the prompt punishments of the people into whose hands he had fallen, to hazard an exposure by any officious boldness. He would greatly have preferred silence and meditation to speech, when a discovery of his real condition might prove so instantly fatal. Unfortunately for this prudent resolution, his entertainers appeared otherwise disposed. He had not long occupied the wisely taken a little in the shade, when another of the elder warriors, who spoke the French language, addressed him:—

"My Canada father does not forget his children," said the chief; "I thank him. An evil spirit lives in the wife of one of my young men. Can the cunning stranger frighten him away?"

Heyward possessed some knowledge of the mummery practised among the Indians, in the cases of such supposed visitations. He saw, at a glance, that the circumstance might possibly be improved to further his own end. It would, therefore, have been difficult, just then, to have uttered a proposal that would have given him more satisfaction. Aware of the necessity of preserving the dignity of his imaginary character, however, he repressed his feelings, and answered with suitable mystery,—

"Spirits differ; some yield to the power of wisdom, while others are too strong."

"My brother is a great medicine," said the cunning savage; "he will try?"

A gesture of assent was the answer. The Huron was content with the assurance, and resuming his pipe, he awaited the proper moment to move. The impatient Heyward, inwardly execrating the cold customs of the savages, which required such sacrifices to appearance, was fain to assume an air of indifference, equal to that maintained by the chief, who was, in truth, a near relative of the afflicted woman. The minutes lingered, and the delay had seemed an hour to the adventurer in empiricism, when the Huron laid aside his pipe, and drew his robe across his breast, as if about to lead the way to the lodge of the invalid. Just then, a warrior of powerful frame darkened the door, and stalking silently among the attentive group, he seated himself on one end of the low pile of brush which sustained Duncan. The latter cast an impatient look at his neighbor, and felt his flesh creep with uncontrollable horror when he found himself in actual contact with Magua.

The sudden return of this artful and dreaded chief caused a delay in the departure of the Huron. Several pipes, that had been extinguished, were lighted again; while the newcomer, without speaking a word, drew his tomahawk from his girdle, and filling the bowl on its head, began to inhale the vapors of the weed through the hollow handle, with as much indifference as if he had not been absent two dreary days on a long and toilsome

hunt. Ten minutes, which appeared so many ages to
Duncan, might have passed in this manner; and the warriors were fairly enveloped in a cloud of white smoke before any of them spoke.

"Welcome!" one at length uttered; "has my friend
found the moose?"

"The young men stagger under their burdens," returned Magua. "Let 'Reed-that-bends' go on the hunting-
path; he will meet them."

A deep and awful silence succeeded the utterance of
the forbidden name. Each pipe dropped from the lips of
its owner as though all had inhaled an impurity at the
same instant. The smoke wreathed above their heads in
little eddies, and curling in a spiral form, it ascended
swiftly through the opening in the roof of the lodge, leaving the place beneath clear of its fumes, and each dark
visage distinctly visible. The looks of most of the warriors
were riveted on the earth; though a few of the younger
and less gifted of the party suffered their wild and glaring
eyeballs to roll in the direction of a white-headed savage,
who sat between two of the most venerated chiefs of the
tribe. There was nothing in the air or attire of this Indian
that would seem to entitle him to such a distinction. The
former was rather depressed, than remarkable for the
bearing of the natives; and the latter was such as was
commonly worn by the ordinary men of the nation. Like
most around him, for more than a minute his look too
was on the ground; but, trusting his eyes at length to steal
a glance aside, he perceived that he was becoming an object of general attention. Then he arose and lifted his
voice in the general silence.

"It was a lie," he said; "I had no son. He who was
called by that name is forgotten; his blood was pale, and

it came not from the veins of a Huron; the wicked Chippewas cheated my squaw. The Great Spirit has said, that the family of Wiss-entush should end; he is happy who knows that the evil of his race dies with himself. I have done."

The speaker, who was the father of the recreant young Indian, looked round and about him, as if seeking commendation of his stoicism in the eyes of his auditors. But the stern customs of his people had made too severe an exaction of the feeble old man. The expression of his eye contradicted his figurative and boastful language, while every muscle in his wrinkled visage was working with anguish. Standing a single minute to enjoy his bitter triumph, he turned away, as if sickening at the gaze of men, and veiling his face in his blanket, he walked from the lodge with the noiseless step of an Indian, seeking, in the privacy of his own abode, the sympathy of one like himself, aged, forlorn, and childless.

The Indians, who believe in the hereditary transmission of virtues and defects in character, suffered him to depart in silence. Then, with an elevation of breeding that many in a more cultivated state of society might profitably emulate, one of the chiefs drew the attention of the young men from the weakness they had just witnessed, by saying, in a cheerful voice, addressing himself in courtesy to Magua, as the newest comer,—

"The Delawares have been like bears after the honeypots, prowling around my village. But who has ever found a Huron asleep?"

The darkness of the impending cloud which precedes a burst of thunder was not blacker than the brow of Magua as he exclaimed,—

"The Delawares of the Lakes!"

"Not so. They who wear the petticoats of squaws, on their own river. One of them has been passing the tribe."

"Did my young men take his scalp?"

"His legs were good, though his arm is better for the hoe than the tomahawk," returned the other, pointing to the immovable form of Uncas.

Instead of manifesting any womanish curiosity to feast his eyes with the sight of a captive from a people he was known to have so much reason to hate, Magua continued to smoke, with the meditative air that he usually maintained, when there was no immediate call on his cunning or his eloquence. Although secretly amazed at the facts communicated by the speech of the aged father, he permitted himself to ask no questions, reserving his inquiries for a more suitable moment. It was only after a sufficient interval that he shook the ashes from his pipe, replaced the tomahawk, tightened his girdle, and arose, casting for the first time a glance in the direction of the prisoner, who stood a little behind him. The wary, though seemingly abstracted Uncas, caught a glimpse of the movement, and turning suddenly to the light, their looks met. Near a minute these two bold and untamed spirits stood regarding one another steadily in the eye, neither quailing in the least before the fierce gaze he encountered. The form of Uncas dilated, and his nostrils opened like those of a tiger at bay; but so rigid and unyielding was his posture, that he might easily have been converted by the imagination into an exquisite and faultless representation of the warlike deity of his tribe. The lineaments of the quivering features of Magua proved more ductile; his countenance gradually lost its character of defiance in an expression of ferocious joy, and heaving a breath from the very bottom of his chest, he pronounced aloud the very formidable name of—

"Le Cerf Agile!"

Each warrior sprang upon his feet at the utterance of the well known appellation, and there was a short period during which the stoical constancy of the natives was completely conquered by surprise. The hated and yet respected name was repeated as by one voice, carrying the sound even beyond the limits of the lodge. The women and children, who lingered around the entrance, took up the words in an echo, which was succeeded by another shrill and plaintive howl. The latter was not yet ended, when the sensation among the men had entirely abated. Each one in presence seated himself, as though ashamed of his precipitation; but it was many minutes before their meaning eyes ceased to roll towards their captive, in curious examination of a warrior who had so often proved his prowess on the best and proudest of their nation. Uncas enjoyed his victory, but was content with merely exhibiting his triumph by a quiet smile—an emblem of scorn which belongs to all time and every nation.

Magua caught the expression, and raising his arm, he shook it at the captive, the light silver ornaments attached to his bracelet rattling with the trembling agitation of the limb, as, in a tone of vengeance, he exclaimed, in English,—

"Mohican, you die!"

"The healing waters will never bring the dead Hurons to life," returned Uncas, in the music of the Delawares; "the tumbling river washes their bones; their men are squaws; their women owls. Go! call together the Huron dogs, that they may look upon a warrior. My nostrils are offended; they scent the blood of a coward."

The latter allusion struck deep, and the injury rankled. Many of the Hurons understood the strange tongue in which the captive spoke, among which number was Magua. This cunning savage beheld, and instantly profited by his advantage. Dropping the light robe of skin from his shoulder, he stretched forth his arm, and commenced a burst of his dangerous and artful eloquence. However much his influence among his people had been impaired by his occasional and besetting weakness, as well as by his desertion of the tribe, his courage and his fame as an orator was undeniable. He never spoke without auditors, and rarely without making converts to his opinions. On the present occasion, his native powers were stimulated by the thirst of revenge.

He again recounted the events of the attack on the island at Glenn's, the death of his associates, and the escape of their most formidable enemies. Then he described the nature and position of the mount whither he had led such captives as had fallen into their hands. Of his own bloody intentions towards the maidens, and of his baffled malice he made no mention, but passed rapidly on to the surprise of the party by La Longue Carabine, and its fatal termination. Here he paused, and looked about him, in affected veneration for the departed, but, in truth, to note the effect of his opening narrative. As usual, every eye was riveted on his face. Each dusky figure seemed a breathing statue, so motionless was the posture, so intense the attention of the individual.

Then Magua dropped his voice, which had hitherto

been clear, strong, and elevated, and touched upon the merits of the dead. No quality that was likely to command the sympathy of an Indian escaped his notice. One had never been known to follow the chase in vain; another had been indefatigable on the trail of their enemies. This was brave, that generous. In short, he so managed his allusions, that in a nation which was composed of so few families, he contrived to strike every chord that might find, in its turn, some breast in which to vibrate.

"Are the bones of my young men," he concluded, "in the burial-place of the Hurons? You know they are not. Their spirits are gone towards the setting sun, and are already crossing the great waters, to the happy hunting-grounds. But they departed without food, without guns or knives, without moccasins, naked and poor as they were born. Shall this be? Are their souls to enter the land of the just like hungry Iroquois or unmanly Delawares; or shall they meet their friends with arms in their hands and robes on their backs? What will our fathers think the tribes of the Wyandots have become? They will look on their children with a dark eye, and say, Go! a Chippewa has come hither with the name of a Huron. Brothers, we must not forget the dead; a redskin never ceases to remember. We will load the back of this Mohican until he staggers under our bounty, and despatch him after my young men. They call to us for aid, though our ears are not open; they say, Forget us not. When they see the spirit of this Mohican toiling after them with his burden, they will know we are of that mind. Then will they go on happy; and our children will say, 'So did our fathers to their friends, so must we do to them.' What is a Yengee? we have slain many, but the earth is still pale. A stain on the name of a Huron can only be hid by blood that comes from the veins of an Indian. Let this Delaware die."

The effect of such an harangue, delivered in the nervous language and with the emphatic manner of a Huron orator, could scarcely be mistaken. Magua had so artfully blended the natural sympathies with the religious superstition of his auditors, that their minds, already prepared by custom to sacrifice a victim to the *manes* of their countrymen, lost every vestige of humanity in a wish for revenge. One warrior in particular, a man of wild and ferocious mien, had been conspicuous for the attention he had given to the words of the speaker. His countenance had changed with each passing emotion, until it settled into a look of deadly malice. As Magua ended he arose, and uttering the yell of a demon, his polished little axe was seen glancing in the torchlight as he whirled it above his head. The motion and the cry were too sudden for words to interrupt his bloody intention. It appeared as if a bright gleam shot from his hand, which was crossed at the same moment by a dark and powerful line. The former was the tomahawk in its passage; the latter the arm that Magua darted forward to divert its aim. The quick and ready motion of the chief was not entirely too late. The keen weapon cut the war-plume from the scalping-tuft of Uncas, and passed through the frail wall of the lodge, as though it were hurled from some formidable engine.

Duncan had seen the threatening action, and sprang upon his feet, with a heart which while it leaped into his throat, swelled with the most generous resolution in behalf of his friend. A glance told him that the blow had failed, and terror changed to admiration. Uncas stood still, looking his enemy in the eye with features that seemed superior to emotion. Marble could not be colder, calmer, or steadier than the countenance he put upon this sudden and vindictive attack. Then, as if pitying a want of skill which had proved so fortunate to himself, he smiled, and muttered a few words of contempt in his own tongue.

"No!" said Magua, after satisfying himself of the safety of the captive; "the sun must shine on his shame; the squaws must see his flesh tremble, or our revenge will be like the play of boys. Go! take him where there is silence; let us see if a Delaware can sleep at night, and in the morning die."

The young men whose duty it was to guard the prisoner instantly passed their ligaments of bark across his arms, and led him from the lodge, amid a profound and ominous silence. It was only as the figure of Uncas stood in the opening of the door that his firm step hesitated. There he turned, and, in the sweeping and haughty glance that he threw around the circle of his enemies, Duncan caught a look which he was glad to construe into an expression that he was not entirely deserted by hope.

Magua was content with his success, or too much occupied with his secret purposes to push his inquiries any further. Shaking his mantle, and folding it on his bosom, he also quitted the place, without pursuing a subject which might have proved so fatal to the individual at his elbow. Notwithstanding his rising resentment, his natural firmness, and his anxiety in behalf of Uncas, Heyward felt sensibly relieved by the absence of so dangerous and so subtle a foe. The excitement produced by the speech gradually subsided. The warriors resumed their seats, and clouds of smoke once more filled the lodge. For near half an hour, not a syllable was uttered, or scarcely a look cast aside; a grave and meditative silence being the ordinary succession to every scene of violence and commotion among those beings, who were alike so impetuous and yet so self-restrained.

When the chief who had solicited the aid of Duncan finished his pipe, he made a final and successful movement towards departing. A motion of a finger was the intimation he gave the supposed physician to follow; and passing through the clouds of smoke, Duncan was glad, on more accounts than one, to be able, at last, to breathe the pure air of a cool and refreshing summer evening.

Instead of pursuing his way among those lodges where Heyward had already made his unsuccessful search, his companion turned aside, and proceeded directly towards the base of an adjacent mountain, which overhung the temporary village. A thicket of brush skirted its foot, and it became necessary to proceed through a crooked and narrow path. The boys had resumed their sports in the clearing, and were enacting a mimic chase to the post among themselves. In order to render their games as like the reality as possible, one of the boldest of their number had conveyed a few brands into some piles of tree-tops that had hitherto escaped the burning. The blaze of one of these fires lighted the way of the chief and Duncan, and gave a character of additional wildness to the rude scenery. At a little distance from a bald rock, and directly in its front, they entered a grassy opening, which they prepared to cross. Just then fresh fuel was added to the fire, and a powerful light penetrated even to that distant spot. It fell upon the white surface of the mountain, and was reflected downwards upon a dark and mysterious-looking being that arose, unexpectedly, in their path.

The Indian paused, as if doubtful whether to proceed, and permitted his companion to approach his side. A large black ball, which at first seemed stationary, now began to move in a manner that to the latter was inexplicable. Again the fire brightened, and its glare fell more distinctly on the object. Then even Duncan knew it, by its restless and sidelong attitudes, which kept the upper part of its form in constant motion, while the animal itself appeared seated, to be a bear. Though it growled loudly and fiercely, and there were instants when its glistening eyeballs might be seen, it gave no other indications of hostility. The Huron, at least, seemed assured that the intentions of this singular intruder were peaceable, for after giving it an attentive examination, he quietly pursued his course.

Duncan, who knew that the animal was often domesticated among the Indians, followed the example of his companion, believing that some favorite of the tribe had found its way into the thicket, in search of food. They passed it unmolested. Though obliged to come nearly in contact with the monster, the Huron, who had at first so warily determined the character of his strange visitor, was now content with proceeding without wasting a moment in further examination; but Heyward was unable to prevent his eyes from looking backward, in salutary watchfulness against attacks in the rear. His uneasiness was in no degree diminished when he perceived the beast rolling along their path, and following their footsteps. He would have spoken, but the Indian at that moment shoved aside a door of bark, and entered a cavern in the bosom of the mountain.

Profiting by so easy a method of retreat, Duncan stepped after him, and was gladly closing the slight cover to the opening, when he felt it drawn from his hand by the beast, whose shaggy form immediately darkened the passage. They were now in a straight and long gallery, in a chasm of the rocks, where retreat without encountering the animal was impossible. Making the best of the circumstances, the young man pressed forward, keeping as close as possible to his conductor. The bear growled frequently at his heels, and once or twice its enormous paws were laid on his person, as if disposed to prevent his further passage into the den.

How long the nerves of Heyward would have sustained him in this extraordinary situation, it might be difficult to decide; for, happily, he soon found relief. A glimmer of light had constantly been in their front, and they now arrived at the place whence it proceeded.

A large cavity in the rock had been rudely fitted to answer the purposes of many apartments. The subdivisions were simple but ingenious, being composed of stone, sticks, and bark, intermingled. Openings above admitted the light by day, and at night fires and torches supplied the place of the sun. Hither the Hurons had brought most of their valuables, especially those which more particularly pertained to the nation; and hither, as it now appeared, the sick woman, who was believed to be the victim of supernatural power, had been transported also, under an impression that her tormentor would find more difficulty in making his assaults through walls of stone than through the leafy coverings of the lodges. The apartment into which Duncan and his guide first entered, had been exclusively devoted to her accommodation. The latter approached her bedside, which was surrounded by females, in the centre of whom Heyward was surprised to find his missing friend David.

A single look was sufficient to apprise the pretended leech that the invalid was far beyond his powers of healing. She lay in a sort of paralysis, indifferent to the objects which crowded before her sight, and happily unconscious of suffering. Heyward was far from regretting that his mummeries were to be performed on one who was much too ill to take an interest in their failure or success. The slight qualm of conscience which had been excited by the intended deception was instantly appeased, and he began to collect his thoughts, in order to enact his part with suitable spirit, when he found he was about to be anticipated in his skill by an attempt to prove the power of music.

Gamut, who had stood prepared to pour forth his spirit in song when the visitors entered, after delaying a moment, drew a strain from his pipe, and commenced a hymn that might have worked a miracle, had faith in its efficacy been of much avail. He was allowed to proceed to the close, the Indians respecting his imaginary infirmity, and Duncan too glad of the delay to hazard the slightest interruption. As the dying cadence of his strains was falling on the ears of the latter, he started aside at hearing them repeated behind him in a voice half human, half sepulchral. Looking around, he beheld the shaggy monster seated on end in a shadow of the cavern, where, while his restless body swung in the uneasy manner of the animal, it repeated, in a sort of low growl, sound, if not words, which bore some slight resemblance to the melody of the singer.

The effect of so strange an echo on David may better be imagined than described. His eyes opened as if he doubted their truth; and his voice became instantly mute in excess of wonder. A deep-laid scheme, of communicating some important intelligence to Heyward, was driven from his recollection by an emotion which very nearly resembled fear, but which he was fain to believe was admiration. Under its influence, he exclaimed aloud—"She expects you, and is at hand;" and precipitately left the cavern.

Hey searces for Alice, Hurons want him to cure sick woman. Magua identifies Uncas + says to be tortured - killed next morning. chief takes ney to cavern @ near mtn. a friendly bear follows them. woman relaxes w/ other woman + Gamut around. Hey sees woman will die w/ or w/o his help.

XXV

"Snug.—Have you the lion's part written? Pray you, if it
be, give it me, for I am slow of study."
"Quince.—You may do it extempore, for it is nothing
but roaring."
A Midsummer Night's Dream[1]

THERE WAS A STRANGE BLENDING of the ridiculous
with that which was solemn in this scene. The beast
still continued its rolling, and apparently untiring movements, though its ludicrous attempt to imitate the
melody of David ceased the instant the latter abandoned
the field. The words of Gamut were, as has been seen, in
his native tongue; and to Duncan they seemed pregnant
with some hidden meaning, though nothing present assisted him in discovering the object of their illusion. A
speedy end was, however, put to every conjecture on the
subject, by the manner of the chief, who advanced to the
bedside of the invalid, and beckoned away the whole
group of female attendants that had clustered there to
witness the skill of the stranger. He was implicitly,
though reluctantly, obeyed; and when the low echo
which rang along the hollow natural gallery from the distant closing door had ceased, pointing towards his insensible daughter, he said,—

"Now let my brother show his power."

Thus unequivocally called on to exercise the functions of his assumed character, Heyward was apprehensive that the smallest delay might prove dangerous. Endeavoring then to collect his ideas, he prepared to perform that species of incantation, and those uncouth rites, under which the Indian conjurers are accustomed to conceal their ignorance and impotency. It is more than probable that, in the disordered state of his thoughts, he would soon have fallen into some suspicious, if not fatal error, had not his incipient attempts been interrupted by a fierce growl from the quadruped. Three several times did he renew his efforts to proceed, and as often was he met by the same unaccountable opposition, each interruption seeming more savage and threatening than the preceding.

"The cunning ones are jealous," said the Huron; "I go. Brother, the woman is the wife of one of my bravest young men; deal justly by her. Peace!" he added, beckoning to the discontented beast to be quiet; "I go."

The chief was as good as his word, and Duncan now found himself alone in that wild and desolate abode, with the helpless invalid, and the fierce and dangerous brute. The latter listened to the movements of the Indian with that air of sagacity that a bear is known to posses, until another echo announced that he had also left the cavern, when it turned and came waddling up to Duncan, before whom it seated itself, in its natural attitude, erect like a man. The youth looked anxiously about him for some weapon, with which he might make a resistance against the attack he now seriously expected.

It seemed, however, as if the humor of the animal had suddenly changed. Instead of continuing its discontented growls, or manifesting any further signs of anger, the whole of its shaggy body shook violently, as if agitated by some strange internal convulsion. The huge and un- wieldy talons pawed stupidly about the grinning muzzle, and while Heyward kept his eyes riveted on its move- ments with jealous watchfulness, the grim head fell on one side, and in its place appeared the honest, sturdy countenance of the scout, who was indulging from the bottom of his soul, in his own peculiar expression of mer- riment.

"Hist!" said the wary woodsman, interrupting Hey- ward's exclamation of surprise; "the varlets are about the place, and any sounds that are not natural to witchcraft would bring them back upon us in a body."

"Tell me the meaning of this masquerade; and why you have attempted so desperate an adventure."

"Ah! reason and calculation are often outdone by acci- dent," returned the scout. "But as a story should always commence at the beginning, I will tell you the whole in order. After we parted I placed the commandant and the Sagamore in an old beaver lodge, where they are safer from the Hurons than they would be in the garrison of Edward, for your high northwest Indians, not having as yet got the traders among them, continue to venerate the beaver. After which Uncas and I pushed for the other en- campment, as was agreed; have you seen the lad?"

"To my great grief! he is captive, and condemned to die at the rising of the sun."

"I had misgivings that such would be his fate," re- sumed the scout, in a less confident and joyous tone. But soon regaining his naturally firm voice, he continued: "His bad fortune is the true reason of my being here, for it would never do to abandon such a boy to the Hurons.

A rare time the knaves would have of it, could they tie
The Bounding Elk and The Long Carabine, as they call
me, to the same stake! Though why they have given me
such a name I never knew, there being as little likeness
between the gifts of 'Killdeer,' and the performance of
one of your real Canada carabynes, as there is between
the natur' of a pipestone and a flint!"

"Keep to your tale," said the impatient Heyward; "we
know not at what moment the Hurons may return."

"No fear of them. A conjurer must have his time, like
a straggling priest in the settlements. We are as safe from
interruption as a missionary would be at the beginning of
a two hours' discourse. Well, Uncas and I fell in with a return party of the varlets; the lad was much too forward
for a scout; nay, for that matter, being of hot blood, he
was not so much to blame; and, after all, one of the
Hurons proved a coward, and in fleeing led him into an
ambushment."

"And dearly has he paid for the weakness!"

The scout significantly passed his hand across his own
throat, and nodded, as if he said, "I comprehend your
meaning." After which he continued, in a more audible
though scarcely more intelligible language,—

"After the loss of the boy I turned upon the Hurons, as
you may judge. There have been scrimmages atween
one or two of their outlyers and myself; but that is neither here nor there. So, after I had shot the imps, I got in
pretty nigh to the lodges without further commotion.
Then what should luck do in my favor, but lead me to the
very spot where one of the most famous conjurers of the
tribe was dressing himself, as I well knew, for some great
battle with Satan—though why should I call that luck,
which it now seems was an especial ordering of Provi-

dence! So a judgmatical rap over the head stiffened the
lying impostor for a time, and leaving him a bit of walnut
for his supper, to prevent an uproar, and stringing him up
atween two saplings, I made free with his finery, and
took the part of the bear on myself, in order that the operations might proceed."

"And admirably did you enact the character; the animal itself might have been shamed by the representation."

"Lord, major," returned the flattered woodsman, "I
should be but a poor scholar for one who has studied so
long in the wilderness, did I not know how to set forth
the movements and natur' of such a beast. Had it been
now a catamount, or even a full-sized panther, I would
have embellished a performance for you worth regarding. But it is no such marvellous feat to exhibit the feats
of so dull a beast; though, for that matter too, a bear may
be overacted. Yes, yes; it is not every imitator that knows
natur' may be outdone easier than she is equalled. But all
our work is yet before us: where is the gentle one?"

"Heaven knows; I have examined every lodge in the
village, without discovering the slightest trace of her
presence in the tribe."

"You heard what the singer said, as he left us,—'She is
at hand, and expects you'?"

"I have been compelled to believe he alluded to this
unhappy woman."

"The simpleton was frightened, and blundered through
his message; but he had a deeper meaning. Here are
walls enough to separate the whole settlement. A bear
ought to climb; therefore will I take a look above them.
There may be honey-pots hid in these rocks, and I am a
beast you know, that has a hankering for the sweets."

The scout looked behind him, laughing at his own conceit, while he clambered up the partition, imitating, as he went, the clumsy motions of the beast he represented; but the instant the summit was gained he made a gesture for silence, and slid down with the utmost precipitation.

"She is here," he whispered, "and by that door you will find her. I would have spoken a word of comfort to the afflicted soul; but the sight of such a monster might upset her reason. Though for that matter, major, you are none of the most inviting yourself in your paint."

Duncan, who had already sprung eagerly forward, drew instantly back on hearing these discouraging words.

"Am I, then, so very revolting?" he demanded, with an air of chagrin.

"You might not startle a wolf, or turn the Royal Americans from a charge; but I have seen the time when you had a better-favored look; your streaked countenances are not ill-judged of by the squaws, but young women of white blood give the preference to their own color. See," he added, pointing to a place where the water trickled from a rock, forming a little crystal spring before it found an issue through the adjacent crevices; "you may easily get rid of the Sagamore's daub, and when you come back I will try my hand at a new embellishment. It's as common for a conjurer to alter his paint as for a buck in the settlements to change his finery."

The deliberate woodsman had little occasion to hunt for arguments to enforce his advice. He was yet speaking when Duncan availed himself of the water. In a moment every frightful or offensive mark was obliterated, and the youth appeared again in the lineaments with which he had been gifted by nature. Thus prepared for an interview with his mistress, he took a hasty leave of his companion, and disappeared through the indicated passage. The scout witnessed his departure with complacency, nodding his head after him, and muttering his good wishes; after which he very coolly set about an examination of the state of the larder, among the Hurons—the cavern, among other purposes, being used as a receptacle for the fruits of their hunts.

Duncan had no other guide than a distant glimmering light, which served; however, the office of a polar star to the lover. By its aid he was enabled to enter the haven of his hopes, which was merely another apartment of the cavern, that had been solely appropriated to the safe-keeping of so important a prisoner as a daughter of the commandant of William Henry. It was profusely strewed with the plunder of that unlucky fortress. In the midst of this confusion he found her he sought, pale, anxious, and terrified, but lovely. David had prepared her for such a visit.

"Duncan!" she exclaimed, in a voice that seemed to tremble at the sounds created by itself.

"Alice!" he answered, leaping carelessly among trunks, boxes, arms, and furniture, until he stood at her side.

"I knew that you would never desert me," she said, looking up with a momentary glow on her otherwise dejected countenance. "But you are alone! grateful as it is to be thus remembered, I could wish to think you are not entirely alone."

Duncan, observing that she trembled in a manner which betrayed her inability to stand, gently induced her to be seated, while he recounted those leading incidents which it has been our task to record. Alice listened with breathless interest; and though the young man touched lightly on the sorrows of the stricken father, taking care, however, not to wound the self-love of his auditor, the tears ran as freely down the cheeks of the daughter as though she had never wept before. The soothing tenderness of Duncan, however, soon quieted the first burst of her emotions, and she then heard him to the close with undivided attention, if not with composure.

"And now, Alice," he added, "you will see how much is still expected of you. By the assistance of our experienced and invaluable friend, the scout, we may find our way from this savage people, but you will have to exert your utmost fortitude. Remember that you fly to the arms of your venerable parent, and how much his happiness, as well as your own, depends on those exertions."

"Can I do otherwise for a father who has done so much for me?"

"And for me too," continued the youth, gently pressing the hand he held in both his own.

The look of innocence and surprise which he received in return convinced Duncan of the necessity of being more explicit.

"This is neither the place nor the occasion to detain you with selfish wishes," he added; "but what heart loaded like mine would not wish to cast its burden? They say misery is the closest of all ties; our common suffering in your behalf left but little to be explained between your father and myself."

"And dearest Cora, Duncan; surely Cora was not forgotten?"

"Not forgotten! no; regretted, as woman was seldom mourned before. Your venerable father knew no difference between his children; but I—Alice, you will not be offended when I say, that to me her worth was in a degree obscured—"

"Then you knew not the merit of my sister," said Alice, withdrawing her hand; "of you she ever speaks as of one who is her nearest friend."

"I would gladly believe her such," returned Duncan, hastily; "I could wish her to be even more; but with you, Alice, I have the permission of your father to aspire to a still nearer and dearer tie."

Alice trembled violently, and there was an instant during which she bent her face aside, yielding to the emotions common to her sex; but they quickly passed away, leaving her mistress of her deportment, if not of her affections.

"Heyward," she said, looking him full in the face with a touching expression of innocence and dependency, "give me the sacred presence and the holy sanction of that parent before you urge me further."

"Though more I should not, less I could not say," the youth was about to answer, when he was interrupted by a light tap on his shoulder. Starting to his feet, he turned, and, confronting the intruder, his looks fell on the dark form and malignant visage of Magua. The deep guttural laugh of the savage sounded, at such a moment, to Duncan like the hellish taunt of a demon. Had he pursued the sudden and fierce impulse of the instant, he would have cast himself on the Huron, and committed their fortunes to the issue of a deadly struggle. But, without arms of any description, ignorant of what succor his subtle enemy could command, and charged with the safety of one who was just then dearer than ever to his heart, he no sooner entertained than he abandoned the desperate intention.

"What is your purpose?" said Alice, meekly folding her arms on her bosom, and struggling to conceal an agony of apprehension in behalf of Heyward, in the usual cold and distant manner with which she received the visits of her captor.

The exulting Indian had resumed his austere countenance, though he drew warily back before the menacing glance of the young man's fiery eye. He regarded both his captives for a moment with a steady look, and then stepping aside, he dropped a log of wood across a door different from that by which Duncan had entered. The latter now comprehended the manner of his surprise, and believing himself irretrievably lost, he drew Alice to his bosom, and stood prepared to meet a fate which he hardly regretted, since it was to be suffered in such company. But Magua meditated no immediate violence. His first measures were very evidently taken to secure his new captive; nor did he even bestow a second glance at the motionless forms in the centre of the cavern, until he had completely cut off every hope of retreat through the private outlet he had himself used. He was watched in all his movements by Heyward, who, however, remained firm, still folding the fragile form of Alice to his heart, at once too proud and too hopeless to ask favor of an enemy so often foiled. When Magua had effected his object he approached his prisoners, and said in English,—

"The pale-faces trap the cunning beavers; but the redskins know how to take the Yengeese."

"Huron, do your worst!" exclaimed the excited Heyward, forgetful that a double stake was involved in his life; "you and your vengeance are alike despised."

"Will the white man speak these words at the stake?" asked Magua; manifesting, at the same time, how little

faith he had in the other's resolution by the sneer that accompanied his words.

"Here; singly to your face, or in the presence of your
nation."

"Le Renard Subtil is a great chief!" returned the Indian; "he will go and bring his young men to see how
bravely a pale-face can laugh at the tortures."

He turned away while speaking, and was about to
leave the place through the avenue by which Duncan
had approached, when a growl caught his ear, and
caused him to hesitate. The figure of the bear appeared
in the door, where it sat, rolling from side to side in its
customary restlessness. Magua, like the father of the sick
woman, eyed it keenly for a moment, as if to ascertain its
character. He was far above the more vulgar superstitions of his tribe, and so soon as he recognized the well-
known attire of the conjurer, he prepared to pass it in
cool contempt. But a louder and more threatening growl
caused him again to pause. Then he seemed as if suddenly resolved to trifle no longer, and moved resolutely
forward. The mimic animal, which had advanced a little,
retired slowly in his front, until it arrived again at the
pass, when rearing on its hinder legs it beat the air with
its paws, in the manner practised by its brutal prototype.

"Fool!" exclaimed the chief, in Huron, "go play with
the children and squaws; leave men to their wisdom."

He once more endeavored to pass the supposed em-
piric, scorning even the parade of threatening to use the
knife, or tomahawk, that was pendent from his belt. Suddenly the beast extended its arms, or rather legs, and in-
closed him in a grasp that might have vied with the
far-famed power of the "bear's hug" itself. Heyward had
watched the whole procedure, on the part of Hawkeye,

with breathless interest. At first he relinquished his hold of Alice; then he caught up a thong of buckskin, which had been used around some bundle, and when he beheld his enemy with his two arms pinned to his side by the iron muscles of the scout, he rushed upon him, and effectually secured them there. Arms, legs, and feet were encircled in twenty folds of the thong, in less time than we have taken to record the circumstance. When the formidable Huron was completely pinioned, the scout released his hold, and Duncan laid his enemy on his back, utterly helpless.

Throughout the whole of this sudden and extraordinary operation, Magua, though he had struggled violently, until assured he was in the hands of one whose nerves were far better strung than his own, had not uttered the slightest exclamation. But when Hawkeye, by way of making a summary explanation of his conduct, removed the shaggy jaws of the beast, and exposed his own rugged and earnest countenance to the gaze of the Huron, the philosophy of the latter was so far mastered as to permit him to utter the never-failing,—

"Hugh!"

"Ay! you've found your tongue," said his undisturbed conqueror; "now, in order that you shall not use it to our ruin, I must make free to stop your mouth."

As there was no time to be lost, the scout immediately set about effecting so necessary a precaution; and when he had gagged the Indian, his enemy might safely have been considered as *hors de combat*.[2]

"By what place did the imp enter?" asked the industrious scout, when his work was ended. "Not a soul has passed my way since you left me."

Duncan pointed out the door by which Magua had

come, and which now presented too many obstacles to a quick retreat.

"Bring on the gentle one, then," continued his friend; "we must make a push for the woods by the other outlet."

" 'Tis impossible!" said Duncan; "fear has overcome her, and she is helpless. Alice! my sweet, my own Alice, arouse yourself; now is the moment to fly. 'Tis in vain! she hears, but is unable to follow. Go, noble and worthy friend; save yourself, and leave me to my fate!"

"Every trail has its end, and every calamity brings its lesson!" returned the scout. "There, wrap her in them Indian cloths. Conceal all of her little form. Nay, that foot has no fellow in the wilderness; it will betray her. All, every part. Now take her in your arms, and follow. Leave the rest to me."

Duncan, as may be gathered from the words of his companion, was eagerly obeying; and as the other finished speaking, he took the light person of Alice in his arms, and followed on the footsteps of the scout. They found the sick woman as they had left her, still alone, and passed swiftly on, by the natural gallery, to the place of entrance. As they approached the little door of bark, a murmur of voices without announced that the friends and relatives of the invalid were gathered about the place, patiently awaiting a summons to re-enter.

"If I open my lips to speak," Hawkeye whispered, "my English, which is the genuine tongue of a white-skin, will tell the varlets that an enemy is among them. You must give 'em your jargon, major; and say that we have shut the evil spirit in the cave, and are taking the woman to the woods in order to find strengthening roots. Practyse all your cunning, for it is a lawful undertaking."

The door opened a little, as if one without was listening to the proceedings within, and compelled the scout to cease his directions. A fierce growl repelled the eavesdropper, and then the scout boldly threw open the covering of bark, and left the place, enacting the character of the bear as he proceeded. Duncan kept close at his heels, and so found himself in the centre of a cluster of twenty anxious relatives and friends.

The crowd fell back a little, and permitted the father, and one who appeared to be the husband of the woman, to approach.

"Has my brother driven away the evil spirit?" demanded the former. "What has he in his arms?"

"Thy child," returned Duncan, gravely; "the disease has gone out of her; it is shut up in the rocks. I take the woman to a distance, where I will strengthen her against any further attacks. She shall be in the wigwam of the young man when the sun comes again."

When the father had translated the meaning of the stranger's words into the Huron language, a suppressed murmur announced the satisfaction with which the intelligence was received. The chief himself waved his hand for Duncan to proceed, saying aloud, in a firm voice, and with a lofty manner,—

"Go; I am a man, and I will enter the rock and fight the wicked one."

Heyward had gladly obeyed, and was already past the little group, when these startling words arrested him.

"Is my brother mad?" he exclaimed; "is he cruel! He will meet the disease, and it will enter him; or he will drive out the disease, and it will chase his daughter into the woods. No; let my children wait without, and if the spirit appears beat him down with clubs. He is cunning, and will bury himself in the mountain, when he sees how many are ready to fight him."

This singular warning had the desired effect. Instead of entering the cavern, the father and husband drew their tomahawks, and posted themselves in readiness to deal their vengeance on the imaginary tormentor of their sick relative, while the women and children broke branches from the bushes, or seized fragments of the rock, with a similar intention. At this favorable moment the counterfeit conjurers disappeared.

Hawkeye, at the same time that he had presumed so far on the nature of the Indian superstitions, was not ignorant that they were rather tolerated than relied on by the wisest of the chiefs. He well knew the value of time in the present emergency. Whatever might be the extent of the self-delusion of his enemies, and however it had tended to assist his schemes, the slightest cause of suspicion, acting on the subtle nature of an Indian, would be likely to prove fatal. Taking the path, therefore, that was most likely to avoid observation, he rather skirted than entered the village. The warriors were still to be seen in the distance, by the fading light of the fires, stalking from lodge to lodge. But the children had abandoned their sports for their beds of skins, and the quiet of night was already beginning to prevail over the turbulence and excitement of so busy and important an evening.

Alice revived under the renovating influence of the open air, and as her physical rather than her mental powers had been the subject of weakness, she stood in no need of any explanation of that which had occurred.

"Now let me make an effort to walk," she said, when they had entered the forest, blushing, though unseen, that she had not been sooner able to quit the arms of Duncan; "I am indeed restored."

"Nay, Alice, you are yet too weak."

The maiden struggled gently to release herself, and Heyward was compelled to part with his precious burden. The representative of the bear had certainly been an entire stranger to the delicious emotions of the lover while his arms encircled his mistress; and he was, perhaps, a stranger also to the nature of that feeling of ingenuous shame that oppressed the trembling Alice. But when he found himself at a suitable distance from the lodges he made a halt, and spoke on a subject of which he was thoroughly the master.

"This path will lead you to the brook," he said; "follow its northern bank until you come to a fall; and mount the hill on your right, and you will see the fires of the other people. There you must go and demand protection; if they are true Delawares, you will be safe. A distant flight with that gentle one, just now, is impossible. The Hurons would follow up our trail, and master our scalps, before we had got a dozen miles. Go, and Providence be with you."

"And you!" demanded Heyward, in surprise; "surely we part not here?"

"The Hurons hold the pride of the Delawares; the last of the high blood of the Mohicans is in their power," returned the scout; "I go to see what can be done in his favor. Had they mastered your scalp, major, a knave should have fallen for every hair it held, as I promised; but if the young Sagamore is to be led to the stake, the Indians shall see also how a man without a cross can die."

Not in the least offended with the decided preference that the sturdy woodsman gave to one who might, in some degree, be called the child of his adoption, Duncan still continued to urge such reasons against so desperate an effort as presented themselves. He was aided by Alice, who mingled her entreaties with those of Heyward that he would abandon a resolution that promised so much danger, with so little hope of success. Their eloquence and ingenuity were expended in vain. The scout heard them attentively, but impatiently, and finally closed the discussion, by answering, in a tone that instantly silenced Alice, while it told Heyward how fruitless any further remonstrances would be,—

"I have heard," he said, "that there is a feeling in youth which binds man to woman closer than the father is tied to the son. It may be so. I have seldom been where women of my color dwell; but such may be the gifts of natur' in the settlements. You have risked life, and all that is dear to you, to bring off this gentle one, and I suppose that some such disposition is at the bottom of it all. As for me, I taught the lad the real character of a rifle; and well has he paid me for it. I have fou't at his side in many a bloody scrimmage; and so long as I could hear the crack of his piece in one ear, and that of the Sagamore in the other, I knew no enemy was on my back. Winters and summers, nights and days, have we roved the wilderness in company, eating of the same dish, one sleeping while the other watched; and afore it shall be said that Uncas was taken to the torment, and I at hand— There is but a single Ruler of us all, whatever may be the color of the skin; and Him I call to witness, that before the Mohican boy shall perish for the want of a friend, good faith shall depart the 'arth, and 'Killdeer' become as harmless as the tooting we'pon of the singer!"

Duncan released his hold on the arm of the scout,

who turned, and steadily retraced his steps towards the lodges. After pausing a moment to gaze at his retiring form, the successful and yet sorrowful Heyward, and Alice, took their way together towards the distant village of the Delawares.

Cheif dismiss women, hey to cure squaw, bear growls, chief leaves in fright, bear removes own head, actually Hawk, Hawk says led Munro + ching to beaver lodge safety, says alice is in this cave, Hey tells alice they'll rescue, dreams of intimacy, Magua comes laughing. Hawk + hey capture him, Heg tells cheif he's taking squaw for cure herbs, says evil spirit in cave + Hurons should stave it off. If it tries to escape, in safe forest, Hawk sends alice + hey to Delaware camp + him to help Uncas

XXVI

"Bot.—Let me play the lion too."
A Midsummer Night's Dream[1]

NOTWITHSTANDING THE HIGH RESOLUTION of Hawk-eye, he fully comprehended all the difficulties and dangers he was about to incur. In his return to the camp, his acute and practised intellects were intently engaged in devising means to counteract a watchfulness and suspicion on the part of his enemies, that he knew were, in no degree, inferior to his own. Nothing but the color of his skin had saved the lives of Magua and the conjurer, who would have been the first victims sacrificed to his own security, had not the scout believed such an act, however congenial it might be to the nature of an Indian, utterly unworthy of one who boasted a descent from men that knew no cross of blood. Accordingly, he trusted to the withes and ligaments with which he had bound his captives, and pursued his way directly towards the centre of the lodges.

As he approached the buildings, his steps became more deliberate, and his vigilant eye suffered no sign, whether friendly or hostile, to escape him. A neglected hut was a little in advance of the others, and appeared as if it had been deserted when half completed—most probably on account of failing in some of the more important requisites; such as food or water. A faint light glimmered through its cracks, however, and announced that, notwithstanding its imperfect structure, it was not without a tenant. Thither, then, the scout proceeded, like a prudent general, who was about to feel the advanced positions of his enemy, before he hazarded the main attack.

Throwing himself into a suitable posture for the beast he represented, Hawkeye crawled to a little opening, where he might command a view of the interior. It proved to be the abiding-place of David Gamut. Hither the faithful singing-master had now brought himself, together with all his sorrows, his apprehensions, and his meek dependence on the protection of Providence. At the precise moment when his ungainly person came under the observation of the scout, in the manner just mentioned, the woodsman himself, though in his assumed character, was the subject of the solitary being's profoundest reflections.

However implicit the faith of David was in the performance of ancient miracles, he eschewed the belief of any direct supernatural agency in the management of modern morality. In other words, while he had implicit faith in the ability of Balaam's ass[2] to speak, he was somewhat skeptical on the subject of a bear's singing; and yet he had been assured of the latter, on the testimony of his own exquisite organs. There was something in his air and manner that betrayed to the scout the utter confusion of the state of his mind. He was seated on a pile of brush, a few twigs from which occasionally fed his low fire, with his head leaning on his arm, in a posture of melancholy musing. The costume of the votary of music had undergone no other alteration from that so lately described, except that he had covered his bald head with the triangular beaver, which had not proved sufficiently alluring to excite the cupidity of any of his captors.

The ingenious Hawkeye, who recalled the hasty manner in which the other had abandoned his post at the bedside of the sick woman, was not without his suspicions concerning the subject of so much solemn deliberation. First making the circuit of the hut, and ascertaining that it stood quite alone, and that the character of its inmate was likely to protect it from visitors, he ventured through its low door, into the very presence of Gamut. The position of the latter brought the fire between them; and when Hawkeye had seated himself on end, near a minute elapsed, during which the two remained regarding each other without speaking. The suddenness and the nature of the surprise had nearly proved too much for—we will not say the philosophy—but for the faith and resolution of David. He fumbled for his pitch-pipe, and arose with a confused intention of attempting a musical exorcism.

"Dark and mysterious monster!" he exclaimed, while with trembling hands he disposed of his auxiliary eyes, and sought his never-failing resource in trouble, the gifted version of the Psalms: "I know not your nature nor intents; but if aught you meditate against the person and rights of one of the humblest servants of the temple, listen to the inspired language of the youth of Israel, and repent."

The bear shook his shaggy sides, and then a well-known voice replied,—

"Put up the tooting we'pon, and teach your throat modesty. Five words of plain and comprehensible English are worth, just now, an hour of squalling."

"What art thou!" demanded David, utterly disqualified to pursue his original intention, and nearly gasping for breath.

"A man like yourself; and one whose blood is as little tainted by the cross of a bear, or an Indian, as your own. Have you so soon forgotten from whom you received the foolish instrument you hold in your hand?"

"Can these things be?" returned David, breathing more freely, as the truth began to dawn upon him. "I have found many marvels during my sojourn with the heathen, but surely nothing to excel this!"

"Come, come," returned Hawkeye, uncasing his honest countenance, the better to assure the wavering confidence of his companion; "you may see a skin, which, if it be not as white as one of the gentle ones, has no tinge of red to it that the winds of heaven and the sun have not bestowed. Now let us to business."

"First tell me of the maiden, and of the youth who so bravely sought her," interrupted David.

"Ay, they are happily freed from the tomahawks of these varlets. But can you put me on the scent of Uncas?"

"The young man is in bondage, and much I fear his death is decreed. I greatly mourn that one so well disposed should die in his ignorance, and I have sought a goodly hymn—"

"Can you lead me to him?"

"The task will not be difficult," returned David, hesitating; "though I greatly fear your presence would rather increase than mitigate his unhappy fortunes."

"No more words, but lead on," returned Hawkeye, concealing his face again, and setting the example in his own person, by instantly quitting the lodge.

As they proceeded, the scout ascertained that his companion found access to Uncas, under privilege of his imaginary infirmity, aided by the favor he had acquired with one of the guards, who, in consequence of speaking a little English, had been selected by David as the subject of a religious conversation. How far the Huron comprehended the intentions of his new friend, may well be doubted: but as exclusive attention is as flattering to a savage as to a more civilized individual, it had produced the effect we have mentioned. It is unnecessary to repeat the shrewd manner with which the scout extracted these particulars from the simple David; neither shall we dwell in this place on the nature of the instructions he delivered, when completely master of all the necessary facts; as the whole will be sufficiently explained to the reader in the course of the narrative.

The lodge in which Uncas was confined was in the very centre of the village, and in a situation, perhaps, more difficult than any other to approach, or leave, without observation. But it was not the policy of Hawkeye to affect the least concealment. Presuming on his disguise, and his ability to sustain the character he had assumed, he took the most plain and direct route to the place. The hour, however, afforded him some little of that protection which he appeared so much to despise. The boys were already buried in sleep, and all the women, and most of the warriors, had retired to their lodges for the night. Four or five of the latter only lingered about the door of the prison of Uncas, wary but close observers of the manner of their captive.

At the sight of Gamut, accompanied by one in the well-known masquerade of their most distinguished conjurer, they readily made way for them both. Still they betrayed no intention to depart. On the other hand, they were evidently disposed to remain bound to the place by an additional interest in the mysterious mummeries that they of course expected from such a visit.

From the total inability of the scout to address the Hurons in their own language, he was compelled to trust the conversation entirely to David. Notwithstanding the simplicity of the latter, he did ample justice to the instructions he had received, more than fulfilling the strongest hopes of his teacher.

"The Delawares are women!" he exclaimed, addressing himself to the savage who had a slight understanding of the language in which he spoke; "the Yengeese, my foolish countrymen, have told them to take up the tomahawk, and strike their fathers in the Canadas, and they have forgotten their sex. Does my brother wish to hear Le Cerf Agile ask for his petticoats, and see him weep before the Hurons, at the stake?"

The exclamation "Hugh!" delivered in a strong tone of assent, announced the gratification the savage would receive in witnessing such an exhibition of weakness in an enemy so long hated and so much feared.

"Then let him step aside, and the cunning man will blow upon the dog! Tell it to thy brothers."

The Huron explained the meaning of David to his fellows, who, in their turn, listened to the project with that sort of satisfaction that their untamed spirits might be expected to find in such a refinement in cruelty. They drew back a little from the entrance, and motioned to the supposed conjurer to enter. But the bear, instead of obeying, maintained the seat it had taken, and growled.

"The cunning man is afraid that his breath will blow upon his brothers, and take away their courage too," continued David, improving the hint he received; "they must stand farther off."

The Hurons, who would have deemed such a misfortune the heaviest calamity that could befall them, fell back in a body, taking a position where they were out of earshot, though at the same time they could command a view of the entrance to the lodge. Then, as if satisfied of their safety, the scout left his position, and slowly entered the place. It was silent and gloomy, being tenanted solely by the captive, and lighted by the dying embers of a fire, which had been used for the purposes of cookery.

Uncas occupied a distant corner, in a reclining attitude, being rigidly bound, both hands and feet, by strong and painful withes. When the frightful object first presented itself to the young Mohican, he did not deign to bestow a single glance on the animal. The scout, who had left David at the door, to ascertain they were not observed, thought it prudent to preserve his disguise until assured of their privacy. Instead of speaking, therefore, he exerted himself to enact one of the antics of the animal he represented. The young Mohican, who at first believed his enemies had sent in a real beast to torment him, and try his nerves, detected, in those performances that to Heyward had appeared so accurate, certain blemishes, that at once betrayed the counterfeit. Had Hawkeye been aware of the low estimation in which the more skilful Uncas held his representations, he would probably have prolonged the entertainment a little in pique. But the scornful expression of the young man's eye admitted to so many constructions, that the worthy scout was spared the mortification of such a discovery. As soon, therefore, as David gave the preconcerted signal, a low hissing sound was heard in the lodge, in place of the fierce growlings of the bear.

Uncas had cast his body back against the wall of the hut, and closed his eyes, as if willing to exclude so contemptible and disagreeable an object from his sight. But the moment the noise of the serpent was heard, he arose, and cast his looks on each side of him, bending his head low, and turning it inquiringly in every direction, until his keen eye rested on the shaggy monster, where it remained riveted, as though fixed by the power of a charm. Again the same sounds were repeated, evidently proceeding from the mouth of the beast. Once more the eyes of the youth roamed over the interior of the lodge, and returning to their former resting place, he uttered, in a deep, suppressed voice,—

"Hawkeye!"

"Cut his bands," said Hawkeye to David, who just then approached them.

The singer did as he was ordered, and Uncas found his limbs released. At the same moment the dried skin of the animal rattled, and presently the scout arose to his feet, in proper person. The Mohican appeared to comprehend the nature of the attempt his friend had made, intuitively; neither tongue nor feature betraying another symptom of surprise. When Hawkeye had cast his shaggy vestment, which was done by simply loosing certain thongs of skin, he drew a long glittering knife, and put it in the hands of Uncas.

"The red Hurons are without," he said; "let us be ready."

At the same time he laid his finger significantly on another similar weapon, both being the fruits of his prowess among their enemies during the evening.

"We will go," said Uncas.

"Whither?"

"To the Tortoises; they are the children of my grandfathers."

"Ay, lad," said the scout in English—a language he was apt to use when a little abstracted in mind; "the same blood runs in your veins, I believe; but time and distance have a little changed its color. What shall we do with the Mingos at the door? They count six, and this singer is as good as nothing."

"The Hurons are boasters," said Uncas scornfully; "their 'totem' is a moose, and they run like snails. The Delawares are children of the tortoise, and they outstrip the deer."

"Ay, lad, there is truth in what you say; and I doubt not, on a rush, you would pass the whole nation; and, in a straight race of two miles, would be in, and get your breath again, afore a knave of them all was within hearing of the other village. But the gift of a white man lies more in his arms than in his legs. As for myself, I can brain a Huron as well as a better man; but when it comes to a race, the knaves would prove too much for me."

Uncas, who had already approached the door, in readiness to lead the way, now recoiled; and placed himself, once more, in the bottom of the lodge. But Hawkeye, who was too much occupied with his own thoughts to note the movement, continued speaking more to himself than to his companion.

"After all," he said, "it is unreasonable to keep one man in bondage to the gifts of another. So, Uncas, you had better take the leap, while I put on the skin again, and trust to cunning for want of speed."

The young Mohican made no reply, but quietly folded his arms, and leaned his body against one of the upright posts that supported the wall of the hut.

"Well," said the scout, looking up at him, "why do you tarry? There will be time enough for me, as the knaves will give chase to you at first."

"Uncas will stay," was the calm reply.

"For what?"

"To fight with his father's brother, and die with the friend of the Delawares."

"Ay, lad," returned Hawkeye, squeezing the hand of Uncas between his own iron fingers; " 'twould have been more like a Mingo than a Mohican had you left me. But I thought I would make the offer, seeing that youth commonly loves life. Well, what can't be done by main courage, in war, must be done by circumvention. Put on the skin; I doubt not you can play the bear nearly as well as myself."

Whatever might have been the private opinion of Uncas of their respective abilities in this particular, his grave countenance manifested no opinion of his own superiority. He silently and expeditiously encased himself in the covering of the beast, and then awaited such other movements as his more aged companion saw fit to dictate.

"Now, friend," said Hawkeye, addressing David, "an exchange of garments will be a great convenience to you, inasmuch as you are but little accustomed to the makeshifts of the wilderness. Here, take my hunting shirt and cap, and give me your blanket and hat. You must trust me with the book and spectacles, as well as the tooter, too; if we ever meet again, in better times, you shall have all back again, with many thanks into the bargain."

David parted with the several articles named with a readiness that would have done great credit to his liberality, had he not certainly profited, in many particulars, by the exchange. Hawkeye was not long in assuming his borrowed garments; and when his restless eyes were hid behind the glasses, and his head was surmounted by the triangular beaver, as their statures were not dissimilar, he might readily have passed for the singer by starlight. As soon as these dispositions were made, the scout turned to David, and gave him his parting instructions.

"Are you much given to cowardice?" he bluntly asked, by way of obtaining a suitable understanding of the whole case before he ventured a prescription.

"My pursuits are peaceful, and my temper, I humbly trust, is greatly given to mercy and love," returned David, a little nettled at so direct an attack on his manhood; "but there are none who can say that I have ever forgotten my faith in the Lord, even in the greatest straits."

"Your chiefest danger will be at the moment when the savages find out that they have been deceived. If you are not then knocked in the head, your being a non-composser will protect you; and you'll then have good reason to expect to die in your bed. If you stay, it must be to sit down here in the shadow, and take the part of Uncas, until such times as the cunning of the Indians discover the cheat, when, as I have already said, your time of trial will come. So choose for yourself,—to make a rush or tarry here."

"Even so," said David, firmly; "I will abide in the place

of the Delaware. Bravely and generously has he battled in my behalf; and this, and more, will I dare in his service."

"You have spoken as a man, and like one who, under wiser schooling, would have been brought to better things. Hold your head down, and draw in your legs; their formation might tell the truth too early. Keep silent as long as may be; and it would be wise, when you do speak, to break out suddenly in one of your shoutings, which will serve to remind the Indians that you are not altogether as responsible as men should be. If, however, they take your scalp, as I trust and believe they will not, depend on it, Uncas and I will not forget the deed, but revenge it as becomes true warriors and trusty friends."

"Hold!" said David, perceiving that with this assurance they were about to leave him; "I am an unworthy and humble follower of One who taught not the damnable principle of revenge. Should I fall, therefore, seek no victims to my *manes*, but rather forgive my destroyers; and if you remember them at all, let it be in prayers for the enlightening of their minds, and for their eternal welfare."

The scout hesitated, and appeared to muse.

"There is a principle in that," he said, "different from the law of the woods; and yet it is fair and noble to reflect upon." Then, heaving a heavy sigh, probably among the last he ever drew in pining for a condition he had so long abandoned, he added, "It is what I would wish to practise, myself, as one without a cross of blood, though it is not always easy to deal with an Indian as you would with a fellow Christian. God bless you, friend; I do believe your scent is not greatly wrong, when the matter is duly considered, and keeping eternity before the eyes, though much depends on the natural gifts, and the force of temptation."

So saying, the scout returned and shook David cordially by the hand; after which act of friendship he immediately left the lodge, attended by the new representative of the beast.

The instant Hawkeye found himself under the observation of the Hurons, he drew up his tall form in the rigid manner of David, threw out his arm in the act of keeping time, and commenced what he intended for an imitation of his psalmody. Happily for the success of this delicate adventure, he had to deal with ears but little practised in the concord of sweet sounds, or the miserable effort would infallibly have been detected. It was necessary to pass within a dangerous proximity of the dark group of the savages, and the voice of the scout grew louder as they drew nigher. When at the nearest point, the Huron who spoke the English thrust out an arm, and stopped the supposed singing-master.

"The Delaware dog!" he said, leaning forward, and peering through the dim light to catch the expression of the other's features; "is he afraid? will the Hurons hear his groans?"

A growl so exceedingly fierce and natural proceeded from the beast, that the young Indian released his hold and started aside, as if to assure himself that it was not a veritable bear, and no counterfeit, that was rolling before him. Hawkeye, who feared his voice would betray him to his subtle enemies, gladly profited by the interruption, to break out anew in such a burst of musical expression as would, probably, in a more refined state of society have been termed "a grand crash." Among his actual auditors, however, it merely gave him an additional claim to that respect which they never withhold from such as are believed to be the subjects of mental alienation. The little knot of Indians drew back in a body, and suffered, as they thought, the conjurer and his inspired assistant to proceed.

It required no common exercise of fortitude in Uncas and the scout, to continue the dignified and deliberate pace they had assumed in passing the lodges; especially as they immediately perceived that curiosity had so far mastered fear, as to induce the watchers to approach the hut, in order to witness the effect of the incantations. The least injudicious or impatient movement on the part of David might betray them, and time was absolutely necessary to insure the safety of the scout. The loud noise the latter conceived it politic to continue, drew many curious gazers to the doors of the different huts as they passed; and once or twice a dark-looking warrior stepped across their path, led to the act by superstition or watchfulness. They were not, however, interrupted; the darkness of the hour, and the coldness of the attempt, proving their principal friends.

The adventurers had got clear of the village, and were now swiftly approaching the shelter of the woods, when a loud and long cry arose from the lodge where Uncas had been confined. The Mohican started on his feet, and shook his shaggy covering, as though the animal he counterfeited was about to make some desperate effort.

"Hold!" said the scout, grasping his friend by the shoulder, "let them yell again! 'Twas nothing but wonderment."

He had no occasion to delay, for the next instant a burst of cries filled the outer air, and ran along the whole extent of the village. Uncas cast his skin, and stepped forth in his own beautiful proportions. Hawkeye tapped him lightly on the shoulder, and glided ahead.

"Now let the devils strike our scent!" said the scout, tearing two rifles, with all their attendant accoutrements, from beneath a bush, and flourishing "Killdeer" as he handed Uncas his weapon; "two, at least, will find it to their deaths."

Then throwing their pieces to a low trail, like sportsmen in readiness for their game, they dashed forward, and were soon buried in the sombre darkness of the forest.

Hawk to camp, gamut scared by bear mask
to main lodge for uncas, uncas hawk + gamut
trade clothes, hawk + uncas to woods, loud cry,
Hurons discover them, think singing will again
save gamut, hawk gets guns + to delaware

XXVII

"Ant. I shall remember:
When Cæsar says Do this, it is performed."
Julius Cæsar[1]

THE IMPATIENCE OF THE SAVAGES who lingered about the prison of Uncas, as has been seen, had overcome their dread of the conjurer's breath. They stole cautiously, and with beating hearts, to a crevice, through which the faint light of the fire was glimmering. For several minutes they mistook the form of David for that of their prisoner; but the very accident which Hawkeye had foreseen occurred. Tired of keeping the extremities of his long person so near together, the singer gradually suffered the lower limbs to extend themselves, until one of his misshapen feet actually came in contact with and shoved aside the embers of the fire. At first the Hurons believed the Delaware had been thus deformed by witchcraft. But when David, unconscious of being observed, turned his head, and exposed his simple, mild countenance, in place of the haughty lineaments of their prisoner, it would have exceeded the credulity of even a native to have doubted any longer. They rushed together into the lodge, and laying their hands, with but little ceremony, on their captive, immediately detected the impo-

sition. Then arose the cry first heard by the fugitives. It
was succeeded by the most frantic and angry demonstrations of vengeance. David, however firm in his determination to cover the retreat of his friends, was compelled
to believe that his own final hour had come. Deprived of
his book and his pipe, he was fain to trust to a memory
that rarely failed him on such subjects; and breaking
forth in a loud and impassioned strain, he endeavored to
soothe his passage into the other world by singing the
opening verse of a funeral anthem. The Indians were
seasonably reminded of his infirmity, and rushing into
the open air, they aroused the village in the manner described.

A native warrior fights as he sleeps, without the protection of anything defensive. The sounds of the alarm
were, therefore, hardly uttered, before two hundred
men were afoot, and ready for the battle or the chase, as
either might be required. The escape was soon known;
and the whole tribe crowded, in a body, around the
council-lodge, impatiently awaiting the instruction of
their chiefs. In such a sudden demand on their wisdom,
the presence of the cunning Magua could scarcely fail of
being needed. His name was mentioned, and all looked
round in wonder that he did not appear. Messengers
were then despatched to his lodge, requiring his presence.

In the meantime, some of the swiftest and most discreet of the young men were ordered to make the circuit
of the clearing, under cover of the woods, in order to ascertain that their suspected neighbors, the Delawares,
designed no mischief. Women and children ran to and
fro; and in short, the whole encampment exhibited another scene of wild and savage confusion. Gradually,

however, these symptoms of disorder diminished; and in a few minutes the oldest and most distinguished chiefs were assembled in the lodge, in grave consultation.

The clamor of many voices soon announced that a party approached, who might be expected to communicate some intelligence that would explain the mystery of the novel surprise. The crowd without gave way, and several warriors entered the place, bringing with them the hapless conjurer, who had been left so long by the scout in duress.

Notwithstanding this man was held in very unequal estimation among the Hurons, some believing implicity in his power, and others deeming him an impostor, he was now listened to by all with the deepest attention. When his brief story was ended, the father of the sick woman stepped forth, and, in a few pithy expressions, related, in his turn, what he knew. These two narratives gave a proper direction to the subsequent inquiries, which were now made with the characteristic cunning of savages.

Instead of rushing in a confused and disorderly throng to the cavern, ten of the wisest and firmest among the chiefs were selected to prosecute the investigation. As no time was to be lost, the instant the choice was made the individuals appointed rose in a body, and left the place without speaking. On reaching the entrance, the younger men in advance made way for their seniors; and the whole proceeded along the low, dark gallery, with the firmness of warriors ready to devote themselves to the public good, though, at the same time, secretly doubting the nature of the power with which they were about to contend.

The outer apartment of the cavern was silent and

gloomy. The woman lay in her usual place and posture, though there were those present who affirmed they had seen her borne to the woods, by the supposed "medicine of the white men." Such a direct and palpable contradiction of the tale related by the father, caused all eyes to be turned on him. Chafed by the silent imputation, and inwardly troubled by so unaccountable a circumstance, the chief advanced to the side of the bed, and stooping, cast an incredulous look at the features, as if distrusting their reality. His daughter was dead.

The unerring feeling of nature for a moment prevailed, and the old warrior hid his eyes in sorrow. Then recovering his self-possession, he faced his companions, and pointing towards the corpse, he said, in the language of his people,—

"The wife of my young man has left us! the Great Spirit is angry with his children."

The mournful intelligence was received in solemn silence. After a short pause, one of the elder Indians was about to speak, when a dark-looking object was seen rolling out of an adjoining apartment, into the very centre of the room where they stood. Ignorant of the nature of the beings they had to deal with, the whole party drew back a little, and gazed in admiration, until the object fronted the light, and rising on end, exhibited the distorted, but still fierce and sullen features of Magua. The discovery was succeeded by a general exclamation of amazement.

As soon, however, as the true situation of the chief was understood, several ready knives appeared, and his limbs and tongue were quickly released. The Huron arose, and shook himself like a lion quitting his lair. Not a word escaped him, though his hand played convulsively with the handle of his knife, while his lowering eyes scanned the whole party, as if they sought an object suited to the first burst of his vengeance.

It was happy for Uncas and the scout, and even David, that they were all beyond the reach of his arm at such a moment; for, assuredly, no refinement in cruelty would then have deferred their deaths, in opposition to the promptings of the fierce temper that nearly choked him. Meeting everywhere faces that he knew as friends, the savage grated his teeth together like rasps of iron, and swallowed his passion for want of a victim on whom to vent it. This exhibition of anger was noted by all present; and, from an apprehension of exasperating a temper that was already chafed nearly to madness, several minutes were suffered to pass before another word was uttered. When, however, suitable time had elapsed, the oldest of the party spoke.

"My friend has found an enemy," he said. "Is he nigh, that the Hurons may take revenge?"

"Let the Delaware die!" exclaimed Magua, in a voice of thunder.

Another long and expressive silence was observed, and was broken, as before, with due precaution, by the same individual.

"The Mohican is swift of foot, and leaps far," he said; "but my young men are on his trail."

"Is he gone?" demanded Magua, in tones so deep and guttural, that they seemed to proceed from his inmost chest.

"An evil spirit has been among us, and the Delaware has blinded our eyes."

"An evil spirit!" repeated the other, mockingly; " 'tis the spirit that has taken the lives of so many Hurons; the spirit that slew my young men at 'the tumbling river'; that took their scalps at the 'healing spring'; and who has now bound the arms of Le Renard Subtil!"

"Of whom does my friend speak?"

"Of the dog who carried the heart and cunning of a Huron under a pale skin—La Longue Carabine."

The pronunciation of so terrible a name produced the usual effect among his auditors. But when time was given for reflection, and the warriors remembered that their formidable and daring enemy had even been in the bosom of their encampment, working injury, fearful rage took the place of wonder, and all those fierce passions with which the bosom of Magua had just been struggling were suddenly transferred to his companions. Some among them gnashed their teeth in anger, others vented their feelings in yells, and some, again, beat the air as frantically as if the object of their resentment were suffering under their blows. But this sudden outbreaking of temper as quickly subsided in the still and sullen restraint they most affected, in their moments of inaction.

Magua, who had in his turn found leisure for reflection, now changed his manner, and assumed the air of one who knew how to think and act with a dignity worthy of so grave a subject.

"Let us go to my people," he said; "they wait for us."

His companions consented in silence, and the whole of the savage party left the cavern and returned to the council-lodge. When they were seated, all eyes turned on Magua, who understood, from such an indication, that, by common consent, they had devolved the duty of relating what had passed on him. He arose, and told his tale without duplicity or reservation. The whole deception practised by both Duncan and Hawkeye was, of course, laid naked; and no room was found, even for the most superstitious of the tribe, any longer to affix a doubt on the character of the occurrences. It was but too apparent that they had been insultingly, shamefully, disgracefully deceived. When he had ended, and resumed his seat, the collected tribe—for his auditors, in substance, included all the fighting men of the party—sat regarding each other like men astonished equally at the audacity and the success of their enemies. The next consideration, however, was the means and opportunities for revenge.

Additional pursuers were sent on the trail of the fugitives; and then the chiefs applied themselves, in earnest, to the business of consultation. Many different expedients were proposed by the elder warriors, in succession, to all of which Magua was a silent and respectful listener. That subtle savage had recovered his artifice and self-command, and now proceeded towards his object with his customary caution and skill. It was only when each one disposed to speak had uttered his sentiments, that he prepared to advance his own opinions. They were given with additional weight from the circumstance that some of the runners had already returned, and reported that their enemies had been traced so far as to leave no doubt of their having sought safety in the neighboring camp of their suspected allies, the Delawares. With the advantage of possessing this important intelligence, the chief warily laid his plans before his fellows, and, as might have been anticipated from his eloquence and cunning, they were adopted without a dissenting voice. They were, briefly, as follows, both in opinions and in motives.

It has been already stated that, in obedience to a policy rarely departed from, the sisters were separated so soon as they reached the Huron village. Magua had early discovered that in retaining the person of Alice, he possessed the most effectual check on Cora. When they parted, therefore, he kept the former within reach of his hand, consigning the one he most valued to the keeping of their allies. The arrangement was understood to be merely temporary, and was made as much with a view to flatter his neighbors as in obedience to the invariable rule of Indian policy.

While goaded incessantly by those revengeful impulses that in a savage seldom slumber, the chief was still attentive to his more permanent personal interests. The follies and disloyalty committed in his youth were to be expiated by a long and painful penance, ere he could be restored to the full enjoyment of the confidence of his ancient people; and without confidence, there could be no authority in an Indian tribe. In this delicate and arduous situation, the crafty native had neglected no means of increasing his influence; and one of the happiest of his expedients had been the success with which he had cultivated the favor of their powerful and dangerous neighbors. The result of his experiment had answered all the expectations of his policy; for the Hurons were in no degree exempt from that governing principle of nature, which induces man to value his gifts precisely in the degree that they are appreciated by others.

But, while he was making this ostensible sacrifice to general considerations, Magua never lost sight of his individual motives. The latter had been frustrated by the unlooked-for events which had placed all his prisoners beyond his control; and he now found himself reduced to the necessity of suing for favors to those whom it had so lately been his policy to oblige.

Several of the chiefs had proposed deep and treacherous schemes to surprise the Delawares, and, by gaining possession of their camp, to recover their prisoners by the same blow; for all agreed that their honor, their interests, and the peace and happiness of their dead countrymen, imperiously required them speedily to immolate some victims to their revenge. But plans so dangerous to attempt, and of such doubtful issue, Magua found little difficulty in defeating. He exposed their risk and fallacy with his usual skill; and it was only after he had removed every impediment, in the shape of opposing advice, that he ventured to propose his own projects.

He commenced by flattering the self-love of his auditors; a never-failing method of commanding attention. When he had enumerated the many different occasions on which the Hurons had exhibited their courage and prowess, in the punishment of insults, he digressed in a high encomium on the virtue of wisdom. He painted the quality, as forming the great point of difference between the beaver and other brutes; between brutes and men; and finally, between the Hurons, in particular, and the rest of the human race. After he had sufficiently extolled the property of discretion, he undertook to exhibit in what manner its use was applicable to the present situation of their tribe. On the one hand, he said, was their great pale father, the governor of the Canadas, who had looked upon his children with a hard eye since their tomahawks had been so red; on the other, a people as numerous as themselves, who spoke a different language, possessed different interests, and loved them not, and who would be glad of any pretence to bring them in disgrace with the great white chief. Then he spoke of their necessities; of the gifts they had a right to expect for their past services; of their distance from their proper hunting-grounds and native villages; and of the necessity of consulting prudence more, and inclination less, in so critical circumstances. When he perceived that, while the old men applauded his moderation, many of the fiercest and most distinguished of the warriors listened to these politic plans with lowering looks, he cunningly led them back to the subject which they most loved. He spoke openly of the fruits of their wisdom, which he boldly pronounced would be a complete and final triumph over their enemies. He even darkly hinted that their success might be extended, with proper caution, in such a manner as to include the destruction of all whom they had reason to hate. In short, he so blended the warlike with the artful, the obvious with the obscure, as to flatter the propensities of both parties, and to leave to each subject of hope, while neither could say it clearly comprehended his intentions.

The orator, or the politician, who can produce such a state of things, is commonly popular with his contemporaries, however he may be treated by posterity. All perceived that more was meant than was uttered, and each one believed that the hidden meaning was precisely such as his own faculties enabled him to understand, or his own wishes led him to anticipate.

In this happy state of things, it is not surprising that the management of Magua prevailed. The tribe consented to act with deliberation, and with one voice they committed the direction of the whole affair to the government of the chief who had suggested such wise and intelligible expedients.

Magua had now attained one great object of all his cunning and enterprise. The ground he had lost in the favor of his people was completely regained, and he found himself even placed at the head of affairs. He was, in truth, their ruler; and, so long as he could maintain his popularity, no monarch could be more despotic, especially while the tribe continued in a hostile country. Throwing off, therefore, the appearance of consultation, he assumed the grave air of authority necessary to support the dignity of his office.

Runners were despatched for intelligence in different directions; spies were ordered to approach and feel the encampment of the Delawares; the warriors were dismissed to their lodges, with an intimation that their services would soon be needed; and the women and children were ordered to retire, with a warning that it was their province to be silent. When these several arrangements were made, Magua passed through the village, stopping here and there to pay a visit where he thought his presence might be flattering to the individual. He confirmed his friends in their confidence, fixed the wavering, and gratified all. Then he sought his own lodge. The wife the Huron chief had abandoned, when he was chased from among his people, was dead. Children he had none; and he now occupied a hut, without companion of any sort. It was, in fact, the dilapidated and solitary structure in which David had been discovered, and whom he had tolerated in his presence, on those few occasions when they met, with the contemptuous indifference of a haughty superiority.

Hither, then, Magua retired, when his labors of policy were ended. While others slept, however, he neither knew nor sought repose. Had there been one sufficiently curious to have watched the movements of the newly elected chief, he would have seen him seated in a corner of his lodge, musing on the subject of his future plans, from the hour of his retirement to the time he had appointed for the warriors to assemble again. Occasionally the air breathed through the crevices of the hut, and the low flames that fluttered about the embers of the fire threw their wavering light on the person of the sullen recluse. At such moments it would not have been difficult to have fancied the dusky savage the Prince of Darkness, brooding on his own fancied wrongs, and plotting evil.

Long before the day dawned, however, warrior after warrior entered the solitary hut of Magua, until they had collected to the number of twenty. Each bore his rifle, and all the other accoutrements of war, though the paint was uniformly peaceful. The entrance of these fierce-looking beings was unnoticed; some seating themselves in the shadows of the place, and others standing like motionless statues, until the whole of the designated band was collected.

Then Magua arose and gave the signal to proceed, marching himself in advance. They followed their leader singly, and in that well-known order which has obtained the distinguishing appellation of "Indian file." Unlike other men engaged in the spirit-stirring business of war, they stole from their camp unostentatiously and unobserved, resembling a band of gliding spectres, more than warriors seeking the bubble reputation by deeds of desperate daring.

Instead of taking the path which led directly towards

the camp of the Delawares, Magua led his party for some distance down the windings of the stream, and along the little artificial lake of the beavers. The day began to dawn as they entered the clearing which had been formed by those sagacious and industrious animals. Though Magua, who had resumed his ancient garb, bore the outline of a fox on the dressed skin which formed his robe, there was one chief of his party who carried the beaver as his peculiar symbol, or "totem." There would have been a species of profanity in the omission, had this man passed so powerful a community of his fancied kindred, without bestowing some evidence of his regard. Accordingly, he paused, and spoke in words as kind and friendly as if he were addressing more intelligent beings. He called the animals his cousins, and reminded them that his protecting influence was the reason they remained unharmed, while so many avaricious traders were prompting the Indians to take their lives. He promised a continuance of his favors, and admonished them to be grateful. After which, he spoke of the expedition in which he was himself engaged, and intimated, though with sufficient delicacy and circumlocution, the expediency of bestowing on their relative a portion of that wisdom for which they were so renowned.

During the utterance of this extraordinary address, the companions of the speaker were as grave and as attentive to his language as though they were all equally impressed with its propriety. Once or twice black objects were seen rising to the surface of the water, and the Huron expressed pleasure, conceiving that his words were not bestowed in vain. Just as he had ended his address, the head of a large beaver was thrust from the door of a lodge, whose earthen walls had been much injured, and which the party had believed, from its situation, to be uninhabited. Such an extraordinary sign of confidence was received by the orator as a highly favorable omen; and though the animal retreated a little precipitately, he was lavish of his thanks and commendations.

When Magua thought sufficient time had been lost in gratifying the family affection of the warrior, he again made the signal to proceed. As the Indians moved away in a body, and with a step that would have been inaudible to the ears of any common man, the same venerable-looking beaver once more ventured his head from its cover. Had any of the Hurons turned to look behind them, they would have seen the animal watching their movements with an interest and sagacity that might easily have been mistaken for reason. Indeed, so very distinct and intelligible were the devices of the quadruped, that even the most experienced observer would have been at a loss to account for its actions, until the moment when the party entered the forest, when the whole would have been explained, by seeing the entire animal issue from the lodge, uncasing, by the act, the grave features of Chingachgook from his mask of fur.

Hurons get Gamut, he sings, they draw back, they find sick dead woman w/ tied Magua, he says how hawk tricked them, Magua says caution, named leader, to Delaware camp; beaver cheif talks to beavers @ pond, big bear comes out, cheif happy, actvally ching after cheif leaves

XXVIII

"Brief, I pray you; for you see, 'tis a busy time with me."
Much Ado about Nothing[1]

THE TRIBE, or rather half tribe, of Delawares, which has been so often mentioned, and whose present place of encampment was so nigh the temporary village of the Hurons, could assemble about an equal number of warriors with the latter people. Like their neighbors, they had followed Montcalm into the territories of the English crown, and were making heavy and serious inroads on the hunting-grounds of the Mohawks; though they had seen fit, with the mysterious reserve so common among the natives, to withhold their assistance at the moment when it was most required. The French had accounted for this unexpected defection on the part of their ally in various ways. It was the prevalent opinion, however, that they had been influenced by veneration for the ancient treaty, that had once made them dependent on the Six Nations for military protection, and now rendered them reluctant to encounter their former masters. As for the tribe itself, it had been content to announce to Montcalm, through his emissaries, with Indian brevity, that their hatchets were dull, and time was necessary to sharpen them. The politic captain of the

Canadas had deemed it wiser to submit to entertain a passive friend, than by any acts of ill-judged severity to convert him into an open enemy.

On that morning when Magua led his silent party from the settlement of the beavers into the forest, in the manner described, the sun rose upon the Delaware encampment as if it had suddenly burst upon a busy people, actively employed in all the customary avocations of high noon. The women ran from lodge to lodge, some engaged in preparing their morning's meal, a few earnestly bent on seeking the comforts necessary to their habits, but more pausing to exchange hasty and whispered sentences with their friends. The warriors were lounging in groups, musing more than they conversed; and when a few words were uttered, speaking like men who deeply weighed their opinions. The instruments of the chase were to be seen in abundance among the lodges; but none departed. Here and there a warrior was examining his arms, with an attention that is rarely bestowed on the implements, when no other enemy than the beasts of the forest is expected to be encountered. And, occasionally, the eyes of a whole group were turned simultaneously towards a large and silent lodge in the centre of the village, as if it contained the subject of their common thoughts.

During the existence of this scene, a man suddenly appeared at the farthest extremity of a platform of rock which formed the level of the village. He was without arms, and his paint tended rather to soften than increase the natural sternness of his austere countenance. When in full view of the Delawares he stopped, and made a gesture of amity, by throwing his arm upward towards heaven, and then letting it fall impressively on his breast.

The inhabitants of the village answered his salute by a low murmur of welcome, and encouraged him to advance by similar indications of friendship. Fortified by these assurances, the dark figure left the brow of the natural rocky terrace, where it had stood a moment, drawn in a strong outline against the blushing morning sky, and moved with dignity into the very centre of the huts. As he approached, nothing was audible but the rattling of the light silver ornaments that loaded his arms and neck, and the tinkling of the little bells that fringed his deer-skin moccasins. He made, as he advanced, many courteous signs of greeting to the men he passed, neglecting to notice the women, however, like one who deemed their favor, in the present enterprise, of no importance. When he had reached the group in which it was evident, by the haughtiness of their common mien, that the principal chiefs were collected, the stranger paused, and then the Delawares saw that the active and erect form that stood before them was that of the well-known Huron chief, Le Renard Subtil.

His reception was grave, silent, and wary. The warriors in front stepped aside, opening the way to their most approved orator by the action; one who spoke all those languages that were cultivated among the northern aborigines.

"The wise Huron is welcome," said the Delaware, in the language of the Maquas; "he is come to eat his 'succotash,' with his brothers of the lakes."

"He is come," repeated Magua, bending his head with the dignity of an Eastern prince.

The chief extended his arm, and taking the other by the wrist, they once more exchanged friendly salutations. Then the Delaware invited his guest to enter his own lodge, and share his morning meal. The invitation was accepted; and the two warriors, attended by three or four of the old men, walked calmly away, leaving the rest of the tribe devoured by a desire to understand the reasons of so unusual a visit, and yet not betraying the least impatience by sign or word.

During the short and frugal repast that followed, the conversation was extremely circumspect, and related entirely to the events of the hunt in which Magua had so lately been engaged. It would have been impossible for the most finished breeding to wear more of the appearance of considering the visit as a matter of course, than did his hosts, notwithstanding every individual present was perfectly aware that it must be connected with some secret object, and that probably of importance to themselves. When the appetites of the whole were appeased, the squaws removed the trenchers and gourd, and the two parties began to prepare themselves for a subtle trial of their wits.

"Is the face of my great Canada father turned again towards his Huron children?" demanded the orator of the Delawares.

"When was it ever otherwise?" returned Magua. "He calls my people 'most beloved.' "

The Delaware gravely bowed his acquiescence to what he knew to be false, and continued,—

"The tomahawks of your young men have been very red."

"It is so; but they are now bright and dull; for the Yengeese are dead, and the Delawares are our neighbors."

The other acknowledged the pacific compliment by a gesture of the hand, and remained silent. Then Magua, as if recalled to such a recollection, by the allusion to the massacre, demanded,—

"Does my prisoner give trouble to my brothers?"

"She is welcome."

"The path between the Hurons and the Delawares is short, and it is open; let her be sent to my squaws, if she gives trouble to my brother."

"She is welcome," returned the chief of the latter nation, still more emphatically.

The baffled Magua continued silent several minutes, apparently indifferent, however, to the repulse he had received in this his open effort to gain possession of Cora.

"Do my young men leave the Delawares room on the mountains for their hunts?" he at length continued.

"The Lenape are rulers of their own hills," returned the other, a little haughtily.

"It is well. Justice is the master of a redskin! Why should they brighten their tomahawks, and sharpen their knives against each other? Are not the pale-faces thicker than the swallows in the season of flowers?"

"Good!" exclaimed two or three of his auditors at the same time.

Magua waited a little, to permit his words to soften the feelings of the Delawares, before he added,—

"Have there not been strange moccasins in the woods? Have not my brothers scented the feet of white men?"

"Let my Canada father come," returned the other evasively; "his children are ready to see him."

"When the great chief comes, it is to smoke with the Indians in their wigwams. The Hurons say, too, he is welcome. But the Yengeese have long arms, and legs that never tire! My young men dreamed they had seen the trail of the Yengeese nigh the village of the Delawares?"

"They will not find the Lenape asleep."

"It is well. The warrior whose eye is open can see his enemy," said Magua, once more shifting his ground, when he found himself unable to penetrate the caution of his companion. "I have brought gifts to my brother. His nation would not go on the war-path because they did not think it well; but their friends have remembered where they lived."

When he had thus announced his liberal intention, the crafty chief arose, and gravely spread his presents before the dazzled eyes of his hosts. They consisted principally of trinkets of little value, plundered from the slaughtered females of William Henry. In the division of the baubles the cunning Huron discovered no less art than in their selection. While he bestowed those of greater value on the two most distinguished warriors, one of whom was his host, he seasoned his offerings to their inferiors with such well-timed and apposite compliments, as left them no grounds of complaint. In short, the whole ceremony contained such a happy blending of the profitable with the flattering, that it was not difficult for the donor immediately to read the effect of a generosity so aptly mingled with praise, in the eyes of those he addressed.

This well-judged and politic stroke on the part of Magua was not without instantaneous results. The Delawares lost their gravity in a much more cordial expression; and the host, in particular, after contemplating his own liberal share of the spoil for some moments with peculiar gratification, repeated with strong emphasis, the words,—

"My brother is a wise chief. He is welcome!"

"The Hurons love their friends the Delawares," returned Magua. "Why should they not? they are colored by the same sun, and their just men will hunt in the same grounds after death. The redskins should be friends, and look with open eyes on the white men. Has not my brother scented spies in the woods?"

The Delaware, whose name in English signified "Hard Heart," an appellation that the French had translated into "Le Cœur-dur," forgot the obduracy of purpose, which had probably obtained him so significant a title. His countenance grew very sensibly less stern, and now deigned to answer more directly.

"There have been strange moccasins about my camp. They have been tracked into my lodges."

"Did my brother beat out the dogs?" asked Magua, without adverting in any manner to the former equivocation of the chief.

"It would not do. The stranger is always welcome to the children of the Lenape."

"The stranger, but not the spy."

"Would the Yengeese send their women as spies? Did not the Huron chief say he took women in the battle?"

"He told no lie. The Yengeese have sent out their scouts. They have been in my wigwams, but they found there no one to say welcome. Then they fled to the Delawares—for, say they, the Delawares are our friends; their minds are turned from their Canada father!"

This insinuation was a home thrust, and one that in a more advanced state of society, would have entitled Magua to the reputation of a skilful diplomatist. The recent defection of the tribe had, as they well knew themselves, subjected the Delawares to much reproach among their French allies; and they were now made to feel that their future actions were to be regarded with jealousy and distrust. There was no deep insight into causes and effects necessary to foresee that such a situation of things was likely to prove highly prejudicial to their future movements. Their distant villages, their hunting-grounds, and hundreds of their women and children, together with a material part of their physical force, were actually within the limits of the French territory. Accordingly, this alarming annunciation was received, as Magua intended, with manifest disapprobation, if not with alarm.

"Let my father look in my face," said Le Cœur-dur; "he will see no change. It is true, my young men did not go out on the war-path; they had dreams for not doing so. But they love and venerate the great white chief."

"Will he think so when he hears that his greatest enemy is fed in the camp of his children? When he is told a bloody Yengee smokes at your fire? That the pale-face who has slain so many of his friends goes in and out among the Delawares? Go! my great Canada father is not a fool!"

"Where is the Yengee that the Delawares fear?" returned the other; "who has slain my young men? who is the mortal enemy of my Great Father!"

"La Longue Carabine."

The Delaware warriors started at the well-known name, betraying, by their amazement, that they now learnt, for the first time, one so famous among the Indian allies of France was within their power.

"What does my brother mean?" demanded Le Cœur-dur, in a tone that, by its wonder, far exceeded the usual apathy of his race.

"A Huron never lies!" returned Magua coldly, leaning his head against the side of the lodge, and drawing his slight robe across his tawny breast. "Let the Delawares count their prisoners; they will find one whose skin is neither red nor pale."

A long and musing pause succeeded. The chief consulted apart with his companions, and messengers were despatched to collect certain others of the most distinguished men of the tribe.

As warrior after warrior dropped in, they were each made acquainted, in turn, with the important intelligence that Magua had just communicated. The air of surprise, and the usual low, deep, guttural exclamation, were common to them all. The news spread from mouth to mouth, until the whole encampment became powerfully agitated. The women suspended their labors, to catch such syllables as unguardedly fell from the lips of the consulting warriors. The boys deserted their sports, and walking fearlessly among their fathers, looked up in curious admiration, as they heard the brief exclamations of wonder they so freely expressed at the temerity of their hated foe. In short, every occupation was abandoned for the time, and all other pursuits seemed discarded, in order that the tribe might freely indulge, after their own peculiar manner, in an open expression of feeling.

When the excitement had a little abated, the old men disposed themselves seriously to consider that which it became the honor and safety of their tribe to perform, under circumstances of so much delicacy and embarrassment. During all these movements, and in the midst of the general commotion, Magua had not only maintained his seat, but the very attitude he had originally taken, against the side of the lodge, where he continued as immovable, and, apparently, as unconcerned, as if he had no interest in the result. Not a single indication of the future intentions of his hosts, however, escaped his vigilant eyes. With his consummate knowledge of the nature of the people with whom he had to deal, he anticipated every measure on which they decided; and it might almost be said, that, in many instances, he knew their intentions, even before they became known to themselves.

The council of the Delawares was short. When it was ended, a general bustle announced that it was to be immediately succeeded by a solemn and formal assemblage of the nation. As such meetings were rare, and only called on occasions of the last importance, the subtle Huron, who still sat apart, a wily and dark observer of the proceedings, now knew that all his projects must be brought to their final issue. He therefore left the lodge, and walked silently forth to the place in front of the encampment whither the warriors were already beginning to collect.

It might have been half an hour before each individual, including even the women and children, was in his place. The delay had been created by the grave preparations that were deemed necessary to so solemn and unusual a conference. But when the sun was seen climbing above the tops of that mountain against whose bosom the Delawares had constructed their encampment, most were seated; and as his bright rays darted from behind the outline of trees that fringed the eminence, they fell upon as grave, as attentive, and as deeply interested a multitude, as was probably ever before lighted by his morning beams. Its number somewhat exceeded a thousand souls.

In a collection of such serious savages, there is never to be found any impatient aspirant after premature distinction, standing ready to move his auditors to some hasty, and, perhaps, injudicious discussion, in order that his own reputation may be the gainer. An act of so much precipitancy and presumption would seal the downfall of precocious intellect forever. It rested solely with the oldest and most experienced of the men to lay the subject of the conference before the people. Until such a one chose to make some movement, no deeds in arms, no natural gifts, nor any renown as an orator, would have justified the slightest interruption. On the present occasion, the aged warrior whose privilege it was to speak, was silent, seemingly oppressed with the magnitude of his subject. The delay had already continued long beyond the usual deliberative pause that always precedes a conference; but no sign of impatience or surprise escaped even the youngest boy. Occasionally, an eye was raised from the earth, where the looks of most were riveted, and strayed towards a particular lodge, that was, however, in no manner distinguished from those around it, except in the peculiar care that had been taken to protect it against the assaults of the weather.

At length, one of those low murmurs that are so apt to disturb a multitude, was heard, and the whole nation arose to their feet by a common impulse. At that the door of the lodge in question opened, and three men, issuing from it, slowly approached the place of consultation. They were all aged, even beyond that period to which the oldest present had reached; but one in the centre,

who leaned on his companions for support, had numbered an amount of years to which the human race is seldom permitted to attain. His frame, which had once
been tall and erect, like the cedar, was now bending
under the pressure of more than a century. The elastic,
light step of an Indian was gone, and in its place he was
compelled to toil his tardy way over the ground, inch by
inch. His dark, wrinkled countenance was in singular
and wild contrast with the long white locks which floated
on his shoulders in such thickness as to announce that
generations had probably passed away since they had last
been shorn.

The dress of this patriarch—for such, considering his
vast age, in conjunction with his affinity and influence
with his people, he might very properly be termed—was
rich and imposing, though strictly after the simple fashions of the tribe. His robe was of the finest skins, which
had been deprived of their fur, in order to admit of a hi-
eroglyphical representation of various deeds in arms,
done in former ages. His bosom was loaded with medals,
some in massive silver, and one or two even in gold, the
gifts of various Christian potentates during the long period of his life. He also wore armlets, and cinctures above
the ankles, of the latter precious metal. His head, on the
whole of which the hair had been permitted to grow, the
pursuits of war having so long been abandoned, was encircled by a sort of plated diadem, which, in its turn, bore
lesser and more glittering ornaments, that sparkled amid
the glossy hues of three drooping ostrich feathers, dyed a
deep black, in touching contrast to the color of his snow-
white locks. His tomahawk was nearly hid in silver, and
the handle of his knife shone like a horn of solid gold.

So soon as the first hum of emotion and pleasure,

which the sudden appearance of this venerated individual created, had a little subsided, the name of "Tamenund" was whispered from mouth to mouth. Magua had often heard the fame of this wise and just Delaware; a reputation that even proceeded so far as to bestow on him the rare gift of holding secret communion with the Great Spirit, and which has since transmitted his name, with some slight alteration, to the white usurpers of his ancient territory, as the imaginary tutelar saint of a vast empire. The Huron chief, therefore, stepped eagerly out a little from the throng, to a spot whence he might catch a nearer glimpse of the features of the man, whose decision was likely to produce so deep an influence on his own fortunes.

The eyes of the old man were closed, as though the organs were wearied with having so long witnessed the selfish workings of the human passions. The color of his skin differed from that of most around him, being richer and darker, the latter hue having been produced by certain delicate and mazy lines of complicated and yet beautiful figures, which had been traced over most of his person by the operation of tattooing. Notwithstanding the position of the Huron, he passed the observant and silent Magua without notice, and leaning on his two venerable supporters proceeded to the high place of the multitude, where he seated himself in the centre of his nation, with the dignity of a monarch and the air of a father.

Nothing could surpass the reverence and affection with which this unexpected visit from one who belonged rather to another world than to this, was received by his people. After a suitable and decent pause, the principal chiefs arose; and approaching the patriarch, they placed his hands reverently on their heads, seeming to entreat a blessing. The younger men were content with touching his robe, or even drawing nigh his person, in order to breathe in the atmosphere of one so aged, so just, and so valiant. None but the most distinguished among the youthful warriors even presumed so far as to perform the latter ceremony; the great mass of the multitude deeming it a sufficient happiness to look upon a form so deeply venerated, and so well beloved. When these acts of affection and respect were performed, the chiefs drew back again to their several places, and silence reigned in the whole encampment.

After a short delay, a few of the young men, to whom instructions had been whispered by one of the aged attendants of Tamenund, arose, left the crowd, and entered the lodge which has already been noted as the object of so much attention throughout that morning. In a few minutes they reappeared, escorting the individuals who had caused all these solemn preparations towards the seat of judgment. The crowd opened in a lane; and when the party had re-entered, it closed in again, forming a large and dense belt of human bodies, arranged in an open circle.

Magua talks to Hard Heart (Delaware orator) @ camp, nothing about Cora, gives gifts, says La Longue Carabine is among them (notorious indian-killer)

XXIX

"The assembly seated, rising o'er the rest,
Achilles thus the king of men addressed."
Alexander Pope, *The Iliad of Homer*[1]

CORA STOOD FOREMOST among the prisoners, entwining her arms in those of Alice, in the tenderness of sisterly love. Notwithstanding the fearful and menacing array of savages on every side of her, no apprehension on her own account could prevent the noble-minded maiden from keeping her eyes fastened on the pale and anxious features of the trembling Alice. Close at their side stood Heyward, with an interest in both, that, at such a moment of intense uncertainty, scarcely knew a preponderance in favor of her whom he most loved. Hawkeye had placed himself a little in the rear, with a deference to the superior rank of his companions, that no similarity in the state of their present fortunes could induce him to forget. Uncas was not there.

When perfect silence was again restored, and after the usual long, impressive pause, one of the two aged chiefs who sat at the side of the patriarch arose, and demanded aloud, in very intelligible English,—

"Which of my prisoners is La Longue Carabine?"

Neither Duncan nor the scout answered. The former,

however, glanced his eyes around the dark and silent assembly, and recoiled a pace, when they fell on the malignant visage of Magua. He saw, at once, that this wily savage had some secret agency in their present arraignment before the nation, and determined to throw every possible impediment in the way of the execution of his sinister plans. He had witnessed one instance of the summary punishments of the Indians, and now dreaded that his companion was to be selected for a second. In this dilemma, with little or no time for reflection, he suddenly determined to cloak his invaluable friend, at any or every hazard to himself. Before he had time, however, to speak, the question was repeated in a louder voice, and with a clearer utterance.

"Give us arms," the young man haughtily replied, "and place us in yonder woods. Our deeds shall speak for us!"

"This is the warrior whose name has filled our ears!" returned the chief, regarding Heyward with that sort of curious interest which seems inseparable from man, when first beholding one of his fellows to whom merit or accident, virtue or crime, has given notoriety. "What has brought the white man into the camp of the Delawares?"

"My necessities. I come for food, shelter and friends."

"It cannot be. The woods are full of game. The head of a warrior needs no other shelter than a sky without clouds; and the Delawares are the enemies, and not the friends, of the Yengeese. Go! the mouth has spoken, while the heart said nothing."

Duncan, a little at a loss in what manner to proceed, remained silent; but the scout, who had listened attentively to all that passed, now advanced steadily to the front.

"That I did not answer to the call for La Longue Carabine, was not owing either to shame or fear," he said; "for neither one nor the other is the gift of an honest man. But I do not admit the right of the Mingos to bestow a name on one whose friends have been mindful of his gifts, in this particular; especially as their title is a lie, 'Killdeer' being a grooved barrel and no carabyne. I am the man, however, that got the name of Nathaniel from my kin; the compliment of Hawkeye from the Delawares, who live on their own river; and whom the Iroquois have presumed to style the 'Long Rifle,' without any warranty from him who is most concerned in the matter."

The eyes of all present, which had hitherto been gravely scanning the person of Duncan, were now turned, on the instant, towards the upright iron frame of this new pretender to the distinguished appellation. It was in no degree remarkable that there should be found two who were willing to claim so great an honor, for impostors, though rare, were not unknown amongst the natives; but it was altogether material to the just and severe intentions of the Delawares, that there should be no mistake in the matter. Some of their old men consulted together in private, and then, as it would seem, they determined to interrogate their visitor on the subject.

"My brother has said that a snake crept into my camp," said the chief to Magua; "which is he?"

The Huron pointed to the scout.

"Will a wise Delaware believe the barking of a wolf?" exclaimed Duncan, still more confirmed in the evil intentions of his ancient enemy: "a dog never lies, but when was a wolf known to speak the truth?"

The eyes of Magua flashed fire; but, suddenly recollecting the necessity of maintaining his presence of mind, he turned away in silent disdain, well assured that the sagacity of the Indians would not fail to extract the real merits of the point in controversy. He was not deceived; for, after another short consultation, the wary Delaware turned to him again, and expressed the determination of the chiefs, though in the most considerate language.

"My brother has been called a liar," he said, "and his friends are angry. They will show that he has spoken the truth. Give my prisoners guns, and let them prove which is the man."

Magua affected to consider the expedient, which he well knew proceeded from distrust of himself, as a compliment, and made a gesture of acquiescence, well content that his veracity should be supported by so skilful a marksman as the scout. The weapons were instantly placed in the hands of the friendly opponents, and they were bid to fire over the heads of the seated multitude at an earthen vessel, which lay, by accident, on a stump some fifty yards from the place where they stood.

Heyward smiled to himself at the idea of a competition with the scout, though he determined to persevere in the deception, until apprised of the real designs of Magua. Raising his rifle with the utmost care, and renewing his aim three several times, he fired. The bullet cut the wood within a few inches of the vessel; and a general exclamation of satisfaction announced that the shot was considered a proof of great skill in the use of the weapon. Even Hawkeye nodded his head, as if he would say, it was better than he had expected. But, instead of manifesting an intention to contend with the successful marksman, he stood leaning on his rifle for more than a minute, like a man who was completely buried in thought. From this reverie he was, however, awakened by one of the young Indians who had furnished the arms, and who now touched his shoulder, saying, in exceedingly broken English,—

"Can the pale-face beat it?"

"Yes, Huron!" exclaimed the scout, raising the short rifle in his right hand, and shaking it at Magua, with as much apparent ease as if it were a reed; "yes, Huron, I could strike you now, and no power of earth could prevent the deed! The soaring hawk is not more certain of the dove than I am this moment of you, did I choose to send a bullet to your heart! Why should I not? Why!— because the gifts of my color forbid it, and I might draw down evil on tender and innocent heads. If you know such a being as God, thank Him, therefore, in your inward soul; for you have reason."

The flushed countenance, angry eye, and swelling figure of the scout, produced a sensation of secret awe in all that heard him. The Delawares held their breath in expectation; but Magua himself, even while he distrusted the forbearance of his enemy, remained immovable and calm, where he stood wedged in by the crowd, as one who grew to the spot.

"Beat it," replied the young Delaware at the elbow of the scout.

"Beat what, fool!—what!" exclaimed Hawkeye, still flourishing the weapon angrily above his head, though his eye no longer sought the person of Magua.

"If the white man is the warrior he pretends," said the aged chief, "let him strike nigher to the mark."

The scout laughed aloud—a noise that produced the startling effect of an unnatural sound on Heyward; then dropping the piece heavily into his extended left hand, it was discharged, apparently by the shock, driving the fragments of the vessel into the air, and scattering them on every side. Almost at the same instant, the rattling sound of the rifle was heard, as he suffered it to fall, contemptuously, to the earth.

The first impression of so strange a scene was engrossing admiration. Then a low, but increasing murmur, ran through the multitude, and finally swelled into sounds that denoted a lively opposition in the sentiments of the spectators. While some openly testified their satisfaction at so unexampled dexterity, by far the larger portion of the tribe were inclined to believe the success of the shot was the result of accident. Heyward was not slow to confirm an opinion that was so favorable to his own pretentions.

"It was chance!" he exclaimed; "none can shoot without an aim!"

"Chance!" echoed the excited woodsman, who was now stubbornly bent on maintaining his identity at every hazard, and on whom the secret hints of Heyward to acquiesce in the deception were entirely lost. "Does yonder lying Huron, too, think it chance? Give him another gun, and place us face to face, without cover or dodge, and let Providence, and our own eyes, decide the matter atween us! I do not make the offer to you, major; for our blood is of a color, and we serve the same master."

"That the Huron is a liar, is very evident," returned Heyward, coolly; "you have yourself heard him assert you to be La Longue Carabine."

It were impossible to say what violent assertion the stubborn Hawkeye would have next made, in his headlong wish to vindicate his identity, had not the aged Delaware once more interposed.

"The hawk which comes from the clouds can return when he will," he said; "give them the guns."

This time the scout seized the rifle with avidity; nor had Magua, though he watched the movement of the marksman with jealous eyes, any further cause for apprehension.

"Now let it be proved, in the face of this tribe of Delawares, which is the better man," cried the scout, tapping the butt of his piece with that finger which had pulled so many fatal triggers. "You see the gourd hanging against yonder tree, major; if you are a marksman fit for the borders, let me see you break its shell!"

Duncan noted the object, and prepared himself to renew the trial. The gourd was one of the usual little vessels used by the Indians, and it was suspended from a dead branch of a small pine, by a thong of deer-skin, at the full distance of a hundred yards. So strangely compounded is the feeling of self-love, that the young soldier, while he knew the utter worthlessness of the suffrages of his savage umpires, forgot the sudden motives of the contest in a wish to excel. It has been seen, already, that his skill was far from being contemptible, and he now resolved to put forth its nicest qualities. Had his life depended on the issue, the aim of Duncan could not have been more deliberate or guarded. He fired; and three or four young Indians, who sprang forward at the report, announced with a shout, that the ball was in the tree, a very little on one side of the proper object. The warriors uttered a common ejaculation of pleasure, and then turned their eyes inquiringly on the movements of his rival.

"It may do for the Royal Americans!" said Hawkeye, laughing once more in his own silent, heartfelt manner;

"but had my gun often turned so much from the true line, many a marten, whose skin is now in a lady's muff, would still be in the woods; ay, and many a **bl**oody Mingo, who has departed to his final account, would be acting his deviltries at this very day, atween the provinces. I hope the squaw who owns the gourd has more of them in her wigwam, for this will never hold water again!"

The scout had shook his priming, and cocked his piece, while speaking; and, as he ended, he threw back a foot, and slowly raised the muzzle from the earth: the motion was steady, uniform, and in one direction. When on a perfect level, it remained for a single moment, without tremor or variation, as though both man and rifle were carved in stone. During that stationary instant, it poured forth its contents, in a bright, glancing sheet of flame. Again the young Indians bounded forward; but their hurried search and disappointed looks announced that no traces of the bullet were to be seen.

"Go!" said the old chief to the scout, in a tone of strong disgust; "thou art a wolf in the skin of a dog. I will talk to the 'Long Rifle' of the Yengeese."

"Ah! had I that piece which furnished the name you use, I would obligate myself to cut the thong, and drop the gourd without breaking it!" returned Hawkeye, perfectly undisturbed by the other's manner. "Fools, if you would find the bullet of a sharpshooter of these woods, you must look *in* the object and not around it!"

The Indian youths instantly comprehended his meaning—for this time he spoke in the Delaware tongue—and tearing the gourd from the tree, they held it on high with an exulting shout, displaying a hole in its bottom, which had been cut by the bullet, after passing through the usual orifice in the centre of its upper side. At this unexpected exhibition, a loud and vehement expression of pleasure burst from the mouth of every warrior present. It decided the question, and effectually established Hawkeye in the possession of his dangerous reputation. Those curious and admiring eyes which had been turned again on Heyward, were finally directed to the weather-beaten form of the scout, who immediately became the principal object of attention to the simple and unsophisticated beings by whom he was surrounded. When the sudden and noisy commotion had a little subsided, the aged chief resumed his examination.

"Why did you wish to stop my ears?" he said, addressing Duncan; "are the Delawares fools, that they could not know the young panther from the cat?"

"They will yet find the Huron a singing-bird," said Duncan, endeavoring to adopt the figurative language of the natives.

"It is good. We will know who can shut the ears of men. Brother," added the chief, turning his eyes on Magua, "the Delawares listen."

Thus singled, and directly called on to declare his object, the Huron arose; and advancing with great deliberation and dignity into the very centre of the circle, where he stood confronted to the prisoners, he placed himself in an attitude to speak. Before opening his mouth, however, he bent his eyes slowly along the whole living boundary of earnest faces as if to temper his expressions to the capacities of his audience. On Hawkeye he cast a glance of respectful enmity; on Duncan, a look of inextinguishable hatred; the shrinking figure of Alice he scarcely deigned to notice; but when his glance met the firm, commanding, and yet lovely form of Cora, his eye lingered a moment, with an expression that it might have been difficult to define. Then, filled with his own dark intentions, he spoke in the language of the Canadas, a tongue that he well knew was comprehended by most of his auditors.

"The Spirit that made men colored them differently," commenced the subtle Huron. "Some are blacker than the sluggish bear. These He said would be slaves; and He ordered them to work forever, like the beaver. You may hear them groan, when the south wind blows, louder than the lowing buffaloes, along the shores of the great salt lake, where the big canoes come and go with them in droves. Some He made with faces paler than the ermine of the forests; and these He ordered to be traders; dogs to their women, and wolves to their slaves. He gave this people the nature of the pigeon: wings that never tire, young, more plentiful than the leaves on the trees, and appetites to devour the earth. He gave them tongues like the false call of the wildcat; hearts like rabbits; the cunning of the hog (but none of the fox), and arms longer than the legs of the moose. With his tongue, he stops the ears of the Indians; his heart teaches him to pay warriors to fight his battles; his cunning tells him how to get together the goods of the earth; and his arms inclose the land from the shores of the salt-water to the islands of the great lake. His gluttony makes him sick. God gave him enough, and yet he wants all. Such are the palefaces.

"Some the Great Spirit made with skins brighter and redder than yonder sun," continued Magua, pointing impressively upwards to the lurid luminary, which was struggling through the misty atmosphere of the horizon; "and these did He fashion to His own mind. He gave them this island as He had made it, covered with trees, and filled with game. The wind made their clearings; the sun and rains ripened their fruits; and the snows came to tell them to be thankful. What need had they of roads to journey by! They saw through the hills. When the beavers worked, they lay in the shade, and looked on. The winds cooled them in summer; in winter, skins kept them warm. If they fought among themselves, it was to prove that they were men. They were brave; they were just; they were happy."

Here the speaker paused, and again looked around him, to discover if his legend had touched the sympathies of his listeners. He met everywhere with eyes riveted on his own, heads erect, and nostrils expanded, as if each individual present felt himself able and willing, singly, to redress the wrongs of his race.

"If the Great Spirit gave different tongues to his red children," he continued, in a low, still, melancholy voice, "it was that all animals might understand them. Some He placed among the snows, with their cousin the bear. Some he placed near the setting sun, on the road to the happy hunting-grounds. Some on the lands around the great fresh waters; but to his greatest, and most beloved, He gave the sands of the salt lake. Do my brothers know the name of this favored people?"

"It was the Lenape!" exclaimed twenty eager voices, in a breath.

"It was the Lenni Lenape," returned Magua, affecting to bend his head in reverence to their former greatness. "It was the tribes of the Lenape! The sun rose from water that was salt, and set in water that was sweet, and never hid himself from their eyes. But why should I, a Huron of the woods, tell a wise people their own traditions?

Why remind them of their injuries; their ancient greatness; their deeds; their glory; their happiness,—their losses; their defeats; their misery? Is there not one among them who has seen it all, and who knows it to be true? I have done. My tongue is still, for my heart is of lead. I listen."

As the voice of the speaker suddenly ceased, every face and all eyes turned, by a common movement, towards the venerable Tamenund. From the moment that he took his seat, until the present instant, the lips of the patriarch had not severed, and scarcely a sign of life had escaped him. He sat bent in feebleness, and apparently unconscious of the presence he was in, during the whole of that opening scene, in which the skill of the scout had been so clearly established. At the nicely graduated sound of Magua's voice, however, he betrayed some evidence of consciousness, and once or twice he even raised his head, as if to listen. But when the crafty Huron spoke of his nation by name, the eyelids of the old man raised themselves, and he looked out upon the multitude with that sort of dull unmeaning expression which might be supposed to belong to the countenance of a spectre. Then he made an effort to rise, and being upheld by his supporters, he gained his feet, in a posture commanding by its dignity, while he tottered with weakness.

"Who calls upon the children of the Lenape!" he said, in a deep, guttural voice, that was rendered awfully audible by the breathless silence of the multitude: "who speaks of things gone! Does not the egg become a worm—the worm a fly, and perish? Why tell the Delawares of good that is past? Better thank the Manitou for that which remains."

"It is a Wyandot," said Magua, stepping nigher to the rude platform on which the other stood; "a friend of Tamenund."

"A friend!" repeated the sage, on whose brow a dark frown settled, imparting a portion of that severity which had rendered his eye so terrible in middle age. "Are the Mingos rulers of the earth? What brings a Huron here?"

"Justice. His prisoners are with his brothers, and he comes for his own."

Tamenund turned his head towards one of his supporters, and listened to the short explanation the man gave. Then facing the applicant, he regarded him a moment with deep attention; after which he said, in a low and reluctant voice,—

"Justice is the law of the great Manitou. My children, give the stranger food. Then, Huron, take thine own and depart."

On the delivery of this solemn judgment, the patriarch seated himself, and closed his eyes again, as if better pleased with the images of his own ripened experience than with the visible objects of the world. Against such a decree there was no Delaware sufficiently hardy to murmur, much less oppose himself. The words were barely uttered when four or five of the younger warriors, stepping behind Heyward and the scout, passed thongs so dexterously and rapidly around their arms, as to hold them both in instant bondage. The former was too much engrossed with his precious and nearly insensible burden, to be aware of their intentions before they were executed; and the latter, who considered even the hostile tribes of the Delawares a superior race of beings, submitted without resistance. Perhaps, however, the man-

ner of the scout would not have been so passive, had he
fully comprehended the language in which the preceding dialogue had been conducted.

Magua cast a look of triumph around the whole assembly before he proceeded to the execution of his purpose. Perceiving that the men were unable to offer any
resistance, he turned his looks on her he valued most.
Cora met his gaze with an eye so calm and firm, that his
resolution wavered. Then recollecting his former artifice, he raised Alice from the arms of the warrior against
whom she leaned, and beckoning Heyward to follow, he
motioned for the encircling crowd to open. But Cora, instead of obeying the impulse he had expected, rushed to
the feet of the patriarch, and raising her voice, exclaimed
aloud,—

"Just and venerable Delaware, on thy wisdom and
power we lean for mercy! Be deaf to yonder artful and
remorseless monster, who poisons thy ears with false-
hoods to feed his thirst for blood. Thou that hast lived
long, and that hast seen the evil of the world, should
know how to temper its calamities to the miserable."

The eyes of the old man opened heavily, and he once
more looked upwards at the multitude. As the piercing
tones of the supplicant swelled on his ears, they moved
slowly in the direction of her person, and finally settled
there in a steady gaze. Cora had cast herself to her knees;
and, with hands clenched in each other and pressed upon
her bosom, she remained like a beauteous and breathing
model of her sex, looking up in his faded, but majestic
countenance, with a species of holy reverence. Gradually
the expression of Tamenund's features changed, and losing their vacancy in admiration, they lighted with a portion of that intelligence which a century before had been

wont to communicate his youthful fire to the extensive bands of the Delawares. Rising without assistance, and seemingly without an effort, he demanded, in a voice that startled its auditors by its firmness,—

"What art thou?"

"A woman. One of a hated race, if thou wilt—a Yengee. But one who has never harmed thee, and who cannot harm thy people, if she would; who asks for succor."

"Tell me, my children," continued the patriarch, hoarsely, motioning to those around him, though his eyes still dwelt upon the kneeling form of Cora, "where have the Delawares camped?"

"In the mountains of the Iroquois, beyond the clear springs of the Horican."

"Many parching summers are come and gone," continued the sage, "since I drank of the water of my own rivers. The children of Minquon are the justest white men; but they were thirsty, and they took it to themselves. Do they follow us so far?"

"We follow none; we covet nothing," answered Cora. "Captives against our wills, have we been brought among you; and we ask but permission to depart to our own in peace. Art thou not Tamenund—the father, the judge, I had almost said, the prophet—of this people?"

"I am Tamenund of many days."

" 'Tis now some seven years that one of thy people was at the mercy of a white chief on the borders of this province. He claimed to be of the blood of the good and just Tamenund. 'Go,' said the white man, 'for thy parent's sake thou art free.' Dost thou remember the name of that English warrior?"

"I remember, that when a laughing boy," returned the

patriarch, with the peculiar recollection of vast age, "I stood upon the sands of the sea-shore, and saw a big canoe, with wings whiter than the swan's, and wider than many eagles, come from the rising sun."

"Nay, nay; I speak not of a time so very distant, but of favor shown to thy kindred by one of mine, within the memory of thy youngest warrior."

"Was it when the Yengeese and the Dutchmanne[2] fought for the hunting-grounds of the Delawares? Then Tamenund was a chief, and first laid aside the bow for the lightning of the pale-faces—"

"Not yet then," interrupted Cora, "by many ages; I speak of a thing of yesterday. Surely, surely, you forget it not."

"It was but yesterday," rejoined the aged man, with touching pathos, "that the children of the Lenape were masters of the world. The fishes of the salt lake, the birds, the beasts, and the Mengwe of the woods, owned them for Sagamores."

Cora bowed her head in disappointment, and, for a bitter moment, struggled with her chagrin. Then elevating her rich features and beaming eyes, she continued, in tones scarcely less penetrating than the unearthly voice of the patriarch himself,—

"Tell me, is Tamenund a father?"

The old man looked down upon her from his elevated stand, with a benignant smile on his wasted countenance, and then casting his eyes slowly over the whole assemblage, he answered,—

"Of a nation."

"For myself I ask nothing. Like thee and thine, venerable chief," she continued, pressing her hands convulsively on her heart, and suffering her head to droop until her burning cheeks were nearly concealed in the maze of dark glossy tresses that fell in disorder upon her shoulders, "the curse of my ancestors has fallen heavily on their child. But yonder is one who has never known the weight of Heaven's displeasure until now. She is the daughter of an old and failing man, whose days are near their close. She has many, very many, to love her, and delight in her; and she is too good, much too precious, to become the victim of that villain."

"I know that the pale-faces are a proud and hungry race. I know that they claim not only to have the earth, but that the meanest of their color is better than the sachems of the redman. The dogs and crows of their tribes," continued the earnest old chieftain, without heeding the wounded spirit of his listener, whose head was nearly crushed to the earth in shame, as he proceeded, "would bark and caw before they would take a woman to their wigwams whose blood was not of the color of snow. But let them not boast before the face of the Manitou too loud. They entered the land at the rising, and may yet go off at the setting sun. I have often seen the locusts strip the leaves from the trees, but the season of blossoms has always come again."

"It is so," said Cora, drawing a long breath, as if reviving from a trance, raising her face, and shaking back her shining veil, with a kindling eye, that contradicted the death-like paleness of her countenance; "but why—it is not permitted us to inquire. There is yet one of thine own people who has not been brought before thee; before thou lettest the Huron depart in triumph, hear him speak."

Observing Tamenund to look about him doubtingly, one of his companions said,—

"It is a snake—a redskin in the pay of the Yengeese. We keep him for the torture."

"Let him come," returned the sage.

Then Tamenund once more sank into his seat, and a silence so deep prevailed, while the young men prepared to obey his simple mandate, that the leaves, which fluttered in the draught of the light morning air, were distinctly heard rustling in the surrounding forest.

Delawares gather to hear Tamenund (100 yrs old), warriors bring Hawk, Cora, Alice + Hey. To protect Hawk, they claims to be la Longue Carabine, Hawk tells truth, stage shooting contest to find true LLC. Hey good, Hawk great, both tied up, Cora tries to get Tamenund to listen to Uncas but he doesn't

XXX

"If you deny me, fie upon your law!
There is no force in the decrees of Venice:
I stand for judgment; answer, shall I have it?"
The Merchant of Venice[1]

THE SILENCE CONTINUED unbroken by human sounds for many anxious minutes. Then the waving multitude opened and shut again, and Uncas stood in the living circle. All those eyes, which had been curiously studying the lineaments of the sage, as the source of their own intelligence, turned on the instant, and were now bent in secret admiration on the erect, agile, and faultless person of the captive. But neither the presence in which he found himself, nor the exclusive attention that he attracted, in any manner disturbed the self-possession of the young Mohican. He cast a deliberate and observing look on every side of him, meeting the settled expression of hostility that lowered in the visages of the chiefs, with the same calmness as the curious gaze of the attentive children. But when, last in his haughty scrutiny, the person of Tamenund came under his glance, his eye became fixed, as though all other objects were already forgotten. Then advancing with a slow and noiseless step up the area, he placed himself immediately before the footstool of the sage. Here he stood unnoted, though keenly observant himself, until one of the chiefs apprised the latter of his presence.

"With what tongue does the prisoner speak to the Manitou?" demanded the patriarch, without unclosing his eyes.

"Like his fathers," Uncas replied; "with the tongue of a Delaware."

At this sudden and unexpected annunciation, a low, fierce yell ran through the multitude, that might not inaptly be compared to the growl of the lion, as his choler is first awakened—a fearful omen of the weight of his future anger. The effect was equally strong on the sage, though differently exhibited. He passed a hand before his eyes, as if to exclude the least evidence of so shameful a spectacle, while he repeated, in his low, guttural tones, the words he had just heard.

"A Delaware! I have lived to see the tribes of the Lenape driven from their council-fires, and scattered, like broken herds of deer, among the hills of the Iroquois! I have seen the hatchets of a strange people sweep woods from the valleys, that the winds of heaven had spared! The beasts that run on the mountains, and the birds that fly above the trees, have I seen living in the wigwams of men; but never before have I found a Delaware so base as to creep, like a poisonous serpent, into the camps of his nation."

"The singing-birds have opened their bills," returned Uncas, in the softest notes of his own musical voice; "and Tamenund has heard their song."

The sage started, and bent his head aside, as if to catch the fleeting sounds of some passing melody.

"Does Tamenund dream!" he exclaimed. "What voice

is at his ear! Have the winters gone backward! Will summer come again to the children of the Lenape!"

A solemn and respectful silence succeeded this incoherent burst from the lips of the Delaware prophet. His people steadily construed his unintelligible language into one of those mysterious conferences he was believed to hold so frequently with a superior intelligence, and they awaited the issue of the revelation in awe. After a patient pause, however, one of the aged men, perceiving that the sage had lost the recollection of the subject before them, ventured to remind him again of the presence of the prisoner.

"The false Delaware trembles lest he should hear the words of Tamenund," he said. " 'Tis a hound that howls, when the Yengeese show him a trail."

"And ye," returned Uncas, looking sternly around him, "are dogs that whine, when the Frenchman casts ye the offals of his deer!"

Twenty knives gleamed in the air, and as many warriors sprang to their feet, at this biting, and perhaps merited retort; but a motion from one of the chiefs suppressed the outbreaking of their tempers, and restored the appearance of quiet. The task might probably have been more difficult, had not a movement made by Tamenund indicated that he was again about to speak.

"Delaware!" resumed the sage, "little art thou worthy of thy name. My people have not seen a bright sun in many winters; and the warrior who deserts his tribe when hid in clouds is doubly a traitor. The law of the Manitou is just. It is so; while the rivers run and the mountains stand, while the blossoms come and go on the trees, it must be so. He is thine, my children; deal justly by him."

Not a limb was moved, nor was a breath drawn louder and longer than common, until the closing syllable of this final decree had passed the lips of Tamenund. Then a cry of vengeance burst at once, as it might be, from the united lips of the nation; a frightful augury of their ruthless intentions. In the midst of these prolonged and savage yells, a chief proclaimed, in a high voice, that the captive was condemned to endure the dreadful trial of torture by fire. The circle broke its order, and screams of delight mingled with the bustle and tumult of preparation. Heyward struggled madly with his captors; the anxious eyes of Hawkeye began to look around him, with an expression of peculiar earnestness; and Cora again threw herself at the feet of the patriarch, once more a suppliant for mercy.

Throughout the whole of these trying moments, Uncas had alone preserved his serenity. He looked on the preparations with a steady eye, and when the tormentors came to seize him, he met them with a firm and upright attitude. One among them, if possible, more fierce and savage than his fellows, seized the hunting-shirt of the young warrior, and at a single effort tore it from his body. Then, with a yell of frantic pleasure, he leaped towards his unresisting victim, and prepared to lead him to the stake. But, at that moment, when he appeared most a stranger to the feelings of humanity, the purpose of the savage was arrested as suddenly as if a supernatural agency had interposed in the behalf of Uncas. The eyeballs of the Delaware seemed to start from their sockets; his mouth opened, and his whole form became frozen in an attitude of amazement. Raising his hand with a slow and regulated motion, he pointed with a finger to the bosom of the captive. His companions crowded about him in wonder, and every eye was, like his own, fastened intently on the figure of a small tortoise, beautifully tattooed on the breast of the prisoner, in a bright blue tint.

For a single instant Uncas enjoyed his triumph, smiling calmly on the scene. Then motioning the crowd away with a high and haughty sweep of his arm, he advanced in front of the nation with the air of a king, and spoke in a voice louder than the murmur of admiration that ran through the multitude.

"Men of the Lenni Lenape!" he said, "my race upholds the earth! Your feeble tribe stands on my shell! What fire that a Delaware can light would burn the child of my fathers," he added, pointing proudly to the simple blazonry on his skin; "the blood that came from such a stock would smother your flames! My race is the grandfather of nations!"

"Who art thou?" demanded Tamenund, rising at the startling tones he heard, more than at any meaning conveyed by the language of the prisoner.

"Uncas, the son of Chingachgook," answered the captive modestly, turning from the nation, and bending his head in reverence to the other's character and years; "a son of the great Unamis."

"The hour of Tamenund is nigh!" exclaimed the sage; "the day is come, at last, to the night! I thank the Manitou, that one is here to fill my place at the council-fire. Uncas, the child of Uncas,[2] is found! Let the eyes of a dying eagle gaze on the rising sun."

The youth stepped lightly, but proudly, on the platform, where he became visible to the whole agitated and wondering multitude. Tamenund held him long at the length of his arm, and read every turn in the fine lineaments of his countenance, with the untiring gaze of one who recalled days of happiness.

"Is Tamenund a boy?" at length the bewildered prophet exclaimed. "Have I dreamt of so many snows— that my people were scattered like floating sands—of Yengeese, more plenty than the leaves on the trees! The arrow of Tamenund would not frighten the fawn; his arm is withered like the branch of a dead oak; the snail would be swifter in the race; yet is Uncas before him as they went to battle against the pale-faces! Uncas, the panther of his tribe, the eldest son of the Lenape, the wisest Sagamore of the Mohicans! Tell me, ye Delawares, has Tamenund been a sleeper for a hundred winters?"

The calm and deep silence which succeeded these words, sufficiently announced the awful reverence with which his people received the communication of the patriarch. None dared to answer, though all listened in breathless expectation of what might follow. Uncas, however, looking in his face with the fondness and veneration of a favored child, presumed on his own high and acknowledged rank, to reply.

"Four warriors of his race have lived, and died," he said, "since the friend of Tamenund led his people in battle. The blood of the turtle has been in many chiefs, but all have gone back into the earth from whence they came except Chingachgook and his son."

"It is true—it is true," returned the sage; a flash of recollection destroying all his pleasing fancies, and restoring him at once to a consciousness of the true history of his nation. "Our wise men have often said that two warriors of the unchanged race were in the hills of the Yengeese; why have their seats at the council-fires of the Delawares been so long empty?"

At these words the young man raised his head, which he had still kept bowed a little, in reverence; and lifting his voice so as to be heard by the multitude, as if to explain at once and forever the policy of his family, he said aloud,—

"Once we slept where we could hear the salt lake speak in its anger. Then we were rulers and sagamores over the land. But when a pale-face was seen on every brook, we followed the deer back to the river of our nation. The Delawares were gone. Few warriors of them all stayed to drink of the stream they loved. Then said my fathers, 'Here will we hunt. The waters of the river go into the salt lake. If we go towards the setting sun, we shall find streams that run into the great lakes of sweet water; there would a Mohican die, like fishes of the sea, in the clear springs. When the Manitou is ready, and shall say "Come," we will follow the river to the sea, and take our own again.' Such, Delawares, is the belief of the children of the Turtle. Our eyes are on the rising, and not towards the setting sun. We know whence he comes, but we know not whither he goes. It is enough."

The men of the Lenape listened to his words with all the respect that superstition could lend, finding a secret charm even in the figurative language with which the young Sagamore imparted his ideas. Uncas himself watched the effect of his brief explanation with intelligent eyes, and gradually dropped the air of authority he had assumed, as he perceived that his auditors were content. Then permitting his looks to wander over the silent throng that crowded around the elevated seat of Tamenund, he first perceived Hawkeye in his bonds. Stepping eagerly from his stand, he made way for himself to the side of his friend; and cutting his thongs with a quick and angry stroke of his own knife, he motioned to the crowd to divide. The Indians silently obeyed, and once more they stood ranged in their circle, as before his appearance among them. Uncas took the scout by the hand, and led him to the feet of the patriarch.

"Father," he said, "look at this pale-face; a just man, and the friend of the Delawares."

"Is he a son of Minquon?"

"Not so; a warrior known to the Yengeese, and feared by the Maquas."

"What name has he gained by his deeds?"

"We call him Hawkeye," Uncas replied, using the Delaware phrase; "for his sight never fails. The Mingos know him better by the death he gives their warriors; with them he is 'The Long Rifle.' "

"La Longue Carabine!" exclaimed Tamenund, opening his eyes, and regarding the scout sternly. "My son has not done well to call him friend."

"I call him so who proves himself such," returned the young chief, with great calmness, and with a steady mien. "If Uncas is welcome among the Delawares, then is Hawkeye with his friends."

"The pale-face has slain my young men; his name is great for the blows he has struck the Lenape."

"If a Mingo has whispered that much in the ear of the Delaware, he has only shown that he is a singing-bird," said the scout, who now believed that it was time to vindicate himself from such offensive charges, and who spoke in the tongue of the man he addressed, modifying his Indian figures, however, with his own peculiar notions. "That I have slain the Maquas I am not the man to deny, even at their own council-fires; but that, knowingly, my hand has ever harmed a Delaware, is opposed to the reason of my gifts, which is friendly to them, and all that belongs to their nation."

A low exclamation of applause passed among the warriors, who exchanged looks with each other like men that first began to perceive their error.

"Where is the Huron?" demanded Tamenund. "Has he stopped my ears?"

Magua, whose feelings during that scene in which Uncas had triumphed may be much better imagined than described, answered to the call by stepping boldly in front of the patriarch.

"The just Tamenund," he said, "will not keep what a Huron has lent."

"Tell me, son of my brother," returned the sage, avoiding the dark countenance of Le Subtil, and turning gladly to the more ingenuous features of Uncas, "has the stranger a conqueror's right over you?"

"He has none. The panther may get into snares set by the women; but he is strong, and knows how to leap through them."

"La Longue Carabine?"

"Laughs at the Mingoes. Go, Huron, ask your squaws the color of a bear."

"The stranger and the white maiden that came into my camp together?"

"Should journey on an open path."

"And the woman that Huron left with my warriors?"

Uncas made no reply.

"And the woman that the Mingo has brought into my camp," repeated Tamenund, gravely.

"She is mine," cried Magua, shaking his hand in triumph at Uncas. "Mohican, you know that she is mine."

"My son is silent," said Tamenund, endeavoring to

read the expression of the face that the youth turned from him in sorrow.

"It is so," was the low answer.

A short and impressive pause succeeded, during which it was very apparent with what reluctance the multitude admitted the justice of the Mingo's claim. At length the sage, in whom alone the decision depended, said, in a firm voice,—

"Huron, depart."

"As he came, just Tamenund," demanded the wily Magua; "or with hands filled with the faith of the Delawares? The wigwam of Le Renard Subtil is empty. Make him strong with his own."

The aged man mused with himself for a time; and then bending his head towards one of his venerable companions, he asked,—

"Are my ears open?"

"It is true."

"Is this Mingo a chief?"

"The first in his nation."

"Girl, what wouldst thou? A great warrior takes thee to wife. Go! thy race will not end."

"Better, a thousand times, it should," exclaimed the horror-struck Cora, "than meet with such a degradation!"

"Huron, her mind is in the tents of her fathers. An unwilling maiden makes an unhappy wigwam."

"She speaks with the tongue of her people," returned Magua, regarding his victim with a look of bitter irony. "She is of a race of traders, and will bargain for a bright look. Let Tamenund speak the words."

"Take you the wampum, and our love."

"Nothing hence but what Magua brought hither."

"Then depart with thine own. The great Manitou forbids that a Delaware should be unjust."

Magua advanced, and seized his captive strongly by the arm; the Delawares fell back, in silence; and Cora, as if conscious that remonstrance would be useless, prepared to submit to her fate without resistance.

"Hold, hold!" cried Duncan, springing forward; "Huron, have mercy! her ransom shall make thee richer than any of thy people were ever yet known to be."

"Magua is a redskin; he wants not the beads of the pale-faces."

"Gold, silver, powder, lead—all that a warrior needs shall be in thy wigwam; all that becomes the greatest chief."

"Le Subtil is very strong," cried Magua, violently shaking the hand which grasped the unresisting arm of Cora; "he has his revenge!"

"Mighty ruler of providence!" exclaimed Heyward, clasping his hands together in agony, "can this be suffered! To you, just Tamenund, I appeal for mercy."

"The words of the Delaware are said," returned the sage, closing his eyes, and dropping back into his seat, alike wearied with his mental and his bodily exertion. "Men speak not twice."

"That a chief should not misspend his time in unsaying what had once been spoken, is wise and reasonable," said Hawkeye, motioning to Duncan to be silent; "but it is also prudent in every warrior to consider well before he strikes his tomahawk into the head of his prisoner. Huron, I love you not; nor can I say that any Mingo has ever received much favor at my hands. It is fair to conclude that, if this war does not soon end, many more of your warriors will meet me in the woods. Put it to your judgment, then, whether you would prefer taking such a prisoner as that into your encampment, or one like myself, who am a man that it would greatly rejoice your nation to see with naked hands."

"Will 'The Long Rifle' give his life for the woman?" demanded Magua, hesitatingly; for he had already made a motion towards quitting the place with his victim.

"No, no; I have not said so much as that," returned Hawkeye, drawing back with suitable discretion, when he noted the eagerness with which Magua listened to his proposal. "It would be an unequal exchange, to give a warrior, in the prime of his age and usefulness, for the best woman on the frontiers. I might consent to go into winter-quarters, now—at least six weeks afore the leaves will turn—on condition you will release the maiden."

Magua shook his head; and made an impatient sign for the crowd to open.

"Well, then," added the scout, with the musing air of a man who had not half made up his mind, "I will throw 'Killdeer' into the bargain. Take the word of an experienced hunter, the piece has not its equal atween the provinces."

Magua still disdained to reply, continuing his efforts to disperse the crowd.

"Perhaps," added the scout, losing his dissembled coolness, exactly in proportion as the other manifested an indifference to the exchange, "if I should condition to teach your young men the real virtue of the we'pon, it would smooth the little differences in our judgments."

Le Renard fiercely ordered the Delawares, who still lingered in an impenetrable belt around him, in hopes he would listen to the amicable proposal, to open his path, threatening, by the glance of his eye, another appeal to the infallible justice of their "prophet."

"What is ordered must sooner or later arrive," continued Hawkeye, turning with a sad and humbled look to Uncas. "The varlet knows his advantage, and will keep it! God bless you, boy; you have found friends among your natural kin and I hope they will prove as true as some you have met who had no Indian cross. As for me, sooner or later, I must die; it is therefore fortunate there are but few to make my death-howl. After all, it is likely the imps would have managed to master my scalp, so a day or two will make no great difference in the everlasting reckoning of time. God bless you," added the rugged woodsman, bending his head aside, and then instantly changing its direction again, with a wistful look towards the youth; "I loved both you and your father, Uncas, though our skins are not altogether of a color, and our gifts are somewhat different. Tell the Sagamore I never lost sight of him in my greatest trouble; and, as for you, think of me sometimes when on a lucky trail; and depend on it, boy, whether there be one heaven or two, there is a path in the other world by which honest men may come together again. You'll find the rifle in the place we hid it; take it, and keep it for my sake; and harkee, lad, as your natural gifts don't deny you the use of vengeance, use it a little freely on the Mingos; it may unburden grief at my loss, and ease your mind. Huron, I accept your offer; release the woman. I am your prisoner!"

A suppressed, but still distinct murmur of approbation, ran through the crowd at this generous proposition; even the fiercest among the Delaware warriors manifesting pleasure at the manliness of the intended sacrifice.

Magua paused, and for an anxious moment, it might be said, he doubted; then casting his eyes on Cora, with an expression in which ferocity and admiration were strangely mingled, his purpose became fixed forever.

He intimated his contempt of the offer with a backward motion of his head, and said, in a steady and settled voice,—

"Le Renard Subtil is a great chief; he has but one mind. Come," he added, laying his hand too familiarly on the shoulder of his captive to urge her onward; "a Huron is no tattler; we will go."

The maiden drew back in lofty womanly reserve, and her dark eye kindled, while the rich blood shot, like the passing brightness of the sun, into her very temples, at the indignity.

"I am your prisoner, and at a fitting time shall be ready to follow, even to my death. But violence is unnecessary," she coldly said; and immediately turning to Hawkeye, added, "Generous hunter! from my soul I thank you. Your offer is in vain, neither could it be accepted; but still you may serve me, even more than in your own noble intention. Look at that drooping, humbled child! Abandon her not until you leave her in the habitation of civilized men. I will not say," wringing the hard hand of the scout, "that her father will reward you—for such as you are above the rewards of men—but he will thank you, and bless you. And, believe me, the blessing of a just and aged man has virtue in the sight of Heaven. Would to God, I could hear one from his lips at this awful moment!" Her voice became choked, and, for an instant, she was silent; then advancing a step nigher to Duncan, who was supporting her unconscious sister, she continued, in more subdued tones, but in which feeling and the habits of her sex maintained a fearful struggle,—"I need not tell you to cherish the treasure you will possess. You love her, Heyward; that would conceal a thousand faults, though she had them. She is kind, gentle, sweet, good, as mortal may be. There is not a blemish in mind or person at which the proudest of you all would sicken. She is fair—O! how surpassingly fair!" laying her own beautiful, but less brilliant hand, in melancholy affection on the alabaster forehead of Alice, and parting the golden hair which clustered about her brows; "and yet her soul is pure and spotless as her skin! I could say much—more, perhaps, than cooler reason would approve; but I will spare you and myself"—Her voice became inaudible, and her face was bent over the form of her sister. After a long and burning kiss, she arose, and with features of the hue of death, but without even a tear in her feverish eye, she turned away, and added, to the savage, with all her former elevation of manner,—"Now, sir, if it be your pleasure, I will follow."

"Ay, go," cried Duncan, placing Alice in the arms of an Indian girl; "go, Magua, go. These Delawares have their laws, which forbid them to detain you; but I—I have no such obligation. Go, malignant monster—why do you delay?"

It would be difficult to describe the expression with which Magua listened to this threat to follow. There was at first a fierce and manifest display of joy, and then it was instantly subdued in a look of cunning coldness.

"The woods are open," he was content with answering. " 'The Open Hand' can come."

"Hold," cried Hawkeye, seizing Duncan by the arm,

and detaining him by violence; "you know not the craft of the imp. He would lead you to an ambushment, and your death—"

"Huron," interrupted Uncas, who, submissive to the stern customs of his people, had been an attentive and grave listener to all that passed; "Huron, the justice of the Delawares comes from the Manitou. Look at the sun. He is now in the upper branches of the hemlock. Your path is short and open. When he is seen above the trees, there will be men on your trail."

"I hear a crow!" exclaimed Magua, with a taunting laugh. "Go!" he added, shaking his hand at the crowd, which had slowly opened to admit his passage,—"Where are the petticoats of the Delawares! Let them send their arrows and their guns to the Wyandots; they shall have venison to eat, and corn to hoe. Dogs, rabbits, thieves— I spit on you!"

His parting gibes were listened to in a dead, boding silence, and, with these biting words in his mouth, the triumphant Magua passed unmolested into the forest, followed by his passive captive, and protected by the inviolable laws of Indian hospitality.

Uncas insults Magua, Tam mad, says to torture Uncas by fire, see Uncas' turtle tattoo, think he's reincarnation of Tam grandpa also called Uncas. Uncas freed, he frees Hawk, Uncas lets Magua keep Cora but realease all other prisoners, Hawk offers to die w/ killdeer for cora. Can't go after him cuz of Tam, but vow to do it soon

XXXI

"Flue.—Kill the poys and the luggage! 'Tis expressly
against the law of arms; 'tis as arrant a piece of knavery,
mark you now, as can be offered in the world."
Henry V[1]

So long as their enemy and his victim continued in
sight, the multitude remained motionless as beings
charmed to the place by some power that was friendly to
the Huron; but the instant he disappeared, it became
tossed and agitated by fierce and powerful passion.
Uncas maintained his elevated stand, keeping his eyes
on the form of Cora, until the colors of her dress were
blended with the foliage of the forest; when he descended, and moving silently through the throng, he disappeared in that lodge from which he had so recently
issued. A few of the graver and more attentive warriors,
who caught the gleams of anger that shot from the eyes
of the young chief in passing, followed him to the place
he had selected for his meditations. After which, Tamenund and Alice were removed, and the women and children were ordered to disperse. During the momentous
hour that succeeded, the encampment resembled a hive
of troubled bees, who only awaited the appearance and

example of their leader to take some distant and momentous flight.

A young warrior at length issued from the lodge of Uncas; and moving deliberately, with a sort of grave march, towards a dwarf pine that grew in the crevices of the rocky terrace, he tore the bark from its body, and then returned whence he came without speaking. He was soon followed by another, who stripped the sapling of its branches, leaving it a naked and blazed trunk. A third colored the posts with stripes of a dark red paint; all which indications of a hostile design in the leaders of the nation were received by the men without in a gloomy and ominous silence. Finally, the Mohican himself reappeared, divested of all his attire except his girdle and leggings, and with one-half of his fine features hid under a cloud of threatening black.

Uncas moved with a slow and dignified tread towards the post, which he immediately commenced encircling with a measured step, not unlike an ancient dance, raising his voice, at the same time, in the wild and irregular chant of his war-song. The notes were in the extremes of human sounds; being sometimes melancholy and exquisitely plaintive, even rivalling the melody of birds— and then, by sudden and startling transitions, causing the auditors to tremble by their depth and energy. The words were few and often repeated, proceeding gradually from a sort of invocation, or hymn to the Deity, to an intimation of the warrior's object, and terminating as they commenced with an acknowledgment of his own dependence on the Great Spirit. If it were possible to translate the comprehensive and melodious language in which he spoke, the ode might read something like the following:

"Manitou! Manitou! Manitou!
Thou art great, thou art good, thou art wise:
Manitou! Manitou!
Thou art just.

"In the heavens, in the clouds, O, I see
Many spots—many dark, many red:
In the heavens, O, I see
Many clouds.

"In the woods, in the air, O, I hear
The whoop, the long yell, and the cry:
In the woods, O, I hear
The loud whoop!

"Manitou! Manitou! Manitou!
Thou art weak—thou art strong; I am slow:
Manitou! Manitou!
Give me aid."

At the end of what might be called each verse he made a pause, by raising a note louder and longer than common, that was peculiarly suited to the sentiment just expressed. The first close was solemn, and intended to convey the idea of veneration; the second descriptive, bordering on the alarming; and the third was the well known and terrific war-whoop, which burst from the lips of the young warrior, like a combination of all the frightful sounds of battle. The last was like the first, humble and imploring. Three times did he repeat this song, and as often did he encircle the post in his dance.

At the close of the first turn, a grave and highly esteemed chief of the Lenape followed his example, singing words of his own, however, to music of a similar character. Warrior after warrior enlisted in the dance, until all of any renown and authority were numbered in its mazes. The spectacle now became wildly terrific; the fierce-looking and menacing visages of the chiefs receiving additional power from the appalling strains in which they mingled their guttural tones. Just then Uncas struck his tomahawk deep into the post, and raised his voice in a shout, which might be termed his own battle-cry. The act announced that he had assumed the chief authority in the intended expedition.

It was a signal that awakened all the slumbering passions of a nation. A hundred youths, who had hitherto been restrained by the diffidence of their years, rushed in a frantic body on the fancied emblem of their enemy, and severed it asunder, splinter by splinter, until nothing remained of the trunk but its roots in the earth. During this moment of tumult, the most ruthless deeds of war were performed on the fragments of the tree, with as much apparent ferocity as if they were the living victims of their cruelty. Some were scalped; some received the keen and trembling axe; and others suffered by thrusts from the fatal knife. In short, the manifestations of zeal and fierce delight were so great and unequivocal, that the expedition was declared to be a war of the nation.

The instant Uncas had struck the blow, he moved out of the circle, and cast his eyes up to the sun, which was just gaining the point, when the truce with Magua was to end. The fact was soon announced by a significant gesture, accompanied by a corresponding cry; and the whole of the excited multitude abandoned their mimic warfare, with shrill yells of pleasure, to prepare for the more hazardous experiment of the reality.

The whole face of the encampment was instantly changed. The warriors, who were already armed and painted, became as still as if they were incapable of any uncommon burst of emotion. On the other hand, the women broke out of the lodges, with the songs of joy and those of lamentation, so strangely mingled, that it might have been difficult to have said which passion preponderated. None, however, were idle. Some bore their choicest articles, others their young, and some their aged and infirm, into the forest, which spread itself like a verdant carpet of bright green against the side of the mountain. Thither Tamenund also retired, with calm composure, after a short and touching interview with Uncas; from whom the sage separated with the reluctance that a parent would quit a long lost and just recovered child. In the meantime, Duncan saw Alice to a place of safety, and then sought the scout, with a countenance that denoted how eagerly he also panted for the approaching contest.

But Hawkeye was too much accustomed to the war-song and the enlistments of the natives, to betray any interest in the passing scene. He merely cast an occasional look at the number and quality of the warriors, who, from time to time, signified their readiness to accompany Uncas to the field. In this particular he was soon satisfied; for, as has been already seen, the power of the young chief quickly embraced every fighting man in the nation. After this material point was so satisfactorily decided, he despatched an Indian boy in quest of "Killdeer" and the rifle of Uncas, to the place where they had deposited the weapons on approaching the camp of the Delawares; a measure of double policy, inasmuch as it protected the arms from their own fate, if detained as

prisoners, and gave them the advantage of appearing
among the strangers rather as sufferers than as men provided with the means of defence and subsistence. In se-
lecting another to perform the office of reclaiming his
highly prized rifle, the scout had lost sight of none of his
habitual caution. He knew that Magua had not come unattended, and he also knew that Huron spies watched
the movements of their new enemies, along the whole
boundary of the woods. It would, therefore, have been
fatal to himself to have attempted the experiment; a warrior would have fared no better; but the danger of a boy
would not be likely to commence until after his object
was discovered. When Heyward joined him, the scout
was coolly awaiting the result of this experiment.

The boy, who had been well instructed, and was sufficiently crafty, proceeded, with a bosom that was swelling
with the pride of such a confidence, and all the hopes of
young ambition, carelessly across the clearing to the
wood, which he entered at a point at some little distance
from the place where the guns were secreted. The instant, however, he was concealed by the foliage of the
bushes, his dusky form was to be seen gliding, like that of
a serpent, towards the desired treasure. He was successful; and in another moment he appeared flying across the
narrow opening that skirted the base of the terrace on
which the village stood, with the velocity of an arrow, and
bearing a prize in each hand. He had actually gained the
crags, and was leaping up their sides with incredible activity, when a shot from the woods showed how accurate
had been the judgment of the scout. The boy answered it
with a feeble but contemptuous shout; and immediately
a second bullet was sent after him from another part of
the cover. At the next instant he appeared on the level

above, elevating his guns in triumph, while he moved with the air of a conqueror towards the renowned hunter who had honored him by so glorious a commission.

Notwithstanding the lively interest Hawkeye had taken in the fate of his messenger, he received "Killdeer" with a satisfaction that, momentarily, drove all other recollections from his mind. After examining the piece with an intelligent eye, and opening and shutting the pan some ten or fifteen times, and trying sundry other equally important experiments on the lock, he turned to the boy, and demanded with great manifestations of kindness, if he was hurt. The urchin looked proudly up in his face, but made no reply.

"Ah! I see, lad, the knaves have barked your arm!" added the scout, taking up the limb of the patient sufferer, across which a deep flesh wound had been made by one of the bullets; "but a little bruised alder will act like a charm. In the meantime I will wrap it in a badge of wampum! You have commenced the business of a warrior early, my brave boy, and are likely to bear a plenty of honorable scars to your grave. I know many young men that have taken scalps who cannot show such a mark as this. Go!" having bound up the arm; "you will be a chief!"

The lad departed, prouder of his flowing blood than the vainest courtier could be of his blushing ribbon; and stalked among the fellows of his age, an object of general admiration and envy.

But in a moment of so many serious and important duties, this single act of juvenile fortitude did not attract the general notice and commendation it would have received under milder auspices. It had, however, served to apprise the Delawares of the position and the intentions of their enemies. Accordingly a party of adventurers, better suited to the task than the weak though spirited boy, was ordered to dislodge the skulkers. The duty was soon performed; for most of the Hurons retired of themselves when they found they had been discovered. The Delawares followed to a sufficient distance from their own encampment, and then halted for orders, apprehensive of being led into an ambush. As both parties secreted themselves, the woods were again as still and quiet as a mild summer morning and deep solitude could render them.

The calm but still impatient Uncas now collected his chiefs, and divided his power. He presented Hawkeye as a warrior, often tried, and always found deserving of confidence. When he found his friend met with a favorable reception, he bestowed on him the command of twenty men, like himself, active, skilful, and resolute. He gave the Delawares to understand the rank of Heyward among the troops of the Yengeese, and then tendered to him a trust of equal authority. But Duncan declined the charge, professing his readiness to serve as a volunteer by the side of the scout. After this disposition, the young Mohican appointed various native chiefs to fill the different situations of responsibility, and the time pressing, he gave forth the word to march. He was cheerfully, but silently, obeyed by more than two hundred men.

Their entrance into the forest was perfectly unmolested; nor did they encounter any living objects that could either give the alarm, or furnish the intelligence they needed, until they came upon the lairs of their own scouts. Here a halt was ordered, and the chiefs were assembled to hold a "whispering council."[2]

At this meeting divers plans of operation were suggested, though none of a character to meet the wishes of their ardent leader. Had Uncas followed the promptings of his own inclinations, he would have led his followers to the charge without a moment's delay, and put the conflict to the hazard of an instant issue; but such a course would have been in opposition to all the received practices and opinions of his countrymen. He was, therefore, fain to adopt a caution that in the present temper of his mind he execrated, and to listen to advice at which his fiery spirit chafed, under the vivid recollection of Cora's danger and Magua's insolence.

After an unsatisfactory conference of many minutes, a solitary individual was seen advancing from the side of the enemy, with such apparent haste, as to induce the belief he might be a messenger charged with pacific overtures. When within a hundred yards, however, of the cover behind which the Delaware council had assembled, the stranger hesitated, appeared uncertain what course to take, and finally halted. All eyes were now turned on Uncas, as if seeking directions how to proceed.

"Hawkeye," said the young chief, in a low voice, "he must never speak to the Hurons again."

"His time has come," said the laconic scout, thrusting the long barrel of his rifle through the leaves, and taking his deliberate and fatal aim. But, instead of pulling the trigger he lowered the muzzle again, and indulged himself in a fit of his peculiar mirth. "I took the imp for a Mingo, as I'm a miserable sinner!" he said; "but when my eye ranged along his ribs for a place to get the bullet in—would you think it, Uncas—I saw the musicianer's blower; and so, after all, it is the man they call Gamut, whose death can profit no one, and whose life, if his tongue can do anything but sing, may be made serviceable to our own ends. If sounds have not lost their virtue, I'll soon have a discourse with the honest fellow, and that in a voice he'll find more agreeable than the speech of 'Killdeer.'"

So saying, Hawkeye laid aside his rifle; and crawling through the bushes until within hearing of David, he attempted to repeat the musical effort, which had conducted himself, with so much safety and *éclat*,[3] through the Huron encampment. The exquisite organs of Gamut could not readily be deceived (and, to say the truth, it would have been difficult for any other than Hawkeye to produce a similar noise), and consequently, having once before heard the sounds, he now knew whence they proceeded. The poor fellow appeared relieved from a state of great embarrassment; for pursuing the direction of the voice—a task that to him was not much less arduous than it would have been to have gone up in the face of a battery—he soon discovered the hidden songster.

"I wonder what the Hurons will think of that!" said the scout, laughing, as he took his companion by the arm, and urged him towards the rear. "If the knaves lie within ear-shot, they will say there are two non-compossers instead of one! But here we are safe," he added, pointing to Uncas and his associates. "Now give us the history of the Mingo inventions in natural English, and without any ups and downs of voice."

David gazed about him, at the fierce and wild-looking chiefs, in mute wonder; but assured by the presence of faces that he knew, he soon rallied his faculties so far as to make an intelligent reply.

"The heathen are abroad in goodly numbers," said David, "and, I fear, with evil intent. There has been much howling and ungodly revelry, together with such sounds as it is profanity to utter, in their habitations within the past hour; so much so, in truth, that I have fled to the Delawares in search of peace."

"Your ears might not have profited much by the exchange, had you been quicker of foot," returned the scout, a little dryly. "But let that be as it may; where are the Hurons?"

"They lie hid in the forest, between this spot and their village, in such force, that prudence would teach you instantly to return."

Uncas cast a glance along the range of trees which concealed his own band and mentioned the name of—

"Magua?"

"Is among them. He brought in the maiden that had sojourned with the Delawares, and leaving her in the cave, has put himself, like a raging wolf, at the head of his savages. I know not what has troubled his spirit so greatly!"

"He has left her, you say, in the cave!" interrupted Heyward; " 'tis well that we know its situation! May not something be done for her instant relief?"

Uncas looked earnestly at the scout, before he asked,—

"What says Hawkeye?"

"Give me twenty rifles, and I will turn to the right, along the stream; and passing by the huts of the beaver, will join the Sagamore and the colonel. You shall then hear the whoop from that quarter; with this wind one may easily send it a mile. Then, Uncas, do you drive in their front; when they come within range of our pieces, we will give them a blow that, I pledge the good name of an old frontiersman, shall make their line bend like an ashen bow. After which, we will carry their village, and take the woman from the cave; when the affair may be finished with the tribe, according to a white man's battle, by a blow and a victory; or, in the Indian fashion, with dodge and cover. There may be no great learning, major, in this plan, but with courage and patience it can all be done."

"I like it much," cried Duncan, who saw the release of Cora was the primary object in the mind of the scout; "I like it much. Let it be instantly attempted."

After a short conference, the plan was matured, and rendered more intelligible to the several parties; the different signals were appointed, and the chiefs separated, each to his allotted station.

Uncas starts war dance to God Manitou (Great Spirit), Hawk sends boy to find rifles, Hurons shoot+wound boy, Uncas plan attack, 20 men each, Gamut comes dressed as Indian, Hawk almost kills him again, Gamut says Magua put Cora in cave near Hurons, Hawk plan: meet w/ Chingt Munro @ beaver pond, then attack+rescue.

XXXII

"But plagues shall spread, and funeral fires increase,
Till the great king, without a ransom paid,
To her own Chrysa send the black-eyed maid."
Alexander Pope, *The Iliad of Homer*[1]

DURING THE TIME Uncas was making this disposition of his forces, the woods were still, and, with the exception of those who had met in council, apparently as much untenanted, as when they came fresh from the hands of their Almighty Creator. The eye could range, in every direction, through the long and shadowed vistas of the trees; but nowhere was any object to be seen that did not properly belong to the peaceful and slumbering scenery. Here and there a bird was heard fluttering among the branches of the beeches, and occasionally a squirrel dropped a nut, drawing the startled looks of the party, for a moment, to the place; but the instant the casual interruption ceased, the passing air was heard murmuring above their heads, along that verdant and undulating surface of forest, which spread itself unbroken, unless by stream or lake, over such a vast region of country. Across the tract of wilderness, which lay between the Delawares and the village of their enemies, it seemed as if the foot of man had never trodden, so breathing and deep was the silence in which it lay. But Hawkeye, whose duty led him foremost in the adventure, knew the character of those with whom he was about to contend too well to trust the treacherous quiet.

When he saw his little band collected, the scout threw "Killdeer" into the hollow of his arm, and making a silent signal that he would be followed, he led them many rods towards the rear, into the bed of a little brook which they had crossed in advancing. Here he halted; and after waiting for the whole of his grave and attentive warriors to close about him, he spoke in Delaware, demanding—

"Do any of my young men know whither this run will lead us?"

A Delaware stretched forth a hand, with the two fingers separated, and indicating the manner in which they were joined at the root, he answered,—

"Before the sun could go his own length, the little water will be in the big." Then he added, pointing in the direction of the place he mentioned, "the two make enough for the beavers."

"I thought as much," returned the scout, glancing his eye upwards at the opening in the tree-tops, "from the course it takes, and the bearings of the mountains. Men, we will keep within the cover of its banks till we scent the Hurons."

His companions gave the usual brief exclamation of assent, but perceiving that their leader was about to lead the way in person, one or two made signs that all was not as it should be. Hawkeye, who comprehended their meaning glances, turned, and perceived that his party had been followed thus far by the singing-master.

"Do you know, friend," asked the scout gravely, and perhaps with a little of the pride of conscious deserving in his manner, "that this is a band of rangers chosen for the most desperate service, and put under the command of one who, though another might say it with a better face, will not be apt to leave them idle. It may not be five, it cannot be thirty minutes before we tread on the body of a Huron, living or dead."

"Though not admonished of your intentions in words," returned David, whose face was a little flushed, and whose ordinarily quiet and unmeaning eyes glimmered with an expression of unusual fire, "your men have reminded me of the children of Jacob going out to battle against the Shechemites,[2] for wickedly aspiring to wedlock with a woman of a race that was favored of the Lord. Now, I have journeyed far, and sojourned much in good and evil with the maiden ye seek; and though not a man of war, with my loins girded and my sword sharpened, yet would I gladly strike a blow in her behalf."

The scout hesitated, as if weighing the chances of such a strange enlistment in his mind before he answered,—

"You know not the use of any we'pon. You carry no rifle; and believe me, what the Mingos take they will freely give again."

"Though not a vaunting and bloodily disposed Goliath," returned David, drawing a sling from beneath his parti-colored and uncouth attire, "I have not forgotten the example of the Jewish boy. With this ancient instrument of war have I practised much in my youth, and peradventure the skill has not entirely departed from me."

"Ay!" said Hawkeye, considering the deer-skin thong and apron, with a cold and discouraging eye; "the thing might do its work among arrows, or even knives; but these Mengwe have been furnished by the Frenchers with a good grooved barrel a man. However, it seems to be your gift to go unharmed amid fire; and as you have hitherto been favored—major, you have left your rifle at a cock; a single shot before the time would be just twenty scalps lost to no purpose—singer, you can follow; we may find use for you in the shoutings."

"I thank you, friend," returned David, supplying himself, like his royal namesake, from among the pebbles of the brook; "though not given to the desire to kill, had you sent me away my spirit would have been troubled."

"Remember," added the scout, tapping his own head significantly on that spot where Gamut was yet sore, "we come to fight, and not to musickate. Until the general whoop is given, nothing speaks but the rifle."

David nodded, as much as to signify his acquiescence with the terms; and then Hawkeye, casting another observant glance over his followers, made the signal to proceed.

Their route lay, for the distance of a mile, along the bed of the water-course. Though protected from any great danger of observation by the precipitous banks, and the thick shrubbery which skirted the stream, no precaution known to an Indian attack was neglected. A warrior rather crawled than walked on each flank, so as to catch occasional glimpses into the forest; and every few minutes the band came to a halt, and listened for hostile sounds, with an acuteness of organs that would be scarcely conceivable to a man in a less natural state. Their march was, however, unmolested, and they reached the point where the lesser stream was lost in the greater, without the smallest evidence that their progress had been noted. Here the scout again halted, to consult the signs of the forest.

"We are likely to have a good day for a fight," he said, in English, addressing Heyward, and glancing his eye upwards at the clouds, which began to move in broad sheets across the firmament; "a bright sun and a glittering barrel are no friends to true sight. Everything is favorable; they have the wind, which will bring down their noises and their smoke too, no little matter in itself; whereas, with us it will be first a shot, and then a clear view. But here is an end of our cover; the beavers have had the range of this stream for hundreds of years, and what atween their food and their dams, there is, as you see, many a girdled stub, but few living trees."

Hawkeye had, in truth, in these few words, given no bad description of the prospect that now lay in their front. The brook was irregular in its width, sometimes shooting through narrow fissures in the rocks, and at others spreading over acres of bottom land, forming little areas that might be termed ponds. Everywhere along its banks were the mouldering relics of dead trees, in all the stages of decay, from those that groaned on their tottering trunks to such as had recently been robbed of those rugged coats that so mysteriously contain their principle of life. A few long, low, and moss-covered piles were scattered among them, like the memorials of a former and long-departed generation.

All these minute particulars were noted by the scout, with a gravity and interest that they probably had never before attracted. He knew that the Huron encampment lay a short half mile up the brook; and, with the characteristic anxiety of one who dreaded a hidden danger, he was greatly troubled at not finding the smallest trace of the presence of his enemy. Once or twice he felt induced to give the order for a rush, and to attempt the village by surprise; but his experience quickly admonished him of the danger of so useless an experiment. Then he listened intently, and with painful uncertainty, for the sounds of hostility in the quarter where Uncas was left; but nothing was audible except the sighing of the wind, that began to sweep over the bosom of the forest in gusts which threatened a tempest. At length, yielding rather to his unusual impatience than taking counsel from his knowledge, he determined to bring matters to an issue, by unmasking his force, and proceeding cautiously, but steadily, up the stream.

The scout had stood, while making his observations, sheltered by a brake, and his companions still lay in the bed of the ravine, through which the smaller stream debouched; but on hearing his low, though intelligible signal, the whole party stole up the bank, like so many dark spectres, and silently arranged themselves around him. Pointing in the direction he wished to proceed, Hawkeye advanced, the band breaking off in single files, and following so accurately in his footsteps, as if to leave it, if we except Heyward and David, the trail of but a single man.

The party was, however, scarcely uncovered before a volley from a dozen rifles was heard in their rear; and a Delaware leaping high into the air, like a wounded deer, fell at his whole length, perfectly dead.

"Ah! I feared some deviltry like this!" exclaimed the scout, in English; adding, with the quickness of thought, in his adopted tongue, "To cover, men, and charge!"

The band dispersed at the word, and before Heyward had well recovered from his surprise, he found himself standing alone with David. Luckily, the Hurons had already fallen back, and he was safe from their fire. But this state of things was evidently to be of short continuance; for the scout set the example of pressing on their retreat, by discharging his rifle, and darting from tree to tree, as his enemy slowly yielded ground.

It would seem that the assault had been made by a very small party of the Hurons, which, however, continued to increase in numbers, as it retired on its friends, until the return fire was very nearly, if not quite, equal to that maintained by the advancing Delawares. Heyward threw himself among the combatants, and imitating the necessary caution of his companions, he made quick discharges with his own rifle. The contest now grew warm and stationary. Few were injured, as both parties kept their bodies as much protected as possible by the trees; never, indeed, exposing any part of their persons except in the act of taking aim. But the chances were gradually growing unfavorable to Hawkeye and his band. The quick-sighted scout perceived his danger, without knowing how to remedy it. He saw it was more dangerous to retreat than to maintain his ground; while he found his enemy throwing out men on his flank, which rendered the task of keeping themselves covered so very difficult to the Delawares, as nearly to silence their fire. At this embarrassing moment, when they began to think the whole of the hostile tribe was gradually encircling them, they heard the yell of combatants, and the rattling of arms, echoing under the arches of the wood, at the place where Uncas was posted; a bottom which, in a manner, lay beneath the ground on which Hawkeye and his party were contending.

The effects of this attack were instantaneous, and to the scout and his friends greatly relieving. It would seem that, while his own surprise had been anticipated, and had consequently failed, the enemy, in their turn, having been deceived in its object and in his numbers, had left too small a force to resist the impetuous onset of the young Mohican. This fact was doubly apparent, by the rapid manner in which the battle in the forest rolled upwards towards the village, and by an instant falling off in the number of their assailants, who rushed to assist in maintaining the front, and, as it now proved to be, the principal point of defence.

Animating his followers by his voice, and his own example, Hawkeye then gave the word to bear down upon their foes. The charge, in that rude species of warfare, consisted merely in pushing from cover to cover, nigher to the enemy; and in this manoeuvre he was instantly and successfully obeyed. The Hurons were compelled to withdraw, and the scene of the contest rapidly changed from the more open ground on which it had commenced, to a spot where the assailed found a thicket to rest upon. Here the struggle was protracted, arduous, and seemingly of doubtful issue; the Delawares, though none of them fell, beginning to bleed freely, in consequence of the disadvantage at which they were held.

In this crisis, Hawkeye found means to get behind the same tree as that which served for a cover to Heyward; most of his own combatants being within call, a little on his right, where they maintained rapid, though fruitless, discharges on their sheltered enemies.

"You are a young man, major," said the scout, dropping the butt of "Killdeer" to the earth, and leaning on the barrel, a little fatigued with his previous industry; "and it may be your gift to lead armies at some future day ag'in these imps the Mingos. You may here see the philosophy of an Indian fight. It consists mainly in a ready hand, a quick eye, and a good cover. Now, if you had a company of the Royal Americans here, in what manner would you set them to work in this business?"

"The bayonet would make a road."

"Ay, there is white reason in what you say; but a man must ask himself, in this wilderness, how many lives he can spare. No—horse," continued the scout, shaking his head, like one who mused; "horse, I am ashamed to say, must, sooner or later, decide these scrimmages. The brutes are better than men, and to horse must we come at last. Put a shodden hoof on the moccasin of a redskin; and if his rifle be once emptied, he will never stop to load it again."

"This is a subject that might better be discussed at another time," returned Heyward; "shall we charge?"

"I see no contradiction to the gifts of any man, in passing his breathing spells in useful reflections," the scout replied. "As to a rush, I little relish such a measure; for a scalp or two must be thrown away in the attempt. And yet," he added, bending his head aside, to catch the sounds of the distant combat, "if we are to be of use to Uncas, these knaves in our front must be got rid of!"

Then turning, with a prompt and decided air, he called aloud to his Indians, in their own language. His words were answered by a shout; and, at a given signal, each warrior made a swift movement around his particular tree. The sight of so many dark bodies, glancing before their eyes at the same instant, drew a hasty, and consequently an ineffectual fire from the Hurons. Without stopping to breathe, the Delawares leaped, in long bounds, towards the wood, like so many panthers springing upon their prey. Hawkeye was in front, brandishing his terrible rifle, and animating his followers by his example. A few of the older and more cunning Hurons, who had not been deceived by the artifice which had been practised to draw their fire, now made a close and deadly discharge of their pieces, and justified the apprehensions of the scout, by felling three of his foremost warriors. But the shock was insufficient to repel the impetus of the charge. The Delawares broke into the cover with the ferocity of their natures, and swept away every trace of resistance by the fury of the onset.

The combat endured only for an instant, hand to hand, and then the assailed yielded ground rapidly, until they reached the opposite margin of the thicket, where they clung to the cover, with the sort of obstinacy that is so often witnessed in hunted brutes. At this critical moment, when the success of the struggle was again becoming doubtful, the crack of the rifle was heard behind the Hurons, and a bullet came whizzing from among some beaver lodges, which were situated in the clearing, in their rear, and was followed by the fierce and appalling yell of the war-whoop.

"There speaks the Sagamore!" shouted Hawkeye, answering the cry with his own stentorian[3] voice; "we have them now in face and back!"

The effect on the Hurons was instantaneous. Discouraged by an assault from a quarter that left them no opportunity for cover, their warriors uttered a common yell of disappointment, and breaking off in a body, they spread themselves across the opening, heedless of every consideration but flight. Many fell, in making the experiment, under the bullets and the blows of the pursuing Delawares.

We shall not pause to detail the meeting between the scout and Chingachgook, or the more touching interview that Duncan held with Munro. A few brief and hurried words served to explain the state of things to both parties; and then Hawkeye pointing out the Sagamore to his band, resigned the chief authority into the hands of the Mohican chief. Chingachgook assumed the station to which his birth and experience gave him so distinguished a claim, with the grave dignity that always gives force to the mandates of a native warrior. Following the footsteps of the scout, he led the party back through the thicket, his men scalping the fallen Hurons, and secreting the bodies of their own dead as they proceeded, until they gained a point where the former was content to make a halt.

The warriors, who had breathed themselves freely in the preceding struggle, were now posted on a bit of level ground, sprinkled with trees in sufficient numbers to conceal them. The land fell away rather precipitately in front, and beneath their eyes stretched, for several miles, a narrow, dark, and wooded vale. It was through this dense and dark forest that Uncas was still contending with the main body of the Hurons.

The Mohican and his friends advanced to the brow of the hill, and listened, with practised ears, to the sounds of the combat. A few birds hovered over the leafy bosom of the valley, frightened from their secluded nests; and here and there a light vapory cloud, which seemed already blending with the atmosphere, arose above the trees, and indicated some spot where the struggle had been fierce and stationary.

"The fight is coming up the ascent," said Duncan, pointing in the direction of a new explosion of fire-arms; "we are too much in the centre of their line to be effective."

"They will incline into the hollow where the cover is

thicker," said the scout, "and that will leave us well on
their flank. Go, Sagamore; you will hardly be in time to
give the whoop, and lead on the young men. I will fight
this scrimmage with warriors of my own color. You know
me, Mohican; not a Huron of them all shall cross the
swell, into your rear, without the notice of 'Killdeer.' "

The Indian chief paused another moment to consider
the signs of the contest, which was now rolling rapidly up
the ascent, a certain evidence that the Delawares triumphed; nor did he actually quit the place until admonished of the proximity of his friends, as well as enemies,
by the bullets of the former, which began to patter
among the dried leaves on the ground, like the bits of
falling hail which precede the bursting of the tempest.
Hawkeye and his three companions withdrew a few
paces to a shelter, and awaited the issue with calmness,
that nothing but great practice could impart in such a
scene.

It was not long before the reports of the rifles began to
lose the echoes of the woods, and to sound like weapons
discharged in the open air. Then a warrior appeared,
here and there, driven to the skirts of the forest, and rallying as he entered the clearing, as at the place where the
final stand was to be made. These were soon joined by
the others, until a long line of swarthy figures was to be
seen clinging to the cover with the obstinacy of desperation. Heyward began to grow impatient, and turned his
eyes anxiously in the direction of Chingachgook. The
chief was seated on a rock, with nothing visible but his
calm visage, considering the spectacle with an eye as deliberate as if he were posted there merely to view the
struggle.

"The time is come for the Delawares to strike!" said Duncan.

"Not so, not so," returned the scout; "when he scents his friends, he will let them know that he is here. See, see; the knaves are getting in that clump of pines, like bees settling after their flight. By the Lord, a squaw might put a bullet into the centre of such a knot of dark skins!"

At that instant the whoop was given, and a dozen Hurons fell by a discharge from Chingachgook and his band. The shout that followed was answered by a single war-cry from the forest, and a yell passed through the air that sounded as if a thousand throats were united in a common effort. The Hurons staggered, deserting the centre of their line, and Uncas issued from the forest through the opening they left, at the head of a hundred warriors.

Waving his hands right and left, the young chief pointed out the enemy to his followers, who separated in pursuit. The war now divided, both wings of the broken Hurons seeking protection in the woods again, hotly pressed by the victorious warriors of the Lenape. A minute might have passed, but the sounds were already receding in different directions, and gradually losing their distinctness beneath the echoing arches of the woods. One little knot of Hurons, however, had disdained to seek a cover, and were retiring, like lions at bay, slowly and sullenly up the acclivity which Chingachgook and his band had just deserted, to mingle more closely in the fray. Magua was conspicuous in this party, both by his fierce and savage mien, and by the air of haughty authority he yet maintained.

In his eagerness to expedite the pursuit, Uncas had left himself nearly alone; but the moment his eyes caught the figure of Le Subtil, every other consideration was forgotten. Raising his cry of battle, which recalled some six or seven warriors, and reckless of the disparity of their numbers, he rushed upon his enemy. Le Renard, who watched the movement, paused to receive him with secret joy. But at the moment when he thought the rashness of his impetuous young assailant had left him at his mercy, another shout was given, and La Longue Carabine was seen rushing to the rescue, attended by all his white associates. The Huron instantly turned, and commenced a rapid retreat up the ascent.

There was no time for greetings or congratulations; for Uncas, though unconscious of the presence of his friends, continued the pursuit with the velocity of the wind. In vain Hawkeye called to him to respect the covers; the young Mohican braved the dangerous fire of his enemies, and soon compelled them to a flight as swift as his own headlong speed. It was fortunate that the race was of short continuance, and that the white men were much favored by their position, or the Delaware would soon have outstripped all his companions, and fallen a victim to his own temerity. But ere such a calamity could happen, the pursuers and pursued entered the Wyandot village, within striking distance of each other.

Excited by the presence of their dwellings, and tired of the chase, the Hurons now made a stand, and fought around their council-lodge with the fury of despair. The onset and the issue were like the passage and destruction of a whirlwind. The tomahawk of Uncas, the blows of Hawkeye, and even the still nervous arm of Munro, were all busy for that passing moment, and the ground was quickly strewed with their enemies. Still Magua, though daring and much exposed, escaped from every effort against his life, with that sort of fabled protection that was made to overlook the fortunes of favored heroes in the legends of ancient poetry. Raising a yell that spoke volumes of anger and disappointment, the subtle chief, when he saw his comrades fallen, darted away from the place, attended by his two only surviving friends, leaving the Delawares engaged in stripping the dead of the bloody trophies of their victory.

But Uncas, who had vainly sought him in the *mêlée*, bounded forward in pursuit; Hawkeye, Heyward, and David still pressing on his footsteps. The utmost that the scout could effect, was to keep the muzzle of his rifle a little in advance of his friend, to whom, however, it answered every purpose of a charmed shield. Once Magua appeared disposed to make another and a final effort to revenge his losses; but, abandoning his intention as soon as demonstrated, he leaped into a thicket of bushes, through which he was followed by his enemies, and suddenly entered the mouth of the cave already known to the reader. Hawkeye, who had only forborne to fire in tenderness to Uncas, raised a shout of success, and proclaimed aloud, that now they were certain of their game. The pursuers dashed into the long and narrow entrance, in time to catch a glimpse of the retreating forms of the Hurons. Their passage through the natural galleries and subterraneous apartments of the cavern was preceded by the shrieks and cries of hundreds of women and children. The place, seen by its dim and uncertain light, appeared like the shades of the infernal regions, across which unhappy ghosts and savage demons were flitting in multitudes.

Still Uncas kept his eye on Magua, as if life to him possessed but a single object. Heyward and the scout still pressed on his rear, actuated, though possibly in a less degree, by a common feeling. But their way was becoming intricate, in those dark and gloomy passages, and the glimpses of the retiring warriors less distinct and frequent; and for a moment the trace was believed to be lost, when a white robe was seen fluttering in the farther extremity of a passage that seemed to lead up the mountain.

" 'Tis Cora!" exclaimed Heyward, in a voice in which horror and delight were wildly mingled.

"Cora! Cora!" echoed Uncas, bending forward like a deer.

" 'Tis the maiden!" shouted the scout. "Courage, lady; we come!—we come!"

The chase was renewed with a diligence rendered tenfold encouraging by this glimpse of the captive. But the way was rugged, broken, and in spots nearly impassable. Uncas abandoned his rifle, and leaped forward with headlong precipitation. Heyward rashly imitated his example, though both were, a moment afterwards, admonished of its madness, by hearing the bellowing of a piece, that the Hurons found time to discharge down the passage in the rocks, the bullet from which even gave the young Mohican a slight wound.

"We must close!" said the scout, passing his friends by a desperate leap; "the knaves will pick us all off at this distance; and see, they hold the maiden so as to shield themselves!"

Though his words were unheeded, or rather unheard, his example was followed by his companions, who, by incredible exertions, got near enough to the fugitives to

perceive that Cora was borne along between the two
warriors, while Magua prescribed the direction and
manner of their flight. At this moment the forms of all
four were strongly drawn against an opening in the sky,
and they disappeared. Nearly frantic with disappointment, Uncas and Heyward increased efforts that already
seemed superhuman, and they issued from the cavern
on the side of the mountain, in time to note the route of
the pursued. The course lay up the ascent, and still continued hazardous and laborious.

Encumbered by his rifle, and, perhaps, not sustained
by so deep an interest in the captive as his companions,
the scout suffered the latter to precede him a little,
Uncas, in his turn, taking the lead of Heyward. In this
manner, rocks, precipices, and difficulties were surmounted in an incredibly short space, that at another
time, and under other circumstances, would have been
deemed almost insuperable. But the impetuous young
men were rewarded by finding that, encumbered with
Cora, the Hurons were losing ground in the race.

"Stay, dog of the Wyandots!" exclaimed Uncas, shaking his bright tomahawk at Magua; "a Delaware girl calls
stay!"

"I will go no farther," cried Cora, stepping unexpectedly on a ledge of rocks, that overhung a deep precipice,
at no great distance from the summit of the mountain.
"Kill me if thou wilt, detestable Huron; I will go no farther."

The supporters of the maiden raised their ready tomahawks with the impious joy that fiends are thought to
take in mischief, but Magua stayed the uplifted arms.
The Huron chief, after casting the weapons he had
wrested from his companions over the rock, drew his

knife, and turned to his captive, with a look in which conflicting passions fiercely contended.

"Woman," he said, "choose; the wigwam or the knife of Le Subtil!"

Cora regarded him not, but dropping on her knees, she raised her eyes and stretched her arms towards heaven, saying, in a meek and yet confiding voice,—

"I am thine! do with me as thou seest best!"

"Woman," repeated Magua, hoarsely, and endeavoring in vain to catch a glance from her serene and beaming eye, "choose!"

But Cora neither heard nor heeded his demand. The form of the Huron trembled in every fibre, and he raised his arm on high, but dropped it again with a bewildered air, like one who doubted. Once more he struggled with himself and lifted the keen weapon again; but just then a piercing cry was heard above them, and Uncas appeared, leaping frantically, from a fearful height, upon the ledge. Magua recoiled a step; and one of his assistants, profiting by the chance, sheathed his own knife in the bosom of Cora.

The Huron sprang like a tiger on his offending and already retreating countryman, but the falling form of Uncas separated the unnatural combatants. Diverted from his object by this interruption, and maddened by the murder he had just witnessed, Magua buried his weapon in the back of the prostrate Delaware, uttering an unearthly shout as he committed the dastardly deed. But Uncas arose from the blow, as the wounded panther turns upon his foe, and struck the murderer of Cora to his feet, by an effort in which the last of his failing strength was expended. Then, with a stern and steady look, he turned to Le Subtil, and indicated by the expres-

sion of his eye, all that he would do, had not the power
deserted him. The latter seized the nerveless arm of the
unresisting Delaware, and passed his knife into his
bosom three several times, before his victim, still keeping his gaze riveted on his enemy with a look of inextinguishable scorn, fell dead at his feet.

"Mercy! mercy! Huron," cried Heyward, from above,
in tones nearly choked by horror; "give mercy, and thou
shalt receive it!"

Whirling the bloody knife up at the imploring youth,
the victorious Magua uttered a cry so fierce, so wild, and
yet so joyous, that it conveyed the sounds of savage triumph to the ears of those who fought in the valley, a
thousand feet below. He was answered by a burst from
the lips of the scout, whose tall person was just then seen
moving swiftly towards him, along those dangerous
crags, with steps as bold and reckless as if he possessed
the power to move in air. But when the hunter reached
the scene of the ruthless massacre, the ledge was tenanted only by the dead.

His keen eye took a single look at the victims, and
then shot its glances over the difficulties of the ascent in
his front. A form stood at the brow of the mountain, on
the very edge of the giddy height, with uplifted arms, in
an awful attitude of menace. Without stopping to consider his person, the rifle of Hawkeye was raised; but a
rock, which fell on the head of one of the fugitives below
exposed the indignant and glowing countenance of the
honest Gamut. Then Magua issued from a crevice, and
stepping with calm indifference over the body of the last
of his associates, he leaped a wide fissure, and ascended
the rocks at a point where the arm of David could not
reach him. A single bound would carry him to the brow

of the precipice, and assure his safety. Before taking the leap, however, the Huron paused, and shaking his hand at the scout, he shouted,—

"The pale-faces are dogs! The Delawares women! Magua leaves them on the rocks, for the crows!"

Laughing hoarsely, he made a desperate leap, and fell short of his mark; though his hand grasped a shrub on the verge of the height. The form of Hawkeye had crouched like a beast about to take its spring, and his frame trembled so violently with eagerness, that the muzzle of the half-raised rifle played like a leaf fluttering in the wind. Without exhausting himself with fruitless efforts, the cunning Magua suffered his body to drop to the length of his arms, and found a fragment for his feet to rest on. Then summoning all his powers, he renewed the attempt, and so far succeeded, as to draw his knees on the edge of the mountain. It was now, when the body of his enemy was most collected together, that the agitated weapon of the scout was drawn to his shoulder. The surrounding rocks themselves were not steadier than the piece became, for the single instant that it poured out its contents. The arms of the Huron relaxed, and his body fell back a little, while his knees still kept their position. Turning a relentless look on his enemy, he shook a hand in grim defiance. But his hold loosened, and his dark person was seen cutting the air with its head downwards, for a fleeting instant, until it glided past the fringe of shrubbery which clung to the mountain, in its rapid flight to destruction.

XXXIII

"They fought, like brave men, long and well,
They piled that ground with Moslem slain,
They conquered—but Bozzaris fell,
    Bleeding at every vein.
His few surviving comrades saw.
His smile when rang their proud hurrah,
    And the red field was won;
Then saw in death his eyelids close
    Calmly, as to a night's repose,
    Like flowers at set of sun."
Fitz-Green Halleck, "Marco Bozzaris"[1]

THE SUN FOUND THE LENAPE, on the succeeding day, a nation of mourners. The sounds of the battle were over, and they had fed fat their ancient grudge, and had avenged their recent quarrel with the Mengwe, by the destruction of a whole community. The black and murky atmosphere that floated around the spot where the Hurons had encamped, sufficiently announced, of itself, the fate of that wandering tribe; while hundreds of ravens, that struggled above the bleak summits of the mountains, or swept, in noisy flocks, across the wide ranges of the woods, furnished a frightful direction to the scene of the combat. In short, any eye at all practised in the signs of a frontier warfare, might easily have traced all those unerring evidences of the ruthless results which attend an Indian vengeance.

Still, the sun rose on the Lenape a nation of mourners. No shouts of success, no songs of triumph, were heard, in rejoicings for their victory. The latest straggler had returned from his fell employment, only to strip himself of the terrific emblems of his bloody calling, and to join in the lamentations of his countrymen, as a stricken people. Pride and exultation were supplanted by humility, and the fiercest of human passions was already succeeded by the most profound and unequivocal demonstrations of grief.

The lodges were deserted; but a broad belt of earnest faces encircled a spot in their vicinity, whither everything possessing life had repaired, and where all were now collected, in deep and awful silence. Though beings of every rank and age, of both sexes, and of all pursuits, had united to form this breathing wall of bodies, they were influenced by a single emotion. Each eye was riveted on the centre of that ring, which contained the objects of so much, and of so common, an interest.

Six Delaware girls, with their long, dark, flowing tresses falling loosely across their bosoms, stood apart, and only gave proofs of their existence as they occasionally strewed sweet-scented herbs and forest flowers on a litter of fragrant plants, that, under a pall of Indian robes, supported all that now remained of the ardent, high-souled, and generous Cora. Her form was concealed in many wrappers of the same simple manufacture, and her face was shut forever from the gaze of men. At her feet was seated the desolate Munro. His aged head was bowed nearly to the earth, in compelled submission to the stroke of Providence; but a hidden anguish struggled about his furrowed brow, that was only partially concealed by the careless locks of gray that had fallen, neglected, on his temples. Gamut stood at his side, his meek head bared to the rays of the sun, while his eyes, wandering and concerned, seemed to be equally divided between that little volume, which contained so many quaint but holy maxims, and the being in whose behalf his soul yearned to administer consolation. Heyward was also nigh, supporting himself against a tree, and endeavoring to keep down those sudden risings of sorrow that it required his utmost manhood to subdue.

But sad and melancholy as this group may easily be imagined, it was far less touching than another, that occupied the opposite space of the same area. Seated, as in life, with his form and limbs arranged in grave and decent composure, Uncas appeared, arrayed in the most gorgeous ornaments that the wealth of the tribe could furnish. Rich plumes nodded above his head; wampum, gorgets, bracelets, and medals, adorned his person in profusion; though his dull eye and vacant lineaments too strongly contradicted the idle tale of pride they would convey.

Directly in front of the corpse Chingachgook was placed, without arms, paint, or adornment of any sort, except the bright blue blazonry of his race, that was indelibly impressed on his naked bosom. During the long period that the tribe had been thus collected, the Mohican warrior had kept a steady, anxious look on the cold and senseless countenance of his son. So riveted and intense had been that gaze, and so changeless his attitude, that a stranger might not have told the living from the dead, but for the occasional gleamings of a troubled spirit that shot athwart the dark visage of one, and the death-like calm that had forever settled on the lineaments of the other.

The scout was hard by, leaning in a pensive posture on his own fatal and avenging weapon; while Tamenund, supported by the elders of his nation, occupied a high place at hand, whence he might look down on the mute and sorrowful assemblage of his people.

Just within the inner edge of the circle stood a soldier, in the military attire of a strange nation; and without it was his warhorse, in the centre of a collection of mounted domestics, seemingly in readiness to undertake some distant journey. The vestments of the stranger announced him to be one who held a responsible situation near the person of the captain of the Canadas; and who, as it would now seem, finding his errand of peace frustrated by the fierce impetuosity of his allies, was content to become a silent and sad spectator of the fruits of a contest that he had arrived too late to anticipate.

The day was drawing to the close of its first quarter, and yet had the multitude maintained its breathing stillness since its dawn. No sound louder than a stifled sob had been heard among them, nor had even a limb been moved throughout that long and painful period, except to perform the simple and touching offerings that were made, from time to time, in commemoration of the dead. The patience and forbearance of Indian fortitude could alone support such an appearance of abstraction, as seemed now to have turned each dark and motionless figure into stone.

At length, the sage of the Delawares stretched forth an arm, and leaning on the shoulders of his attendants, he arose with an air as feeble as if another age had already intervened between the man who had met his nation the preceding day, and him who now tottered on his elevated stand.

"Men of the Lenape!" he said, in hollow tones that sounded like a voice charged with some prophetic mission; "the face of the Manitou is behind a cloud! His eye is turned from you; His ears are shut; His tongue gives no answer. You see Him not; yet His judgments are before you. Let your hearts be open and your spirits tell no lie. Men of the Lenape! the face of the Manitou is behind a cloud."

As this simple and yet terrible annunciation stole on the ears of the multitude, a stillness as deep and awful succeeded as if the venerated spirit they worshipped had uttered the words without the aid of human organs; and even the inanimate Uncas appeared a being of life, compared with the humbled and submissive throng by whom he was surrounded. As the immediate effect, however, gradually passed away, a low murmur of voices commenced a sort of chant in honor of the dead. The sounds were those of females, and were thrillingly soft and wailing. The words were connected by no regular continuation, but as one ceased another took up the eulogy, or lamentation, whichever it might be called, and gave vent to her emotions in such language as was suggested by her feelings and the occasion. At intervals the speaker was interrupted by general and loud bursts of sorrow, during which the girls around the bier of Cora plucked the plants and flowers blindly from her body, as if bewildered with grief. But, in the milder moments of their plaint, these emblems of purity and sweetness were cast back to their places, with every sign of tenderness and regret. Though rendered less connected by many and general interruptions and outbreakings, a translation of their language would have contained a regular descant, which, in substance, might have proved to possess a train of consecutive ideas.

A girl, selected for the task by her rank and qualifications, commenced by modest allusions to the qualities of the deceased warrior, embellishing her expressions with those oriental images that the Indians have probably brought with them from the extremes of the other continent, and which form of themselves a link to connect the ancient histories of the two worlds. She called him the "panther of his tribe"; and described him as one whose moccasin left no trail on the dews; whose bound was like the leap of the young fawn; whose eye was brighter than a star in the dark night; and whose voice, in battle, was loud as the thunder of the Manitou. She reminded him of the mother who bore him, and dwelt forcibly on the happiness she must feel in possessing such a son. She bade him tell her, when they met in the world of spirits, that the Delaware girls had shed tears above the grave of her child, and had called her blessed.

Then, they who succeeded, changing their tones to a milder and still more tender strain, alluded, with the delicacy and sensitiveness of woman, to the stranger maiden, who had left the upper earth at a time so near his own departure, as to render the will of the Great Spirit too manifest to be disregarded. They admonished him to be kind to her, and to have consideration for her ignorance of those arts which were so necessary to the comfort of a warrior like himself. They dwelt upon her matchless beauty, and on her noble resolution, without the taint of envy, and as angels may be thought to delight in a superior excellence; adding, that these endowments should prove more than equivalent for any little imperfections in her education.

After which, others again, in due succession, spoke to the maiden herself, in the low, soft language of tenderness and love. They exhorted her to be of cheerful mind, and to fear nothing for future welfare. A hunter would be her companion, who knew how to provide for her smallest wants; and a warrior was at her side who was able to protect her against every danger. They promised that her path should be pleasant, and her burden light. They cautioned her against unavailing regrets for the friends of her youth, and the scenes where her fathers had dwelt; assuring her that the "blessed hunting-grounds of the Lenape" contained vales as pleasant, streams as pure, and flowers as sweet, as the "heaven of the pale-faces." They advised her to be attentive to the wants of her companion, and never to forget the distinction which the Manitou had so wisely established between them. Then, in a wild burst of their chant, they sang with united voices the temper of the Mohican's mind. They pronounced him noble, manly and generous; all that became a warrior, and all that a maid might love. Clothing their ideas in the most remote and subtle images, they betrayed, that, in the short period of their intercourse, they had discovered, with the intuitive perception of their sex, the truant disposition of his inclinations. The Delaware girls had found no favor in his eyes! He was of a race that had once been lords on the shores of the salt lake, and his wishes had led him back to a people who dwelt about the graves of his fathers. Why should not such a predilection be encouraged! That she was of a blood purer and richer than the rest of her nation, any eye might have seen; that she was equal to the dangers and daring of a life in the woods, her conduct had proved; and now, they added, the "wise one of the earth" had transplanted her to a place where she would find congenial spirits, and might be forever happy.

Then, with another transition in voice and subject, allusions were made to the virgin who wept in the adjacent lodge. They compared her to flakes of snow; as pure, as white, as brilliant, and as liable to melt in the fierce heats of summer, or congeal in the frosts of winter. They doubted not that she was lovely in the eyes of the young chief, whose skin and whose sorrow seemed so like her own; but, though far from expressing such a preference, it was evident they deemed her less excellent than the maid they mourned. Still they denied her no meed her rare charms might properly claim. Her ringlets were compared to the exuberant tendrils of the vine, her eye to the blue vault of the heavens, and the most spotless cloud, with its glowing flush of the sun, was admitted to be less attractive than her bloom.

During these and similar songs nothing was audible but the murmurs of the music; relieved, as it was, or rather rendered terrible, by those occasional bursts of grief which might be called its choruses. The Delawares themselves listened like charmed men; and it was very apparent, by the variations of their speaking countenances, how deep and true was their sympathy. Even David was not reluctant to lend his ears to tones of voices so sweet; and long ere the chant was ended, his gaze announced that his soul was enthralled.

The scout, to whom alone, of all the white men, the words were intelligible, suffered himself to be a little aroused from his meditative posture, and bent his face aside, to catch their meaning, as the girls proceeded. But when they spoke of the future prospects of Cora and Uncas, he shook his head, like one who knew the error of their simple creed, and resuming his reclining attitude, he maintained it until the ceremony—if that might be called a ceremony, in which feeling was so deeply imbued—was finished. Happily for the self-command of both Heyward and Munro, they knew not the meaning of the wild sounds they heard.

Chingachgook was a solitary exception to the interest manifested by the native part of the audience. His look never changed throughout the whole of the scene, nor did a muscle move in his rigid countenance, even at the wildest or the most pathetic parts of the lamentation. The cold and senseless remains of his son was all to him, and every other sense but that of sight seemed frozen, in order that his eyes might take their final gaze at those lineaments he had so long loved, and which were now about to be closed forever from his view.

In this stage of the funeral obsequies, a warrior much renowned for deeds in arms, and more especially for services in the recent combat, a man of stern and grave demeanor, advanced slowly from the crowd, and placed himself nigh the person of the dead.

"Why hast thou left us, pride of the Wapanachki?" he said, addressing himself to the dull ears of Uncas, as if the empty clay retained the faculties of the animated man; "thy time has been like that of the sun when in the trees; thy glory brighter than his light at noonday. Thou art gone, youthful warrior, but a hundred Wyandots are clearing the briers from thy path to the world of spirits. Who that saw thee in battle would believe that thou couldst die? Who before thee has ever shown Uttawa the way into the fight? Thy feet were like the wings of eagles;

thine arm heavier than falling branches from the pine; and thy voice like the Manitou when he speaks in the clouds. The tongue of Uttawa is weak," he added, looking about him with a melancholy gaze, "and his heart exceeding heavy. Pride of the Wapanachki, why hast thou left us?"

He was succeeded by others, in due order, until most of the high and gifted men of the nation had sung or spoken their tribute of praise over the *manes* of the deceased chief. When each had ended, another deep and breathing silence reigned in all the place.

Then a low, deep sound was heard, like the suppressed accompaniment of distant music, rising just high enough on the air to be audible, and yet so indistinctly, as to leave its character, and the place whence it proceeded, alike matters of conjecture. It was, however, succeeded by another and another strain, each in a higher key, until they grew on the ear, first in long drawn and often repeated interjections, and finally in words. The lips of Chingachgook had so far parted, as to announce that it was the monody[2] of the father. Though not an eye was turned towards him, nor the smallest sign of impatience exhibited, it was apparent, by the manner in which the multitude elevated their heads to listen, that they drank in the sounds with an intenseness of attention, that none but Tamenund himself had ever before commanded. But they listened in vain. The strains rose just so loud as to become intelligible, and then grew fainter and more trembling, until they finally sank on the ear, as if borne away by a passing breath of wind. The lips of the Sagamore closed, and he remained silent in his seat, looking, with his riveted eye and motionless form, like some creature that had been turned from the Almighty hand with the form but without the spirit of a man. The Delawares, who knew by these symptoms that the mind of their friend was not prepared for so mighty an effort of fortitude, relaxed in their attention; and, with an innate delicacy, seemed to bestow all their thoughts on the obsequies of the stranger maiden.

A signal was given, by one of the elder chiefs, to the women who crowded that part of the circle near which the body of Cora lay. Obedient to the sign, the girls raised the bier to the elevation of their heads, and advanced with slow and regulated steps, chanting, as they proceeded, another wailing song in praise of the deceased. Gamut, who had been a close observer of rites he deemed so heathenish, now bent his head over the shoulder of the unconscious father, whispering,—

"They move with the remains of thy child; shall we not follow, and see them interred with Christian burial?"

Munro started, as if the last trumpet had sounded in his ear, and bestowing one anxious and hurried glance around him, he arose and followed in the simple train, with the mien of a soldier, but bearing the full burden of a parent's suffering. His friends pressed around him with a sorrow that was too strong to be termed sympathy—even the young Frenchman joining in the procession, with the air of a man who was sensibly touched at the early and melancholy fate of one so lovely. But when the last and humblest female of the tribe had joined in the wild, and yet ordered array, the men of the Lenape contracted their circle, and formed again around the person of Uncas, as silent, as grave, and as motionless as before.

The place which had been chosen for the grave of Cora was a little knoll, where a cluster of young and healthful pines had taken root, forming of themselves a melancholy and appropriate shade over the spot. On reaching it the girls deposited their burden, and continued for many minutes waiting, with characteristic patience, and native timidity, for some evidence that they whose feelings were most concerned were content with the arrangement. At length the scout, who alone understood their habits, said, in their own language,—

"My daughters have done well; the white men thank them."

Satisfied with this testimony in their favor, the girls proceeded to deposit the body in a shell, ingeniously, and not inelegantly, fabricated of the bark of the birch; after which they lowered it into its dark and final abode. The ceremony of covering the remains, and concealing the marks of the fresh earth, by leaves and other natural and customary objects, was conducted with the same simple and silent forms. But when the labors of the kind beings who had performed these sad and friendly offices were so far completed, they hesitated, in a way to show that they knew not how much further they might proceed. It was in this stage of the rites that the scout again addressed them:—

"My young women have done enough," he said; "the spirit of a pale-face has no need of food or raiment, their gifts being according to the heaven of their color. I see," he added, glancing an eye at David, who was preparing his book in a manner that indicated an intention to lead the way in sacred song, "that one who better knows the Christian fashions is about to speak."

The females stood modestly aside, and, from having been the principal actors in the scene, they now became the meek and attentive observers of that which followed. During the time David was occupied in pouring out the pious feelings of his spirit in this manner, not a sign of surprise, nor a look of impatience, escaped them. They listened like those who knew the meaning of the strange words, and appeared as if they felt the mingled emotions of sorrow, hope, and resignation, they were intended to convey.

Excited by the scene he had just witnessed, and perhaps influenced by his own secret emotions, the master of song exceeded his usual efforts. His full, rich voice was not found to suffer by a comparison with the soft tones of the girls; and his more modulated strains possessed, at least for the ears of those to whom they were peculiarly addressed, the additional power of intelligence. He ended the anthem, as he had commenced it, in the midst of a grave and solemn stillness.

When, however, the closing cadence had fallen on the ears of his auditors, the secret, timorous glances of the eyes, and the general, and yet subdued movement of the assemblage, betrayed that something was expected from the father of the deceased. Munro seemed sensible that the time was come for him to exert what is, perhaps, the greatest effort of which human nature is capable. He bared his gray locks, and looked around the timid and quiet throng by which he was encircled with a firm and collected countenance. Then motioning with his hand for the scout to listen, he said,—

"Say to these kind and gentle females, that a heartbroken and failing man returns them his thanks. Tell them that the Being we all worship, under different names, will be mindful of their charity; and that the time shall not be distant when we may assemble around his throne without distinction of sex, or rank, or color."

The scout listened to the tremulous voice in which the

veteran delivered these words, and shook his head slowly when they were ended, as one who doubted their efficacy.

"To tell them this," he said, "would be to tell them that the snows come not in the winter, or that the sun shines fiercest when the trees are stripped of their leaves."

Then turning to the women, he made such a communication of the other's gratitude as he deemed most suited to the capacities of his listeners. The head of Munro had already sunk upon his chest, and he was again fast relapsing into melancholy, when the young Frenchman before named ventured to touch him lightly on the elbow. As soon as he had gained the attention of the mourning old man, he pointed towards a group of young Indians, who approached with a light but closely covered litter, and then pointed upward towards the sun.

"I understand you, sir," returned Munro, with a voice of forced firmness; "I understand you. It is the will of Heaven, and I submit. Cora, my child! if the prayers of a heartbroken father could avail thee now, how blessed shouldest thou be! Come, gentlemen," he added, looking about him with an air of lofty composure, though the anguish that quivered in his faded countenance was far too powerful to be concealed, "our duty here is ended; let us depart."

Heyward gladly obeyed a summons that took them from a spot where, each instant, he felt his self-control was about to desert him. While his companions were mounting, however, he found time to press the hand of the scout, and to repeat the terms of an engagement they had made, to meet again within the posts of the British army. Then gladly throwing himself into the saddle, he spurred his charger to the side of the litter, whence low and stifled sobs alone announced the presence of Alice. In this manner, the head of Munro again dropping on his bosom, with Heyward and David following in sorrowing silence, and attended by the aide of Montcalm with his guard, all the white men, with the exception of Hawkeye, passed from before the eyes of the Delawares, and were soon buried in the vast forests of that region.

But the tie which, through their common calamity, had united the feelings of these simple dwellers in the woods with the strangers who had thus transiently visited them, was not so easily broken. Years passed away before the traditionary tale of the white maiden, and of the young warrior of the Mohicans, ceased to beguile the long nights and tedious marches, or to animate their youthful and brave with a desire for vengeance. Neither were the secondary actors in these momentous incidents forgotten. Through the medium of the scout, who served for years afterwards as a link between them and civilized life, they learned, in answer to their inquiries, that the "Gray Head" was speedily gathered to his fathers— borne down, as was erroneously believed, by his military misfortunes; and that the "Open Hand" had conveyed his surviving daughter far into the settlements of the "pale-faces," where her tears had at last ceased to flow, and had been succeeded by the bright smiles which were better suited to her joyous nature.

But these were events of a time later than that which concerns our tale. Deserted by all of his color, Hawkeye returned to the spot where his own sympathies led him, with a force that no ideal bond of union could bestow. He was just in time to catch a parting look of the features of Uncas, whom the Delawares were already inclosing in his last vestments of skins. They paused to permit the longing and lingering gaze of the sturdy woodsman, and when it was ended, the body was enveloped, never to be unclosed again. Then came a procession like the other, and the whole nation was collected about the temporary grave of the chief—temporary, because it was proper that, at some future day, his bones should rest among those of his own people.

The movement, like the feeling, had been simultaneous and general. The same grave expression of grief, the same rigid silence, and the same deference to the principal mourner, were observed around the place of interment as have been already described. The body was deposited in an attitude of repose, facing the rising sun, with the implements of war and of the chase at hand, in readiness for the final journey. An opening was left in the shell, by which it was protected from the soil, for the spirit to communicate with its earthly tenement, when necessary; and the whole was concealed from the instinct, and protected from the ravages of the beasts of prey, with an ingenuity peculiar to the natives. The manual rites then ceased, and all present reverted to the more spiritual part of the ceremonies.

Chingachgook became once more the object of the common attention. He had not yet spoken, and something consolatory and instructive was expected from so renowned a chief on an occasion of such interest. Conscious of the wishes of the people, the stern and self-restrained warrior raised his face, which had latterly been buried in his robe, and looked about him with a steady eye. His firmly compressed and expressive lips then severed, and for the first time during the long ceremonies his voice was distinctly audible.

"Why do my brothers mourn!" he said, regarding the dark race of dejected warriors by whom he was environed; "why do my daughters weep! that a young man has gone to the happy hunting-grounds; that a chief has filled his time with honor! He was good; he was dutiful; he was brave. Who can deny it? The Manitou had need of such a warrior, and He has called him away. As for me, the son and the father of Uncas, I am a blazed pine, in a clearing of the pale-faces. My race has gone from the shores of the salt lake, and the hills of the Delawares. But who can say that the Serpent of his tribe has forgotten his wisdom? I am alone—"

"No, no," cried Hawkeye, who had been gazing with a yearning look at the rigid features of his friend, with something like his own self-command, but whose philosophy could endure no longer; "no, Sagamore, not alone. The gifts of our colors may be different, but God has so placed us as to journey in the same path. I have no kin, and I may also say, like you, no people. He was your son, and a redskin by nature; and it may be that your blood was nearer—but if ever I forget the lad who has so often fou't at my side in war, and slept at my side in peace, may He who made us all, whatever may be our color or our gifts, forget me! The boy has left us for a time; but, Sagamore, you are not alone."

Chingachgook grasped the hand that, in the warmth of feeling, the scout had stretched across the fresh earth, and in that attitude of friendship these two sturdy and intrepid woodsmen bowed their heads together, while scalding tears fell to their feet, watering the grave of Uncas like drops of falling rain.

In the midst of the awful stillness with which such a

burst of feeling, coming, as it did, from the two most renowned warriors of that region, was received, Tamenund lifted his voice to disperse the multitude.

"It is enough," he said. "Go, children of the Lenape, the anger of the Manitou is not done. Why should Tamenund stay? The pale-faces are masters of the earth, and the time of the red-men has not yet come again. My day has been too long. In the morning I saw the sons of Unamis happy and strong; and yet, before the night has come, have I lived to see the last warrior of the wise race of the Mohicans."

Funeral for Cora + Uncas, chant that C+U will be together in "the Happy Hunting Ground" + Ching sings song of dad to dead son, bury Cora. Munro ask Hawk to tell Indians 2 hopes: God won't forget the Delawares niceness + they'll all be together 1 day where race doesn't matter. Hawk says no + just thanks them for brave. Whites leave w/o Hawk, Uncas traditional burial. Ching feels alone, Hawk says Uncas only left him for a time. Tam says he has lived to see the last warrior of the race of the Mohicans.

NOTES

Chapter I

1. **"Mine ear . . . my kingdom lost?":** From William Shakespeare's *Richard II*, Act III, scene ii. King Richard tells Sir Stephen Scroop that he is prepared to hear the worst about his cousin Henry Bolingbroke's plans to usurp his lands and his throne. Eventually, Bolingbroke becomes King Henry IV of England.
2. **husbandman:** Farmer.
3. **Montcalm:** Louis-Joseph, Marquis de Montcalm, was the general who led the French and Indian forces against the British.
4. **"numerous as the leaves on the trees":** Cooper's variation of a quotation taken from David Humphrey's *An Essay on the Life of the Honourable Major-General Israel Putnam: Addressed to the State Society of the Cincinnati in Connecticut and Published by Their Order* (1788). Putnam was an English

army officer who, during the French and Indian War, was captured and tortured. The Humphrey quotation refers to General Montcalm's vast manpower and actually reads: "M. de Montcalm informed Major Putnam, when a prisoner in Canada, that one of his running Indians saw and reported this movement; and upon being questioned relatively to the numbers, answered in their figurative style, 'if you can count the leaves on the trees, you can count them.'"

5. **Munro:** The historical figure George Munro was a lieutenant colonel in the English forces and commander of Fort William Henry. He is also the father of Alice and Cora Munro. Scholars still debate whether the "real" Munro had daughters.

6. **leagues:** A league is equal to roughly three miles.

7. **nankeen:** A type of durable cloth, yellowish in color and made of cotton. The name is a derivation of Nanking, a region in China where the fabric has been made dating back to the Silk Road.

8. **both havens:** This reference notes the cities of New London and New Haven, Connecticut, two active ports bringing trade to the newly developing colonies. A militia of New Haven settlers joined the British army against the French and the Indians. New Haven was the co-capital of Connecticut, along with Hartford. New London was an important port of entry, at a point where the Long Island Sound meets the Atlantic Ocean.

Chapter II

1. **"Sola, sola . . . sola!":** From Shakespeare's *The Merchant of Venice*, Act V, scene i, a greeting to grab

someone's attention. Because this chapter intro-
duces David Gamut, jovial psalmodist and comic relief, the quotation may reflect the merry appearance
of this new character.

2. **Narragansett:** A reference to the Narragansett
Pacer, a breed of horse that vanished after the Revolutionary War. The Narragansett was known for its
easy gait, small stature, surefootedness, and speed.
Later, Duncan tells Hawkeye that the horses "come
from the shores of Narragansett Bay, in the small
province of Providence Plantations, and are celebrated for their hardihood."

3. **castor:** A hat made of beaver pelt.

4. **psalmody:** The act of singing songs or hymns.

5. **" 'hath music in his soul' ":** Cooper revises this
quotation from *The Merchant of Venice* also as the
quotation used in the epigraph for this chapter, taken
from Act V, scene i: "The man that hath no music in
himself,/Nor is not mov'd with concord of sweet
sounds,/Is fit for treasons, stratagems, and spoils."
Such a man cannot be trusted and is as dark in spirit
as the underworld.

6. ***The Psalms, Hymns . . . in New England:*** The Pu-
ritans used this book, nicknamed the *Bay Psalm
Book*, as the basic resource for psalmody. "Standish,"
below, refers to the name of a particular hymn.

7. **unknown engine:** A pitch pipe.

Chapter III

1. **"Before these fields . . . in the shade":** From the
poem "Indian at the Burial Place of His Fathers" by
William Cullen Bryant (1824). Bryant and Cooper

met in New York City after the publication of
Cooper's *The Pioneers*. The novel inspired Bryant's
poem, in which an Indian laments the loss of his an-
cestral lands to the colonizers. This stanza follows:

Those grateful sounds are heard no more,
The springs are silent in the sun;
The rivers, by the blackened shore,
With lessening current run;
The realm our tribes are crushed to get
May be a barren desert yet.

2. **Maquas:** Maquas belong to the same larger tribe of
people as the Mohawks and the Iroquois. *Maqua* is a
perjorative term for Mohawk used by the Mohicans.

3. **Dutch:** The Dutch arrived in what is now New York
City in the early seventeenth century.

4. **sagamore:** Head of a North American tribe, usually
of the second position rather than the primary leader.

Chapter IV

1. **"Well, go thy way ... for this injury":** From
Shakespeare's *A Midsummer Night's Dream*, Act II,
scene i, when the king of the fairies, Oberon, asks his
queen, Titania, to give him her changeling boy, and
she denies him.

2. **Mingo:** Hawkeye uses the term *Mingo* to refer to
members of the Iroquois nation. Historically, however, the Mingo did not belong to the same tribe but
were groups of Indians belonging to different com-
munities in West Virginia and Ohio who were subject
to Iroquois rule and custom. The Mingo allied with
the French during the war.

Chapter V

1. **"In such a night . . . ere himself":** From Shakespeare's *The Merchant of Venice*, Act V, scene i, a scene of wooing between Lorenzo and Jessica. The name Thisbe refers to the Ovidian myth of Thisbe and Pyramus, young star-crossed lovers.

2. **Glenn's:** Glens Falls, New York, which in real life is a halfway point between Fort William Henry and Fort Edward. South Glens Falls is now home to Cooper's Cave, the spot where Cooper was inspired to write the novel in 1825. Cooper accompanied Edward Stanley, future prime minister of Great Britain, to the cavern beneath the falls, where Stanley suggested that a romance be set. Cooper began to think about his previous *Leatherstocking* characters, and the novel was born.

Chapter VI

1. **"Those strains . . . with solemn air":** Lines from Robert Burns's poem "The Cotter's Saturday Night" (1785). The poem depicts a scene of domestic idyll in the country.

2. **Connecticut levy:** Those youths levied by Connecticut to serve in the army.

Chapter VII

1. **"They do not sleep . . . see them sit":** From "The Bard: A Pindaric Ode" (1757), by Thomas Gray.

Chapter VIII

1. **"They linger yet ... their native land":** More lines from Gray's poem "The Bard." The two lines that follow and finish the stanza echo the themes of the novel:

     With me in dreadful harmony they join,
     And weave with bloody hands the tissue of thy line.

Chapter IX

1. **"Be gay securely ... thy clear brow":** From Thomas Gray's incomplete verse drama, *Agrippina* (1775).
2. *patois:* A nonstandard language or provincial dialect.

Chapter X

1. **"I fear we shall ... have overwatched!":** From Shakespeare's *A Midsummer Night's Dream,* Act V, scene i. Bottom asks Theseus if he wants to see an epilogue to the play-within-the-play or a dance. Theseus chooses the dance, then claims it is time for bed after a night of entertainment.
2. *manes:* Latin: the divine souls or spirits of the dead.
3. **Sir William Johnson:** Superintendent of Indian Affairs for British North America, Johnson began his relationship with the Native Americans when he was a young colonist building a community of settlers on his father's land in the Mohawk River Valley. Johnson's experiences in trade, expansion, and social poli-

tics laid the foundation for his role as "Colonel of the Forces to Be Raised out of the Six Nations."

Chapter XI

1. **"Cursed by . . . forgive him"**: The line is spoken by Shylock, in *The Merchant of Venice*, Act I, scene iii. Bassanio asks Shylock for a loan, using Antonio's credit to bind the deal. Shylock lends him the money but cannot forgive Antonio, whom he dislikes, particularly since the man "hates [Shylock's] sacred nation," the Jews, and calls Shylock a "cut-throat dog." Cooper changes the word *be* to *by*, which changes the meaning of the phrase.
2. **" 'city of cannon' "**: Nickname for Quebec. Fearing attack from the British, Count Frontenac ordered Quebec to be fortified immediately with walls and a strong battery. In 1690, when the British attacked the port, the Quebecois let loose their cannon fire and sank the enemy ships. After the battle, the French strengthened the fort further, adding a Royal Battery.
3. **on the shores of the great lake:** Huron lands that stretched north of Lake Ontario.
4. **withes:** A band or rope made of twisted twigs, vines, or stems.
5. **riving:** Ripping violently.

Chapter XII

1. **"Clo.—I am gone . . . with you again"**: From Shakespeare's *Twelfth Night*, Act IV, scene ii. The farewell is sung by a Clown who, as a joke prompted by Sir Toby and Maria, is disguised as a priest and

misleads the imprisoned Malvolio into thinking he is mad.

2. **Major Effingham:** British army officer Major Oliver Effingham appears near the end of Cooper's novel *The Pioneers* (1823). He is nicknamed Fire-Eater by Chingachgook (or John Mohegan) and adopted as his son. Effingham employed Natty Bumppo (Hawkeye/Leatherstocking) as a servant before Bumppo took to the woods. Bumppo cared for the man in secret when he became old and impoverished.

Chapter XIII

1. **"I'll seek a readier path":** A line from the poem "A Night Piece on Death," by Thomas Parnell. The quotation is taken from the first stanza:
   By the blue taper's trembling light,
   No more I waste the wakeful night,
   Intent with endless view to pore
   The schoolmen and the sages o'er;
   Their books from wisdom widely stray,
   Or point at best the longest way.
   I'll seek a readier path, and go
   Where wisdom's surely taught below.

2. **war of their own waging:** In the mid-seventeenth century, the Mohican (also called Mahican) and Mohawk tribes fought the Beaver Wars over power brought by fur trade with the Dutch. The Dutch favored the Mohicans, but the Mohawk eventually won the conflict. The Mohicans began to move west after the defeat.

3. **Albany Patteroon:** A country manor belonging to the Rensselaer family. Stephen Van Rensselaer became the lord of the manor at age five. However, the property was the principal landmark of a town called West Manor and was not identified as part of Albany until 1815. *Patroon* refers to the proprietor of a manor as noted by the Dutch governments of New York and New Jersey during the colonial years.

4. **bivouac:** A temporary military campsite.

Chapter XIV

1. **"Guard.—Qui est là? . . . de France":** In English, "Who is there? Peasants, poor French people." This quotation from Shakespeare's *Henry VI, Part I,* Act III, scene ii, is taken from the moment Joan La Pucelle (Joan of Arc) and a few soldiers come to the city gates disguised as beggars selling corn and ask for entry. They intend to take the city of Rouen.

2. **licks:** A salt or mineral deposit that animals lick to acquire certain needed nutrients.

3. **Dieskau:** Jean-Armand Dieskau was the French commander of the French regulars being sent to Canada. Dieskau was defeated by Sir William Johnson during a battle on September 8, 1755. After learning about Johnson's plan to attack Fort Frederic, a French holding, Dieskau decided to confront his troops before they reached the fort with his own force of 220 regulars, 680 Canadians, and 600 Indians. Although the French appeared to be winning the fight early on, Dieskau's tactic to face the British head-on cost him his men and the fight. Dieskau

tended to his own leg wounds in England but eventually went home to France.

4. **that little pond:** The "Bloody Pond" incident occurred after Dieskau's defeat. Two hundred men from New Hampshire and New York, under the leadership of Captains Folsom and McGinnis, spied a camp of 300 Canadians and Indians near Lake George, New York. The struggle ended with the French defeat and more than 200 men leaving the water "colored with blood." This incident is directly noted several pages below, by the notation "bloody pond."

5. **"Qui vive?":** "Who lives?" This was a standard question from a sentry to approaching strangers, a way of querying their loyalty, i.e. "Long lives *which* king?"

6. **"D'où venez-vous . . . bonne heure?":** "Where do you come from—where are you going, at this good hour?"

7. **"Je viens de . . . me coucher":** "I am coming from an exploration, and I'm going to bed."

8. **"Etes-vous officier du roi?":** "Are you a king's officer?"

9. **"Sans doute . . . au général":** "Of course, my comrade; you take me for someone provincial! I am leader of a regiment on horseback; I have here, with me, the daughters of the commander of this fort. Aha! You hear what I'm saying! I've had them in my custody since close to the other fort, and I am escorting them to the general."

10. **"Ma foi! . . . avec les dames":** "My faith! Ladies; I apologize . . . but—luck of the war! you will find our general a brave man, and well-mannered around the ladies."

11. **"C'est le caractère . . . à remplir":** "Men of war have that kind of character. . . . Good night, my friend; I wish you a more pleasant duty to fulfill."

12. **"Bonne nuit, mon camarade":** "Good night, my comrade."

13. **Vive le vin, l'amour:** "Long live wine, love." A song from the comic opera *Le Deserteur* (1769), by Pierre-Alexandre Monsigny and the librettist Michel-Jean Sedaine.

14. **"Qui va là?":** "Who goes there?"

15. **"C'est moi":** "It's me."

16. **"Bête!—qui?—moi!":** "Beast!—who?—me!"

17. **"Ami de la France":** "Friend of France."

18. **"Tu m'as pleu . . . camarades, feu!":** "You seem more like an *enemy* of France; stop! Or by God I will make you a friend of the devil. No! Fire, comrades, fire!"

19. **"Point de quartier aux coquins!":** "No mercy to the rogues!"

20. **glacis:** A long, open bank below the ramparts, which allows attackers no cover.

21. **sally-port:** A well-fortified side point of entry, which enables defending troops to exit protected.

Chapter XV

1. **"Then go we in . . . a word of it":** The Archbishop of Canterbury speaks these lines from Shakespeare's *Henry V*, Act I, scene i. The greedy archbishop plans to attend a meeting with the French ambassador and King Henry, who plots to invade France. Canterbury has his own plot: to stop Henry from confiscating church lands for the war efforts, he will raise funds

from other members of the clergy to aid Henry in his cause.

2. **fortress of Ticonderoga:** The French, in 1755, built Fort Carillon on the Ticonderoga peninsula because of its strategic location on Lake Champlain. Fort Carillon served as the base for General Montcalm's attack on Fort William Henry in 1757. In 1758, the battle for the fort began; the French, though outnumbered, found success in the fight, but the next year, they surrendered the fort to the British after a siege by General Jeffrey Amherst. However, before relinquishing the territory, the French blew up a powder magazine. This action forced the British to repair the fort in order to use it successfully. By the Revolutionary War in 1777, the fort was under American command. As part of his Saratoga campaign, British General John Burgoyne and his troops positioned a cannon at the top of Mount Defiance, and the Americans withdrew from the fort.

3. **those artificial waters:** The Erie Canal, begun in 1808, finished in 1825, links Lake Erie to the Hudson River.

4. **he of Lothian:** The Marquess of Lothian, a member of Scottish nobility.

5. **Woolwich Warren:** A collective of military buildings in Woolwich, England, now known as the Royal Arsenal. Founded in 1716, Woolwich Warren was the base for "gunners," as the Warren was founded on two companies of artillery.

6. **Earl of Loudon:** John Campbell, fourth Earl of Loudon (1705–1782), left his position as commander-in-chief of the British troops in December 1757 and was replaced by General James Abercrombie.

7. **marquee:** A pavilion or large tent.
8. **plains of Abraham:** Montcalm's French forces fell in this battle in Quebec City on September 13, 1759, as British troops commanded by General James Wolfe and Vice Admiral Charles Saunders sailed north past the city, scaled the cliffs, and sent in their organized army on foot. Wolfe and Montcalm were injured in this defining siege.
9. **"Monsieur . . . cet interprête":** "Sir . . . I take great pleasure in—bah!—where is that interpreter?"
10. **"Je crois . . . un péu Français":** "I believe, sir, that that will not be necessary. . . . I speak a little French."
11. **"Ah! j'en suis. . . . Eh, bien! monsieur":** "Ah! I feel at ease. . . . I hate those knaves; one never knows if they are on the right foot with them. Ah, well, sir."
12. **Salique laws:** A code of French royal laws, written between 476 and 496, which state that no daughter shall inherit land unless the sons of the family are dead.

Chapter XVI

1. **"Edg.—Before . . . this letter":** From Shakespeare's *King Lear*, Act V, scene i, said at a British camp near Dover as they are preparing to fight the French. Edgar, disguised as Poor Tom the beggar, delivers to Albany a letter he intercepted, written from Goneril to Edmund. The letter contains Goneril's request for Edmund to kill Albany.
2. **sugar-hogsheads:** Barrels in which to store sugar.
3. **thistle:** Refers to the Order of the Thistle, a Scottish order of knighthood.

4. *nemo me impune lacessit:* Latin for "No one provokes me with impunity." Motto of the Order of the Thistle.

5. **Monsieur Vauban:** Sebastien de Vauban, a military engineer for Louis XIV, was an expert on fortifications and siege-craft, the art of creating the strategy and equipment needed to lay siege to a fort.

6. **"En arrière . . . un peu":** "Get behind me, my children—it's hot; get back a little."

Chapter XVII

1. **"Weave we . . . is done":** From "The Bard," by Thomas Gray, section 123.

2. **"Le mot d'ordre?":** "The password?"

3. **"La victoire":** "Victory."

4. **"C'est bien . . . matin, monsieur!":** "Very well . . . walk well this morning, sir."

5. **"Il est . . . mon enfant":** "It is necessary to be vigilant, my child."

6. **"Il faut . . . dort jamais!":** "One must be vigilant, in truth! I believe that we have there, a lance corporal who never sleeps!"

7. **cross of St. Louis:** A medal belonging to the Order of St. Louis, a military order founded by French King Louis XIV and awarded to exceptional officers.

8. **" 'Why rage the heathen furiously!' ":** From the *Bay Psalm Book*, Psalm 2.

9. **sick and wounded:** Historically, the sick and the wounded who could not be moved were left to the French; however, once the British left the fort, the Indians "butchered" them, according to John In-

glis's work on "Colonel George Monro and Fort William Henry," written April 10, 1916.

10. **he dashed the head . . . her very feet:** This incident, though dramatic, depicts the event as noted in the *New York Mercury*, August 22, 1757: "The Children were taken by the Heels and their Brains beat out against the Trees and Stones."

Chapter XVIII

1. **"Why, anything . . . all in honor":** From Shakespeare's *Othello*, Act V, scene ii. Othello speaks with Lodovico and decides to kill himself rather than be put on trial for murder.

Chapter XIX

1. **"Salar.—Why . . . my revenge":** From Shakespeare's *The Merchant of Venice*, Act III, scene i. Shylock talks to Salario about the pound of flesh he intends to collect from Antonio.

Chapter XX

1. **"Land of Albania! . . . savage men!":** From the poem "Childe Harold's Pilgrimage," by Lord Byron, published between 1812 and 1818.

2. **Jarmans on the Mohawk:** German Protestants who settled in "German Flatts," or the town of Herkimer, New York.

Chapter XXI

1. **"If you find . . . flea's death"**: From Shakespeare's *The Merry Wives of Windsor*, Act IV, scene ii. Mistress Ford and her husband converse about her honesty and his suspicions when he suspects her of having an affair with Falstaff.
2. **alluvion:** A deposit of sediment or soil created by the flow and current of water.

Chapter XXII

1. **"Bot.—Are we . . . for our rehearsal":** From Shakespeare's *A Midsummer Night's Dream*, Act III, scene i. Bottom gathers with the other members of the play-within-the-play to rehearse in the woods.
2. **wish-ton-wish:** Cooper uses the word to mean "whippoorwill," though the term is also known to mean "prairie dog" in Pawnee. Cooper's intention has been debated by scholars.

Chapter XXIII

1. **"But though . . . trapped or slain?":** From the poem "The Lady of the Lake," by Sir Walter Scott (1810).
2. **termagant:** A derogatory term for a woman, meaning a shrew or nag.

Chapter XXIV

1. **"Thus spoke . . . their chief obey":** From Alexander Pope's epic translation, *The Iliad of Homer*

(1713), which chronicles the final year of the Trojan War.

Chapter XXV

1. **"Snug.—Have you . . . nothing but roaring"**: From Shakespeare's *A Midsummer Night's Dream*, Act I, scene ii. Quince, Snug, Bottom, Flute, Snout, and Starveling, a company of players, discuss the plot and characters of their play-within-the-play.
2. *hors de combat:* French for "outside of combat."

Chapter XXVI

1. **"Bot.—Let me play the lion too"**: From Shakespeare's *A Midsummer Night's Dream*, Act I, scene ii (see note 1, chapter XXV).
2. **Balaam's ass:** During the time of Moses, King Balak of Moab ordered Balaam to come and help defeat the Israelites who threatened to usurp his power. Balaam refused, telling the king that, in a dream, God instructed him not to go. The king promised to reward Balaam, and Balaam agreed and, now with God's permission, headed for the kingdom. Along the way, an angel appeared to the donkey he rode, prompting the animal not to travel further. When Balaam became upset with the donkey, the donkey spoke, complaining about the punishment. At this point, Balaam saw the angel, who informed him that the donkey was the only reason the angel did not kill Balaam.

Chapter XXVII

1. **"Ant. I shall . . . it is performed"**: From Shakespeare's *Julius Caesar*, Act I, scene ii. Antony is about to run a foot race. Caesar instructs him to touch Calpurnia as he sets off, since infertile women who were touched by runners were believed to become fertile.

Chapter XXVIII

1. **"Brief, I pray . . . with me"**: From Shakespeare's *Much Ado about Nothing*, Act III, scene v. Dogberry, a policeman, wants to speak with Leonato, who has little time to spare. Dogberry wishes to tell the governor about two men he and Verges arrested the previous evening.

Chapter XXIX

1. **"The assembly . . . of men addressed"**: From Alexander Pope's translation of *The Iliad*.
2. **the Yengeese and the Dutchmanne:** The English and the Dutch fought during the mid-seventeenth century over commerce, though the battles were mostly between their respective navies. The prize was territory, including the Delaware Valley.

Chapter XXX

1. **"If you deny . . . shall I have it?"**: From Shakespeare's *The Merchant of Venice*, Act IV, scene i. Shylock is demanding his pound of flesh from Antonio.

2. **"Uncas the child of Uncas":** Cooper wrote, in the Preface to his work *The Wept of Wish-ton-Wish* (1829), that he chose the name Uncas because it seemed like a "sort of synonym for chief with the Mohegans, a tribe of the Pequods, among whom several warriors of this name were known to govern in succession." In fact, Uncas was a rebellious Pequot chief in the early seventeenth century and allied with the English against the Dutch in their trade conflicts. He, with a small band of Mohegan warriors, eventually fought with the English against the Pequots and the Narragansetts.

Chapter XXXI

1. **"Flue.—Kill the poys...in the world":** From Shakespeare's *Henry V*, Act IV, scene vii. Fluellen and Gower, on the battlefield against the French, discuss King Henry's order to kill the French prisoners.
2. **"whispering council":** A war strategy by which chiefs gather in secret locations, protected by sentinels. Then "they separate and remain hidden, till intelligence from their spies authorises an attack," as told by John Dunn Hunter in his *Memoirs of a Captivity among the Indians of North America* (1824).
3. ***éclat:*** French for "brilliance" or "conspicuousness."

Chapter XXXII

1. **"But plagues ... black-eyed maid":** From Alexander Pope's translation of *The Iliad* by Homer, Book I.

2. **Shechemites:** Residents of Shechem, first capital of the kingdom of Israel.
2. **stentorian:** Booming or loud.

Chapter XXXIII

1. **"They fought . . . set of sun":** From Fitz-Green Halleck's poem "Marco Bozzaris" (1825), about a brave Greek revolutionary who died in 1823 while attacking the Turks.
2. **monody:** Musical term meaning a line sung by a single voice.

INTERPRETIVE NOTES

The Plot

Set in the rugged wilderness of upper New York State three years into the French and Indian War, this novel has become the most popular and memorable of Cooper's *Leatherstocking Tales*.

On the way to Fort William Henry, where Colonel Munro is fighting the French, Major Duncan Heyward, David Gamut, and the Munro sisters, Cora and Alice, are misdirected by their Huron guide, Magua. When the traveling party meets frontier woodsman Hawkeye and two Mohicans, Chingachgook and Uncas, Magua escapes. As the group heads for hidden caves, the party is attacked by a band of Hurons. With their ammunition running low, Hawkeye, Uncas, and Chingachgook decide to leave the travelers and find reinforcements. David, Heyward, and the sisters are captured. Magua, infatuated with Cora, tells her that he will set Heyward and Alice free if she marries him. Her refusal—accompanied by an unusual moment of defiance by Alice—angers Magua, who attempts to kill both Alice and Heyward. Hawkeye, Uncas, and Chingachgook arrive in the nick of time and attack the Hurons. Magua slips away again. Hawkeye and his companions lead the group through the woods to the fort, barely avoiding death at the hands of the French and their Native American allies. Along the way, Uncas develops feelings for Cora, while Heyward expresses interest in Alice.

At the fort, Colonel Munro decides to surrender to the French, since General Webb plans not to send any reinforcements. When the English prepare to leave the fort according to the terms of the French agreement, the Indians attack. Magua kidnaps the sisters and David Gamut. Hawkeye, Uncas, Chingachgook, Heyward, and Colonel Munro pursue Magua. During the chase, Uncas is captured by the Hurons, but Hawkeye rescues him. The men go to the village, where Cora is held captive. Tamenund, the tribe patriarch, permits Magua to keep Cora as prisoner. A battle ensues, and the protagonists defeat their enemies, yet Magua and two warriors leave the fighting and drag Cora away into the woods. The struggle to free Cora continues, and in the violence, Cora, Uncas, and Magua are killed. Chingachgook and Hawkeye speak intimately, and the wise leader reveals his sadness that he is alone. Tamenund reveres the noble race of Mohicans and laments the future of his people.

Characters

Hawkeye. Often considered the main protagonist of the novel, Nathaniel "Natty" Bumppo goes by the adopted name of Hawkeye. A resourceful woodsman, hunter, and scout in the tradition of Daniel Boone, Hawkeye is also known as La Longue Carabine, or the Long Rifle. Hawkeye represents a successful and idealistic merging of worlds; although he is white, he lives and identifies with the Native American community. Additionally, he symbolizes the new American individual, as he forges his own path through settlement and savagery.

Chingachgook. Father of Uncas and an old friend of Hawkeye, Chingachgook, also called Le Gros Serpent (the Great Snake), is the last Mohican chief. Wise, level-headed, and unfazed by dangerous circumstances, he inspires reverence for the Indian way of life. He is a man of few words.

Uncas. Close friend of Hawkeye and son of Chingachgook, Uncas also fulfills the title role in the novel. He essentially symbolizes the last of the Mohicans, a people on the brink of extinction. Uncas also reflects the common image of the "noble savage" as he combines strength, ferocity, and compassion.

Magua. On the surface, Magua, a chief in the Huron tribe, is the villain of the novel. However, a closer read shows Magua's motivation and ambition as a visceral reaction to both the violent colonization of his world and his attempt to find his place within that world. He has suffered at the hands of white men, which lightens the dark edge of his character and allows for reader sympathy. His nickname is Le Renard Subtil, or the Sly Fox.

Duncan Heyward. A major in the English army, Duncan takes seriously his mission to protect the daughters of Colonel Munro but cannot fully adapt to or understand the ways of the frontier. In this way, Heyward serves as Hawkeye's foil, as Hawkeye thrives in unpredictable, uncivilized circumstances. Heyward often must rely on Hawkeye or Uncas to save his life. He falls in love with Alice, Colonel Munro's younger daughter.

Cora Munro. Cora, Alice's older half-sister, is the woman of reason. Bold, forthright, and nurturing, she represents the new woman of the frontier, particularly since her opinions on race and culture are modern and open-minded. Her mother was part "Negro," so, like Hawkeye, she represents the cultural and racial mixing of the New World. She attracts both Uncas and Magua.

Alice Munro. The opposite of her older sister, Cora, Alice is fair-skinned and highly emotional. Prone to fainting, crying, and trembling, Alice adheres to the expectations of a "civilized" damsel in distress. However, though she often seems weak and helpless, Alice does exhibit conviction and courage, particularly when she chooses death over freedom in suggesting that Cora refuse to become Magua's wife.

Colonel Munro. Commander of the British forces, he leads his troops with optimism yet is unsuccessful in his approach to frontier maneuvers. Munro was married twice, once in the West Indies to Cora's mother, who died, then to Alice's mother, his sweetheart in Scotland. Although he loves his daughters and is fueled by a grand patriotism, Munro makes an ineffectual leader.

General Montcalm. Officially named Marquis Louis Joseph de Saint-Véran, Montcalm commands the French forces, with the help and knowledge of Indian warriors. Shrewd and strategic, Montcalm also demonstrates his merciful side when he offers fair and honorable terms for English surrender.

David Gamut. Early in the novel, David appears as a random musician who encounters Duncan and the sisters in the woods. Despite his seemingly superficial and comedic role, David serves the plot later in the novel as he aids in rescuing Uncas and Hawkeye. As a religious character, David also generates thought about the place of Christianity in this "savage" world and provides an interesting complement to Hawkeye, who claims no religion.

Tamenund. The sage of the Delaware tribe, Tamenund earns his people's respect with his even-handed judgment and insight.

Major Themes

The Savage versus the Civilized

All the characters in the novel participate in this conflict, those who are allied with a particular side as well as those who try to understand and accept the ways of both adversaries. For example, Duncan Heyward is a highly trained and educated soldier devoted to upholding the honor of the English army. While he shows diplomacy at times when remarking on the skill of his Mohican guides, he dismisses Native American beliefs, customs, and tactics in favor of those he formally learned. His lack of knowledge of his environment places him in dangerous situations, and often his life depends on those "schooled" on the frontier, such as Hawkeye or Uncas. Heyward is a gentleman and, as such, subscribes to the code of battle, which offers the "fair fight."

In contrast, Magua, highly trained and educated in the Huron fashion of warfare, is motivated by revenge, which Hawkeye deems strictly a Native American way of thinking. His passionate hatred for Colonel Munro, combined with a strategy of deception, violence, and treachery, seems to mirror for Heyward the savagery of the frontier. But Magua's approach has grown from European encroachment on the New World. Magua seeks retaliation for his humiliation and punishment at the hands of Colonel Munro, who accused him of public drunkenness and tied him to a whipping post. Magua blamed the colonel, and the English, for the incident that led to his wife leaving him for another man. Yet, in effect, the white man did bring alcohol to the Native American world, providing the means for Magua's moral deterioration.

Hawkeye, as white man, woodsman, and Mohican ally, treads the boundary between savage and civilized. He claims that some Native Americans, those other than the Delawares and Mohicans, are liars and "varlets" yet at the same time respects their beliefs. He realizes that the white settlers and explorers have invaded Native American lands. Yet Hawkeye views the white man's culture as somewhat more elevated than the Native Americans', particularly the white man's values. White men, for instance, are not motivated by revenge, according to

Hawkeye. In this way, Hawkeye conforms to Heyward's type of integrity and honor system. But he does not shy from a confrontation, as shown by his relationship with his rifle, "Killdeer."

The omniscient narrator plays a vital role in establishing the conflict between the savage and the civilized. Cooper's third-person narrative does not hold an unbiased opinion and, in fact, depicts the Native American characters as good and evil depending on how vicious or how noble they are. While Uncas is shown as a "young warrior" with a "quiet smile," Magua is as cunning as his nickname, the "Sly Fox," suggests, with "cold contempt" and a "ferocious smile." Chingachgook, with his calm, thoughtful ways, cannot possibly lead a band of dark, savage "conquerors," as Magua can.

Cultural Blending

Both Cora and Hawkeye are characters whose identities fall outside the normal categories. In the white man's "civilized" world, Cora, with her mixed heritage and outspoken tendencies, would not be accepted as a proper lady. Colonel Munro addresses this possibility when Heyward expresses interest in Alice rather than Cora: "You scorn to mingle the blood of the Heywards with one so degraded—lovely and virtuous though she be?" Munro accuses Heyward of prejudice, which Heyward vehemently denies, but Munro's suspicion mirrors social tendencies. Cora is admired in the Indian world by Magua and Uncas but chooses to die rather than live in the "savage" Magua's world. In a sense, there is no place for Cora, since she does not belong in either society.

Hawkeye chooses to live with Native Americans yet

holds fast to some of the "white man's" ideas. He has adapted to the frontier code and scoffs at formal education. He rejects the regimented, regulated world to which, according to the color of his skin, he should belong. At the same time, he recognizes that he does not have the same instinct or keen eye as Uncas and can never be a Mohican. He is an outsider.

The Frontier as Both Heaven and Hell

In *The Last of the Mohicans*, Cooper depicts the American frontier as both violent and idyllic. Since the vast landscape and seemingly endless frontier were such prominent features of the first two hundred years of American history, much of American literature focuses on "interpreting" the wilderness.

European colonists came to the New World specifically to find a "promised land," a "New Canaan"; Instead, they discovered a hostile, brutal land. Interestingly, the view of the wilderness was regional, with many of the Puritanical New Englanders seeing the dark forests as the devil's lair and the more adventurous "Southern" colonists willing to brave the sinful thickets to make a new home for themselves. Nevertheless, the notion of the frontier as something to be tamed, controlled, and purified of evil was held by most, particularly in light of native attacks, as well as captivity tales told by those who survived the ordeals. The representation of wilderness as hellfire is illustrated by the 1636 entry included in the *Journal of John Winthrop*, in which Indians "cut off [a man's] hands . . . and afterwards cut off his feet" for simply hunting birds; and *A Narrative of the Captivity and Restauration of Mrs. Mary Rowlandson*, the woman's personal story about her harrowing experience in 1676. For many of Cooper's characters, the wilderness is a threat to their bodies and souls.

In Cooper's time, the Romantic movement in art and literature had begun to cast the wilderness in a new light. It was not dark and evil but innocent and sublime, a source of inspiration. Cooper's novel seems to straddle the Puritan and Romantic positions. Early on in *The Last of the Mohicans,* he shows "a human visage, as fiercely wild as savage art and unbridled passions could make it peer[ing] out" from the "branches of the bushes that formed the thicket"; this type of scene is common in the novel, as Indians hide in the dark brush, watch, and wait. However, Cooper also paints a serene picture of the great outdoors, with "the cooler vapours of the springs and fountains [rising] above their leafy beds," "the heavens . . . studded with stars," and "the clouds of high vapour . . . rising in spiral wreaths from uninhabited woods, looking like smokes of hidden cottages." For Cooper, the frontier is both hell and heaven on earth, two mythical places colliding and claiming the space for their own—essentially capturing the moment before Paradise is lost.

CRITICAL EXCERPTS

Biographical Studies

Ringe, Donald. *James Fenimore Cooper*. New York: Twayne Publishers, 1962. Updated edition, 1988.

Ringe uses biographical materials to accompany a thorough exploration of Cooper's literary achievements, as well as providing an overview of Cooper scholarship in the span of decades between the early 1960s and the late 1980s.

This book intends quite frankly to state the case for James Fenimore Cooper. It agrees with Marius Bewley that Cooper has long been undervalued as an artist, and with Charles A. Brady that his case should be reopened and judged once again. Thus, although it recognizes his well-known faults and failures, it chooses not to emphasize them, but to stress instead the thematic interpretation of his tales and the means, sometimes highly successful, by which he gave his themes expression. It asks the reader, therefore, to lay aside his preconceptions, to see the novels in their own terms, and to seek the meaning that they, like all works of literary art, will yield if carefully read for themselves alone. The purpose is to understand the tales that they may be evaluated in the light of that knowledge.

Franklin, Wayne. *James Fenimore Cooper: The Early Years*. New Haven, Connecticut: Yale University Press, 2007.

Franklin compiled this detailed chronicle of Cooper's "early years," from childhood through his mid-thirties, from his extensive and careful study of Cooper's family papers, which in the past often have been misread, misunderstood, and/or edited in ways that limited a complete perspective of the famous author. Scholars consider this book a major contribution in the field of Cooper studies, which deepens our understanding of a mythic American writer who fathered the "the Western, the sea tale, the Revolutionary romance." Franklin demonstrates how Cooper's life reflects, through his literature and other public endeavors, the American quest for independence and foreshadows the future power and progress of a burgeoning republic.

Cooper was, in this as in so many ways, deeply typical of the early Republic. His sense of the strengthening influence of the market in social relations, of the role in the law as itself an element of economic warfare, and of the threat of wealth to democracy, even his enduring tendency to view America's social landscape as a collection of tattered surfaces and wishful incompletions—as with the frontier village of Templeton in *The Pioneers*—suggest the degree to which his social ethos and his aesthetic vision were shaped by the chaotic situation so many other men and women faced during that period.

Person, Leland S. *A Historical Guide to James Fenimore Cooper*. New York: Oxford University Press, 2007.

Using a conversational tone and an engaging approach, Person places Cooper's life and works within a social and historical context. The book, while devoting a chapter to a "brief biography" and billed as a "historical guide," offers a well-rounded picture of the "robust-souled" Cooper through its exploration of the author's literary imagination and impact. Additionally, the book attempts to show how his writing tackled cultural, racial, political, and gender issues, positioning Cooper as more than a writer of frontier myth. Articles include "Cooper's Europe and His Quarrel with America" by J. Gerald Kennedy and "Race Traitor: Cooper, His Critics, and Nineteenth Century Politics" by Barbara Alice Mann.

Even though Cooper overdoes the conversations in many of his novels, especially in the frontier romances, he had a good ear for the controversies of the day, and he consistently showed his interest in debating them in his fiction. Considering that a primary goal of this historical guide is to situate Cooper in the cultural context in which he wrote and was read, that feature of his writing constitutes one of his most important achievements.

Early Reviews and Interpretations

Gardiner, W. H. "Cooper's Novels," *North American Review*. January 1826.

This long, detailed review of the popular "American novelist" addresses Cooper's readership and acknowledges that some readers may not admire his complexity or his penchant for "groundwork." The review also dismisses some of Cooper's underdeveloped characters, a few unconvincing plot points, and awkwardness in writing technique. In his conclusion, the reviewer that the believes that Cooper could be a better novelist if he corrected the "numerous defects" in his style. Nevertheless, the reviewer encourages readers to sit back and enjoy "disentangling the thread of narrative" and enjoy the main characters, as well as the "romantic incidents."

Indeed, if we are called upon to state what, in our judgment, constitutes the characteristic excellence of this writer, we should say, without hesitation, that it is exhibited in the rapidity of his incidents, the vividness of his action, and the invention of the machinery of the piece by which we mean all that answers in the modern novel as a substitute for the mythological divinities of the ancient epopeia, or the giants and enchanters, fairies and weird sisters of Runic poetry and the elder romance; those subtile agents bordering upon the preternatural, who weave, and, at pleasure, unravel the mysteries of the plot, and effect such surprises of the imagination as are essential to its dramatic effect.

Unsigned reviewer. *Monthly Review*, June 1826.

The author of this review gives Cooper a positive reception, remarking on his attention to detail, complimenting his skill for suspense, and demonstrating the success of the novel with a summary accompanied by personal commentary.

The structure of the tale itself is sufficiently simple, but the narrative is frequently worked up to an intensity of horror and an agony of suspense which are really much more than interesting: the anxiety of the reader becomes engrossed, and his imagination excited, in many of the situations of the story, to a degree which is absolutely painful. Indeed it is a positive fault in the romance that the personages, for whom our sympathies are keenly awakened, encounter one unrelieved and perpetual crisis of terrific danger through three whole volumes of adventure. They are never for an instant secured from the appalling contingencies of a conflict with the Indian.

Twain, Mark. "Fenimore Cooper's Literary Offences." *North American Review*, July 1895.

Although this review is primarily about *Deerslayer*, Twain is Cooper's most ardent—and famous—critic. His argument revolves around Cooper breaking eighteen out of nineteen "rules governing literary art in the domain of romantic fiction" and suggests that the "Leather Stocking series ought to have been called the Broken Twig series" because of its reliance on dramatic clichés. Twain's tone is conversational, sarcastic, and pointed, with animated details and references to Cooper's work.

Cooper's gift in the way of invention was not a rich endowment; but such as it was he liked to work it, he was pleased with the effects, and indeed he did some quite sweet things with it. In his little box of stage properties he kept six or eight cunning devices, tricks, artifices for his savages and woodsmen to deceive and circumvent each other with, and he was never so happy as when he was working with these innocent things and seeing them go. . . . He prized his broken twig above the rest of his effects, and worked it the hardest. It is a restful chapter in any book of his when somebody doesn't step on a dry twig and alarm all the reds and whites for two hundred yards around.

Critical Interpretations: Mid-Twentieth Century

Smith, Henry Nash. *Virgin Land: The American West as Symbol and Myth*. New York: Vintage, 1950.

Virgin Land discusses the myth of the West, beginning with explorers' quest for a "Passage to India" and ending with the "civilization" of the American frontier. Chapter four discusses Cooper's *Leatherstocking Tales* and their relationship to the myth of Daniel Boone.

The similarities between Boone and Leatherstocking were analyzed at length by a perceptive writer in *Niles' Register* in 1825, when Leatherstocking had appeared in only one novel, *The Pioneers*. The critic points out that both these heroes love the freedom of the forest, both take a passionate delight in hunting, and both dislike the ordinary pursuits of civilized men. As testimony to the fidelity of Cooper's characterization, the writer quotes a letter from a traveler through the Pennsylvania mountains who came upon herdsmen and hunters reminiscent both of Boone and of Leatherstocking. One of their number, celebrated throughout the West as having once been a companion of Boone, had set out for Arkansas when he was almost a hundred years old, and was reported to be still alive, a solitary hunter in the forest. A nephew of the emigrant who remained in Pennsylvania, himself athletic and vigorous at the age of seventy, shared Leatherstocking's love of hunting and his antipathy for "clearings" to such a marked degree that the traveler felt he must have sat as a model for Cooper.

Darnell, Donald. "Uncas as Hero: The Ubi Sunt Formula in *The Last of the Mohicans*." *American Literature* 37 (1965): 259–66.

Darnell sets out to prove why Uncas should be considered the main hero in the novel, through the exploration of particular scenes, descriptions, and theme. Darnell suggests Uncas reaches "true tragic stature" in the novel with his death.

Thus, when Uncas makes his appearance at the Delaware village, he has a past filled with heroic deeds. But it is not his past that warrants Uncas's role as the hero, but rather the bright destiny legend has predicted for him.

To understand the significance of Uncas the history of his race must be known.

Martin, Terence. "From the Ruins of History: *The Last of the Mohicans.*" *Novel* 2 (Spring 1969): 221–29.

Martin demonstrates how Cooper strategically and stylistically moves the narrative of the novel from romance to a history of sorts. Cooper's characters exist in a world based on both actual and fictional events, events shaped and revised by Cooper's personal commentary.

> At times clumsily, at times adventitiously, Cooper has taken us in *The Last of the Mohicans* from conventional romance to a moment of history which, by means of violence and atrocity, burns itself to ruins. Then, with all preparations made, he has led us from the ruins of history to mourn the death of Uncas in the most exalted world of romance of which he was capable.

Baym, Nina. "The Women of Cooper's Leatherstocking Tales." *American Quarterly* 23 (December 1971), 696–709.

Baym writes about the vital role of women in Cooper's popular series, despite the fact they may appear inconsequential and/or one-dimensional. Baym concludes, however, that Cooper's women are stunted by social limitations and order.

> I would argue, however, that the place of women in the Leatherstocking Tales relates directly to Cooper's main themes: contrasting modes of thought as they are brought into play in the establishment of an American civilization.

Critical Interpretations: 1990s and Beyond

Peck, Daniel. *New Essays on "The Last of the Mohicans."* New York: Cambridge University Press, 1992.

Part of the "New Essays" series by Cambridge, this book offers new interpretation of the way Cooper uses language, discusses the novel's criticism since its publication, and presents new arguments on race and gender. Essays include "The Wilderness of Words in *The Last of the Mohicans*" by Wayne Franklin and "How Men and Women Wrote Indian Stories" by Baym. An excerpt from Baym's essay discussing the literary echoes between male and female writers of the "Indian" genre follows:

> The self-conscious merging of gender and Indian issues may be seen when we put *The Last of the Mohicans* in its historical network of men and women's Indian stories that revised each other from gendered perspectives. Two Indian stories by men—the epic poem *Yamoyden* (1820) by James W. Eastburn and Robert C. Sands, and *The Pioneers* by James Fenimore Cooper (1823)—inspired Lydia Maria Child's *Hobomok* (1824); this novel in turn affected Cooper's next Indian book, *The Last of the Mohicans* (1826); and *The Last of the Mohicans* spurred Catharine Maria Sedgwick to write *Hope Leslie* (1827).

Rosenwald, Lawrence. " 'The Last of the Mohicans' and the Languages of America." *College English* 60: (January 1998), 9–23.

Rosenwald discusses the representation of language in *The Last of the Mohicans* and discusses how the way

Native American languages are represented can radically alter a writer's and a reader's perspective of a particular character.

Cooper's account of Uncas's war-song makes us raise the questions we would ask about any complex linguistic performance, for instance: What are formal patterns and conventions of such songs? Where and how has Uncas learned them? And raising these questions means seeing how Cooper's novel, in its truncated representation of Native American linguistic performance, has made it impossible for us to answer them. Reading the account of Hawk-eye's bad translation makes us skeptical of all translations. What else, we wonder, has Hawk-eye gotten wrong? What distortions might characterize the "translations" of Delaware utterances that Cooper has been offering us throughout the novel?

Pitcher, E. W. "The 'Hapless Babes' of the Frontier: Ovid, *The History of Maria Kittle,* and *The Last of the Mohicans.*" ANQ: A Quarterly Journal of Short Articles, Notes, and reviews 13 (Summer 2000), 33–37.

Pitcher compares scenes in *The Last of the Mohicans* to Ovid's *Metamorphoses* and highlights the parallels between the ancient classic and Cooper's mythical tale.

In *The Last of the Mohicans,* Cooper embellished his remarkably accurate depiction of the 1757 battle for Fort William Henry by reporting events through the eyes of his fictional cast of characters and by inserting sentimentalized, dramatic illustrations of general terror and tragedy following the march out of the surrendered fort. The murder of helpless children was epitomized in the scene in chapter 17 of the babe torn from his mother's grasp, held by the feet over the head of a "wild" Huron, then its head "dashed . . . against a rock" and its "quivering remains" thrown at the feet of the distracted mother (Cooper 175). Several analogues have been cited by scholars as sources for Cooper's horrid imaging, but a relevant parallel in Ovid's *Metamorphoses* has gone unnoticed.

Smith, Lindsey Claire. "Cross-cultural Hybridity in James Fenimore Cooper's *The Last of the Mohicans*." *ATQ (The American Transcendental Quarterly)* 20.3 (September 2006).

Smith's article focuses on the cultural hybridity of *The Last of the Mohicans* to reveal the contemporary social relevance of the novel.

Cooper's Leatherstocking novels will never be the authority on American Indians of the eighteenth century or their contact with other peoples in the formative years of the United States. For accuracy and relevancy in understanding the experiences of America's indigenous peoples during earlier centuries, it is imperative that students and scholars turn their attention to the early writings of American Indians such as Samson Occum, William Apess, John Rollin Ridge, Sarah Winnemucca, Charles Alexander Eastman, and Elias Boudinot. However, *The Last of the Mohicans* is nonetheless worthy of study because of its unique fictional emphasis on the convergence of black, Indian, and white peoples, a cross-cultural contact that highlights key concerns such as integration, land and ecology, and identity, in the American imagination.

Questions for Discussion

The Last of the Mohicans begins with an epigraph from Shakespeare's *Richard II*. Find out more about this play. Why does Cooper start the novel with this quote? What parallels does he want to reader to draw? Throughout the novel, Cooper quotes Shakespeare's *The Merchant of Venice* repeatedly. Find out more about this play. Why do you think Cooper made such frequent allusions to it?

Cooper polarizes his Native American characters, portraying them as either good or evil. How does this stereotype the Native American cultural identity? What other characters does Cooper stereotype, and how?

Cora and Alice represent two very distinct types of women, as emphasized by their physical features. How does the classic conflict of brunette versus blonde stereotypes play into the development of each sister's character?

The novel's setting plays an important role in the story. Cooper provides keen detail about the wilderness and, in some instances, shows human beings at odds with nature. More than a century later, how does Cooper's message resound? Can you see similarities between how humans treat nature today and how they treated nature during Cooper's lifetime? Can you think of ways in which humans cannot conquer nature, even today?

Frequently in the novel, Hawkeye suggests that schooling would not have prepared him for the conflict at hand, especially since he is a "warrior of the wilderness." How do you think education has prepared you for your life? Can you name some experiences you have had in which "bookish knowledge did not carry you through harmless"? In those situations, what did you need to know that was not taught through books and formal schooling?

In writing this novel, as well as the others in the *Leatherstocking Tales* series, Cooper fictionalized some of the events of the French and Indian War. Think of other works you have read or films you have seen that fictionalize historical events and/or people. Do you think this approach to real-life occurrences diminishes the event or person in any way? Do you think the event, through its revised depiction, becomes less important? Or do you think fictionalizing history makes the actual event more interesting and memorable to a reader or viewer?

SUGGESTIONS FOR THE INTERESTED READER

If you liked *The Last of the Mohicans*, you might also be interested in the following:

Montcalm and Wolfe, by Francis Parkman. This book, originally published in 1884, encompasses volumes six and seven of Parkman's series on the conflict between the English and the French in North America. A revered American historian, Parkman pulls facts and events together into a compelling narrative, creating what some consider a "work of literary art."

Daniel Boone: The Life and Legend of an American Pioneer, by John Mack Faragher. Since mythic woodsman Daniel Boone has been called the inspiration for Cooper's character Natty Bumppo (or Hawkeye), readers may enjoy this biography, published in 1993, which uses popular narrative, public record, Boone's personal documentation, and oral storytelling to depict the legendary figure.

Blood Meridian, by Cormac McCarthy. Set near the Texas-Mexico border in the 1850s, the 1985 novel is a bloody tale of bounty hunters on their quest for Indian scalps, yet it reflects the style and conventions of the frontier genre. The book was hailed by critics as an "American classic" upon its publication, both for its gripping and grizzly story and for McCarthy's breathtaking stylistic skill.

The Last of the Mohicans, VHS, DVD, 1992. This film, starring Daniel Day-Lewis as Hawkeye, Madeleine Stowe as Cora, Russell Means as Chingachgook, and Eric Schweig as Uncas, revises the novel into a story of passion, longing, and romance. Some details of Cooper's novel have been omitted, combined, or changed to reflect director Michael Mann's particular vision; for example, in the film, Heyward falls in love with Cora, rather than Alice, while Uncas develops feelings for Alice. In the book, Uncas and Magua struggle over the elder, darker sister. This movie adheres more to a plot revised for a 1936 film version starring Randolph Scott.

BESTSELLING ENRICHED CLASSICS

JANE EYRE
Charlotte Brontë
0-671-01479-X
$5.99

WUTHERING HEIGHTS
Emily Brontë
0-7434-8764-8
$4.95

THE GOOD EARTH
Pearl S. Buck
0-671-51012-6
$6.99

*THE AWAKENING AND
SELECTED STORIES*
Kate Chopin
0-7434-8767-2
$4.95

*HEART OF DARKNESS
AND THE SECRET SHARER*
Joseph Conrad
0-7434-8765-6
$4.95

GREAT EXPECTATIONS
Charles Dickens
0-7434-8761-3
$4.95

A TALE OF TWO CITIES
Charles Dickens
0-7434-8760-5
$4.95

*THE COUNT OF
MONTE CRISTO*
Alexandre Dumas
0-7434-8755-9
$6.50

10210 (1 of 2)

Available in paperback from Pocket Books wherever books are sold.

Not sure what to read next?

Visit Pocket Books online at
www.simonsays.com

Reading suggestions for
you and your reading group
New release news
Author appearances
Online chats with your favorite writers
Special offers
Order books online
And much, much more!